Jilly Cooper is a well-known journalist, writer and media superstar and the author of many number one bestselling novels. Her novels include *Riders*, *Rivals*, *Polo*, *The Man Who Made Husbands Jealous*, *Appassionata*, *Score!* and *Pandora*. She and her husband live in Gloucestershire with several dogs and cats.

POLO

'Another massive, unputdownable saga of sweaty horse-flesh, adulterous bonking and beautiful people with posh voices . . . within its genre it is a work of towering genius' Kate Saunders, *Evening Standard*

'An exuberant tale of handsome players, spoiled women and rich barons, spiced with plenty of illicit sex' *Cosmopolitan*

'A tale of lust which only just stops short of frightening the horses' *The Times*

'Chukkas, jodhpurs, marquees . . . plenty of sex . . . people are bankable and bonkable. The Prince of Wales slips in and out of the text . . . close both to reality and the secret of life of our imaginations . . . the essence of a good blockbuster' *Guardian*

D1331601

By Jilly Cooper

FICTION

Pandora
The Rutshire Chronicles:
Riders
Rivals
The Man Who Made Husbands
  Jealous
Appassionata
Score!

NON-FICTION

Animals in War
Class
How to Survive Christmas
Hotfoot to Zabriskie Point
  (with Patrick Lichfield)
Intelligent and Loyal
Jolly Marsupial
Jolly Super
Jolly Superlative
Jolly Super Too
Super Cooper
Super Jilly
Super Men and Super Women
The Common Years
Turn Right at the Spotted Dog
Work and Wedlock
Angels Rush In
Araminta's Wedding

CHILDREN'S BOOKS

Little Mabel
Little Mabel's Great Escape
Little Mabel Saves the Day
Little Mabel Wins

ROMANCE

Bella
Emily
Harriet
Imogen
Lisa & Co
Octavia
Prudence

ANTHOLOGIES

The British in Love
Violets and Vinegar

JILLY COOPER

POLO

A LEGEND OF
FAIR WOMEN AND BRAVE MEN

CORGI BOOKS

POLO
A CORGI BOOK : 0 552 15057 6

Originally published in Great Britain by Bantam Press,
a division of Transworld Publishers

PRINTING HISTORY
Bantam Press edition published 1991
Corgi edition published 1992

13 15 17 19 20 18 16 14 12

This book was set in Plantin by
Chippendale Type Ltd, West Yorkshire.

Corgi Books are published by Transworld Publishers,
61–63 Uxbridge Road, London W5 5SA,
a division of The Random House Group Ltd,
in Australia by Random House Australia (Pty) Ltd,
20 Alfred Street, Milsons Point, Sydney, NSW 2061, Australia,
in New Zealand by Random House New Zealand Ltd,
18 Poland Road, Glenfield, Auckland 10, New Zealand
and in South Africa by Random House (Pty) Ltd,
Endulini, 5a Jubilee Road, Parktown 2193, South Africa.

Printed and bound in Great Britain by
Cox & Wyman Ltd, Reading, Berkshire.

To Felix
with all love

AUTHOR'S NOTE

To avoid confusion, I should point out that although *Polo* brings back many of the characters from my earlier books *Riders* and *Rivals*, it is not, in the strictly chronological sense, a sequel. The story begins in the very early 1980s, a year after *Riders* ended and Rupert Campbell-Black split up from his wife Helen. It finishes in the late 80s, two years after the end of *Rivals*.

A word of explanation is in order about the handicapping system in polo which is at least as complicated as A level maths.

A full game of polo consists of six chukkas of approximately seven minutes each. There are four players in each team: a forward at No. 1, two midfield players at Nos. 2 and 3 and a back at No. 4. Every player has a rating known as a 'handicap', which is reassessed by the polo authorities twice a year. These handicaps reflect individual ability and range from minus two for an absolute beginner up to a maximum of ten for the very best players. No Englishman has been rated at ten since the Second World War.

The term 'high-goal polo' in England means that the aggregate handicap of a team entered for a particular tournament must be between 17 and 22. A 22-goal team, for example, could be composed of a forward with a handicap of two, two midfield players, each on eight, and a back on four. In Palm Beach, where the standard is higher, the ceiling for a high-goal side is 26, and in Argentina as high as the ultimate 40, with each of the members of the team on ten. No player can take part in high-goal polo unless he has at least a handicap of one.

In medium-goal matches the aggregate handicap of the team is normally between 16 and 12 and in low goal between 8 and 0.

Most tournaments are based on handicap. Thus the team with the higher aggregate concedes goals at the start of a match to the other side.

ACKNOWLEDGEMENTS

One of the joys of writing this book has been the friends I made during my research. I have seldom encountered more charming or helpful people than among the polo community. Travelling alone to strange places can be very daunting. I am therefore eternally grateful to Ronald Ferguson and Pilar Boxford for opening so many doors for me and, above all, to Geoffrey and Jorie Kent in Palm Beach and Jean-Jacques and Zou Zou de Wolff and their family in Argentina for offering me endless hospitality, the run of their yards, introductions to top-class players, grooms and ponies alike, and transforming what might have been a terrifying ordeal into a great adventure.

Many other people helped me. Like those referred to above, they are all skilled in their own fields, but, as I was writing fiction, I only heeded their advice in so far as it fitted my story. The accuracy of the book in no way reflects their expertise or their views. They include:

Anthony and Mary Abrahams, Sally Armstrong, Paula Atkins, Susan Barrantes, Garth and Diana Bearman, Steve and Sandi Berg, Garth and Pat Booth, Michael Brown, Nene Martinez Castro, Peter Cadbury, Johnnie Cahen-D'Anvers, Alina Carter, Charles and Tita Carter, Sarah Clark, Louise Cooper, Richard and Rosie Costelloe, Leone Cran, Francis Craven, John and Liza Crisp, Robert Cudmore, Kuldip Singh Dhillon, Gabriel Donoso, Richard Dunhill, Taylor Duvalle, John Ellis, Tom and Gilly Emerson, Susan Ferguson, Tom Fletcher, Tracy Forman, Edward Fursden, Cecil Gifford, Martin Glue, Peter and Elizabeth Grace and their daughters Jane, Pippa, Victoria and Katie, Edward Green, Janet Greep, Terry Hanlon, Ritchie Harrison, Anthony and Sue Hayden-Taylor, Felicity Higson, Howard and Camilla Hipwood, Julian and Patricia Hipwood, John Horswell, John Hunter, Richard Jarvis, Gregg Keating, Chrissie and Brett Kiely, Dee Kiely, Alan and Fiona Kent, Kate Kavanagh, Robert and Sandi Lacey, Manuel Lainez, Mary Latz, Philippe Leopold-Metzger, Robert and Barbara

Lindemann, Norman and Aly Lobel, Stewart Lodge, Dora Lowenstein, William Lucas, Cassandra MacClancy, Stuart and Chrissie Mackenzie, the late Charles Mackenzie-Hill, Anthony Marangos, Cassandra Marchessini, David Marchwood, Ted Marriage, Gil Martin, Sherry Merica, George and Sarah Milford-Haven, Edgar Miller, Sheila Murphy, Caroline Neville, Alex Olmos, Joan Pardey, Andrew Parker-Bowles, David Phillips, Hilary Pilkington, Mike Ponting, Billy and Dawn Raab, Laura Lee Randall, Timmy Roach, Derek Russell-Stoneham, Edwina Sandys, Maggie, Allan and Warren Scherer, Andrew Seavill, Anthony Sebag-Montefiore, Sam and Angie Simmonds, J.P. Smail, Adam Snow, Scott Swedlin, Harriet Swift, Peter Thwaites, Henry and Mandy Tyrone, Andrea Vianini, Walter Wade Welsh, Alana Weston, Caroline Wheeler, Jack and Marjory Williams, Nick, Ginny, Zoe and Rod Williams, Francis Willey, and Paul Withers.

Nor as a writer does one automatically expect generosity from one's own profession, but few could have been kinder or more unstinting with encouragement, time and advice than William and Lilo Loyd, John and Lavinia Watson, John and Cilla Lloyd, Hugh and Maria Ines Dawnay, and Michael Hobday.

Although I enjoyed hospitality in polo clubs internationally, I am especially privileged to live near one of the loveliest polo clubs in the world, Cirencester Park. I would therefore like to thank the Earl and Countess Bathurst, The Hon. Mark and Rosie Vestey and, particularly, Douglas and Sally Brown, Ronnie and Diana Scott, Alison Roeves, Eika Clark, Claire Millington, Sarah Ridley, Ted Allen and all the other staff and members of the club for all their tolerance, friendliness and co-operation.

I must also stress that *Polo* is a work of fiction, and none of the characters is based on anyone, except when they are so famous or so central to the polo world – as Ronald Ferguson or Terry Hanlon are – that they appear as themselves. Any resemblance to any living persons or organizations is purely coincidental and wholly unintentional. The polo world, however, is full of legends and wonderful anecdotes, and if an incident or a line of dialogue is attributed to a character in the book, this character is on no way intended to portray the original subject of the anecdote or the speaker of the line of dialogue.

Polo took a long time to write. I am therefore deeply grateful to my publishers at Transworld: Paul Scherer, Mark Barty-King, Patrick Janson-Smith, and all their staff for their kindness and encouragement. I also had marvellous editorial help from Diane Pearson, Broo Doherty and Tom Hartman.

In addition I am immeasurably lucky to have Desmond Elliott not only as my literary agent, but as my best friend.

Polo is a very big book and consequently I owe a vast debt of gratitude to Annette Xuereb-Brennan, Annalise Dobson and Anna Gibbs-Kennet, who bravely deciphered my ghastly handwriting and typed great chunks of the manuscript; and also to Beryl Hill, Diane Peter, Jane Brooks, Chris Ingersent, Verity Tilling and Catherine Parkin, who all typed individual chapters. Thanks should also go to Tony Hoskins and Diane Stevens for driving me to numerous polo matches.

Nor could the book ever have been written without the stoical back-up of Ann Mills, whose obstacle race over the piles of books and papers to clean my study resembled participation in the Grand National rather than a polo match, or Jane Watts, my PA, who spent hours collating manuscripts, transcribing corrections and generally providing cheer and comfort when I despaired the book would ever be finished.

It is not easy living with a writer, who is totally absorbed when a book is going well and suicidal when it is going badly. Therefore the lion's share of my gratitude must go to my family, including my mongrel Barbara and her agent Gypsy (who met a very nice class of dog at polo matches) for their endless understanding and good cheer.

Finally, I would like to pay tribute to all the gallant ponies who take part in the game and to the grooms who spend such long hours looking after them.

CHARACTERS

BART ALDERTON	An American airplane billionaire. Polo patron of the Alderton Flyers.
GRACE ALDERTON	His second wife.
LUKE ALDERTON	Bart's son by his first wife. A professional polo player.
RED ALDERTON	Bart's and Grace's son. An unprofessional polo player.
BIBI ALDERTON	Bart's and Grace's daughter – a poor little rich girl.
THE HONOURABLE BASIL BADDINGHAM	English polo player, jack of all trades.
PHILIP BAGLEY	A vet.
DREW BENEDICT	English polo player and a dashing Captain in the Welsh Guards.
SUKEY BENEDICT	His wife. An English heiress and jolly good sort.
JAMES BENSON	A smooth private doctor.
MRS BODKIN	Rupert Campbell-Black's housekeeper.
MARGIE BRIDGWATER	An American lawyer.
JAIME CALAVESSI	An Argentine polo player.
RUPERT CAMPBELL-BLACK	Show-jumping ace, later MP for Chalford and Bisley and Minister for Sport.
TABITHA CAMPBELL-BLACK	His daughter.
BRIGADIER CANFORD	Chairman of the Pony Club and later of the British Polo Association.
DOMMIE AND SEB CARLISLE	English polo players – known as the Heavenly Twins.
WINSTON CHALMERS	A shit-hot American lawyer.
LUCY CHALMERS	His ravishing much younger wife.
DORIS CHOW	A Chinese hooker.

11

KEVIN COLEY	A petfood billionaire and polo patron of Doggie Dins.
ENID COLEY	His awful wife.
TRACE COLEY	His daughter.
CONCHITA	Bart Alderton's maid.
CAMERON COOK	Director of Programmes at Corinium Television.
JACKIE COSGRAVE	Hippy painter and art lecturer. Also proficient in the art of lechery.
BRAD DILLON	Team manager of the American polo team.
RICKY FRANCE-LYNCH	A nine-goal English polo player, nicknamed *El Orgulloso* – the proud one – by the other players.
CHESSIE FRANCE-LYNCH	His bored, but exquisitely beautiful, wife.
WILLIAM FRANCE-LYNCH	Their three-year-old son.
HERBERT FRANCE-LYNCH	Ricky's father. A tartar and former nine-goal polo player.
FRANCES	Ricky France-Lynch's head groom.
DINO FERRANTI	American show-jumper. Sales Director of Ferranti's Inc.
BOBBY FERRARO	An American polo player.
COMMANDER 'FATTY' HARRIS	Club Secretary of Rutshire Polo Club.
SIMPSON HASTINGS	A lethal American journalist.
PAUL HEDLEY	A member of the crack South Sussex Pony Club team.
BRIGADIER HUGHIE	Chairman of Rutshire Polo Club and the club bore.
MRS HUGHIE	His wife.
INOCENTA	A misnamed Argentine beauty.
JESUS	A nine-goal Chilean polo player given to telephonitis and treble-dating patrons.
JOEL	Ricky France-Lynch's farm manager.

BEATTIE JOHNSON	A seductive, unprincipled, Fleet Street columnist.
JOSÉ	A glamorous Mexican ringer.
VICTOR KAPUTNIK	A Hungarian pharmaceutical billionaire, patron of the Kaputnik Tigers.
SHARON KAPUTNIK	A nymphomaniac night-club hostess later married to Victor.
MARMADUKE KEMPTON	A tobacco baron.
AURIEL KINGHAM	A very famous American film star.
MISS LEDITSKY	Bart Alderton's secretary.
BILLY LLOYD-FOXE	Ex-England show-jumper and BBC Sports Presenter.
JANEY LLOYD-FOXE	A national newspaper columnist.
MISS LODSWORTH	Commissioner for Rutshire Girl Guides, hoary polo groupie and a rip-roaring busybody.
JUSTIN AND PATRICK LOMBARD	Brothers and members of Rutshire Pony Club polo team.
LOUISA	One of Ricky France-Lynch's grooms.
HAMISH MACLEOD	A television producer.
DAISY MACLEOD	His wife, a painter.
PERDITA MACLEOD	Daisy's daughter.
VIOLET MACLEOD	Hamish's and Daisy's daughter.
EDDIE MACLEOD	Hamish's and Daisy's son.
BRIDGET MACLEOD	Hamish's mother, an absolute bitch.
'DANCER' MAITLAND	A cockney rock star. Lead singer of Apocalypse.
LIONEL MANNERING	A goaty psychiatrist.
PHILIPPA MANNERING	His man-eating wife.
MANUEL	Bart Alderton's groom.
LANDO MEDICI	A bent polo patron.

ALEJANDRO MENDOZA	A ten-goal Argentine polo player, the greatest back in the world.
CLAUDIA MENDOZA	His wife.
LORENZO, LUIS AND PATRICIO MENDOZA	Alejandro's elder sons. All polo players.
CASSANDRA MURDOCH	Luke Alderton's girlfriend.
BEN AND CHARLES NAPIER	Eight-goal English polo players and brothers known as the Unheavenly Twins.
SHARK NELLIGAN	A nine-goal American polo player.
SETH NEWCOMBE	An ace American bone surgeon.
JUAN O'BRIEN	A ten-goal Argentine polo player. David Waterlane's hired assassin.
MIGUEL O'BRIEN	Juan's elder brother. Another ten-goal polo player and David Waterlane's second hired assassin.
TINY O'BRIEN	Juan's wife known variously as Sitting Bully and the Policia.
ROSIE O'GRADY	A comely nurse.
DECLAN O'HARA	An Irish television megastar.
MAUD O'HARA	His actress wife.
PATRICK O'HARA	His son.
TAGGIE O'HARA	His elder daughter. An angel.
CAITLIN O'HARA	His younger daughter.
MRS PAGET	A committee member of a London Adoption Society.
HAL PETERS	An American automobile billionaire and born-again Christian. Polo patron of Peters' Cheetahs.
MYRTLE PETERS	His wife.
RAIMUNDO	Alejandro's *peticero* and Master of the Horse.

SAMANTHA	Shark Nelligan's glamorous groom.
RANDY SHERWOOD	A Pony Club Adonis, member of the crack South Sussex polo team.
MERLIN SHERWOOD	Randy's younger brother, another Adonis, playing for South Sussex.
MRS SHERWOOD	Their glamorous mother.
ANGEL SOLIS DE GONZALES	An Argentine polo player and Falklands war pilot, whose brother Pedro was shot down and killed.
BETTY SOLIS DE GONZALES	Angel's aunt.
UMBERTO	Alejandro's groom.
HELMET WALLSTEIN	Chief Executive, Euro-Electronics.
GISELA WALLSTEIN	His wife.
SIR DAVID WATERLANE, BART	Owner of Rutminster Hall, patron of Rutshire Hall polo team.
CLEMENCY WATERLANE	His wandering wife.
MIKE WATERLANE	His son, also a polo player.
WENDY	Hamish Macleod's PA.

1

Queen Augusta's Boarding School for Girls has a splendid academic reputation, but on a sweltering afternoon in June one of its pupils was not paying attention to her English exam. While her classmates scribbled away, Perdita Macleod was drawing a polo pony. Outside, the scent of honeysuckle drifted in through the french windows, the cuckoo called from an acid-green poplar copse at the end of the lawn. Perdita, gazing out, thought longingly of the big tournament at Rutshire Polo Club where the semi-finals of the Rutshire Cup were being played. All her heroes were taking part: Ricky France-Lynch, Drew Benedict, Seb and Dommie Carlisle, the mighty Argentines, Miguel and Juan O'Brien, and, to crown it, the Prince of Wales.

Fretfully, Perdita glanced at her exam paper which began with a poem by Newbolt:

'And it's not for the sake of a ribboned coat,' she read,
*'Or the selfish hope of a season's fame,
But his Captain's hand on his shoulder smote –
Play up! Play up! and play the game!'*

'Are Newbolt's views of team spirit outdated?' asked the first question. Perdita took a fresh sheet of paper and wrote 'Yes' in her disdainful blue scrawl, 'the schoolboy in the poem must be an utter jerk and a poofter to boot to prefer his captain's hand on his shoulder to a season's fame and a ribboned coat.'

She put down her pen and thought how much she'd like a ribboned coat, one of those powder-blue blazers, braided with jade-green silk. Hamish, her ghastly stepfather, never gave her nearly a large enough allowance. Then she thought of fame. Perdita wanted to be a famous polo player more than anything else in the world. Being at a boarding school, she could not play in the termtime and had so far only achieved the first team of a suburban pony club of hopelessly low standard. When her family moved to their splendid new house in Rutshire in the autumn, however, she'd be able to have a pony and join a good club like Rutshire or Cirencester just over the border.

God, she was bored with this exam. She lit a cigarette, hoping it would encourage her form-mistress, who was adjudicating, to expel her. But, despite the furious wavings of paper by the swot on her right, her form-mistress didn't react. She was far too engrossed in Perdita's Jackie Collins, which she'd confiscated the day before and round which she'd now wrapped the dust jacket of Hilary Spurling's biography of Ivy Compton-Burnett.

Perdita took another drag and glanced at the next question: 'Do you find the poems of Thomas Hardy unduly preoccupied with death?'

It wasn't an afternoon for death. Perdita slid through the french windows across the sunlit lawn. Once out into Rutminster High Street, she tugged out the tails and undid the top buttons of her shirt, hitched up her navy-blue skirt a few inches and wrinkled her navy-blue socks. Conscious that men fancied schoolgirls, she left on her black and pink striped tie, but loosened her hair from its tortoiseshell clasp so it cascaded white-blond down her back, eliciting wolf-whistles from two workmen mending the road.

Perdita stuck her nose in the air; her sights were set higher than roadmenders. She was a big girl for fourteen, tall and broad in the shoulder, with pale, luminous skin and a full, sulky mouth. A long Greek nose and large, very wide-apart eyes, as dark as elderberries, gave her the look of a creature of fable, a unicorn that might vanish at any moment.

The main gates of Rutshire Polo Club were swarming with police because of the Prince's visit. Taking a short cut, Perdita clambered over a wall to the right, fighting her way through the undergrowth, scratching her legs on brambles and stinging nettles, until she reached the outskirts of the club. A vast emerald-green ground stretched ahead of her. On the right were the pony lines, where incredibly polished ponies, tied to iron rails in the shade of a row of horse chestnuts, were stamping, nudging, flattening ears at each other and aiming kicks at any fly eating their bellies.

God, they were beautiful, thought Perdita longingly, and curiously naked and vulnerable with their hogged manes and bound-up tails.

Beyond the pony lines stood the little clubhouse with its British, American and Argentine flags. Beyond that reared the stands and the pink-and-white tent for the sponsors' lunch before Sunday's final. Cars for today's semi-final already lined both sides of the field. Polo fever had reached an all-time high this season due to the Prince's impending wedding to Lady Diana Spencer.

Ringing Ground One and Ground Two behind the clubhouse were massive ancient trees, their wonderful variety of green occasionally interrupted by the rhubarb-pink of a copper beech. With their lower branches nibbled level by itinerant cows, they looked like an army of dowagers in midi-dresses. To the north, through this splendidly impressive backdrop, could be glimpsed the rose-pink roof of Rutminster Hall, a charming Queen Anne manor house, home of Sir David Waterlane, a polo fanatic who owned the surrounding nine hundred acres.

Perdita scratched her nettle stings. The moment she was famous, she decided darkly, as an orange and black striped helicopter landed on the greensward behind the clubhouse, she would go everywhere by air. Envy turned to excitement as the helicopter doors burst open and two young players, both in evening shirts and dinner jacket trousers, jumped out. Instantly Perdita recognized Seb and Dommie Carlisle, otherwise known as the Heavenly Twins. Vastly brave, blond and stocky like two golden bear cubs, it was said that any girl in the twins' lives, and there were legions, had to play second fiddle to polo and the other twin.

Next moment a small, fat, bald man with the tiny mean eyes and wide jaw of a bilious hippo, who was wearing an orange-and-black polo shirt and straining white breeches, charged up bellowing, 'For Christ's sake, hurry up. The umpires are waiting to go on. We should have started five minutes ago. Why are you so late?'

'We started late,' said Seb Carlisle, putting his arm round the fat man's shoulders. 'Dommie had this terrific redhead.'

'No, Seb had this terrific brunette,' came the muffled tones of Dommie Carlisle. Having whipped his shirt over his head to reveal a bronzed and incredibly muscular back, he nearly collided with the little fence round the clubhouse as he desperately tried to undo his cufflinks from the outside.

'Well, if I can be on time, I can't see why you bloody can't,' shouted the fat man, whom Perdita now identified as Victor Kaputnik. Originally Hungarian, Victor was a pharmaceutical billionaire and famous polo patron who employed the twins as professionals and whose helicopter and fuel had just transported them from London.

Polo players are rated by handicap, which ranges from minus two goals, which means an absolute beginner, to ten goals for the very top-class player. This has nothing to do with the number of goals they may score, but is an indication of their ability. Although only twenty, the twins already had four-goal handicaps. Much of their energy was spent ripping off Victor Kaputnik. Longingly, Perdita watched them sprint into the clubhouse.

Outside, people carrying glasses of Pimm's or beer were drifting towards the stands. Perdita was dying for a Coke and a sandwich, but she hadn't brought any money. She lit another fag to take the edge off her appetite. Looking at the scoreboard, she saw that today's first semi-final was a needle match between Victor's team, the Kaputnik Tigers, who were wearing orange-and-black shirts, and the Alderton Flyers, in duck-egg blue, who were all four sitting near a Lamborghini parked under a chestnut tree, zipping up their boots. There was The Hon. Basil Baddingham, a notorious roué with patent-leather hair and a laughing, swarthy face, who gave Perdita a terrific eyemeet, and Drew Benedict, a dashing blond captain in the Welsh Guards, with very regular features and eyes to match his blue shirt. And there, Perdita caught her breath, was her utter, utter God: Ricky France-Lynch, grimly fastening on his kneepads and refusing to exchange banter with the others. Ricky, who had the beautiful, lean, powerful body, the coarse, black curls and the sensitive, yet virile, features of a Russian ballet dancer, was the best-looking player in England, and had a nine-goal handicap. The most talented and dedicated player, he was also the most tricky.

Not for nothing had the Argentine players nicknamed him *El Orgulloso*, the proud one.

Standing slightly apart from the other three, swinging a polo stick furiously round and round, and champing to get into the fray, was their patron, Bart Alderton. An American airplane billionaire and the owner of television stations and newspapers, Bart was a still strikingly handsome man in his late forties, with thick grey hair, tinged with red like a wolf's pelt and a belligerent suntanned face. One of the most renowned and feared predators in the world markets, where he snapped up companies before they could even blink, Bart had houses and strings of polo ponies in five countries. Known as the artful tax dodger, he seldom paid tax in any of them.

Today Bart was determined to wipe the floor with his old rival Victor Kaputnik, whom Bart had taken a girl off many years ago, and who in revenge last year had appealed to the Monopolies Commission and blocked Bart's taking over a leading British airplane manufacturer.

Victor had brought down a new bimbo who he was keen to impress and was equally anxious to win.

Bart had Drew Benedict, Basil Baddingham and Ricky France-Lynch on his team for the English season. Bart liked Drew and Bas, who were amateurs, suitably deferential and prepared to socialize with him for the sake of having all their bills picked up. Ricky, who earned a long salary playing for Bart as a professional, was an entirely different proposition. Bart resented Ricky's arrogance and detachment. He was incommunicative before matches and disappeared home like smoke afterwards. Today he'd even refused to have a team meeting, arguing that there was no point when Bart never did anything he was told.

It further irritated Bart, as the teams walked down to the stretch of green behind the back line where the grooms were warming up their ponies for the first chukka, that all the girls gazed at Ricky, not at him.

The Alderton Flyers were shortly joined on the field by the Kaputnik Tigers, who consisted of Victor Kaputnik, who'd just taken out his teeth and had a slug of brandy to steady his nerves, the Carlisle twins, who erupted on to the field as joyous as otters, and a nine-goal Chilean player called Jesus, who lived in Victor's house and coached him

21

every day and with whom Victor had just had a blazing row, because the Chilean had run up a £5,000 telephone bill, ringing his girlfriend in Chile.

'Talk about Chile con carphone,' said Seb Carlisle, collapsing with laughter, as the two sides formed up on the halfway line.

A second later the umpire, in his striped shirt, had thrown the white ball in, sticks slashed and cracked, stirrups chinked and expletives flew as the players struggled to get it out, followed by a hailstorm of hooves on the dry ground as everyone hurtled towards goal.

Blocking a cut-shot from Jesus, Ricky took the ball back upfield, changing direction three times to fox the opposition. As he hurtled towards goal in a cloud of dust, the obvious pass was to Drew on his right. Looking towards Drew, Ricky flicked a lovely under-the-neck shot round to Bas, who slammed the ball between the posts.

'Bloody marvellous,' screamed Perdita, jumping up and down. The rest of the crowd clapped languidly.

As the Tigers edged ahead, however, it was plain to Perdita, who was watching every stroke, that Bart was a much better player than Victor, who despite the Chilean's coaching, just cantered about getting in everyone's way. Ricky, she realized, was much the best player, but his team-mate, the blue-eyed Drew Benedict, normally the most dependable of players, must have been celebrating too heavily last night. Missing pass after pass, he was having the greatest difficulty in controlling the Chilean's dazzling aggression.

2

Sitting in the stands with the sun behind them, sat the wives and girlfriends of the players, but all wearing dark glasses, so no one could see if they were bored. Bart Alderton's wife, Grace, a puritan mother in her forties, had breeding and old money and did a huge amount for charity. Marrying her after ditching his loyal and loving first wife had given Bart the connections and the extra cash to turn him into a billionaire. Described by Basil Baddingham as the only social grace Bart had acquired on the way up, Grace was wearing a Cartier watch, a string of pearls and a purple silk dress printed with pansies. Her dark hair was drawn back in a bun, and a straw hat with a purple silk band shaded her austere but beautiful face. Grace considered suntans both vulgar and ageing. In her soft white hands lay a red notebook in which she kept the score and recorded every botched shot and missed penalty during the game and the name of the Alderton Flyer responsible.

Next to Grace sat Sukey Elliott, who'd got engaged to Drew Benedict the day before – hence Drew's hangover. She seemed to remember every match played and goal scored by Drew in the last two seasons. A keen horsewoman herself, Sukey was the sort of girl who could get up and do the ponies if Drew had a hangover. Sukey had a neat, rather than an exciting, figure, and a horsey, not unattractive, face. Her light brown hair was taken off her forehead by a velvet bow. She was wearing a blue-spotted shirt-waister dress for the party Lady Waterlane always gave in her beautiful house across the park on the Thursday evening of Rutshire Cup Week.

Sukey would make the perfect army wife, always showing a charming deference to the wives of superiors, in this case Grace Alderton. But even more valuable in Drew's eyes, Sukey possessed a hefty private income which, after marriage, would enable him to resign his commission and play polo full time.

'We're thinking of having our wedding list at either the General Trading Company or Peter Jones or Harrods. Which would you suggest?' Sukey asked Grace.

On Sukey's left in the row below sat Victor's bimbo, a red-headed night-club hostess called Sharon, whose heavy eye make-up was running and whose uplifted breasts were already burning.

'Blimey it's 'ot,' she said to Sukey. 'Why do the 'orses keep bumpin' into each uvver?'

Grace would have ignored Sharon, regarding her as both common and part of the opposition. Sukey was kinder and enjoyed imparting information.

'It's called a ride-off,' she explained. 'When a ball is hit, it creates its own right of way, and the player who hit it is entitled to hit it again. But if another player puts his horse's shoulder in front of that first player's horse's shoulder, and a good horse will feel the pressure and push the other horse off the line, then the second player takes up the right of way. If you cross too closely in front of another rider – like someone shooting out in front of you on the motorway – it's a foul.'

'Ow, I see,' said Sharon, who plainly didn't. 'And why does the scoreboard say Victor's team's winning when there seem to have been more goals down the uvver end?'

'That's because they change ends after each goal,' said Sukey kindly, 'so no-one gets the benefit of the wind.'

'I could do with the benefit of some wind,' said Sharon, fanning herself with her programme. 'It's bleedin' 'ot.'

'It is,' agreed Sukey. 'Would you like to borrow my hat?'

Grace Alderton thought Sukey was a lovely young woman who would make a splendid wife for Drew. She did not feel at all the same about Chessie France-Lynch who rolled up halfway through the fourth chukka in a coloured vest, no bra, frayed denim bermudas and torn pink espadrilles, clutching a large glass of Pimm's and a copy of *Barchester Towers*. Chessie, who had bruised, scabious-blue eyes, and looked like a Botticelli angel who'd had too much nectar at lunchtime, made no secret of the fact that she found polo irredeemably boring. Being stuck at home with a three-year-old son, William, polishing silver cups and taking burnt meat out of the oven, because Ricky hadn't got back from a match or was coping with some crisis in the yard, was not Chessie's idea of marriage.

'You've missed an exciting match, Francesca,' said Grace pointedly.

'I'd have been on time,' grumbled Chessie, 'if that goon in the bar didn't take half an hour to make a Pimm's.'

'Better go and help out,' said Commander Harris, the club's secretary, known as 'Fatty', waddling off to the bar.

'To help himself to another drink, the disgusting old soak,' said Chessie. 'Congratulations,' she went on, sitting down next to Sukey. 'When are you getting married?'

'In September, so that Drew can finish the polo season.'

'When did he propose?'

'On Sunday. It was so sweet. He asked me to look after his signet ring before the match, then put it on my wedding-ring finger, and said would I, and now he's bought me this heavenly ring.'

'Nice,' said Chessie, admiring the large but conventional diamond and sapphires. 'Drew must have had to flog at least one of Bart's ponies to pay for that.'

Grace's red lips tightened, and even more so when the players, who always seemed to be playing on some distant part of the field, for once surged over to the four-inch-high wooden boards (as the sidelines are known in polo) near the stands. Ignoring Ricky's yells to leave the ball, Bart barged in, missed an easy shot and enabled Seb Carlisle to whip the ball away to Dommie, his twin, who took it down the field and scored.

'When I say fucking leave it, Bart, for fuck's sake leave it,' Ricky's bellow of exasperation rang round the field, eliciting a furious entry in Grace's red book and an extremely beady glance from Miss Lodsworth, a local bossy boots and one of the whiskery old trouts always present at polo matches.

'It was my ball,' shouted Bart. 'I paid for this fucking team, and I'm going to hit the goddam ball . . . '

To lighten the atmosphere, as the players cantered back to change ponies after the fourth chukka, Sukey warmly informed Chessie that Ricky had already scored two splendid goals.

'Good,' said Chessie lightly. 'We might not have black gloom all the way home for a change. He still won't talk, mind you. Even if he wins, he's too hyped up to say anything.'

Sukey's total recap of the match was mercifully cut short by the arrival of one of Bas Baddingham's gorgeous mistresses, a long-haired blonde called Ritz Maclaren. She and Chessie proceeded to gossip noisily about their friends until Grace hushed them reprovingly and asked Chessie what she intended to wear for Lady Waterlane's party that evening.

'What I've got on,' said Chessie. 'Until Ricky's father relents and gives us some cash, or Ricky gets his polo act together, I can't see myself ever affording a new dress. It's the ponies that get new shoes in our house' – she waved a torn espadrille hanging on the end of a dusty foot at Grace – 'not me.'

'It's not very respectful to Lady Waterlane not to change,' reproved Grace. To which Chessie replied that Clemency Waterlane would be so busy wrapped round Juan O'Brien, her husband's Argentine pro, that she would hardly notice.

'I can't think why David Waterlane doesn't boot Clemency out,' said Ritz Maclaren, who was calmly removing her tights.

'Terrified Juan would go as well,' said Chessie. 'David told Ricky there was no problem getting another wife, but he'd never find another hired assassin as good as Juan.'

'Oh, good shot, Ricky,' cried Sukey. 'Do watch, Chessie; your husband's playing so well.'

As the bell went to end the fifth chukka, Perdita raced down to the pony lines to catch a glimpse of Matilda, Ricky France-Lynch's legendary blue roan, whom he always saved for the last chukka.

Ponies that had played in the fifth chukka, which, except for Victor's, had had every ounce of strength pushed out of them, were coming off the field, drenched in sweat, nostrils blood-red as poppies, veins standing up like a network of snakes. Bart's horse, having been yanked around, was pouring blood from a cut mouth, sending scarlet froth flying everywhere.

Grooms instantly went into a frenzy of activity, untacking each pony, sponging it down, throwing water over its head, taking down its tail. Other grooms were loading already dried-off ponies from earlier chukkas into lorries for the journey home, while still others were leading them round, or just holding them as they waited to go on, quivering with pitch-fright, while their riders towelled off the sweat and discussed tactics for the last chukka.

'That Ricky France-Lynch's got a wonderful eye,' said the security man who was looking after the Prince's Jack Russell.

He's got wonderful eyes, thought Perdita wistfully. Deep-set, watchful, dark green as bay leaves and now, as they lighted on Matilda, his favourite pony, amazingly softened.

Before a game Matilda got so excited that her groom could hardly hold her. Snorting, neighing shrilly, kicking up the dust with stamping feet, watching the action with pricked ears, her dark eyes searched everywhere for Ricky. As he walked over, she gave a great deep whicker of joy. They had hardly been separated a day since she was a foal. She was the fastest pony he'd ever ridden, turned at the gallop, and once, when she'd bucked him off in a fit of high spirits, had raced after the rider who had the ball and blocked the shot. There wasn't a player in the world who didn't covet Matilda. And now Ricky was going to need all her skills: the Alderton Flyers were three down.

The last chukka was decidedly stormy. Ricky scored two goals, then Drew and Bas one each, putting the Flyers ahead. Then Bart, frantic he was the only member of the team without a goal, missed an easy shot and took his whip to his little brown pony.

'It was your bloody fault, not the pony's,' howled Ricky, to the edification of the entire stand, 'and for Christ's sake get back.'

Evading Drew's clutches yet again, Jesus, the Chilean, thundered towards goal. In a mood of altruism and probably seeing a chance to be forgiven for the £5,000 telephone bill, he put the ball just in front of Victor, his patron, who, connecting for the first time in the match, tipped it between the posts and levelled the score to cheers and whoops from all round the ground. Victor immediately waved his stick exuberantly at his red-headed night-club hostess, who was just thinking how much better looking every man in the field was than Victor.

'Why's Victor's 'orse wearing so many straps? It looks like a bondage victim,' she asked Sukey.

'The saddle has to hold if you're going to lean out of it,' explained Sukey patiently.

'Ride hard, hit hard, and keep your temper,' said Brigadier Hughie, the club chairman and bore who'd just arrived.

Contrary to this advice, Bart, incensed that Victor had scored, proceeded to ride the fat little Hungarian off the ball at such a dangerous angle that Bart was promptly fouled and the Tigers awarded a forty-yard penalty. Bart then swore so hard at the umpire that the penalty was upped to thirty yards, which Jesus had no difficulty driving between the posts, putting the Tigers ahead again.

27

In the closing, desperately fought seconds of the game Jesus got the ball and set off for goal, his bay mare's hooves rattling like a firing squad on the dry ground. Ricky, on Matilda, belted after him and had caught up when the bay mare stumbled. As the bell went Matilda cannoned into her and ponies and riders crashed to the ground in front of the stands to the horrified gasps of the crowd. As the dust cleared, Ricky and Jesus could be seen to have got to their feet. The Chilean's bay mare got up more slowly and, after an irritated shake, set off at a gallop for the pony lines. Matilda, however, made several abortive attempts and, when she finally lurched up, her off fore was hanging horribly.

Oblivious of the whiskery old trout Miss Lodsworth complaining noisily about the disgusting cruelty of the game, Perdita watched helplessly, tears streaming down her face. On came the vet's van; the crowd fell silent. As screens were put round the pony, Fatty Harris, the club secretary, somewhat unsteadily joined the little group. Victorious but grim-faced, with Dommie Carlisle unashamedly wiping his eyes, the Kaputnik Tigers rode back to the pony lines where the grooms of the great Argentines, Juan and Miguel O'Brien, and their patron, Sir David Waterlane, were warming up ponies for the next match in which they were playing with the Prince of Wales.

Behind the screen, however, an argument was raging.

'You're not putting Mattie down,' hissed Ricky. 'If it's a cannon bone, we can slap her into plaster. I want her X-rayed.'

'She'll be no use for polo,' protested the vet.

'Maybe not, but I'm bloody well going to breed from her. It's all right, lovie,' Ricky's voice softened as he stroked the trembling mare.

'Give her a shot of Buscopan,' advised Fatty Harris.

'Don't be fucking stupid,' snapped Ricky. 'If you kill the pain, she'll tread on it and make it worse.'

'Got to get her off the field, Ricky,' said Fatty fussily, his breath stale from too many lunchtime whiskies. 'Prince's match is due to start in ten minutes. Can't hold it up.'

Utterly indifferent to the fact that in the end he held up the Prince's match for half an hour, and that most of the spectators and some of the players regarded him as appallingly callous for not putting Matilda out of her agony, Ricky, helped by Drew and Bas, gently coaxed the desperately hobbling mare into a driven-up horse box. Ricky would stay inside with her, while one of his grooms drove them the eight miles home, to where the vet would bring his X-ray equipment.

Green beneath his suntan, shaking violently and pouring with sweat, Ricky spoke briefly to his wife Chessie when she came over and hugged him. Chessie had often been jealous of Matilda in the past; now she could only pity Ricky's anguish.

'I'm desperately sorry, darling. When'll you be back?'

'Probably not at all. I'll ring you.'

'But what about Lady Waterlane's reception?' asked an outraged Bart, who had just joined them. 'You can't miss that.'

Ricky looked at Bart uncomprehendingly.

'B-b-bugger Lady Waterlane,' he said coldly.

Ricky had just climbed in beside the mare when a ripple of excitement ran through the crowd as a dark man in a cherry-red polo shirt pulled up his pony beside the lorry. His hazel eyes were on a level with Ricky's as he called out: 'Desperately sorry, Ricky. Ghastly thing to happen. Always liked Matilda – great character. Hope you manage to save her.'

Touched by the expression of genuine sympathy on the Prince's face, Ricky forgot to bow.

'Thank you, sir.'

Bart and Grace, who'd also joined him on the field, shot forward expectantly, avid to be presented, but it was too late.

Shouting back to Ricky to let him know the result of the X-ray, the Prince had moved off, hitting a ball ahead of him, cantering across the pitch and out of Bart's life.

'Why the hell didn't you introduce us?'

'It seemed irrelevant.'

As they raised the ramp of the horse box and shot the bolts, Bas and Drew shook their heads. They knew how devastated Ricky was, but he was pushing his luck.

Aubergine with rage, Bart turned to Chessie.

'What the fuck does your husband think he's playing at?'

'Polo,' said Chessie bitterly. 'Absolutely nothing else.'

29

3

Bart's resentment against Ricky was in no way abated when the Prince regretfully decided he wouldn't have time to look in at Lady Waterlane's party because his match had been delayed. Lady Waterlane, who didn't find Latins at all lousy lovers, was so preoccupied with Juan O'Brien, her husband's Argentine professional, that she hardly noticed the Prince's absence.

A rather too relaxed hostess, besides feeding and watering her guests and giving them free access to the bedrooms where the four-posters hadn't been made for weeks, Lady Waterlane expected people to get on with it.

Totally confident in the business world, Bart felt an outsider among the raffish and sometimes aristocratic members of the polo community who knew each other so well. He had expected Ricky to introduce him to everyone. Chessie, furious at having forked out for a baby-sitter and determined to stay for the party, could easily have fulfilled this function, but Bart had been so rude to her about Ricky's arrogance, and the fact that she was dressed like a tramp, that she had stalked off to comfort Jesus the Chilean who was mortified his pony had caused Matilda's fall.

Bart, however, was not left alone for long. June and July (when the mid-season's handicaps were announced) were the months when dissatisfied patrons started looking round and wondering which players they would hire to make up their teams for next year.

Apart from the occasional amateur, like Bas and Drew, there are two kinds of players in polo – the patrons who have the money and the professionals who earn money playing for them. Professional players are only as good as their last three games; contracts rarely extend beyond a season. There is therefore collossal pressure to perform well. But, with one's future at stake, diplomacy is almost more important than performance. Patrons not only like to win, but also to be taken to parties and treated as one of the boys.

During the season everyone had noticed the *froideur* between Ricky and Bart. Miguel O'Brien, known as the Godfather because he controlled the other Argentine players like the Mafia, was also grimly aware that with his handsome brother Juan constantly wrapped round Clemency Waterlane, David Waterlane might not be overkeen to employ them to play for Rutminster Hall next year. David was tricky and also very mean. Looking round the beautiful drawing room, Miguel's conniving, dark little eyes noticed the damp patches on the faded yellow wallpaper and the tattered silk chaircovers, and saw that David's ancestors on the walls could hardly see out through the layers of grime. He knew, too, that David owed thousands to Ladbroke's and the taxman. Thinking how agreeable it would be next year to be sponsored by Bart's millions, Miguel started chatting him up.

'You ride very well for the leetle time you 'ave learn,' purred Miguel. 'Wiz zee right coaching you could be miles bettair, but success in polo is eighty per cent zee good 'orses.'

He hoped Bart and his beautiful wife would come and stay at his *estancia* in Argentina and try out some of the family's superb ponies. Bart was flattered. Imagine the kudos of having the great O'Brien brothers playing on his team both in England and Palm Beach.

The Napier brothers, Ben and Charles, known as the Unheavenly Twins because of their cadaverous appearance, who'd been beaten by the O'Briens, David Waterlane and the Prince in the second match, were also at the party. Cruel to their horses and even crueller to their patron, a petfood billionaire who they'd ripped off so unmercifully that he was threatening to quit polo, the Napiers also tried to make their number with Bart during the evening. But they were pre-empted by Seb and Dommie Carlisle, who, having got drunk and appropriated Perdita after the match, came rushing up to Bart: 'Oh, Mr Alderton, could you please take us into a corner and chat us up like mad, so Victor will get appallingly jealous and offer us three times as much next year?'

Bart was amused. The twins, he decided, would be far more fun to play with than Ricky or the Napiers.

Drew Benedict couldn't stay long at the party, as he had to dine with Sukey's parents, his future in-laws, but, ever

31

diplomatic, he found time to talk to Bart, his patron, telling him how well he had played and how the team would never have reached the semi-finals without him.

'It's disappointing we didn't make the finals, but a good thing from my point of view,' added Drew philosophically. 'I'm supposed to be guarding some nuclear weapons this weekend, and I'd have had difficulty getting leave on Sunday.'

Having mugged up on the *Wall Street Journal* and the *Financial Times* every day, Drew was also able to comment on the progress of Bart's latest take-over. Admiring Drew's well-worn but beautifully cut suit, his striped shirt and blue silk tie, and his dependable handsome face with the turned-down blue eyes and juttingly determined jaw, Bart thought that he was quite the best kind of Englishman – a sort of butch Leslie Howard. Briefly he touched Drew's pin-striped arm with the back of his hand, the nearest he ever got to intimacy with men.

'The Army's loss'll be Sukey's gain,' he said roughly. 'She's a very lucky young woman.'

Drew grinned. 'London's fortune-hunters are out to lynch me.'

Having taught himself Spanish because he realized what an advantage it would be understanding what the Argentines were gabbling to each other on and off the field, Drew had also overheard Miguel talking to Juan. Before he left, he took Chessie on to the terrace. The setting sun was turning the house a warm peach and gilded the lake around which cows were lying down. Catmint brushed against Chessie's legs as Drew adjusted the shoulder-strap of her coloured vest which had flopped down her arm.

'As your husband's best friend . . .'

' . . . You want me to stop flirting with Jesus!'

'That too,' said Drew. 'Look I've just overheard that oily sod Miguel telling Juan that Bart's fed up with Ricky and things look rosy for next year. Ricky should be here guarding his patch.'

'Well, he's not,' snapped Chessie. 'When did a party ever come before a pony? He's just rung up to say they've X-rayed Matilda's leg and it's a cannon bone, so they're going to slap it in plaster and then sling her up.'

32

'Thank Christ, so he'll be here soon.'

'Some hope,' said Chessie bitterly. 'He prefers to stay with Mattie. He's already collected Will from the baby-sitter. He's so bloody arrogant, he'll never dance to Bart's tune.'

'He who pays for the Piper Heidsieck calls the tune,' said Drew, deheading a rose.

'Drew-hoo, Drew-hoo,' Sukey was calling from the french windows.

'Shades of the prison-house begin to close,' mocked Chessie.

'Don't be subversive,' said Drew, kissing her on the cheek. 'You'd better chat up Bart instead of Jesus, or your husband's on a collision course.'

The party roared on. Coronation chicken was served, although Seb Carlisle was heard to remark that it was debatable whose coronation it was celebrating. A few bread rolls were thrown. Dommie Carlisle added to the rising damp by filling a condom with water and spraying it round the drawing room. All the players' dogs, which followed them everywhere, lay around panting, finishing up the food and being tripped over.

In a dark corner Juan O'Brien, a beautiful animal with big, brown eyes, long, black curls and a vast, slightly bruised, lower lip, was gazing limpidly at Clemency Waterlane: 'You haf the most wonderful eyes in the world. My best mare in Argentina ees due to foal soon. Eef it's a filly, I shall call her Clarissa after you.'

'Actually my name's Clemency,' said Lady Waterlane, 'but it's awfully sweet of you, Juan.'

Victor Kaputnik, the pharmaceutical billionaire, bald pate gleaming in the candlelight, black chest-hair spilling out of his unbuttoned shirt, was boasting in his thick Hungarian accent about his prowess as a businessman.

'I have discovered a cure for the common cold,' he was telling Fatty Harris, the club secretary.

'I wish he'd find a cure for the common little man,' muttered Seb Carlisle. 'He's an absolute pill.'

'No, he makes pills,' giggled Dommie, shooting a jet of water into the round red face of Fatty Harris who was too drunk to realize where it had come from.

Bart's mood was not improving. Once a heavy drinker, he had cut out booze almost entirely, to improve his polo, but now really longed for a huge Scotch. Desperately dehydrated after the game, he had already drunk two bottles of Perrier. He was livid they'd lost the match, livid that Victor had scored that goal, which he was boasting to everyone about, livid that Victor had got into the final with the Prince, and might well appear photographed with the Prince and Lady Diana on the front of Monday's *Times*, and livid that Victor was now dancing with his red-headed night-club hostess, his six o'clock shadow grating the sunburnt cleavage of her splendid breasts.

And there was Clemency Waterlane wrapped round Juan, and that ravishing schoolgirl bopping away with Dommie and Seb. Bart knew that Grace was a wonderful wife, but he had never forgiven her for being from a better class than him, and was fed up with her criticizing his polo, pointing out that if he hadn't bumped Victor so hard today Jesus would never have been awarded that penalty. Now she was being charming to that old bore Brigadier Hughie, and his wife.

'I've broken m'right leg twice, m'left leg once, my right shoulder three times, cracked three ribs and dislocated m'thumb and m'elbow,' droned on Hughie.

'Polo players are very brave people,' said Mrs Hughie, who looked like an eager warthog.

'Brave enough to face the Inland Revenue every year,' drawled Chessie on her way to the bar.

Ignoring Chessie, Grace listened politely, thinking how dirty Clemency Waterlane's house was and how much better she, Grace, could have arranged the flowers. Then, noticing Bart pouring himself a huge Scotch, she left Mrs Hughie in midflow, as she strode across the room.

'Baby, we weren't going to drink. Look, I'm exhausted. Shall we go?'

Bart said he wasn't tired, and still had some business to discuss with Miguel. Why didn't the pilot fly Grace home and come back for him in an hour.

Chessie France-Lynch, rather drunk, sat in the depths of a sofa, letting conversations drift over her. From a bench on the terrace, she heard an outraged squawk as

Victor's pudgy hand found the soft flesh between Sharon's stockings and her suspender belt.

'Hey, d'you fink I'm common or somefink, Victor? Tits first, please!'

In front of the fireplace still full of ash from a fire last March, four young bloods were discussing next week's tournament in Cheshire.

'Seb and Dommie are definitely coming and they're mounted.'

'Who's going to mount Drew?'

'Simon can't, because he's mounting Henry. Bas is mounting himself.'

'Well, Bas will have to mount Drew too then.'

Nor did the young men deflect in the slightest from their conversation when David Waterlane, having found Juan mounting his beautiful wife in an upstairs four-poster, was forced to expel the frantically protesting Argentine from the house.

Clemency was sniffing in an armchair and receiving a pep talk from Brigadier Hughie, who felt that, as chairman of the club, he should provide moral guidance. 'D'you really feel, Clemency, m'dear, that it's worth leaving a tolerant husband, three lovely children and nine hundred acres for the sake of six inches of angry gristle?'

Clemency sniffed and said yes she did, that David could be very intolerant, and Juan's gristle wasn't angry and was considerably more than six inches.

Chessie found herself giggling so much that she had to leave the room and went slap into Bart Alderton, who was clutching another large Scotch. Chessie updated him on the Juan-Clemency saga.

'She's crazy,' went on Chessie. 'David puts up with murder, even if he is stingy, and he *is* loaded.'

'Unlike your spouse,' said Bart pointedly.

'Ghastly word,' said Chessie. 'And I hear you're not espousing his cause next year.'

Bart took her arm and frogmarched her outside on to the long grass beyond the lawn, away from a scuffling Victor and Sharon.

'Who told you that?' he said sharply.

'Miguel was overheard boasting to Juan. I wish you the luck of them. Miguel will fleece you and Juan will no doubt offer Grace a good deal more than six inches. At least Ricky's honest and hasn't jumped on Grace.'

'Why's he so broke?' snarled Bart. 'He's paid enough.'

Chessie put a hand on a stone lion. Though the sun was long set, it was still warm. The scent from a clump of philadelphus was almost overwhelming.

'Stymied by a massive overdraft,' she said. 'He's spent so much on the yard and ponies and a stick-and-ball field. And he's no good at selling ponies on at a wicked profit like some people. He gets too fond of them, and always justifies not selling them by claiming they'll go for three times as much next year, when he's put more work into them. His father used to help him, but they fell out.'

'Can't say I blame his Daddy,' said Bart heavily. '*El Orgulloso*, indeed.'

'Actually Ricky's very shy and introverted,' protested Chessie. 'He's Aquarius you know – aloof glamour, but has difficulty expressing himself.'

'What sign d'you think I was born under?' asked Bart.

Chessie laughed. 'A pound sign, I should think. I want another drink.'

Shrieks were coming from the swimming-pool as people, fully dressed, jumped into the icy water, which David Waterlane had been too mean to turn up until that morning.

Inside, Bart poured a glass of wine for Chessie and more whisky for himself.

'I'm not sponsoring Ricky next season,' he said brutally. 'I'm crazy about my polo, but not with him. It's costing me a million dollars a year, none of it disposable. Victor scores a goal today and all I get is abuse.'

'He droppeth as the gentle rain from heaven,' said Chessie. Seeing her face was quite expressionless, Bart said, 'He neglects you too.'

'He prefers polo to sex,' said Chessie flatly, 'but what player doesn't?'

'I don't,' said Bart roughly, stroking her slender brown arm with the back of his hand. 'I wouldn't neglect anything as precious as you.'

'Put me in a packing chest with the rest of your Renoirs, would you?' taunted Chessie.

The Waterlanes' ancient gramophone was now playing 'Anything Goes'. Bart took Chessie off to dance.

'Where's Grace?' murmured Chessie, deciding that Bart was rather excitingly built.

'Gone home, she was pooped.'

'Leaving you on the loose? That's unwise.'

'Unwise of Ricky and Grace,' said Bart, drawing her close.

For the first time he looked her straight in the eye and kept on looking. Her skin was translucent, her hair tousled, her wanton sleepy eyes as violet as the shadows beneath them.

'You could strip a man's aftershave off with a look like that,' said Bart.

'Wish I could strip off Victor's chest-hair. At least he has the manners to dance with his hostess,' said Chessie drily as Sharon and Victor quickstepped past.

Gathered round a billiard table in the next room, Jesus, who'd just spent half an hour on David Waterlane's telephone ringing Chile, Seb, Dommie and Perdita, who still hadn't returned to her boarding school, were demonstrating polo plays with sugar lumps.

'At the hit-in you should have tapped the ball to Seb and he'd have hit it to me,' said Dommie, moving a sugar lump. 'I was here.'

'No, you was 'ere,' said Jesus, moving it to the right.

'And you should have been here,' said Perdita, moving it back to the left.

'You seem to know more about it than us,' said Dommie, squeezing her waist.

'I ought to go,' said Perdita ruefully. 'They lock the fire escape at midnight. We've got biology first thing tomorrow, and I haven't revised at all.'

'If you're weak on the subject of human reproduction,' said Seb, starting to plait her long, blond mane, 'Dommie and I could give you a quick crash course. There are plenty of beds upstairs. How old are you?'

'Fourteen,' said Perdita.

'Gaol bait as far as we're concerned,' sighed Dommie. 'Come back in two years' time. What are you going to do when you grow up?'

'Play polo.'

'You'd do better as a stockbroker or a soccer player,' said Seb. 'There's no money in polo.'

'I know,' said Perdita, 'but at least I'd rub up against all the richest, most powerful men in the world.'

'Like Mrs France-Lynch,' said Dommie, watching Chessie rotating her flat, denimed belly against Bart's crotch. 'That looks like trouble to me.'

'Bloody 'ell,' said Jesus ruefully. If he hadn't spent so long on the telephone, he might have scored there. He toyed with the idea of cutting in, then decided he might want to play for Bart one day.

Aware that they were being watched, Bart and Chessie retreated to David Waterlane's study. Tearing himself away from the photographs of ponies and matches on the wall, Bart discovered Chessie looking down her vest examining her breasts.

'Whaddyer doing?'

'They say everything you touch turns to gold. I wondered if I had.'

'Let me try again.' Bart slid his hands inside her vest. 'Christ, you're sexy.'

They were interrupted by Mrs Hughie, who, like the Brigadier, rather ineffectually tried to act as a custodian of morals at polo parties, and was now trying to foist strong black coffee on unwilling guests.

'Hello, Chessie,' she said, averting her eyes as Chessie re-inserted her left breast. 'Jolly bad luck about Matilda. Ricky's been playing so superbly too. I was trying to remember, what's his handicap?'

'His personality,' said Bart bleakly.

'Oh, I wouldn't say that.' Mrs Hughie gave a nervous laugh as she handed Chessie a cup.

'D'you take sugar?'

Chessie looked straight at Bart.

'Only in Daddies,' she said softly.

'I actually came to find you,' said Mrs Hughie hastily, as the whoops increased next door. 'I'm awfully fond of Seb and Dommie, but they have had a bit too much to drink, and they're with a dear little soul called Perdita Macleod, who's boarding at Queen Augusta's. Could you possibly drop her off on your way home, Chessie?'

'Thereby killing two birds who might otherwise get stoned,' said Chessie.

Bart was absolutely furious, but as she and Perdita left the floodlit house for the moonlit night, Chessie reflected that Bart would be more likely to renew Ricky's contract if she held out.

Storming up Ricky's drive, twenty minutes later, twitching with desire and frustration, she was alarmed to find the house in darkness. Even worse, the front door was open and no-one was at home.

Panic turned to rage, however, when she discovered Ricky still in his breeches and blue polo shirt, fast asleep in the stable next to Matilda's. Will, also asleep, lay in his arms. They were surrounded by two Labradors, a whippet, the stable cat, assorted plastic guns and dinky toys and a copy of *Thomas the Tank Engine*. The Labradors blinked sleepily and thumped their tails. Matilda, hanging from her sling, looked up watchfully. In Chessie she recognized a rival. But Ricky and Will didn't stir.

4

Chessie woke at noon feeling hungover and guilty. She shouldn't have got tight or off so publicly with Bart. Gossip spread round the polo community like napalm. If Ricky didn't know by now, his grooms certainly would. Her fears were confirmed when Will wandered in later from playgroup, bearing paintings to be admired, stories to be read, and his hands crammed full of yellow roses pulled off by the head for her.

Stocky as a Welsh cob, Will had a round pink face and dark brown slanting eyes with long curly lashes tipping the blond fringe of his pudding-basin hair. No child could be more edible, even allowing for a mother's bias. How could she have dallied with Bart and jeopardized this, thought Chessie, hugging him fiercely.

'Did you bring me a present?' demanded Will.

'I didn't go anywhere I could get you one,' said Chessie. 'Who brought you home from playgroup?'

'Fuckies,' said Will, who couldn't pronounce Frances, the head groom's name. 'Fuckies say Mummy got pissed up last night.'

'Mummy did not.'

'Mattie got sore leggie,' went on Will.

'As if I didn't know,' snapped Chessie.

'Want some crisps.'

'Ask Daddy.' Chessie snuggled down in bed.

'Daddy gone to London.'

'Don't be ridiculous. Daddy loathes London.'

Ricky avoided London at all costs. Only his passion for Chessie after they'd first met had dragged him up to her flat in the Cadogans, and then he'd always got lost. As Will pottered off crispwards, Chessie thought about Bart. He reminded her of all those rich, ruthless, cynical, invariably married men whom she'd met and had affairs with when she used to cook directors' lunches in the City. One of them had been about to set her up in her own restaurant in the Fulham Road, called Francesca's, when she had met Ricky.

It had been at her rich grandparents' golden wedding. With an eye to inheriting loot rather than a sense of duty, Chessie had reluctantly driven down from London expecting to be bored rigid. Instead she found that her plain, horsey cousin Harriet, who at twenty-five had never had a boyfriend, had turned up looking almost pretty and bursting out of her brown velvet dress with pride because she had Ricky in tow. Despite having absolutely no small talk and the trapped ferocity of a tiger whipped into doing tricks at the circus, he was the most attractive man Chessie had ever seen. It took her exactly fifteen minutes to take him off her poor cousin Harriet, gazing sleepily at him across the gold candles throughout dinner, then dancing all night with him. The chuntering of outraged relations was so loud, no-one could hear the cracking of poor Harriet's heart.

Offhand with people to cover up his feelings, unused to giving or receiving affection, Ricky had not had an easy life. The France-Lynches had farmed land in Rutshire for generations. Horse-mad, their passion for hunting had been exceeded at the turn of the century by a passion for polo. Herbert, Ricky's father, the greatest polo player of his day and a confirmed bachelor, had suddenly at fifty-five fallen madly in love with a twenty-year-old beauty. Sadly she died giving birth to Ricky, leaving her arrogant, crotchety, heartbroken husband to bring up the boy in the huge, draughty Georgian house, which was called Robinsgrove, because the robins in the woods around were supposed to sing more sweetly there than anywhere else on earth. Ricky needed that comfort. Determined that his son should follow in his footsteps, Herbert was appalled to discover that the boy was left-handed. This is not allowed in polo. Consequently Herbert spent the next years forcing Ricky to do everything right-handed to the extent of tying his left arm to his side for hours on end. As a result Ricky developed a bad stammer, for which he was terribly teased at school.

Although Herbert adored the boy, he couldn't show it. Only by playing better polo could Ricky win his father's approval. Herbert went to every match, yelling at Ricky in the pony lines. The cheers were louder off the field than on when Ricky started yelling back. Herbert's vigilance was rewarded. At just twenty-three, when he met Chessie, Ricky's handicap was six and he had already played for England.

To Chessie he was unlike anyone she had ever met. In the middle seventies, when men were getting in touch with their feelings and letting everything hang out, Ricky gave nothing away. A tense uncompromising loner, lack of love in his childhood had made him so unaware of his charms that he couldn't imagine anyone minding being deprived of them.

Chessie had had to make all the running. Smitten by her, Ricky was terrified to feel so out of control and went into retreat. He was always away playing in matches or searching for new horses. He never rang because he was shy about his stammer, and he knew it would wreck his polo career to marry when he needed all his concentration to make the break. Gradually, persistently, Chessie broke down his resistance.

Herbert had been violently opposed to the marriage, but when the tetchy old eccentric met Chessie he was as bowled over as his son, even to the extent of moving out of Robinsgrove, which had grooms' flats, stabling for twenty horses and four hundred acres of field and woodland, and moving into the Dower House two miles away, to make way for her and Ricky. At first the marriage was happy.

41

Herbert went to matches with Chessie and enjoyed her cooking at least once a week, and when Chessie produced an heir two years later the old man was happier than he'd ever been.

But although Herbert had initially settled £200,000 on Ricky, Chessie, used to having her bills picked up and being showered with presents by besotted businessmen, soon went through it. The land, which included a large garden, a tennis court and a swimming-pool, needed maintaining and the house, with its vast rooms, needed a gas pipe direct from the North Sea to keep it warm.

Also Ricky's dedication, aloofness and incredible courage on the field, which had attracted Chessie madly in the beginning, were not qualities she needed in a husband. Ricky adored Chessie, but he was far too locked into polo, and after the first two years too broke, to provide her with the constant approval, attention and material possessions she craved.

Resentful that Ricky wouldn't pay for a nanny, Chessie was always palming Will off on his grooms. Most top-class players employ one groom to three ponies; Ricky's grooms had to look after five, even six, but they never minded. They all adored Ricky who, beneath his brusqueness, was fair, kind and worked harder than anyone else, and they were proud to work for such a spell-binding player.

Chessie, a constant stranger to the truth, had also failed to tell Bart at the Waterlanes' party that she had caused Ricky's rift with his father. Gradually Herbert had recognized Chessie for what she was: selfish, manipulative, lotus-eating, narcissistic, unreliable and hopelessly spoilt. One rule in the France-Lynch family was that animals were fed before humans. Horrified one day when Ricky was away that the dogs had had no dinner by ten at night and the rabbit's hutch hadn't been cleaned out for days, Herbert had bawled Chessie out. Totally unable to take criticism, Chessie complained to Ricky when he came home, wildly exaggerating Herbert's accusations, triggering off such a row between father and son that Herbert not only stopped the half-million he was about to settle on Ricky to avoid death duties, but cut Ricky out of his will.

Although both men longed to make it up, they were too proud. Ricky, whose family had always been the patrons, was forced to turn professional. Incapable of the tact needed to massage the egos of businessmen, desperately missing Herbert's counsel, appallingly strapped for cash – Bart's £25,000 for a season went nowhere when you were dealing with horses – Ricky threw himself more into polo and devoted less time to Chessie.

In Chessie's defence, with a less complex man she might have been happy. She loved Ricky, but she burned with resentment, hating having to leave parties early because Ricky was playing the next day. Why, too, when there were ten other bedrooms in Robinsgrove with ravishing views over wooded valleys and the green ride down to the bustling Frogsmore stream, did Ricky insist on sleeping in the one room overlooking the stables? Here the window was always left open, so if Ricky heard any commotion he could be outside in a flash.

As she staggered downstairs to make some coffee, on every wall Chessie was assaulted by paintings of polo matches and photographs of Ricky, Herbert and his brothers, leaning out of their saddles like Cossacks, or lined up, their arrogant patrician faces unsmiling, as their polo sticks rested on their collar bones. Going through the dark, panelled hall, she glanced into the library and was reproached by a whole wall of polo cups grown yellow from lack of polish.

Oh God, thought Chessie hysterically, polo, polo, polo. Already on the wall was the draw of the British Open, known as the Gold Cup, the biggest tournament of the year. Starting next Thursday and running over three weeks, it would make Ricky more uptight than ever.

At least marriage had taught him domesticity. In the kitchen his white breeches were soaking in Banish to remove brown bootpolish and the grass stains from yesterday's fall. From the egg yolk on the plates in the sink, he had obviously cooked breakfast for Will and himself, but Chessie only brooded that she was the only wife in polo without a washing-up machine. On the table was a note.

'Darling,' Ricky had written with one of Will's crayons. 'Gone to London, back late afternoon, didn't want to wake you, Mattie's bearing up. Love, Ricky.'

43

Other wives, thought Chessie, scrumpling up the note furiously, went to Paris for the collections. Ricky was so terrified of letting her loose in the shops, he wouldn't even take her to London. At least it was a hot day. She might as well get a suntan. Going upstairs to fetch her bikini, she heard the telephone and took it in the drawing room. It was Grace, probably just back from a shopping binge at Ralph Lauren, sounding distinctly chilly. Learning Ricky was in London, she asked to 'speak with Frances'.

'Speak *to*, not *with*, you silly cow,' muttered Chessie. 'Doesn't trust me to pass on messages.'

She was about to go in search of Frances when she noticed a lighter square in the rose silk wallpaper above the fireplace. It was a few seconds before she realized that the Munnings had gone. Valued at £30,000, it had been given to them as a wedding present and was a painting of Ricky's Aunt Vera on a horse. Ricky must be flogging it in London in order to buy another pony.

'I don't believe it,' screamed Chessie, storming into the hall, where she found Will applying strong-arm tactics to the frantically struggling stable cat as he tried to spray its armpits with Right Guard.

'Stop it,' howled Chessie, completely forgetting about Grace at the other end.

Ricky returned around six. He had managed to get £10,000 for the Munnings. He knew it was pathetically little, but at least it had enabled him to buy from Juan a dark brown mare called Kinta who'd previously been a race horse, whom he'd always fancied and with whom Juan had never clicked.

He felt absolutely shattered. Now yesterday's adrenalin had receded, he could feel all the aches and pains. He was in agony where Jesus had swung his pony's head into his kidneys and where a ball had hit his ribs. His stick hand was swollen where Victor had swiped at him, and there was a bruise black as midnight in the small of his back where Jesus's bay mare had lashed out at him scrabbling to regain her feet after that last fall.

Chessie waited for him in the drawing room, fury fuelled by his checking Mattie and the other ponies before coming into the house.

'Hi, darling,' he said, ignoring the gap above the fire-place, 'I've got another pony.'

'How dare you flog Aunt Vera?' thundered Chessie. 'Half of that money belongs to me, how much did you get?'

'Ten grand.'

'You were robbed.'

At that moment Will erupted into the room.

'Daddy bring me a present?'

'Yes, I did,' said Ricky, handing him a half-size polo stick for children.

Will gave a shout of delight, and, brandishing it, narrowly missed a Lalique bowl on the piano.

'Just like Daddy now.'

Chessie clutched her head. 'Oh, please, no,' she screamed.

5

Chessie's *froideur* with Ricky didn't melt. But he was kept so busy getting acquainted with Kinta, now known as the 'widow-maker', tuning her and the other ponies up for the first Gold Cup match next Thursday, playing in medium-goal matches and worrying about Mattie, who didn't seem to be responding to treatment, that he hardly noticed until he fell into bed. Then, when he was confronted by the Berlin Wall of Chessie's back, he tended, after his hand had been shuddered off, to drop into an uneasy sleep, leaving Chessie twitching with resentful frustration all night.

Grace made it plain that she was livid with Chessie for leaving her hanging on the telephone. Bart had made absolutely no attempt to get in touch with Chessie – perhaps he was still sulking because she had thwarted his plans by giving Perdita a lift home. Surprised how anxious she was to see him again, Chessie went along to the Thursday match and deliberately dressed down, in a collarless shirt and frayed Bermudas, held up with Ricky's red braces, to irritate Grace. Alas, the grooms were all tied up with the ponies and her baby-sitter had gone to Margate, so she was forced to take Will and his new, short polo stick with her.

Will was a menace at matches. Having grabbed a ball, he proceeded to drive it into Fatty Harris's ankles, Brigadier Hughie's ancient springer, David Waterlane's Bentley, and finally a lot of little girls playing with a doll's pram, who all burst into noisy sobs. This was drowned by Will's even noisier sobs when he saw his father umpiring the first match between the Kaputnik Tigers and Rutminster Hall. Wriggling out of Chessie's grasp, he rushed on to the field and was nearly run down by Jesus the Chilean. Juan and Miguel were on epic form, and after a frenzied last chukka of bumps and nearly fatal falls, Rutminster Hall ran out the winners by 10-6.

Victor Kaputnik, whose gloating when he won was only equalled by his rage when he lost, could be heard yelling furiously at the twins and Jesus as they came off the field. Chessie was about to wander down to the pony lines in search of Bart when he emerged out of a duck-egg blue helicopter, followed by Grace, extremely chic in brown boots, a brown trilby and a fur-lined trench coat, her glossy, dark hair drawn back in a French pleat.

After last week's heatwave, a bitter north wind was flattening the yellowing corn fields, turning the huge trees inside out, driving icy rain into the eyes of the players and horses, and putting the easiest penalty in jeopardy. Despite this, there was a good crowd to watch the second match between the Alderton Flyers and the Doggie Dins Devils, who included the notorious Napier brothers, an underhandicapped Australian and Kevin Coley, their appalling petfood billionaire patron.

Not being able to face an hour with Grace, Chessie was thankful when the Carlisle twins bounded up, teeth brilliantly white in their mud-spattered faces, and insisted she watch from their car. Will, who adored the twins, immediately stopped crying.

'Aren't you flying home with Victor?' asked Chessie.

'No, he's pissed off with us because we were late. I'll go and get us a drink,' said Seb.

As the Alderton Flyers rode on to the field, all wearing polo-necked jerseys under their shirts, Chessie was glad of the warmth of the twins' Lotus. Listening to the whistling kettle sound of Victor's black-and-orange helicopter soaring out of the trees, she turned to Dommie: 'I don't

46

know why you're looking so smug about losing.'

'Oh, we'll catch up,' said Dommie. 'There are four more matches in the draw. Don't tell Victor. He thinks we were late because of the traffic. Actually we were selling a pony for about three thousand pounds more than it's worth. Seb had just lied that its grandsire was Nijinsky when I walked in and said it was Mill Reef, but we got over that hurdle.'

'Who bought it?' asked Chessie idly.

'Phil Wedgwood.'

'Bloody hell,' said Chessie. 'He rang Ricky yesterday. Said he'd just sent the mare Ricky sold him in May to the knackers because she had back trouble and could he buy another. Ricky loved that mare so much he hung up on him. Now Phil's bought one from you – Jesus!'

'I don't think your husband's got his act together commercially,' said Dommie. 'He's got to learn to care less about ponies and more about patrons. Victor is so thick we sold one of his own ponies to him the other day. Quick! Duck! Here comes the Head Girl!'

Through the driving rain, both suitably clad for the weather, came Sukey and Grace going towards Bart's limo, which had been driven independently to the match for them to sit in. Grace nodded coolly. Sukey, who was carrying a camera, tapped on the window: 'I was hoping to video the match, so Drew could isolate his mistakes afterwards, but the visibility's so awful. Bad luck on losing, Seb.'

'I'm Dommie.'

'Oh, sorry. I can never tell you two apart.'

'I've got the bigger cock,' said Dommie.

Chessie giggled. Sukey firmly changed the subject. 'We've had the *Daily Express* at home all morning, doing a feature on Drew. You'd never dream how many rolls of film they used.'

'They wanted to do Ricky and me,' said Chessie furiously, 'but Ricky was far too uptight to let them in on the morning of a match.'

'Oh, Drew's managed to conquer his nerves,' said Sukey. Then, looking at Chessie: 'Aren't you frozen?'

'Not with me around,' said Dommie, running his hands up and down her bare legs.

Before Sukey had time to look old-fashioned, Seb had arrived holding three Bloody Marys and a Coke in his hands, and a packet of crisps between his teeth for Will.

'Christ, this weather's awful. D'you want a drink, Sukey?'

'No thanks, I've just had a cup of tea. There's the throw-in. I must go and watch with Grace. Such a wonderful lady.'

'Silly bitch,' muttered Chessie, putting the Bloody Marys on the dashboard as Seb got in beside her. Next minute Bart thundered past them, eyes screwed up against the rain, swiping at the ball and missing completely. He was so bad, reflected Chessie, it was a turn-off to watch him. But not as bad as the petfood billionaire Kevin Coley, who was simultaneously hitting his poor pony round the legs with his stick, tugging on its mouth, and plunging huge spurs into its sides.

'Dreadful rider,' winced Seb.

'He's just given me a book on dog breeds,' said Dommie, getting it out of his Barbour. 'Seb and I are thinking of getting a pit bull.'

'Jesus's game is distinctly off today,' said Seb.

'Baby Jesus is a little bugger,' said Will, his mouth full of crisps.

The conditions were worsening, the pitch was a black sea of mud. Beyond the clubhouse the pink-and-white sponsors' tent strained at its moorings. By the third chukka the Alderton Flyers were leading by 8-4, not because of superior play, but because Juan, who was umpiring, was so anxious to curry favour with Bart that he hadn't blown a single foul on him.

'God,' said Seb, as Bart crashed into Charles Napier at ninety degrees, 'that should have been a goal to the other side.'

'Shall we get a white or a brindle one?' asked Dommie.

'How's your ravishing schoolgirl?' asked Chessie.

'Expelled, poor darling. We tried to take her out on Sunday. We were going to Windsor and thought she'd like a jaunt, but they wouldn't even give us a forwarding address.'

'Oh, she'll turn up,' said Chessie. 'Those sort of girls always do.'

'Ready for another drink?' asked Seb, as the half-time bell went.

'I quite like Basenjis,' said Dommie, 'but they don't bark.'

He ran his hand down Chessie's bare leg again.

'Honestly, Mrs F-L, if you weren't married to Ricky, I'd make such a play.'

'Feel free,' said Chessie, then jumped at a tap on the window.

'Divot-stomping time, Francesca,' ordered Grace Alderton, looking disapprovingly at the row of glasses on the dashboard.

Dommie lowered the window a centimetre.

'It's too cold. Mrs F-L isn't dressed for treading in, and we've just got warm for the first time today.'

Grace didn't actually flounce, but her body stiffened as she stalked off on to the pitch.

'Good period, baby,' she shouted to Bart, as he cantered back, muddy but elated, having scored a goal.

'Can we get our diaries together when we get back to the car?' Sukey asked Grace, as they trod back the divots. 'I don't want to have our wedding on a day when you won't be in England.'

Will took a great slug of Dommie's second Bloody Mary and started on a bag of Maltesers Seb had brought him.

'Don't let him eat them all,' said Chessie. 'He'll be sick.'

Will ate four, then put the rest in the breast pocket of his shirt. 'Allbody will think I've grown a tit.'

The twins roared with laughter.

Ricky's breeches were black with mud as he came out for the fifth chukka. His spare sticks were in front of Dommie's car, leaning against the little fence that ran along the edge of the pitch. Some players used the same length stick for every pony, but Ricky preferred longer sticks for taller ponies, and Kinta, the new dark brown thoroughbred was nearly sixteen hands. If he broke a stick, he expected Chessie to run out and hand him a new one.

'Those are the fifty-ones on the left, and the fifty-twos on the right,' he shouted to her as he cantered back for the throw-in.

'Are you going to Deauville?' Chessie asked the twins.

'Shut up,' said Seb. 'I want to see how Ricky goes on Juan's pony, and you can get your nose out of that book, Dom.'

Ricky was used to riding with his reins completely loose, the slightest pressure on his horses' necks turning them to the left or right. Kinta, however, coming from the race track where horses are only expected to go one way and used to being yanked around by Juan, pulled like an express train and was almost impossible to stop.

'Christ, Ricky won't have any arms left,' said Dommie, as Kinta easily outstripped Charles Napier's fastest pony. 'But she's going bloody well for him. Juan must be as sick as a baby with its first cigar.'

Both sides were now squelching around the Doggie Dins' goal. Bart should have dropped back and marked Ben Napier, but, instead, rushed into the mêlée and, losing control of his pony, mis-hit.

'Get back, you stupid fucker,' howled Ricky.

'Interesting your husband never stammers when he's shouting abuse,' said Seb.

As Will took another slug of Bloody Mary, Ricky and Ben Napier both bounded forward trying to prise the ball out of the mud. There was a crack as Ricky's stick broke. Swinging round, he galloped towards the boards.

'He wants another stick,' said Seb.

Reluctantly Chessie climbed out into the stabbing rain. Only the fence and the row of cars stopped Kinta.

'Fifty-two,' yelled Ricky.

'Are you trying to tell me your age?' drawled Chessie.

'Give me my fucking fifty-two.'

'Say please!'

'Chess-ee, come *on*,' said Seb disapprovingly.

'Sthop sthouting, Daddy,' said Will.

'For Christ's sake,' howled Ricky.

'Don't be infantile,' said a furious Grace, running forward and handing the stick to Ricky. Seizing it, he hurtled back into the game. But it was too late. Despite Kinta's phenomenal speed, Doggie Dins had taken advantage of Ricky's absence to score a goal.

'Sthop sthouting,' said Will, filling up his water-pistol from Seb's Bloody Mary.

As the bell went for the end of the fifth chukka, Chessie caught sight of Grace's face and was about to belt back into the smoky warmth of the twins' car.

'May I speak with you, Francesca?'

'Shall we have a word after the match? I'm watching Ricky.'

'Not noticeably.'

'Wee-wee,' clamoured Will.

'I've got to take Will to the loo,' said Chessie.

'Why don't you let him pee in Fatty Harris's rain gauge?' said Dommie.

'Then Fatty will be so horrified by the amount of rainfall, he'll cancel Sunday's match and we'll have a day off,' said Seb.

'I quite like Rottweilers,' said Dommie.

'Wee-wee,' said Will, dropping his Maltesers in the mud as he scrambled out of the car.

If Grace hadn't been present, Chessie would have picked the Maltesers up. As she dragged Will away, he burst into tears.

'I'll take him to the lav,' said Sukey. 'Then you and Grace can chat.'

'He won't go with you,' protested Chessie.

'Come along, Will,' said Sukey briskly. To Chessie's amazement, Will trotted off with her.

'You only have to use the right tone of voice,' said Grace.

'Do look,' said Seb, nudging Dommie. 'Grace is about to urge Mrs F-L to exercise a little decorum.'

'Decorum's a nice name for a dog,' said Dommie. 'Then I could exercise it.'

Inside Bart's limo the new leather smelt like a tack shop. Grace had been a good wife to Bart. Twenty-one years ago, she had taken this roaring roughneck and turned him into a tycoon. She had provided him with the contacts, the friendships, the staff, the right silver and china at her dinner parties, where important people met the important people they wanted to meet. Grace was acutely aware of the social advantages of polo. She longed to invite the Prince to dine at one of her five houses, as much as she wanted her two children to make brilliant marriages. Grace's every action, whether she was fund-raising at a calorie-conscious teetotal buffet lunch or reading biographies of famous people as she pedalled away on her exercise bicycle, was geared towards improvement.

She couldn't understand Chessie's lack of motivation, and had spent a lot of time this summer discussing both Chessie's and Ricky's shortcomings with Bart. But in the last week she had noticed Bart was slagging off Chessie less and less. He was even talking about bringing her and Ricky over to Palm Beach for the polo season in January. Having herself dreamt about Ricky last night, rather a disturbing dream, Grace had now decided that he was terribly misunderstood, and took a positive pleasure in giving his wife a pep talk.

'Are you supporting Doggie Dins, Francesca?'

'Of course not,' snapped Chessie.

'One could be fooled into thinking so. A married couple is two people, half a polo team, and you're intelligent enough to know that you only win at polo and in life if you play as a team and support each other. Your behaviour towards Ricky is flip, destructive and totally unsupportive.'

Chessie yawned. 'You've no idea how tricky he is. Women are always on Ricky's side because he's so good-looking.'

'I am not *Women*,' said Grace icily. 'How many times have you failed to pass on messages, turned up late at matches, and showed no interest in the game? Look at you today, egging on the twins, dressed like a tramp, and now not giving Ricky his fifty-two. If the Flyers lose this match it'll be entirely your fault. You're twenty-seven, not seventeen, Francesca.'

'When Ricky signed his contract with you,' said Chessie furiously, 'there was absolutely no clause about my turning up in a ball dress at every match. You've no idea what it's like living with a man who's totally obsessed with polo.'

'If your husband's going to succeed,' Grace looked at Chessie's mutinous profile, 'you have to put up with loneliness. When Bart was building up the business, he often didn't come home till two o'clock in the morning.'

'Not surprised,' said Chessie, 'if you bent his ear like this.'

'Don't be impertinent.'

'I don't want to hear any more. You can buy Ricky but not me.' Scrambling out of the limo, Chessie went slap into Sukey and Will who was still clutching his water-pistol.

'All better,' said Sukey. 'Such a jolly little chap, I waited outside and didn't miss a minute. Oh, well played, Drew darling, oh go on, go on.'

'Stick 'em up,' said Will, his eyes squinting through his blond fringe.

'Don't point guns at people, dear,' said Grace.

Next minute Will had emptied a pistol full of Bloody Mary into her cream silk shirt. Grace gave a scream. Chessie made the mistake of laughing.

'If you'd take your nose out of that book for one second,' said Seb to Dommie, 'you'd see Ricky finally losing his patron.'

As Chessie dragged Will off in search of Ricky, she could hear Sukey comforting Grace. 'I'm sure Mrs Beeton will know how to get tomato juice out.'

Suddenly Chessie stopped laughing and started to cry. 'That was naughty,' she screamed at Will. 'You may have been defending my honour but your methods were very extreme.'

'Hi, honey,' said a voice. 'You're getting soaked.'

It was Bart, coming off the field.

Delighted to have scored two goals and trounced Doggie Dins, he was in exultant form. Then he realized that the rain pouring down Chessie's face was tears.

'Hey – what's the matter?'

'Your ghastly wife's been giving me a dressing-down for not dressing up, telling me what an awful wife I am.'

The icy wind was sweeping the drenched striped shirt against her breasts. 'I tell you the only reason Frankenstein was a monster was because he was frank,' she added furiously.

Just for a second they were hidden from the pitch by a home-going horse box. Bart put a warm sweating hand on Chessie's neck and she felt her stomach disappear.

'I've tried to put you out of my mind,' he said roughly, 'but I didn't manage it. Grace and I are going back to the States tomorrow – for a wedding – one of the Biddles' – even in the pursuit of love Bart had to name-drop – 'I'll be back on Wednesday. How about lunch on Thursday?'

'All right.'

'Meet me at Rubens' Retreat at one o'clock,' said Bart and rode on.

Grace came forward as he reached the pony lines: 'Well played, baby.' Then, consulting her red book, 'but you were loose in the fifth chukka.'

'How dare you chew out Chessie France-Lynch?' snarled Bart. 'I run this team, OK, and don't you forget it.'

6

Grace's pep-talk only intensified Chessie's desire to take her husband off her. The weather continued windy and very cold, and Chessie spent the next week sourly watching her suntan fade and thinking up alibis for Thursday lunchtime. Fortunately Ricky was being paid £1,000 to play in a charity match at the Guards Club that day, on the understanding that he stayed behind for drinks and allowed himself to be gawped at by all the sponsors' rich clients. This meant he wouldn't be home much before eight.

Ricky was loath to go. He was desperately worried about Mattie, who'd stopped eating and kept biting listlessly at her plaster. Her eyes were dull – always the first sign of pain in a horse. He was sure the plaster was beginning to smell, a sinister indication that infection or, even worse, gangrene, was setting in.

'Pooh,' said Will, coming into Chessie's bedroom with his new polo stick, and breathing in the collective reek of Duo Tan, Immac and nail polish.

'Don't touch,' screamed Chessie as he trotted purposefully towards the make-up bottles on her dressing table. She loathed being distracted when she was getting ready – it was all Ricky's fault for not being able to afford a nanny. Nor could she start washing her hair until he'd gone. Then she found the water hadn't been turned on. She also dried her hair upside down too long so it stood up like a porcupine. She didn't know if she was more nervous of seeing Bart or Ricky finding out. It was so cold, she put on a pale pink cashmere dress, which was near enough flesh tones in colour, to make her look as though she was wearing nothing at all. Sticking her tongue out at Herbert's portrait, she ran down the stairs.

Out in the yard, she was relieved to find that Louisa, Ricky's youngest and most amenable groom, had been left in charge. Plump, pink-faced, always smiling, Louisa had been described by Chessie in a bitchier moment as looking like a piglet who'd just won the pools. She was a complete contrast to Ricky's head groom, Frances, who, scrawny, angry and equally obsessed with Ricky and the horses, was always finding fault with the other grooms' work. Chessie had nicknamed Frances and Louisa 'Picky and Perky'. Perky was now trying to coax Mattie to eat a carrot.

'Can you look after Will for a couple of hours?' Chessie asked her. 'I'm just popping out to lunch with a girlfriend.'

'Pooh,' said Will. 'Mattie's leg smells awful.' Then, realizing Chessie was getting into the car without him, started to cry.

'Mummy won't be long. I'll bring you a present,' called Chessie as she drove off.

'Girlfriend indeed,' muttered Louisa, catching a whiff of Diorissimo. 'Mummy's gone a-hunting.'

Ten miles from Robinsgrove the wind dropped, the sun came out and the temperature rocketed, shrivelling the wild roses hanging from the hedgerows. Chessie could see her face reddening in the driving mirror and feel the sweat trickling down her ribs. It was all Ricky's fault for not being able to afford a car with air-conditioning. There were no shops on the way for her to buy something cooler. Her mouth tasted acid with nerves.

Rubens' Retreat, once a large country house, now an hotel, was set in lush parkland. Reputed to have the best food and the softest double beds in England, it was a favourite haunt of the rich and libidinous. Inside it was wonderfully cool. Chessie nipped into the Ladies to remove her stockings, tone down her flushed face and clean her teeth.

'I've just had gastric flu and keep getting this terrible taste in my mouth,' she explained to the attendant who'd seen it all before.

She found Bart in an alcove, screened by huge plants. On the telephone, he only paused to kiss her and wave her to the chair beside him. He was very brown and wearing a cream silk shirt, a pin-striped suit and an emerald-green tie, which matched the greensward on which naked ladies were sporting with cherubs on the mural round the walls.

'I don't care if the price is rising, keep buying, but spread it around; we should have control by tomorrow lunchtime,' ordered Bart, waving to the waiter to pour Chessie a glass of champagne.

While half his mind wrestled with the complicated finances of one of the fiercest take-overs Wall Street had ever known, his eyes ran over Chessie. She was as flushed as a peony, that pink dress emphasized every curve like a second skin. As the waiter laid a dark green napkin across her crotch, it was as though he was putting on a fig leaf. Bart wanted to take her upstairs and screw her at once.

'Sorry about that,' he said as he came off the telephone.

'Aren't you drinking?' asked Chessie, noticing his glass of Perrier.

'I'm driving.'

'Perrier don't make you merrier,' said Chessie idly.

'Just looking at you makes me drunk,' said Bart. 'Where does Ricky think you are?'

'At home. I was terrified the match might be cancelled.'

'It isn't. I checked it out,' said Bart. 'How is he?'

'Preoccupied. Mattie's deteriorating; Kinta won't stop.'

'Sure he hasn't got a bit on the side?' asked Bart as they studied the menu.

Chessie laughed sourly. 'The only bits Ricky's interested in go in horses' mouths.'

'How was he when you got home after Lady Waterlane's reception?'

'Asleep in the hay beside Mattie.'

'That figures. He thinks he's Jesus Christ anyway.'

The telephone rang.

'Choose what you want to eat,' said Bart picking up the receiver. 'I'd like poached salmon, zucchini and no potatoes,' he told the waiter.

'Why are you so keen to take over this company?' asked Chessie, as he came off the telephone five minutes later.

'Chief Executive, Ashley Roberts, blackballed me at the Racquet Club ten years ago.'

'You *are* into revenge,' said Chessie, taking a slug of champagne.

'Never forget a put-down. That all right?' He brandished his fork in the direction of Chessie's fish pâté.

'Fraction too much fennel,' said Chessie. 'OK, OK, that wasn't a put-down. I used to cook for a living before I got married. I'll cook for you one day.'

Bart massaged her arm. 'I sure hope so. I'm sorry about Grace.'

'Did the Bloody Mary come out of her shirt?'

'No. She called Ralph. He's making her another one.'

'I suppose that's what shirty means. How was the wedding? Is Grace still Biddling while Rome burns?'

Bart tapped her nose with his finger. 'You must not take the piss.'

'How did you two meet?' asked Chessie as the waiter took away her hardly touched pâté.

'I was a test pilot at NASA. Great life, none of us thought we'd live beyond thirty. You can't imagine the joy of testing an airplane, learning its personality, talking to it, poking and probing, finding new things. I was a little boy from nowhere, but when I flew I felt like a god.'

He blushed, ashamed of betraying emotion. 'Grace came to visit the plant, and that was that. She grounded me but she backed me.'

Chessie was fascinated: 'How come you got so rich?'

Bart shrugged. 'I build the best airplanes and helicopters in the world and I bought land when it was worth $300 an acre. Now it's going for $10,000. All markets go in cycles, the skill is knowing when to get in and when to get out.'

Chessie breathed in the sweet scent of white freesias and stocks in the centre of the dark green tablecloth.

'How were your children when you went back?'

'OK.' Quite unselfconsciously Bart got photographs out of his wallet.

'That's Luke. He's twenty-two.'

'Nice face,' said Chessie.

'Comes from my first marriage. Doesn't live with us. He's been working his way up as a groom in a polo yard. Very proud. Won't accept a cent from me.'

'Sounds like Ricky.'

'More sympatico than Ricky,' said Bart flatly. 'This is Red.'

Chessie whistled. 'Wow, that's an even nicer face. He really is beautiful.' Then, sensing she'd said the wrong thing: 'Nearly as good-looking as his father.'

Bart looked mollified: 'All the girls are crazy for Red. He's kinda wild. He got looped at the wedding, and threw his cookies all over his granny's porch. Plays polo like an angel. If he'd quit partying he'd go to ten. And here's my baby, Bibi.' Bart's voice softened.

'Now she *is* like you,' said Chessie. 'What a clever, intelligent face.'

No one could call her pretty with that crinkly hair and heavy jaw.

'Bibi is super-bright. Harvard Business School, only one interested in coming into the business. She's Daddy's girl. Doesn't get on with Grace. She might relate to a younger woman,' he added pointedly.

He is definitely putting out signals, thought Chessie, as their second course arrived.

'D'you often have affairs with men who aren't your husband?' said Bart, forking up poached salmon.

'Not since I was married. And you?'

'Occasionally. They weren't important.'

Chessie examined the oily sheen on a red leaf of radicchio. 'Is this?'

'I guess so. That's why I didn't call you before.'

Elated, Chessie regaled him with scurrilous polo gossip, knowing it would delight him to know how other players ripped off their patrons. Aware she was dropping the twins in it, and not caring, she told him about them selling one of Victor's own horses back to him.

'Are you going to Deauville?' asked Bart as he came off the telephone for the third time.

'Not unless Ricky forks out for a temporary nanny. The grooms get so bolshy about baby-sitting and Deauville's no fun unless you can go out in the evening. We haven't had a holiday since we were married,' said Chessie bitterly and untruthfully.

Bart traced the violet circles under her eyes.

'You need one. Don't you ever get any sleep?'

'Not since I met you,' said Chessie, who had drunk almost an entire bottle of champagne.

It excited her wildly that this man at the same time as dealing in billions of dollars could give her his undivided attention. All her grievances came pouring out: 'Having been dragged up by a succession of nannies himself, Ricky thinks Will ought to be brought up by his mother.'

'Will's a nice kid,' said Bart. 'He's only whiny, over-adrenalized and super-aggressive because he's picking up tensions from your marriage. You're both too screwed up to give him enough attention.'

'That's not true.' Chessie dropped her fork with a furious clatter. 'If you're going to talk to me like that, I'm going.'

Bart caught her wrist, pulling her back.

'Stop over-reacting,' he said sharply. 'You haven't done anything wrong. Will's playing up because you're miserable.'

'Does your son Red throw up in porches and no doubt in Porsches because you and Grace aren't happy?' spat Chessie.

'Grace no longer excites me. Let's go upstairs,' said Bart calmly and he opened a door hidden in the romping nymphs behind him which led straight into a lift. 'The beauty of this place is you don't have to go through Reception to get to the bedrooms.'

It was a most unsatisfactory coupling. Bart was too anxious to get at her. Chessie was too angry and uptight to get aroused. Despite her moans and writhings, Bart knew she hadn't come. Sick with disappointment and frustration, she got dressed. Here was just one more failure because she was not able to tell people what she liked, that she never came from straight screwing, and never with Ricky.

'Poor little Rick's girl,' said Bart, kissing her forehead.

It's all over, thought Chessie miserably.

As they went outside, Bart's telephone rang again. He talked so long that Chessie was about to wander off without even saying goodbye when he hung up in jubilation.

'I've got forty-nine per cent. By tomorrow lunchtime I'll have nailed him.'

'What's your next take-over target?' asked Chessie sulkily.

'You are,' said Bart. He glanced at his watch. 'They'll just be throwing-in. We're going for a ride.'

Like all polo players, he drove too fast, overtaking with split-second timing, one hand on the wheel, the other resting on Chessie's thigh. As the limo swung round the hangar, the helicopter standing on the apron was as blue as the Flyer's polo shirts and as the sky above. On its side

59

in dark blue letters was written: 'Alderton – your friend in high places'.

Chessie sat in the passenger seat with the full flight harness biting into her pink dress. Having gone round turning on switches and tightening screws as a pre-flight check, Bart had taken off his jacket and his green silk tie, and was secured by just a seat belt round his waist.

Satisfied everything was in order, he started up the engine. There was a thrilling roar as the jets took a grip on the rotors which quickly accelerated to their operating speed. With a last look round to see everything was clear, Bart alerted the control tower, who asked for his destination and initial reading.

'We're going to do local flying towards the south-east, not above a thousand feet,' said Bart.

As they flew over yellowing fields and rain-drenched woods and villages, Chessie gave a scream of joy.

'Isn't it heaven, just like a child's farm? If you picked up the houses they'd be hollow underneath.'

She longed to run her hand up and down Bart's pin-striped thigh, hard as iron like Ricky's.

'There's David Waterlane's place,' said Bart. 'You can see them stick and balling.'

Down below Chessie could see the dark, silken flash of the lake flecked with duck, and the dark brown oval of the exercise ring.

'If you look closely,' she said, 'you may see Clemency sunbathing in the nude, or Juan getting his back brown on top of her. Talk about One flew over the Cuckold's Nest.'

Bart laughed. The sun was beating down on the glass bubble. Oh hell, I'm getting too hot again, thought Chessie.

Five minutes later Bart pointed out a beautiful, white house with a green roof, set in a clearing thickly ringed with woodland. He flew so low that Chessie could see the cars glittering outside the front door and white figures leaping on the tennis court. The swimming-pool glittered in the sunshine like an aquamarine.

'Gorgeous place,' breathed Chessie.

'Belongs to Ashley Roberts,' Bart's voice thickened with excitement. 'When I take him over tomorrow and fire him later this year, he'll be forced to put it on the market. How'd you like to live there?'

Chessie went very still.

'We rattle enough in our present house,' she said lightly.

Ahead loomed a huge, apparently substantial, white-and-mushroom-brown cloud which had formed into turrets, icebergs and snow drifts.

'Let's go through that archway,' said Bart, not even touching the snow-white edges. Now he was flying alongside a massive, pinky cliff, just clipping it, laughing as Chessie flinched away. 'I used to play around for hours like this when I was a boy. Now I'm going right into this cloud. This is the most scary feeling in the world,' he added, as they were enveloped in dense fog. 'Even after years of flying it still scares the shit out of me. You can't figure if you're upside down. You have a total disregard of what the brain is telling you. It's completely disorientating.' Then, as he came out into brilliant sunshine, he smiled at her, powerful as he was handsome. 'Pretty much like meeting you.'

He does like me, thought Chessie in ecstasy, and I'm mad about him. He's tied up in a mega-take-over, and he's fooling around in the air with me.

The sun was beating down on the bubble again. The shimmering fields and woods seemed to stretch for ever. Sheep huddled under the trees like lice.

'I'm baking,' gasped Chessie, wishing she could find some shade like them.

'Take your dress off,' said Bart idly. 'Just undo the harness and take it off.

'Ker-ist,' he said a moment later, as Chessie threw the dress behind her seat. 'Oh, Christ.'

She was only wearing a pair of rose-patterned white pants. The slenderness of her waist emphasized the fullness of her thighs, and her breasts soft and white-gold in the sunshine with the nipples pink and spread. Her cheeks were very flushed, her eyelids drooped over eyes leaden with lust.

She'd put Victor's bimbo in the shade, thought Bart. She was more beautiful than any of the girls his son Red attracted.

'Two joysticks,' murmured Chessie, putting her hand on his cock. 'I know which one I'd like best.'

Bart wanted her now, but, even on automatic pilot, making love in a helicopter is not in the flight manual.

61

'We're over Victor's land,' he said in amusement. 'There's a clearing in the wood where we can land. No one will find us. I'll just tell them I'm going down.'

'On me I hope,' whispered Chessie.

Having cleared with flight control, Bart eased the power and headed for the trees. Chessie saw the clearing, a little sage-green disc, cut in half by a winding stream, flanked by willows. There were no houses near by. Switching off, Bart allowed the blades to stop before opening the door and jumping on to the lush green grass. Next moment he'd walked round to the other door, and his arms were deliciously full of Chessie.

'Jesus, you're lovely,' he murmured, carrying her to the shade of a large oak tree. This time he was going to take it very slowly.

'Why did you pretend you came before?' he asked, as he laid her gently down in the groin of two huge roots.

Chessie opened her eyes in terror. 'I didn't,' she stammered, 'I came beautifully.'

'Liar!' Peeling down her pants, he slid his fingers into the oily cavern. 'That's better. I should put you across my knee for distracting me at nine hundred feet.'

Instantly, her breath quickened, her eyes went dull, her legs widened ecstatically. So that's it, Bart thought in triumph, she wants to be treated like a naughty little girl. His hand slid to her bottom, exploring gently but persuasively.

'Is that what you like?' he whispered. 'Your butt paddled?' Repelled but wildly excited, Chessie squirmed against him.

'Ricky's too straight, huh?'

Chessie nodded helplessly. 'I can't talk to him.'

Slipping his hand under her buttocks, between her legs, he fingered the bud of her clitoris, and felt the flood of wetness as she gasped and came.

The sun had dropped behind the trees as he pulled out of her for the last time.

'The skill,' said Chessie, mocking to hide how moved she felt, 'is knowing when to get in and when to get out.'

They didn't talk on the way home. Mist was rising from the river. Bart dropped her off where her car was, at Rubens' Retreat.

'You're going to be very late. What movie have you been to see?'

'*Gone with the Wind*,' said Chessie, 'twice round.'

'I guess this take-over's going to take up so much of my time I won't go to Deauville,' said Bart. Then, getting a jewel box out of his briefcase, 'I've got you a present.'

Chessie wasn't really into costume jewellery, but for paste the diamonds were certainly beautifully set, and looked pretty round her neck in the driving mirror. She supposed the rich didn't dare wear real jewels any more.

'Thank you,' she said, trying to simulate enthusiasm.

'Are you going to be able to hide them from Ricky?' asked Bart, cupping her groin with his hand.

Chessie glanced down.

'I'd better shove them up there,' she said bitterly. 'That's one place Ricky won't look.'

7

As Ricky rode off the field at the end of the match at the Guards Club there was a message to ring Louisa.

'Mattie's worse,' she said, trying to hold back the tears. 'Her leg smells awful and her eyes are dead. Phil Bagley's out on his rounds, but I got him on his bleeper. He's coming as soon as possible.'

Mercifully, Major Ferguson, the Deputy Chairman and Polo Manager, understood.

'Course you must go at once. I'll explain to the sponsors.'

'I'm s-s-sorry,' mumbled Ricky. 'S-s-suppose I shouldn't have tried to save her.'

'Done just the same myself,' said Major Ferguson. 'Mattie's a legend – give anything for one of her foals. I'll ring you in the morning – love to Chessie.'

If only Ricky'd had Bart's helicopter. Limited in the horse box to forty miles an hour, going slap into rush-hour traffic, and trapped between returning tractors and hay lorries, he didn't get home until nearly eight. Please God, save her, he prayed over and over again.

Phil Bagley was already in Mattie's box. The stink of putrefaction was unmistakable, Mattie hung leaden in her

63

sling. For the first time since she was a tiny foal, she didn't whicker with delight to see Ricky. Phil Bagley looked up, shaking his head.

'The leg's completely cold below the plaster,' he said brusquely, to hide his feelings. He loved Mattie, having treated her since she was a foal, and had rejoiced in her dazzling career. 'I've been sticking needles in and she doesn't feel anything, and her temperature's right up, which indicates secondary infection as well as gangrene.'

Ricky crouched down beside Phil Bagley, feeling Mattie's skin which had gone hard and crisp like parchment.

'Is she in pain?'

'Yup – considerable I'm afraid.'

'There's no way we can take off the plaster and clean it up?'

'We can have a look.'

Ricky held Mattie's head. Although her breath quickened, she made no attempt to fight, as Phil got to work. He only had to saw a few inches – the stink was appalling.

'I'm sorry, Ricky. It's completely putrid. If she were a dog or a human we could amputate.'

The fiercely impassive Frances, who was looking over the stable-door, gave a sob.

'Of course.' Ricky deliberately kept his voice steady. 'You must do it at once.' Then, without turning, 'Frances, can you ask Louisa to see that Will's well out of the way?'

As Phil went off for the humane killer, Ricky put his arms round Mattie's neck, running his hand up the stubble of her mane.

'Sorry I put you through it, sweetheart,' he muttered. 'I only wanted to save you.' His voice broke, as she gently nudged him as if in forgiveness. Shutting his eyes, he scratched her gently behind the ears, putting his lips to the white star between her eyes, where the humane killer would go, until he felt Phil's hand on his shoulder.

The sun had set but there was still a fiery glow in the West as Chessie stormed up the drive. Dog daisies lit up the verges and the air was heavy with the sweet scent of the lime tree flowers. She had hidden Bart's necklace in the lining of her bag and, buying a *Rutshire Echo*, had memorized the synopsis of the Robert de Niro film she was supposed to have seen. Sober now, her earlier bravado evaporated, she was twitching with nerves. As she drew closer, she heard a muffled explosion and slammed her foot on the accelerator. The house was in darkness. Perhaps Will had got hold of one of Ricky's guns. Then she saw the lorry parked crooked across the yard and panicked. Ricky was home already. Outside Mattie's box, he was holding Frances in his arms.

'Oh, charming,' said Chessie acidly, 'I thought you were wowing sponsors at Guards.'

Ricky looked round, his face ashen, his eyes huge, black holes. Then Chessie saw that Frances's normally accusing, disapproving face was a blubbered, disintegrating mass of tears.

'What on earth's the matter?'

'I've just put Mattie down,' said Phil Bagley in a tight voice, as he emerged from Mattie's box. 'I'm terribly sorry.'

'Oh, God,' said Chessie, not knowing what to say, but feeling passionate relief that no-one would bother where she'd been. 'For a terrible moment I thought it was Will.'

Shooting her a look of pure hatred, Ricky walked past her into the night. In the kitchen she found Will patting the plump shoulder of a frantically sobbing Louisa.

'Mummy,' he turned in delight, 'Louisa crying. Did you bring me a present?'

'Delicious sweeties,' said Chessie, producing a handful of Rubens' Retreat's *petits fours* out of her bag.

'Ugh,' said Will spitting a marzipan banana out all over the floor.

Ricky didn't come back all night. Chessie thought he must have gone to his father's, until the telephone woke her at eight o'clock next morning.

'Herbert here,' barked a voice. Trust the old bugger not to apologize for ringing so early, or after so long. 'Can I speak to Ricky?'

'He's not here.'

'Well, tell him I've just heard about Mattie. Bloody shame. I'm very sorry.'

It must have cost Herbert a lot to ring, but Chessie decided not to pass on the message. She didn't want him back in their lives, hanging around, restricting her freedom. Looking out of the window, she saw Ricky was back and with a couple of men from the village, was digging a grave in the orchard, where generations of dogs and stable cats had been buried. The two Labradors, tails wagging, were trying to join in, frantically scrabbling the earth with their paws. Wayne, Ricky's second favourite pony, a custard-yellow gelding with lop ears who'd been devoted to Mattie, stood by the paddock gate, neighing hysterically.

Keen to escape such a house of mourning, longing to be alone to think about Bart, Chessie drove into Rutminster on the pretext of doing the weekend shopping. Out of curiosity, on the way home, she stopped off at a jeweller to get Bart's necklace valued. The bumpy, veined, arthritic hands trembled slightly as they examined the stones.

'Very, very nice,' said the jeweller in reverent tones. 'I'd be surprised if you'd get much change out of £100,000, might be even higher. Pretty stones, for a pretty lady,' he added with a smile at Chessie's gasp of amazement.

Chessie was so stunned she went straight out and committed the cardinal indiscretion of ringing Bart at home from a call box.

'Pretend I'm a wrong number. Look, I'm sorry I was so horribly ungrateful. I'd no idea those diamonds were real.'

'Like my love for you,' said Bart softly. 'I can't talk now,' and hung up.

'Did you bring me a present?' said Will when she got home.

Joyfully Chessie gathered him up, and swung him round till he screamed with laughter.

'I've got a hunch,' she murmured. 'I may have got you a new Daddy.'

Bart rang her later. 'Can you talk?'

'I could talk when I was eighteen months,' said Chessie, 'but I'm precocious.'

Out of the window, she could see Louisa wiping her eyes with the back of her hand, as she planted primroses round Mattie's grave.

'Mattie had to be put down,' she told Bart.

'I'm sorry – she was a helluva horse. How's Ricky taking it?'

'Bottling it up as usual.'

'Any repercussions last night?'

'Ricky was too shell-shocked even to realize I'd been away. I forgot to ask yesterday. Are you still going to drop him?'

'I guess I'm going to drop Ricky *and* Grace,' said Bart.

The polo community were flabbergasted when Bart didn't come to Deauville and allowed the team that he was forking out so much for to play without him. His place was taken by an underhandicapped Australian who interchanged so dazzlingly with Ricky that the Alderton Flyers clinched the French Championships after a very close fight against David Waterlane and the O'Brien brothers. Kinta, suddenly clicking with Ricky, won the Best Playing Pony award, to Juan's fury. So much were the Flyers on form they were hotly tipped to win the French Gold Cup next Sunday.

Although Ricky desperately missed Mattie, he felt his luck was changing. During the endless barbecues and parties, the racing and gambling which characterize Deauville, players and patrons who aren't rushing home every evening get a chance to talk. Ricky spent a lot of time with David Waterlane, and his son, Mike, a raw, silent, spotty youth, back from Harrow for the holidays. Hopelessly inhibited by his father, Mike showed considerable promise. Feeling the boy's relationship with David was very like his own with Herbert, Ricky immediately struck up a rapport with Mike. They exercised their horses at dawn every day in the surf and stick and balled together. Mike's game improved dramatically, and as a result David signed Ricky up as his senior pro for the next year. He and Ricky had been to the same school and understood each other. David was sick of the double-dealing and histrionics of the O'Briens.

Ricky had to confess that to the abscess-draining bliss of Bart's absence was added the relief of not having Chessie with him. He could concentrate on his game, and not worry the whole time whether she was bored, or spending too much money, or sulking because she wasn't spending money. He was well aware that his marriage was going badly, but being used to cold war over the years with Herbert, he didn't feel it was the end of the world.

After drinking at least a bottle and a half of champagne after the French Championships, Ricky tried to ring home, but the telephone was dead – probably been cut off. Suddenly, missing Chessie like hell, he decided to accept Victor Kaputnik's offer of a lift back to the Tiger's yard at Newbury. Sukey and Drew, who were coming too, had parked their car there, and could give him a lift back to Rutshire. Buoyed up by champagne, ecstatic with victory, he bought a dark green cashmere jersey for Chessie, a cowboy suit for Will, and stopped off at the supermarket and loaded up with garlic sausage, salami, Toblerone, huge tomatoes, and the cheese which smelt like joggers' socks which Chessie adored so much.

Victor's helicopter seated eight, so drinking continued on the flight, and Sukey, who didn't drink, drove Drew and Ricky back to Rutshire, so they were able to carry on boozing, reliving every chukka. Next Sunday's Gold Cup seemed well within their grasp now. Ricky sat in the back addressing occasional fond and drunken remarks to the huge silver cup which he would have to hand over to Bart tomorrow.

'We're going to spend the second half of our honeymoon in Argentina and find Drew some really good ponies,' said Sukey as she turned off the M4.

It must be nice having a wife who acted as chauffeur and remembered every shot you'd ever scored, thought Ricky. But he didn't think he could bring himself to sleep with Sukey. He was overwhelmed again with longing for Chessie. He should have forked out for a temporary nanny. They needed to spend more time together.

My luck has turned, he told himself again, as Sukey drove up the lime avenue. I'm going to be a better husband from now on. Robinsgrove was in darkness. Perhaps Chessie'd gone to stay with her mother. As he stood reeling uncertainly in the yard, he suddenly felt a sword-thrust of misery that Mattie wasn't there to welcome him. Then a white ghost shot out of the grooms' flat. Millicent the whippet, frisking round his legs, was overjoyed he was home. She was shortly followed by the two Labradors, and

Louisa, who was spilling out of a yellow sundress. Sounds of revelry were going on behind her.

'Whatever are you doing back?' she asked in horror.

'Just for the night,' said Ricky, clanking bottles as he searched in the carrier bag. 'We won.'

'Ohmigod, how wonderful,' said Louisa, flinging her arms round his swaying body. He was absolutely plastered, bless him.

'And Kinta won Best Playing Pony. Any problems?'

'No, everything's fine. They're all turned out except Wallaby, and his hock's much better. Come and have a drink to celebrate.'

The whoops and howls were increasing.

'Who the fuck's that?' shouted a voice.

'No thanks,' said Ricky, handing Louisa a garlic sausage, and a bottle of Cointreau. 'For you, where's Chessie?'

Louisa looked guilty. Ricky thought it was because he'd caught her having a party.

'Gosh thanks, she's left a note on the kitchen table. Millicent hasn't been eating,' she called after Ricky, as he tottered towards the house. 'But she will now you're home.'

Ricky realized how drunk he was when he tripped up the back doorstep, and nearly dropped the cup. God, that cheese stank. There was no moon, so he spent ages finding his keys.

The kitchen was incredibly tidy. Usually by Sunday night it was a tip. He dumped the carrier bags on the table, poured himself a large whisky, and was just about to open a tin of Chappie for Millicent, when he saw Chessie's letter. How odd, she'd put it in an envelope.

'Dear Ricky,' he read, 'I'm leaving you. I can't put up with a miserable, totally meaningless marriage any more. I'm taking Will. My lawyers will be in touch. Don't try and find me. Yours, Chessie.'

Very carefully he spooned the contents of the Chappie tin into Millicent's bowl and, putting it down, sprinkled biscuits over it. Then, as he walked towards the telephone and realized he'd scattered biscuits all over the floor, he started to shake, his thighs suddenly seemed to have a life of their own, leaping and trembling. His heart was crashing against his rib-cage.

The telephone was dead, so he went over to Louisa's flat, where he found a young man in pink boxer shorts brandishing the garlic sausage, like a large cock, at a frantically giggling Louisa. Her giggles died when she saw Ricky.

'Can I use your telephone?'

Louisa nodded. 'Use the one in the bedroom.'

'Chessie's left me,' Ricky told Drew over the telephone.

'Christ – I am sorry.'

'Did you know anything?'

'I'd heard rumours.'

'Why the fuck didn't you warn me?'

'I hoped it would blow over.'

'Who's the man?'

'You're not going to like this,' Drew paused. 'Bart Alderton.'

'Bart,' said Ricky incredulously, 'but he's old enough to be . . .'

'Her sugar daddy; that's what attracted her. Look, I'll come over.'

'No – I'm going round to kill him.'

'For Christ's sake, you're in no condition.'

But Ricky'd hung up.

Louisa was standing in the doorway, her eyes filled with tears.

'I'm so sorry,' she stammered. 'You oughtn't to drive. Wait till morning.'

But Ricky pushed straight past her. Millicent, having wolfed her dinner and hoovered up the biscuits on the floor, was determined not to be left behind and jumped belching into the now mended BMW.

It was a warm night. The clouds had rolled back leaving brilliant stars and a rising moon. As Ricky couldn't find the top of the whisky bottle, he wedged it in the side pocket, taking repeated slugs as he drove. He covered the twenty miles in as many minutes, overtaking two cars at once on the narrow roads, shooting crossroads. A cold rage had settled in. It wasn't Chessie's fault. Bart Alderton could corrupt anyone.

The electric gates had not yet been installed, so Ricky was able to open the iron ones. Deer and sheep blinked in the headlights as he drove up an avenue of chestnut trees. As he rattled over the second sheep grid, where the drive opened up into a big sweep of gravel, the beautiful seventeenth-century manor house, with its ruff of lavender and white roses clambering to the roof, was suddenly floodlit.

Little Millicent quivered in the back as four Rottweilers came roaring round the side of the house, fangs bared, growling horribly, scrabbling at the car's paintwork with thick black claws. Taking another slug of whisky, Ricky got out of the car and, because he was totally unafraid, only stopping to pat a sleek, snarling head or mutter a casual 'good dog', was able to walk unscathed through the pack and ring the door bell.

A security guard answered. His shoulders seemed to fill the door.

'Mrs France-Lynch?' said Ricky.

'You've got the wrong house, buddy.'

'I'm coming in to wait for her.'

'Who's that?' called Chessie's voice.

For a second the security man was caught on the hop. Shoving him aside, Ricky walked into the house. Chessie looked floodlit too. She was wearing a red silk dress, long-sleeved, high-necked and slinky, black shoes with four-inch heels, and huge rubies at her ears, neck and wrists. Her hair had been newly streaked, cut shorter and swept off her flawless face. Ricky caught his breath. She looked staggering. The tramp had become a lady.

'How dare you barge in here?' Radiant with spite, Chessie moved towards him. 'Get out. Bart'll be back in a minute, then we're going out – to Rubens' Retreat.' It was as though she was outlining the evening's whereabouts for a baby-sitter.

'How long's this been going on?'

'My being miserable? Since I met you, I guess.'

'You're coming home.'

'To that dump! I'm bloody not.'

She caught a waft of whisky. Ricky was wearing a crumpled dark blue shirt and jeans. Unshaven, very brown, his black hair falling over his forehead, he looked savage and dangerous.

Ricky dropped his eyes first and, aware of the hovering guard, turned left into the drawing room which had been

71

exquisitely furnished in soft corals and yellows by Grace. All the cushions looked as if they had been blown up with bicycle pumps.

'L-l-look, I know things have been difficult, but I love you.'

'Do you now?'

'I've been spending so much time on the ponies, so we could get straight. Things'll get better.'

'Bullshit,' screamed Chessie hysterically. 'Polo's a drug only curable by poverty or death, and you're hooked.'

'We won today.'

'So fucking what?' sneered Chessie. 'Bart's still going to drop you.'

Ricky bit his lip. 'David's going to sponsor me next year, and I've almost certainly got a patron for Palm Beach.'

'That still won't be enough to live on.'

'I'll tap my father.'

'Your father's a disgusting, crabby old man,' taunted Chessie, 'and you're getting more like him every day. I'm not having you damaging Will, like Herbert damaged you, making you incapable of showing affection for anything but a horse. I'm surprised you noticed we'd gone.'

Under the chandelier in the centre of the room, he could see she was uncharacteristically wearing a lot of make-up – making her look much harder. Bart's influence was already working.

'And you think Bart's the answer,' said Ricky slowly. 'I was fooled at the beginning. He'll crucify you; he's only interested in conquest. He beats up his horses; soon he'll do the same to you.'

He already has, thought Chessie, stretching voluptuously. She could hardly sit down after Bart had spanked her that afternoon.

'Bart's the most considerate man I've ever met.' Then, as Ricky raised his eyebrows, 'and the best lover. He could give you a bit of coaching. I'm fed up with being married to a failure in and out of bed.'

Ricky clenched his fists. For a second Chessie thought he was going to hit her. Mocking him with her enhanced beauty, she sauntered over to the drinks trolley, and with a totally steady hand poured herself a vodka and tonic. Her dress was so low-cut at the back that Ricky could see a violet bruise above the cleft of her buttocks.

'I'll make a bargain with you,' she said, swinging round. 'I'll come back to you the day you go to ten *and* win the Gold Cup.' She ticked the conditions off with long, scarlet nails. '*And* the day England win back the Westchester.'

It was virtually an impossibility. No English player had gone to ten since before the war, and the Westchester Cup, the Holy Grail of Anglo-American polo, had remained uncontested in American hands since 1939.

'You bitch,' whispered Ricky.

'I agree, it's highly unlikely,' said Chessie. Her laugh sounded horrible, almost mad.

'Daddy! Daddy!' Woken by the din, frightened by the shouting, Will, in pale blue pyjamas, trailing a huge, white, fluffy monkey, obviously the result of a trip to Harrods, ran into the room and threw himself into Ricky's arms. He was so excited he couldn't speak. Ricky clung on to his warm, chunky body, which smelt of talcum powder and shampoo, seeking sanity and comfort. This couldn't be happening. He couldn't let Chessie take Will away.

'Did you bring me a present?'

The cowboy suit was at home. Putting his hand in his jeans' pocket, Ricky pulled out a little silver pony with a detachable saddle and bridle that he'd been given as an extra prize for captaining the winning team. 'Here you are.'

'Horsie,' said Will, enraptured. 'Horsie like Mattie.' Then, turning to Chessie: 'Daddy stay the night?'

'Daddy's going,' said Chessie icily, reaching for the bell.

'Let me keep him for tonight.'

'No,' said Chessie alarmed. 'You'll kidnap him.'

'What are you planning to do with him?'

'Take him back to America of course, but we'll be back and forth to England all the time. Bart does so much business. I'm sure the lawyers will grant you visitation rights.'

'Visitation rights?' said Ricky, enraged. 'You're even talking like a fucking American now. He's my child, and I'm not having that bastard bringing him up. We're going home,' he said, pushing Will's blond fringe out of his eyes. Then, when Will looked doubtful: 'Millicent's in the car and you can see Louisa.'

Aware of the security man hovering in the hall, Ricky made a dive for the french windows.

'No,' screamed Chessie.

'Mummy,' bellowed Will, suddenly scared.

'Stop him,' yelled Chessie.

But Ricky was already sprinting across the lawn, with Will bawling his head off, and next minute the BMW was careering down the drive, scattering Rottweilers. They met Bart coming the other way and had to mount the verge to pass him. Ricky was in luck. Bart, because he was coming to pick up Chessie, had left the gates open. Poor Millicent was bouncing around in the back.

As stone walls and dusty August trees flashed by, Ricky knew he ought to fasten Will's seat belt, but all that seemed important for the moment was putting as much distance as possible between himself and Bart. There was a crossroads in half a mile where he could lose him. In mounting the verge he had spilt the whisky and the car reeked of drink.

'Want Mummy!' howled Will. 'Want Mummy!'

'It's all right, darling, you're safe. Daddy loves you, you'll see Mummy soon. I've got a present for you at home.'

Will's sobs subsided a little. Ahead the River Fleet gleamed in the moonlight. As they hurtled towards the bridge, Ricky put a hand on Will's leg to steady and reassure him. Next moment the moon slid behind a big, black cloud. Too late, he saw, in the pale glow of the headlights, a fox cub racing down the middle of the bridge towards him, its eyes yellow and panic-stricken. Instinctively Ricky swung to the left and hit the side of the bridge head on. Over the almighty crunch, he heard Will scream, felt an agonizing pain in his elbow and then blackness.

The two speed cops reached him before Bart. Millicent was whimpering in the back. Will was killed outright, his neck broken by the impact of the dashboard. Ricky was unconscious, the gash down the side of his face pouring blood, his right arm in a curiously vulnerable position. You could smell whisky all over the car.

'Plastered,' said one of the traffic cops, shaking his head, 'and neither of them wearing seat belts.'

Then, as the moon came out, he noticed the polo stickers on the windscreen and the little silver pony clutched in Will's hand.

'Christ, it's Ricky France-Lynch,' he said.

As his companion rang for an ambulance, he tried to coax Millicent out of the back. Seeing Ricky's licence on the floor, he flipped through it.

'Thought as much,' he muttered. 'Two drunk-driving charges already. They'll clobber him for manslaughter, poor sod. He thought the world of that kid, poor little bugger.'

8

Nearly four months after William France-Lynch was killed in a car crash and his father arrested on charges of manslaughter and drunken driving, Perdita Macleod broke up for the Christmas holidays. Having been expelled from Queen Augusta's for carousing with the Carlisle twins and walking out of her English exam, she had been dispatched to an even stricter and more expensive boarding school. Only the threat that she wouldn't be given a polo pony for Christmas had prevented her running away.

To the bliss of breaking up was the added thrill that her mother and stepfather had at last moved into Brock House, a rambling medieval rectory on the Rutshire-Gloucestershire border. Six miles from Rutshire Polo Club, it was, even more excitingly, only two miles from Eldercombe, the village in which Ricky France-Lynch lived. Although the poor darling, Perdita reflected bitterly, was still cooling his heels in Rutminster gaol awaiting trial.

Terrified lest her mother would be eccentrically dressed or, even worse, blub in 'Oh, Little Town of Bethlehem', Perdita had failed to send home the invitation to the end-of-term carol service, merely telling her to pick her up afterwards. Perdita was normally too idle to lift anything heavier than a cigarette, but today, in the hope of a lightning getaway, she had lugged her trunk, her record player, carrier bags full of posters, dirty washing, polo magazines, holiday work (some hope), Vivaldi the hampster and a yucca called Kevin down three flights of stairs and piled them up outside her school house.

Alas, just as everyone was spilling out of chapel – identikit mothers in on-the-knee suits, identikit fathers in fawn coats with brown velvet collars – Perdita's mother, Daisy, rolled up in an absolutely filthy, falling-apart Mini and immediately started tooting and waving like a rainbow windmill. Abandoning the car and blocking everyone's way, she ran across the tarmac to fling her arms round her daughter.

Finally Perdita, crimson in the face, was able to wriggle free and start hurling carrier bags into the car, as the held-up traffic tooted and everyone, particularly the fawn-coated fathers, stared in amazement.

Why, thought Perdita savagely, does my mother have to be so wacky, and so demonstrative, and, even worse, look half the age of any of the other mothers? Daisy in fact looked adorable. In her early thirties, she had the round, grave, dark brown eyes, the rosy cheeks, the long, straight, shiny brown hair parted in the middle, and gaudy taste in clothes of a Matrioska doll.

But when she stopped worrying and smiled, her eyes had the joyous sparkle and her mouth the dark pink bewitching softness of Hogarth's Shrimp Girl. Today she was less gaudy than usual. Trying to catch a landscape in a certain light before she left, she had forgotten to take off her painting smock or wash the Alizarin crimson off her hands and looked as if she'd been killing a pig. On her left cheek was a large splodge of burnt sienna, which she'd used to capture the faded ginger of the oak woods beneath the new house.

'Oh look, there's Blue Teddy,' cried Daisy, in her slightly breathless voice which squeaked when she got excited. She propped Perdita's ancient teddy bear up between Kevin the yucca and the record player. 'Now he can see out of the window, it's such a ravishing drive home. Oh, there's Miss Osbourne,' went on Daisy, scrabbling in the back as she saw Perdita's house mistress bearing down on them. 'I bought her a bottle of Bristol Cream.'

'No, Mum, she's an old bitch,' hissed Perdita. 'For Christ's sake, get in, we're holding up the traffic.'

'Hi, Perdita! Have a good Christmas.' A group of classmates, to whom Perdita, with her beauty, outward insouciance and murderous wit, was a source of constant fascination, peered in through the window.

'Are you Perdita's friends?' asked Daisy, who'd never been allowed to meet any of them. 'How lovely! We've just moved to Rutshire. Perhaps you'd like to come and stay in the holidays.'

The tooting was getting deafening.

'Mum, for God's sake,' shrieked Perdita.

'By-ee,' shouted Daisy, windmilling to Miss Osbourne and the group of girls as she set off in a succession of jerks down the drive, narrowly avoiding ramming the car in front as she stopped to admire the trailing yellow twigs of a willow tree against an angry navy-blue sky.

'Can't think what's wrong with the car,' said Daisy as it ground to a halt and died just inside the school gates. The tooting became even more acrimonious as she frantically tried the ignition.

'Need any help?' The father of Lucinda Montague, Perdita's sworn enemy, reeking of brandy from his office party, popped his head inside the car.

'It won't budge,' said Daisy helplessly.

''Fraid you've run out of petrol.'

Daisy, who always found the wrong things funny, went off into peals of laughter. Perdita put her head in her hands. It was not until four fathers, all roaring with laughter, who'd also obviously been to office parties, lifted the Mini out of the way and Miss Osbourne had provided a can of petrol, and they'd reached the slow lane of the motorway, and Daisy'd apologized a hundred times, that Perdita thawed enough to light a cigarette and ask what the house was like.

'Oh, gorgeous,' said Daisy, thrilled to be forgiven. 'You cannot believe the views. This morning the whole valley was palest cobalt green with frost, and the shadows of the bare trees were . . . '

'Do Eddie and Violet like it?' interrupted Perdita who was bored rigid by 'Nature'.

'Adore it! There's so much space after London.'

'I bet they've bagged the best rooms.'

'Every room is best. We're going to be so happy. You've already been asked to a Pony Club Barn Dance.'

'I wouldn't be seen dead,' said Perdita scornfully. No-one who'd bopped the night away with Jesus and the Carlisle twins would lower herself to a Pony Club hop. 'When can we get my pony?'

'Well, I rang the twins as you suggested. They're in Argentina, but their groom put me on to a man outside Rutminster, who's got a bay mare. If you like her, subject to a vet's certificate, you should be able to have her right away, although Daddy may think you should wait till Christmas Day.'

'That's stupid. Christmas isn't for ten days. I could be schooling or even hunting her by then. How much are you prepared to pay?'

'I can't see Daddy going much above £500.'

'You won't get a three-legged donkey for that,' snapped Perdita, stubbing out her cigarette and lighting another one.

'The move's been dreadfully expensive,' began Daisy hopefully. 'Perhaps if your report's good . . . '

'Don't be fatuous. Daddy doesn't give a shit about my reports! Now if it were Violet or Eddie . . . '

'That's not true,' protested Daisy, knowing it was.

'When's Granny Macleod arriving?'

'Twenty-third,' said Daisy gloomily.

'That's all we need. Now she's a widow, she'll be more ghastly and self-obsessed than ever.'

Daisy knew she ought to reprove Perdita, but she had never got on with her mother-in-law herself and was dreading having her for Christmas. Bridget Macleod, in her turn, had never forgiven her daughter-in-law for having what she referred to as 'a past'.

Nearly sixteen years ago, when she was only seventeen, Daisy had become pregnant while she was at art college. Her parents were so appalled when they learned the circumstances in which the baby was conceived that they threw Daisy out. Eventually Daisy gave birth to a daughter, and called her Perdita – 'the lost one' – because she knew she couldn't afford to keep her. In utter despair, while going through the legal process of adoption, Daisy had met a trainee barrister, Hamish Macleod. Hamish was one of those stolid young men who grew a beard and had a flickering of social conscience during the sixties, which was firmly doused by the economic gloom of the seventies.

Moved by Daisy's plight, rendered sleepless by her beauty, Hamish asked her to marry him so that she could keep the baby. Daisy had accepted with passionate gratitude. Hamish was good-looking and seemed kind; she was sure she could grow to love him – anything to keep Perdita. Hamish's family – particularly his mother, Bridget – were appalled. Scottish, lower-middle class, rigidly respectable, they branded Daisy a whore who had blighted their only son's dazzling career at the Bar. They had threatened to black the wedding unless Daisy put on a wedding ring and pretended that she was a young widow whose husband had been killed in a car crash.

Daisy, after fifteen years of marriage, still looked absurdly young. Kind, sympathetic, dreamy, hopelessly disorganized, she had become increasingly insecure, because Hamish, who had now left the Bar and become a successful television producer, never stopped putting her down and complaining about her ineptitude as a mother, her lack of domesticity and her lousy dress sense. Subconsciously, he'd never forgiven her for having Perdita illegitimately and hit the roof if she looked at other men at parties. He also ruthlessly discouraged her considerable gifts as a painter, because they reminded him of her rackety art-student past and because he considered there was no money in it.

Nor could he ever forgive Perdita for her strange beauty, her bolshiness and her dazzling athletic ability. Throughout the marriage he had pointedly lavished affection on the two children, Violet and Eddie, now aged thirteen and eight, whom he and Daisy had had subsequently. Less glamorous than Perdita, they were sweeter-tempered and better-adjusted.

Daisy's fatal weakness was a reluctance to hurt anyone. She had tried and tried to screw up the courage to tell Perdita the truth about her birth, but, terrified of the tantrums this would trigger off, she had funked it, feeding her the official line that her father had been killed in a car crash. 'We were so in love, darling, but he never knew I was pregnant.'

Daisy dreaded the day when Perdita might want to know the name of her real father. At least her blinkered obsession with polo and ponies had some advantages. Aware, however, that Hamish didn't love her, Perdita tried to trigger off a response by behaving atrociously. Matters weren't helped by Bridget Macleod's ability to beam simultaneously at Hamish, Violet and Eddie, and freeze out Daisy and Perdita. This reduced Daisy to gibbering sycophancy and Perdita to utter outrageousness.

Dark thoughts about her mother-in-law's impending visit occupied Daisy until darkness fell, by which time they had reached the village of Appleford where several cottages in the High Street already sported holly rings and the village shop window was bright with crackers and Christmas puddings. Brock House lay a quarter of a mile on, its gates flanked by pillars topped by stone badgers. Bumping down the pitted drive Daisy reached a fork. To the left, past vast unkept rose bushes and a dovecote, lay farm buildings which had been converted into garages, stables and a tackroom with paddocks behind. To the right, flowerbeds edged with box and a paved terrace led down stone steps to the back of Brock House. Shaggy with creepers, long and low, with its little lit-up windows, the house had a secretive air. On the far side, beyond a large lawn edged with herbaceous borders, the land dropped sharply into the Appleford Valley, thickly wooded with oaks and larches, and famous for its badger sets.

Inside was chaos. Daisy had made heroic attempts to get straight after moving, but now the children had come home bringing their own brand of mess. Violet and Eddie were in the kitchen, and greeted their elder sister guardedly.

'What's for supper?' asked Eddie, who was circling advertisements in *Exchange and Mart*.

'Chicken casserole and chocolate mousse to celebrate Perdita's first night home,' said Daisy.

'There was,' said Violet. 'You left the larder door open and Gainsborough got at the chicken. Then he was sick. I cleared it up, and I got some sausages from the village shop.'

Thank God for Violet, thought Daisy. Violet Macleod had inherited Daisy's sweet nature and round face and Hamish's solid figure, freckles and curly, dark-red hair, which clashed with her high colour when she blushed. She also had beautifully turned-down amethyst eyes, which, she pointed out ruefully, matched her plump purple legs. Less bright than Perdita, she did much better at school because she was hard-working and methodical and because she knew you needed straight 'A's to become a vet. Violet spent much of her time sticking up for her father and grandmother and protecting her mother from Perdita's tantrums. She was now combing the recently sick, long-haired ginger tomcat, Gainsborough, who was mewing horribly.

'Stop it,' said Violet firmly. 'You know fur balls make you sick.'

Eddie, at eight, looked not unlike a bouncer in a nightclub. Slightly dyslexic, hugely entertaining, he was interested in making a fast buck and enjoying himself. He had already found another prep schoolboy across the valley with whom to spend his time. His current ambition was to have a gun for Christmas. Daisy was dragging her feet because she felt Eddie might easily murder his elder sister.

'Give us a fag, Perdita,' said Eddie as Perdita got out a packet of Silk Cut.

'Eddie!' said Violet, shocked. 'You are much too young.'

'Want us to show you round?' asked Eddie.

Unloading the car, listening to the thundering feet and yells of excitement as the children raced along the passages, Daisy prayed that in this house they would at last be a really happy family.

'The stables are fantastic,' said Perdita with rare enthusiasm when she returned twenty minutes later with the others.

When the telephone rang, Daisy answered. From the way their mother stiffened and her voice became nervous and conciliatory, the children knew it was their father. Now she was apologizing for forgetting to get his suit back from the cleaners.

'I'll pick it up first thing in the morning. Perdita's home. Would you like a word?' For a second Perdita's normally dead-pan face was vulnerable and hopeful.

'Well, you'll see her later. Oh, I see, you must be frantic. See you tomorrow night then. He's not coming home,' explained Daisy, putting down the receiver.

'Because he knows I'm back,' said Perdita flatly.

'Nonsense,' blustered Daisy. 'He sent tons of love.'

All three children knew she was lying.

'He's only got love for Eddie,' sneered Perdita, 'and not-so-shrinking Violet. Can I have a vodka and tonic? I am fifteen now.'

'Oh, all right,' said Daisy. Anything to keep the peace.

9

'Dark, dark, dark,' wailed Daisy a week later. 'The Hoover's gone phut, the washing machine's broken down, Hamish says the place is a tip, and the kitchen brush has alopecia.'

'I'm off.' Perdita, dressed for hunting in boots, skin-tight breeches and a dark blue coat, went straight to the house-keeping jar.

'What are you doing?' asked Daisy.

'I need money for the cap.'

'You took a tenner yesterday.'

'I'll pay you back out of my Christmas present money,' said Perdita, rushing off towards the stables.

'Where's my dark green sweater?' bellowed Hamish from upstairs. 'There are two buttons missing off my blazer and why the hell isn't there any loo paper?'

Daisy sighed. Hamish had come back exhausted after a week's filming last night to watch one of his programmes – a documentary on road haulage. Daisy hadn't helped matters by falling asleep because it was so boring. The moment the final credits went up, Hamish's mother was on the telephone telling him how wonderful it had been. When no-one else rang, Hamish, who was pathological about his beauty sleep, retired to bed. The telephone then started up again, but instead of being congratulations from Jeremy Isaacs and Alasdair Milne, it was friends of the children, catching up on gossip and wondering what life in the country was like, until Hamish was screaming with irritation.

Now he was downstairs bellyaching because Perdita had whipped the last of the housekeeping money. 'I told you to always keep a float. I don't know them well enough in the village shop to ask them to cash a cheque. What time's *Peter Pan*?'

'Oh, Christ,' said Daisy hysterically. 'I'd forgotten all about *Peter Pan*. I can't go. I've got to get everything ready for your mother tomorrow, and do all the cooking, and shopping, and buy the stocking presents, and I haven't wrapped any of the other presents, and I've got to stay in for the washing-machine man. We haven't got any clean sheets.'

Hamish looked at her pityingly. 'I can't understand why you can't treat Christmas like any other weekend. I suppose you've got your period coming.'

'I've got your bloody mother coming,' muttered Daisy into the sink.

'Wendy can do the shopping,' said Hamish loftily, '*and* the stocking presents. Give me the list.'

'But she must be frantic,' protested Daisy. Wendy was Hamish's PA, who seemed to work for him twenty-four hours a day.

'It's always the busiest people who find the time,' said Hamish sanctimoniously. 'Wendy can take the children to *Peter Pan*. I'll bring them and the shopping home afterwards. I hope,' he added ominously, 'you're going to get things shipshape for Mother. She's had a very stressful year and needs a rest.'

In the past, on hearing Hamish's car draw up outside, Daisy had been known to take mugs out of the dish washer and frantically start washing them up in the sink, so much did Hamish hate to see her inactive. He was a successful film producer because he was good at keeping costs down, finicky about detail, and had brilliant empathy with his leading ladies who found him attractive because, to use one of his favourite phrases, he 'targeted' on them. Hamish, in fact, looked rather like an Old Testament prophet who regretted shaving off his beard for a bet. Copper-beech red hair rippling to his collar, a wide noble forehead, smouldering hazel eyes beneath jutting black brows, and a fine, hooked nose with flaring nostrils lapsed into a petulant mouth and a receding chin. Hamish also loved the sound of his own voice, which reminded him of brown burns tumbling over mossy rocks in the Highlands. Having muscular hips and good legs, he also wore a kilt on every possible occasion.

He was now, however, soberly dressed in grey flannels, and applying a clothes brush to the small of his blazered back, as he grumbled about cat hair. The moment he'd borne Eddie, Violet and the shopping list off to work, Daisy felt guilty about making such a scene. With the pressure off, she started reading the *Daily Mail*.

'I believe it is possible,' a young American girl was quoted as saying, 'to have a caring, supportive husband, cherishing children, and a high octane career.'

I have none of these things, thought Daisy, I only want to paint.

Later that evening she and Violet decorated the house. Violet organized a bucket of earth and red crêpe paper for the tree, and Daisy was comforted by the rituals of hanging up the same plastic angel with both legs firmly stuck together and the tinsel with split ends and the coloured balls which had lost their hooks, and had to be tucked into the branches until they fell prey to Gainsborough.

In the alcove by the front door they set up the crib, which had been in the Macleod family for generations. There had nearly been a divorce the year Daisy painted the plain wooden figures, putting Mary in powder blue and Joseph in a rather ritzy orange.

'Did you enjoy *Peter Pan*?' asked Daisy, as she arranged straw from the stables in Baby Jesus's manger.

'It was fun,' said Violet. 'I'd forgotten Captain Hook went to Eton. Daddy loved it too.'

'Daddy came with you?' said Daisy in amazement.

'Wendy got an extra ticket,' explained Violet, standing on a chair to tie mistletoe to the hall light. 'He gets on awfully well with Wendy. They're always laughing.'

That's nice, thought Daisy wistfully. Hamish seldom laughed at home.

'The lost boys reminded me of Perdita,' said Violet.

Life would be so peaceful, thought Daisy, if it were just her and Violet. Now they were alone, she could tell Violet how wonderful her report was.

Daisy also felt guilty that Perdita's new pony had cost £1,500. A beautiful bay mare called Fresco, she had arrived with a saddle and a pound note tucked into her bridle for luck, which Perdita had nailed to the tackroom wall.

But that was only the beginning. Fresco's trousseau of rugs, so new they practically stood up by themselves, and headcollars and body brushes and curry combs, not to mention feed, had cost a fortune. At least Perdita was blissful. Having established an instant rapport with the pony, she was totally organized and reliable about looking after her. It was such a relief having her in a good mood and out of the house, hunting and exploring the countryside, particularly near Ricky France-Lynch's land, but Daisy still felt she ought to buy better presents for the other two children.

Hamish had violently discouraged Daisy against taking any interest in money, on the grounds that she was too stupid to understand it. But she had felt mildly alarmed when he told her they were only going to rent Brock House, because he had invested almost the entire proceeds from the London house in a co-production with the Americans. The resulting movie, he assured her, would be such a sure-fire hit he'd recoup his original stake five times over and be able to buy Brock House or something far grander in a year or two. The spare cash left over gave Daisy the illusion that for once they were flush. She must find something more exciting for Violet than that Laura Ashley dress. Suddenly she had a brainwave.

At least Bridget coming made her tidy up, thought Daisy the following day, as she plumped the cushions in the drawing room and used eight fire-lighters and all yesterday's *Mail* and *Telegraph* to light the logs Hamish had grudgingly chopped that morning. And at least they weren't going to Bridget's for Christmas. With a shiver, Daisy remembered the year when baby Eddie and Violet, and particularly Perdita, had trodden Lindt kittens into Bridget's carpet and sacked her ultra-tidy house more effectively than any Hun or Visigoth.

Going into the garden to pick some pinched pink roses and winter jasmine for Bridget's bedroom, Daisy breathed in the sweet, just freezing air, the acrid smell of bonfires and leaves moulding into the cocoa-brown earth.

The red had gone out of the woods now; they were uniformly dun and donkey brown, with the traveller's joy glittering silken over the tops of the trees in the setting sun.

In a fringe of beeches across the valley, rooks grumbled like waves scraping on shingle.

It was so beautiful. If *only* she could paint, but Hamish would be driving Biddy, as his mother was nicknamed, down from the airport now. I must try to be efficient and nice to her and forget about painting until she leaves, Daisy told herself firmly. I must be grateful for the millionth time to Hamish for saving me from solitary evenings in peeling bedsitters with one bar on the fire, and a forty-watt bulb and no money. And look at Perdita whom Hamish had enabled to live in this glorious house and hunt this wonderful pony. Every Macleod had a silver lining.

As always, she felt even guiltier when Hamish came through the door with his mother, such a frail little person with tears in her eyes who smelt of Tweed cologne and brought home-made fudge and shortbread and a bottle of whisky for Hamish.

How could I have turned her into such a monster, thought Daisy as she put on the kettle. There was a clatter of hooves outside and Perdita appeared at the back door.

'I suppose there's no hope the Glasgow shuttle crashed with no survivors?' she asked.

'Hush, she's arrived,' said Daisy. 'You must try and be nice to Granny, and for God's sake, tidy your room when you've sorted out Fresco. Daddy's bound to show her round the house. Did you have a good day?'

'Brilliant, we got three foxes. I got a brush.' Perdita's face was muddy, but her pale cheeks were for once flushed with colour and her dark eyes sparkled like jet.

'Rupert Campbell-Black was out. Christ, he's good-looking. He gave me several swigs of brandy, and Billy Lloyd-Foxe too; he's really nice and gave me two fags, and they both said it wouldn't hurt Fresco to hunt her and play polo. Hunting was the best way to get used to a young horse, and Rupert told me he was going to have one more crack at the World Championships next year, and then give up show-jumping. And Drew Benedict was there, and the twins. They're off to Palm Beach just after Christmas, but we're going to get together in the spring holidays, and Fresco jumped a bullfinch at least six foot high, and that journalist Beattie Johnson came to the meet. She said she was getting material for an in-depth interview with Ricky. Rupert pissed her up and said he was only interested in in-depth intercourse. Of course she was only digging up dirt. Evidently Ricky's taken Will's death terribly hard, and that bitch Chessie buggered off with all the France-Lynch jewellery, and when you think how rich Bart is. It's all right, I'm coming, sweetheart,' she turned back to Fresco. 'I can't tell you how much I like living in Rutshire. Rupert and Billy gave us a lift home in their lorry. We really must get a trailer.'

'Not at the moment,' said Daisy, coming out to give Fresco a piece of carrot.

'Where's the newly-wid now?' asked Perdita.

'She's upstairs,' Daisy giggled. 'You mustn't be naughty. It must be awful being widowed.'

'Bet she's knocked out. She can't have loved Grandpa, the way she bossed him around. The poor old sod must be having the best Christmas ever, first time he's rested in peace for forty years.'

By the time Biddy Macleod had expressed joy and amazement at the increased growth and splendour of Violet and Eddie, and at Hamish's taste in putting up pictures (none of them Daisy's) and arranging the furniture, although Aunt Madge's chest of drawers in the spare room could do with a 'guid' polish, and come downstairs having unpacked – 'I'm not happy till I get straight' – and how it was late for tea at five, although flying made one work up a thirst, and what a nice young fellow had insisted on carrying her hand luggage at the airport, Daisy had decided Biddy was an absolute monster again.

And she didn't look remotely frail any more – just a bossy old bag with mean little eyes like burnt currants, a tight white perm and a disapproving mouth like a puckered-up dog's bum. She doesn't mind being widowed at all, thought Daisy. It leaves her free to indulge her real passion: Hamish.

The first black Daisy put up was to forget Biddy had lemon in her tea.

'Trust Hamish to remember,' said Biddy, smiling mistily.

Chuntering, Daisy belted back to the kitchen, but got distracted. Through the clematis and winter jasmine which framed the hall window, she could see the red afterglow of the sunset, blackly striped by a poplar copse. I must remember it just like that, she thought, it wouldn't be a cliché with the picture frame of creeper.

'Mummy!' called Violet. 'You were getting Granny some lemon. Mummy was looking out of the window,' she explained to her grandmother and Hamish. 'She finds things so beautiful sometimes she forgets what she's doing.'

Hamish's and Biddy's eyes met.

'I must get that creeper cut back, it's ruining the brickwork,' said Hamish.

'I got seventy-five Christmas cards,' Biddy was boasting as Daisy came back having scraped the mould off a wizened slice of lemon. 'I'd prefer it black,' Biddy said pointedly.

'Can't you remember anything?' snapped Hamish, glaring at Daisy.

'As long as it's wet and warm,' said Biddy with a martyred sigh. 'I was saying I got seventy-five Christmas cards. So many people wrote saying such nice things about your father, Hamish, I brought them with me.'

'We didn't get many this year,' said Hamish petulantly. 'Daisy was so late in sending out the change of address cards.'

As Daisy was clearing away the tea things and Biddy had been poured a wee glass of sherry, Hamish suddenly went to the gramophone and put on a record that had just reached Number One in the charts.

'I must just play you this lovely record, Mother.'

It was some choirboy singing a poignant solo beginning, 'If onlee your Christmas could be my Christmas,' and going on to expound on the loneliness of being separated from loved ones during the festive season.

'But you don't like pop music, Daddy,' said Violet in amazement.

'I know, but I heard it on the car radio and fell in love with it. It's great isn't it, Mother?'

'Very moving,' said Biddy. 'I love the sound of choirboys' voices.'

At that moment Perdita walked in. Still flushed from hunting, still in her white shirt, tie, breeches and boots, she looked utterly ravishing. Surely Biddy will concede that, thought Daisy.

'Hello, Granny,' said Perdita guardedly, making no attempt to kiss her grandmother.

'You've shot up,' said Biddy accusingly. 'I hear your father's bought you a pony. I hope you realize what a lucky girl you are.'

'She's lovely,' agreed Perdita. 'What's for supper, Mum? I'm starving.'

Going to the drinks tray, she poured herself a large vodka and tonic.

'What the hell are you doing?' thundered Hamish.

'Mum always lets me.'

Biddy's dog's-bum mouth puckered up even more disapprovingly.

'How's your new school?'

'Horrific.'

'And have you decided what you're going to do when you grow up?'

Perdita smiled. 'I'm going to get divorced.'

'I beg your pardon?'

'I'm going to marry a mega-rich businessman, catch him cheating on me, and take him to the cleaners. Mum, I truly am going to need a trailer. The meets after Christmas are too far away to hack to.'

Biddy's and Hamish's simultaneous explosions were diverted by the doorbell. Thankful to escape from the fray, Daisy fled to answer it.

'Oh, the little duck,' they could hear her saying from the hall. 'Violet darling, I'm sorry you had to have her before Christmas, but here's your present.'

The next moment an English setter puppy had padded happily and confidently into the drawing room. She had a black patch over one eye like Nelson, black ears, a lean speckled body like a baby seal, and a tail which hadn't unfurled its feathers, but which shook her whole body every time she wagged it.

'Oh, Mummy,' gasped Violet as the puppy joyfully licked her bright pink face. 'She's the loveliest thing in the world. I can't believe it. Is she really mine? Oh, I love her.'

'And who is going to look after her when Violet goes back to school?' said Hamish furiously.

'I am,' said Daisy. 'Then I won't be lonely when you're away so much. I've had a lot of dropped telephone calls this week, which I'm sure must be burglars checking up – a large dog's a terrific deterrent.'

It was hard to tell who looked more disapproving, when having rushed round in excitement, and tried to snatch Biddy's knitting, the puppy peed on the rug in front of the fire.

'That rug was a wedding present from the McGaragles,' thundered Hamish.

'I'll get a cloth,' said Violet. 'Oh, thank you, Mum, she's the best present I've ever had.'

By the time Ethel, as the puppy was now called, had rampaged round the house, chased Gainsborough up the tree with subsequent loss of glass balls, peed again twice, had a bowl of scrambled egg, and fallen asleep on a cushion by the Aga, Daisy had managed to get supper ready.

It was the first time they had eaten in the dark green dining room with the big window looking over the valley and the red berries of the holly tucked behind every picture gleaming in the candlelight. Daisy had taken a lot of trouble to make *coq au vin* and a meringue and ice-cream pudding with raspberry purée. Hamish wasn't going to have a public row with Daisy about the puppy; instead he pointedly ignored her, making no comment about the food and telling his mother at great length about the new film he was making on Robert Burns.

'I've got no airpetite since your father passed away, but I must keep my strength up,' said Biddy, piling a Matterhorn of mashed potato on to her plate. She had always been the most demonstrative leaver, always taking too much so she could leave a lot. Worst of all, she ate terribly slowly. Violet, who longed to play with the puppy, and Perdita and Eddie, who wanted to watch television, were nearly going crazy and only waited because they wanted some pudding.

Perdita lit a cigarette.

'Put it out,' thundered Hamish.

Perdita pretended to snore. Eddie got the giggles. Violet went bright crimson trying not to giggle. Daisy had to rush out of the room to get the pudding.

'It's absolutely yummy,' said Violet, accepting a second helping.

'Can we have it instead of Christmas pudding?' asked Eddie.

Biddy Macleod said nothing. She wanted to leave it, but she was too greedy.

'You must be tired, Mother,' said Hamish. 'Early bed with a hotty, I think.'

Biddy, who loved it when her son was masterful, admitted she was a little weary. 'But before I turn in, I'd love to see your road haulage film again.'

'But *International Velvet*'s on,' protested Perdita.

'You can watch it in your bedrooms,' said Hamish heavily.

'But we can't tape it,' wailed Eddie, 'and my television shows snow storms on all four channels.'

'Mine's broken,' said Perdita.

'If your mother occasionally saw fit to get anything mended,' said Hamish nastily, 'you wouldn't be in this predicament. For once you are not going to do everything you want.'

Biddy smiled at Violet. 'Would you kindly make me a cup of Horlicks? I brought my own jar. It's on the hall table. I didn't think you'd have any here, although Hamish used to love a drink of Horlicks.'

Ignoring Perdita, who was looking at her with horror, a cold, blank stare coming straight off the North Pole, Biddy added, 'And if you're coming up, Eddie, there's no waste-paper basket in the guest room, nor toilet paper in the guest bathroom.'

'Where is Ethel going to sleep?' said Daisy, as she wearily finished clearing up.

'In my room,' said Violet, who was gently teasing the diving, biting Ethel with an old slipper.

'She is *not*,' thundered Hamish, who had just dispatched Biddy to bed. 'I am not having this house reduced to a urinal. How *could* you introduce a puppy at Christmas?' he added to Daisy. 'All the dog charities say it's the worst time. She will sleep in the stables.'

Because he doted on Violet, he relented enough to allow Ethel to sleep in the kitchen with a ticking clock wrapped in a towel to simulate her mother's heartbeat.

'We must start as we mean to go on,' said Hamish, getting into bed with his pyjamas buttoned up to the neck, and pointedly turning out the light on his side of the bed. A great howl rent the air.

'Christ,' said Hamish.

'Oh, I love the sound of puppies' voices,' said Perdita from the television room, as an even more piteous howl rent the air.

'Silent night, silent night,' giggled Eddie from his bedroom.

'Oh, poor Ethel,' said Violet, from the landing, trying not to cry.

'Typical,' exploded Hamish. 'My mother has come here for a rest, I am totally exhausted and have to be on location at six tomorrow, and you introduce that incontinent beast. I think you do these things deliberately.'

'I truly don't,' said Daisy humbly. 'I just thought Violet deserved something special.'

'Because you've bankrupted me buying that pony for Perdita.'

Ethel's howls were growing in volume.

'Let Violet get her, just for tonight,' pleaded Daisy.

'No,' said Hamish. 'Will no-one listen to the voice of common sense? I hope you're satisfied you're ruining mine and my mother's Christmas. There's no way I'll get to sleep now.'

As Daisy lay twitching in the darkness, waiting for the next explosion, Hamish started snoring. Unheard by her father, Violet had tiptoed downstairs and carried a delighted, wriggling Ethel upstairs to bed with her.

In the television room, unconcerned by any of the rumpus she had caused earlier, Perdita lit a cigarette and put in a tape of last year's Polo International, freezing it every time Ricky hit the ball. One day she'd have a swing as good as his.

Christmas Eve started badly. Hamish buzzed off humming 'If Onlee', leaving Daisy with a mass of food to buy, all the presents to wrap up and dispatch, and Biddy Macleod to entertain. A hard overnight frost symbolized Biddy's mood and put paid to any hunting, so Perdita was hanging around winding everyone up. The ever-tactful Violet took Biddy on an extended tour of the house. As some sort of death-wish, afterwards Daisy couldn't resist showing Biddy the stables. Surely the old bag could find something nice to say about the immaculate tack room, and the gleaming, contented Fresco, fetlock deep in clean straw. But Biddy merely remarked it was a pity Perdita didn't keep her bedroom like that and how 'all that equipment must have cost puir Hamish a fortune'.

Daisy bit her lip.

'But Fresco's been a huge success, Perdita's been so much easier since she's got a real interest, and the children are fighting so much less,' she protested.

'Mummy, Mummy,' yelled Violet from her bedroom window. 'Quickly, Perdita's killing Eddie.'

'Whatever for?' said Daisy, racing over the gravel.

'He's recorded *The Wizard of Oz* over her International tape.'

Christmas Eve deteriorated. After lunch Biddy solemnly rootled out Hamish's mending and sourly sewed to the Festival of Nine Lessons and Carols. Ever-placating, Daisy kept rushing in, putting more logs on the fire and offering cups of tea. Hamish should have been back after lunch, but didn't return until seven, singing 'If Onlee' and sucking extra strong mints.

'At least, have a rest tomorrow and Boxing Day,' Biddy implored him.

'I'll have to go in on Boxing Day and look at the rushes.'

'You work too hard.'

Out of despair and to get her through the nightmare of packing presents, Daisy got stuck into the vodka and orange much too early. She made heroic attempts to have dinner bang on eight, leaving a beef casserole in the slow oven of the Aga. Then she discovered to her horror at ten to eight that Perdita had replaced the beef with some barley she was boiling overnight for Fresco.

'You did it on purpose,' yelled Hamish.

'I did not,' screamed Perdita. 'I didn't know it was for tonight.'

Daisy burst into tears. Biddy, who'd set like a jelly all day, suggested she rustle something up. Instead Hamish, with an air of martyrdom, swept Biddy, Violet and Eddie out to supper at the local pub, saying they'd go on to Midnight Mass afterwards. He refused to take Perdita. Seeing Perdita's white, set face, Daisy said she had all the stockings to do and she'd skip supper and walk down to Midnight Mass later.

Upstairs in her bedroom, with a bottle of Benedictine, she started frantically cocooning presents with Sellotape. Biddy would be shocked; she believed in recycled paper and string.

It was past eleven-thirty by the time Daisy had finished the stockings. It's the only time fat, lumpy legs are acceptable, she thought, laying them on the bed. She ought to get ready for church but she couldn't find her boots anywhere.

Looking for them downstairs, she found Ethel crunching something up in the hall. She was so adorable with her thumping tail and speckled head. Then, as Ethel coughed up a piece of wood, which was definitely orange, Daisy let out a moan.

'What's up?' said Perdita, who was eating Philadelphia cheese with a spoon in the kitchen.

'Ethel's eaten St Joseph,' wailed Daisy. 'Granny'll have a heart attack.'

'Hooray,' said Perdita. 'I've bought her the *Jane Fonda Work Out Book* for Christmas. Hopefully it'll finish her off. It's nearly midnight, let's go out and see if Fresco's kneeling down to honour the birth of Christ.'

The grey, lurex lawn crunched beneath their feet. Jupiter, Orion, Capella and the Dog Star blazed overhead. There were never such stars in London, thought Daisy. Fresco gave a low, deep whinny of welcome, but didn't bother to get up as Perdita sat down beside her.

'That means they're happy and relaxed,' said Perdita proudly. 'If they lie down. Isn't she beautiful? She's the best friend I've ever had, thank you so much, Mum. I'll be a great polo player one day, and then I can support you.'

Unbelievably touched, tight from tiredness and Benedictine, Daisy wandered away from the stable door. Then, behind her, from the black church spire, she heard the mad, romping din of the bells echoing down the white frozen valley, celebrating the birth of Christ.

The hopes and fears of all the years, thought Daisy, overwhelmed with a wave of loneliness and despair. How wonderful to love and be in love at Christmas. Then, wiping away the tears, she chided herself. How ridiculous to think there was more to life than a husband, children and a lovely house.

'I do love you,' she mumbled much later when Hamish came to bed.

'Is that because you've drunk half a bottle of Benedictine? D'you want some sex, Daisy?'

Daisy didn't. She was absolutely knackered, but she thought it might cheer Hamish up. Sex with him was always the same. Hand straight down to the clitoris, rubbing it until she was wet enough for him to go in, then ten brisk thrusts before he came.

10

Daisy's hangover did not enhance Christmas morning for her. Nor did Eddie playing a computer game he'd got in his stocking, which squawked every time the monkey grabbed the banana on the palm tree, nor did Biddy yakking on and on and letting her croissant get cold.

Biddy had made a little stocking for Hamish, filled with socks, underpants, shaving soap, disposable razors and initialled handkerchiefs and, finally, a fawn jersey which he was now wearing – 'All the things I know you need,' Biddy had added pointedly.

Daisy, who longed to get everyone out of the kitchen so she could stuff the turkey, clutched her head as the telephone rang. Swearing and falling over the puppy, Hamish grabbed the receiver. It was his leading lady in the Robert Burns film, who'd found a tax bill among her Christmas cards.

Hamish turned on the charm. 'But, darling, you'll get repeat fees.'

And I ought to get re-heat fees, thought Daisy, as she shoved Biddy's cooling croissant back in the oven for the third time.

'That was Melanie,' said Hamish coming off the telephone, switching on the kettle and dropping another herbal teabag into his cup.

'Even on Christmas Day they pester you,' sighed Biddy. 'And you ought to eat a proper breakfast. You've lost so much weight.'

'Seven pounds,' said Hamish, smugly patting his concave stomach, then snatching up the telephone as it rang again.

'Hamish Macleod, oh, hello, hello.' Turning towards the window, Hamish hunched his broad shoulders over the telephone, jumping as Biddy leapt up to tuck in the Marks and Spencer tag sticking up from his jersey collar.

'How are *you*?' he went on. 'No, not yet, we open ours at teatime. Lovely, it's awfully sweet of you. I'll try. Happy Christmas.'

Trying not to smirk, he put down the receiver. 'Isn't that sweet? That was Wendy ringing to wish us all Happy Christmas. She sent special love to you and Violet,' he added to Eddie, 'and hoped you enjoyed *Peter Pan*. She's my PA,' he added to Biddy. 'Absolutely first rate. I hope you get a chance to meet before you go back.'

They were late opening their presents because Daisy was still stuffing the turkey and edging it into the Aga, which was harder than parking the Mini in Cheltenham on Christmas Eve.

'Make a list,' said Hamish bossily, as the children fell on their presents, 'or we'll never remember who gave who what, and get a bin for all the paper we can use again, and get that dog out of here,' he added as Ethel pitched in joyously.

Biddy Macleod gave Eddie a camera, Violet a Walkman and Hamish some gold cufflinks to replace the ones Daisy had lost in the laundry. She gave Daisy a set of cake forks and Perdita two padded, satin coathangers.

'Judging by your room, I thought you needed something to hang your clothes on,' she told Perdita.

Daisy, shopping at the last moment, had overspent appallingly. Eddie was overwhelmed with the airgun.

Violet was too sweet not to pretend to be enchanted with the Laura Ashley dress, but Hamish wasn't remotely pleased with his Barbour and green gumboots nor his silk shirts (after all it was his money Daisy was squandering), and when Biddy opened the box with the beautiful, pale grey silk nightie, she merely said, 'Thank you,' very quietly and put it to one side. She made no comment about the *Jane Fonda Work Out Book*, but went into raptures over Eddie and Violet's massive box of chocolates, 'I'm going to have one now,' and then there was all the palaver of identifying a coffee creme from the chart.

'Oh, come on,' said Perdita.

Biddy went into orbit when Hamish handed her an envelope which told her that the tapes of all his programmes, including *Road Haulage*, and a video machine, would be waiting for her in Glasgow when she got home.

'One more present,' said Daisy, handing Biddy an unwieldy red parcel cocooned in Sellotape. 'It says "Biddy love from Ethel".'

In the end Hamish had to help Biddy rip it open. She gave a gasp as she extracted a pair of dusty, ancient, down-at-heel boots, one with a piece of chewing gum sticking to the toe.

'What is the meaning of this?'

'They're Mummy's boots,' said Violet. 'She's been looking for them all day.'

'I must have packed them by mistake,' said Daisy in a small voice.

Everyone dressed for dinner. Daisy only had time to wriggle into an old purple-and-red caftan and tone down her scarlet cheeks. Perdita, in a black skirt and shirt that Daisy had given her, came into the kitchen as Daisy was draining the sprouts. Her clean white-blond hair hung in a long plait. With that lovely smooth, white forehead, and long, long, dark eyes, and the Greek nose, and the tiny, upper lip curving over the wonderful passionate mouth, she was pure Picasso, thought Daisy.

'You look gorgeous,' she said.

'I wish Daddy and Granny thought so. That was inspired giving boots to an old boot.'

'Hush,' hissed Daisy. 'It was totally unintentional.'

Violet, loyally wearing her new Laura Ashley, which was quite the wrong colour, and embarrassingly emphasized her emergent bust, was doing valiant work with Biddy Macleod in the sitting room. Biddy, who'd been down since half past seven, pointedly refused a second glass of sherry: 'There'll be wine at dinner.'

Violet admired Biddy's shoes – black glacé kid with high heels to show off Biddy's tiny feet.

'I thought I disairved a treat.'

At that moment Hamish walked in expecting praise. He was wearing a frilly shirt, a black-velvet coat with silver buttons, a sporran, a heavy, closely pleated kilt, neat buckled shoes, and a silver dirk in his socks.

'Oh, Hamish, you look glorious,' said Biddy. '"Thou mindst me of departed joys, departed never to return".' She applied a handkerchief to her burnt currant eyes. 'You look the image of your father.'

'I didn't mean to upset you, Mother.'

'No, it makes me happy to see you carrying on the tradition.'

'You look lovely in your scarlet, too.'

'I didn't want to spoil the feast,' said Biddy.

'What feast?' said Hamish, looking at his watch. 'It's nearly nine o'clock. Are we ever going to eat?' he demanded, marching into the kitchen, just as Daisy was carrying a swimming-pool of turkey fat to the sink. Her hair was dank with sweat, her cheeks carmine, only the dead white rings under her eyes showed how tired she was.

'We'll be about quarter of an hour.'

'But everyone's starving.'

'Look at Dirk Bogarde,' said Perdita, who was lounging against the Aga. 'You should have put Man Tan on your knees.'

Hamish's lips tightened. 'You ought to be helping your mother.'

'So ought you. I thought modern husbands were supposed to share the cooking.'

'Few husbands work the hours I do. Ouch!' screeched Hamish, as Ethel goosed him liberally.

'You'll never guess what Ethel's done, Granny,' said Perdita dreamily as they sat down to dinner. 'She's chewed up St Joseph.'

'But that crib's been in the family for generations,' spluttered Biddy. 'Is this true?'

'Mary's a single parent now,' said Perdita. 'Very topical, although I suppose God the Father's floating about overseeing things so she's not quite alone. I wonder how God impregnated her. AID or just miracles?'

'Perdita,' snarled Hamish, handing a large plate of breast to Biddy.

'I wouldn't mind God as a father,' went on Perdita. 'Just think of the things he could do: magic me up a trailer, flatten the top paddock into a stick-and-ball field; exterminate certain people.' She smiled sweetly at Granny Macleod.

'Be quiet,' thundered Hamish, putting down the carving knife with a clatter. 'I am going to beat that dog.'

'Oh, no, Daddy,' Violet turned pale. 'She chewed it up yesterday. She'll have no idea what she's being beaten for. It is Christmas.'

Not a word of praise passed Biddy Macleod's lips throughout Christmas dinner, although a great deal of food did. Now they were pulling crackers and Hamish was checking the angle of his blue paper Admiral's hat in the big mirror over the fireplace. He had hardly eaten a thing.

Perdita pulled a cracker with Eddie and disappeared under the table to get the rolled-up hat and the motto. She emerged a minute later, elderberry dark eyes glittering, looking dangerously elated. Oh help, thought Daisy, I've seen that look before. Violet noticed it too and exchanged uneasy glances with Eddie who was on his fourth satsuma. Hamish poured glasses of brandy for himself and Biddy, and a very small one for Daisy.

'We don't want a repeat of last night. To absent friends,' said Hamish raising his glass.

'Indeed,' said Biddy, 'To my dear, dear Lochlan.'

Perdita refilled her glass with red wine.

'To Ricky France-Lynch,' she said and drained it.

Biddy's mouth vanished and never came back.

'I hope he gets ten years for merdering that poor wee bairn.'

'He did not murder him,' said Perdita ominously.

'Perdita,' murmured Daisy. Why, she wondered, was she frightened of everything, and Perdita of nothing – not bullfinches out hunting, nor Biddy Macleod.

'Drunk driving to my mind is murder,' went on Biddy. 'No-one has any right to drive when they're off their head with drink.'

'He'd been celebrating,' snapped Perdita. 'He'd just won one of the biggest tournaments in the world.'

'All polo players are the same to my mind,' replied Biddy. 'Spoilt, jet set, indulging airvery gratification.'

'Rubbish,' said Perdita furiously. 'I bet if Grandpa Macleod had run off with some tart, taking Hamish with him when he was two, and you'd been to some Hogmanay piss-up, you'd have jumped into your Austin Seven and tried to get him back, and not given a stuff about drunk driving.'

Mouthing furiously, Biddy was too outraged to speak.

'Go to your room,' thundered Hamish, then turning to Daisy: 'Will you control your child.'

'She doesn't have to,' said Perdita, picking up her cigarettes. 'I'm going. I'm not having anyone slagging off Ricky, that's all. You shouldn't judge people you don't know.'

Pushing back her chair, she picked up the new black shoe which Biddy had kicked off because it was murdering her corns from under the table and threw it among the cracker remnants. The toe had been completely chewed off by Ethel. Biddy burst into tears and Ethel was shut howling in the utility room.

Daisy went out to the stable where she found Perdita mutinously cuddling Fresco.

'Darling, how could you?'

'How could I not? The bloody bitch, poor Ricky.'

'She is Daddy's mother.'

'She's your husband's mother. Do you know what she said to Violet in the sitting room? "Isn't it a funny thing, none of my grandchildren have fair hair like I did," and Violet said: "But Perdita does". And Bloody Macleod said smugly: "I mean my real grandchildren."'

'How horrible,' said Daisy, totally unnerved by talk veering towards Perdita's origins. 'She's never liked me, and secretly I think she's jealous because you're so much prettier than all her other grandchildren.'

Perdita waited until much later in the evening when Daisy and the children were watching *The Magnificent Seven*.

'Mummy says Granny's jealous because I'm so much better looking than you or Eddie.'

'Oh, shut up,' said Violet, who was red-eyed from Ethel's banishment. 'Mummy wouldn't say a thing like that, would you, Mummy?'

'Well,' stammered Daisy. 'Oh God, you're a bitch sometimes, Perdita.'

On Boxing Day Hamish, reeking of Paco Rabanne, went off to the office. Another frost ruled out hunting. Instead Perdita, practising her swing on a tea chest on the lawn, hit a ball straight through the stained-glass window halfway up the stairs. Daisy forgot she'd put a chicken in the Aga for lunch, so it emerged as a charred wren and they had cold turkey and salad instead.

Swelling with turkey leftovers and righteous indignation, Biddy darned Hamish's socks. If her beloved son was in financial straits, it was entirely due to Daisy's mismanagement and extravagance.

The sky outside was turning yellow, the forecast said snow.

'Wouldn't it be lovely,' said Violet, 'if we got snowed up and you couldn't go home, Granny?'

Daisy turned pale. Like an addict needing a fix, she thought she'd go mad if she didn't paint. While Biddy had her sleep after lunch, she surreptitiously got out the sketch book Violet had given her for Christmas and drew Ethel and Gainsborough on their backs in front of the fire. Nor could she resist a quick sketch of Biddy Macleod, mouth open and snoring, chin doubled, two tweed spare tyres, legs apart showing three inches of doughy, white thigh between lisle stockings and wool knickers.

'Christ, that's good,' said Perdita, creeping up. 'Best thing you've done in years. You shouldn't have flattered her so much.'

'Hush,' Daisy giggled, and, as Biddy was stirring, hid the drawing in the desk and went off to put the kettle on.

Away from the fire, she started shivering. She hoped she wasn't getting 'flu. She was just bringing in the tea things when she heard Perdita saying, 'Do look at this really good drawing Mum's done of you.'

'It's not you,' squeaked Daisy, nearly dropping the tray. 'It's supposed to be an old girl who lives in the village.'

But Biddy Macleod had put on her spectacles.

'I see,' she said quietly. 'Now I know what you really feel about a defenceless old woman, Daisy. But I shall behave with dignity, I'm going to pack my suitcase.'

'Oh, please,' gabbled Daisy, utterly distraught. 'It wasn't meant to be a likeness. Look at Picasso; look at Francis Bacon.'

'There's no need to explain yourself, Daisy.'

'At least have a cup of tea.'

'I don't want anything.' Slowly Biddy went out of the room.

'That was stirring it,' Daisy shouted at Perdita.

'I don't care. With any luck, we've got shot of her.'

When Biddy came downstairs with her suitcases she insisted on waiting in the hall for Hamish as the wind whistled through the broken stained-glass window. She had a long wait. Hamish, desperately late, sucking extra strong mints, took in the situation at once, led his mother into the study and left the door ajar.

'I feel so unwelcome,' sobbed Biddy. 'It's not you or Violet or little Eddie, but Daisy and that wicked, wicked girl.'

Hamish persuaded her to stay on.

'Now you see what I have to put up with, Mother,' Daisy heard him saying. 'Please don't go. I need you.'

11

Hostilities had to be suspended the following night because they had been asked to a party in Eldercombe by a bearded psychiatrist called Lionel Mannering, and Philippa, his rapacious wife. Daisy dreaded parties. In the past Hamish had got so insanely jealous if she spoke to other men that she'd completely lost the art of chatting anyone up. She also had a raging sore throat, and was so cold and shivery that she put on a crimson and white striped dress (which she'd never worn because it was too low-cut) and put a crimson mohair polo neck over the top as a suck-up gesture because Biddy had once knitted it for her. Unable to wash her hair because Biddy and Hamish had hogged the hot water, she decided to put it up.

'You look great, Mother,' said Hamish, helping Biddy out of the icy wind into the front seat of the car.

Sepia clouds raced across a disdainful white moon. Sitting in the back, Daisy, who was beginning to feel really ill, felt sweat cascading down her sides and soaking her fringe.

It was a large, noisy party with all the women in taffetas, satins and beautiful silk shirts. There were also loads of good-looking men for Daisy to avoid. The moment Hamish entered the room, he was off, delighted to be with his peers, as he called them, telling everyone he was in television, dumping Biddy on the hostess's mother, and chatting up all the Rutshire wives, who were delighted to have some new talent, and even more delighted when Hamish's busty wife with the red, shiny face in the awful clothes was pointed out to them.

The lean, rapacious hostess whisked everyone round introducing them as if she were doing a grand chain in an eightsome reel. Daisy talked to a sweet girl who was giggling with nervous relief because she'd just got rid of her mother-in-law. 'I'm going to get seriously drunk.'

'I can't. Mine's over there,' said Daisy regretfully.

'There's Basil Baddingham. Look at the colour of him – he must've been skiing or playing polo abroad,' said the girl. 'He'll know the latest on Ricky.' Then, as all the Rutshire wives converged, shrieking, on Bas: 'He's so wicked, he must have had every woman in the room.'

'Not me,' said Daisy, almost regretfully.

The girl laughed. 'It's only a matter of time.'

Daisy was comforted to see people's eyes glazing over at Biddy's monologue.

'My son's in television,' held them for five minutes, until they discovered Hamish wasn't producing *Rumpole* and then drifted off. 'This is my first Christmas as a widow,' at least held the women for another five.

Daisy was so hot she thought she was going to faint. As Hamish was the other end of the room, she took off her crimson polo neck, which wiped off all her make-up and pulled the pins out of her hair, so it cascaded around her shoulders and splendid cleavage.

Bas, a connoisseur both of horse and female flesh, crossed the room. Hastily, Daisy slung the crimson polo neck round her shoulders, hiding her cleavage with the sleeves.

'Shame to cover it up,' said Bas, whose height gave him a good view. 'You're living in Brock House, aren't you? I've seen you in the village, and I've met Perdita hunting. Christ, she's pretty. Rupert and the twins and I are all drawing lots to take her out on her sixteenth birthday.'

'That's nice,' said Daisy. 'You'll have to wait till next November.'

'I like things on slow burn,' said Bas idly. 'I can see where Perdita gets her looks.'

'Do you live near here?' said Daisy hastily. He was so attractive, but it was difficult concentrating when little black spots seemed to be taking away half of his wickedly smiling face.

'In Cotchester. I've got a wine bar. You must come and dine there one evening – er – when your husband's away.'

It was definitely a come-on.

'How's Ricky France-Lynch?' said Daisy, to change the subject.

Bas shook his head. 'Fucking brave. I thought he'd top himself cooped up like that, and he's already had three operations on his elbow.'

Daisy winced. 'Will he be able to play again?'

Bas shrugged. 'Won't get much chance to find out if he's convicted. The trial starts next month. I say, are you all right?' He put a suntanned hand on Daisy's forehead, then ran his fingers lingeringly down her cheek. 'You're absolutely baking. You ought to be in bed, preferably with me.'

As Daisy swayed, he pushed her gently down on the sofa. 'Philippa,' he yelled to his hostess, 'have you got a thermometer?'

Turning round a couple of minutes later to check whether Biddy was all right, Hamish saw Daisy sitting on a sofa with a thermometer in her mouth, exposing her entire bosom to a tall, dark and very handsome man who was stroking her pulse. Hamish was across the room in a flash.

'What's going on?' he said furiously.

'*You're* a lousy husband,' accused Bas. 'No, don't try to talk,' he chided Daisy. 'You haven't had it under your tongue for a minute.'

Through feverish, red-veined eyes Daisy looked beseechingly up at Hamish.

'Why are you making a fuss, Daisy?' asked Hamish coldly.

'It's no fuss,' said Bas, whipping out the thermometer. 'See for yourself, it's nearly 104.'

'You must take her home at once,' insisted Philippa. 'Poor darling, I expect you're exhausted by Christmas and just moving in,' then adding, as Biddy bustled up, 'what a good thing you've got Mummy staying. You must keep her tucked up warm, Mummy, and not let her do a thing.'

Daisy didn't dare look at Biddy.

'See you when you're better, darling,' said Bas.

'Do come back when you've dropped her and Mummy,' Daisy heard Philippa say to Hamish.

Four days later, on New Year's Eve, Daisy staggered up – only slightly comforted that she had lost seven pounds. Clutching on to the bedroom window, she could see Perdita stick and balling on the lawn in the fading light. She had used two of Eddie's cricket stumps as goal posts. Now she was galloping flat out, then stopping, pirouetting Fresco round on her hocks, and shooting off in another direction, both their pony tails flying. On the last gallop, Fresco didn't manage to stop and flat-footed all over the herbaceous border. Hamish would do his nut.

Jumping off, Perdita stuffed the pony with carrots, hugging her and covering her face with kisses. She's never loved a human like that, thought Daisy sadly. If only Hamish ever showed a flicker of interest in her.

Clinging on to the banisters, Daisy staggered downstairs to an unrecognizable kitchen. Every surface was stripped and gleaming. Even the azalea Daisy's mother had sent her from the alcoholic's home looked quite sprightly. Drying-up cloths boiled briskly on top of the Aga, grey scum trembling on top. Humming 'If Onlee', Biddy was ironing a new emerald-green shirt which had somehow found its way into Hamish's wardrobe. On the memo pad by the telephone, Biddy had jotted down Ajax, Domestos, Blue Loo, Shake and Vac, Freshaire x 3.

'I can't thank you enough for taking over,' said Daisy as she collapsed into a chair.

'Someone had to,' said Biddy tersely.

'Goodness, you iron well.'

Biddy had finished the green shirt and had started on Hamish's Y-fronts. There was something obscene in the loving way she slid the hot iron with a hiss of steam into the crotch. Daisy could feel the sweat drenching her forehead.

'I'm afraid I don't bother to iron pants and socks,' she mumbled apologetically. 'Where's Ethel?'

'In her kennel outside, where she should be,' said Biddy. 'That'll be Hamish.' Her face really lit up as she heard wheels on the gravel.

Hamish, looking pale but elated, reeked of extra strong mints again.

'You are a miracle,' he said, kissing Biddy on the cheek. 'Only you could get a polish like that on the front-door handle. We've sent your black shoes back to the manufacturers and asked them to find an identical pair. Feeling better?' he added turning to Daisy, but not looking at her. 'You look *much* better.'

'How was your day?' asked Biddy. 'Were you pleased with the rushes?'

'Green grow the rushes oh, I love the lassies oh,' said Daisy dreamily.

'Better than I thought,' said Hamish ignoring Daisy. 'The bad news is that Melanie's got flu, so we probably won't be able to start shooting on Monday. The good news is that Wendy's asked us to supper.'

Oh no, thought Daisy, I'm simply not up to it.

'But Wendy's been working all day,' she protested. 'She won't want to be bothered.'

'Course she will,' said Hamish briskly. 'I've accepted anyway. Good for you to get out, and Mother certainly needs a break.'

There was a mini-tantrum before they left because Gainsborough had shed ginger fur over the new green shirt which Biddy had ironed specially. Biddy also huffed and puffed because her stack-heeled brown shoes were less dressy with the red dress than the glacé kid.

Daisy knew she should have washed her hair but she felt too exhausted.

If Wendy had been working all day, reflected Daisy, it had been on the dinner party. The flat was gleaming, full of freesias, more tinselled and red-ribboned than Santa's grotto in a department store, and the food exquisite and consisting of all Hamish's favourite things.

Hamish, who'd brought lots of bottles, kept leaping up and filling glasses and clearing away as he never did at home. Wendy, whom Daisy vaguely remembered as a raver in black leather and chain belts, was dressed in a grey wool midi-dress with a white collar. Her long, dark hair, so shiny Biddy might have been polishing it all day, was held back by a black velvet ribbon. All evening she 'targeted' on Biddy, flattering her preposterously, laughing at her frightful jokes and displaying an encyclopaedic knowledge of Hamish's work.

'*Burns* is going to be a seminal work, of course, but I think *Haulage* is my favourite,' she was now saying, as Biddy greedily scraped up the remains of a second helping of passion fruit mousse. 'Hamish is a cut above other producers because he's so caring – not just for actors and directors, but the crew as well.'

And for you too, thought Daisy, watching Hamish's enraptured face. Hamish had been given to crushes throughout their marriage, but Daisy had never seen him so besotted. Nor did Wendy make the mistake of ignoring Daisy. She kept suggesting other food when Daisy couldn't manage to eat anything, bringing her into the conversation as a coarse fisherman occasionally pulls on a spare rod.

'What a lovely meal,' said Biddy, folding her napkin.

'As it's Hogmanay I should have served you haggis,' said Wendy, 'but I couldn't get one. "Great chieftain of the pudding race",' she added skittishly to Hamish.

'I see you know your Burns,' said Biddy approvingly.

'The Hag is astride, this night for a ride,' muttered Daisy.

'I really like that young person,' yelled Biddy, when Wendy, refusing any help, went next door to make coffee.

'What a poppet,' yelled Wendy, as Biddy went off to the loo.

Daisy only started getting jumpy when Wendy, having asked Biddy if she'd like some background music, put on 'If On-lee'.

'I really love this tune,' Wendy said, dancing a few steps. Her eyes shining, she couldn't have been prettier.

If on-lee, sighed Daisy, I was at home in bed, but I suppose we'll have to see in the New Year. Hamish, however, was most solicitous about getting her home early and sending her straight to bed.

Next morning Biddy left, hardly saying goodbye to Daisy or Perdita, but kissing Violet and Eddie very fondly.

'I feel so much happier about things now,' Daisy heard her saying to Hamish.

Daisy felt jumpy, but for the next few days screaming matches over thankyou letters and getting three trunks packed left her little time to think. Neither Violet nor Eddie wanted to go back to school and loathed being parted from Ethel and the airgun respectively, but Perdita was worst of all, clinging round Fresco's neck, sobbing and sobbing. 'I can't leave her, Mum, please let me go to the local comprehensive. I promise I'll work and pass my O levels.'

Once they were back, it was reversed-charge calls three times a day to see if Fresco and Ethel and the airgun were OK, driving Hamish demented.

The Sunday after term began the sky turned the colour of marzipan and it started to snow. By teatime it was drifting. Appleford was completely cut off and Hamish couldn't get home for ten days. It was very cold, but Daisy lived on tins, Ethel tourneyed with the drifts, and fat Gainsborough tiptoed along the white fences using his ginger tail as a rudder. Daisy also painted maniacally and joyfully. Brought up in London, she was unused to snow like this.

The thaw brought a telephone call from Hamish, saying snow had held up filming, but he'd be back at the weekend. More sinister, the postman got through again, staggering under a pile of brown envelopes.

Daisy left them for Hamish as usual. Then a letter arrived to both of them, complaining that none of last term's school fees had been paid and requesting settlement for the spring and winter terms at once. Pickfords were also agitating to be paid for the move. Even more alarming, all the cheques Daisy had written for Fresco and Ethel and Hamish's silk shirts came winging back. Daisy rang up the bank manager.

'I'm afraid there's nothing to honour the cheques, Mrs Macleod, and now you've sold the London house, no security.'

'I'll talk to my husband this evening,' whimpered Daisy.

In panic, detesting herself, Daisy went to Hamish's desk and went through his bank statement – £35,075 in the red. How on earth had the penny-pinching Hamish managed that?

With frantically trembling hands, hating herself even more, Daisy went through Hamish's American Express forms, and nearly fainted. The restaurant and hotel bills were astronomical, and he must have spent more at Interflora in a year than she'd spent on Perdita's pony. She supposed leading ladies had to be kept sweet and suppressed the ignoble thought that Hamish had paid for all those freesias banked in Wendy's flat.

There was also a £500 bill from Janet Reger for December, of which Daisy had never seen the fruits. Her heart cracking her ribs, she looked at the minicab bills. Hamish, terrified of losing his licence, never drove if he'd been drinking. Daisy went cold. The December account was for £450. Nearly every journey was to or from Wendy's flat.

Hamish was always saying he had a bed in the office. Maybe he regarded Wendy's flat as his office. She mustn't over-react. But if she'd known how desperately they were in debt, she'd never have spent so much money at Christmas. She jumped guiltily as the telephone rang.

It was an old friend, Fiona, who'd always bossed Daisy about at school.

'Can I come and spend the weekend?'

'Of course.' Daisy quailed at how irritated Hamish would be. 'Did you have a good Christmas?'

'Course not. You don't if your lover's married.'

Wendy seemed to manage, thought Daisy.

'Fiona, have you heard anything about Hamish?'

'Well, one's heard he's keen on some PA. But let's face it, Hamish has always liked ladies. And no doubt in the end he'll get as bored sexually with her as he did with you. Sit tight, don't rock the boat. I'll see what I can suss out before the weekend.'

Daisy sat down and cried, and Ethel, who'd been disembowelling one of Biddy's stuffed coathangers, leant against her and licked her face. Daisy wasn't raging with jealousy. Hamish had 'stood by her' as the papers called it for fifteen years. She couldn't expect him to always lie on top of her as well. Then Hamish rang to tell her he didn't want any supper, and not to wait up.

Next morning Daisy sat hunched over a cup of coffee, trying not to think about Wendy, listening to Hamish's bath running out. Gainsborough was chattering at the window, crossly watching robins, tits and sparrows feeding on the bird table. Then a predatory magpie swooped down and they all scattered. 'One for sorrow,' said Daisy, crossing herself with a shiver. 'Good morning Mr Magpie, how are your wife and children – and your mistress?' she added as an afterthought.

Turning to the front page of the *Daily Mail*, she saw that Ricky France-Lynch had been sent down for manslaughter.

'*Orgulloso Gets Two Years*,' said the headline.

Bastard, thought Daisy, looking at the sensual yet implacable face of the judge.

'*Sir Anthony Wedgwood QC, defending*,' read Daisy, '*said that his client had had extreme provocation. A wife he worshipped was taken off him by his patron, and he has been punished a million times by the death of a son he adored, and terrible injuries which have almost certainly put an end to his polo career.*'

If that hasn't, thought Daisy furiously, two years in jug certainly will.

The judge sounded just like Biddy Macleod.

'*The defendant*,' he had told the jury, '*is a member of the jet set, the* jeunesse dorée, *who raised a thousand pounds a match playing for his patron. He may just have been left by his wife, but he was used to living in the fast lane, and already had convictions of speeding and drunken driving. I feel*,' went on the judge, '*there should be some redress for his young wife, who has sustained the terrible loss of a child. Nor do I believe there should be one law for the rich.*'

There were pictures of Ricky looking stony-faced and much, much thinner, arriving at court and, on the inside pages, of a bewitchingly glamorous Chessie and the adorable little boy, and also of Ricky's friends: Basil

Baddingham, Rupert Campbell-Black, David Waterlane and the twins, all looking boot-faced after the verdict.

Daisy's eyes filled with tears. Poor Ricky, he was far, far worse off than she was. Outside the sky was leaden grey and a bitter north wind ruffled the hair of the wood, but at least the hazel catkins hung sulphur-yellow like a Tiffany lamp. Ricky can't see any of that, thought Daisy, incarcerated in Rutminster prison.

'Ricky France-Lynch got two years,' she told Hamish, as she handed him a cup of herbal tea.

Hamish glanced at the paper. 'He's already done six months' remand. If he behaves himself he'll be up before the parole board in a few months. He'll probably only do a year in the end.'

'You are clever to know things like that.'

'Wife's bloody good-looking. I don't blame Bart Alderton,' said Hamish, helping himself to muesli.

Daisy was so busy reading all the details of the trial, and that Rupert and Bas were going to appeal, and wondering whether to send Ricky a food parcel, that it was a few minutes before she noticed two suitcases in the hall.

Oh God, Hamish must be off to recce some new film, and she'd been so preoccupied with penury and painting, she didn't know what it was. He was bound to have told her, and he'd be livid because she hadn't listened. She must be a better wife.

Putting his muesli bowl in the sink, Hamish removed some bottles of whisky and gin, given him by hopeful theatrical agents for Christmas, from the larder and asked Daisy if she'd got a carrier bag.

'Here's one from Liberty's, rather suitable if you're wanting your freedom,' Daisy giggled nervously. 'Going anywhere exciting?'

'Very,' said Hamish calmly. 'I'm leaving you. I'm moving in with Wendy.'

For once the colour really drained from Daisy's rosy cheeks.

'For g-g-good?' she whispered.

'For my good,' said Hamish. 'I'm afraid I've come to the end of the road.'

Like Harry Lauder, thought Daisy wildly, Hamish should be wearing his kilt.

'I can't cope with your hopeless inefficiency any more,' he went on. 'The house is a tip. You never diary anything or pick up my cleaning. The children, particularly Perdita, are quite out of control. Their rooms are like cesspits. I owe it to my career. I can never invite backers or programme controllers, or anyone that matters, to the house. You can't even cope with Mother for a few days. It isn't as though you even worked.'

To justify leaving her, Hamish was deliberately pouring petrol on resentment that must have been smouldering for years.

'I'm sorry,' mumbled Daisy, 'I will try and be more efficient, I keep thinking about painting.'

'One wouldn't mind,' said Hamish with chilling dismissiveness, 'if you were any good. I married you fifteen years ago because I felt sorry for you. I feel I deserve some happiness.'

He's enjoying this, thought Daisy numbly. She could see Biddy Macleod crouched on top of the fridge like an old Buddha applauding him. Picking up her coffee cup she found the washing-up machine already full and clean, and started unloading it.

'Until I met Wendy, I didn't know what happiness was,' said Hamish sententiously. 'She makes me feel so alive.'

'Alive, alive oh-ho,' mumbled Daisy. 'Cock-ups and muscles, alive, alive oh.' I'm going mad, she thought, I can't take this in.

'Wendy's so interested in everything I do.'

Easy to be interested when you're in love, thought Daisy sadly. Trying to take ten mugs out of the machine, one finger through each handle, her hands were shaking so much, she dropped one on the stone floor.

'See what I mean, you're so hopeless,' said Hamish smugly.

Sweeping up the pieces, Daisy cut herself and wound a drying-up cloth round her hand.

'And frankly,' glancing in the kitchen mirror Hamish extracted a piece of muesli from his teeth, 'I can't put up with Perdita any more. I have forked out for that little tramp till I'm bankrupt.'

'Perdita,' said Daisy, losing her temper, 'would have been OK if you'd ever been nice to her.'

'Mother thinks she's seriously disturbed. There must be some bad blood somewhere.'

'That was definitely below the belt.' Daisy started throwing forks into the silver drawer.

'*That* is family silver,' said Hamish.

'Not my family any more,' screamed Daisy, and picking up the drawer she emptied it into the Liberty's carrier bag beside the whisky and the gin. 'Take the bloody stuff away. So you're leaving me because I'm lousy at housework, and don't help your career, and you can't stand Perdita, and Wendy makes you feel so alive. Why can't you tell the truth and just say you enjoy screwing Wendy.'

'I knew you'd resort to cheap abuse.'

'Nothing cheap about those bills. Minicabs must have found their way blindfold to Wendy's and you must have kept Interflora in business. It ought to be re-named "Inter-Wendy" – you certainly were.'

'You've been snooping,' sighed Hamish. 'I was trying to conduct this with dignity. I had hoped to avoid animosity for Eddie's and Violet's sake.'

Daisy's eyes darted in terror. 'You're not going to take them away . . . ?'

'Only if you really can't cope,' said Hamish loftily. 'We'll have them at weekends and for a good chunk of the holidays. You can certainly have custody of Perdita and that appalling dog.'

'She's not appalling,' said Daisy, throwing Ethel a Bonio from the red box on top of the fridge. 'What about the house? We've only just moved in, and until we pay Pickfords I don't think they'll move us again.'

'You'll have to rent somewhere cheaper.'

Watching Ethel slotting the Bonio between her paws and eating it like an ice-cream, Daisy wished Violet could see her. 'What about the children?'

'Wendy and I told Eddie and Violet last night. We drove over to see them.'

'How did they take it?' whispered Daisy. The blood was beginning to seep through the drying-up cloth.

'Very calmly, as I expected. Once they realized they'd still see a great deal of me, they stopped worrying.' He peered into the machine and picked out the potato peeler. 'Wendy's doesn't work, so I'll take this one.' He dropped it into the carrier bag. 'And how many times have I told you not to put bone-handled knives in – oh, what does it matter?'

Fluttering on the bottom window pane, Daisy suddenly saw a peacock butterfly which had survived the winter. Trying not to bruise it with her shaking hands, she let it out of the window.

It was Hamish's calmness that paralysed her. He might have been explaining to his leading lady that he was dropping her mid-film. Wendy would be so much better in the part.

'But I don't know anything about money,' she said in terror.

'You better learn. It's time you grew up.'

'And we're dreadfully overdrawn.'

'Whose fault is that?' said Hamish, gathering up his suitcases in the hall. 'You didn't exactly pull in your horns over Christmas. I can't afford you, Daisy. You can contact me through my lawyers.'

Daisy started to shake.

'Why didn't you tell me you wanted a divorce, before we went through all this hassle of moving?'

'I doubt if you'd have listened. You were so anxious to get here so Perdita could have her pony and you could paint, you couldn't think about anything else.' And he was gone.

The drying-up cloth round her hand was soaked with blood now. Looking out of the window, she gave a scream as Gainsborough pounced on the peacock butterfly and gobbled it up. It was no more good at coping with the outside world than she was.

12

Fifteen years of marriage to Hamish had made Daisy feel a total failure as a wife, but they had equipped her even less for a divorce. Hamish had never let her pay a bill, renew a car licence or an insurance policy or look at a tax document. The first crushing blow on visiting her solicitors was to discover that the Hollywood co-producers had decided to ground Hamish's movie project and his entire £200,000 investment had gone up in smoke. A visit to the bank manager confirmed that there was not only no money, but massive debts. Hamish was OK. The co-producer of the movie, feeling guilty about Hamish's losses, offered him work in LA for at least a year and had also taken on Wendy as a PA. This took Hamish outside the jurisdiction of the courts, so it would cost Daisy a fortune in lawyers' fees to get a penny out of him.

Cruellest of all, now that Hamish had dumped Daisy, Biddy Macleod was quite prepared to subsidize him. For a start she was going to pay Violet's and Eddie's school fees and give them a fat allowance, but she refused to fork out anything for Perdita, which meant Perdita would have to leave her current boarding school – who were kindly allowing her to stay on until the end of term in late March.

As the creditors moved in, Daisy's jewellery, the silver and pictures and the better pieces of furniture all had to be sold. The owner of Brock House, who lived abroad, said Daisy could stay until April, but he must have his rent. Investigating the possibility of a council house, Daisy was told she was at the bottom of the list.

Locals tended to ignore her, not knowing what to say. A few London friends rang for grisly details and gave her more grisly details of the women, usually themselves, that Hamish had tried to get into bed. Then they shrugged their shoulders. Daisy was always losing things; why not her husband as well?

'Do ring us if you need us,' they said.

But Daisy didn't ring. However miserable she was inside, she projected an image of cheerfulness. Like her namesake already dotting the lawn outside, however much you mowed her down, she would pop up the next day.

Just before half-term Fresco's owner, Tim Jeddings, came to re-possess her because she hadn't been paid for either. Daisy couldn't watch as the pony was loaded into the trailer. Merry-eyed, muddy, a little fat from no exercise, she had brought so much happiness.

Daisy's plan had been to tell Perdita on the drive home, when no eye contact would make it easier. Then Perdita got a lift home with a schoolfriend, and instead of running into the house, headed straight for the stable, extracting a Granny Smith from her school skirt and joyfully screaming for Fresco.

It was a glorious day. The sun was lighting up the crimson buds on the beech trees; snowdrops spread like the Milky Way across the lawn.

'Fresco, Fresco,' Perdita's cries rang round the valley, bouncing off stone walls and trees. By now, greedy and loving, Fresco should have been belting up the field. A minute later, Perdita had burst into the kitchen, her breath coming in great gasps, shuddering and shaking from head to foot.

'Fresco must have jumped out of her field. We must get her a friend. Ring the police at once.'

'Darling, I'm afraid she's gone.'

'What d'you mean, gone?'

'Tim Jeddings took her back. The cheque bounced. We haven't got enough money to pay for her.'

For a second Perdita stared at her, her face changing from alabaster to putty. 'I don't believe you. There must be money from selling this house.'

'It's only rented.'

'You could have taken me away from school, I'd have got the money from somewhere. What about your jewels?'

Daisy held out her ringless hands. 'They've all gone.'

Then Perdita screamed and screamed.

'She's gone to a wonderful home up North,' babbled Daisy. 'I didn't want to tell you while you were at school.'

'But I never said goodbye,' screamed Perdita. 'I don't believe Tim's sold her yet.'

Rushing into the hall, she found the telephone book. She was shaking so badly, she mis-dialled three times. 'Mr Jeddings, Mummy's lying. You haven't sold Fresco on yet.'

There was a long pause. Perdita slumped against the wall.

'You rotten bastard,' she screeched and crashed down the receiver.

Hearing the din, Ethel came rushing in with a muddy nose and a dug-up dahlia root in her mouth, and threw herself delightedly on Perdita.

'Go away,' yelled Perdita, shoving Ethel violently away. 'Why haven't you sold her as well? Because she's darling Violet's dog, I suppose. Why the fuck can't you go out to work and earn some money like everyone else's

116

mother, instead of producing crappy, awful paintings no-one wants?'

For half an hour she was so hysterical that Daisy was about to ring the doctor. Then she went silent, and wouldn't talk to Daisy or the other children when they came home. Nor would she eat. After she'd taken all three children back to school on Tuesday night, Daisy went into Perdita's room. Every cutting of Ricky France-Lynch, every photograph of Fresco, was ripped into tiny pieces all over the floor.

'Oh God, what have I done,' moaned Daisy, bursting into tears. She was interrupted half an hour later by the door bell. Imagining it was some creditor, she was just sidling downstairs intending to bolt the door when it opened and Basil Baddingham walked in. He looked so opulent with his patent leather hair and his even suntan and his wide, wolfish smile showing his perfect teeth, that he seemed to have come from another planet.

'Please go away,' said Daisy, clapping her hands over her blubbered, swollen face. 'It's not a good time.'

'Always a good time for a drink,' said Bas. Brandishing a bottle of Dom Perignon, he set off purposefully towards the kitchen where lunch still lay on the table and Gainsborough was thoughtfully licking up Perdita's untouched shepherd's pie.

'I'm really not up to it,' mumbled Daisy.

'Get some glasses,' said Bas, removing the gold paper from the bottle. 'I am your knight in shining armour.'

'I had one of those,' said Daisy, 'but he walked out because I didn't keep it shining enough.'

'I know. You've had a rotten time. But you're well shot of him. I'd have been round sooner, but I've been in Palm Beach. Have you found somewhere to live?'

'There's a flat on the Bledisloe Estate.'

'Won't do, far too rough,' said Bas. 'You and Perdita'd be sitting ducks for all the yobbos.'

At the pop of the champagne cork, Gainsborough shot out of the room, sending the remains of the shepherd's pie crashing to the floor.

'Let's go and sit somewhere slightly more comfortable,' said Bas, filling up their glasses. There was still a sofa in the drawing room, but it was bitterly cold.

117

'Bailiffs do this?' asked Bas, then, as Daisy nodded: 'You poor old thing.'

Under his gentle questioning, Daisy told him about the selling of Fresco and Hamish's departure.

'I know it seems like the end of the world,' said Bas, 'but you're an extremely pretty lady, and scores of men are going to come running after you once you've got your confidence back, including me.'

Daisy giggled, feeling slightly happier.

'I've got a much better idea,' Bas went on. 'You can't move into the Bledisloe Estate. One of Ricky's tenants finally kicked the bucket during the big freeze. He lived in a lovely little house, Snow Cottage, on the edge of Ricky's land. Been there for thirty years. Only paid ten pounds a week. Ricky was too soft to put up the rent. Now he wants me to sell the house to some rich weekenders. It's a bit tumbledown, but there are three bedrooms and an orchard, and the same stream that runs through Rupert's land, so you'll have condoms flowing past your door. The only problem is you'll also have Philippa and Lionel Mannering – I met you at their party – gazing down at you from their awful house. But come the summer they won't be able to see through the trees. Anyway, she'll be far too interested in Ricky when he comes out of prison to waste much time on you.'

'Won't Ricky mind us living there?' asked Daisy, hardly daring to hope.

'He's not minding anything much at the moment, poor bastard, except Will dying and Chessie buggering off. I'm sure he'll let you stay for a year while you sort yourself out. I see no reason to alter the rent.'

'But I thought he was desperately short of cash. Oughtn't you to sell it for him?'

'Certainly not,' said Bas, filling up her glass. 'It's insane to sell anything at the moment. Since the Prince of Wales moved into the area, property's going to quadruple in Rutshire over the next few years. I'll take you to see it tomorrow.'

'It's a heavenly cottage,' said Daisy brightly as she drove a stony-faced Perdita home at the beginning of the school holidays. 'I know we're all going to be terribly happy there.'

'You said the same thing about Brock House,' snapped Perdita.

She looked pinched and miserable, her hair had lost all its sheen, her eyes their jetty sparkle.

'How many bedrooms are there?'

'Three, so someone will have to share; perhaps you and Violet.'

'We will not!'

'Well, there's a room off the sitting room we can use,' said Daisy placatingly, wistfully bidding goodbye to a possible studio, 'and it's surrounded by fields, so perhaps one day we'll be able to afford a pony again.'

Perdita shot her mother a black stare of hatred.

'Shut up about that,' she hissed.

The holidays were a nightmare. Daisy was so broke that they were living virtually on bread and jam, and Perdita's hatred corroded everything. Although she had grumbled in the past about her boarding schools, she bitterly resented being sent to a comprehensive and was absolutely mortified that Biddy was forking out for Violet and Eddie.

Daisy felt awful and wished she could raise two fingers to Biddy and send all the children to the local comprehensive, but to make ends meet she was due to start a job as a filing clerk at a nearby Christmas pudding factory at the beginning of May, and she thought Eddie and Violet were too young to come home to an empty house every evening.

Besides, the women's magazines all advised one to leave children at their schools: 'At the time of divorce, school is often the only continuity.'

The day before Violet went back, she and Perdita had a terrible row. Perdita had just endured a week at her new school, where her strange set face and uppity manners had done nothing to endear her to her classmates. One boy had called her Turdita, and when she screamed at him, the others had taken up the refrain. Getting home, Perdita took it out on Violet, who'd just had a letter from Hamish announcing that Wendy was pregnant.

'Disgusting letch,' screamed Perdita. 'Wendy's a whore. And now she's got a bun in the microwave, Hamish'll favour the new brat and lose interest in you.'

119

'Rubbish,' said Violet furiously. 'At least we know who our father was.'

'What d'you mean?' snarled Perdita.

'Nothing,' said Violet, realizing she'd gone too far.

'My father was killed in a car crash.'

'Of course he was,' mumbled Violet. 'I must go and finish packing.'

Half an hour after her mother had gone to bed that night, Perdita began searching. It had grown much colder, the wind had risen and creepers rattling long fingers against the windows kept making her jump. Her heart was beating so hard she felt it must wake her mother. The blood was pounding in her ears, her whole body was throbbing, as she crept downstairs into the study.

At least we know who our father is? What had Violet meant? What poison had she been fed by Hamish? Bugger, the overhead bulb had gone and they'd been too poor to replace it. Perdita crept round the room groping like a blind man, tripping over a small stool, at last finding the side light by the desk which was too eaten by woodworm for the bailiffs to take.

Only yesterday she'd come in and found her mother crying over a letter which Daisy had quickly stuffed into one of the drawers. Everything was in a frightful mess, but Perdita could only find bills and business correspondence. Her hands moved around, pressing drawers and shelves, frantic to find the pulse point that opened the secret drawer. At last her fingers rubbed against a little switch on the inside right of the top shelf, and the centre of the desk swung round. In a small drawer at the back was a bundle of papers tied up with a green ribbon. Icy with sweat, Perdita collapsed on to the wooden wing chair to read them.

On top was a photograph of Daisy in her teens. Even allowing for changes in fashion, she was unbelievably pretty, with her dark hair longer than her mini skirt. There were also some photographs of herself as a baby, and then a snapshot of a man surrounded by a group of students. On the back, Daisy had written, 'Jackie being admired'. Her father had been called Jackie. Was that him? Perdita examined the man's face again. It was handsome, slightly weak. Her hands were trembling so much she nearly tore the cutting from the *Guardian*. It was a review of Jackie Cosgrave's exhibition. The reviewer thought well of his work. 'Bold, brave and starkly original.' The review contained another photograph of Jackie. He *was* handsome. Was that her name, Perdita Cosgrave?

Next she found a marriage certificate between Daisy James and Hamish Macleod on 14 December 1966, at Ayrshire Register Office. That was only fifteen years and four months ago. They'd certainly lied about the length of their marriage. A picture of Daisy and Hamish on their wedding day showed Hamish, with a beard, in an awful kilt, looking surprisingly happy and proud. Daisy looked awful, very peaky and thin in a ghastly pale coat and skirt, her hair tucked into an unbecoming hat. And here was a birth certificate.

'Perdita James, born 6 November 1966.' Her heart seemed to be pounding in her throat now. 'Mother, Daisy James, father unknown.'

Perdita gave a croak of misery. At the bottom of the pile was a yellowing, torn, tear-stained letter dated 13 December 1966, which was from Hamish.

'Darling Little Daisy,' so he was capable of tenderness, 'Tomorrow we will be married. Please don't worry, my family will come round when they realize how adorable you are, and how happy you're going to make me. Don't torture yourself over Perdita's parentage.' The letter was shaking so much now she could hardly read. 'It doesn't matter, she's the bonniest wee bairn in the world. I'll be her father, and love her far more than whoever he is would ever have done. I will take care of you always, Hamish.'

The next minute, the outside drawer, which had been on her knee, crashed to the ground, scattering papers everywhere. There was a muffled bark from Daisy's bedroom overhead.

Jumping up with the letter in her hand, Perdita thought she was going to black out. 'Don't torture yourself over Perdita's parentage.' Had her mother lied to Hamish about Jackie Cosgrave, had she been a prostitute or a nympho who'd bedded so many men she didn't know who the father was? The next moment Perdita jumped out of her shuddering skin as a reluctant Ethel, shoved by a terrified Daisy, burst into the room.

'We've got nothing for you to burgle,' began Daisy, brandishing Eddie's airgun – 'Darling, what *are* you doing?'

'What were you doing,' hissed Perdita, 'sixteen years ago? You told me Jackie had been killed in a car crash.'

'He was,' stammered Daisy, looking far more scared than by any burglar.

'Don't lie to me, or were you lying to Hamish to get him to marry you, poor sod? Who was my father?' her voice rose to a shriek.

Daisy had gone deathly pale. Her teeth were chattering. 'Shall we have a drink?'

'No. For once we're going to talk.'

'I tried to tell you,' sobbed Daisy. 'Hamish thought it better not when you were younger, and then it was too late.'

'You'd better tell me now.' Perdita's black brows were pulled right down over her furious, hating eyes. 'Were you on the game, or raped by a gang of louts?'

'No, no,' Daisy shook her head. She was wearing a peach woollen nightdress she'd got for 20p in a jumble sale. Her hair was dragged back with an elastic band, her eyes popping out huge like a rabbit with myxomatosis. Ethel, gazing at them both soulfully, started to scratch.

'I was just seventeen when I went to art college,' mumbled Daisy. 'Jackie was my art master. I fell madly in love with him. He was so frightfully attractive, all the class, irrespective of sex, had crushes on him, but for some reason he chose me. He was a very good painter.'

'I saw the cutting.'

'He was also divorced, heavily into drugs and the king of the swingers. He didn't love me but he was flattered by my hero-worship. One evening he took me to a party in Chelsea. I'd never seen such people, only about a dozen of them, but so beautiful, sophisticated and jet set. They were all rock stars, actors and polo players. I was desperately shy. I'd hardly touched drink before, and never, never drugs. But I took both to please Jackie to show I was up to it and got absolutely stoned.' Her voice faltered, so low now Perdita could hardly hear it over the moan of the wind. 'I'm sorry to shock you, but I was very young.'

'About a year and a half older than me,' said Perdita spitefully.

'The p-p-party degenerated into what people talk about as a typical sixties orgy,' stammered Daisy. 'At least it was the only one I ever went to. Everyone was, er, making love to everyone.'

'Don't you mean fucking?' sneered Perdita.

'Yes,' whispered Daisy. 'I know it's awful, but I was so stoned I don't remember anything about it.'

'Inconvenient,' said Perdita, lighting one cigarette from another. The wind was screaming down the chimney, thorns from the climbing rose outside were scraping the window-pane like fingernails.

'I woke up next morning with a terrible hangover, lying on the host's hearth rug, utterly appalled by what I remembered doing. Then horror turned to panic when I discovered I was pregnant. I went to Jackie. He refused to accept any responsibility.'

'Can't say I blame him,' said Perdita tonelessly. 'Any of the guys at the party could have been my father.'

'I'm sorry.' Daisy hung her head.

'What happened then?'

'I was devastated. I loved Jackie so much, I hoped he'd come round. I put off telling Granny and Granddaddy James because I was so frightened.'

'Same old story,' blazed Perdita. 'You're too worried to let down Jackie at the orgy, too wet to tell me about Fresco or my father, too wet to tell your parents – till it's too fucking late.'

Daisy's voice broke: 'Granny and Granddaddy were sweet at first. They just couldn't cope with me not knowing who your father was. They said I must have you somewhere else. So I went to this unmarried mothers' home in Scotland.'

Huge tears were pouring down Daisy's face now. 'You were so beautiful, I wanted to keep you so badly. Then one bitterly cold day there was this big pond frozen over beside the unmarried mothers' home. I looked out as I was feeding you. All the children were skating with their parents. One little girl was just sliding along shrieking with joy while her father held her hands. I felt it was so selfish to deprive you of two parents, and I must let you be adopted. There was this wonderful couple who wanted you, they were so longing to have a child. I

123

knew I was going to lose you, that's why I called you Perdita.'

'The Lost One,' said Perdita tonelessly.

'Hamish's firm was overseeing the adoption. He sought me out at the unmarried mothers' home and offered to marry me. He was different in those days. He had ideals, he was so kind and so good-looking, I was sure I could grow to love him. Anyway I'd have married the devil, I was so desperate to keep you.'

'No wonder Biddy looked so sour at the wedding,' said Perdita savagely. 'Did you tell her I was a little orgy bastard? No wonder she loathes me. What chance did I ever have? Hamish took me on because he had the temporary hots for you. Once he got bored, he got fed up with me.'

'It's all my fault and I'm sorry,' sobbed Daisy. 'I love you more than anything in the world. Please forgive me.' Getting up, stumbling over a pile of art magazines, she fell towards Perdita, holding out her arms, frantic to comfort and be comforted. But Perdita, who'd always detested physical contact, shoved her away.

'Don't touch me, you disgusting slag. All those men in one night. I bet you loved it, and what's more Violet knows.'

'She doesn't,' said Daisy aghast. 'I swear it.'

'Bloody does. Biddy or probably Hamish tipped her off.'

'Oh my God,' whispered Daisy. 'Oh, darling, I'm so sorry.'

'Why the fuck didn't you let that wonderful couple adopt me?' hissed Perdita. 'They'd have given me a much better life than you or Hamish have.'

13

For such a solitary and reserved introvert as Ricky France-Lynch prison was slightly less crucifying than it might have been because it made him feel in some infinitesimal way that he was atoning for the terrific wrongs he had done Chessie. Not only had he killed her child, but he was convinced she'd never intended to stay with Bart and could now only be miserable living with such a monster.

Even while recovering from horrific operations on his

right elbow in the prison hospital, he wrote her endless letters with his left hand, begging, in a rare dropping of his guard, for her forgiveness and her return. Chessie answered none.

The one glimmer of cheer was that Herbert, his father, felt so sorry for Ricky that he changed his will yet again, leaving everything to Ricky instead of the local hunt, who were absolutely furious, which at least meant the bank came sweet and Ricky could turn his ponies out instead of selling them.

After the relative freedom of being on remand, where he could wear his own clothes, have visitors and go for walks outside, his worst time inside was the month after his conviction when for twenty-two hours a day with lights out at six, he was 'banged up' in a tiny cell in Rutminster Prison, with a burglar, a murderer and a GBH case.

He was next moved to Greenwood, an open prison on the Rutshire—Wiltshire border. The drive, with the sun warming the bare trees and snowy fields sparkling against a delphinium-blue sky, was tantalizingly beautiful. Near the prison was a large Elizabethan manor house with ramparts of yew overlooking a great frozen lake, which belonged to some cousins Herbert had fought with. What would they think, wondered Ricky, if he climbed over the wall and dropped in on them for tea?

The prison governor was a raging snob.

'We've got six millionaires, four old Etonians, three Radleans, two solicitors, an archdeacon and a rock star, the lead singer of Apocalypse, in at the moment,' he told Ricky, 'so you're pretty small fry. The rock star gets so much fan mail, he ought to be sewing his own mail bags. Sorry about your arm, bad business. We'll find you something not too taxing to do, the library or the art department or a bit of gardening. I'm a racing man myself, but evidently the Scrubs has got a table completely set aside for polo players. Never knew there were so many bad hats in the game.'

Queueing up for lunch, Ricky felt sick. He dreaded having to adjust to a new set of people. He'd grown fond of his three previous cellmates, who'd been very tolerant, when, impossibly run down, he had kept them awake with his incessant coughing or his screaming nightmares.

Nor had he ever been intimidated at Rutminster. Just behind him in the queue on his first day, however, was a fat little man with strands of dyed black hair oiled across his bald patch and a puffy complexion like marshmallow. Flanked by four huge minions, he was making a lot of noise. Irritated that Ricky was ignoring him, he poked him in the ribs.

'Howdya get that?' He pointed at Ricky's elbow. 'Is that sling 'olding up a limp wrist, or did we 'urt it raising our glass once too often to our mouth? Drunk driving wasn't it? I 'ear we plays polo wiv Prince Charles.'

Ricky said nothing and, deciding against dishcloth-grey mutton and flooded yellow cabbage, helped himself to mashed potato.

'Off our nosh, are we?' went on the fat little man, drawing so close that Ricky could smell breath like too sweet cider. 'Ay suppose we're used to creamed potatoes at Buck House. Won't be playin' polo for a bit, will we? WILL WE?' his voice rose threateningly.

For a second Ricky considered ramming the plate of mashed potato in his face. Instead he said, 'Why don't you piss off?'

'Piss orf,' mimicked his tormentor, turning to his four huge minions who shook with sycophantic laughter. 'Oh, we are an 'ooray 'enry, aren't we? Did we pick up that posh accent from Prince Charles? We better learn some manners.' And mindful of his beefy entourage, he punched Ricky in the kidneys.

Not for nothing did Ricky have the fastest reflexes in polo. He was also instinctively left-handed. Next minute a left hook had sunk into the fat man's marshmallow jaw and sent him flying across the canteen crashing to the ground. Strolling across the room, Ricky hauled him to his feet and smashed him against the wall.

'Don't ever speak to me like that again,' he said softly, 'or I'll really hurt you,' and dropped him back on the floor.

There was a stunned silence. Not a screw nor a minder moved.

'More of an 'ooray 'enry Cooper,' drawled a camp cockney voice.

Everyone cracked up and bellowed with approval as

the fat little man struggled to his feet and shuffled out, threatening vengeance.

'Dancer Maitland', the owner of the camp cockney voice, held out a long, pale hand to Ricky. 'Welcome to Greenwood.'

Ricky knew nothing of the music business, but the tousled mane of streaked shoulder-length hair, darkening at the roots and scraped back into a pony tail, and the heavily kohled, hypnotically decadent, frost-grey eyes hidden behind dark glasses told him at once that this must be the rock star of whom the governor had boasted.

Thin to the point of emaciation, in jeans and a black jersey, Dancer had a long mournful clown's face, a pointed chin and a big pale mouth like a lifebelt. Intensely theatrical, giving off a suggestion of tragi-comic heights, he moved with feet turned out and pelvis thrust forward with the fluid grace of a ballet dancer. Gathering up Ricky's plate of cooling mashed potato, he bore it off to a far table and, sitting down, patted the seat beside him. Unwilling to be charmed, Ricky sat opposite.

''Ooray 'enry, 'ip, 'ip, 'ooray. The 'ole prison will put up a plaque to you for flooring that fat queen.'

'Who is he?'

'You didn't know? Marmaduke Kempton. That's not his real name. Bent property developer. Terrorized the East End. In 'ere he's a tobacco baron, known as the Duke, carrying on his reign of terror. Most powerful guy in the nick, or he was till you floored him. Now eat up your spuds,' went on Dancer reprovingly, 'although your strength doesn't seem to need keeping up. The food's atrocious in 'ere, but I've got a pet screw who smuggles fings in for me.'

Gazing at the night-black glasses, Ricky said nothing.

'We've got Judge Bondage-Smith in common,' drawled Dancer. Ricky looked blank.

'He sent me down too – month before you. Made the same crack about living in the fast lane, "Who are Apocalypse" indeed?' Dancer peered over his glasses, imitating the Judge. 'Fucking 'ell, you'd have thought everyone 'ad 'eard of us.'

'I hadn't,' confessed Ricky, straightening a prong of his fork.

Dancer grinned. His mouth, with its exquisitely capped teeth, seemed to light up his sad clown's face like a semi-circle of moon.

'You're better looking than Bondage-Smith, so I'll forgive you. We're in the same dormitory by the way. Very Enid Blyton – I didn't bag you a bed by the window. The draught'd have given you earache.' Then, seeing the wary expression on Ricky's face, 'I know you're dyin' to know what I was brought in for, but it ain't that. Sex offenders and long-term murderers are all tucked away in another dorm, stockbrokers and accountants in the next.'

Encouraged by the slight lift at the corner of Ricky's mouth, Dancer went on. 'I was busted smuggling cocaine and heroin into England. Shame really. I'd gone cold turkey six months before; gone through all the screaming heeby-jeebies of coming off. I was just bringing in the stuff for a friend.'

'What's it like in here?' Ricky removed a long, dark hair from his potato and put down his fork.

'Triffic contacts,' said Dancer. 'My shares have rocketed. An' the screws'll do anything for a bit of dosh. You won't have any 'assle with the inmates now you've taken out the Duke. The Padre's a bugger, literally. Loves converting straight blokes, so keep your ass superglued to the wall when he's around.'

'You don't seem to eat much either,' said Ricky, looking at Dancer's congealing mutton.

'I'm so anorexic I have midnight fasts,' said Dancer.

'Have you – er – had lots of hits in the top twenty?'

'Five number ones, the last one for twelve weeks, and fourteen weeks in the States,' sighed Dancer, shaking his head. 'Who are Apocalypse? indeed. My solicitor's comin' in 'ere for a stretch next week. No wonder I didn't get off.'

Dancer saved Ricky's sanity. He made him laugh and later he made him talk about polo, and slowly about Chessie, but never about Will. In return Dancer was incredibly frank about his own sexuality and the problems of a deprived childhood, followed by fame and colossal riches too early.

'I was an East End kid. Suddenly we had a break. I was going everywhere, staying at the best hotels, meeting the best people, birds throwing themselves at me, smart parties. I got so I had to be high to go on stage, then I was getting so high on coke, I started taking heroin to calm me down, and ended up addicted to that as well.

'You've gotta talk, Rick. Bottle it up and it comes out in uvver directions. The night my auntie died, my uncle went straight up the pub. Two months later, he went off his 'ead, and died of an 'eart attack.'

'Thanks,' said Ricky.

Anyone, claimed Evelyn Waugh, who has been to an English public school, feels comparatively at home in prison. For Ricky it was better. He'd been bullied at school. Here he was very popular. The inmates liked him because he didn't show off or drop names or grumble, and because beneath his aloof, impassive manner, his grief was almost palpable. Once he started giving racing tips that worked, even the Duke forgave him and started asking him what Prince Charles was really like, and if he'd ever clapped eyes on Princess Diana.

There were terrible moments. He was plagued by feelings of utter worthlessness. He slept appallingly, still wracked by insomnia, followed by nightmares. He was consumed with desire for Chessie. He was crucified by the knowledge that Will's last terrifying memory must have been Chessie and he screaming at each other, and being gathered into a car and hurtled to his death. He was also worried stiff about his arm. He still couldn't move his fingers or pick up anything heavy.

But there were small victories, captaining the prisoners' bowls team to a win against the screws, watching the wallflowers and forget-me-nots he'd planted come out in the bed by the visitors' check-in gate.

All his free time was spent with Dancer. Mostly they talked about polo. Insatiable for knowledge, Dancer would demand again and again to hear how Mattie had died, and how Wayne, Mattie's half-brother, had let himself out of his box and flooded the yard, and how Kinta, thundering unstoppable down the field at Deauville, enabled Ricky to score the winning goal. Night after night, with four white chess pieces for one team, and four black for the other, Ricky taught Dancer the rudiments of the game.

One late April evening when they could hear the robins singing outside, reminding Ricky unbearably of home, they got out the board and the eight black-and-white pieces.

'Show me some sneaky moves,' said Dancer.

'Well, if black hits the ball upfield,' began Ricky, 'and the opposing white back and the black number one are in pursuit of the ball riding each other off,' Ricky moved the black-and-white bishops forward so they clashed into each other, 'if black number one judges himself beaten, he should move to the left and draw white off the line. Black number two, watching the play, charges up the line – Dancer, are you listening to me?'

'I was finking how nice it'd be if you said Apocalypse instead of black.'

'You thinking of taking up polo?'

'I've got a lot of money I want to get rid of.'

'If you teach me to make money,' said Ricky, 'I'll teach you to play polo.'

'Apocalypse is a great name for a polo team,' said Dancer.

That night Ricky told Dancer about Chessie's parting jibe: 'She says she'll only come back to me if I go to ten, and win the Gold Cup and England win back the Westchester.'

'Piece a cake,' said Dancer airily. 'You said the teams with the longest purses win. I was goin' to retire, but I'll write anuvver song. It'll go to number one, because everyone's missed me while I've been inside. Then I'll take up polo, and wiv me as your patron, we'll take everyone out.'

Good as his word, Dancer abandoned his autobiography which he'd been scribbling in a red notebook and wrote a song called 'Gaol Bird' about a robin trapped in a cage. The tune was haunting. In the right mood, Dancer would sing it suddenly in bed at night. Few prisoners threw shoes at him, the words spoke for all of them.

In April they were all distracted by the Falklands War. A man in the dormitory had a son in the Paras. Ricky was worried about Drew Benedict who had resigned his commission and was due out of the Army in August, but who was now steaming out with the task force. Drew had the kind of crazy courage and lack of nerves to get himself killed. Ricky dropped a line to Sukey, who was no doubt now diligently schooling Drew's new Argentine ponies and watching every bulletin.

In early May Ricky got a letter from his solicitor requesting a visit. The night before, he was lounging on his bed, watching the trees thickening with young leaves against a pale pink sunset. Dancer, peering in the mirror, was grumbling about his roots.

'I wish you'd first seen me on stage wiv my hair all wild, and my make-up on, Rick. How can anyone operate wiv no eyeliner? Can't even get your eyelashes dyed in this dump. When you were at boarding school did you try anyfink with blokes?'

'Once or twice.'

'You enjoy it?'

'Not much,' said Ricky, who was now concentrating on *Polo* magazine. 'Better than nothing I suppose, staved off the loneliness.'

'Might be better than nuffink here.' Dancer put a hand on Ricky's shoulder. 'Want to try it sometime?'

There was a long pause. The prison building was turning a pale rose madder in the sun which was sinking like a blazing ruby into the far blue horizon. Chessie was wearing rubies the night Will died.

'Not really,' said Ricky. 'I'm still married.'

'Don't mind my asking?' Dancer's drawl had a slight tremor.

'Not at all. I just want Chessie back. But you've been fucking good to me, Dancer. I wouldn't have survived the last months without you.'

The sunset was no longer responsible for the red glow which suffused Dancer's long, sad face.

'Now that is Enid Blyton,' he said sardonically. 'Ian's coming to see me tomorrow. That's why I'm uptight.' Then, when Ricky raised his eyebrows, 'Ian's the bloke I smuggled the coke in for.'

There was no sun the next day. Thick mustard-yellow fog hung round the prison. The visitors' room, with its potted plants and its bright mural of a farmyard and 'No Smoking beyond this point' sign, was a bit like an airport lounge. Children played underfoot. Wives and girlfriends with dyed hair, short skirts, no stockings and very high heels held hands with inmates, but said little. The screws delivered coffee and tea at 20p a cup. Martin, Ricky's solicitor, in his dark grey suit, clinging to his ox-blood briefcase for extremely dear life, looked out of place.

'No sugar for me,' he said, dropping saccharin in his cup. 'I envy you your waistline,' he added heartily, privately thinking how thin and drawn Ricky looked, hoping he hadn't caught something nasty in prison.

Across the room Ricky was aware of Dancer, coiled into a relaxed theatrical pose, hand exaggeratedly cupping his pointed chin to hide the tension as he chatted to a thickset, blond young man with a sulky face. This must be Ian. He was quite unlike the birds of paradise with their rainbow hair and tight leather trousers who usually visited Dancer.

'The news is not exactly good,' Martin was saying as he opened his briefcase. 'I'm afraid Chessie's filed for divorce. In fact I've got the papers and a letter for you here.'

Ricky went very still, but felt his heart was leading some crazed life of its own, trying to fight its way out of his ribs. The letter was written from Bart's New York flat. The Palm Beach season would be over. Chessie's small, almost illegible, writing only covered a quarter of the page.

'Dear Ricky, Please sign these papers and give me a divorce. I think you owe it to me. I need to forget and everything about you reminds me of Will. I'm sorry. Yours, Chessie.'

Yours, Chessie, thought Ricky dully, what a ridiculous way to end a letter when she's not mine any more. Borrowing Martin's gold Cartier pen, he signed the papers.

'I'm afraid the other bad news, which Frances told me to tell you, is that Millicent's dead. She was run over.'

It seemed a kinder way than to tell Ricky the little whippet had simply stopped eating.

Christ, thought Ricky, another death. Dancer was always saying they went in threes: Matilda, then Will, now Millicent.

'It was very quick – no one's fault.'

Ricky put his head in his hands. He'd missed Millicent more than the ponies – the way she'd curled her silken body almost inside him, snaking her head into his hand, shivering with nerves and adoration. She was the thing he'd most looked forward to coming out to.

After that the fog seemed to invade his brain so he took in nothing, particularly that Bas in some ludicrous Robin Hood gesture had let Snow Cottage to someone called Daisy Macleod.

'Ridiculous when your plan was to redecorate and sell it as soon as the existing tenant died,' said Martin, thinking of his huge unpaid bill.

'What's up?' said Dancer afterwards.

'Nothing. How did it go?'

'I wouldn't give him any more dosh, so he got nasty, and said he'd got someone else. A plague on both your arses, I said. Fanks to you, Ricky, I don't feel nuffink for him any more. What did your bloke say? You look as though your 'ouse burnt down.'

Ricky shrugged. 'He brought divorce papers. I signed them.'

He couldn't tell even Dancer about Millicent. He was terrified of breaking down.

'Divorce is nuffink,' said Dancer furiously. 'Just a piece of paper. How can you fight when you're stuck in here. But I promise you, Ricky, when we get out of 'ere we'll buy the best ponies in the world and outmount everyone.'

In late August the Hon Basil Baddingham dropped in on his old friend, Rupert Campbell-Black, curious to see how Rupert was coping with one of his first surgeries as the new MP for Chalford and Bisley. Even before entering the constituency office, Bas was assaulted by wafts of scent. Being an expert on such matters, he identified Femme, Fracas, Joy and Diorella, before they all merged into one, totally eclipsing the tobacco-sweet smell of the large buddleia outside the door, although the dozens of peacock and tortoiseshell butterflies cruising over the long amethyst flowers, reflected Bas, were not unlike the gaudy constituents who thronged the waiting room, patting their hair and powdering their noses.

Bas had expected the people haunting MPs' surgeries to be largely pensioners seeking smaller electricity bills and quicker hip replacements. This lot looked as though they needed a husband replacement, and as Rupert had just divorced his wife Helen, they must have high hopes. Some were very pretty. Perhaps I ought to go into politics, thought Bas.

'I'm afraid if you haven't an appointment there's no way Mr Campbell-Black can see you,' said the thoroughly flustered agent. 'It's like the first day of the sales here.'

'I only dropped in socially,' said Bas. 'Just tell him I'm here.'

Finding himself a corner on the dark green leather seat, Bas picked up a July *Horse and Hound* which had a large photograph of himself, Kevin Coley of Doggie Dins and the disgusting Napier brothers jubilantly hoisting the Gold Cup above their heads.

'Basil Baddingham, playing well above his handicap,' said the copy, *'found the flags twice in the crucial fifth chukka.'*

Bas smirked and, glancing up, saw several of the occupants of the waiting room eyeing him with great interest. He smiled back at the prettiest one, who dropped her eyes, then looked again when she thought he wasn't looking. Just back from Deauville, Bas was very brown.

Women got awfully restless in August, he thought. It was an awareness of summer running out and lovers being away with their wives and seemingly unending school holidays. The pretty one, who was wearing a pink cotton jersey cardigan and jeans, had just been summoned to see Rupert. She had a glorious bottom.

Bas was an 'Hon' because his official father had been ennobled for his work as a munitions manufacturer during the war. After twenty-three years of utter fidelity to Lord Pop Pop, as he was known, Bas's mother had had a mad fling with an Argentine polo player. The result was Bas, who had inherited both his father's amorous and equestrian skills. A very early marriage had ended in divorce and no children. Having no intention of getting caught again, at thirty-four Bas dabbled in property, ran a very successful wine bar, hunted all winter, played polo and was known, after Rupert Campbell-Black, as the worst rake in the West of England.

Having spent many happy autumns buying ponies and playing polo in the Argentine, Bas's loyalties had been torn apart by the Falklands War. He had loathed seeing his second fatherland so humiliated. But Bas was a commercial animal and he was even more irritated that he was banned from buying Argentine ponies any more.

He had also recently bought a large tract of land round Rutshire Polo Club, on which he intended to build upmarket polo yards with glamorous houses attached, and flog them at a vast profit to poloholics like Victor Kaputnik and Bart Alderton. Unfortunately Rutshire Polo Club was not the draw it should have been. The bar was useless. The Argentine players, who had added such glamour, had been forced to turn back in mid-flight, and with Drew Benedict away in the Falklands and Ricky in prison, the attendance had dwindled drastically.

The scented ladies were getting restless. The girl in the pink cardigan had been in with Rupert for ages. When she came out, Bas's expert eye noticed the flushed face and the buttons done up on the wrong holes.

'Mr Baddingham,' said the agent.

'I was next,' thundered a big woman in dungarees.

'I'm afraid Mr Campbell-Black can't see anyone else today,' said the agent, desperately trying to stem the storm of protest. 'He had to return to London for a crucial meeting with the PM.'

Grinning, Bas slid into Rupert's office.

'Bloody good winning the Gold Cup,' said Rupert.

'Bloody marvellous winning the World Championships,' said Bas. 'The ideal moment to retire.'

'Not sure I should have done,' said Rupert, looking ruefully at the pile of papers. 'Show-jumping's much easier than this. Facts at your fingertips indeed. My fingertips are more used to pleasuring other things.'

Rupert's suntan from the World Championships didn't altogether hide the dark circles under his eyes. Too much sex, recent divorce or withdrawal symptoms at announcing his retirement, wondered Bas.

'I've only got ten minutes,' said Rupert. 'I'm going back to London.'

'On a Friday night? She *must* be special. Who is she?'

'Beattie Johnson.' Rupert was unable to resist boasting. Bas whistled. 'Is that wise?'

'Sensational in bed,' said Rupert.

135

'And utterly unscrupulous in print,' said Bas disapprovingly.

'It's all right. She's abandoned *The Scorpion* for six months to ghost my memoirs.'

'A house ghost!' said Bas. 'Look, Ricky's coming out of prison next month.'

Rupert raised his eyes to heaven: 'Christ! Having jacked in show-jumping, I know exactly how he must feel not being able to play polo. We ought to join Hooked on Horses Anonymous.'

'Wasn't so bad in prison,' said Bas. 'He had a routine and people all round him. He liked the people.'

'Well, he was brought up on a large estate,' said Rupert. 'He should know how to get on with the working classes.'

'How's he going to cope when he gets out?' asked Bas. 'That bloody great house, no Chessie, no Will. Look, I want to show you an amazing girl.'

'I've got one.' Rupert looked at his watch. 'In London.'

'It's on your way,' said Bas.

Down at Rutshire Polo Club, the huge trees in their midi-dresses were turning yellow. A scattering of mothers lined Ground Two.

'This is the Pony Club,' said Rupert, outraged. 'I'm off.'

'One chukka,' said Bas soothingly. 'Watch number three in the black shirt on the dark brown mare with the white blaze.'

Only the narrowness of the waist, the curl of the thigh and the slight fullness in the T-shirt indicated that the player was a girl.

Next moment Perdita had tapped the ball out of a jumble of sticks and stamping ponies' legs, ridden off the opposing number three, dummied past the white number four and scored. Two minutes later she scored again with an incredible back shot from twenty yards.

'Not only does she get to the ball in time to examine it for bugs,' said Bas, 'but she plays with five times more aggression than any of the boys.'

'Not bad,' said Rupert grudgingly. 'In fact she's almost as good as I was when I started. But the competition's pathetic. She wouldn't stand up even in low goal.'

'Would if she were properly taught. She's fantastic-looking close up. Just think what a draw she'd be here in a few years' time. A really stunning good girl player.'

'Just because you want to push up the price of the land round the club.'

'You can buy in too,' said Bas.

Thundering down the field, Perdita caught one of the opposition on the hop.

'Get off my fucking line, you creaming little poofter,' she screamed and, whipping the ball past him, flicked it between the posts.

'Fine command of the English language,' said Rupert, 'and that's an exceptionally nice mare.'

'It's Ricky's,' said Bas. 'Since he's been in prison his ponies have been turned out and Perdita's been borrowing them all summer without asking. That happens to be Kinta; Best Playing Pony at Deauville last year.'

Rupert took another look at Perdita as she lined up for the throw-in.

'Didn't she come out with the East Cotchester last year?'

'That's the one. Father walked out, lost all their money. Girl like that ought to be sponsored. She's bankable – and bonkable. Has the Ministry for Sport got any spare cash?'

'None,' said Rupert, getting into his car. 'Polo's too elitist. Everything's going to the Olympic Fund.'

'Well, at least let's give her to Ricky. He can't play for ages because of his elbow. He can't drive or go abroad for a year. If he's not going to drink himself insensible, we've got to find him an interest.'

14

To avoid the press, Ricky was let out of prison by a side door two hours early. His tweed jacket hung off him, the faded brown cords were held up by an old school tie, the cuffs of his check shirt slipped over his knuckles like mittens. Once through the door, he took a great shuddering breath. A thrush was singing in the sycamores. The sun had just risen in a tidal wave of rose and turquoise, but dense inky blue storm clouds gathered menacingly in the West.

Ricky was expecting Joel, his farm manager, with the Land-Rover. Instead, spotlit against this thunderous backdrop, lounging around a vast open Bentley, like characters out of Scott Fitzgerald, were Rupert, Bas, Drew and a tousled but undeniably desirable blonde who was wearing Rupert's dinner jacket over her rose-printed silk dress.

Bas, being half-Latin and the most demonstrative, came straight up, put his long muscular arms round Ricky and kissed him on both cheeks.

'Welcome back, dear boy,' he murmured in his husky, caressing, almost exaggeratedly English accent.

Drew, very brown from the troopship, but more reserved, relieved Ricky of his suitcase. Rupert, his blue eyes bloodshot and slightly off centre, lipstick all over his evening shirt, put an arm round Ricky's shoulder, leading him to the car: 'You made it, you poor sod. Christ, I'm glad you're out.' Then, drawing forward the tousled blonde, 'This is Beattie Johnson.'

Ricky stiffened, his eyes wary and hostile. Beattie Johnson had written some vicious lies about him and Chessie during the trial.

'It's OK,' said Rupert quickly. 'She's off duty.'

Although Rupert had kissed off all her make-up and reddened her face with his stubble, she was even sexier close up. Curling her arms round Ricky's neck, she kissed him on the edge of his mouth.

'You poor old thing, the nightmare's over. I have to tell you, you're much more glamorous in the flesh.'

Beattie's flesh, in its clinging softness, reminded Ricky agonizingly of Chessie. Beneath the sharp tang of her scent, he caught the unmistakable fishlike reek of sex and nearly blacked out.

'Leave him alone, Beattie,' snapped Bas. 'You sit in the front, Ricky. Isn't this a truly terrific motor car?'

'We decided it wasn't worth going to bed,' said Rupert, as he headed towards the motorway. 'We thought we'd all have breakfast at Sheepfield Chase. Bas got them to lay on a private room, so you won't get gorped at.'

'And the uncondemned man is going to eat a hearty breakfast,' said Beattie, putting her hands on Ricky's shoulders. Ricky tried not to freeze away. Having taken a large swig out of a bottle of Krug, Bas handed it forward to him. Ricky shook his head.

'Go on,' chided Beattie. 'You're about three bottles behind the rest of us.'

'No thanks,' said Ricky. Looking down he saw Beattie's rather dirty toe-nailed foot edging down the gear lever to rub against Rupert's black thigh. Putting down a hand, Rupert caressed her instep.

'Bugger off now,' he said to her, 'or I'll be done for drunk driving. And for Christ's sake, get that black tie off, Bas.'

Ricky wished he could go straight home. He needed to touch base, but it had been so kind of them to turn up, he must make an effort. He turned to Drew. 'Glad you got back safely.'

'Bloody nuisance missing a whole season,' said Drew.

'It must have been wonderful all those cheering crowds welcoming you back,' gushed Beattie.

'We'd no idea of the strength of feeling back home,' said Drew. 'It was a complete surprise. We were overwhelmed.'

'How did you feel when the truce was finally signed in Port Stanley?' went on Beattie. 'Did you have a fantastic piss-up?'

'No,' said Drew. 'We were simply glad to be alive.'

He's changed, thought Ricky. The golden boy's grown up and been jolted out of his habitual sang-froid.

'Drew's being recommended for an MC,' said Bas.

'Sukey must be thrilled,' said Ricky.

They've all done so well, he thought wistfully – World Champions, Gold Cups, MCs.

The conversation inevitably got on to polo and what a bore it was not being able to buy ponies from Argentina any more.

'I'm getting some from Australia,' said Bas, 'and the Prince of Wales.' Then, realizing Beattie was listening, he started gabbling away in Spanish to Drew.

'Speak English,' said Beattie furiously, hearing the words, 'Charles and Diana'. 'It's bloody rude.'

When she could get no change out of either Drew or Bas, she turned back to Ricky.

'Did they give you a hard time inside because you were a gent?'

'No.'

'How was Dancer Maitland?'

'Great.'

'Did he make a pass at you?'

'Oh, shut up, Beattie,' said Bas.

'Well, he is a screaming pouf. I'd have made a pass at Ricky if I'd been in prison.'

'Dancer's f-f-fine,' said Ricky, wanting to strangle Beattie. 'He's a lovely man. Everyone adored him.'

Out of the corner of his eye, he could see Beattie writing 'lovely man' on her wrist with eye pencil. The inky black cloud had spread over the whole sky. They only just managed to reach the hotel and get the roof up when the heavens opened.

'I guess MP stands for Moderately Pissed,' said Rupert, as ravishing waitresses, hand-picked by Bas, brought more bottles of Krug into the private room. Ricky put his hand over his glass.

'Go on,' said Bas. 'You must celebrate today.'

'Honestly, I've given it up.'

'That's ridiculous,' said Rupert. 'You used to drink for Rutshire.'

'I don't *want* a drink,' said Ricky through gritted teeth. Then, lowering his voice, 'I'm sorry, I just feel I owe it to Will.'

'Ah,' said Rupert, also dropping his voice, 'I understand. Sorry. But don't punish yourself too hard. Christ, look at the tits on that waitress.'

Attack came next from Ricky's left.

'You mustn't be sad,' said Beattie, pouring him a cup of coffee. 'Spare men are at such a premium these days, you'll be snapped up in a trice. I've got some stunning girlfriends. You must make up a four with Rupert and me.'

Her hot, brown eyes ran over him, telling him what fun they could have together. She's not sure of Rupert and is trying to make him jealous, thought Ricky. God knows, he'd be impossible to hold.

'Is it true,' asked Beattie, 'that Chessie said she'd only come back to you if you went to ten and won the Westchester?'

'For fuck's sake, shut up,' snarled Rupert; then, turning back to Bas, 'No, it definitely half-brother to Nijinsky.'

140

Breakfast arrived – eggs, bacon, sausages, kidneys, cold ham and a mountain of kedgeree.

'I'll help you,' said Beattie, piling up Ricky's plate. 'You definitely need feeding up.'

Then they all watched in horror as Ricky tried to cut up a piece of ham. His right arm simply wasn't up to it.

'I'll do it for you,' said Drew, taking Ricky's knife and fork.

The prettiest waitress was already sitting on Bas's knee, feeding him fried bread spread with marmalade.

'They're all booked for the morning,' murmured Rupert, who had his hand halfway up Beattie's skirt. 'I'd go for that redhead over there.'

'I've found an amazing girl for you to teach polo to,' Bas called across the table.

'Smile, please,' said Beattie, who had suddenly produced a camera.

Ricky got to his feet, fried egg churning in his stomach. He only just reached the lavatory in time, then it was mostly bile he threw up. Drew was waiting as he came out, the blue eyes matter-of-fact, but not insensitive.

'I'm sorry, we thought you needed cheering up. We went about it the wrong way. I'll run you home.'

On the motorway the windscreen wipers fought a losing battle with the downpour and Drew talked idly about the Falklands.

'Once we reached the actual island, I had the somewhat unenviable task – because I speak Spanish – of debriefing the Argie POWs. One of their pilots, shot down in the sea, was actually a polo player. Arrogant sod, although I must say British methods of obtaining information are somewhat reprehensible.'

'So are Beattie Johnson's,' said Ricky. 'Christ, she's awful.'

'Awful,' agreed Drew. 'Ever since Rupert packed in show-jumping he's been drinking and screwing his brains out. I had a look at your ponies, by the way. They look very well. A season off's probably done them good.'

'I don't know if I'm going to be able to . . . ' Ricky's voice trailed off.

'Course you will. You've got to get to ten.'

141

Frances, the head groom, and Joel, Ricky's farm manager, were furious to be caught on the hop. Not expecting Ricky for hours, and by then absolutely plastered, they hadn't swept the yard. There was hay and straw everywhere, floating in huge puddles. Louisa was just furious that she'd failed to keep up the crash diet she'd started every morning for the last month in anticipation of Ricky's return. But Ricky didn't seem to notice anything. Having patted the Labradors, he said he wanted to be on his own for a bit and he'd see them later.

Inside the house, the emptiness hit him like a boxing glove. No silken whippet coiled herself round him, jumping for joy. His one craving was to look at Will's photographs again. The one in his wallet had cracked and almost disintegrated. But on the piano in the drawing room he found only empty silver frames. Shaking, he opened the photograph album and found every picture of Will had been removed, and where there had been photographs of Ricky and Chessie together, Chessie had cut out herself.

As he looked round the room, he noticed pieces of furniture missing, pictures taken from the walls, huge gaps in the bookshelves. Churning inside, feeling bile rising in his mouth again, he raced upstairs. Someone had tactfully removed the child gate from across the top stair, but the rocking-horse with most of its paint chipped away by Will's polo stick still stood on the landing.

Will's bedroom had obviously been tidied up. Opening a drawer, he found the policeman's helmet Will had been wearing when he squirted Grace with Bloody Mary. There were all the Dinky cars Will so adored. Snoopy lay spread-eagled on the bed, with his vast inflated belly.

'Oh God,' groaned Ricky, finding Will's piggy bank empty on the window sill. Chessie'd even broken into that.

Stumbling into his dressing room, he found the photographs of his ponies still up, but the pictures of Chessie and Will once again removed. Next door, in the bedroom, he nearly fell over Millicent's basket lined with his old dressing gown, but found all Chessie's clothes and her jewellery gone. And there, mocking him, was the huge four-poster with its blue chintz curtains covered in pink peonies and roses – he remembered how she'd accused him in that terrible last row of being such a failure in bed. Hopelessly overexcited by her, he supposed he had often come too quickly. The glow-stars Chessie had stuck on the ceiling had long since lost their luminosity. Howling like a dog, Ricky threw himself down, burying his face in the pillow for some faint trace of the Diorissimo she always wore, but there was nothing.

15

Later in the day Ricky pulled himself together and had a bath. Outside the rain had stopped and everything dripped and sparkled in the hopelessly overgrown garden. Tortoise-shell butterflies rose indignantly as he picked Michaelmas daisies, honeysuckle and roses to put on Will's grave in the little churchyard at Eldercombe, where generations of France-Lynches had been buried.

William Richard France-Lynch, 1978–81, said the newest headstone. The vicar, toddling past to choir practice, was about to stop and speak to Ricky, but, seeing his face, moved quickly away.

Towards sunset, missing Dancer's prattle and overcome by restlessness, Ricky told Frances to saddle up Donaghue, his old hunter. Now was as good a time as any to see if he'd lost his nerve. Once mounted, the ground seemed miles away, the saddle impossibly slippery, so he tried to concentrate on his surroundings. Joel had got very slack; the fences were in a terrible state.

Bypassing the orchard and a field of stubble, he set out to look at his ponies which were turned out in the watermeadows at the bottom of the valley. After the rain, the ground steamed like a Grand National winner. The sinking yellow sun was turning the steam amber gold. Flocks of gulls were returning to the Bristol Channel after a day's looting in the newly ploughed fields.

With only one arm working, Ricky had difficulty open-ing the gate leading to the valley. But Donaghue stood like a statue. Checking the sheep grid alongside the gate, Ricky was pleased to see that at least the wooden ramp which enabled field mice or hedgehogs to clamber out was still in position. The view down the valley, as always, took his breath away. On each steep side dense ashwoods plunged to fringes of reddening bracken, then into a green ride which was divided by a stream which hurtled down through caverns of wild rose, hawthorn and the elders the valley was named after, then raced on to meet the Frogsmore Stream where it flowed under Snow Cottage.

At least this is all still mine, thought Ricky, kicking Donaghue into a canter. Thank God there wasn't anyone around to see him clinging to the horse's mane. Relief on reaching the more level watermeadows turned to joy and a great lump rose in his throat as he saw Kinta, who'd kept carting him last summer, and Wayne, Mattie's hideous custard-yellow admirer and the yard escapologist, standing together idly chewing and scratching each other's necks. Their tails and their punk, growing-out manes were full of burrs. Then Ricky froze, for, on a stretch of grass eaten flat by sheep, some strange female was riding Pilgrim, his finest mare from Argentina. She was cantering bareback with just a headcollar, and with a polo stick, was tapping a ball in and out of a row of stones, presumably pinched from one of his walls. For a second, he was transfixed with pleasure by how well she rode, then as he drew nearer, and the ponies stopped grazing and looked up, he realized she was only a schoolgirl, with her skirt tucked into dark blue wool knickers, and her platinum-blond pony tail tied back with her school tie. For a further few seconds, he watched her execute a perfect figure of eight, changing legs in and out of a couple of stones. Then he flipped. 'What the fuck do you think you're doing?'

The roar was loud enough to send the ponies scuttling away, almost to start an avalanche of ash trees. Turning, the girl gave a gasp of horror, then swinging Pilgrim round, set off at a gallop up the valley. Ricky gave chase, all thought of his damaged arm forgotten. Donaghue was bigger and had a longer stride than Pilgrim, but the girl was lighter, and God, she made the pony shift. Oblivious of stones and rabbit holes, jumping over fallen logs, she reached the top of the hill and thundered towards the sheep grid.

'Come back,' howled Ricky. 'Don't be a bloody idiot.'

Perdita ignored him. Digging her heels into Pilgrim's heaving sides, she put her straight at the sheep grid. For a second, the pony hesitated, then the iron bars flew beneath her and she had landed safely on the other side. By the time Ricky had gone through the side gate, he found Pilgrim running around the barley stubble, and the girl vanished into the beech woods like a gypsy's lurcher.

Pilgrim was gratifyingly delighted to see her master, digging him in the ribs and searching his pockets for Polos, whickering with joy, until Donaghue was squealing and snapping with jealousy.

By some miracle Pilgrim seemed all right, but, as Ricky ran his hands down her delicate dark brown legs, he shuddered at the thought of them snapped by those murderous iron bars. Grimly he rode back to the stables to tell Joel what had happened.

'Sounds like Perdita Macleod,' said Joel.

'Who the hell's she?'

'Daisy Macleod's daughter. They've rented Snow Cottage.'

'They what? I know nothing about it.'

'You do,' said Joel. 'You signed the lease the day Martin came to see you. I guess you had a lot on your mind.'

'Well, they're not living there much longer,' snapped Ricky.

'I'd no idea she was riding the ponies,' said Joel. 'I haven't been down that end of the valley for a few days.'

'Well, you should have been; half the fences and walls are down.'

'She's a stuck-up bitch, that Perdita.' Joel hastily changed the subject, 'They can't stand her at the village shop.' Then, because he wanted an excuse to go and see Daisy, added, 'I'll pop down and have a word with her mother.'

'I'm going to talk to her mother,' said Ricky grimly.

'I'll drive you,' said Joel.

'No. I'll walk down through the woods.'

Daisy Macleod had had a gruelling day. She absolutely loathed her new job. Her boss, Mr Bradley, the Christmas pudding manufacturer, was a revolting thick-voiced, pot-bellied letch, who was constantly chiding her because her typing and filing, particularly in her current state of post-divorce shock, were not up to scratch. Almost worse, he insisted she wore high heels and dresses to the office, adding that as a 'Caring Chauvinist', he was only making her dress as femininely as possible for her own good, so that she might one day attract a new husband. He made Daisy's flesh creep, but she put up with it because she desperately needed the money, and the factory, on the far side of Eldercombe Village, was in walking distance, so she could rush home and take Ethel out during her lunch hour.

Now Eddie and Violet had gone back for the autumn term, Daisy had hoped Perdita would be less disruptive. She had got straight 'U's in her O levels, but any remonstrance from Daisy triggered off a storm of abuse. Then on the first Friday of term she was suspended for a week for punching a girl in the playground.

'At least I wasn't being laid by the art master,' she screamed at Daisy when she got home. 'I don't take after you that much.'

Daisy knew that when Perdita was frightened she became more abusive – but it didn't make things easier. Now, a fortnight later, Perdita should have been back at school, but, to the intense irritation of the Caring Chauvinist, the switchboard at the Christmas pudding factory had been besieged by calls all day – from mothers complaining that Perdita had terrorized their children, from the village shop grumbling that Perdita had walked out twice without paying and asking Daisy to settle a horrifying drink-and-cigarette bill, and, worst of all, from Perdita's form mistress saying Perdita hadn't been near the school since Tuesday and was supposed to be retaking her O levels, which didn't bode well.

Walking wearily home along the cart track which ran alongside Ricky's woods and at right-angles to the Eldercombe valley, Daisy kicked off her shoes. Although sharp pebbles cut her bare feet, anything was better than those punishing high heels. Even the undeniable prettiness of Snow Cottage didn't cheer her up, because she was so aware of crumbling mossy walls that should be pointed, and hart's tongue ferns growing out of the roof, and the hayfield of a lawn, and a door bell that didn't work, and red apples littering the orchard floor, reproachfully waiting to be turned into pies.

There was no sign of Perdita, but at least Daisy got a wonderful welcome from Ethel, who whimpered and moved from foot to foot with joy, then bounded straight into the stream, splashing about, then shaking herself all over Daisy.

Daisy's love for Ethel had deepened almost into idolatry over the last months, despite her frightful naughtiness and her great destructive paws. Ethel never seemed to mind how much Daisy sobbed into her shaggy shoulder, and this morning, to cheer Daisy up, she had even chewed up Hamish's copy of Robert Burns.

Turning on the washing-up machine and looking out into the red twilight, Daisy decided that too many evenings since she moved in had been spent drinking too much vodka, when the budget ran to it, and trying to change television channels on the cordless telephone. Nor had she painted since she moved in, her inspiration seeming to have dried up. Tonight she would do something practical. Perdita was always grumbling she had nowhere to put her clothes. A cupboard on the landing was full of the children's old toys. If Daisy put them in plastic bags they could be stored in the attic and Perdita would have a new cupboard.

Daisy had a bet with herself: a large vodka and orange if she could empty the cupboard in half an hour. But then the memories came flooding back of a time when Hamish and she had seemed happy, as she found corn dollies never made up, kites never built, jigsaws of Windsor Castle never even opened. She was so busy trying on Mickey Mouse masks, and plugging in clacking false teeth, and turning soapy liquid into a stream of bubbles, she didn't notice Ethel beating a retreat downstairs with a large stuffed panda.

And there was one of Eddie's all-time best presents – the plastic, bloodstained knife which hooked round the back, but looked as though it was going through the head. Putting it on, catching sight of herself in the landing mirror, Daisy burst into tears.

Wiping her eyes and rushing downstairs to answer the telephone, she found Perdita's headmistress on the line. Her first fears were that Perdita had been expelled. Instead the headmistress gave her a pep-talk.

'We don't feel, Mrs Macleod, that Perdita is getting quite the right home back-up. It's very hard being a latch-key child *and* the victim of a broken home. We do realize you have to earn your living, but I gather that Perdita never sees her father.'

'They really don't get on,' said Daisy apologetically.

'Are you sure you're not letting your animosity towards your ex-husband poison your judgement? Perdita's not a stupid child, just very disturbed. Perhaps if you could spend more time talking to her.'

Instead of slumped in front of the telly with a bottle of vodka, thought Daisy. In despair at the prospect of finding Perdita another school, she noticed the washing-up machine had stopped. It was so ancient, the door kept opening. Seeing Gainsborough sitting on the kitchen table with his back paw in the air like a leg of mutton, Daisy grabbed her sketching pad. Keeping the door of the washing-up machine shut with her bottom, she started drawing frantically. Next moment Ethel gave a bark of delight and Daisy steeled herself for another frightful row with Perdita. Instead, through the kitchen door, hardly knocking, came the most ravishing-looking man. Gosh, she thought, my luck has changed. Then as he turned towards her she noticed the long, livid scar running down the side of his face and realized to her horror that he must be Ricky France-Lynch, her landlord.

'Oh dear,' said Daisy, 'I thought you were Perdita.'

'It's her I've come to talk about,' said Ricky bleakly.

'Join the queue,' said Daisy helplessly, as the washing-up machine, changing direction, gave a great dragon's roar. 'What's she done now?'

Stammering, Ricky told her about riding Pilgrim and jumping the sheep trap. 'She could have killed herself and £10,000 worth of pony.'

'I didn't know she'd been riding them,' said Daisy appalled. 'I'm terribly sorry.'

'She's also been taking them to the pony club all summer.'

'Oh my God,' gasped Daisy. 'She's not here at the moment, but I promise it won't happen again.'

'I'll t-t-take her to court if she doesn't stop.'

'I don't blame you,' said Daisy. 'Look, do sit down.'

As she moved forward the washing-up machine stopped. 'You have to lean against it,' she explained. Then, her eyes falling on the breakfast and last night's supper washing-up in the sink: 'I'm afraid it's an awful tip. Look, do have a drink, I've got some vodka, and I know Perdita's got the remains of a bottle of Malibu. She certainly owes it you.'

Ricky shook his head. Just for a second he looked slightly less grim. 'D'you always go around with knives through your head?'

'I expect Perdita wishes I did.' Crimson with embarrassment, Daisy tore the knife off. 'I was sorting out the children's toy cupboard. Oh hell, poor panda,' she pointed helplessly at black-and-white fur and blue foam rubber littering the hall.

'We've got so little space,' she went on, 'and you know how hopeless children are at allowing anything to be thrown away.'

'Yes,' said Ricky.

'Oh, heavens,' said Daisy, mortified as she remembered about Will. 'I'm so sorry.'

'It's all right. Mind if I look round?'

Quailing, Daisy nodded. The only thing she'd done to the house was to put rose-printed paper up in Violet's room, and the damp had come straight through.

'We love it so much here.' Her voice trailed off as she thought of the dreadful mess he'd find in the children's bedrooms. Mindlessly, she drew in some whiskers on Gainsborough's face and thickened his tail. It was no good, she'd have to have a drink. As she was tugging the ice tray out of the hopelessly frozen ice box, Ricky came downstairs looking grimmer than ever. 'This place is an absolute disgrace.'

'It is,' agreed Daisy humbly. 'Anarchy somehow broke out after my husband walked out.'

'No, the state of it,' said Ricky. 'There's damp in every room. That sink's coming away from the wall. You need bookshelves and cupboards fitted in all the rooms. I've got builders starting in the yard tomorrow. I'll send a couple down here to sort things out. They can probably mend the washing-up machine.'

'Oh, thank you.' Daisy had great difficulty not bursting into tears again. 'Are you sure you don't want a drink?'

Ricky shook his head. 'I don't – not since Will . . . '

'Oh, how stupid of me,' said Daisy, appalled. 'How could I be so crass?' And how awful too, she thought, for Ricky to be reminded of Will's death by that scar every time he looked in the mirror.

She was amazed when he sat down at the kitchen table and started stroking Ethel's lovely speckled head.

'Why's Perdita so screwed up?'

And he listened without interrupting while she told him about the failed O levels and having to sell Fresco, the first thing Perdita had really loved, and about Hamish never loving her and spoiling the other two.

'He wasn't Perdita's father,' Daisy blurted out.

'Who was?' asked Ricky.

'Some other man,' said Daisy, going scarlet. 'But because aunts and grandmothers and teachers and family friends all prefer Violet and Eddie, I sort of over-compensate to make it up to her. You give in because it's easier than facing one of her tantrums.'

Getting up, she put two pieces of melting ice into her glass of vodka, then, going to a yellow tin on the shelf, took out a tea bag and put it on top of the ice, then, unseeingly gazing out into the darkening garden, she switched on the kettle.

Taking the glass from her, Ricky removed the tea bag, switched off the kettle and, looking in the fridge and not finding any tonic, added orange juice to the vodka before handing it back.

Here's someone in an even worse state than I am, he thought. To his amazement, he found himself saying, 'Bas has already spoken to me about Perdita. He thinks she's got fantastic potential. If she promises not to bunk out of school any more, and tries to get her O levels, I'll give her a weekend job working in the yard. If she takes that seriously, and passes her O levels, I'll teach her to play polo.'

For a second Daisy's face quivered; then she blew her nose noisily on a piece of kitchen roll.

'Are you sure it won't be a bore?'

Ricky shook his head. 'The probation officer's keeping tabs on me, I can't drive or leave the country for a year. Give me something to do.'

'That is the nicest thing that's ever happened,' said Daisy slowly. Like a golden retriever searching for a sock to give a returning master, she looked frantically round the room. Then, ripping the drawing of Gainsborough from her sketching pad, she thrust it into his hand.

Perdita came in ten minutes after Ricky had left. She looked pale, truculent and dangerous.

'Something wonderful's happened,' said Daisy.

'You've found a lover,' spat Perdita. 'So what else is new?'

Daisy winced. 'Ricky France-Lynch came round.'

'So?' For a second, Perdita looked terrified, then resumed her normal expression: furious dark eyes in a white, cold stony face.

'You're to go and see him at eleven on Saturday.'

'Whatever for?'

'He's going to offer you a part-time job. And if you work hard and get your O levels, he'll take you on full time.'

'After the way he swore at me this afternoon I'm not sure I want it,' said Perdita coldly.

Daisy resisted a desire to shake her. Instead, she asked what she wanted for supper.

'I'm not hungry,' snapped Perdita. Stepping over the toys Daisy had turned out, she flounced into her bedroom and slammed the door. Waltzing deliriously round the room, she pulled out the only photograph of Ricky she hadn't ripped up and, whispering, 'At last, at last,' started covering it with kisses.

16

At a quarter to eleven next morning Perdita sauntered downstairs, reeking of the remnants of Daisy's last bottle of Je Reviens. Her deliberately dishevelled, newly washed hair fell halfway down her back. Her normally alabaster skin was smothered in bronze base to hide two spots which had sprung up overnight on her nose and chin out of nerves. An excess of royal-blue eyeliner and mascara ringed her angry eyes. She wore no bra. Her breasts, as rounded as scoops of ice-cream, were emphasized by the tightest royal-blue T-shirt. No pants line marred the impossibly stretched navy-blue jodhpurs. Flicking her whip against gleaming brown boots, she posed in front of Daisy.

'Dressed to kill,' she said sarcastically.

Certain to kill any passion in Ricky, thought Daisy. Perdita was much too beautiful to smother herself in that muck, and the twelve pounds missing from the house-keeping must have paid for that T-shirt.

'If I look like a whore,' said Perdita, reading her mother's thoughts, 'I'm only taking after you. I've no idea when I'll be back, if ever.'

Outside it was still hot. The sun had dried the dew, but the fields were still strewn with cobwebs. Forget-me-nots and jade-green watercress choked the stream. At the top of the ride Ricky's house skulked like a grey battleship in its ocean of turning beech trees.

'This should be fun,' said Frances to Louisa, as Perdita strolled into the yard, cigarette still hanging from her lips. 'Is she applying for a job as a hooker?'

The ponies, peering out over their bottle-green half-doors, however, made no secret of their delight at seeing Perdita, who had been stuffing them with carrots nicked from Philippa Mannering's garden all summer.

'It'll be interesting to see how fit you've got them,' said Frances nastily. 'And I'd put that out,' she added, pointing to a 'No Smoking' sign over the tack room door.

Chucking her lighted cigarette in a dark green tub of white geraniums, ignoring Frances's look of disapproval, Perdita went up to each pony, hugging them and pulling their ears. Even Kinta, known to bite everyone, rested her face against Perdita's, leaving a blob of green slime on her right nipple just as Ricky came out of the tack room. Yesterday his face had been animated with rage. Today it had resumed its normal impassivity. Close up, Perdita noticed the putty-grey pallor, the black hair flecked with grey, the livid scar running from right eyebrow to jawbone. His mouth had vanished in a grim line. Neither the thick, curly eyelashes nor the black rings underneath them tempered the bleak animosity of the slanting dark eyes above the hard Slav cheekbones.

Perdita felt a strange mixture of passion and compassion. I'll make him better, she thought. He's going to be my lover and the father I never had. I'm going to be the love of his life and the child he lost.

Ricky looked at Perdita. Even the crude make-up and the obscenely tight clothes could not really detract from her beauty. Yet in her wanton, blatant sexuality, she was terrifyingly close to both Beattie Johnson and Chessie. A waft of Je Reviens reached him, sickly sweet amid the stable smells of horse sweat, leather, straw and droppings. He was overcome with revulsion.

'Tack up Sinatra,' he said to Louisa.

Louisa and Frances exchanged awed but gleeful glances. Sinatra was the most difficult ride in the yard. He had to be gagged up to the eyeballs for anyone to control him. Bred in Kentucky, his coat had the mushroom-fawn silkiness of a Weimaraner. Brilliant on his day, he bucked under the saddle and pulled like the Inter-City to London.

'Leave off the running reins – and he doesn't need a double bridle or that martingale,' ordered Perdita, following Frances into Sinatra's box.

'We're the best judge of that,' snapped Frances. 'He throws his head when he stops.'

'I've been riding him in a headcollar all summer.'

'On your swollen head be it. My God, is Ricky ever going to knock *you* into shape.'

'Talking of shapes,' drawled Perdita, staring contemptuously at the scrawny, hipless, bustless Frances, 'yours leaves a great deal to be desired.'

Ricky made no comment about the lack of martingale, but handed her a hat as soon as she was mounted.

Aware it would flatten her hair, Perdita grumbled that she didn't want to look like Mrs Thatcher going down a mine.

'Put it on,' said Ricky sharply.

Ricky stood in the middle of a sandy, oblong corral which was enclosed by post-and-rail fencing except for a gate at one end and a stretch of wall at the other. For a start he made her circle on different legs, leading to small circles, then into figures of eight. Each time Sinatra changed legs perfectly.

'Blimey,' said Louisa.

'Keep your weight on the inside leg,' said Ricky. 'Now circle the ring at a gallop, then turn at the top sharply, changing legs.'

Knowing this was the most important move in polo,

Perdita cantered round sweetly, calmly, then leaning right forward, she sent Sinatra thundering down the side of the ring, only just preventing him crashing into the wall. Going into a lightning turn which nearly brought the pony down, before Ricky could stop her, she careered back to the other end, executing a turn so sharp that Sinatra's fawn nearside should have been full of splinters.

'Stop showing off,' howled Ricky.

'Just proving he's better in a snaffle.'

'He only stopped to avoid c-c-concussing himself.'

'Crap,' said Perdita rudely, and, swinging round, galloped back, pulling Sinatra up five yards in front of the wall, turning so fast that for a second both pony and rider vanished in a cloud of brown dust. Emerging, she thundered up to Ricky, slithering to a halt three feet away from him, running her hand up and down Sinatra's bristly poll to show him her appreciation.

'Well?' she taunted Ricky.

'Your weight's too far forward.'

'It can't be.'

'Bloody can. If you hadn't anticipated those stops, you'd have been right over his neck.'

After a quarter of an hour on Sinatra, by which time his silken coat was dark brown with sweat, Ricky changed her on to Kinta, the widow-maker, who required the brute strength of a Juan O'Brien to halt her wilful stampede.

'This should be even more fun,' hissed Frances to Louisa.

'She rides jolly well,' conceded Louisa.

'Ricky'll never put up with this kind of lip.'

Perdita's method of stopping Kinta was simple. She rode her flat out at the brick wall at the end, which must have been five foot high. Sitting still in the saddle, she made no attempt to pull her up. Unable to stop, Kinta had no option but to hoist herself over the wall, just catching it with a cannon bone and pecking on landing.

'I think we'll walk back, you stupid bitch,' Perdita chided the hobbling pony as she opened the gate and returned to the ring.

'What the fuck d'you think you're playing at?' White with rage, Ricky bent down to examine Kinta's leg.

'Teaching her a lesson. Look how she's learnt it.'

Swinging Kinta round, she hurtled her towards the wall.

'Stop,' yelled Ricky too late.

As if she were doing a dressage test, Kinta swivelled round, changing legs perfectly, hurtled down to the far corner and turned again.

'Blimey cubed,' said Louisa in amazement.

'You keep forgetting to stop in a straight line,' said Ricky, determined not to praise her, 'and you never look round to check who's behind you. Anyone coming down the line would take you clean out.'

'Nobody here,' shrugged Perdita.

'It's got to be instinctive for when there is someone,' said Ricky. 'Look, look and keep looking into the distance, never at your hands.'

At that moment a yellow-and-crimson hot-air balloon came over the hill, letting out a great recharging snort. Kinta, nervy at the best of times, jerked up her head, hitting Perdita smartly on the nose.

Totally unsympathetic, Ricky ordered her to go on circling the ring, doing small turns. For Perdita, frantically wiping away blood as it splattered her and Kinta, the session deteriorated sharply. Ten minutes more on Kinta were followed by twenty minutes on Wayne, Ricky's favourite pony, still circling, turning, then swinging round and putting her left hand on Wayne's custard-yellow right quarter at the trot, until her face and neck were streaming with sweat and blood, and her mascara and eyeliner were smeared and making her eyes sting.

Wayne flattened his big donkey ears and rolled his bruised dark eyes in martyrdom. Like an instinctive footballer who doesn't need to train, he was appalled to be subjected to such boring manoeuvres. The sun grew hotter.

'I will not give in, I will not give in,' said Perdita through clenched teeth. Her tits were agony, bouncing around. But just as she was about to crack, Ricky signalled to Frances to bring in a bucket of polo balls. Wayne perked up as Ricky smoothed out the pitted sand in the centre with his boot and put down a ball.

'We'll start off with the nearside forehand, so you want him on the nearside leg.'

Desperate to show what she could do, Perdita completely mis-hit three balls in a row.

'You're not watching the ball.'

Wayne, getting crafty, skedaddled so near the ball that she couldn't hit it without bashing his legs. She missed again.

'Fucking hell,' she screamed.

'Now she'll go to pieces,' said Frances happily.

'Come here,' said Ricky.

Dripping with sweat and blood, make-up streaking her face like a clown caught in a deluge, Perdita rode sulkily up to him.

'Calm down,' he said gently. 'You're going too fast and getting uptight, and he knows it. And keep at him with your left leg or he'll move in.'

Back she went, chattering with rage and panic. 'Please God, or he'll never take me on.'

Slowly Ricky took her through it. 'Don't cut the corner; up out of the saddle; bend over; look at the ball; begin your swing; keep watching the ball; head over the ball.'

Crack! Stick and ball connected in an exquisitely timed shot.

'Bingo!' Perdita threw her stick into the air, ten feet high, and caught it. 'That was perfect.'

'You hit it too late, and don't throw your stick in the air. It's dangerous.'

'Better a stick in the air than a stick-in-the-mud!'

The galloping fox weather-vane was motionless in the swooning heat. Beneath it the stable clock said two fifteen. She had been riding for two hours, nearly twice the length of a normal match.

'We'll try one more thing,' said Ricky.

Louisa led out two ponies – Willis, a huge bay, invaluable because he had the best brakes in Rutshire, and Hermia, a little chestnut mare Ricky had bought in Argentina in 1981, who was very green and terrified of everything.

Ricky mounted Willis. Perdita clambered wearily on to Hermia. Her ribs and shoulders were agony, her back ached, her thighs were raw where the sweating jodhpurs had rubbed them. Her hands could hardly hold Hermia's reins as she followed Ricky a hundred yards down a wooded lane, past an empty, leaf-strewn swimming-pool. Here, in two and a half acres of lush, green grass, framed by midge-filled trees, lay Ricky's stick-and-ball field.

Next year's tiny catkins were already forming on the hazels. Ricky noticed the reddening haws and remembered how little Millicent used to shut her eyes to avoid the prickles as she delicately picked the berries off the thorn trees. Overwhelmed with bitterness at the hand fate had dealt him, he saw no reason why he should show others any mercy.

'Now, do everything I tell you,' he yelled to Perdita as he kicked Willis into a gallop. The big bay's stride was longer than Hermia's and Perdita had to really motor to keep up. Halfway up the field, Ricky shouted, 'Turn!'

'He's crazy,' raged Frances in anguish. 'If he has a fall, his arm's buggered for good.'

Four times Ricky raced up and down the field, executing sharper and sharper turns. Now he was hurtling towards two orange-and-white traffic bollards which served as goal posts up the other end.

'Ride me off,' he bellowed.

Perdita spurred Hermia on, but she was just too far behind. Ricky's knee and the shoulder of his horse hit Hermia so hard that she seemed to fly four feet through the air. Perdita was still reeling when Ricky turned and was riding back. 'Ride me off again.'

The fourth time Perdita was knocked clean out of the saddle and only stayed mounted by clinging to the mare's neck.

'Bastard,' she screamed as she righted herself.

But by now Ricky had reached the opposite end of the field. 'Now ride towards me. Towards me! Towards me! Don't duck out! Keep going!'

The mighty Willis was thundering at them like a Volvo on the motorway. Perdita could feel Hermia quailing and about to bolt. It was all she could do to keep her on course.

She could see Willis's red nostrils as big as traffic lights, his white-edged eyes, the flashing silver of his bit. They must crash, they must.

'Stop,' yelled Ricky, swinging Willis to the left. Obedient to their masters, Willis and Hermia skidded to a halt, so close that Hermia's head brushed Willis's quarters, and Perdita was deposited on the grass, all the breath knocked out of her aching body.

'You bloody fool,' she croaked.

'I told you not to sit so far forward. Get up, you're not hurt.'

'I know I'm bloody not, but *you* might have been. You risked a head-on collision and wrecking your arm for ever, just for the sake of putting me down. You're crazy.'

Just for a second Ricky smiled.

'At least you've given me back my nerve. Go and have a shower and we'll have lunch.'

'Doesn't look so sexy now, does she?' said Frances spitefully, as a dusty, blood-stained Perdita hobbled into the yard, wincing as she led Hermia.

'Oh, I don't know,' said Joel.

'She's jolly brave,' said Louisa. Kind-hearted and admiring, she followed Perdita into Hermia's box.

'You OK?'

'Fine.' Perdita leant against the wall, fighting back the tears.

'I'll see to Hermia,' said Louisa, 'and show you where the shower is.'

After she'd found Perdita a towel and some soap, she handed her a pair of pants and a long, white T-shirt with bananas and oranges embroidered on the front.

'I thought you might want to change.'

'Thanks,' said Perdita slowly. 'Sorry I was bloody beforehand. I was absolutely shit-scared.'

'Needn't have been,' said Louisa. 'Joel and I thought you did brilliant. The hot water's erratic, but there's plenty of cold.'

Twenty minutes later Perdita joined Ricky in the kitchen. He was drinking Coke, eating a slice of ham between two pieces of white sliced bread and reading *The Times* sports page. He rose six inches from his chair as she came in. At least he recognizes I'm female, thought Perdita, encouraged.

Louisa's T-shirt, several sizes too big for her, fell to a couple of inches above her knees. Her hair, wet from the shower, was slicked back, the alabaster skin was without a scrap of make-up. Her nose was swollen, her big curved mouth looked as though bees had stung it, and her wary, dark eyes were still bloodshot from the dust.

'That's better. You look like a human,' said Ricky. 'If you ever turn up tarted up like that again, you go straight back to your play-pen. What d'you want to drink?'

'Vodka and tonic,' said Perdita, chancing her arm.

'Not if you're going to play polo. Most top players hardly drink or smoke,' he added, removing her packet of cigarettes and throwing it in the bin.

'There were four in there,' said Perdita, outraged. 'Anyway, the twins smoke.'

'They're not top players – yet.'

Armed with a glass of Perrier and a ham sandwich, Perdita wandered round the kitchen, stopping before a photograph of Herbert on a pony.

'Who's that?'

'My father.'

'Any good?'

'He was a nine,' said Ricky. 'Won the Inter-Regimental Cup seven times in a row and played in the Westchester.'

'Oh,' sighed Perdita.

'Why d'you want to learn polo?'

'I want to go to ten,' said Perdita simply.

Looking down at the remains of his ham sandwich, Ricky found he was suddenly not hungry and threw it in the bin.

'I don't think it's possible,' he said. 'With timing and skill a girl could hit the ball as far as a man. You could train your ponies even better, but it's the riding-off and the violence that's the problem.'

'I'm nearly five foot seven,' protested Perdita. 'That's bigger than lots of the Mexicans or Argentines.'

The telephone rang. One of the grooms must have picked it up because next moment a boot-faced Frances had put her head through the window.

'It's Philippa Mannering,' she snapped at Ricky. 'Would you like to go to kitchen supper tonight?'

'No, thanks.'

'Tomorrow? The next day?'

'Sorry, I can't.'

Frances shrugged her shoulders and disappeared.

'Ghastly old bag, that Philippa,' said Perdita. Then, when Ricky didn't react, 'Her house overlooks ours. She's always peering through the trees with her binoculars. She

159

wouldn't suit you. She's a nympho, wear you out in a week.'

'Thank you for the advice,' said Ricky tartly.

I fancy him so much, thought Perdita, I'll never be able to eat again.

As if reading her mind, Ricky said, 'Get one thing straight, I'm not interested in you sexually. If you work here, it's as a groom.'

'Are you after my mother?' hissed Perdita.

'Hardly. She's not in a fit state to have anyone after her at the moment.'

'You need a dog round here,' said Perdita fretfully, as she also threw her uneaten ham sandwich in the bin. 'It's a crime to waste scraps like that.'

She gazed at Herbert's unsmiling face again. 'You've got to beat your father and go to ten too.'

Ricky thought of his damaged elbow which was now hurting like hell, and didn't seem to be getting any better.

'Yes,' he said bleakly.

Because he wants Chessie back, thought Perdita, but I'll get him long before that.

17

Alone in his large draughty house, mourning Will, desperate for Chessie, panicking about his arm, Ricky's hatred for Bart, obsessive, primeval, poisoning, living deep within him, grew like a beast. And so he took it out on Perdita. She didn't mind him making her clean all the tack, or skip out the horses, or scour the fields for lost balls, or even put all the bandages and saddle blankets through the ancient washing machine that kept breaking down. But sometimes he seemed to invent tasks deliberately, scrubbing the inside and outside of buckets, and even cleaning the bowl of the outside lavatory. Worst of all, he wouldn't let her near a polo stick.

Perdita raged inside and took it out on Daisy at home. But at the yard she behaved herself, knowing it was her only chance. Once a week, too, the sullen, protective, scrawny Frances drove Ricky to Rutminster to see his probation officer, which gave Perdita the chance to stick and ball on the sly, while Louisa kept *cave*. Louisa and Perdita had become inseparable.

In the spring Perdita retook and passed seven O levels. As a reward, Ricky allowed her to help Louisa get the ponies fit for the coming season, riding them up and down the steep Rutshire hills, trotting them along the winding country lanes.

One April afternoon they were exercising ponies along the chocolate-brown earth track which ran round the huge field of young barley which Perdita had escaped into after jumping the sheep grid the year before. It was a still, muggy day. Wild garlic swept through the woods like an emerald-green tidal wave. The sweet scent of primroses and violets hung on the air.

'No one's ever loved anyone as much as I love Ricky,' said Perdita restlessly.

'He's thirty and you're sixteen,' protested Louisa.

'I don't care. I'm still going to marry him when he grows up. Christ, look at that.'

Perdita took hold of little Hermia who was still very nervous and even Wayne rolled his black-ringed eyes and raised his donkey ears a centimetre as a vast black helicopter chugged up the valley. Almost grazing the tips of the ash woods, it flew round the paddocks, over the stick and ball field and circled the battlements of Robinsgrove like a malevolent crow.

Coming out of the forage room holding a bucket of stud nuts, Ricky, in a blinding flash of hope, thought it might be a returning Chessie. Then he saw the four horsemen of the Apocalypse on the side of the helicopter as it dropped into a paddock beyond the corral, scattering ponies.

As the rotors stilled, the door flew open and out stepped a lean, menacing figure, entirely clad in zips and black leather. Heavily suntanned, his eyes were hidden behind dark glasses and his blond-streaked mane far more teased and dishevelled than Perdita's.

'Blimey,' squeaked Louisa. 'It's Dancer Maitland. Why didn't I stick to that diet?'

Dancer was followed by two heavies in tweed suits, with bulging muscles and pockets, who had great difficulty squeezing out of the door. As he reached Ricky, Dancer removed his dark glasses. His heavily kohled, brilliant grey eyes glittered with excitement.

'From you 'ave I been absent in the spring,' he drawled, ' "Gaol Bird" was number one on the US charts this morning, so I fort it was 'igh time I took up polo.'

Ricky just gazed at him.

'Knew you'd get a shock when you saw me done up,' said Dancer, raking a heavily metalled hand through his blond curls. Then he put his arms round Ricky and hugged him.

'Grite to see you, beauty.'

'It's w-w-wonderful to see you,' stammered Ricky.

' 'Ave you missed me?'

Ricky nodded. 'To tell the truth I bloody have.'

'This is Paulie and this is Twinkle,' said Dancer, waving airily at the two heavies who were gazing hungrily at Perdita. 'Them's my minders. Very amenable, if I feed them fresh Rottweilers every morning. This place is somefink else. The 'ouse, and all the trees and that ravine.' He gazed down the valley.

'We 'ad a cruise round,' he went on. 'Who owns the big house on the edge of the village?'

'Eldercombe Manor?' asked Ricky. 'Some awful old fossil called Bentley.'

'How much land?'

'About two hundred acres, including the village cricket pitch.'

'Perfect,' said Dancer. 'Now I want to see all the ponies. That's Wayne wiv the floppy ears, an' Kinta wiv the bad-tempered face and li-el Hermia, she's the shy one. You see, I remember everyfink you told me.'

But when Ricky took him into a nearby paddock where a dozen ponies came racing up and, at the sight of Ricky's bucket of stud nuts, started flattening their ears, barging and kicking out at each other, Dancer edged nervously closer to Ricky.

'Can we get a taxi back to the yard?'

'They won't hurt you, although they might hurt each other,' said Ricky. 'Stop it,' he snapped, punching Willis on the nose as the big bay lashed out at little Pilgrim.

Once he was safely on the other side of the post and rails, Dancer said that, now he was here, it was time for his first lesson. Four or five minutes later he emerged from the house with his hair tied back in a pony tail, wearing a black shirt, breeches and boots.

'Look at the length of those legs,' sighed Louisa, 'I'm going to convert him.'

'I'm surprised Ricky hasn't ordered him to take off his make-up,' snapped Perdita, who felt wildly jealous of Dancer.

'Potential patron,' explained Louisa. 'Ricky wouldn't mind if he wore blusher and a miniskirt.'

'These boots 'ave never been on an 'orse before, and neither 'ave I,' boasted Dancer, as Ricky took him through a games room, crammed with golf clubs, ski boots, tennis rackets and polo sticks, to a room with netting walls and floors sloping down to a flat oblong on which stood a wooden replica of a horse. Every time the ball was hit it rolled back so it could be hit again. Before he jiggered his arm, Ricky would spend half an hour a day in here practising his swing. Dancer on the wooden horse was a revelation – long legs gripping the slatted barrel, new boots in the stirrups, shifting effortlessly in the saddle. He had a marvellous eye and sense of timing; he met the ball right every time.

'Cowdray an' ten goal 'ere I come,' he screamed, getting more and more excited. 'I can fucking do it! We can start getting some ponies right away. Now let's try a real 'orse.'

'You may not find it quite so easy,' said Ricky gently. 'Tack up Geoffrey,' he added to Perdita.

Geoffrey was known as the 'hangover horse' because he was the kindest, easiest ride in the yard and from the days when Ricky used to drink heavily, had always seemed to know when his master was somewhat the worse for wear. You could trust a dead baby on Geoffrey.

'All right, gimme a stick,' said Dancer, when Perdita had lengthened his stirrup leathers.

'Try without one to begin with,' advised Ricky.

'Don't be daft, I've cracked it,' said Dancer, riding into the corral.

Even on the gentle Geoffrey, however, he fell off seven times, with escalating screams of rage and elation.

'I can't control this fucking machine,' he yelled at Ricky. 'It's got no steering, no brakes, and I can't get my foot off the accelerator. Give me another one.'

163

'Just walk to start with,' shouted Ricky, and, as Geoffrey jerked his black head to avoid being hit in the eye, he added, 'Stop brandishing that stick like Ian Botham. You've got to take it slowly.' He grabbed the relieved pony's bridle and removed Dancer's stick. 'There's no problem teaching you to play polo, but you've got to spend the next six months learning to ride. The aim is to keep the patron out of traction. Now get your ass down in the saddle, get your heels down and your knees in.'

By the end of an hour Dancer had fallen off twice more, was bruised as black as midnight and utterly hooked.

'What d'you fink?' he asked Perdita, as he rode into the yard. 'Am I going to make it?'

'Gaol Bird' was blaring out of the tack room wireless.

'You couldn't be a worse polo player than you are a singer,' snapped Perdita.

Back in his black leather trousers, wearing two of Ricky's jerseys, Dancer prowled round the drawing room, clutching a huge Bacardi and Coke and looking at the cups and the photographs.

'What an 'eritage! Christ, I ache all over, you fucker. When can we go and buy some ponies?'

'We can't yet.' Ricky put another log on the fire. 'We've got enough ponies here. If you're serious we can spend the summer teaching you to ride, and if it works out, see about buying ponies in the autumn.'

'You're stalling,' said Dancer, shivering and edging towards the fire. 'Arm still playing up?'

Ricky shrugged. 'I've still got no feeling and no strength in my last three fingers.'

'I've got just the bloke for you.'

'I've seen three specialists,' said Ricky wearily. 'They all say rest it.'

'You could fucking rest it for ever,' said Dancer. 'We've got to get you to ten an' get the Westchester back, an' you're not getting any younger. My friend Seth Newcombe practises in New York, best bone man in the world.'

'I can't leave the country.'

'Mountain better come to Mahomet,' said Dancer. 'Seth'll fly over if I ask him nicely. He's been after me for years.'

164

'I'm not being carved up by some old queen,' said Ricky outraged.

'Think he might deflower you under the anaesthetic?' said Dancer. 'Don't be so pig-'eaded.'

Seth arrived in England by private jet the following Saturday. Dancer's helicopter transported him and his X-ray equipment to Robinsgrove. A charming WASP with the gentlest hands and the whitest cuffs Ricky had ever seen, he examined Ricky's arm for ten minutes, then said he'd like to operate immediately.

'I think there's a trapped nerve. You must be in a lot of pain.'

'Can you guarantee a one hundred per cent success rate?' asked Ricky belligerently.

'No, but you won't get the strength or feeling back into your hand if you just leave it. And you'll certainly never get to ten, or nine, or eight, or even seven. I know a bit about polo. I used to play at the Myopia Club in Boston for years.'

'Christ, I hope he wears spectacles when he carves me up,' said Ricky.

A week later Ricky went into a clinic in Harley Street. The operation took several hours. Dancer and Perdita waited in a private room so Dancer wouldn't get mobbed and, as the day wore on, Perdita's animosity evaporated and she and Dancer clung to each other for reassurance. Perdita, despite Ricky's admonition, smoked one cigarette after another. Dancer, stuck into Bacardi and Coke, was in an even worse state.

'What happens if he's really fucked up?'

'Seth seth he won't,' said Perdita.

'He's such a sod, I don't know why we love him so much.'

'I ache for him in bed every night,' sighed Perdita.

'I ache every night from falling off his bloody 'orses.'

'Pity Seth can't give him a heart transplant at the same time to get him over Chessie,' said Perdita. 'I'm sorry I didn't like you to begin with. I guess I was jealous.'

'I like you,' said Dancer. 'You're going to play on my team when Ricky gets better. Black's a great colour wiv your eyes.'

Both jumped as Seth came into the room still in his green gown. He looked elated but desperately tired, his eyes were bloodshot beneath the green cap.

'Well, we untrapped the nerve – that prison hospital made the most godawful cock-up – and re-set the elbow. Touching wood,' he leant down to touch the table and, realizing it was veneer, shuddered and touched a picture frame, 'he should get back all the strength of his fingers and make a one hundred per cent recovery.'

Dancer burst into tears.

'Can we see him?' asked Perdita, as she and Seth mopped him up.

'No point. He'll be out like a light for the next few hours.'

'When can he play again?'

'Well, he'll have to be patient. A little low goal next year, high goal perhaps in 1985.'

While Ricky was in hospital, Dancer had not been idle. Rolling up at his bedside a few days later, he looked very smug.

'Well, I've got my yard,' he said, putting a large jar of caviar and a bunch of yellow roses down on the bed.

'Where is it?' snapped Ricky.

'Eldercombe Manor.'

'Jesus! How did you fiddle that?'

'I went to see Lady Bentley. Nice lady. Said she was fed up wiv providing tea for all the villagers and their visiting teams every Sunday. I told her, "That's the trouble wiv noblesse oblige, it flamin' nobbles you." Anyway your mate Basil Baddingham has been very co-operative. He's 'andled the deal and says I'll get planning permission for everyfing.'

Ricky groaned. 'You're crazy.'

'No, we're not. All we need is a stack of brown envelopes filled wiv dosh. Bas says the Council's completely bent, that's why they're called Councillors because they counts the money they get in bribes every day.' Dancer roared with laughter.

'How much did they sting you?' asked Ricky, disapprovingly.

'Nearly a million, but Bas reckons it'll be worf four million by the end of the eighties. There's rooms we can knock froo for a recording studio, and uvver rooms we can knock froo for parties. An' a nice piece of flat land where we can build a polo field.'

'The village have been playing cricket on that for generations.'

'Well, they'll have to watch polo now.'

'And Miss Lodsworth, the village bossyboots, will be next door marshalling the Parish Council like a tiger. She's not going to like her girl guides being corrupted by all your musicians.'

Dancer grinned. 'Sounds kind of fun. Bas didn't mention any incentives in the hand-out about under-age schoolgirls. And talking of schoolgirls, I just love that Perdita. I watched her stick and balling this morning. Never missed the goal posts once.'

'She is *not* supposed to be playing.'

'You can't hold her back,' protested Dancer. 'Why are you so foul to her?'

'Got to bash the stems of roses to get the water in,' said Ricky flatly.

'She told me about losing 'er pony,' said Dancer. 'Fort I might buy her another one.'

'You will *not*,' snapped Ricky, suddenly looking pale and tired. 'I can only just control her as it is. I got complaints about her from Miss Lodsworth only last week – taking seven ponies up Eldercombe High Street to save making two journeys so she could get back and stick and ball. And she gives them too much road work, so they won't get dirty and she won't have to waste time scraping off the mud. Every time my back's turned, she picks up a stick.'

'Probably want to sleep wiv her,' said Dancer slyly. 'That's why you're so 'orrible.'

'The only thing I'm interested in is getting Chessie back,' snapped Ricky.

He was bitterly ashamed that, having been assured by Seth that his arm would recover, he was still overwhelmed with black gloom.

The day before Ricky was due home the ancient washing machine finally croaked because Perdita had overloaded it with saddle blankets and Frances had made such a scene that Dancer whipped Perdita off to Rutminster to buy Ricky a new one as a welcome-home present.

'We don't want him any crosser wiv you than he already is,' said Dancer, as they stormed back to Eldercombe along the motorway.

Perdita adored Dancer's car, a gold Ferrari, fitted with all the latest gadgets including a synthesizer, a CD player, whose speakers were blaring out 'Gaol Bird', and two telephones.

'Let's try ringing each other up,' she suggested; then she gave a scream. 'Look! There's a little dog running along the verge. It must have been dumped. Stop, for Christ's sake!'

'Can't stop 'ere,' protested Dancer.

'You bloody can. Get in the left-hand lane.'

Then, for a second the traffic slowed down to allow cars to turn off at Exit fifteen and Perdita was out of the Ferrari, narrowly avoiding being run down by a Lotus, and on to the grass track in the centre of the motorway. Tears streaming down her face, she belted back the way they had come, looking desperately for the little dog. Cars were hurtling past her in both directions. How could the little thing possibly survive? Her heart was crashing in her ribs as she stumbled over the uneven divots.

Just when she felt she couldn't run another step, she saw the little dog again. He had huge terrified eyes with bags under them like a basset, and one ear that stuck up and the other down, and a long, dirty grey body and stumpy legs. He wore no collar, and was poised, absolutely terrified, on the far side of the right-hand traffic lane. Perdita didn't call to him, but, seeing her, he suddenly dived into the traffic, narrowly missing a milk lorry and a BMW and only avoiding a Bentley because it swerved to the left, causing great hooting and screaming of brakes. Now the dog was racing down the green track ahead of her. Two hundred yards away loomed a Little Chef restaurant.

'Oh, please God, let him make it,' sobbed Perdita.

Stumbling on, ignoring the wolf whistles and yells of approval from passing drivers, she watched in anguish as the dog decided to make a dive and plunged into the traffic again. Trying to avoid a Volvo going at 100 m.p.h. he was hit by the front of an oil lorry which knocked it on to the hard shoulder.

Perdita gave a scream of horror, which turned into joy as the dog stumbled on to three legs and dragged himself into the safety of the restaurant.

Oblivious of cars, forgetting Dancer, Perdita somehow crossed the road and sprinted the last hundred yards. The dog was nowhere to be seen but, following a trail of blood, Perdita found him underneath a parked lorry. His eyes were terrified, his lip curling, his little back leg a bloody pulp.

'It's all right, darling.' Gradually she edged towards him, but when she put out her hand, he snapped and cringed away. Perdita tried another tack. Crawling out, she explained what had happened to the driver of the lorry and asked if she could have a bit of his lunch. Grinning, he gave her half a pork pie. At first the dog looked dubious, then slowly edged forwards and gobbled it up, plainly starving.

'More,' yelled Perdita.

By the time the dog had finished the pork pie and eaten three beef sandwiches, several drivers were gathered round admiring Perdita's legs.

'You've got to help me catch him,' she said, peering out, her cheeks streaked with oil. 'He'll bleed to death if we don't get him to a vet.'

The dog was finally coaxed out with a bowl of water, so frantic was his thirst. The first lorry driver gave Perdita an old blanket to wrap him in, the second offered to drive her to the nearest vet and went off to borrow the Yellow Pages from the restaurant. The third was suggesting the RSPCA might be better when Dancer screamed up in his Ferrari.

'Fuckin' 'ell, Perdita, fort you'd been totalled.'

All the drivers had to have Dancer's autograph for their wives and tell him what a bleedin' shame he'd been put inside before he and Perdita finally set off for the vet's. Perdita had to hold on to the little dog very tightly as he shuddered in her arms. Despite the blanket, he bled all over Dancer's pale gold upholstery. Mercifully the vet was at the surgery. Putting the dog out, he operated at once. The leg needed sixty stitches. Once again Dancer and Perdita waited.

'He won't have to lose the leg,' said the vet as he washed his hands afterwards, 'but he'll have very sore toes for a bit. You can pick him up tomorrow.'

'What are you going to do with him?' Dancer asked Perdita.

'Give him to Ricky. He's got to learn to love something new.'

Getting home to find Little Chef, as he was now known, *in situ*, Ricky was absolutely furious.

'I do *not* want another dog, and, if I did, it would be a whippet. That must be the ugliest dog I've ever seen.'

'He's sweet,' protested Perdita. 'He's had a bad time' – like you have, she nearly added.

'A dog is a tie.'

'Not a very old school one in Little Chef's case,' admitted Perdita. 'But mongrels are much brighter than breed dogs and you need something to guard the yard. Frances is getting very long in the tooth.'

Little Chef hobbled towards Ricky. The whites of his supplicating, pleading eyes were like pieces of boiled egg. His tail, instead of hanging between his legs, was beginning to curl.

'I don't want a dog,' said Ricky sulkily. 'It broke Millicent's heart every time I went away. I'm not into the business of heart-breaking.'

'Could have fooled me,' drawled Dancer. 'I've gotta go. I've got a concert.'

'So have I. Dancer's got me a ticket,' said Perdita, scuttling out after him. 'See you tomorrow. Just give him a chance.'

Left alone with Ricky, Little Chef limped to the door and whined for a bit. When it was time to go to bed, Ricky got Millicent's basket down from the attic and put it in front of the Aga.

'Stay,' he said firmly.

Little Chef stayed.

Upstairs he had difficulty getting out of his clothes. Across the yard, he could see a light on in Frances's flat. She'd be across in a flash if he asked her. Since the operation he'd had terrible trouble sleeping. To get comfortable he had to lie on his back with his left hand hanging out of the bed.

His body ached with longing for Chessie. For a second he thought of Perdita, then slammed his mind shut like a

170

dungeon door. That could only lead to disaster. Frances's scrawny body was always on offer, but on the one night when despair had driven him to avail himself of it he hadn't even been able to get it up. That was why she was so bitter.

He turned out the light, breathing in the sweet soapy smell of hawthorn blossom. Through the open window the new moon was rising like a silver horn out of the jaws of the galloping fox weather-vane. Before he had time to wish, he jumped out of his skin as a rough tongue licked his hand. In the dim light he saw Little Chef gazing up at him beseechingly.

'Go away,' snapped Ricky. Then, as the dog slunk miserably away, 'Oh all right, just this once.'

But when he patted the bed, Little Chef couldn't make it, so Ricky reached down and helped him up. Immediately he snuggled against Ricky's body, giving a sigh of happiness. For the first time in years, both of them slept in until lunchtime.

18

Within a week Little Chef was running the yard, bringing in the ponies from the fields, doing tricks for pony nuts, retrieving lost balls from the undergrowth, then running on to the field and dropping them when there was a pause in play.

He also learnt not to scrabble Dancer's leather trousers and who was welcome in the yard, biting the ankles of visiting VAT men, growling at Philippa Mannering when, ever hopeful, she dropped in on Ricky, and lifting his leg on the probation officer's bicycle.

He adored Perdita, but Ricky was his great love, and gradually as the ugly little dog limped after him, barking encouragement during practice chukkas, and even hitching a lift on the back of a pony in order not to be separated, Ricky succumbed totally to his charms.

And when the vet came to take out Little Chef's stitches, it was Ricky who held the wildly trembling dog in his arms. Any visiting player who was foolish enough to make eyes at Perdita, or disparaging cracks about Little Chef's appearance, got very short shrift.

By the beginning of August Ricky's arm was so much better that he was able gently to stick and ball. By the end of August so excessive had been the overtime paid the builders and excavators that Dancer and his gaudy retinue were able to move into Eldercombe Manor.

Miss Lodsworth had a busy summer. When she wasn't inveighing against cruelty to ponies and disgusting language at Rutshire Polo Club, and furiously ringing up Ricky to complain about Perdita thundering ponies five abreast down Eldercombe High Street, she was writing to Dancer, to grumble about cheeky builders, truculent security guards, and Alsatians chasing her cat, Smudge. Nor was she amused by helicopters with flashing lights landing like fireflies at all hours, nor the deafening boom of all-night recording sessions.

Worst of all, some sadist of a landscape designer had slapped down Dancer's stick-and-ball field right next to her house, so she not only had fairies at the bottom of her garden, but also a microcosm of Rutshire Polo Club. As Commissioner for Rutshire, how could she hold dignified get-togethers with her guides when expletives and polo balls kept flying over her hawthorn hedge?

Nor did any of the rest of the Parish Council come to her aid. The Vicar, who was a closet gay, and the local solicitor, who reckoned that such development would triple the price of his house, both thought Dancer was splendid.

Dancer, however, was warned well in advance that Miss Lodsworth would be holding an All-Rutshire Jamboree in her garden on the first Saturday in September and had promised there would be no stick and balling that afternoon. A perfect day dawned. Rising early, Miss Lodsworth prayed that it would continue fine and her guides would find enjoyment as well as fulfilment in their Jamboree. Believing in economy, Miss Lodsworth had already baked rock and fairy cakes and spread hundreds of sandwiches with crusts still on with Marmite and plum jam which was cheaper than strawberry. Nor was Coca Cola or Seven-Up allowed. Her guides would have lemon squash because it was better for them and less expensive.

Creaking up from her knees, Miss Lodsworth snorted with indignation. Even on a Saturday Dancer's bulldozers were still knocking down trees and flattening hillocks to extend one of the loveliest cricket grounds in England into a polo field. Just after lunch, as she was wriggling into her guide uniform, which had grown somewhat tight, Miss Lodsworth looked out of the window and saw a girl not wearing a hard hat clattering five ponies down the High Street.

It was that fiendish Perdita Macleod. Now she had pulled up outside the village shop and was yelling to them to bring her out an ice-cream. The Vicar's wife, who had parked on a yellow line while her gay husband went into the shop to get a treacle tart, got such a shock when Wayne stuck his big, hairy white face in through the window that she jumped out and ran away. A traffic warden, finding an empty car, gave the Vicar a parking ticket.

Clattering on, trying to hold five ponies and eat an ice-cream, Perdita was not amused to hear whoops and noisy hooting behind her. It was Seb and Dommie Carlisle packed into their Lotus, with two sumptuous brunettes, and a bull terrier spilling out of the luggage compartment.

Aware that she was hot and sweaty and her hair was escaping from its towelling band, Perdita greeted them sulkily.

'We're going to see over Dancer's *palazzo*,' yelled Seb, 'and swim in his pool, which is even bigger than Loch Lomond. Why don't you come over?'

'I haven't got a bikini.'

'That's the last thing you'll need. See you later.'

When she got back to the yard, however, Ricky had other ideas.

'What the fuck were you doing taking out five ponies at once? I've just had Miss Lodsworth *and* the Vicar's wife on the telephone. If you step out of line once more you're fired. And don't think you're going to turn them out and slope off. I want each pony washed down and *all* the sweat scraped off. I'm going out to look at a pony, and don't forget to double-lock Wayne's door.'

The Jamboree was in full swing. Guides were marching, pow-wowing, flag-waving and singing stirring songs as Dancer showed the twins over a totally transformed Eldercombe Manor. As they progressed through the great hall, which was now a recording studio, and practice rooms and six master bedrooms, with bathrooms and jacuzzis *en suite*, and an intercom service so Dancer's retinue could chatter to each other all night, the twins' whoops of laughter and excitement grew in volume.

'I want a mistress bedroom,' said Seb, bouncing on one of the huge double beds.

Outside they admired a pink brick yard for twenty ponies, which looked like three sides of a Battenburg cake, and an indoor school, completely walled with bullet-proof mirrors.

'Bas said it looked like a tart's bedroom,' said Dancer cheerfully.

'He's seen enough of them,' said Dommie. 'How the hell did you get planning permission?'

'Bas and I gave a little drinks party for all the local planning committee. An' greased their palms so liberally their glasses kept sliding out of their 'ands.'

'And there were German Shepherds abiding in the fields,' said Seb, keeping a close hold on Decorum, his bull terrier, as Twinkie the security guard prowled past with an Alsatian. 'But this is designated an Area of Outstanding Natural Beauty.'

'It will be when my ponies arrive next week,' said Dancer cosily.

Soon the twins and their brunettes and various glamorous hangers-on were all stripped off round the pool. Miss Lodsworth, exhorting her guides to greater endeavour in this modern world, was having great difficulty making herself heard over the din of Dancer's group, who were warming up in the recording studio.

Seb, standing on the top board with binoculars, was peering into Miss Lodsworth's garden in excitement.

'That blonde one looks very prepared to me. Lend a hand, darling,' he shouted. 'Isn't that what girl guides are supposed to do?'

'I wish someone would lend me a farm hand,' said Dancer's interior designer sulkily. 'Wilhelm won't speak to me since I chucked his Filofax in the jacuzzi. *He's* nice,' he added, as one of Dancer's workmen went past wielding his JCB like Ben Hur.

'Now they're doing semaphore,' said Seb. 'Get me a goal flag, Dancer, then I can signal, "Do you screw?" to that blonde.'

'She'll tie a clove hitch in your willy if you're not careful,' said Dommie.

'Then it'll be a guided missile!' Collapsing off the diving board with laughter at his own joke, Seb just managed to keep the binoculars above the water level.

Meanwhile over in Snow Cottage, Daisy Macleod, trying to fill up her painting jar, found there was no water in the tap. In the house above her, Philippa Mannering, who wanted to wash her hair before the dinner party to which Ricky had refused to come yet again, found not only no water in the tap but that the washing-up machine had stopped in mid-cycle. Over at Robinsgrove, finding no water to hose down the ponies, Perdita put them in their boxes and, having given them their hay nets and filled up the water buckets from the water trough, raced off to Dancer's for a swim.

Wayne, Ricky's favourite pony, had such a low threshold of boredom that he had a special manger hooked over the half-door so he could eat and miss nothing in the yard at the same time. The yard escapologist, he had been known to turn on taps and flood the yard and, even worse, let other ponies out of their boxes when he got bored. At matches he had to be watched like a hawk in case he wriggled out of his headcollar, and set off for the tea tent, where his doleful yellow face and black-ringed eyes could coax sandwiches and cake out of the most stony-hearted waitress. Left to his own vices, deserted even by his friend Little Chef, who'd gone with Ricky, Wayne started to fiddle with the bolt.

At the Jamboree it was time for tea. The Marmite and plum jam sandwiches were already curling on the trestle table under the walnut tree. The guides were hot and thirsty, but as Miss Lodsworth went to the kitchen tap for water to fill up the jugs of concentrated lemon squash, only a trickle came out of the tap.

'Please, Miss Lodsworth,' said a pink-faced Pack Leader, 'the upstairs toilet isn't flushing.'

'Nor's the downstairs,' said her friend.

Looking out across Dancer's emerging polo fields, Miss Lodsworth first thought how beautiful as a huge fountain of water gushed a hundred feet into the air, throwing up rainbow lights in the sunshine against the yellowing trees.

Picking up the telephone, she was on to Dancer in a trice.

'D'you realize,' she spluttered, 'that your bulldozers have gone slap through the chief water main? The whole village will be cut off, and my guides have nothing to drink.' She couldn't mention the question of lavatories to Dancer.

Round the pool they were all having hysterics as Dancer tried to calm her down.

'I'll get on to the emergency services immediately. Of course they work on a Saturday. An' if it gets too bad, your little girls can come and drink out of the swimming-pool. And we've got plenty of Bourbon if you're pushed.'

He had to hold the telephone away from his ear.

An hour later Perdita sidled into the yard with wet hair to be confronted by Frances quivering with ecstatic disapproval.

'Why the hell didn't you bother to dry off the ponies?'

'I just nipped over to Dancer's for a swim.'

'Can't keep away from the boys, can you? Did you turn Wayne out?'

'No. Yes, I must have done.' Perdita always blinked when she was lying. 'Oh Christ, he must be in one of the paddocks or the garden.'

'He isn't, I've looked,' sneered Frances. 'Thank God Ricky'll come to his senses and sack you now.'

'Oh, please don't tell him,' pleaded Perdita. She hadn't realized quite how much Frances detested her.

'You stay here.' Frances handed her Hermia's lead rope. 'I'll take my car and go and look for him.'

'I'll go,' sobbed Perdita, and, leaping on to Hermia's back, she clattered off down the drive.

Perdita couldn't get any sense out of the gaudy retinue round Dancer's pool. They were all drunk or stoned.

'Wayne's gone missing,' she screamed. 'Please someone come and help me look for him.'

'Probably gone to the Jamboree,' said Dommie, looking up from his brunette. 'Miss Lodsworth'll be teaching him how to untie clove hitches.'

'Don't be so fucking flip.'

Pulling on a pair of Garfield boxer shorts, grumbling Dommie tiptoed barefoot across the gravel out to his Lotus.

'You go west, I'll go north.'

'Have you seen a yellow pony with a white face? Have you seen a yellow pony with a white face?' Getting more and more desperate, Perdita stopped at every house and scoured every field. Ricky would go apeshit if anything happened to Wayne. Then, as she entered Eldercombe Village, she saw a pile of droppings in the middle of the road.

'Looking for a pony?' said an old man. 'He went into that garden.'

Perdita went as green as the guides' unconsumed lemon squash. For there in the gateway, framed in an arch of clematis as purple as her face, stood Miss Lodsworth. She'd had to buy all her guides Coca Cola from guiding funds, and send them home early in a hired bus in case they electrocuted themselves storming the gates of Eldercombe Manor in search of Dancer. She would be eating Marmite sandwiches and rock buns for months.

'Dancer Maitland has wrecked my Jamboree,' roared Miss Lodsworth. 'Your pony has wrecked my garden. He's trampled on my alstroemerias and my dahlias, kicked out my cucumber frame and broken down the fence into the orchard.'

'I'm terribly sorry. I'll pay,' begged Perdita. *'Please* don't ring Ricky.'

'I'm going to ring my solicitor.'

Wayne was enchanted to see Hermia and Perdita, and gave the appearance of having been searching for them all day. As she only had one lead rope, Perdita had to walk both ponies the mile and a half back to Robinsgrove. At the bottom of the drive, Wayne started to totter, and his yellow belly gave such a thunderous rumble, he started looking round at it in surprise and reproach.

Oh God, colic, thought Perdita; perhaps he's eaten something he shouldn't, I must get him home.

Halfway up the drive, Wayne started pawing his belly and rolling the whites of his eyes. Soon he was cannoning off lime trees and, as they passed the second gates, crashed into the left-hand gatepost. By the time he had staggered into the yard he could hardly stand up, hitting the ancient, mossy mounting block and tripping over one of the green tubs filled with white geraniums, as Little Chef came bounding out to lick him on the nose.

177

Perdita had never known Ricky so angry. Taking one look at the swaying Wayne, he yelled at Frances to ring Phil Bagley, the vet.

'Tell him it may be a heart attack, or colic, or twisted gut. He could even have been hit by a car. Tell him to fucking hurry.'

Then, turning on Perdita: 'You stupid b-b-bitch, I told you to double-bolt those doors.'

'I know. I forgot.'

'Well, you've forgotten once too often. Get out, you're fired.'

'Please let me see what Phil says,' whispered Perdita, whose face was now as white as Wayne's.

'Get out,' hissed Ricky, who needed all his strength to guide the staggering, crashing Wayne into his box. 'Just fuck off.'

Phil Bagley arrived in a quarter of an hour.

'I was delivering one of Mark Phillips' calves,' he said indignantly. 'The things I do for you, Ricky. Now, where's this pony?'

As he went into his box Wayne was still pawing his belly. Then, slumping against the wall, he crashed to the ground.

'I'll give him a massive jab of vitamin B,' said Phil when he'd examined him, 'and some Buscopan. It's obviously hurting him. Then we'd better get some fluids inside him. I guess it's twisted gut. Where's he been?'

'Escaped to Eldercombe, got into Miss L-L-Lodsworth's garden.'

'Jesus, you'd think he'd been programmed.'

As Phil loaded his syringe and Ricky tried to calm the terrified pony, whose eyes were quite glazed now, they heard frantic barking outside.

Next minute Miss Lodsworth's head appeared over the half-door, looking even more like a horse than Wayne.

'I've come to make a complaint.'

'Not now,' said Phil, who was holding the needle up to remove the air bubbles.

'Piss off,' muttered Ricky under his breath.

'I must speak to someone.'

'Can you wait somewhere else?' snapped Phil. 'I'm sorry, but we've got a critically sick horse here.'

'Sick, my eye,' thundered Miss Lodsworth, 'That horse isn't sick, it's dead drunk. It's just eaten all my cider apples.' There was a long pause. Crouching down, Phil sniffed Wayne's breath.

'I do believe you're right. How many apples d'you reckon he ate?'

'Close on a hundred.'

Ricky never thought he'd want to hug Miss Lodsworth.

'Are you sure?' he said, getting to his feet.

As he plunged the needle into Wayne's shoulder, Phil started to laugh. A second later, Dommie Carlisle, shivering slightly in just boxer shorts, appeared beside Miss Lodsworth.

'You've found him. Thank Christ. I've been looking everywhere. What's the matter with him?'

'Pissed as a newt,' said Ricky.

'I'm surprised you treat the matter so lightly,' bristled Miss Lodsworth. 'What about my apples?'

'He ought to have some painkillers,' said Phil, 'and we ought to get some fluids into him. Don't want him to wreck his liver.' But Wayne was sleeping peacefully.

'Better lay on some Fernet Branca for the morning,' said Dommie. 'I think I deserve a drink, Ricky.'

'You *all* deserve a drink,' said Ricky turning to Miss Lodsworth. 'I'm frightfully s-s-sorry. I'll refund you for the apples, and any other damage. I haven't got any cider, but I can offer you plenty of whisky.'

Miss Lodsworth had had a long day. 'Oh all right, I haven't been inside this house since I used to come here to dances when your father was a boy. Not that he ever danced with me.'

After Ricky'd settled them in the drawing room with drinks, he went in search of Perdita. She wasn't on the wooden horse or in the yard or in the tack room. Little Chef tracked her down in the pink dusk at the bottom of the garden, with her arms round an apple tree, sobbing her heart out.

'Please God, make Wayne better,' she was saying over and over again, then started as Little Chef stood up on his stumpy back legs to lick her hand.

'I'm so sorry,' she wailed. 'Please give me another chance. I love it here so much. I promise not to cheek

179

Frances and cut corners. I just love the ponies and Cheffie – and you – so much,' she couldn't stop herself adding.

In a year of working for him she had never cried or apologized. She looked so forlorn, so utterly defeated, her head drooping like a snowdrop, her wonderfully lithe body clinging almost orgiastically to the tree trunk. Ricky had to steel himself not to take her in his arms, but he would have been putting a match to a petrol-soaked bonfire, and he didn't want to hate himself any more than he did already.

'It's OK,' he said gently. 'He's not ill, just drunk. He'd helped himself to Miss Lodsworth's cider apples.'

'Oh, my God! Will he be OK?'

'Fine, except for a thumping hangover. But you can't afford to make mistakes like that. He might have got on to the motorway.'

'Like Little Chef,' shuddered Perdita, starting to cry again. 'That's what makes it so awful.'

'I over-reacted,' said Ricky dropping a hand on her hair. 'You can start full time next week if you like.'

'Oh, you are lovely.' Seizing his hand, Perdita covered it with kisses. 'I could make you better. I really do love you.'

Ricky felt dizzy. It was so long since he'd wanted someone like this.

'No, you don't,' he said firmly. 'You ought to be meeting more boys your own age, not lechers like Bas and the twins. If you're coming to work here full time, you're bloody well going to join the Pony Club.'

19

Polo is largely a matter of pony power. Having left the Army, Drew Benedict had spent a great deal of Sukey's money buying really good ponies. With these he turned his game around and was gratified when his handicap was raised to eight in the autumn listings a year later. The following year, after an excellent May and June playing for David Waterlane, Drew felt he ought to put something back into the game. He therefore agreed to coach the Rutshire Pony Club for the polo championships, the finals of which were held at Cowdray at the end of July. Drew also quite liked an excuse to get away from Sukey on summer evenings. Used to commanding platoons, he was determined to knock the Rutshire teams into shape. One of his crosses was Perdita Macleod, who had now been working full time for Ricky for nine months and felt she knew everything.

Perdita, on the other hand, even though she was playing with seventeen to twenty-one year olds, regarded playing for the Pony Club as deeply *infra dig*. She loathed being parted from Ricky for a second, and Felicia, the ponies Ricky and Drew had lent her were still very green

Consequently she never stopped bellyaching to Daisy about how all the other Pony Club members had at least three ponies, and how humiliating it was having to hack to meetings when everyone else rolled up either in the latest horse boxes with grooms, or driving Porsches with telephones. Nor, she told Daisy, did that 'bloody old geriatric' Drew Benedict ever stop picking on her, and all the other boys in the team were such wimps. 'One of them started crying yesterday, when I hit him with my stick. It was only because he was using his elbows all the time. I tried to explain to Drew, but he just sent me off.'

'Aren't any of the boys attractive?' enquired Daisy hopefully.

'Not compared with Ricky,' snapped Perdita, 'and they all think Drew's absolutely marvellous, because he's an eight and a Falklands hero and all. He's such a bastard.'

'You're always saying that about Ricky,' said Daisy reasonably.

'But I'm madly in love with Ricky, so I put up with it.'

It was nearly two and a half years since Hamish had walked out on Daisy and she could no longer claim to be madly in love with him, but she missed the presence of a man in her life, and her self-confidence was in tatters. By some miracle she had hung on to her job with the Caring Chauvinist, but she found it exhausting coping with that, and running the house, and looking after Perdita, and more and more after Violet and Eddie. Now Wendy had a daughter, called Bridget, after Biddy Macleod, Hamish seemed less interested in his older children. Snow Cottage simply wasn't big enough for all of them, particularly when Perdita, who still hadn't forgiven her mother, was always banging doors and making scenes.

Daisy, ever hopeful and optimistic, however, still made heroic efforts to win Perdita round. She couldn't afford a car yet, but on the day of the final trials for the Pony Club Championships, which were held at Rutshire Polo Ground, she and Ethel took two buses and walked a mile in pouring rain to lend Perdita support.

Perdita, however, was deeply embarrassed to see her mother arriving in unsuitably colourful clothes and dripping wet hair, like a superannuated hippie. Why the hell couldn't she turn up in a Barbour, a headscarf and a Volvo like everyone else's mother? Nervous because she was due to play in two chukkas' time, Perdita refused even to acknowledge Daisy's presence.

Momentarily the rain had stopped. It was a hot, very muggy evening. The sun, making a guest appearance between frowning petrol-blue clouds, floodlit the dog daisies and hogweed in the long grass and turned the pitch a stinging viridian. A sweet waft of lime blossom mingled with the rank, sexy smell of drying nettles and elder flowers.

Daisy had brought her sketch pad, but found it difficult to capture the action and hold on to a straining Ethel. Perhaps she could let Ethel off. There seemed to be an awful lot of dogs around for her to play with. Liberated, Ethel frisked with a Jack Russell in a red, spotted scarf and wolfed up a half-eaten beefburger bun. Then, as the players came thundering down the boards, she joined the stampede, trying to steal the ball and nearly bringing down the pony of a fat child with pigtails, whose mother promptly started yelling at Daisy.

Fortunately her torrent of abuse was diluted by a downpour of even more torrential rain. All the mothers raced for their Volvos as the players struggled over to another part of the field. Sheltering her sketch pad under her shirt, Daisy looked helplessly around. She had no mackintosh. She'd just managed to catch a joyously soaked Ethel when a blond man with a flat cap pulled over his straight nose asked her if she'd like to sit in his Land-Rover.

'It's all right. I don't mind the dog.'

Ethel clambered into the back and slobbered down his neck.

'You are kind,' said Daisy gratefully. 'Being a Pisces, I

normally love rain, but this shirt's a bit see-through when it's wet.'

She was wearing a fringed dark purple midi-skirt and a pink muslin shirt from the early seventies, which had tiny mirrors sewn into it, and which was clinging unashamedly to her breasts. Her dark hair fell damp and straight, just grazing her nipples.

'You look like Midi Ha Ha,' said the blond man, smiling slightly, but when Daisy unearthed a bottle of made-up vodka and orange from the chaos of her bag he shook his head.

Helping herself, Daisy noticed he never took his eyes off the play and was now turning on the windscreen wipers to watch a dark-haired boy coax a fat roan pony down the field. 'That child's definitely team potential, but the pony's an absolute bitch, I must have a word with his parents. And Christ, that pony's improved since last year.' Then, consulting a list on the dashboard, 'No, it hasn't, it's another pony. Do you want my coat?'

'I'm fine.' Daisy took another swig out of her bottle. 'Midi Ha Ha. Laughing Vodka. At least I can't be done for being drunk in charge of a setter.'

'Nice dog,' said the blond man, putting back a hand and rubbing Ethel behind the ears.

'Isn't she?' agreed Daisy, who was beginning to perk up.

She noticed that the man was very handsome in a stolid, heavy-lidded, way. She would have to mix Manganese blue with a little Payne's grey to get the colour of his eyes. He had a lovely mouth and lovely muscular thighs. Daisy suddenly wanted to check her face, and when he went off at the end of the chukka to talk to the next group playing, which included Perdita, she toned down her rosy cheeks and drenched her neck with Je Reviens, but failed to put the top back on properly, so it stank out the Land-Rover.

'Je Reviens,' said the blond man, sniffing as he got back inside. 'And I did.'

'You're too young to have a child playing?' asked Daisy, fishing.

'Yes.' Checking the list of players again, he opened the car door, yelling, 'For Christ's sake, Mark, you're not on your man.'

'Ought to be called Un-Mark,' said Daisy, taking another swig. 'I'm dying to find out which is Drew Benedict.'

'Really?'

'Ghastly old fossil,' went on Daisy happily. 'He's giving Perdita such a hard time. I would have thought having worked for Ricky for nearly two years, she might be allowed to evolve her own style.'

She offered the diminishing bottle to him again.

Again he shook his head.

'How'd you get on with Ricky?' he asked.

'Never see him. I just pay his farm manager our rent. He rides past occasionally. He still looks pretty miserable, but Dancer seems to have cheered him up, and the specialist says he'll definitely be playing again next year.'

'Then we'll all have to look to our laurels,' said the blond man, 'but he's not a good teacher. Too impatient and introverted, too obsessed with his own game.'

He's got a sexy voice, thought Daisy, soft and very quiet. She wished she knew if he were married.

'There are lots of boys playing,' she said in surprise. 'Perdita seems to be the only girl.'

'Boys tend to avoid the Pony Club, because they're always being told to keep their toes up and clean tack. Give them a stick and ball and it's a different story. Some of them are pretty bloody impossible when they arrive. No idea how to play as a team or to think of other people. Most of them get far too much pocket money.'

'Not Perdita's problem,' said Daisy.

'Nor enough discipline. Parents' marriages are so often breaking up.'

'Hum – Perdita's problem,' sighed Daisy whose tongue had been totally loosened by drink on no lunch. 'Everyone keeps telling me she needs a father. But it's tricky if you're a single parent – isn't that a ghastly expression? If you go out at night looking for a father for your children, everyone brands you a whore. People like Philippa Mannering and Miss Lodsworth. D'you know them?'

'Only too well.'

'And if you're too miserable because you've been deserted, people think you're a drag and don't ask you to parties. And if you're too jolly, wives think you're after their husbands. I feel like taking a pinger to parties to stop myself talking to anyone's husband longer than two minutes. Even girlfriends I know really well get insanely jealous. Mind you, the husbands think you're after them as well. If you don't have a man, even the plainest ones think you're dying for it.'

'And are you?' asked the blond man, who was watching Perdita jump the boards and execute a particularly dazzling back shot. 'Good girl, she kept her head down.'

'Not really, but on lovely days you're suddenly overwhelmed with longing to be in love again.'

He turned and looked at her. Did she detect compassion or was it slight wistfulness in those incredibly direct blue eyes? She was just thinking how easy he'd be to fall in love with, and that she really mustn't start cradle-snatching when he said, 'Perdita's seriously good. She's already been picked for the Jack Gannon, that's the eighteen to twenty-one group. But she ought to apply for a Pony Club polo scholarship.'

'What'd that entail?'

'Six months in New Zealand or Australia. The BPA pay for her ticket out there and put her in a yard. She'd get pocket money. In return she'd look after the ponies, school them and play polo.'

'Oh, how wonderful,' sighed Daisy, thinking longingly of the peace at home; then added hastily, 'For Perdita, of course.'

'They have to be heavily vetted beforehand, so they don't let the side down. Some winners in the past have been temperamental and failed to get up in the morning, but on the whole they go out as boys and come back as men.'

'I hope Perdita doesn't grow hairs on her chest,' giggled Daisy. 'Sorry, I'm being silly. It's a wonderful idea, but I'm sure Drew Benedict won't allow it.'

'Why not?'

'He thinks she's useless.'

The blond man looked faintly amused. 'There's the bell,' then, as a woman strode past in plus fours with an Eton crop, added, 'and there's the DC. I'd better go and have a word with her.'

'Looks more AC to me,' said Daisy, draining the last of the vodka and orange.

The sinking sun had appeared again, gilding the wheat

fields and splodging inky shadows in the rain-soaked trees. Daisy got unsteadily out of the Land-Rover. Next moment Ethel nearly pulled her over as Perdita galloped up.

'Hello, Mum. You've got tomato skin on your front tooth. What on earth were you talking to Drew about for so long.'

'Drew?' said Daisy faintly. 'But you said he was old.'

'So he is, at least twenty-nine, but I really like him now. He's picked me for the Jack Gannon, and I'm four months under age, and he says Hermia's really improved.'

Daisy was almost too embarrassed to accept a lift home from Drew.

'I had no idea,' she mumbled.

'I'll have to be a bit nicer to Perdita in future,' he said drily.

Perdita was in such a good mood that she and Daisy actually had supper together for the first time in months.

'Er – is Drew Benedict married?' asked Daisy as she mashed the potato.

'To a terrific Sloane called Sukey,' said Perdita, not looking up from *Horse and Hound*. 'She's just had a baby – it popped out during the semi-finals of the Queen's Cup. If it had been a girl, Drew wanted to call her Chukka. Bas said it ought to be called Chuck-up because it's always being sick.'

Daisy added too much milk to the potatoes. 'Is she pretty?'

'Sukey? No-oo,' said Perdita scornfully. 'Drew married her for her money.'

'I thought he was gorg – I mean quite attractive,' said Daisy.

'Too straight for me,' said Perdita. 'I wonder if I ought to take up weight-lifting.'

Daisy nearly said Perdita could start off by weight lifting some of her belongings upstairs, but desisted because it was such heaven to be on speaking terms again.

Encouraged by Drew, Daisy applied for a Pony Club scholarship for Perdita, and they were duly summoned to Kirtlington to meet the Committee in early July. As their appointment wasn't until the afternoon, Sukey

Benedict asked them to lunch beforehand. To the Caring Chauvinist's extreme irritation, Daisy took the day off and hired a car.

Very out of practice at driving, she had several near-misses on the motorway and her nerves weren't helped by Perdita spending most of the journey with her hands over her eyes, as Daisy ground recalcitrant gears and proceeded in a succession of jerks down the High Streets of Oxfordshire villages.

Having thought about Drew Benedict rather too much in the last fortnight, Daisy was fascinated to see what Sukey was like. But, as she came down the steps of the beautiful russet Georgian house, first impressions were very depressing. Only five weeks after having a baby, Sukey's figure was back to an enviable slimness. The perfect pink-and-white skin had no need of make-up. Her collar-length, mousey hair was drawn off her forehead. She wore a blue denim skirt on the knee and a striped shirt with the collar turned up. Noting the lack of creases, the air of calm efficiency, the brisk, high-pitched voice, Daisy thought gloomily that Sukey couldn't be more different from her. If this was Drew's type, she didn't stand a chance. Then she felt desperately guilty. Who was she, who'd been crucified by Hamish's departure, to hanker after someone else's husband?

Escaping into the downstairs loo, which had photographs of Drew in various polo teams all over the walls, Daisy repaired her pink, shiny face. It was so hot outside that she had settled for an orange cheesecloth caftan, which she'd jacked in with a belt of linked gold hippos. The gathers over the bosom made her look as though she was the one breast-feeding. She wore brown sandals, and tried to arrange the cross-gartering over two scabs where she'd cut herself shaving. The telephone had rung just as she'd finished washing her hair, so it had dried all wild and was now held back with an orange-and-shocking-pink striped scarf, off which Ethel had chewed one of the corners. Gold-hooped earrings completed the picture. I look awful, thought Daisy, particularly as Perdita, who'd be expected to ride, looked absolutely ravishing in a dark blue shirt and white breeches.

Coming out of the loo, she found Drew, looking equally

ravishing in a blue striped shirt rolled up to show very brown arms. He had that high-coloured English complexion, which looks so much better with a suntan.

He took her into the sitting room, which Daisy was comforted to see was absolute hell – far too much eau-de-Nil and yellow and ghastly paintings of polo matches interspersed with some excellent watercolours. Over the fireplace was a very glamorized portrait of Sukey in a pale blue ball dress and some very good sapphires. Over the desk was a portrait of Drew, probably painted in his late teens. He was wearing an open-necked shirt, and his blond hair flopped over his eyes, which were smiling with a lazy insolence.

'Johnny Macklow?' said Daisy, impressed.

Drew nodded. 'Good girl. Only had one sitting, spent the whole time fending the old bugger off. Refused to go back for any more. My mother was furious. Vodka and orange, wasn't it?'

'Not too large,' chided Sukey. 'She's got to talk sense to the Committee later.'

'Need a stiff one to cope with that lot,' said Drew.

Having handed the glass to Daisy, he turned to Perdita: 'Like to come and see the yard?'

'Lunch at one fifteen on the dot. Don't be too long,' ordered Sukey.

After they'd gone Sukey paced up and down sipping Evian water. Out of the window, Daisy admired the incredibly tidy garden. Not a weed dared to show its face. Beyond, a heat haze shimmered above the fields which sloped upwards to a wood which seemed about to explode in midgy darkness. On the piano was a picture of a baby in a silver frame.

'He's sweet,' said Daisy.

'Just beginning to smile,' said Sukey, her voice softening.

'And you've got your figure back so amazingly.'

'Exercise and not drinking helps.'

'It must,' said Daisy guiltily, taking a huge gulp of her vodka and orange.

Sukey had reached the window in her pacing and was about to start on the return journey.

'Look, I hope you don't mind my saying so, but I know Drew's frite-fly keen for Perdita to get this scholarship.'

'He's been so kind,' mumbled Daisy.

'But the Committee are really rather stuffy.' Sukey was like a comely steamroller. 'I honestly think you ought to wear something more conventional. That orange dress would be lovely at a party, but it makes you look a bit arty and hippy. And you should wear tights.'

'They all had holes,' said Daisy, flushing.

'Let's just pop upstairs and see if we can find something more suitable.'

'But you're miles thinner than me.'

Before she knew it Daisy was upstairs in the tidiest bedroom she had ever seen. Even the few pots of make-up on the blue-flowered dressing table seemed to be standing to attention. The double bed was huge too. Lucky thing to be made love to by Drew on it, Daisy was appalled to find herself thinking.

'When I was having Jamie, I had this lovely dress, which I hardly got out of,' said Sukey, raking coat hangers along a brass bar. 'Ah, here it is.'

Triumphantly she extracted a navy-blue cotton dress with a big white sailor collar, presumably to distract from the bulge.

'Oh, I couldn't,' protested Daisy.

But, as if mesmerized, she found herself getting out of her orange caftan and darting almost minnow-like into the navy-blue dress, so ashamed was she of the greyness of her pants, which had practically detached themselves from the elastic.

'It really isn't me,' she protested.

'It is. You need the whole look,' insisted Sukey bossily. 'Here's a pair of tights. They've even got a darn; the Committee'll like that and these shoes will be perfect. I love flatties, don't you? But a little heel's better for this dress. They do fit well. And the earrings don't really go, or the scarf. Just let me brush your hair back and put on this Alice band. There! Don't you look charming? Neat but not gaudy.'

Daisy gazed at herself in the mirror. Her forehead was unnaturally white where her fringe had been drawn back. She suppressed a terrible desire to fold her arms and break into a hornpipe.

'It's truly not me.'

'It'll *certainly* be the Committee,' said Sukey firmly.

'You want Perdita to get this scholarship, don't you?'

There was a knock and a Filipino maid put a shiny dark head round the door.

'It's ready, is it, Conchita? We'll be down in a sec. Can you tell Mr Benedict?'

Drew didn't recognize Daisy when she crept in.

'Where's Daisy got to?' he said, breaking off a grape.

'Christ!' said Perdita. 'You've been Sloaned, Mum.'

'Doesn't she look nice?' said Sukey.

'She looks gross.'

Sukey's lips tightened. Drew looked at Daisy incredulously, torn between rage and a desire to laugh. 'But that's your maternity dress,' he added to Sukey.

'And as my disgusting stepfather walked out two and a half years ago,' pointed out Perdita, 'the Committee are going to think it pretty odd that Mum's got a bun in the oven.'

'She doesn't look at all pregnant,' said Sukey.

'She looks like Jolly Jack Tar,' snapped Perdita. 'Shiver your timbers, Mum.'

'Shut up, Perdita.' Fighting a fearful urge to burst into tears, Daisy giggled instead.

'Daisy looked lovely before,' said Sukey, plunging a knife into the yellow, red and green surface of the quiche, 'but you know how stuffy Brigadier Canford and Major Ashton are.'

'Charlie Canford's such a DOM he'd have much preferred Daisy as she was,' said Drew coldly.

No-one could have told from his face that he was absolutely livid with Sukey, but he didn't want a row, which would upset Daisy and gee Perdita up before the interview.

Patting the chair beside him, he told Daisy, 'If Perdita gets the scholarship, Sukey and I may well be going out to New Zealand at the same time to buy some ponies, so we can keep an eye on her.'

'Not if you're going to dress me in sailor suits,' said Perdita, giving a bit of pastry to Drew's slavering yellow Labrador.

'I don't think Perdita ought to have wine if she's going to ride,' said Sukey. 'Would you like salad with or after, Daisy?'

Ignoring her, Drew filled up Perdita's glass, then, seeing

Daisy's eyes had suddenly filled with tears, asked her if she'd like another vodka and orange.

'Another thing to remember at the interview,' said Sukey pointedly, 'is to let Perdita do the talking. Some mothers answer all the time for the children, which makes the Committee think the child lacks initiative.'

'What have you done to my Mum, Suke,' sang Perdita.

'Shut up, Perdita,' said Drew and Daisy simultaneously.

'And do try and appear really keen, Perdita,' advised Sukey. 'The Committee loves enthusiasm.'

The interview lasted half an hour. Very kindly, they asked Daisy about her financial circumstances. She stuck out her darned leg, hoping to give an impression of genteel poverty, smiled so much her face ached and, despite Sukey's warnings, found herself talking too much to compensate for Perdita's bored indifference.

Brigadier Canford, who was indeed a lover of pretty girls, looked at Perdita's impassive, dead-pan face, and had a strange feeling he'd seen her before somewhere.

'And what d'you want to get out of polo?'

'I want to go to ten.'

'Bit ambitious. Nearest a woman's ever got is five.'

Out of the window Perdita could see children riding in pairs and dribbling balls in and out of soap boxes.

'I know, but there was a piece in a polo magazine the other day saying many women were ten in beauty, but never could be ten in polo. Fucking patronizing.'

'Perdita,' murmured Daisy.

'I hope you wouldn't use language like that in New Zealand, young lady,' said the Brigadier. 'You'd be representing your country, you know.'

'Still patronizing.'

Later they watched her playing a chukka with seven other contenders for the scholarship.

Brigadier Canford admired the lightning reflexes, the way she adjusted to a not-very-easy pony in seconds and showed up the others as she ruthlessly shoved them out of the way and cat-and-mouse-whipped the ball away just as they were about to hit it.

'Wow,' he said, turning to Drew. 'I'm not sure she couldn't go to ten, and she'd certainly be ten in looks if she smiled more often.'

Puzzled, he shook his pewter-grey head. 'I can't think where I've seen her before.'

Apart from Perdita, the Rutshire team for the Jack Gannon Cup consisted of Justin and Patrick Lombard, farmer's sons who'd spent their lives in the saddle and who made up for lack of finesse with dogged determination, and David Waterlane's son, Mike, now nearly twenty-one, who played like an angel when his father wasn't on the sideline bellowing at him.

In an exhausting, exhilarating fortnight, they moved round the country triumphing gloriously at Cheshire, being demoralized at Cirencester, where they drew against a vastly inferior team, cockahoop at Kirtlington, and nearly coming unstuck at Windsor, where Perdita was sent off for swearing, so Rutshire had to play the last chukka with only three men, and only just won.

On the first Friday in August they finally reached Cowdray and won the semi-finals by the skins of their gumshields. The Quorn, opposing them, had rumbled Drew's Exocet weapon, and spent the match giving Perdita so much hassle that she only hit the ball twice. The Lombard brothers and Mike Waterlane, however, scored a goal apiece to put Rutshire into Sunday's final against the mighty South Sussex, who hadn't been beaten for three years.

The entire Championships were being sponsored by petfood billionaire and fitness freak, Kevin Coley, Chairman of Doggie Dins, Moggie Meal and the newly launched Fido-Fibre. Kevin had formerly sponsored show-jumping, but five years ago had run off with Janey, the wife of Billy Lloyd-Foxe, one of his professionals and Rupert Campbell-Black's best friend. After Janey went back to Billy, Kevin had patched up his differences with his wife, Enid, but one of the conditions had been that Kevin would sponsor polo instead of show-jumping to avoid bumping into Janey on the circuit, and because their daughter, Tracey, would meet a nicer class of young man in polo. Trace – as she liked to be called – at eighteen was playing in the crack South Sussex team against Rutshire in the final. If she wasn't quite up to her other team-mates, her presence there vastly increased her father's generosity. The whole South Sussex team had been driving round the country in a vast aluminium horse box, evidently the latest thing in America, and Kevin had provided each player with four top-class ponies.

The South Sussex team was also more than compensated by the rock solidarity of a boy called Paul Hedley at back, and the dazzling Sherwood brothers, Randolph and Merlin, who'd pulled out of high goal polo for a fortnight to piss it up with the Pony Club.

Randy Sherwood, who was known as the Cock of the South, had a handicap of two and was so glamorous with his long, long legs and curly hair that fell perfectly into shape, that girls clamoured to groom for him for nothing. Merlin, who was quieter, but just as lethal, had pulled a different groupie every night of the Championships. Randy, going amazingly steady for him, had spent the fortnight screwing Trace Coley, who was as pretty as she was spoilt, because he'd heard rumours that Kevin was thinking of including him in his team next year.

Perdita and Trace had detested each other on sight and, together with Randy, Trace spent a lot of time when they weren't screwing, winding Perdita up. Not only did they drench her in a water fight when she didn't have a change of clothes and throw her on the muck heap, but on Friday evening offered her a roll filled with Doggie Dins, so she spent the rest of the night throwing up. Perdita reacted with screaming tantrums. Trace, suspecting Randy's incessant baiting might have some basis in desire, stepped up the spite.

And now it was Finals' Day and the number two Ambersham ground at Cowdray was a seething mass of caravans, tents, trailers, canvas loose-boxes for 200 ponies and rows of cars belonging to team managers and exhausted parents. Breakfast of sausage, egg and chips was sizzling over camp-fires. The mobile loos had worked until the day before, but now each bowl was an Everest of Bronco and the stench was getting worse.

With fifty teams present, there had also been one hell of a party the night before. Now, revellers nursed their hangovers. All the Beaufort and the VWH had been penalized for skinny-dipping. One of the Quorn had been discovered in a very loose-box with a girl from the Cotswold and dropped from his team. Perdita, not in a party mood, had stayed in her tent reading *The Maltese Cat*.

Daisy, having taken a fortnight's holiday to drive Perdita around in yet another hired car, had never felt so shattered in her life. She spent the morning scrubbing out the ponies' boxes because the Rutshire team manager, miffed that Drew seemed to have utterly taken over, threatened dire reprisals if a blade of straw was left on the floor. In despair at the greasiness of her hair, Daisy had washed it in the river – how the hell had women coped in biblical times? – and it had dried all crinkly. The cornflower-blue dress she had brought to wear at the finals had been slept on by Ethel and was impossibly creased, as was her face after two nights sleeping in the car. Her legs, not brown enough, were becoming bristly.

She was miserably aware of getting on Perdita's nerves, and, as all the fathers had rolled up, of the loneliness of being a woman on one's own. She was almost abject with gratitude to Drew who'd insisted she use his Land-Rover as her base, and who'd come up specially that morning to invite her to lunch and to watch the match with him and Sukey.

Among the Pony Club, Daisy noticed, Drew was a Superman. A fortnight ago he had played for England against America in the annual International. Only his two hard-fought goals and grimly consistent defence had prevented the game turning into a rout. Now he couldn't move twenty yards without signing autographs. In his cool way Drew found this gratifying.

Marrying Sukey had admittedly enabled him to buy a string of cracking ponies and build a much-envied yard, but he was increasingly irked by the curbs on his freedom. Sukey raised eyebrows when he ordered rather too good a bottle of claret in restaurants. She winced at the size of his tailor's bill and questioned him going to Harley Street to replace two teeth knocked out in the Gold Cup when there was a perfectly good National Health dentist down the road. And just because Miguel O'Brien had switched to a new, ludicrously expensive, lightweight saddle, why did all Drew's ponies need one too?

Drew had never been extravagant, but he couldn't see the point of parsimony for parsimony's sake, so he had decided to look for a patron, some ignoramus who would pay him a long salary to coach him and look after his ponies. Kevin Coley was rumoured to be fed up with the dreadful Napiers and looking for a new senior professional. Trace Coley was impossibly spoilt, but Drew felt he could handle her. It was therefore in his interest to be the coach responsible for toppling South Sussex this afternoon.

While the South Sussex team, by invitation of Kevin, were all lunching on lobster, gulls' eggs, out of season strawberries and champagne in the Doggie Dins' Tent, half a mile away in one of Lord Cowdray's cottages, the Rutshire were having a team meeting. The curtains were drawn so they could see the video that Drew was playing of their semi-final against the Quorn. Drew leant against the wall, his thumb on the control button.

'Today we have one problem – you have to mark the other guys or we'll lose. You should never be more than two horse-lengths away from your man at any time. You *must* concentrate. Justin. You were loose in the first chukka, so were you, Patrick.' Drew froze the picture for a second. 'Their Number Three was all on his own. If Randy Sherwood gets loose with the ball we're lost. Trace Coley's their weak link. You won't have any trouble with her, Mike, so give Patrick all the back-up he needs and both mark the hell out of Randy.'

'I'll try,' said Mike, who had a hoarse voice like a braying donkey, the gentle timidness of a Jersey cow, and blushed every time he was spoken to.

Drew turned to Perdita, who was deciding whether to race to the loo and be sick again.

'Remember you're playing polo, not solo, Perdita. Their back, Paul Hedley, is quite capable of storming through and scoring, so stay with him. And, above all, no tantrums. South Sussex may be ludicrously over-confident, but we can't beat them with three players.'

Then, to Perdita's squirming embarrassment, he replayed the clip of her rowing with the umpire three times, freezing the frame of her yelling with her mouth wide open, until her team-mates were howling with laughter and rolling round on the floor. A shaft of sunlight coming through the olive-green curtains wiped out the picture.

'Let's go and have lunch,' said Drew.

Daisy hung about until Drew and the team came back to the Land-Rover. Sukey had done everyone proud, and the Lombard boys, who were Labradors when it came to food, were soon wolfing smoked salmon quiche, marinated breast of chicken, mozzarella in brown rolls, ratatouille and potato salad made with real mayonnaise.

Mike, who'd gone greener than the minted melon balls provided for pudding, and Perdita, who was lighting one cigarette from another, couldn't eat a thing.

'You must get something inside you,' insisted Sukey bossily, 'and you too, Daisy.'

I'd like your husband's cock inside me, Daisy was absolutely horrified to find herself thinking. It was only because Drew had remembered she liked vodka and orange and had poured her two really strong ones. In her present vulnerable state she was hopelessly receptive to kindness.

'Oh, where's Ricky?' moaned Perdita for the millionth time.

'Don't be too upset if he doesn't come,' said Drew in an undertone. 'I know he wants to, but all these children riding and such family solidarity may be too much for him.'

He's so sweet to her, thought Daisy gratefully, getting out her sketchbook as Drew took the team off to the pony lines to tack up.

Sukey firmly screwed the top on the vodka. 'You're driving. I expect you'd like coffee now instead of another drink.'

'Aren't you nervous?' said Trace Coley fondly, as Randy accepted a glass of brandy.

'Don't be ridiculous. Mike Waterlane's their only decent player, and he'll go to pieces as soon as his father turns up.'

David Waterlane drove his Rolls-Royce with the leaping silver polo pony on the front towards Cowdray. He had made the mistake of going via Salisbury because his bride of six months, who was twenty years younger than him, wanted to look at the cathedral. As they drove through rolling hills topped by Mohican clumps of trees and moved into the leafy green tunnels of Petersfield, his bride, who'd been primed by Drew, put her hand on her husband's cock and suggested that it would be more fun to stop and have their picnic in a field than join the crowds at Cowdray. It was only two o'clock, they'd seen the parade many times before, and Mike's match wouldn't start before 4.15.

Ponies tacked up in the pony lines yawned with boredom as their owners gave them a last polish. Mothers cleared up the remnants of picnics. Fathers looked up at the uniform ceiling of grey cloud and decided to put on tweed caps instead of panamas.

Mrs Sherwood, Randy's and Merlin's mother, divorced, with a Brazilian lover, and too glamorous for words in a peach suede suit, was talking to Kevin Coley, who looked like a pig with a thatched, blond tea-cosy on its head. Kevin, in turn, was being watched by his wife, Enid, who had gaoler's eyes, was more regal than the Queen, and in her spotted dress looked like a Sherman tank with measles. Daisy marvelled that she and Kevin could produce a daughter as pretty as Trace.

Cavalcades were riding quietly down to the ground, past trees indigo with recent rain, and cows and horses grazing alongside the faded grey ruins of the castle with its crenellated battlements and gaping windows. Of the fifty teams taking part in the parade, only eight were playing in the four finals, but there was still the prize for the best-turned-out team to be won.

The ground, a huge stretch of perfect emerald turf, was bordered to the north by fir trees and to the south by mothers having fearful squawking matches about the authenticity of various junior teams who weren't allowed to ride bona fide polo ponies.

'Tabitha Campbell-Black's pony played high goal at Cirencester!'

'No, it didn't!'

'Yes, it did!'

Brigadier Canford, Chairman of the Pony Club, and lover of pretty girls, was less amused to be stampeded by Valkyries.

'The Beaufort are cheating. They've back-dated membership of their Number Four. He's American and only been in the country two weeks.'

'The Bicester are cheating too. I've just caught them trying to ditch their weak link and import a brilliant boy from Rhinefield Lower who doesn't have a team.'

'Ladies, ladies,' said Enid Coley, joining the group of howling mothers. 'Polo is only a game.'

'And she'll have the South Sussex team manager stoned to death at dawn with vegetarian Scotch eggs if they don't win,' murmured Bas Baddingham who'd just rolled up and was kissing Daisy.

At two forty-five the parade began. On they came: chestnut, bay, dark brown, dappled grey, palamino, the occasional extravagantly spotted Appaloosa, ears pricked, tack gleaming, stirrups and bits glittering.

Daisy marvelled at the shifting kaleidoscope of coloured shirts, and the great, ever-moving millipede of ponies' legs in their coloured bandages. Many of the riders wore face-guards like visors in some medieval contest. Daisy wished she could paint it, but you'd need to be Lady Butler to capture that lot. Fatty Harris, Rutshire's club secretary, seconded for the day to do the commentary, had had rather too good a lunch in the Doggie Dins' Tent and was waxing lyrical over the ancient names.

'Here comes the Beaufort, the Bicester, the Cotswold, the Vale of the White Horse, the Craven, the Shouth Shushex Shecond Team.'

'Thought he'd have trouble with that one,' said Bas.

'And a big cheer for the Rutshire,' went on Fatty Harris, 'today's finalists in the Jack Gannon.'

On came the Rutshire in their Prussian-blue shirts, Prussian-blue bandages on their ponies' gleaming legs. Little Hermia, a changed pony after a fortnight's attention from Perdita, danced and snatched at her bit in excitement.

'She should have ridden Felicia in the parade,' said Sukey disapprovingly. 'Hermia doesn't need hotting up.'

But Hermia's the nearest she can get to Ricky, thought Daisy, and she's still hoping he'll turn up.

Next to Perdita rode Mike Waterlane on Dopey, a deceptively sleepy-looking pony, who was faster than a Ferrari and nipped all the opposition ponies in the line-out. Beyond him rode the Lombard brothers grinning broadly and enjoying themselves.

'Oh, don't they look lovely?' Suddenly the tears spurted out of Daisy's eyes and she had to turn away and bury her face in Drew's Land-Rover. Next moment a large piece of kitchen roll had been shoved into her hand. A minute later, when she'd got control of herself, Drew was back with another glass of vodka and orange.

A great cheer rang out as Cowdray, the home team, came on in their orange shirts.

'And here we have the other finalists in the Jack Gannon, unbeaten for the last three years, the South Shushex.' Fatty Harris got it half right this time.

Randy, Merlin, Paul and Trace rode with a swagger and there was no doubt their ponies were the sleekest, fittest and most expensive of all.

'I'm sure you all know that Trace Coley, the daughter of Kevin Coley, Chairman of Doggie Dins and our sponsor, is South Sussex's Number One in the final today,' announced Fatty Harris.

Kevin raised both clasped hands in a salute to acknowledge luke-warm cheers; Trace lifted her whip.

'She's left her hair loose, the little tart,' said Perdita contemptuously. 'That'll cost them the turn-out prize even if they win everything else. Oh, I wish Ricky was here.'

'Ladies and gentlemen,' said Fatty Harris, 'I give you the Pony Club.'

At the sight of these serried, beautifully turned-out ranks, this huge army with their polo sticks on their collarbones like bayonets, a deafening cheer went up. Fathers rushed about with video cameras, mothers wiped their eyes. Randy and Merlin Sherwood's beautiful mother adjusted her mascara in the driving mirror and eyed Rupert Campbell-Black who'd just rolled up alone in a dark green Ferrari to watch his daughter, Tabitha, play in the first final for the under-fourteens. Rupert, who'd just been appointed Tory Minister for Sport, eyed Mrs Sherwood back.

Then, suddenly, out of the sky like a vast whirring hornet came a black helicopter. Perdita gave a gasp as it landed to the west of the pitch. The door flew open and, like a page from Nigel Dempster, out jumped the Carlisle twins, Seb carrying Decorum, their bull terrier, and Dommie helping out a redhead and a blonde whose skirts immediately blew above their heads to show off wonderful suntanned legs.

They were followed by Dancer in dark glasses and black leather, Twinkle and Paulie, each with an Alsatian, and finally – Perdita gave a scream of delight – by Ricky with Little Chef in his arms.

'Now, members of the Pony Club, will you please walk off the pitch,' exhorted Fatty Harris. 'We owe it to the Cowdray ground and to Lord Cowdray to walk off.'

In the past the temptation to gallop across the hallowed Cowdray turf, which so many of them were not going to have the chance to play on, had been too much for the teams. Dreadful stampedes had resulted, with the whole field being cut up before a ball had been hit, which had resulted in turn in threats of not being allowed back. The sight of Ricky, however, was too much for Perdita.

'I'm here,' she screamed, and digging her heels into Hermia, went straight into a gallop towards the helicopter, followed by 199 yelling Pony Club members, who fortunately veered off to the left, and didn't trample the new arrivals to death.

'Disgraceful,' spluttered Sukey. 'She should lose her scholarship for that.'

Drew shrugged. 'The sooner she's packed off to New Zealand away from Ricky the better.'

Seeing her master, Hermia ground to a halt and whinnied with pleasure. Little Chef leapt up and licked her nose.

Jumping off, Perdita threw herself into Dancer's arms, hugged the twins, and then turned more shyly to Ricky. Her heart was crashing around like Big Ben about to strike.

'Thank you so much. I never thought it'd make so much difference,' she gabbled.

Ricky put up a hand and touched her cheek.

'Hermia looks well,' he said, 'and much h-h-happier.'

'She shakes hands for a Polo now,' said Perdita.

'You'd better win. We've all got money on it,' said Dancer. 'Can you get that crate of Moët out?' he added to Twinkle.

The twins, who had only left the Pony Club two years ago, pushed off to see their old chums. Everyone else landed up beside Drew's Land-Rover. Soon the autograph hunters were swarming round Drew, Bas and Dancer. It broke Perdita's heart that Ricky, who'd only been out of top-class polo for three years, was totally ignored.

'What a lovely shirt,' said Sukey to Bas. 'Where did you get it?'

'Marks and Spencer, I think,' said Bas.

'There, you see,' Sukey chided Drew. 'I'm always telling you there's no need to go to Harvie and Hudson.'

Seeing the flash of anger in Drew's eyes, Bas tactfully enquired after the baby. He'd forgotten what sex it was.

'Oh, Jamie's at home,' said Sukey. 'I'm amazed how Drew dotes on him. Men love having a boy, don't they?' She turned to Ricky. 'It matters so much to a man having an heir.'

For a second, as Ricky's face went dead, Bas and Dancer exchanged horrified glances.

'Isn't that Tabitha Campbell-Black playing for the East Cotchester?' said Bas, as a tiny figure, jaw thrust out, white stick-like legs flailing, thundered down the boards. 'Come on, Tabitha.'

'Man, man, man,' screamed the tiny figure to the East Cotchester Number Three. 'Take the fucking man, for Christ's sake.'

The umpire blew his whistle. 'That'll be forty against you for swearing, young lady. Consider yourself lucky you haven't been sent off.'

Bellowed on by her father, Tabitha scored three goals and East Cotchester won the Handley Cross.

Leaning against the Land-Rover, Daisy drew Rupert. Goodness, he had a beautiful face. Then she drew Ricky with his sombre, slanting dark eyes and then Drew twice, trying not to make him too handsome. In pencil, she could never capture the blueness of his eyes. Having sketched Bas as a merry Restoration rake, she had a crack at Sukey. Not easy – Sukey's charm was all in her colouring. She had a long face and such a naked forehead, Daisy found herself turning her into a polo pony.

'I'd hide that if I were you.'

Looking up with a start, Daisy saw that Ricky was actually smiling.

'Oh my God.' Daisy ripped out the page.

'Very appropriate,' said Ricky, taking it from her. 'I'm sure Sukey turns on sixpence.'

'She has a turn if Drew spends sixpence,' said Bas, peering over Ricky's shoulder. 'Bloody good, that's brilliant of Rupert. I'm much better looking than that.'

Giggling, Daisy stuffed the page into her pocket.

'I've done a couple of Hermia, in fact several,' she shoved the book at Ricky. He really was the most shy-making man.

Ricky flicked through, really looking. 'You've got her, even that little scar over her eye. They're marvellous.'

'Keep them,' said Daisy, blushing.

'I framed your cat. You must come and see it.'

'You must come and have supper sometime,' Daisy was staggered to hear herself saying. It must be the vodka.

'I'd like that,' said Ricky.

And he always says no to Philippa Mannering, thought Daisy. Perhaps if he fancied Perdita he saw her as a potential mother-in-law.

'Hello, Ricky,' said a shrill voice. Grinning up at him, her two front teeth missing, was Tabitha Campbell-Black.

'Hello, Tab. D'you know Mrs Macleod?'

'You played very well,' said Daisy.

'I know. None of the others did.' Tabitha, who had all the beauty and arrogance of her father, was now gouging out the centre of Sukey's home-made fruitcake with both hands.

'Have you had a good camp?' asked Ricky.

'Great. I haven't cleaned my teeth for a week.'

'They'll fall out.'

'No, they're used to it.'

'Where's your father?'

'Chatting up Randy Sherwood's mother. He's given Beattie Johnson the push, which is a shame. She never minded me getting into bed with her and Daddy.'

'Has he bought any new horses?'

'Yes, a stallion called Lord Thomas. He's so good, I hold the mares when he mates with them. Lord Thomas is the perfect gentleman, he always licks the mares afterwards.'

'Unlike his father,' murmured Ricky to Daisy, as Tabitha scampered off.

21

The Rutshire and the South Sussex were warming up their ponies for the Jack Gannon. The long wait had told on Perdita's nerves.

'Think positive,' she said through clattering teeth.

Mike Waterlane was grey. 'I don't know what's happened to Daddy.'

'Hopefully, he's had a shunt,' said Patrick Lombard, tightening his girths.

The pale yellow flowers of the traveller's joy entwined in the hedgerows brought no happiness to David Waterlane stuck behind a convoy of cars on the Midhurst Road which was held up by a huge lorry with a sign saying 'Horses' on the back.

'Bound to be show-jumpers – bloody yobbos,' said David Waterlane apoplectically.

There was no way he was going to reach Cowdray nor his son's match for the throw-in. The new Lady Waterlane, having drunk three-quarters of a bottle of Bollinger and achieved two and a half orgasms, was well content.

'Go for the girl,' ordered Randy Sherwood, as South Sussex rode on to the field. 'Mark her stupid, bash the hell out of her. Once she loses her rag, they'll all go to pieces.'

'I want 5-0 on the scoreboard by half-time,' Drew told Rutshire, 'and don't let Randy get loose.'

'My son is one,' announced a large mother, whose red veins matched her dress.

'That's a lovely age. Is he crawling?' asked Seb Carlisle's girlfriend.

'She's talking about his handicap,' said Sukey in a low voice, and looked very disapproving when Daisy started to laugh.

To a whirring of cine-cameras and a gratifying clicking of Nikons, Enid Coley progressed graciously into the stands. No-one could see a thing round her big spotted hat. Kevin Coley was busy supervising four different video cameramen to capture Trace's every stroke of genius on the field. Seeing Dancer and Drew talking to Mrs Sherwood and Rupert and, being a terrible star fucker, he barged into the group.

'Let the best man win,' he smirked at Drew.

'Well, it certainly won't be you,' drawled Rupert.

Mrs Sherwood turned and smiled at Kevin. After all, he was picking up her sons' expenses. 'Do you know

Dancer Maitland and Rupert Campbell-Black, Kevin?'

'Rather too well,' said the new Minister for Sport, his eyes like chips of ice.

'Shut up,' said Drew out of the corner of his mouth. 'I hope he's going to sponsor me.'

'I wouldn't advise it,' went on Rupert, not lowering his voice at all. 'Kevin sponsored a friend of mine a few years ago and took over his wife. If you're going into business with Kev, I'd slap Sukey into a chastity belt pronto.'

'That is quite uncalled for,' spluttered Kevin.

'They're about to throw-in. Come on, Rutshire,' shouted Bas, filling up everyone's glasses.

'Why are you wearing that wrist brace?' Merlin asked Randy as he lined up behind Justin Lombard.

'Too much wanking,' said Mike Waterlane, going bright pink at his own daring.

'I don't need to wank, you little pipsqueak,' snapped Randy, nodding and smirking in Trace's direction. 'I've got the real thing.'

'I hope she's better at screwing than polo,' hissed Perdita, who, like a cat waiting to spring, was watching the umpire's hand.

'You bitch,' squealed Trace.

The umpire, who was having great difficulty controlling his dapple-grey pony, hurled the ball in. Hermia hated throw-ins. It took all the strength of Perdita's frantically squeezing legs to stop her ducking out. Reaching over, however, she managed to hook Randy's stick, so Mike was able to tap the ball away. Thundering towards the centre of the field, giving two South Sussex players the slip, Perdita picked up a beautiful pass from Mike, skedaddled easily round Paul Hedley, hit two glorious offside forehands towards goal, before cutting the ball perfectly through the buttercup-yellow goal posts. Up went the yellow flag.

'That'll teach you to booze at lunchtime,' she said sweetly to Randy as she cantered back.

After that Randy really had it in for her. Taking a pass from Patrick during the next chukka, she set out once more for goal.

'Leave,' brayed a hoarse donkey voice behind her, 'leave, you bloody idiot.'

For a fatal second Perdita paused, thinking it was Mike shouting. Turning her head, she saw it was Randy Sherwood imitating Mike to muddle her, and that he was the only player in pursuit and had now gained valuable distance. The ball was ahead on her left. As she stood up in her stirrups, stretching over Hermia's nearside shoulder to hit the forehand, her right leg automatically swivelled up in the air. Lined up along the south of the field, the crowd could only see her left side. One umpire was up the other end, the other was too busy controlling his refractory pony to watch what Randy was up to. A second later he had neatly kicked her right stirrup out. Perdita mis-hit wildly, and only by some miracle stayed in the saddle, by which time Randy had backed the ball upfield to Merlin, who scored.

'Bastard,' screamed Perdita, racing down the field, twirling her stick in the air, which was against the rules.

She also knew that she should have reported the foul to Mike, who would then make an official complaint to the umpire, but she was too angry.

'The fucking, cheating bastard,' she screamed. 'He kicked out my stirrup.'

'I what?' asked Randy, the picture of innocence.

The umpires conferred, then, like Tweedledum and Tweedledee in their striped shirts, cantered over to the third man in the stands, who'd been gazing at Mrs Sherwood at the time and missed the incident altogether, and who now waved his down-turned palms back and forth to indicate no foul.

'You've got to be joking,' said Perdita hysterically. 'Bloody, dirty cheat.'

The umpires awarded a thirty-yard penalty to South Sussex.

At the slowest, most mocking hand-canter Randy Sherwood circled and stroked the ball between the posts.

'You're making things seriously easy for us,' he told a raging Perdita as he cantered back.

Despite dogged marking by Rutshire, the superior pony power of South Sussex was beginning to tell. They were six-five ahead and Drew and Ricky had their heads together at half-time. Then, as the Rutshire ponies' girths were loosened and they were washed down, scraped and walked round by the grooms, Drew called a brief team meeting.

'I'm going to swap you over,' he said. 'You're going to Number Four, Justin, and you're moving up to Number Two, Mike.'

Mike lowered the can of Coke which he'd been emptying down his parched throat.

'I couldn't. I'll never hold Randy.'

'Randy's got a slower pony in this chukka, who won't like Dopey taking a piece of him in the line-out one bit.'

It was a wise change. Randy's late night and heavy lunch were telling on him. He was not seeing the ball so well. Like a fly on an open sore, Mike harassed him, the way Randy had harassed Perdita earlier, and was too busy to notice that his father had finally arrived. Randy got so mad, he slashed Mike across the knuckles with his stick. The umpire, who'd finally got control of his pony, gave Rutshire a penalty. Taking it, Mike hit the post, but a hovering Patrick Lombard slammed it in. Six all. The cheering was now non-stop.

Perdita had the line and was cantering a wilting Hermia down the boards, her roan coat turned the colour of red cabbage with sweat, her breath coming in huge gasps. Ahead, the ball was bumping and slowly losing momentum over the divots, and Paul Hedley, the South Sussex Number Four, was galloping over to ride her off and back the ball up the field. What was that fake she'd practised with Ricky and Dancer last week? She checked a grateful Hermia. Paul checked his big, black thoroughbred. Perdita checked Hermia even harder, Paul followed suit. Filled with the devil, Perdita swung Hermia even closer to the boards, so the ponies' nearside hooves were scraping the paint off, and Paul, who'd been instructed to mark Perdita at all costs, stayed with her.

For a second his mind was off the ball, leaving it free for Patrick Lombard to belt in and whip it away, dribbling it for a few yards, then powering it to Mike, who, relishing his new freedom at Number Two, took it up field.

Merlin, who'd been covering for Paul and protecting the South Sussex's goal, cleared once again, but Perdita blocked his shot. She could have tried for goal, but Mike had an easier shot so she gave him a lightning, nearside, under-the-neck pass. The whole ground groaned as Mike hit the post. Like Chrissie Evert executing an effortless backhand crosscourt volley at Wimbledon, Perdita shot forward and whacked the ball home. Seven-six, Rutshire were in the lead – the ground erupted, flat caps were being hurled in the air. Horns tooted. There were fifteen seconds left of play.

'We can't go to extra time,' Drew muttered to Ricky. 'Our ponies have had it.'

Realizing this, Randy shook off Mike at the throw-in and raced off to level the score.

'Look at the ground opening up for Randy Sherwood,' said Fatty Harris. 'Watch him going into overdraught, whoops, I mean overdrive. Can Randy make it seven all?'

Randy felt he could. With Sherwood arrogance, he lifted his stick for the copybook cut shot. Next moment Perdita, streaking down the field, had thrown herself out of the saddle and clinging with her left hand round Hermia's damp hot neck, hooked Randy as the final bell tolled for South Sussex. The crowd went crazy.

'Ouch,' howled Ricky.

'Oh my God,' gasped Daisy, letting him go. 'Was that your bad arm?'

'Nothing's bad at this moment,' said Ricky triumphantly.

'Bloody marvellous,' yelled Drew.

'I knew they'd win easy,' crowed Dancer.

'Swap jerseys with me, I dare you,' said Merlin Sherwood to Perdita. Without missing a beat, she whipped off her Prussian-blue shirt to show a flash of white breast and browny-pink nipple before she dived into Merlin's olive-green jersey.

'Did you see that?' said Sukey in a shocked voice to Brigadier Canford.

'Indeed I did,' said the Brigadier. 'Wish I'd brought binoculars. Damn fine little player.'

Stripped to the waist, brown from the Zimbabwe sun, Randy rode up to Perdita to shake her hand. Grabbing it, he pulled her towards him. For a second she felt his hot, strong sweaty body against hers, then he kissed her.

'Well played, you stuck-up little bitch,' he whispered. 'I'll get you in the end.'

Next minute Perdita had slapped him across the face.

'Fuck off, you great oaf,' she screamed.

Laughing, Randy cantered off. Trace Coley, who'd lost a match and a lover in as many minutes, burst into tears.

Dismounting to rest Hermia, Perdita walked off the field straight up to Ricky.

'Was it OK?'

It was the first time she'd seen him look really happy.

'It was f-fucking wonderful.'

Oh God, thought Daisy, he mustn't smile at her like that, he's utterly irresistible.

Kevin and Enid Coley were slightly compensated by the barrage of cameramen, particularly one from *The Tatler*, who photographed them talking to Lord Cowdray, and later handing out prizes and cups.

Tabitha Campbell-Black was livid because she won a bag of Bailey's Performance Mix horse feed rather than a T-shirt with a picture of a polo pony on the front.

'I'm sure your performance isn't at all mixed,' murmured Rupert to Mrs Sherwood who seemed to have accepted South Sussex's defeat with great equanimity. The Brazilian lover was looking increasingly disconsolate.

The prize-giving was supposed to be compèred by Fatty Harris, but having taken so many nips while he was commentating, he had to pop into the Portaloo immediately after the match. He then had the humiliation of being locked in and towed away, with all the Pony Club screaming with delight at the sight of his vast red-nosed, anguished face and hammering fists at the window.

Horse boxes and cars were already driving off as Trace Coley, looking sexy in her father's panama, sauntered up to receive a body brush and a blue rosette as one of the runners-up in the Jack Gannon.

Hastily scribbling out his copy for *The Times* on the bonnet of his car, J.N.P. Watson wrote:

'The star of the side, however, was seventeen-year-old Perdita Macleod, the Rutshire Number One, who scored three goals. Working at Richard France-Lynch's yard for the past two years, she showed much of the old France-Lynch magic, and must be regarded as high goal potential.'

'And finally,' announced Brigadier Canford, 'we come to the Mary Tyler Award for the most promising girl player.'

Daisy watched an expectant Trace Coley re-arranging her panama in the driving mirror of her father's Rolls as Brigadier Canford put on his spectacles to have a better look. Then he beamed with delight. 'Which goes to Perdita Macleod.'

For a second Perdita froze as the reluctant cheers began to crescendo and stuffed her fists in her eyes, fighting back the tears. Then, immediately pulling herself together, she strolled up and thanked Kevin and Brigadier Canford very sweetly for her polo stick, before flicking a very obvious V-sign at Trace on the way back. Immediately Drew took her aside. 'Will you bloody well pull yourself together. Non-stop swearing, stripping off on the field, making V-signs at the sponsor's daughter. I saw you. Do you want that scholarship or not? After all the trouble your mother's taken driving you round the country, why the hell are you deliberately trying to hurt her?'

'So we'll no more go a-Land-Roving so late into the night,' sang Daisy five minutes later, as, dizzy with pride and vodka, she weaved back to Drew's boot looking for her bag and went slap into Drew.

'The Coleys have asked us back for drinks at Château Kitsch – that's worth seeing anyway,' he said, 'but lots of potential patrons will be there and the Pony Club Committee, so it could be useful to Perdita. They've just confirmed her scholarship by the way, but don't tell her or she might blow it. It's nothing to cry about.'

'I don't know how to thank you, and I've got nothing to wear,' mumbled Daisy.

'You look fine. No one'll change.'

Daisy wished just for once that Drew could see her when she wasn't looking awful.

'Are Ricky and Dancer going?'

'They've gone home. Ricky's just been even ruder to Kevin than Rupert was. Told him he didn't want to accept hospitality from patrons who go round cuckolding their players. It gave him a ghastly feeling of *déjà vu*.'

'Does Kevin know what *déjà vu* means?'

'He does now. And Enid's hopping.'

Half an hour later Enid had calmed down, at least on the surface, and changed into her aquamarine lurex hostess gown. As her hair had been squashed down by her David Shilling spotted hat, she put on her prettiest blond wig with the tendrils over the forehead. Drenched in Shalimar, wearing her pearls, because her diamonds might make people who'd been unable to change feel under-dressed, Enid awaited her guests, radiating regality.

'I didn't realize it was going to be a tented wank,' said Drew, as Sukey applied a dash of pink lipstick. It was not yet dusk, but the drive up to Kevin's mock Tudor house was lined with lit-up toadstools. The front door was flanked with the famous Moggie Meal cat and the Doggie Dins terrier. Six foot high and floodlit, they winked, mewed and yapped when the door bell was rung. Inside, maids in black took coats for tickets, and told everyone to go through the lounge as Mrs Coley was receiving in the pool area.

Perdita listened to her mother grinding gears and going on and on and on about how marvellously Perdita had played and how it had been the proudest moment of her life, and how everyone from Rupert to Brigadier Canford said what a great future she had and Drew this and Drew that. And of course, being Daisy, she was quite unable to resist telling Perdita the thrilling news which she mustn't tell *anyone*, that she'd got the scholarship.

'Just think,' she raved on, as they drove past honey-suckled hedges and trees covered with reddening apples, 'six months in New Zealand. Hot springs and Kiwis and,' Daisy couldn't remember anything else about New Zealand, 'oh yes, Maoris, of course.'

'Maori, Maori quite contrary,' said Perdita gloomily.

Why wasn't she flying back to Robinsgrove with Dancer and Ricky? She didn't want to go to New Zealand. She'd die if she was parted from Ricky for five minutes. He'd been so lovely, and her shoulder still burned where he'd put a hand on it after the game. If she stayed in England with him, she'd learn much faster than shovelling horse-shit in New Zealand and being made to get up early in the morning. Getting up early was only worth it if she were going to see Ricky.

'I wonder if you'll be in South Island or North Island,' said Daisy, narrowly avoiding ramming the car in front which had braked suddenly.

'Oh, shut up, Mum, I want to think.'

By the pool at Château Kitsch, which was as blue as Enid Coley's hostess gown, Trace, who'd changed into a slinky

210

black dress, was having a row with Randy Sherwood.

'How dare you kiss Perdita Macleod in front of everyone?' she hissed.

'Because I want to screw her,' said Randy unrepentantly. 'I bet she's a virgin, and she'd be volcanic in the sack.'

Perdita had just walked in. She was still wearing muddy breeches, black socks and Merlin's polo shirt. Her hair was scraped back in a pony tail, her face was smeared with mud. What was the point of tarting up if Ricky wasn't there? Ignoring Randy's imperious wave, she walked over to talk to Mike Waterlane.

On the edge of the pool, knowing there was a possibility of Kevin sponsoring Drew, Sukey was chatting up Enid Coley. Perdita remembered Sukey being just as deferential to Grace Alderton three years ago, the first time she'd seen Ricky in the flesh. I can't go to New Zealand, she thought.

The food being handed round was quite awful – muesli sticks, unsalted nuts, prunes, figs, sliced bananas. Huge jugs of fruit juice were being pressed on guests, rather than booze.

Randy Sherwood edged up to Perdita.

'My mother's just gone off with Rupert Campbell-Black,' he said. 'I think he is the coolest guy in the world, and the richest. I wouldn't mind him as a stepfather.'

Reaching out for a vegetarian Scotch egg, and hurling it at his brother, Randy added casually, 'Will you have dinner with me tonight?'

But Perdita wasn't listening; she was far too engrossed in Sukey's conversation with Enid Coley.

'When one thinks of the number of miserably displaced children from broken homes who've been given a sense of purpose by the Pony Club,' Sukey was saying, then, lowering her voice, 'take Perdita Macleod. She was a little horror when Drew took her over – but look how she played today.'

'Given one or two shocking lapses of behaviour,' snorted Enid Coley. 'Mind you, it can't have helped working all this time for Ricky France-Lynch. He is the rudest, most arrogant man I've ever met. I mean, who does he think he is? I totally understand his little wife going off with Bart Alderton. Kevin and Bart do a lot of business together.'

'He did lose a child,' said Sukey.

'Because he was drunk. From all Bart says, he was rude and arrogant before that. That's what stopped him getting to the top.'

'What did you say?' said an icy voice.

Beneath the mud smears, Perdita was as white as a new polo ball. She was shaking with rage, there was fifth-degree murder in her eyes.

Sukey started. 'Oh, Perdita, I'd no idea you were there.'

'We were saying,' said Enid, without looking over her hefty lurex shoulder, 'that Ricky France-Lynch's personality stopped him getting to the top.'

'Well, you're going to the bottom, you disgusting old bag,' screamed Perdita, and the next moment she had butted Enid in the small of a very large back right into the swimming-pool. Jumping in after her, Perdita pulled off Enid's wig to reveal scant grey wisps and pushed her under the water, where the aquamarine hostess gown billowed up to display fawn pop socks at the end of fat, purple legs.

'How dare you slag off Ricky?' screamed Perdita. 'How dare you? How dare you?'

Everyone was shouting. There were even some cheers. Next minute, Kevin, Drew and Randy Sherwood, who was laughing his handsome head off, had jumped into the pool and were trying to prise Perdita away.

'Stop it,' said Drew, pinning her arms behind her back and grimly increasing the pressure until she gasped with pain and let go.

'Did you hear what she was saying about Ricky?' she cried hysterically.

'You're not helping him by behaviour like this,' snapped Drew.

For a second Perdita struggled with him, then watched with mixed emotions by Sukey, Daisy and a drenched Randy Sherwood, she collapsed sobbing in his arms. 'No one understands Ricky like I do.'

22

Ricky was so furious with Perdita for deliberately sabotaging her scholarship that he gave her the sack.

Even the sight of Little Chef and the ponies longingly looking out for her every morning didn't make him relent.

'He's a hard man,' said plump Louisa, who also missed Perdita dreadfully. Only the sullen, scrawny Frances was delighted.

At home Perdita behaved more atrociously than ever before, storming round the house, refusing to get a job and screaming at Violet and Eddie when they returned bronzed from a month in LA with Hamish and Wendy. Nor were matters helped by Violet gaining ten 'A's in her O levels, losing a stone and getting her first boyfriend, who rang her constantly at all hours of the night from Beverly Hills. Violet and Eddie then went back to their respective boarding schools, paid for by Granny Macleod, which only stepped up Perdita's paranoia and jealousy.

At the end of September Violet came home for a long weekend and Perdita was so bloody-minded that in despair Daisy escaped to Harvest Festival for an hour of peace. Eldercombe Church was packed. Miss Lodsworth, who organized the flower rota, had excelled herself. Huge tawny chrysanthemums big as setting suns, gold dahlias like lions' manes, yellow roses, sheaves of corn, briar and elder glowing with berries all brought a glow to the ancient yellow stone. Every window-ledge was crammed with apples gleaming like rubies, vast vegetable marrows and pumpkins and, more prosaically, tinned fruit, sardines and baked beans. Some joker had even added a tin of Doggie Dins.

Daisy also noticed, as she slid into an empty pew at the back, that the church was unusually full of attractive women. There was Philippa Mannering looking avid in a beautifully cut check suit and a brown beret at a rakish angle. There was the pretty girl from the village shop wearing an emerald-green dress more suited to a wedding. Exotic scent mingled with the more religious smells of incense, furniture polish and veneration. Putting paid to Daisy's hour of peace were also hoards of children clambering over pews, chasing each other down the aisles, punching their mothers, and having to be repeatedly hushed for talking. Not children used to being brought to church, thought Daisy. Then she realized she'd forgotten to kneel down when she came in, and blushing, sank to her knees.

Oh, please God, she prayed, shake Perdita out of this ghastly mood and make her happy again, and look after darling Violet and Eddie, and Gainsborough and Ethel, and please God, if you think it's right, let me fall in love with a man who isn't married, who falls in love with me and don't make it too long.

Hell, she'd picked a pew next to the radiator. She'd be as red as those beetroots in the window in a minute. Please God, don't make me so vain, she asked, scrambling to her feet with the rest of the congregation as the organ launched into 'We plough the fields and scatter'.

Then Daisy twigged the reason for all those glammed-up women. Far ahead, in the France-Lynch pew, poignant because he was the sole inhabitant, stood Ricky. He was looking unusually smart in a pin-stripe suit and a black tie which was the only colour he'd worn since Will died. With the pile of huge marrows, the whole service seemed like some ancient fertility rite, with Ricky the unattainable corn king whom everyone wanted.

'*He only is the maker of all things near and far,*' bellowed Miss Lodsworth, totally out of tune. '*He paints the wayside flower, He lights the evening star.*'

Daisy's eyes filled with tears. What beautiful words. Would she ever find time to paint wayside flowers again? Ricky certainly lit the Evening Star for Perdita. She *must* ask him round for a drink.

The gay Vicar, who loved the sound of his own voice, took a long time over the service and Daisy's thoughts started to wander. Tears filled her eyes again as she thought of the little gravestone in the churchyard: In loving memory of William Richard France-Lynch, 1978-81.

Oh, poor Ricky. Daisy blew her nose on a piece of blue loo paper. She felt even sorrier for him with that stammer when he went up to read the first lesson, and had to announce that it came from the eighth chapter of Deuteronomy, a word which took him four goes. His face was impassive, his hands steady. Only the long pin-striped right leg, shuddering uncontrollably, betrayed his nerves. Now he was wrestling with the bit about '*God leading thee into the w-w-wilderness for forty years to humble thee and to p-p-prove thee.*'

Comparing his grey frozen features with the carved stone

angel beside the lectern, looking at the long lit-up scar, and the furrowed forehead as he wrestled with the difficult words, Daisy thought he didn't need to humble or prove himself any more. She supposed because he was ostensibly Lord of the Manor, he felt he had to do it. Dancer would have had much more fun.

Daisy was sweating for him, and as he stumbled over the word '*pomegranates*', she could feel the collective goodwill of the painted ladies in the congregation urging him home like the favourite in the Grand National.

The Vicar then took the text for his sermon from the second lesson, 'God loveth a cheerful giver', and was so carried away by his own rhetoric that he absent-mindedly helped himself to most of the grapes hanging down from the top of the pulpit.

Daisy was screwing up her courage to accost Ricky and ask him for a drink after church when the Vicar launched into the final prayer about being made flesh, and she suddenly remembered the vast ox heart cooking in the oven for Ethel, which would burn dry if it wasn't taken out, so she belted home. Anyway Ricky had been buttonholed outside the church by the gay Vicar and scores of eager ladies.

'Come to dinner this evening, just kitchen sups,' Philippa was saying.

'I'm afraid I've got to work,' Ricky said brusquely.

'*I'd* simply love to,' said the Vicar.

Daisy was still giggling when she got home to Snow Cottage and made the mistake at lunch of telling Perdita that Ricky had read the lesson.

'Did you speak to him?' demanded Perdita, dropping her forkful of braised fennel with a clatter. 'What did he say about me? Did you ask him for a drink?'

'I didn't get near him. He was surrounded . . . ' Daisy was about to say 'by women', but hastily changed it to 'by members of the congregation as I was leaving, and I had to get back for Ethel's heart.'

'What about my fucking heart?' screamed Perdita. 'You don't give a shit that it's broken. You're so bloody wet, one could grow waterlilies all over you,' and, storming out of the kitchen, slammed the door behind her.

'Why don't you stand up to her, Mum?' asked Violet.

I must not cry, Daisy gritted her teeth. After she'd

cleared up lunch she hoisted Ethel's huge ox heart out of its water on to the chopping board. Usually she got through cutting it up by fantasizing that she was Christian Barnard saving the life of Francis Bacon or Lucian Freud. Today it didn't work, the tears started flowing again. I mustn't go to pieces, she whispered, tomorrow I'll be brave, and ask Ricky round for a drink.

Fortunately the Caring Chauvinist was away the following day, but Ricky's number was always engaged. Only when she checked with directory enquiries did she learn that the receiver was off the hook.

Getting home from the office, she found Violet and Perdita having another screaming match.

'I'm not coming home at half-term if she's here, Mum,' complained Violet. 'She's destroying all of us.'

Having cleaned her teeth, washed, put on a bit of make-up and brushed her hair, Daisy set out up the ride to Robinsgrove. The sun was sinking in a red glow, the lights were coming out in Eldercombe Village. Once more Daisy was knocked out by the fecundity of everything, the black-thorn purple with sloes, plump hazel nuts already shredded by squirrels, elderberries shiny as caviar hanging like shower fittings from their crimson stems. She ought to make elderberry wine, then she wouldn't spend so much on vodka.

Ethel bounced ahead, crashing joyfully through the russet bracken, then splashing and rolling in the stream, spooking as ponies loomed out of the dusk. Ahead towered Robinsgrove – such a large house for one unhappy man.

I must be brave for Perdita's sake, said Daisy through chattering teeth as she pressed the door bell. He can only tell me to eff off. Inside she heard frantic barking. The door opened an inch.

'Yes,' said an incredibly unfriendly voice.

Little Chef had other ideas. Barging through the gap, he hurled himself on Ethel in a frenzy of tightly curled tail-wagging. Then, on tiptoe with excitement, he danced round her licking her eyes and ears.

'Oh, it's you,' said Ricky. 'C-come in.'

'Ethel's soaking.'

'She's OK. Little Chef seems to like her.'

Following him through the dark, panelled and tapestried

hall, Daisy noticed the telephone off the hook in the drawing room, then froze. Ahead on the kitchen table lay a twelve bore. Ricky must be about to commit suicide. She must get him out of the house.

'I came to ask you to supper,' she babbled looking back into the drawing room. 'You must come at once. Autumn's awfully depressing, it affects lots of people. I'm sure things'll seem better tomorrow.'

Ricky followed her gaze.

'Oh, that accounts for the peace today. I must have left it off the hook this morning. Rupert rang about a pony. I went out to the yard to check some detail.'

He replaced the receiver. Instantly it rang – Philippa trying to fix up a dinner date.

'I'm working tonight,' snapped Ricky, 'and next week I'm going to Argentina.' He slammed down the receiver. 'Fucking woman.'

He was going to shoot himself and Little Chef, thought Daisy numbly.

'I don't think you should be on your own,' she said in what she hoped was a calming voice. 'I know you'll never get over what's happened. But nice things do happen. They played "Invitation to the Waltz" on Radio 3 this morning' – she was speaking faster and faster, edging towards the gun – 'such a heavenly tune, I played it at school, and suddenly found myself waltzing round the kitchen, then Ethel leapt up and waltzed with me, and I thought perhaps there is a life after Hamish. If you came to supper now, you could watch television, and Violet learnt how to play poker in California, she's teaching me, we could have a game and Perdita would love to see you.' Her voice trailed off when she saw Ricky looking at her in utter amazement.

'What *are* you going on about?'

Daisy pointed nervously at the gun. 'I think you should put that horrid thing away.'

Suddenly Ricky smiled with genuine amusement. It was as though the carved angel by the lectern had suddenly come to life.

'You thought I was going to top myself. I've been shooting partridge with Rupert. I was cleaning my gun. Look.' He held up his oily hands.

'Oh, gosh,' said Daisy appalled. 'How stupid of me!'

'Anyway, you can't commit suicide with a twelve bore, although they're always doing it in books. Look.' He picked up the gun, and held it to his temples, 'One's arms simply aren't long enough to pull the trigger.'

Daisy had gone absolutely scarlet.

'I was just worried, with the telephone off the hook and all.'

'I'm quite OK,' said Ricky, slotting the gun back in its case, 'and I would like to come to supper.'

'You would?' Daisy's jaw dropped. All they had in the house was six eggs for scrambling and the remains of Ethel's heart. As if reading her thoughts, Ricky said, 'Better still, we'll go out.'

'Oh, no,' said Daisy, appalled. 'I didn't mean that. I wouldn't dream of foisting myself on you. And the children . . .'

'Are quite capable of looking after themselves. I got my licence back last week, so it's a treat to drive someone.'

'I'm not dressed.'

'Nor am I.' He was wearing faded olive-green cords, a check shirt and a dark brown jersey.

Daisy would so like to have got tarted up, but at least her hair was newly washed that morning and her teeth were clean. But Perdita would never forgive her for going out with Ricky.

'I'll just wash,' he said, 'and you can ring home.'

Daisy was desperately relieved to get Violet, who was wildly encouraging. 'Go for it, Mum, he's gorgeous. Got yourself a decent date at last.'

Ricky took her to a French restaurant in Rutminster with low beams, scrubbed pine tables, sawdust on the floor, rooms leading one into another and mulberry red walls covered with hunting prints. The head waiter, enchanted to see Ricky after three years' absence, kissed him on both cheeks, enquired after his elbow, and found him a quiet corner.

Daisy was mildly encouraged that Ricky deliberately sat on her right, on his non-scar side. He ordered her a large vodka and orange and Perrier for himself. At first the pauses were dreadfully long.

'D'you miss not drinking very much?'

He nodded. 'I'm lousy at small talk, and it helped.'

'Couldn't you just drink occasionally when you need it – like at parties?'

'Once I start I can't stop – like Kinta.' He uncrossed a pair of knives.

'I suppose you feel it's a way of making sure it never happens again.' She flushed as red as the mulberry walls. 'I'm sorry. I shouldn't remind you.'

Ricky broke up a piece of brown bread, but didn't eat it.

'Does it get better?' asked Daisy.

'Not much.'

The flame from a scarlet candle lit up the stubble darkening his chin and the even blacker rings under his eyes.

Oh, Christ, that's torn it, thought Daisy.

'Are you ready to order, Meester France-Lynch?' asked the head waiter. 'The *moules marinières* are very very nice.'

'I'll have that,' said Ricky, then turned to Daisy.

Oh help, she thought. One of the things that had driven Hamish crackers was her inability to make up her mind.

'No hurry,' said Ricky. 'Give us a few more minutes.'

'I'd like mushrooms *à la grecque*,' said Daisy quickly,

'And to follow, *les perdreaux sont superbes*. We serve them stuffed with foie gras and cooked in Madeira.'

'Partridge,' explained Ricky. 'They do them very well here.'

Daisy nodded hastily. 'I'd like that.' Anything not to irritate.

'And don't overcook them,' said Ricky. 'And we'll have a bottle of the Number Fourteen.'

'I'll be plastered,' said Daisy, aghast.

'No-one could accuse me of being a half-b-b-bottle man,' said Ricky. 'What was your husband like?'

'Very half-bottle, very noble-looking, very serious. He thought I was too silly for words, but he made it possible for me to keep Perdita, so I'll always be grateful.'

'You miss him?'

'I miss all the things he did – like policies and banks and keeping the children in order. And I miss having a pair of arms round me. It's like being a house without a roof.'

She was boiling. She'd have to take off her thick blue jersey soon, and she couldn't remember how many buttons had come off the shirt underneath, and it was sleeveless, and she hadn't shaved her armpits since Philippa asked her to supper last week.

'It's such a pity,' she gabbled on, 'one can't go out and buy a new husband or wife the next day, like you do with puppies or kittens. I'm sure it'd be much easier to help one get over things.'

'I don't want a new wife,' said Ricky flatly.

'No,' said Daisy humbly, thinking of poor Perdita. 'I can see that. Chessie was so beautiful. I've seen pictures.'

'Better in the flesh. Her colouring was so p-p-perfect. It was my fault I neglected her. I was foul-tempered and arrogant and polo-mad. I never had any money to buy her the things she wanted.'

She had you, Daisy wanted to say. It was no good, she'd have to take her jersey off. Horrors, two middle buttons were missing to show an ancient grey bra. Hastily she breathed in and clamped her arms to her sides to hide the stubble. Then, seeing Ricky looking at her in amazement, said quickly, 'Bart Alderton sounds hell.'

'He's a sadist,' said Ricky as the waiter arrived with their first course. 'That's why I must get her back.'

And while the black mussel shells rose in the spare plate, like cars on a scrap heap, he told Daisy about Chessie's last taunt.

'But that's wonderful,' said Daisy, 'so romantic. You can win the Gold Cup and the Westchester, and go to ten like the labours of Hercules. I'd rather do that than kill the Hydra. You must do it.'

Ricky passed Daisy a mussel. 'They're very good. I will if Dancer has anything to do with it. Now they've lifted the ban on my going abroad, I'm off to Argentina next month to squander his millions on some really good ponies.'

'Perdita adored Dancer,' said Daisy. 'These mushrooms are bliss. In fact, the whole thing is a real treat.' She took a huge gulp of wine.

'How is she?' asked Ricky casually.

'Suffering from massive withdrawal symptoms. She misses you – all,' she added hastily.

'I miss her,' said Ricky. 'She's a menace, but she makes me laugh.'

'I wish she occasionally made us laugh at home,' sighed Daisy.

'Giving you a hard time, is she?' Ricky filled up Daisy's glass.

It was not in Daisy's nature to bitch, but faced with Ricky's almost clinical detachment, everything came pouring out – Perdita's endless tantrums, her impossible demands, her spite to the other children.

'I haven't got many wits, but I'm at the end of them. That was lovely.' She handed her plate to the waiter. 'Hamish going affected her dreadfully. They fought the whole time, but underneath she was frantic for his love and approval.'

'Who was her father?'

'It's so shaming,' whispered Daisy.

'Can't be that bad.'

She was saved by the waiter shimmying up with the partridges, making a great show of how pink they were inside, pointing out the foie gras stuffing, the celeriac purée and the exquisitely dark and glistening Madeira sauce. But the moment he left Ricky returned to the attack.

'So, what happened?'

Being Daisy, she blurted it all out. 'I should have told Perdita years ago, but I'm such a drip I funked it.'

Tears were flooding her face and she wiped them frantically away with the sleeve of her jersey. Aware a drama was taking place and dying to know if this was Ricky's latest, the waiter sidled over.

'Everything all right, Meester Franch-Lynch?'

'Perfect, now push off.' Ricky put a hand over Daisy's, a large rough hand with callouses beneath the base of each long finger from endlessly holding a polo stick.

'You are a good mother,' he said gently. 'I can read between Perdita's lies. I know what sacrifices you've made, working in that ghastly Christmas pudding factory, not buying any new clothes for years.' He picked up the frayed, very pointed collar of her shirt.

'I didn't know I was going out to dinner,' said Daisy defensively.

'Course you didn't.'

'I don't know what to do with her.' Daisy blew her nose on her red-checked table napkin, then realized what she'd done. 'Oh God, I'll wash it and send it back.'

'She needs polo,' said Ricky, 'but serious polo. She ought to be playing ten chukkas a day with really good players,

221

and she ought to get miles away from you so she can't kick the shit out of you.' As he filled her glass again he knocked over the salt cellar and quickly chucked the spilt salt over his left shoulder. 'Are you painting?'

'Not much.' Daisy was pleating the edge of the tablecloth. 'All my inspiration seems to have dried up since Hamish left and I seem to have lost all my confidence as a woman. Not that I had much, anyway.'

'In what way?' Ricky was stripping the partridge leg with his teeth, very white and even except a front one chipped by a polo ball. 'Come on, eat up.'

It is quite difficult cutting up a partridge when your elbows are glued to your ribs. Daisy started forking up celeriac.

'Last week I went to dinner at Philippa's. She insisted she'd got a lovely man for me. But it was just as an excuse to get her latest lover into the house. He wasn't remotely interested in me and brought Philippa some goat's cheese that looked like Tutankhamun's brain. They disappeared for hours to look at some rare book and Lionel insisted on seeing me home.' Her lip trembled. 'I'm sorry, this is awfully boring.'

'Horror films aren't boring,' said Ricky.

'And suddenly he leapt on me.'

'Disgusting old goat!' Ricky was comfortingly furious.

'Appropriate, really! He tasted of goat's cheese. I've never been very good at rejecting people, so I told him I was frigid. He just leered and said, "I'm a psychiatrist, little girl. I can cure that." ' Daisy gave a shudder.

'I'll chuck them out,' said Ricky angrily.

'Joel says they're model tenants,' said Daisy. 'They're always cutting their lawn.'

'Can't imagine Lionel modelling anything. You're not to have anything more to do with them. Understand?'

Ricky put his knife and fork together. 'Let's get back to Perdita. I'll take her to Argentina with me next week. No, it's a good idea. You know Alejandro Mendoza?' Then, with incredulity, 'But he's the greatest back in the world. The Mendozas are blood rivals of the O'Brien brothers, Juan and Miguel, who used to play for David Waterlane before the Argies were banned. They invariably end up on opposite sides in the Argentine Open. I'm going out to buy ponies from Alejandro. He takes a few players every year on his *estancia*. They bring on the young ponies and in return he teaches them. My handicap went up in twos the winters I spent with him. There are always young boys hanging round the place. Perdita needs a boyfriend. I'll leave her with Alejandro till Christmas.'

'We couldn't possibly afford the plane fare,' mumbled Daisy.

'Dancer'll pick that up,' he said. 'He wants Perdita to play for him next year. She'll add some much-needed tone. He's been nagging me to take her back for weeks. He can just advance her some salary. There's no need to cry.'

'I'm sorry.' Daisy wiped her eyes on her sleeve again. 'I ought to get the Niagara Falls Award for bawling. I'm just not used to lucky breaks. Are you sure?'

'Positive. Now Rupert's Minister for Sport, he can fiddle her a visa.' As he smoothed back his dark hair, his signet ring caught the light.

'What's your motto?' she asked.

'Never surrender,' said Ricky bleakly.

And he won't until he gets Chessie back, thought Daisy. Three-quarters of a bottle of wine had loosened her tongue.

'I've been moaning on about Perdita all evening, but at least she's alive, whereas Will . . . '

' . . . isn't,' said Ricky watching the bubbles rise in his glass of Perrier. 'Suffering's supposed to make you nicer. Didn't work for me. That's probably why I've been so bloody to Perdita. The guilt still knocks me sideways – just being alive. Sometimes I panic because I can't remember what he looked like. Chessie took all the photographs. She needed them. He'd be six now, old enough to start hitting a ball around. It comes in waves, doesn't it?' He glared at her. 'Look, I really don't want to talk about it.'

'I just think you ought to try and forgive yourself,' mumbled Daisy. We're like two chickens side by side trying to defrost, she thought.

'When are you coming back to England?'

'February or March. I can't stand another English winter. Dancer's fixed up for me to make a bomb coaching movie stars in Palm Springs. My elbow still plays up when I play too long.'

After that they talked about Dancer and Ethel and Little

Chef and Ricky's ponies, and drank so many cups of coffee and Daisy even had a *crème de menthe frappé* that it was long after midnight when they left.

'The colandered Barbour,' said Ricky, holding out her coat for her. 'You've been crawling through my barbed wire!'

Outside, in the back of the BMW, Ethel's great spotted goofy face was grinning out. Beside her, his front paws on her shoulder, tail wagging his small body into a frenzy, was Little Chef.

'It's easy for dogs,' said Daisy with a hiccup. 'I've had such a lovely time,' she said as Ethel fell on her in ecstasy, 'and Ethel's lick is much more efficient than cleansing cream.'

'This road is awful,' said Ricky as they bounced down the rough track to Snow Cottage. 'I must get it fixed before the winter.'

Seeing all the lights on, Daisy quailed. Surely Perdita wouldn't kick up when she knew she was going to Argentina. Desperate Ricky shouldn't think she was giving him the come-on, she had the door open before the car stopped.

'Do come in and tell Perdita. She'll be so excited,' she called back as she scuttled up the path. If Ricky was there Perdita might not make a scene, but he had paused to look at the front gate which needed mending.

Perdita sat on the kitchen table dressed all in black. She looked like a hell cat, sloe eyes glittering, teeth bared in a terrifying rictus grin, body rigid with loathing.

'Darling – the most heavenly news,' said Daisy.

'How dare you go out to dinner with Ricky?' screamed Perdita. 'I bet his telephone wasn't off the hook at all. You just wanted an excuse to vamp him. You can't do without it, you bloody old tart, can you? I bet you asked *him* out.'

Next minute Ricky had walked into the room and slapped her across the face. 'Don't you ever talk to your mother like that again, you revolting little bitch,' he howled. 'Now go to bed!'

Perdita gazed at him, her white left cheek slowly turning bright scarlet, her eyes widening in horror.

'Nothing wrong with your elbow if you can hit like that,' she spat. 'She's poisoned you against me, I knew she would.'

'I said go to bed,' said Ricky harshly. 'Go on, bugger off.'

With a stifled sob Perdita stumbled upstairs, slamming the door so hard that every ornament in the house shook.

There was a pause, then both Ricky and Daisy jumped at the sound of clapping. Slowly Violet walked into the room.

'I always heard how marvellous you were,' she said to Ricky, 'but I'd no idea *how* marvellous. I've been waiting for years for someone to do that.'

'Good,' said Ricky, unmoved.

Then, slowly, he looked round the kitchen and the sitting room at the flowers painted all over the pale green walls, like a meadow in summer, at the dark green ivy crawling up the stairs and the bears and tigers and dragons decorating every piece of furniture.

'Christ,' he said in amazement.

'I can always paint over it,' said Daisy hastily.

'It's stunning. You said you hadn't been painting. Stop shaking. It'll be all right.'

'Should I go to her?'

'Leave her to stew,' said Violet and Ricky in unison.

'Oh, and by the way, Mum,' went on Violet, 'Philippa rang and said could you man the bric-à-brac stall on Saturday.'

'No, she can't,' snapped Ricky.

'I said you couldn't,' said Violet gleefully. 'I told her you'd gone out to dinner with Ricky. She sounded put out.'

'Oh goodness,' said Daisy.

'I've been hearing how marvellous you are,' said Ricky drily to Violet, 'but I'd no idea how marvellous. Might put the bloody nympho off.'

After he'd had another cup of coffee, he went up to see Perdita. She was crying great wracking despairing sobs into her pillow. Ricky sat down on her bed.

'Fuck off.'

'It's me, Ricky.'

'Fuck off even more. I hate you.'

'You better stop sulking and apologize to your mother or I won't take you to Argentina.'

'I'll never apologize to her,' said Perdita tonelessly. 'What did you say? How? When?'

'Week after next, to stay with Alejandro. He'll teach you a few manners and how to play polo properly.'

'Oh, thank you!' Perdita flung her arms round his neck.

He could feel her hot soaked cheeks, her wet hair, her lips against his cheek, the bars of her ribs, the softness of her breasts, the contrasting bullet hardness of her nipples.

'And then can I come back to Robinsgrove?'

'If you behave yourself.'

Still she clung. He could feel her heart pounding. She was so like Chessie. He'd never wanted to screw anyone more in his life, but gently he disengaged himself.

'Go and apologize to your mother.'

Next day the weather turned cold, bitter winds systematically stripping the trees. Walking through Ricky's woods, Daisy noticed ruby-red sticky buds thrusting out on the chestnuts, although many of the trees still clung on to their shrivelled brown leaves. Like Ricky and me clinging on to the past, thought Daisy.

Ten days later Ricky and Perdita left for Argentina.

'I want to ask two f-f-favours,' said Ricky as he put Perdita's suitcases in a boot crammed with polo sticks. 'Could you possibly put flowers on Will's grave sometimes for me? And if Little Chef goes into a real decline will you promise to ring me?'

Perdita hardly bothered to kiss her mother goodbye. She hadn't forgiven her her night out with Ricky. The wireless blared 'I just called to say I love you' as Daisy went back into the house. She couldn't help envying Perdita.

It was a terribly long journey, even though they broke it in Florida. Ricky hardly took his nose out of a Frederick Forsyth novel. Perdita, bra-less, in a T-shirt and a skirt that buttoned up the front for easy access, writhed and burned beside him. She cleaned her teeth every three hours and had Juicyfruit continually at the ready in case he wanted to kiss her. She deliberately got a bit drunk at dinner and when the lights were switched out let her head fall on to his shoulder.

'I'm cold,' she murmured.

'I'll get you another blanket.'

As he would for any of his ponies, thought Perdita bitterly.

'I'm still cold,' she whispered half an hour later.

Ricky put an arm round her shoulders, but made no pass and eventually she fell asleep. Ricky gazed out of the window at stars as sleepless as himself. If he slept he might have nightmares about Will and Chessie. He couldn't bear to wake up screaming on the plane as he so often did alone at night at Robinsgrove.

23

Ricky got very uptight at Miami Airport when his polo sticks were nearly put on a plane to Hawaii by mistake.

'Expect the poor things needed a holiday. You work them hard enough,' said Perdita. But even Ricky telling her not to be bloody silly couldn't douse her sudden euphoria at the sight of the BA stickers being stamped on their luggage. She was going to Argentina, home of the greatest polo players and ponies in the world.

The Buenos Aires flight was delayed and the plane horribly hot, but this didn't upset the passengers who seemed delighted to be going home. The men, very handsome and as many of them blond as dark, gathered at the back of the plane, embracing each other and eyeing Perdita with approval and chattering like a great drinks party. After a shamingly large second supper of chicken, sweetcorn and cake, a vast vodka and tonic and half a bottle of red wine, at one o'clock in the morning the chatter suddenly turned into the Frogsmore Stream running under Snow Cottage and she fell asleep until six to find the chatter going on as loud as ever.

Women passengers who'd nodded off in full make-up emerged with faces crumpled and ankles swollen. For breakfast they were offered cake again, this time with salt and pepper.

'Bearing in mind the vast divide between rich and poor in Argentina, they presumably let them eat cake all the time,' said Perdita.

Ricky didn't smile. He'd had another sleepless night and ahead lay customs, who couldn't be expected to be exactly pro-British, and because of post and telephone strikes in Argentina, he hadn't been able to confirm the flight with

227

Alejandro, so they'd have to go through the hassle of hiring a car to drive the 330 kilometres out to his *estancia*.

Perdita, however, was excitedly looking down on vast faded pink rivers curling through spinach-green forest, and the blue shadow of their plane lying across Buenos Aires. Now she could see red houses, swimming-pools, race tracks, skyscrapers sticking up like teeth, and roads and railways so uniformly crisscross they seemed like tiles on a vast kitchen floor.

Rupert had also pulled some powerful strings. After a lightning whip through immigration, an official located all their luggage and polo sticks and whizzed them through customs. As they came through the exit doors, Ricky looked wearily round for an Avis sign. Perdita, in a faded purple T-shirt and sawn-off pale pink jeans, was pleasantly aware of all the men staring unashamedly at her. Then a young man in a blue shirt rushed up to his arriving girlfriend with a huge bunch of hyacinths and daffodils. Abandoning the English winter, Perdita realized she and Ricky had gone slap into the Argentine spring.

Next minute a tall, blond boy with a bull-dog jaw and massive shoulders walked up to them, looking slightly apprehensive.

'Hi, Ricky,' he said in a deep Florida drawl. 'Don't know if you remember me, Luke Alderton. If you want to hit me across the airport, I'll understand, OK, but I'm staying with Alejandro. Thought you might like a ride out to the *estancia*.'

For a second, Ricky glared at him, then he smiled. 'I never had any fight with you, Luke. It's incredibly kind of you to meet us on the offchance. This is Perdita.'

Perdita found her hand being engulfed in an incredibly strong grip, and Luke looked down at her, grinning lazily and appreciatively.

'What are you doing here?' asked Ricky.

'Being used as cheap labour to break Alejandro's ponies,' said Luke, taking Perdita's suitcases from her, 'in return for picking up a few tips from the master.' (He pronounced it masster.)

'Thank Christ for that,' said Ricky. 'You can look after Perdita.'

'Shouldn't be too much of a hardship,' said Luke, then eyeing Perdita's slender arms, 'but she better start pumping iron if she's going to play high goal.'

As he sorted out the porter with amazingly fluent Spanish, Perdita noticed he was wearing a bomber jacket with US Open printed on the back.

'Who's he?' she whispered to Ricky.

'Bart's son by a previous marriage,' said Ricky. 'Potentially the best back in the world.'

Within seconds they'd piled into a battered Mercedes and were fighting their way out on to the airport road. Luke pointed to a red spotted scarf gathering dust up on the dashboard.

'You may want to put that over your eyes, the driving's kinda crazy here,' he said as ten cars hurtled forward with absolutely no lane discipline, and all went straight through a red light with furious honking. Next moment a huge bus with Jumbo El Rapido on the side tore past overtaking and cutting in front.

'Christ,' muttered Perdita.

'Good training for the polo here,' said Luke. 'The Carlisle twins and my brother Red were down here last week with Victor Kaputnik. They came out of a restaurant and had a race with Juan O'Brien and two of his cousins. Victor nearly had a triple by-pass. He jumped out of Red's car yelling, "Taxi, taxi". He was so frightened he wouldn't let the driver go across a green light in case he hit Red and the twins coming the other way.' Luke shook with laughter.

'Who's staying with Alejandro?' asked Ricky.

'Well, one guy couldn't stand the pace and Ray Walter broke his wrist and went home, and there's an Argie, Angel Solis de Gonzales, ex-Mirage pilot, trying to make it as a pro. Not wildly pro-Brit understandably.'

'Any good?' asked Ricky.

'Awesome. He's only been playing seriously for a couple of years,' said Luke, hardly flinching as a car cut right in front of him, missing them by millimetres. Leaning out of the window, he let loose a stream of abuse.

'How come you speak such good Spanish?' asked Perdita.

'Last time I was here it rained for forty days. The only answer was to learn Spanish. They say my accent is 'orrible, but at least I can understand what they're saying on the pitch and suss out their Machiavellian little games.'

They were into flat, open country now. Perdita looked at the huge puddles reflecting a vast expanse of sky.

'I'm really, really here.'

Luke smiled. 'You will fall madly in love with Argentina,' he said in his deep husky voice, which had a slight break in it, 'with the wild life, the birds, the open spaces. But you will find it unconquerable, the extremes, the ferocity, the apparent heartlessness, the hailstorms that can wipe out a crop in half an hour. People own masses of land, not developing it or working it. It's just there.'

'How very un-American,' said Perdita.

Looking sideways at Luke, she decided that he wasn't at all good-looking but definitely attractive. A tawny giant with shoulders and arms like a blacksmith's, he had lean hips, more freckles than a gull's egg, a snub nose, sleepy honey-coloured eyes, Bart's pugnacious jaw and red-gold hair sticking up like a Dandy brush. He was also attractive because he was so reassuring.

On top of the dashboard was a poem called *Martin Fierro* and a Spanish dictionary lying with its spine up, to which he must have been referring as he waited.

'It's the great Gaucho poem,' he told her. 'Martin Fierro's aim in life was to sleep on a bed of clover, look up at the stars, and live as free as a bird in the sky. He put his horse and his dog a long way before his wife.'

'You don't look as though you read poetry,' said Perdita in amazement, 'and Martin's a very naff name for a Gaucho.'

Ricky, sharing the back with two polo helmets, a new saddle and numerous carrier bags of shopping, was beginning to relax.

'How's Alejandro?'

'Probably had ten more kids since you were last here. Argentines adore their kids,' Luke told Perdita. 'Their big interest is the family. They won't pay taxes, and they never stop at red lights.' He put out a huge hand to shield Perdita as a car shot out.

'Who are you playing for next year?' asked Ricky.

'Hal Peters – the automobile king – nice guy,' said Luke. 'Thought about nothing but cars for the first twenty-five years of his life, now he thinks about nothing but polo. He's given me a free hand to buy horses. But every time I show any interest Alejandro quadruples the price. I guess I'm lucky to be working. Young American players are really feeling the cold at the moment. They can't get sponsorship, because all the patrons think it's chic to have an Argie on their side.'

'Your father has three,' said Ricky bleakly. 'What's Red's handicap now?'

'Six, should be higher. He hates to stick and ball. His mother allowed him to sit out college for a year and he never went back. He won MVP awards – Most Valuable Player,' he explained to Perdita, 'all summer, then blows it by testing positive for drugs the day before the US Open. Gets suspended and fined $5,000.'

'Is he coming down here?'

'Well, he's always expected, like the Messiah,' Luke grinned at Perdita. 'My kid brother's kind of wild. Like Richard Cory he glitters and flutters pulses as he walks. Look, heron on the edge of that alfalfa field.'

With the amazing eyesight that had helped him become a great player, Luke pointed out egrets, storks and even a snake that whisked into its hole before Perdita could see it.

Passing through a town, Perdita noticed someone had painted a blue-and-white flag and a 'Malvinas belong to Argentina' slogan on the plinth of a statue of a general.

'For Christ's sake, keep your trap shut about the Falklands when we get there,' said Ricky.

'Alejandro's not anti-Brit,' said Luke. 'He likes anyone he can sell horses to. He still talks mistily about Cowdray, and Guards and the parties, and the hospitality, and the women you didn't have to date twenty-two times before laying them.'

They were deep in the country now, driving through absolutely flat land like a table top. Slowly Perdita was trying to absorb the immensity of the pampas. The vast unclouded duck-egg-blue semi-circle of sky, like a protractor on the horizon, was only broken by the occasional windmill or fringe of acid-yellow poplars or milk-green gum trees. The grass seemed to flow on for ever like a millpond sea. Occasionally, like a liner, they passed an *estancia* with stables and a drive flanked by poplars and sailed on. At last Luke swung on to a dirt road potted with huge holes. His left elbow, sticking out of the window, was soon spattered with mud as they shattered vast puddles reflecting the blue of the sky.

'Sorry,' he said as Perdita nearly hit the ceiling. 'You should have taken a sleeping pill.'

On the right was a sunlit village with square white houses like a Western shanty town.

'This place is called General Piran after some top brass who defended his country against the marauding British. It's the nearest civilization to Alejandro's place,' explained Luke. 'That's the phone exchange which never works. That's the fire station. They've got two fire stations, but all the houses are so far away they never get there in time. The teachers are all on strike, hardly surprising when they're only paid a hundred dollars a month, so all Alejandro's kids are at home getting under their mother's feet.'

He is nice, thought Perdita. How did anyone as vile as Bart produce a son like that?

'Alejandro's land begins here at the water.' He pronounced it 'wott-urr'. 'He owns everything in front of us as far as the eye can see.'

They had swung into an avenue lined with gums, their stark, white trunks rising like pillars. At the end on the left was a stick-and-ball field, a polo field covered with gulls, paddocks full of polished horses, then a group of red modern buildings. 'Barns to the right, grooms' quarters to the left, Alejandro's straight ahead,' said Luke as he drove up to a large ugly mulberry-red house with flowerbeds full of clashing red tulips, primulas and wallflowers, and a water tower completely submerged in variegated ivy.

Instantly out of the front door charged a man a foot smaller than Luke, but with a barrel-chest as big. He had a huge Beethoven head of black curls, a brown face scorched with wrinkles by an unrelenting sun, small dark eyes and a smile like a slice of water melon, which showed a lot of gold fillings. He wore old jeans, espadrilles and a torn blue T-shirt through which spilled a lot of black chest-hair. Throwing open his arms, he gave a great roar of laughter.

'*El Orgulloso*,' he shouted, '*El Orgulloso*. Mountain Everest, he come to Mahomet at last,' and he folded

Ricky in a vast hot embrace. 'Welcome, we are so please to see you.'

Then, peering round the side of Ricky's arm, he caught sight of Perdita and his little black eyes brightened even more.

'And this is Perdita. She is certainly very OK.' Seizing her hand, he looked her up and down. 'Why you waste your life on polo? Find a nice billionaire instead.'

'I want both,' said Perdita.

Alejandro gave another bellow of laughter.

'Good girl, good girl. I speak very well English, don't you theenk? Come and see my ponies.' About to lead them back towards the stables, he lowered his voice and said to Luke, 'Did you get it?'

Luke nodded and, getting a red jewel box out of his jeans' pocket, handed it to Alejandro just before a beautiful woman came out of the house. She had heavy lids above huge, dark, mournful eyes, a wonderful sculptured, aquiline nose, a big, sad, red mouth and long, shiny, blond hair with dark roots showing down the middle parting. She also had a wonderful bosom, a thickening waist and very slim brown legs in leather sandals.

'Reeky,' she hugged him. 'It has been so long, and this must be Perdita.' A shadow of apprehension crossed her face, immediately replaced by a warm and welcoming smile. 'What a beauty,' she said, kissing Perdita on both cheeks. 'I am Claudia, Alejandro's wife. Let me show you your room. You must be tired.'

'Nonsense,' said Alejandro.

'She 'as come 'alfway across the world,' protested Claudia.

'To see my horses,' said Alejandro.

They went across a lawn down an avenue of mulberry trees, past a thickly planted orange grove.

'To 'ide the chickens,' explained Alejandro.

To the right, a lot of youths building a swimming-pool eyed Perdita with interest. Alejandro snapped at them to get on with their work. The stables were far more primitive than Perdita expected. A few words in Spanish had been painted on the tack-room roof.

'It says, "Please don't tether any horses to this roof, or they'll pull it off",' translated Luke.

Dancer's latest hit single, 'Girl Guide', was belting out of the tack room. A pack of emaciated lurchers with burrs in their rough dusty coats charged forward, whimpering and weaving against Perdita's legs. But as she bent to cuddle them a small boy, brushing down a pony, picked up a lump of mud and hurled it at the dogs to drive them off. Perdita was about to yell at him when her attention was distracted by a man with a cruel leathery face wearing gaucho pants and a white shirt who was galloping a pony very fast round a tiny corral. The horse's nostrils were vastly inflated and it was panting rhythmically as its hooves struck the hard ground. The man's control was undeniable. She could hear the horse groan as he squeezed it with his calves.

'That's Raimundo the *peticero*, master of the horse,' said Luke, with a slight edge to his voice.

'Looks a nasty piece of work.'

'Work isn't the operative word. He's acting busy because Alejandro's here.'

In the yard an old man in a beret was clipping a pony's mane. The pony was rolling its eyes but stood motionless because a young boy relentlessly twisted its ear. Other horses wandered loose among the gum trees, while still others were muzzled and tied up. They looked very thin, but well-muscled.

'They're playing this afternoon,' explained Luke. 'Argentines don't feed or water their horses eight hours before a match. I guess they are thin, but again Argentines don't like their horses to carry a lot of weight.'

Perdita grew increasingly boot-faced when every pony she tried to cuddle cringed away with terror.

'They're all headshy,' she complained furiously.

'Shut up,' said Luke. 'You're here to learn not beef.'

Fortunately Alejandro was concentrating on Ricky, boasting that every pony in the yard had been entirely responsible for clinching last year's Argentine Open. They were distracted by a boy in his twenties cantering into the yard on a beautiful red chestnut. He had a bony, tortured face, angry, slanting peacock-blue eyes, bronze curls and a sallow complexion.

Wow! thought Perdita.

'Angel,' yelled Alejandro, 'breeng that mare 'ere. I want Reeky to see 'er.' Then with a touch of malice, 'These are

234

my friends, Reeky and Perdeeta. Isn't she beautiful? Won't she need the charity belt?'

Angel pulled up in horror and a cloud of dust, growled something incomprehensible, but undeniably insulting, threw down the reins, kicked his right foot out of the stirrup and, swinging it over the horse's withers, jumped to the ground and ran into the house.

'Zat is Angel,' said Alejandro with a shrug, 'still fighting zee Falklands War.'

Amazing cooking smells were drifting from the kitchen. Seeing Perdita beginning to wilt, Luke took her back to the house.

Ricky and Alejandro had to be dragged away from the horses to a lunch laid out on a blue-and-white checked tablecloth under the gum trees. They needed two tables to accommodate the ten children.

Ranging from twenty-one downwards, there were three boys, Patricio Maria, Luis Maria and Lorenzo Maria, followed by three ravishing plump girls, followed by four more boys, the youngest being little Pablo, who was three. All had the dark eyes and dark curls of their father.

Claudia exclaimed in delight over the presents Ricky had brought, which included a dark red cashmere jersey, a length of Harris Tweed, a striped silk Turnbull and Asser dressing gown and a Herbert Johnson tweed cap for Alejandro. Then she introduced her children to Perdita.

'Don't warry,' said Alejandro with his great laugh. 'I don't recognize them myself sometime.'

'Only the ones that play polo,' said Claudia without rancour.

'Have a wheesky, Ricky,' said Alejandro, brandishing Ricky's duty-free Bourbon. Then, when Ricky shook his head, 'But you used to dreenk half a bottle before chukkas. It was your petrol.'

'I've changed.'

'Luke?' asked Alejandro.

'Not if I've gotta play this afternoon,' said Luke, sitting down next to Perdita.

'You are, because I'm not,' said Alejandro, splashing whisky into his glass. 'The opposition's very weak today,' he explained to Ricky, 'but Luke is a good back. I must look after my laurel.'

Two silent maids served them. Perdita felt too tired to eat, but when she tried her steak it was pure poetry, tender as velvet, juicy as an orange, and so exploding with flavour that she was soon piling her plate with potato purée, tomato salad and geranium-red barbecue sauce.

'I can't believe this food,' she said to Claudia five minutes later. 'It's wonderful.'

'We in Argentina are very like the Breetish except in their cooking, which is 'orrible,' said Alejandro, who was now wearing both his new dressing gown and the tweed cap over his black gollywog curls. 'I like to dress like an Englishman.'

The talk was all of polo. Claudia didn't contribute and concentrated on the younger children.

'I love to play again in England,' Alejandro said to Ricky. 'When you theenk the ban will be lifted?'

'I don't know,' sighed Ricky, who was eating hardly anything. 'Prince Charles is Colonel of the Welsh Guards, which makes it very difficult for him. And there's the security problem.'

'That is a point,' said Alejandro, looking round. 'Where's Angel?'

'Not 'ungry,' said Claudia, trying to force potato purée into little Paolo.

'Not 'ungry, angry. Angel,' he explained to Ricky, 'was an ex-Mirage pilot. He 'ate the English, but when he gets to know Perdita,' Alejandro smiled at her from under the peak of his cap, 'he will forgeeve.'

Perdita, having taken far too much, was now feeding the rest of the steak to the shaggy lurchers who ringed the table, but kept their distance.

'They're so thin,' she protested to Alejandro.

'Raimundo don't feed them. They live on hares and badgers they catch out in the pampas.'

Perdita didn't think she could eat another thing, but the figs in syrup that followed were so delicious she was soon piling on great dollops of cream.

'Angel is stupid,' went on Alejandro. 'The rest of us in Argentina 'ave forgiven you for the Falklands War.'

'Oh good,' said Perdita, brightening up. 'Why is that?'

'Because of Benny Hill,' said Alejandro. 'We love heem, and all those lovely girls with no clothes on. I love Eenglish

236

programmes, *Upper Stairs, Down Stairs*. The only thing I watch else is polo on cable, and we've got a veedeo of last year's Open. I'll show it to you, Reeky.'

'And you can point out all the ponies you've just showed me who allegedly played in it,' said Ricky drily.

Alejandro giggled. 'Some was previous year.'

'Our doctor has tiny plane that was conscripted during the Malvinas War,' said Claudia. 'The military say they want to fly rockets on it, but when they see 'ow small it was, it didn't get called up.'

'All the food parcels people sent us from abroad was stolen by the post office,' said Alejandro.

What heavenly people, thought Perdita. They're so merry and funny.

The spear-shaped leaves of the gum tree were dappling their faces as the sun moved towards the Andes. A dragonfly was bombing the table. Luke pointed out a stork, black and white between the silver trunks. Beyond, the pampas seemed to swim in the midday heat.

'Ow long are you weeth us, Reeky?' asked Claudia, who'd had a secret crush on him in the old days and was appalled to see how grey and tense he looked.

'Probably the day after tomorrow.'

'But you said you'd stay a week,' said Perdita in horror.

'Where are you going next?' asked Luke.

'Palm Springs.'

'That's great,' said Luke. 'My half-sister Bibi's out there. Working in LA. You must call her. She doesn't get out enough. She's on a zero handicap, but she'd play super if she played more.'

'Who's your patron now, Reeky?' asked Alejandro.

'Dancer Maitland,' chipped in Perdita proudly.

Alejandro nearly fell off his seat. All the Mendoza children were roused out of their pallid apathy.

'You get his autograph?'

'You send us records?'

'He numero uno this week.'

'Is he nice? Please breeng 'im 'ere.'

'He's a sweet man,' admitted Ricky. 'But he's very busy, and has difficulty even finding time to stick and ball. You stupid bitch,' he murmured furiously under his breath to Perdita, 'now Alejandro'll quadruple his prices.'

'Please stay, Reeky,' pleaded Claudia. 'You need a holiday. Let us pamper you.'

'Let them pampas you,' said Perdita bitterly.

She loves him, thought Luke. Perdita was very pale now, her skin the parchment colour of her white-blond mane. She'll be like a little palomino when she turns brown, he thought.

'Have a siesta,' Claudia urged her as they'd finished coffee.

'No, I want to look at the ponies with Ricky,' said Perdita, frantic not to miss a minute.

'Just for an hour. We all do,' said Claudia soothingly.

Upstairs, feeling utterly suicidal, Perdita looked round her tiny bare room. The only furniture was a wardrobe, a chest of drawers with no lining paper, a straight-backed wooden chair and a narrow single bed with a carved headboard. There was an overhead light with no lampshade and a bedside lamp on the floor which didn't work. The only colour came from a picture of a gaucho cracking a whip, a tiny red mat and a shocking pink counterpane. She ought to unpack, but she only got as far as getting out Ricky's photograph in its blue silk frame and putting it beside the bed. The thought of all those blonde movie stars in Palm Springs pursuing him made her feel quite sick. She'd gone off Luke since he suggested Ricky ring his sister.

She'd just lie on the bed for a minute. Did she imagine it or did a head of bronze curls pop round the door, and were a pair of peacock-blue eyes gazing at her with implacable hatred? Then the door slammed shut and next moment she was asleep.

24

Waking the next morning, she was outraged that they'd left her to sleep. Luke and Alejandro's three eldest sons had won their match. The teachers had suddenly ended their strike, and the four youngest children had gone back to school. Ricky, exhausted but elated after haggling all night with Alejandro, had bought eight horses.

Perdita, not in the best mood after a cold shower, found him having breakfast.

'You promised to wake me.'

'You needed sleep.'

He poured her some black coffee. Sulkily she added milk and buttered a croissant.

'Nice family,' said Ricky.

'Very,' said Perdita. 'I'm not sure about that Angel. He looks as though he wants to Exocet me.'

'Luke'll look after you,' said Ricky. 'Look, I'm leaving at teatime – catching the eight o'clock flight.'

'You can't,' said Perdita hysterically.

'I've got the horses I need. Luke's going to get them into America. From there we'll fly them to England.'

'But why so early, for Christ's sake?'

'Alejandro's got business in Buenos Aires. He's giving me a lift to the airport.'

Whatever Alejandro's business was in BA, it necessitated a silk shirt, light grey trousers, a jacket hanging from a coathanger in the back of the car, his Herbert Johnson cap and about fifteen pints of Aramis.

Perdita cried unashamedly after they left, fleeing to her bare room and hurling herself down on the pink counterpane. Half an hour later there was a knock on the door.

'Bugger off,' she howled.

It was Luke. 'Poor baby. Feeling homesick?'

'No, Ricky sick,' sobbed Perdita. 'I can't live without him.'

Luke sat down on the bed and put a huge arm round her.

'You'll see him in less than three months.'

'That's a whole school term. I don't *want* it,' she snapped as he handed her a large vodka and tonic, then took such a huge gulp that she nearly choked.

'Isn't Ricky kind of old to play Florizel?' asked Luke.

'Not having a father, I'm only attracted to older men,' said Perdita.

'I used to hero-worship the guy when he played for my father,' said Luke. 'He was awesome. I watched him yesterday. He'll be as good as ever when his elbow heals. He must go to ten.'

'All he's interested in is getting bloody Chessie back.'

'She's not bloody.'

'How's she getting on with your ghastly father?'

'Pretty happy, I guess. Doesn't appear to be in any hurry to quit.'

Perdita sat up, blew her nose and looked at him with red, swollen eyes.

'Jolly odd having a stepmother the same age as you. D'you fancy her?'

'Couldn't help it at first, but we've become friends. Her marrying Dad didn't screw me up like the other two. Red and Bibi have given her hell.'

'Serve her right.'

'She lost a kid,' said Luke reasonably.

'Does she still miss Will?'

'Yeah, but she won't show it.'

'Like Ricky. He's so good at bottling things up, he ought to work in a ketchup factory.'

Luke picked up Ricky's photograph. 'You gotta treat being down here as a chance to learn polo. Meet them halfway and you'll improve out of all recognition. And you'll like it here; it's kinda fun.'

'How come you're so nice?' asked Perdita.

Luke yawned. 'My brother Red's better-looking than me. He gets all the girls – very good for the character. Dinner's about ten, I'll boil up some water so you can have a shower.'

'What time do we get up here?'

'Six o'clock. And on the horses by seven.'

'God!' said Perdita, appalled. 'What else do we have to do?'

'Shift the cattle, work the horses, stick and ball, come back for lunch, an hour's siesta, and you go out like a light I can tell you, then we play chukkas in the afternoon. At least you won't be roped in to build the swimming-pool.'

He left her not much happier. She tried to sleep, but she was desperately nervous about tomorrow. What if she made a complete fool of herself and let Ricky down? At least he wouldn't be here to witness it. She felt twitchy about that vile Angel who hovered shadowy in the background, waiting to perform some dreadful mischief. She started violently at a knock on the door. Frantically wiping her eyes, she went to answer it and found Luke with only a small towel round his waist. For a terrifying moment

Perdita thought he was going to pounce on her. Instead the bull-dog face creased into a huge smile.

'Honey, I am absolutely shit-scared of spiders, and there's the biggest son-of-a-bitch in the shower. Could you possibly remove it for me?'

Giving a scream of laughter, Perdita felt better.

Luke Alderton had been only three years old when Bart dumped his mother for Grace and his first memories were of tears and endless shouting. Grace had proceeded to have two children, Red and Bibi, whom she and Bart adored and spoilt impossibly. Grace, however, tended to ignore Luke when he came to stay, doing her duty without love or warmth. Then his mother had married again, to a PT instructor who beat Luke up so badly that a court ruled he should go and live with Bart full time. Here he had always felt an outsider.

At eighteen, because they wouldn't let him read Polo at Yale, he chucked up any thought of an academic career. Determined to be utterly independent of Bart, he slowly worked his way up, starting as a groom and finally getting his own yard, buying ponies cheap off the race track, or from other players who couldn't get a tune out of them, making them, and selling them on, which he detested because he got so fond of them. Invariably riding green ponies, his handicap at six was lower than it should have been. He didn't have the natural ability of his brother, Red, but he was bigger and stronger. You didn't want to be in the way when Luke hit the ball.

Because he'd missed out on higher education, and because he could seldom afford to go out on the town with the other players, he spent his evenings listening to music and devouring the classics. On long journeys in the lorry he'd keep the rest of the team entertained reciting great screeds of poetry, Longfellow, Macaulay, whole scenes from Shakespeare, now even bits of *Martin Fierro*, in an 'orrible accent.

All the Argentines adored him and nicknamed him Señor Gracias because he was so grateful for the smallest favour. It was the same in the States. He was always in work because he was cheerful, absolutely straight and very good company. But although he smiled in the face of the direst provocation, underneath he was as determined as Ricky to go to ten.

After such a lousy start in life, and not a penny of the Alderton millions, people often expressed amazement that he was so unchippy. The answer was always the same. 'There's nothing to be gained from blaming your background or other people. You've got to get out and help yourself.'

A second after Perdita fell asleep, it seemed Luke was banging on the door telling her to get up and to wear a sweater as it was cold first thing. Out in the yard, Alejandro had turned from the charming rogue of yesterday into a roaring tyrant, bellowing instructions to all the boys. In the corral the ponies waited, mostly chestnut, all young and timid, ducking nervously behind each other to avoid being caught. When Alejandro yelled at Perdita to tack up a little chestnut gelding, she was so nervous she could hardly do up the throat lash or adjust the stirrups. Once up, she felt she was straddling an eel. Every male from the neighbouring *estancias*, except Luke, who was off moving the cattle, seemed to be gathered round the paddock to watch her as she set off in the milky, misty morning light towards a row of poplar trees. Alejandro shouted after her to do turns at the canter.

'I'll show them,' she thought, shoving her nose in the air. 'Don't jibe at me, Argentina.'

Reaching the middle of the field, she laid the nearside rein on the chestnut's neck to tell him to go right. Instantly he did a lightning U-turn and set out back to the stables, leaving Perdita swearing on the stone-hard ground while all the onlookers roared with laughter and Alejandro shouted in broken English at her. She had three more falls before she and a handful of other players started stick and balling. She was just getting used to the chestnut when Alejandro moved her on to a dark brown mare who, when it wasn't bucking, shied at the ball, and then on to another chestnut, whom she had great difficulty in holding.

She was also staggered by how energetically the Argentines played, hitting balls up in the air, juggling and tapping them, twisting, turning and stopping, followed by Ferrari bursts of acceleration before circling again. Then they did the whole thing all over again without stirrups, and all the time talking and shouting to one another. She was also aware of Angel, the Brit-hater, who hadn't once eaten at the same table as her since she arrived, who was now riding harder and turning faster than any of the others, urging his pony on with great pelvic thrusts. It seemed he was deliberately galloping very close past her to upset her chestnut mare, who kept taking off into the pampas.

She had fallen off twice more and ridden twelve different ponies by lunchtime and was so tired she could hardly eat. Although Luke translated the whole time for her, she felt desperately isolated and sick with longing for Ricky. He must have nearly reached Palm Springs by now.

Tugged out of her siesta like a back tooth, she staggered groggily out to the yard. The sun was shining platinum rather than gold now, and beating down on her head. To her intense humiliation, Luke, Angel, Alejandro, three of Alejandro's sons, and two of their friends who'd come to lunch were playing on one pitch while Perdita had been put on another with Alejandro's three younger sons and four of their cousins – none of them a day over twelve.

'Talk about going back to playgroup,' snarled Perdita.

The ponies were tied up in the shade to the branches of a row of gum trees which divided the two pitches. Gulls flapped around uttering their strange cry of 'Tero, Tero', and swooping down to scavenge whenever play moved on. A strong lemon smell, from a local herb known as black branch, hung on the hot steamy air. The mosquitoes went to work on any available flesh. After the throw-in the ball came out miraculously in Perdita's direction.

Now I'll show them, she thought, lifting her stick for a flawless offside drive. Next second she gave a scream of rage as she was hooked by an eleven-year-old cousin, who then proceeded to whip the ball away down field. One of Alejandro's sons playing back rode him off for the backhand and hit it up the field to his brother who dribbled it a few yards, then sliced it to Perdita. Instantly an eleven-year-old cousin pounced on her, shielding her from the ball and riding her off.

All of them played with such ferocious energy and skill that, for the next nightmarish seven minutes, she didn't touch the ball.

'*Faulazo*,' they yelled, as they teased her into crossing in front of them.

'*Dejala*,' they yelled as she rode in for the big swipe and missed it.

'*Hombre, hombre, hombre*,' they chorused, urging her to take her man, and '*Que lenta*,' they screamed when she failed to catch up with her number four, and he went up the field and scored to loud cheers. A huge cow bell was rung at the end of the chukka, but the boys went on playing.

'Perdita,' yelled Alejandro, 'change the horse.'

'Better change the rider,' said Perdita, fighting back the tears. She was sore all over, out of breath, pouring with sweat, and there were three more chukkas to go. 'I don't want to play with kids,' she screamed at Luke. 'They're all laughing at me.'

'Not at you,' said Luke soothingly, while saddling up a black mare with a white star for her. 'They always talk and joke among themselves. You're over-reacting. This pony's much easier. She follows the ball and positions herself for every shot. Just leave it to her.'

Perdita was settling down and had even hit a respectable forehand which only just missed the goal when Alejandro, out of some devilry, swopped one of his sons and a cousin for Luke and Angel.

Angel proceeded to put on an incredible display of histrionics, peacock-blue eyes flashing, nostrils flaring above his furiously pouting mouth, as he shouted and swore at Alejandro.

'What's he saying?' Perdita asked Alejandro's twelve year old, who blushed. 'He say he no want to play with Eeenglish – er – scum.'

'Charming,' snapped Perdita.

'*Choto*,' Angel swore at her as he galloped past to defend his goal and, however much Luke set up shots for her, Angel rode her off. Then, after a whispered word with one of the cousins, Angel and he galloped up on either side of her and neatly lifted her off the little black mare.

'Bastards,' howled Perdita, sitting on the painfully hard ground, and bashing it with her stick, 'fucking bastards.'

'No understand Eeenglish,' mocked Angel. 'Go back home,' and launched into a stream of expletives in Spanish. Perdita replied in equally basic English.

Next minute Luke had cantered up with Perdita's black pony. 'I'm not going to translate for either of you,' he said softly. Then, turning furiously on Angel, 'For Chrissake, pack it in.'

Five minutes later Luke blocked a brilliant goal from the youngest cousin and cleared. Christ, he really can smite the ball almost the length of the pitch, marvelled Perdita. Angel, racing towards the enemy goal, tried to intercept with an air shot. Missing, he swung his pony round in pursuit, and when it didn't turn quickly enough, clouted it very hard round the head with his stick. In a flash Perdita closed on him and bashed him across the knuckles with her stick.

'You triple bastard! I'll report you to the RSPCA.'

Turning, realizing it was Perdita, Angel gave a howl of rage and set off in pursuit. So blackly venomous was his expression that Perdita fled towards the next pitch, scattering the polo balls which lay like a hatch of goose eggs near the goal posts. Angel, on a faster pony and using his whip, had nearly caught her up when Luke thundered up and rode him off. Such was the force of the bump that Angel's horse crashed to the ground, temporarily winded.

Leaping to his feet, Angel charged Luke, about to drag him off his horse.

'I wouldn't,' said Luke raising his stick. 'Stop behaving like a two year old. She's a woman.'

'She's a beetch, and English beetch, like Margaret Thatcher,' growled Angel. 'I keel her when I catch her.'

'You've been winding her up all day,' shouted Luke. 'D'you want to put her off completely?'

'Yes,' hissed Angel, looking at his bleeding knuckles. 'Then she'll go home for good.'

For a second they glared at each other. Then Angel vaulted back on to his pony, which had just tottered groggily to its feet, and galloped back to the stables.

Back in her room, Perdita fell on her bed, too despairing and exhausted even to cry. She'd been a disaster and let Ricky down. They'd pack her back to England.

There was a knock on the door. It was Luke again.

'Baby, it's OK.' He took her in his arms.

'Ouch,' grumbled Perdita. 'You've got hands like sandpaper.'

'To rub off all your rough edges,' said Luke.

'I made such an idiot of myself. Those were children. The standard is ludicrous. I'll never cope.'

'Hush, hush,' said Luke. 'Argentines learn polo like a language. Those boys have been playing with a short mallet since they were two. By the time they're ten or eleven they're on a six handicap. Look, you're jet lagged. You couldn't understand what they were saying. There's hours till dinner. Let's go into General Piran and I'll buy you a drink.'

It was so hot that Perdita would have liked to have worn shorts or a dress, but her mosquito bites had come up in huge red bumps and were oozing and itching like mad, so she settled for her pale pink jeans and a dark blue shirt. A huge yellow sun was gilding the puddles and turning the poplars the colour of lemon sherbets. A cloud like a fluffy white crocodile basked at the bottom of the vast open fan of fading turquoise sky. Luke drove slowly to avoid the potholes, just two thumbs on the steering wheel.

'I had one hell of a hassle when I first came out. I was used to riding with my reins hanging in festoons. Alejandro and his son all stop horses with five-inch curbs and send them on with spurs about the same length. I kept being carted all the way to Buenos Aires.'

Perdita stared moodily at the horizon.

'You'll be playing in matches soon. You'll enjoy that. You can't go back to England without taking some Argentine silver.'

'Some hope!'

To distract Perdita's attention from a terrified stray dog that was cringing on the right of the road, Luke pointed out three tumbledown houses on the left.

'Known as Death Row. In that house lived a bricklayer who murdered the baker because he thought he'd stolen one of his pigs. Then four brothers turned up in a bus and killed three brothers who lived in that house next door. Then the grocer who lived in the third house shot himself.'

'If you hadn't bumped that sodding Angel there'd have been another murder this afternoon,' said Perdita sulkily.

'What a dinky little country this is. What a dump,' she added as they entered the village.

Luke pointed out the little white church, with its red corrugated roof, that was always having its windows broken by the football pitch next door.

'At least it provides air-conditioning in summer,' he went on. 'And that's the gas station. The prettiest girl works there. Angel's dating her and spends his time filling up Alejandro's truck. The gasoline bill at the end of the month is going to be something else!' He shook with laughter.

'Does he put draw reins and a five-inch curb on her?' spat Perdita. 'I'm surprised he didn't break that pony's jaw this afternoon.'

Because of the mosquitoes they sat inside the bar.

'Señor Gracias, *buenas noches*,' said the owner as he took Luke's order for a vodka and tonic and a Bourbon.

'I'll pay for it,' said Perdita, defiantly brandishing a $100 bill. She was in no mood to accept charity from anyone. 'How much is this worth?'

'About fifteen dollars. Put it away.'

'D'you want water?' asked Perdita, reaching for the jug on the bar counter.

Luke grinned and shook his head. 'I'm a tidy person, I like my whisky neat.'

On the wall was a gaudy oil painting of a bull pouring blood with pics sticking out of it like a pincushion. A smirking matador, with a pink satin bottom even tighter and more uppity than Angel's, was lifting his jewelled sword for the kill.

'God, they're cruel. They never speak to their ponies except to curse them.'

'They're different from us,' said Luke. 'If Americans – and particularly the Brits – have a horse or a dog that behaves badly – they admit the fact, and rather celebrate and make a joke of it, right? Whereas to an Argentine, it's a matter of pride never to have a horse or dog that's anything less than perfect. They can't understand anyone not minding losing and they want to shine individually. My buzz is being on a team. I don't give a shit about not scoring goals. If I've set up the play that leads to goals, that's OK by me.'

'You're too fucking Christ-like,' snapped Perdita. 'You get no prizes for coming second.'

Luke picked up his whisky, his freckled hand was so big you could hardly see the glass. He didn't tell her it broke his heart every time the Argentines hurt a horse or he saw a terrified stray dog racing by the side of the road. He knew the cruelty she was going to witness over the next three months would be agony for her because, for some reason, she trusted animals far more than humans, but, like a nurse looking after animals in a vivisection clinic, he couldn't prevent her pain, only alleviate it as much as possible.

'There's certainly a degree of roughness with horses,' he admitted. 'The Argies have so many, they can afford to dispense with them. When Red and I were kids we had races jumping on ponies in the fields and galloping them round a tree and back without a bridle. We could never do that with Argentine ponies: they just bolted in terror. The Argentines break them by fear and pain, but they get results. Look at those kids today.'

'Look at Angel clouting that sweet little mare with his stick – the fucker.'

She was paler than ever and, Luke noticed, that in that shirt, her eyes were more navy blue than black.

'He's OK Angel,' he said, 'Argentine saying – never judge a man until you have walked two moons in his shoes.'

'Well, he needn't take it out on me. I wasn't part of the bloody task force.'

Back in his bare, little room, Angel lay on his bed smoking one cigarette from another. He should have been with the girl from the petrol station half an hour ago, but he was too eaten up with jealousy that his dear *amigo*, Luke, had taken that white-haired she-devil out for a drink.

On the wall was a painting of a Mirage wheeling away from a flaming British aircraft carrier, with the sea and sky incarnadined by the blaze. On the chest of drawers was a photograph of his elder brother Pedro in uniform, his pale patrician face the image of Angel's, except for a black moustache. There were also photographs of his weak and charming father, who had read *Pravda* and the *Daily Telegraph* every morning, and his beautiful feckless mother, who'd run off with an Italian and now lived in some *palazzo* in Rome, and of the huge house in which he'd been brought up.

Besides these photographs were Pedro's polo helmet, which now had a map of the Malvinas stamped on the front (which Angel always wore in matches), and a jar of earth he'd dug up from the Islands on the day he'd been sent home as a prisoner of war.

The Solis de Gonzales family, eight-generation Irish intermarried with Spanish, were immensely rich. Angel had had a magical childhood, bucking the system at the smart Buenos Aires boys' school of Champagnat and living during the termtime in a large house in the Avenidad del Libertador. Let loose on the family *estancia* during the holidays, he and Pedro had played cops and robbers on horses, and later polo with his cousins, who all came from large houses near by.

In their teens Angel and Pedro had hung around the polo grounds, waiting for players to fall off, so they could substitute for them. Angel had never had a lesson; he played as naturally as he walked.

Angel's branch of the Solis de Gonzales, however, were no good at looking after their business affairs. His father, separated from his mother, lived six months of the year in Paris. Every so often the camp manager would telephone from the *estancia*: 'We have no more money.'

'Then sell some land,' Angel's father would say, and go back to his latest mistress or the gambling tables or the racecourse at Longchamps. He never took care of the land, nor did he put anything back.

Denied parents for so much of the year, Angel had idolized Pedro. On the polo field they had been dynamite and almost telepathetic in anticipating each other's moves. But there had been no question of them taking up polo professionally. Polo was all right as a hobby, but for a living, as Angel's father, who prided himself on his English had pointed out, it was distinctly 'Non-U'.

He disapproved almost as much when Pedro, who was mad about flying, but unable to afford a plane, had joined the air force in the late seventies to be followed, two years later, by Angel. Disapproval turned to horror when both boys set off in their Mirages for the Falklands. Both were brilliant pilots, having the same reckless flamboyant courage and ability to get the last ounce out of their ancient machines in the air as their ponies on the field.

A fortnight after Pedro's plane plunged flaming into the sea, Angel was shot down behind British lines and escaped with a smashed kneecap and concussion. When he came round, he was interrogated by one particularly phlegmatic, poker-faced Guards Officer, a polo player who spoke fluent Spanish. To someone as proud as Angel, this, and the result of the war, had been the ultimate humiliation. But, even knowing how strong the British now were, he would give up polo tomorrow and climb back into his cockpit and resume the attack on Port Stanley. Returning home with the other prisoners of war, he found his father had died of a heart attack.

It is Argentine law that when a man dies his estate must be divided equally between his children. Angel's father had inherited 4,000 acres, but had sold off so much that only 800 acres were left for Angel and his three sisters. The sisters, who had all married well, were unconcerned that Angel, with only 200 acres of grazing land in the middle of his rich cousins' estates, had been left to pay his father's debts. His mother, happy with her Italian, was not interested. His grandmother, living in luxury in the Plaza Hotel in Buenos Aires and grumbling because she had to wash her own stockings, claimed she had no money even to pay her own bills.

In despair, Angel had gone to his rich cousins, pleading that unless they helped him out he would be forced to sell the land to an outsider, a property developer who wanted to build houses there. The rich cousins, thinking he was bluffing, ignored him; then, when he sold the land, they were absolutely furious and banished him from their houses.

Angel was now desperately trying to make his way as a professional polo player. His secret ambition was for the Argentine ban to be lifted so he could get to England and avenge Pedro's death by taking out the English and especially one poker-faced Guards Officer.

Alejandro wouldn't help him. He was jealous of new blood, particularly when it was as blue as Angel's, but Luke, who knew how hard it was to get established, had recognized Angel's talent. Before Perdita arrived he and

Angel had spent hours talking in the evenings trying to improve each other's English and Spanish. Luke realized that, beneath his corroding bitterness and pyrotechnic bursts of Latin temperament, Angel was by nature merry, with a kind heart and an even greater sense of the ridiculous. The latter had for the moment deserted him. The Brits had taken Pedro, now this blonde witch had stolen Luke. Angel was biding his time.

25

Perdita refused to admit it, but she was terribly homesick. There was no post nor telephone because of the strike, and she was tormented by fantasies of Ricky being ridden off by starlets in Palm Springs. Used to smothering any animal she met with love, she felt dreadfully deprived when the Argentine ponies flinched away from her. Only Raimundo's lurchers responded when she combed the burrs out of their coats and fed them bits of meat.

Visiting players, Raimundo, the grooms and Alejandro looked at her with ill-concealed lust, but her dead-pan hauteur and Señor Gracias' large, looming presence kept them at bay. Angel smouldered at a distance, losing no chance to bitch her up. She was aware that none of the men except Luke took her seriously as a player.

Claudia was enchanting, endlessly kind and sympathetic, but, beneath her pre-occupation with her children, Perdita sensed a deep sadness. Her daughters were also charming with their big dark eyes and exuberantly glossy hair and breasts rising like pomegranates, and they giggled in amazed delight when Perdita swore and yelled at the grooms and even screamed at their father. Heavy chaperonage, too, seemed to enhance their value, like jewellery locked in glass cases rather than scrambled in trays on the counter. But to Perdita they appeared curiously passive, sitting and waiting for some man to make them unhappy.

Luke was her salvation. The Argentine night came down like a blind, but, when it was too dark to ride, he seldom took a siesta, struggling instead through *Martin Fierro*, *Don Quixote*, or *El Cid* with the aid of a Spanish dictionary, or listening to music, mostly Mozart. But he was always prepared to turn off the tape and listen to her ranting on about how she missed Ricky and how bloody the Argentines were being to her and to their horses. An inspired listener, he seldom volunteered information about himself.

'Have you got a girlfriend?' she asked him once.

'Yeah.'

'Are you going to marry her?'

'Nope.'

'Why not?'

'Not in love with her, I guess. There's only one reason to get married, because you can't not. And I've seen too much unhappiness caused by broken marriages. I want mine to stick.'

A few weeks later Perdita sat under a jacaranda tree which was scattering purply-blue petals all over the parched brown ground. At least the drought had driven off the mosquitoes.

'Darling Ricky,' she wrote, 'David Waterlane's been here today. He brought a letter from Mum. He's going on to New York, and promises to post this for me. He bought four ponies, all of which Alejandro swore played in the final of last year's Open. That makes over fifty ponies he's sold this year that he claims took part. He must have changed ponies an awful lot. How are you getting on? Have you been signed up to star in a film yet? Has Luke's bloody sister been in touch with you? Do you miss me a bit? I think I'm getting a bit better at polo. There is a beautiful little iron-grey mare here that Alejandro has frightened out of her wits and says is too wet for polo. I wish you'd bought her, I think she's brilliant. If you send me the money, I think we could get her for $1,000.

'Christ, the Argentines are cruel. Last week they started breaking the wild three year olds and goodness, Raimundo and the grooms adored it, treating it like some macho game. Did you realize they drive the ponies into a corral, then tie them to a stake in the burning sun for five days with no food or water? Alejandro caught me stealing out to water them the first night. We had a frightful row. He said the English were fine ones to bang on about cruelty when they sent little boys off to boarding school when they were eight. I said it had done Eddie a power of good. Anyway after that he put Raimundo on guard with a gun. I wouldn't mind being shot, but I'm sure

252

Raimundo would insist on raping me first. He's such a lech.

'Anyway on the sixth day, it's really horrific. I came back from moving the cows, and found Raimundo and his merry men engaged in breaking proper. Five of them to one desperately weakened pony with sunken eyes and ribs you could play tunes on – lassoing it with weighted thongs, and pulling it over and over on the desperately hard ground, until it was crapping everywhere in terror. God, I loathe Alejandro for allowing it.

'Finally on the seventh day, I thought that, being Catholic, they'd rest, but still unfed and unwatered, each pony was blindfolded and tacked up, and Raimundo got on each one's back, and whipped it and whipped it out into the pampas, until the pony's spirit was completely broken, and it'll never argue with man again. How can any horse fail to be screwed up, when its first contact with man is fifth degree burns, starvation, and flagellation? No wonder they're terrified.

'I kicked Raimundo in the shins – there was a bit of a row. Alejandro wouldn't let me stick and ball for a week. And it's not just the animals they're cruel to. Claudia was crying the other morning and I caught Luke hugging her. He said he was comforting her. Utterly bloody Alejandro has a mistress in BA. He went to see her that day he took you to the airport. According to Luke, Argentine men feel they've failed to demonstrate their virility unless they have a mistress, and that only their wives get married, they remain single. Christ, what an attitude, just like Rupert Campbell-Black's when he was married.

'I hate Argentine men, particularly that Angel. All they're interested in is screwing and thumb-screwing. And as there isn't an Inquisition any more, they take it out on the horses. If Luke wasn't here, I'd go crackers. God, he's nice, and he really works at his polo, every evening, lining up ball after ball, and practising penalties.

'He's a brilliant teacher too. Alejandro gets pissed off and shouts if you don't do the right thing straight away. Luke tells you what to do all the time, but quietly, and he never loses his temper, except if he thinks you're not trying.

'Please, please write. I hope your elbow's better now. Think of me sometimes. I must go, as David W is leaving in half an hour. All my love, Perdita.'

Having handed over her letter and waved goodbye, Perdita wandered down to the stables. The sun, which had burnt the stick-and-ball field and the pitches to a dusty liver chestnut, had now set, but it was still impossibly hot. She could hear whoops of laughter. What devilish torture had Raimundo dreamed up now? Running through the orange grove, which already had little green oranges on, past the chickens, she froze with horror. In the middle of the yard the little pony Alejandro regarded as useless stood quivering with terror.

Her iron-grey coat was black with sweat and dust, her thin sides heaving, her eyes rolling. Umberto, Alejandro's laziest groom, was holding tightly on to her, while Raimundo, who was wearing a leather apron to protect his gaucho pants, his little eyes glinting with pleasure and cruelty, was attaching a long lead rope to her headcollar. He then took the rope through her front and back legs and tied it firmly to the back bumper of the Mercedes, which Angel had backed into the yard. Angel was now sitting in the driving seat, a fag hanging out of his sulky mouth, revving up the engine.

'What the hell's going on?' exploded Perdita.

Angel looked round. 'Your little darling won't back,' he sneered. 'This lesson should teach 'er,' and he revved the engine even more loudly.

'Right,' yelled Raimundo.

Umberto leapt clear, the grey pony made a bolt for freedom.

'Stop it,' screamed Perdita, making a lunge at Angel. But she was too late. He had rammed his foot down on the accelerator, the Mercedes shot forward, the little grey's neck jerked frantically and she cartwheeled violently in the air crashing to the ground, to be dragged ten feet before Angel braked.

The surrounding grooms roared with laughter and cheered. Picking his way over the diarrhoea, which had splattered all over the ground and avoiding the frantically flailing hooves of the shocked, utterly terrified, pony, Raimundo grasped her headcollar and, aided by Umberto and the other grooms, yanked her to her feet. Four of them hung on to her. She made a frantic leap to shake them off, as they lifted her back and front nearside feet over the rope and positioned her with her back to the revving Mercedes again.

'Three or four goes should make up the mind for her,' said Raimundo evilly, as Perdita picked herself up off the dusty ground.

Angel crouched over the wheel. That should teach that stuck-up bitch to fall in love with ponies. He wished it were Perdita at the end of the rope, he'd like to see her crashing to the ground over and over again. But with her, he'd keep on driving.

Raimundo was taking his time. Angel glanced round and gave a shout of warning. Too late – Perdita, her face ashen, her black eyes blazing, had a pitchfork poised a foot from Raimundo's capacious buttocks. Next second she had plunged it into them.

Giving a bellow of pain and rage, Raimundo jumped a foot in the air and let go of the pony, who took off, jerking to a halt as the slack of the rope ran out.

'Leave her alone, you bastard, or I'll kebab you,' screamed Perdita.

All the grooms doubled up with laughter. Swinging round in a fury, Raimundo was about to leap on Perdita when she brandished the fork in his face.

'D'you want your eyes gouged out, you fucking sadist? Untie that pony.'

Raimundo's sallow face had turned a dark red.

'*La puta que te pario*,' he spat at her, but backed away as the evil-looking prongs stroked his eyelashes.

'Get her off me,' he bellowed at the other grooms. But, enjoying the sport too much, they continued to barrack and laugh.

'Olé,' shouted Umberto.

Then, out of the corner of her eye, Perdita saw Angel approaching. There was murder in his eyes; the beautiful pouting mouth had disappeared completely.

'Don't you come near me,' hissed Perdita, rage driving out all fear, flickering the pitchfork like an adder's tongue between him and Raimundo. 'No wonder you lost the Falklands War. Bullies are always cowards. You run away from real men, so you take it out on horses, you lousy Latin creeps.'

Clenching his fists, rigid with rage, Angel advanced on her, translating what she had said for the others. Perhaps she had better make a bolt for it.

'I keel you, English beetch.' Angel's grey shirt was touching the pitchfork now.

Perdita had drawn it back to ram it into him when suddenly she found her arms gripped from behind.

'Drop,' thundered Luke.

'Fuck off,' screamed Perdita. 'Don't bloody interfere.'

'Drop!' Luke tightened his grip on her and the pitchfork clattered to the ground.

'That hurt,' shouted Perdita. 'Are you on those bastards' side?'

Just as Angel was about to leap on her, Luke picked her up and carried her yelling into the house. Desperately she kicked backwards like a buck rabbit, trying to get him in the groin.

'Let me go, put me down,' and when he wouldn't, she tried to plunge her teeth into his arms which were clamped round her like steel bands. The next second he had put her under the shower and turned on the cold tap. For once it decided not to have cystitis and gushed out like the Victoria Falls funnelled through a hose pipe.

'Had enough?' he said fifteen seconds later.

Gasping, choking, spluttering, she struggled to escape.

'Are you going to behave yourself?' He pulled her away from the driving jet of water.

'No,' screamed Perdita, aiming a kick at his shins. 'Now I know how Enid Coley felt.'

'Well, go back under again.'

Her drenched hair stranded her face, her pale lilac dress clung to her body, her eyelashes divided like a starfish as he pulled her out a second time. As she opened her mouth to shriek, he grabbed a green towel hanging over the shower rail and slapped it over her mouth.

'Pack it in,' he said sharply. 'D'you want to get sent home?'

'I don't care,' mumbled Perdita, trying to bite him through the towel. 'Bastards, how can you stand there and not mind?'

'Of course I mind, but we're here to learn, Miss McEnroe.'

'Don't call me that, you great jerk,' said Perdita, hammering her fists against his chest, which was as hard as the ground outside. 'They're going to break that pony's leg.'

256

'Or teach it to rein back,' said Luke. He drew back the dingy plastic curtains covering the small window overlooking the yard.

'Angel's on her back now, and she's reining back pretty good. Their methods are cruel, but they get results.'

'I hate this bloody country,' hissed Perdita.

Luke made an attempt at levity. 'There are good things about it. Polo boots are three times cheaper than they are in the UK.'

'Oh, shut up.' Out of the window, she could see a huge pink moon, like the inside of a guava, climbing out of the gum trees.

'Even the moon's blushing at the horrible way they treat ponies,' she snarled. 'Why's it that stupid colour anyway?'

'Catching the last of the sun's rays,' said Luke. 'Sun's rising in the East now; gone to shine on your Mom.'

Suddenly Perdita had a vision of Daisy, kind, scatty, busty, in her awful clothes, constantly making concessions, whom she hadn't written to since she'd arrived. Glaring at Luke, she burst into tears.

'Hush, honey, hush, I hate it too,' he murmured, enfolding her in his arms and stroking her sopping hair. 'I know it's awful. I guess I wanta play polo better so I can beat the shit out of them on the field.'

One moment she was sobbing her heart out, then, lulled by the bearlike warmth of his chest and the comforting shelter of his great arms and shoulders, she had fallen asleep like a child. Gazing down, Luke thought how beautiful she was despite the tear-stains and the swollen eyelids. She hardly stirred as he pulled off her lilac dress and carried her in her bra and pants into her bedroom. Laying her gently on the bed, he removed the dark red blanket from his bed and put it over her.

Perdita woke at two in the morning. Slowly the events of the previous evening re-assembled themselves. Had it been a nightmare? No, her bra and pants were still wet. Luke must have put her to bed.

Oblivious of any guards, she stole downstairs. Outside, huge stars blazed like shaggy white chrysanthemums; the moon had stopped blushing and was now flooding the pampas with ghostly silver light. A warm breeze ruffled the leaves of the gum trees, which cast a thousand ebony shadows on the burnt dusty yard, which was now palest grey instead of brown. She could hear the occasional snort and stamp of a pony, then jumped out of her skin, as something cold and snakelike was thrust into her hand. It was the wet nose of one of Raimundo's shaggy lurchers, who was frantically waving her long crooked tail.

'Sweet thing,' Perdita crouched beside her, stroking her rough fur, as the bitch writhed against her in delight. Both jumped as a great snore rent the air. Umberto, tonight's guard, was slumped against the bottom of a tree, an empty bottle at his feet.

Now was her chance. Out in the corral, tied so tight to the big stake in the centre that the Argentines call a *palemque* that she couldn't even move her head, was the little grey pony.

'You poor little duck,' said Perdita gently.

Nearly breaking her neck, the pony pulled away in panic, the whites of her eyes glinting in the moonlight, coat curled with dried sweat like an Irish Water Spaniel.

At first, when Perdita held out the bucket, she was too frozen with fear to drink. But when her muzzle was dunked in the water almost over her nostrils, the temptation became too much. Sucking in great drafts, she drained one bucket and then half another.

Watching her fondly, Perdita was reminded of Fresco. If only she could jump on her back and not stop galloping until she got to Ricky and Palm Springs. As she laid her hand on the little mare's neck, she quivered violently, but didn't move away.

'I'm going to call you Tero,' she whispered, 'because you and I are going to fly away from this hellhole.'

Loosening the rope so the mare's nose could reach the ground, she left her with a pile of hay.

Next morning the post strike ended, bringing five letters from Daisy, none of which Perdita opened. She was in a black gloom because not even a postcard had arrived from Ricky.

Alejandro, having been out on the bat the night before, returned at breakfast time with the pallor and red eyes of a white rat. He was then thrown into a frenzy by a letter announcing the impending arrival of Lando Medici, the richest of American patrons who always paid for ponies in readies out of a Gladstone bag.

Soon Alejandro was venting his hangover on all the staff, yelling at them to tidy up the place and all the ponies.

'Where's Raimundo?' he shouted at a wincing Umberto.

'He sick,' said Umberto.

'Well, get him up.'

'What's the matter with him?' demanded Perdita, who was busy trimming the hairy fetlocks of a gelding that resembled a Clydesdale more than a polo pony.

Just for a second Umberto forgot his own hangover. 'Señor Gracias give heem the eye black.'

'He what?' gasped Perdita.

'Raimundo was in the bar with his friends last night. Señor Gracias come in and talk to eem very quietly, then he heet him across the room. Everyone cheer. They no like Raimundo – very hard man.'

'What did Raimundo do?' asked Perdita in awe.

'He run away,' said Umberto with a grin. 'He leave very quick. Señor Gracias – how you say? – too beeg to tango with. Angel was in the bar too. Upchatting girl from the gas station. Señor Gracias turned towards him and Angel ran away too – all down the road like Carl Lewis. He was very frightened. He not drive car tied to pony again in an 'urry.'

Later Perdita cornered Luke. He looked tired and his eyes were bloodshot from the dust.

'I thought we were here to learn not to criticize,' she said sternly. Then that wonderful once-a-year smile split her face in two. 'You have definitely won the Man of the Macho Award.'

Standing on tiptoe, she kissed him on the cheek. Luke blushed beneath his freckles and his heart jumped several beats. It's only because there's a dearth of available women out here, he told himself sternly.

Alejandro, fed up with Raimundo's laziness and his exorbitant whining demands, was put in such a good mood when he saw the black eye that he agreed that Perdita could take over the breaking of little Tero.

'She no good for polo, too cheeken, but eef you want to waste your time.'

259

26

Luke had temporarily routed Raimundo and Angel, but
their animosity towards Perdita, if less overt, was in no way
abated. To give Perdita a break, Luke took her away the
following Saturday to see a high goal match at the famous
Hurlingham Club which left her speechless with wonder,
then on to Buenos Aires to an English production of *The
Merchant of Venice* throughout most of which she slept.

Her only comments at dinner afterwards as she gorged
herself on tournedos, raspberries and cream and St Emilion
were that Shylock was almost as beady about money as
Alejandro and that Bassanio was a wimp.

'Portia'd have done much better with that suitor who
talked about his horse all the time. At least he'd have given
her some decent ponies.'

Luke, who knew the play backwards, had been moved
to tears by the moonlit love scene between Lorenzo and
Jessica. A lemon-yellow half-moon was hanging overhead
as he and Perdita left the restaurant. But any hope he might
have had of sliding his arm round her and trying a tentative
first kiss on the drive home was scotched when she fell
asleep the moment she got into the car.

Her white dress had fallen off the shoulder nearest
him, her skirt was rucked up to mid-thigh, her hair
rippled silver. With her scornful mouth softened by sleep
and pale eyelids hiding her furious eyes, she looked as
vulnerable as she did desirable. Wracked with longing,
Luke drove through the grey lunar landscape, only broken
by occasional white towns or ebony clumps of trees.

Up at five and sleeping badly of late, Luke kept his mind
off Perdita and himself awake on the long straight roads,
as he had done so often in the past, by concentrating on a
particular horse. This time it was Maldita, a grey mare who
had slipped into the yard already broken as part of a job lot
a few weeks ago.

Alejandro was allergic to greys, particularly the whiter
ones. His father had been paralysed by a fall from a white
stallion. On the one recent occasion when the Mendoza
family had got near winning the Argentine Open, it had

been on a grey mare that Alejandro had missed the clinching penalty. His phobia had spread to his grooms when Raimundo's even crueller predecessor had broken the leg of a grey filly, hurling it to the ground for branding, and the following day he had died of snake bite. Whenever they passed a grey on the road, the grooms crossed themselves.

The iron grey, Tero, got by because her coat was almost black, but Maldita was so dazzlingly white, except for a sprinkling of rust-brown freckles on her belly, that she looked as though she'd been through the car wash. At fourteen hands she was on the small side for polo, with a lovely intelligent head, wide-apart dark eyes, clean legs and a smooth, effortless stride. Unfortunately she was as bitchy as she was beautiful, lashing out with teeth and hooves at any human who came near her, and bucking them off if they tried to get on her back. Even when Raimundo strapped one of her back legs to her belly to stop her kicking, she struck out with the other leg and, crashing to the ground, laid about her with her front legs and teeth.

Alejandro was all for putting a bullet through this she-devil's head and dispatching her to the nearest abattoir. Luke, however, who was a genius with difficult horses, begged to be allowed to have a crack at her.

He had begun by putting Maldita in a stable with no straw and taking water and feed to her every eight hours, then, when she went for him, immediately removing them. After twenty-four hours she was so hungry that she dived her pale pink nose into the bucket instead of at him. Two days later she allowed him to stand in her stable while she ate. Starving her until the next evening, he coaxed her with pony nuts into a stall which Raimundo used for branding and saddling bigger horses, which was so narrow she couldn't turn round. Tying her lead rope so tightly she couldn't move her head, Luke had climbed up and approached her from above. Talking softly the whole time, he slowly ran his hands over her, caressing, gentling and scratching up and down her mane where once her mother would have lovingly nibbled her, then progressing to her back and flanks. After the first minutes of trembling outrage, Maldita had stopped behaving as though his fingers were red-hot pokers and reacted almost voluptuously to his touch. Luke wished Perdita were as responsive. At the end of half an hour, back in her box, he rewarded her with hay and water.

After a week of such treatment, he mounted her, sending her into the same orgy of bucking that had dislodged the grooms and all the Mendoza boys. Finding she couldn't unseat him, she paused for breath, anticipating her next devilry. She was so small, and Luke so long in the leg, he looked like some father riding a seaside donkey to amuse his children.

'You won't need a mallet on that one,' shouted Alejandro. 'You can kick the ball with your feet, or if you miss, that beetch will kick it for you.'

Unnerved by Alejandro's great roar of laughter, Maldita had taken off into the pampas, somehow miraculously missing rabbit holes and fallen logs as she hurtled along. Luke sat still and gave her her head, amazed that the more she warmed up, the faster she went, staggered by the distance she could carry his 190-pound bulk in the burning sun.

After nearly four miles she ran into the river that bordered Alejandro's land, which was so deep she was forced to swim. On the opposite bank, Luke rolled off her back and lay on the grass. The heaving mare glared back at him, too exhausted to move. Afterwards he hacked her quietly home and was further amazed that she responded to his legs and hands and had the perfect mouth and balance of a made polo pony. It didn't stop her lashing out at him with her teeth and back legs as he unsaddled her, but he felt he was making progress and, the next day, stick and balling her he found she was a natural. In her dark-eyed pallor and arrogant bloody-mindedness, she reminded him of Perdita. If she could trust one human, he felt, she could achieve anything. Driving home from the theatre he pondered his next move. Seeing General Piran ahead, he decided to try her in practice chukkas tomorrow.

It was past three o'clock, but the tack room light, besieged with huge crashing moths, was still on. Raimundo's shaggy lurchers swarmed round Perdita as she staggered groggily out of the car.

'I've never been so exhausted in my life. Christ, what's that?' she shrieked, as fat Umberto, clearly drunk and absolutely terrified, lurched out of the shadows brandishing a gun.

'What in hell's the matter?' said Luke, taking the gun from him.

'Maldita, she is dead,' gabbled Umberto in Spanish.

'What!' howled Luke.

Raising his hands in panic, begging Señor Gracias not to shoot him, Umberto whimpered that Maldita had developed colic that morning.

'We fight all day to save her.'

'What did you try?' demanded Luke furiously.

'Everything, enemas, catheters, fluids to hydrate her. All impossible, she more busy fight us than the colic. She get up, she get down, she roll, she kick the stomach, like crazy woman. We try real hard.' Then, seeing the expression on Luke's face, Umberto indignantly lifted his loose trousers up above his boots to display two huge purple bruises: 'What you think these are, love bites?'

'What did the vet say?'

'A lump of sand block her gut.'

'When did he last come?'

'This afternoon. He no come back. His daughter getting married this evening.'

'Then where the fuck's Alejandro? Humping in BA, I suppose.'

'He didn't even went,' explained Umberto, who couldn't ever have imagined Señor Gracias being so angry about anything. 'He go to wedding of vet's daughter.'

'Along with everyone else, I guess,' said Luke. 'Why didn't anyone take her to the veterinary hospital? They could have operated.'

'Alejandro say she too weak,' said Umberto, leaving unspoken the truth that Alejandro would be too mean to fork out the equivalent of $5,000 for a green and vicious mare.

'Where is she?' asked Luke.

'In the first paddock under the gum trees. Alejandro tell me shoot her if pain get too bad. He say best stable for that mare is a coffin.' Umberto crossed himself. 'But bad luck to kill white horse. Anyway she already die, she not move for twenty minutes.'

Followed by Perdita, who only half understood what was going on, Luke sprinted out to the paddock. Although the moon had set, they could see Maldita's ghostly white body slumped in the corner like a cast-off shroud.

'Poor little bitch.' Luke was shaking with rage. But as he put his hand beneath her nearside elbow, he felt the faintest heartbeat and, to his joy, the mare struck feebly out at him with her off-fore and gave a half-whicker of recognition which turned into a groan. Her white coat was drenched with sweat, her belly horribly distended.

'Put some rugs on her,' he ordered Perdita, as he raced back into the house. Under his bed he had a complete medicine chest, full of stuff given him by a veterinary friend in Palm Beach. There was one thing that might save the mare, and that was only a 10,000 to 1 chance.

Back in the paddock he was greeted by a stream of expletives. Even in her hopelessly weakened condition, Maldita had lashed out when Perdita tried to put a rug on her.

'What are you giving her?' asked Perdita as Luke plunged the needle into the mare's neck.

'Neostymine. Push her into internal contractions. It'll either kill her or make her pass the sand.' The mare writhed and groaned as another spasm of pain shook her body.

'She's in such agony,' stormed Perdita, 'why don't we just put her out of her misery?'

'We're giving her a chance,' said Luke curtly. 'Now help me get her to her feet.'

They both jumped as a black shadow fell across the mare's contorted body. It was little Tero, turned out in the same paddock, offering silent sympathy.

Round and round they staggered like the end of some ghastly marathon, Luke dragging Maldita upright and along by her headcollar, supporting her with his body, Perdita propping up her other side. Tero followed them at a distance, watching her new friend with sorrowful anxious eyes. Luke could have done with more help, but Umberto had barricaded himself into the tack room with another bottle.

After twenty minutes Luke felt his titanic strength was supporting both Maldita and a buckling Perdita, and ordered the latter to bed. When she refused, flopping with exhaustion by the gate, he threw a spare rug over her.

The huge expanse of sky was lightening now, the stars growing pale, a far cry from Lorenzo's 'patines of bright gold'. Occasionally a farm dog barked, a frog croaked by the water trough gleaming in the half-light, a rabbit caught by some predator shrieked in terror, a distant pounding of pop music indicated that the wedding of the vet's daughter was still being celebrated.

Twice Maldita collapsed. It was hard to tell now if it was Luke's sweat or hers that drenched her rug. Occasionally she groaned and made half-hearted kicks at her agonizingly swollen belly.

Walking her round, Luke was reminded of his school-friend Spike, who'd been caught in the locker room with another boy. Terrified that the publicity could ruin his father, who was a senator running for president, Spike had OD'd on barbiturates. By talking to him all night and keeping him on his feet, Luke had saved Spike's life, only to have him try again success-fully a week later when the story finally hit the press. Somehow Luke felt he owed it to Spike's memory to save the mare.

'Come on, baby,' he urged her. 'You gotta pull through. Just try and crap, then you'll feel better.'

To keep them both awake, he reeled off endless poetry; Shakespeare, Hiawatha, then because Maldita might prefer her own language, he started on *Martin Fierro*.

Afterwards he couldn't tell if he had dreamed it, but he was sure little Tero drew close to Maldita several times, trying to prop her up, and twice he felt Tero's timid nudge of encouragement in his back when he was buckling with exhaustion.

By the time the stars had faded, Maldita's heart had rallied, beating almost as fast as her pounding little hooves had on the pampas. Her belly gave a massive rumble.

'Come on, honey,' mumbled Luke. 'If you pull through, I swear I'll take you to Palm Beach, Windsor, Cowdray and Deauville. You'll have a life without winters, playing the best polo in the world.'

But the mare was arching her back and groaning in such agony now that Luke only just managed to keep her on her feet. It was as though Vesuvius had erupted inside her. He could see a faint pink glow in the East. From the tack room Umberto's snores rent the air. In a distant field a mare whinnied, and a stallion whinnied back. Luke staggered. His strength was giving out.

'Come on, Spike baby,' he muttered. 'Don't die, you've gotta see another sunrise.'

Waking very cold and aching, Perdita saw little red flames flickering across the great blue arch of sky and thought for a terrified second that she was in the middle of a forest fire. Then she became conscious of a vast blood-red sun warming the pampas. The trunks of the gum trees soared bright pink, the tack room windows flared crimson and all the birds in the world seemed to be singing for joy. Sitting up stiffly, Perdita gave a gasp, for in the corner beside Tero, a beautiful rose-red mare, her coat mackerelled with dried sweat, was quietly grazing. Fast asleep against the fence slumped Luke, his face as rumpled as an unmade bed, his shirt, as Perdita shook it, drenched with dew.

'Maldita,' whispered Perdita incredulously, 'she's OK?'

Luke opened a bloodshot eye and grinned triumphantly.

'She passed the sand. What a mare! If she can fight off that medication, she'll take on the whole world.'

Hearing Luke's voice, Maldita glanced up, gave a whicker of joy and, a little unsteadily walked towards him, pressed her nose against his shoulder and breathed lovingly down his neck.

'She knows you saved her life,' said Perdita in awe.

But, as she stretched out a hand to stroke the mare, Maldita moved even closer to Luke, flattening her ears and lashing out at Perdita protectively with a hind leg.

Umberto, snoring in the tack room, barricaded against ghoul and hobgoblin by one of the feedbins, was woken to a punishing hangover by the increasingly irritated din of muzzled horses kicking their water buckets. Peering through the cobwebs at the stable clock, Umberto realized he should have been up an hour ago. Any minute Alejandro would be back from the wedding breathing fire and brandy fumes. Alejandro didn't like dead mares around; it looked

266

bad if potential buyers dropped in. He'd better get that she-devil shifted.

Clutching his head, Umberto set out to rouse the other grooms. The sun had now lost its rosy tinge and shone extremely painfully into his eyes. Next moment, he nearly died of fright. For, ghostly in the pale light, glaring through the fence at him, was a dazzling white Maldita.

'*Fantasma*! *Aparecido*!' he shrieked. Frantically crossing himself over and over again, he fled screaming towards the grooms' quarters as fast as his fat legs would carry him.

'What's up with him?' asked Perdita in amazement.

Luke shook with laughter. 'He left her for dead. He figures she's a ghost.'

'Figured she didn't have a ghost of a chance,' giggled Perdita. 'Why don't you call her Fantasma? It's a much prettier name than Maldita.'

And so Maldita the malevolent became Fantasma the fantastic. Within a few days she had recovered enough to play practice chukkas, going straight into fast polo as though she'd played it all her life. She adored the game so much, Luke only had to shift his weight or touch her mouth to get her to do what he wanted, and she was so competitive she would bump anyone, at first even riding off ponies on her own side. She was still bitchy. If Luke were grooming her, she lashed out if he brushed her belly or round her ears, and went for anyone else who came near her. But she could sense when he was getting her ready for a match and stood like a statue, even dropping her head for him to clip her mane.

The only other being Fantasma adored was Tero. The two mares had become inseparable and cried bitterly if they were parted, Fantasma even bashing down fences to get at her friend. Alejandro was so staggered by Fantasma's progress that he decided to waive his prejudice against greys; not so much that he was prepared to get on her back, but he spent a considerable time wondering how he could flog Fantasma to a rich patron without them finding out how vicious and unmanageable the mare could be when she was away from Luke.

27

One of the great debates raging through the Argentine polo world was whether Alejandro Mendoza was a greater player than the mighty O'Brien brothers, Miguel and Juan. Certainly the Mendoza family's ambition in life was to beat the O'Briens. Over twenty years the two great polo dynasties had battled it out in the Argentine Open at Palermo. In the eighties the O'Briens, with Juan and Miguel on ten and their two cousins on nine, had predominated. The Mendozas, however, were biding their time. Alejandro had married at twenty. In two or three years Luis, Patricio and Lorenzo would be catching up with Miguel's cousins, and by this time Miguel, who drank and ate too much, might well be over the top. And Juan – as Alejandro (who as one who lived in a glass house and was in no position to hurl polo balls) pointed out – might well have died of sexual excess.

Hardly an evening passed without one of the Mendozas gnashing their teeth over old videos of the Open and swearing: Death to the O'Briens. Alejandro was also very jealous that Miguel and Juan, aided by Bart Alderton's fat salary, had started their own polo club, buying much of the adjoining land and selling plots to polo enthusiasts at vastly inflated prices.

Another hotly contested tournament was the Copa de Republic, a vast knock-out competition which went on all over the country from November to April. Played entirely on handicap, it meant that a team like the O'Briens, the aggregate of whose handicaps added up to thirty-eight goals, could be pitted against a team whose goals only totalled eight. This year, by some freak of fate, the Mendozas had drawn the O'Briens in the first round, and were due to play them at the latter's new polo club forty miles away on the first Saturday in December.

On the Thursday Luis Mendoza pulled a groin muscle, so Luke had to take his place. On the Friday Lorenzo Mendoza lost his temper with a pony that kept going up with him. Pulling it over to frighten it, he failed to jump clear and the pony fell on him, smashing his thigh. Sobbing with pain and rage, he was carted off to hospital by an ashen Claudia and the family doctor, who'd been presented with a horse every time he delivered a Mendoza baby. Now Angel would have to substitute for Lorenzo. As a result, Alejandro, reluctant to face a rout, ducked out on Saturday morning complaining of an ancient back injury.

Perdita, covering the bottom of the lorries with straw to protect the ponies' feet, suddenly heard Alejandro shouting that she better dig out a pair of clean breeches and polish her boots, as she'd be playing in the match that afternoon. Perdita went into shock horror. In five hours she'd be marking Miguel O'Brien – a gnat trying to curb an elephant. Her confidence was further eroded by both Patricio and Angel launching into a flurry of Latin hysterics that all the press would be there and why should the humiliation of a certain Mendoza defeat be quadrupled by having a stupid girl on the team. Whereupon Luke lost his temper and told them not to be such fucking chauvinists.

As a final straw, on going to change Perdita discovered she'd got the curse, which was invariably as bloody as Culloden on the first day. How ghastly if she bled through her breeches. The O'Briens' club was far too new to have a Ladies' Loo, and she was nearly out of Tampax. Storming out of her room, she went slap into Luke.

'I'll polish your boots,' he offered.

'I can't play.'

'Sure you can. Unknowns are always discovered in the Copa de Republic. It's your big break.'

'How can I play against Angel and Patricio as well as the O'Briens?'

'Hush, hush.' Luke drew her to him. As always his vast warmth steadied her. 'Think how proud Ricky would be.'

Burying her face in Luke's chest to hide her blushes, Perdita asked him if he knew the Spanish for Super Tampax, and if they could stop for some on the way.

'I guess so,' said Luke, putting a hand down to stroke her aching, knotted belly, 'and some Buscopan too if you need it. Stop worrying – we're on twelve, they're on thirty-eight. All we've gotta do is stop them scoring twenty-six goals.'

They took two lorry-loads of ponies including Fantasma. Little Tero whinnied hysterically when she discovered she was being left behind. Angel drove the first lorry. Perdita sat between him and Luke, who was busy working out who

269

should ride which pony in each chukka. A compulsive polo watcher, he was familiar with many of the O'Briens' horses and would probably have to rearrange the list when he saw which ones they were playing.

'You've gotta mark Juan,' he told Angel. 'He ought to be a twelve or a thirteen, he's so good. He's on to the ball before anyone else, but he conserves the energy of his horses.'

'Unlike Reeky,' taunted Angel, 'who do too much and exhaust his horses.'

'Don't talk crap,' said Perdita furiously.

'Pack it in,' snapped Luke, 'and drive a bit slower. We don't want to go up the ass of that flour lorry in front.'

Angel's fingers drummed angrily on the steering wheel as he gazed moodily at the long, straight road ahead of them. Suntanned now, he no longer looked as though he was dying of jaundice. Bronze tendrils stuck to his forehead. Lean jaws, continually chewing gum, were covered in stubble. He might have shaved for a match, thought Perdita; the girl in the petrol station must have a skin like garlic sausage.

'Look at those sheep grazing under that pylon,' said Luke quickly, trying, too late, to distract Perdita's attention from another dumped dog, cringing and terrified, at the side of the road.

'Stop!' she screamed in anguish. 'We can't leave him.'

Hunched over the wheel, Angel accelerated.

'Aren't there any Dogs' Homes in this shitty country?' demanded Perdita.

'We don't need them,' snarled Angel. 'As a nation, we drive very fast which solve the problem. *Perdida* means stray in Spanish,' he added contemptuously.

Rigid with hatred, they sat a foot apart, with Perdita rammed against Luke. But, as her shirt grew soaked in sweat, she was obliged to edge nearer Angel, who looked at her as if she were a tarantula.

Realizing they were both going through the roof with nerves, Luke put down his notes and tipped his battered panama over his snub nose.

'*Listen, my children, and you will hear,*' he began in his deep husky drawl, '*of the midnight ride of Paul Revere,
On the eighteenth of April in Seventy-five.*

Hardly a man is now alive
Who remembers that day and that year.'
'Put a sock in it,' grumbled Perdita.
'Spik Spanish,' said Angel fretfully.

A grin spread across Luke's freckled face. 'You'll love this poem, Angel. It's all about a crushing Brit defeat.
'A hurry of hooves on the village street,' he went on,
'And beneath from the pebbles in passing a spark
Struck out by a steed flying fearless and fleet.
That was all! and yet through the gloom and the light
The fate of a nation was riding that night.'

As he related the heroic tale of Paul Revere's gallop through the night to alert the Americans to the arrival of the British Redcoats, the forty miles flew by and Perdita and Angel strained to catch every word.

'That was great,' said Perdita in amazement when he'd finished. 'Where d'you learn that stuff?'

'In school when I had time to kill.'

'Give us something else.'

Luke laughed and put on an English accent:
'We few, we happy few, we band of brothers;
For he today that sheds his blood with me
Shall be my brother, be he ne'er so vile
This day shall gentle his condition.'

'Nice,' said Perdita. Then under her breath, 'But nothing's going to gentle Angel!'

The ponies, who always had an uncanny knowledge that they'd reached their destination, were stamping and scraping the floor in the back.

'And here's Le Cloob O'Brien,' announced Angel.

They turned into a dirt track flanked by very young gum trees. On either side in various stages of development were yellow houses with crinkly red roofs like Swiss chalets. The club house, which looked like a turreted Ruritanian castle, had white walls, grey roofs, flawless pitches front and back, but as yet no windows, nor, as Perdita suspected, a Ladies' loo, or changing room. She changed in the lorry with Martina, a sorrel mare with four white socks, who was never let out until the last moment, as she was driven so crazy by the flies. Perdita was trembling so badly that she could hardly zip up her boots. She felt a stone overweight with the Super Tampax and all the Kleenex stuffed inside herself. The once-crocus-yellow polo shirt, now faded to primrose with a huge maroon satin Number One on the back, was almost falling to pieces. It had been worn the last time the Mendozas beat the O'Briens in the Open and on every occasion they had met since. Trying to put her head through a sleeve, Perdita nearly ripped it further.

Luke let her out. The primrose yellow suited him, she thought. It emphasized the sleepy honey-coloured eyes in his brown face and the yellow streaks in his reddy-gold hair. He looked in terrific shape too. The massive shoulders and chest tapered down to the lean cowboy hips and long legs.

The O'Briens looked in even greater shape. Everywhere, Perdita seemed to see the emerald-green colours they had chosen to emphasize their Irish origins, which were worn by players, grooms and supporters alike. Both their lorries were green, and so were their lead reins, anti-sweat sheets, buckets and bandages, and there were green braids on their splendid horses' tails, which were left down until the last moment to protect them from the flies.

Perdita felt her stomach disappear. There was Miguel, huge and thick-set with a permanently hard ugly smirk on his face, and lithe, handsome Juan, whom she'd last seen being forcibly ejected for bonking his host's wife at the Waterlanes' party, both swinging their sticks round and round to loosen up their shoulders.

Then she noticed a vast woman with a swarthy dead-pan face and black hair drawn back into a bun, who was standing near the O'Briens with grimly folded arms.

'Who's Sitting Bully?' she asked Luke.

'Juan's wife.' Then, at Perdita's look of incredulity, 'Known as the Policia. When she accompanies him to Palm Beach, he drops all his girlfriends, goes to church and prays, and becomes the model husband. The moment she leaves, he's back with a blonde on each arm.'

Perdita started to laugh.

'The good news,' went on Luke, 'is that, because she's around, Juan hasn't been able to have his extra-marital pre-match hump, which miraculously lifts his game. Instead he and Juan lunched with Victor and Sharon Kaputnik. Victor's thinking of buying a dozen horses off them, unless he sees something he fancies better at Alejandro's tomorrow. They're not playing their best horses today. They're saving them for the Open.'

'So they have no doubt about wiping the floor?'

'None,' said Luke. 'Let's hope pride comes before several falls.'

'Will you do up my kneepads?' asked Perdita. 'I don't want anyone, particularly Angel, to see how much I'm shaking.'

'The bad news,' went on Luke, tucking a strap into a buckle, 'is that one of today's umpires, Jaime Calavessi, bumped one of the O'Brien boys wrong last week. After the match, "Tiny", as Mrs Juan is euphemistically known, and her three sons chased Jaime round the field and nearly broke his jaw. So any decisions he makes today will be nervously pro-O'Brien. The other umpire is Juan's brother-in-law, so he won't be un-biased either.'

A large crowd had gathered, giving a great air of carnival. Little boys raced about hitting balls with short mallets. Young players sat inside the boards, anxious to get as near their gods as possible. Voluptuous girlfriends, sisters and mothers constantly turned against the hot dusty wind to secure their cascading glossy hair with plastic bull-dog clips. Perched on bonnets of cars, smoking and chattering non-stop, they were getting high on tins of diet Coke.

Spectators, wandering along the pony lines, were amused to watch Fantasma, who'd been muzzled to stop her savaging anyone, standing on her two front legs and lashing out with both back ones.

A ripple of excitement went through the crowd as Miguel's wife, who was small, dark, and as pretty as Mrs Juan was ugly, rolled up with Victor and Sharon Kaputnik. Victor, fatter and balder and more like a bilious little hippo than ever, was obviously enjoying playing the O'Briens off against the Mendozas.

'In Chile they like you anyway,' he was saying loudly. 'In Argentina they cheat you and laugh all the way to the bank. They only entertain you if they know you're going to buy their ponies.'

'Bloody rude,' said Perdita, furiously. 'How dare he bitch about Argentina? And, my God, Sharon's been gentrified!'

When Perdita last saw her as Victor's bimbo in 1981, Sharon's hair had been dyed the colour of strawberry jam, her splendid breasts had floated like beachballs out of her skin-tight polyester dress and her six-inch spike heels must have terrorized any lurking moles as she tripped on to the Rutshire pitch at treading-in time.

Today her hair, the discreetest palest auburn, curled softly on her collar and she was wearing a white muslin midi-dress, white stockings and flat white pumps. Vast pearls, which some poor oyster must have needed an epidural to produce, circled her neck and wrists. The bracelet had gone from her ankle, the heavy make-up from her eyes. The graciousness of her entrance, however, was somewhat marred. Clinging on to her big picture hat with one hand and holding up her white parasol with the other, there was nothing left to prevent the hot wind from the Andes blowing her dress over her head, to reveal a white suspender belt and French knickers.

'My people used to have an *estancia* in Chorley Wood,' she was telling an uncomprehending Mrs Miguel. 'Oh, best of luck, Hoo-arn,' she cried, priding herself on her pronunciation, as Juan cantered on to the field, followed by a cloud of dust and the eyes of every woman round the pitch.

Impossibly arrogant and handsome, teeth flashing beneath his ebony moustache, so much copied by the young Argentine bloods, black curls flowing from under a very unIrish tartan hat, Juan's long thighs gripped a bay mare who was so glossy he could have checked his reflection in her quarters. A great cheer went up as he started hitting the ball around, the merest tap sending it miles across a field as brown as Raimundo's goatskin apron.

'*Idolo*, my hero, I am 'ere!' yelled a busty blonde through cupped hands, earning herself a wave from Juan and dirty looks from both Sharon and Mrs Juan, who had stationed themselves grimly on the halfway line, surrounded by supporters.

'That bay Juan's riding is very powerful,' Luke told Angel. 'Three days without oats and she can still play, but Juan has trouble stopping her, don't forget. He'll also try and hit you too late.'

Knowing the others were depending on him, Luke kept his nerves to himself as he went round checking girths and bandages. To give Perdita confidence in her first chukka, he'd put her on a dark brown pony called Chimango (which meant bird of prey), who was as steady as a rock, but who swept down on the ball like a hawk.

'Luke,' shouted Juan. Cantering up, he bent down and gave Luke a great hug. 'My dear friend, 'ow are you? How is Alejandro? Still bent as a paper cleep?'

'No more than you,' said Luke. 'We hear you've been selling Victor carthorses. Did you wax their fetlocks beforehand?'

'No, we use ladies' razor,' giggled Juan. 'Your father is very well. He ring me tomorrow wiz zee 'andicap listings. If he go up, we 'ave to look for another ringer.'

Under Juan's pony's elegant hooves, the ground was cracking and blowing away in clouds of dust. 'I 'ear you reduce to playing wiz girls. Alejandro must be sleeping,' he said.

'He is not,' said Perdita, outraged.

'He means slipping,' Luke reassured her.

'That's even worse.'

'This is Perdita,' said Luke.

'Ay, ay, ay,' sighed Juan, peering under her hat. 'You are twelve goal in looks, *señorita*; what does it matter about zee polo?'

'Bloody sexist,' muttered Perdita, as Juan rode off.

'He's pissed,' said Luke.

'We'll show him,' said Perdita as she mounted Chimango.

Angel and Patricio were about to ride on to the field.

'Wait!' Perdita leant forward and removed a piece of straw from Angel's pony's eyelashes.

'Put on the Rimmel mascara next,' said Angel sarcastically.

'Oh, fuck off.'

'Knock it off,' said Luke, picking up his stick. 'Now come on, you guys. We may be the underdogs, but we're gonna fight like pit bulls.'

28

And fight they did. The O'Briens, expecting a canter over, were unpleasantly surprised to find themselves pegged. Both Juan and Miguel had lunched not wisely but too well. Under a punishing overhead sun, lobster, steak tournedos and *dulce de leche* churned uneasily in their bellies. Not used to drinking, Juan was seeing the ball, if not double, at least one and a third, which led to a lot of misses and botched shots at goal.

The crowd, expecting a bloodbath, were captivated by such a young and aggressive side. Perdita goaded Miguel like an angry wasp. Angel, turned on by the odds stacked against him, hurled himself on Juan as though he was a Mirage pilot once again. He was also brilliantly interchanging with Patricio as Luke constantly fed them with passes, while doggedly taking out one O'Brien player after another as they thundered towards goal.

The *cognoscenti*, however, noticed that, although Perdita was often in a position to score goals, Angel and Patricio never passed to her and that Alejandro's ponies, enjoying Luke's light hands and sympathetic riding, were going really well. The girls noticed Angel's hawklike good looks. Studying their score sheets and not realizing that he was a poor relation of the Solis de Gonzales, they were turned on by his ancient name. They were soon even more excited by his clowning. Miguel, sobering up and getting paunchy, was deeply unamused by this new young stag entering the forest.

Just as Angel was throwing himself out of his saddle for a nearside forehand Miguel put his knee under Angel's knee so he overbalanced and tumbled off his pony. Next second Angel had leapt to his feet, belted after the pony and jumped on again before Miguel's brother-in-law, the umpire, could whistle 'Man Down'.

'*Idolo*,' shouted Juan's busty blonde admirer, transferring her loyalties.

This piece of circus produced roars of laughter from the crowd and seemed to shatter the O'Briens' concentration. Juan throughout the first half was noticeably eyeing Sharon

Kaputnik, who was standing behind Victor coyly resting her pointed chin on his bald head which enabled her to eye anyone she chose. At the beginning of the third chukka, Luke came out on Fantasma, whose beauty drew all eyes like the rising moon. She was so quick at the throw-in that Luke immediately got the ball out, lofting it upfield over Patricio's head, so he was able to ride Miguel off and score. Two minutes later Miguel, one of those aggressive backs who got bored hanging around the back line and irritated because Luke was playing so well, came roaring down with the ball. Tearing after him, Perdita lurched forward to hook his stick. A second later, to her utter humiliation, he had blasted the ball, taking Perdita's stick, and very nearly Perdita, with him. Acutely aware of Angel and Patricio raising their eyes to heaven, Perdita had to decide whether to dismount and pick up her stick or race to mid-field where Raimundo was brandishing another one. She opted for the latter. As Angel careered down the boards to stand in for her and bump Miguel, Miguel clouted the ball straight at Angel's face. Seeing it coming, Angel threw himself off his pony.

'Get back on that horse,' screamed Patricio as Miguel picked up the ball again and took it towards the Mendozas' goal-mouth.

'I don't want to be killed,' yelled back Angel. Once more the crowd howled with laughter.

Fortunately Fantasma believed in defending her goal-mouth as ferociously as she protected Luke or even a bucket of pony nuts. Seeing Miguel hurtling towards the goal, she calmly sent his much larger pony flying, stumbled and miraculously righted herself. Then, positioning herself perfectly for Luke to hit the backhand, she instantly wheeled round and displayed a staggering burst of acceleration which enabled Luke to power the ball upfield.

Juan's umpiring brother-in-law was so struck with admiration that his whistle dropped out of his mouth.

What a horse, thought Luke exultantly.

Devastating the O'Briens' defence with an offside forehand, he put the ball twenty yards in front of a remounted Angel. Only Perdita and an O'Brien cousin were between Angel and the goal now. Angel didn't want to pass to Perdita, but as a hundred and fifty-five pounds of O'Brien cousin with razor-sharp elbows hurtled towards him, it seemed the easier option. The sweat cascading into her eyes made it difficult for Perdita to see the ball.

'Aim for the left goal post; don't go to pieces,' she told herself frantically as she scooped up the ball and tapped it into position.

'You're going to be hooked,' bellowed Luke.

Glancing round she saw Juan thundering down on her, a predatory smile on his handsome face. Lowering her stick, aware of Angel on her left, she flicked the ball to him under her pony's neck, and with a lovely click of his mallet, Angel stroked in an exquisite nearside cut shot making the score 28-9 to the Mendozas on the half-time bell.

'Well played, Angel,' said Patricio, falling on his neck as they cantered off the field.

Bastards, thought Perdita, patting her pony over and over again. We made that goal.

Back at the pony lines, morale in the Mendoza camp was sky high. The O'Briens might have scored nine goals, but they had all been penalties. It was only when she stopped playing that Perdita realized how hot it was. Towelling the sweat off her face, she wrung out her wet shirt. She would have liked to have drunk a whole bottle of Evian but limited herself to a few gulps, which she immediately spat out. Angel's olive skin had hardly changed colour, but Luke rode up with his face brick red from the heat and delighted that Fantasma and his team had played so brilliantly.

'Well played, you guys. They're mad now. They're rowing amongst themselves. That was a helluva shot, Angel, and from you, Patricio. You're making Juan look as though he's never been on a horse before.'

Then, taking a swig of diet Coke, he turned to Perdita.

'Well done, baby! You made that last goal, setting up the shot for Angel.'

Perdita could have wept with gratitude, particularly when he turned on the others: 'You gotta give Perdita more work. She's dying of loneliness and heat stroke out there.' For a brief minute he massaged her shoulders, pressing his thumbs in, unknotting the muscles. 'And I hope you notice she's covering for you whenever you get loose.'

278

Patricio put a perfunctory hand on Perdita's shoulder, which was an amazing concession, but Angel's eyes were still as cold as an Alaskan lake.

'Christ, I wish there was a Ladies' loo,' said Perdita, taking a swig of Luke's diet Coke and rubbing ice all over her burning face.

'Use the Men's room,' said Luke. 'I'll keep guard, but be quick.'

Perdita was in such a hurry that at first she didn't notice the gasps and groans that were coming from the next-door cubicle, the walls of which seemed to be heaving as violently as Fantasma's sides after the last chukka. Then, overwhelmed by curiosity, she climbed on to the lavatory seat and, peering over, had to stifle a scream of laughter. For there was Sharon, her big hat lying like a whole Brie on the floor, her parasol neatly folded in the corner, and her muslin skirt and silk petticoat once more over her head, while Juan, bronzed hands clamped to her snow-white bottom, drove in and out with far more energy than he'd shown on the field.

'Oh, Hoo-arn, Hoo-arn,' gasped Sharon, as one of his brown hands disappeared into her bush, 'ay'm comin'.'

Glancing out of the glassless window, Perdita saw a grim-faced Mrs Juan advancing towards the Gents, and not wanting to be blamed, shot out of the door. Hysterical with giggles, she told Luke.

'Sharon's umbrella is down – probably thinks it's un-lucky indoors – but Juan is definitely up.'

'Pity,' grinned Luke. 'There'll be no holding him now.'

'Sharon was certainly holding him just then,' said Perdita, doubling up with laughter again. 'Talk about Long Dong Juan! Shall we tip off Victor? Then he won't buy any of Juan's ponies.'

'Come on,' said Luke, trying to be serious. 'Get back on Chimango. We've got a match to win.'

'Thank God my father isn't playing,' murmured Patricio to Angel as, aware of the admiration of the crowd, they rode back on to the field. 'I love my father, but Señor Gracias is better captain. He doesn't shout all the time and he puts us on the right horses.'

'I hope he stops that shit Miguel killing me,' said Angel, chucking away his cigarette. 'I can't believe we're so much ahead.'

'And can beat them,' said Patricio.

But as they went into the fatal fourth, the sun went behind a donkey-grey cloud and everything went wrong. Angel, trying to block a shot, went straight across Juan, who was given a thirty-yard penalty, which Miguel tipped between the posts. Patricio, at last obeying Luke's nagging, gave Perdita a lovely pass just in front of goal, which she promptly hit wide; then down the other end Angel backed the ball by mistake to Miguel, who promptly scored.

'I know about zee horses,' sighed Raimundo at mid-field, 'but not about zee players.'

Two more dubious fouls were called against the Mendozas and then Juan, liberated by his bang in the loo, suddenly woke up. Eyes sparkling, medallion glittering in the returned sunlight, he went into an orgy of brilliance notching up nine goals in one chukka.

'Hoo-arn has not lost his touch,' said Sharon smugly, as Juan swaggered back to the pony lines acknowledging the cheers with his stick.

'Steady down, steady down. We can do it, we can do it,' urged Luke, walking round banging his right fist into the open palm of his left hand. 'Juan's on a really fast pony this chukka, Angel. Don't get into a horse race with him. You gotta outfox him and not let him get the ball.'

But nothing could stop Juan and his magic mallet now. Tapping in four goals in as many minutes, he levelled the score. Getting the ball out yet again, he set off upfield.

'*Vamos, vamos,*' yelled the crowd as Angel whipped and spurred his slower pony after him. Luckily the ball hit a divot, Juan missed it and Angel checked his pony for the backhand. Instantly Miguel crashed into him broadside, ramming him so hard that the pony swung round 180 degrees, totally winded. Up went the sticks of the Mendozas.

'*Faulazo,*' they yelled.

'*Faulazo,*' yelled Claudia and the Mendoza supporters.

'*Faulazo,*' yelled almost the entire crowd.

Jaime, the umpire, shot a nervous glance at Mrs Juan, who folded her arms implacably and shook her head. Jaime was just awarding against Angel for crossing Miguel when

Perdita took matters into her own sweaty hands. Charging up to Miguel, she bashed him on the wrist with her stick.

'Stop it, you great bully,' she screamed. 'That's the third time you've tried to kill Angel.'

'For Chrissake, Perdita,' roared Luke.

Lifting his stick, Miguel would have clouted her back if the O'Brien brother-in-law hadn't bravely ridden between them. Giving Perdita a bollocking, he awarded the O'Briens a free goal.

'Why you do that?' Angel asked her in amazement.

'I hate you,' spat Perdita, 'but I hate dirty play even more.'

Unfortunately Alejandro had chosen the worst possible time to arrive and witnessed the whole incident. Guilty at rolling up so late after a little detour to Buenos Aires and expecting carnage, he was irritated to see how staggeringly well his team had done without him. Stopping only briefly to kiss Sharon's hand and embrace Victor and make sure they would be staying the night in General Piran, he went off to shout at his team.

'You're all loose. Stop tapping and 'eet it. You change wiz Angel, Luke, so you can mark Juan, and as for you,' he turned, roaring, on Perdita, ''ow dare you 'it Miguel? You should 'ave been sent off. I said we shouldn't 'ave played her,' he added to Luke.

Finally, glancing at the four ponies being walked round for the last chukka, he bellowed that they were the wrong ones and ordered Raimundo to tack up others, immediately.

Luke had gone very still.

'Leave those ponies as they are,' he said softly to Raimundo, then, taking Alejandro by the arm, drew him away from the others.

'You asked me to captain this side because you were too goddam lazy to play and you don't like being pussy-whipped. They played like angels, right, and unless you want my fist in your fucking face, get off my case.'

Alejandro was so flabbergasted that he sauntered off to regain some ascendancy by extravagantly complimenting Sharon.

'Now, calm down,' said Luke, turning back with a grin to his astounded team. 'They're only two goals ahead and we're younger, fitter and braver. Let's bury them.'

Seeing Juan mounting a black thoroughbred who could have won the Kentucky Derby, he put Angel up on a very fast dark brown mare he'd intended to ride himself. Then he had a battle with his conscience. If he rode Fantasma again, they had twice as good a chance of winning, but if Victor and Sharon took another look at such a showy, beautiful horse they might want to buy her. He glanced over at Fantasma who was dying to get back into the action. Standing gazing at the pitch, her dark eyes wide with excitement, scraping up the dust with her hooves, she ran her muzzled nose restlessly along Umberto's arm until he cursed her as he led her round. Luke went over and tightened her girths. He'd have to find more money from somewhere else.

Perdita was now riding a beautiful chestnut called Cuchilla.

'Good milk, Perdita,' Angel called to her as they cantered upfield for the throw-in. Perdita ignored him.

'I say, good milk, Perdita.'

'Oh, fuck off,' she snapped. She assumed it was some beastly crack implying that she should be breast-feeding rather than playing.

Somehow in the last chukka the Mendozas steadied. But it was a pandemonium of frantic swordplay and scrimmaging around the Mendoza goal-mouth until it seemed impossible that the goal-hungry green-and-white posts hadn't swallowed the ball. Finally, taking a fearful risk, Luke left his back door open and took the ball upfield, outrunning Juan, snaking Fantasma past the two O'Brien cousins, then passing to Angel. Once again only Perdita, who was glued to Miguel, stood between him and goal. Aware there was no way Angel would give Perdita the chance to score, Miguel galloped forward to bump him off the ball. Discounted, ignored, Perdita waited despondently behind him. Good milk indeed. Then, to her amazement, Angel had passed Miguel with a ravishing offside forehand landing right at her feet. For a second she froze as Miguel yanked his horse round so violently that he cut its mouth and pounded towards her. Then, with her back to the goal and no time to position herself, she executed that most foolhardy of shots, known as the millionaire's, because only a rich man can afford to jeopardize his pony in this way. Pulling the ball towards her, she slammed it between Cuchilla's beautifully clean front and back legs and under her bound-up tail. Having miraculously missed any limbs, the refractory ball hit the posts and bounced back.

'Bad milk, Perdita,' shouted Angel, then galloped up screaming, '*Dejala, dejala, dejala.*'

Next moment he had scored and the crowd went wild. Only one goal behind with two minutes left.

'Bad milk, Perdita,' said Angel, riding up to her as they cantered back for the throw-in.

Jaime Calavessi, who longed for an O'Brien victory to get him off the hook, hurled the ball in. Taking no chances, Juan tapped it away and set out, like Paul Revere, on his thoroughbred black pony Glitz. As he galloped down the boards Patricio raced alongside him waiting for a chance to ride him off and pinch the ball. Failing to tempt Patricio on to his line, Juan suddenly pulled Glitz up in a frenzy of outrage, twirling his stick to indicate he'd been crossed.

'Manufactured,' yelled Luke, Patricio, Angel and Perdita in unison. Then, advancing on a cringing Jaime, 'That foul was manufactured.'

'*Faulazo,*' yelled the O'Briens, closing in on Jaime.

Jaime fingered his aching jaw. Glancing up, he saw an unsmiling Mrs Juan draw her finger across her throat. In a superb display of arrogance, Miguel walked his pony off to a spot thirty yards from the Mendozas' goal as though the penalty was a *fait accompli*. Jaime awarded the penalty to the O'Briens.

'It's not bloody fair,' said Perdita as they lined up behind their back line. 'This whole game is rigged and why does that bastard Angel keep saying good and bad milk to me?'

Luke was revving Fantasma up to block Miguel's shot, but suddenly he laughed. 'The word *leche* means milk *and* luck in Spanish. I guess Angel was trying to wish you luck.'

Jaime's conscience was troubling him. There was only a minute left and Miguel was messing around joking with the other umpire, his brother-in-law, making a great play of teeing up the ball. Jaime caught sight of Perdita's anguished face. She'd played so well and she was so much prettier than Mrs Juan – and he was, after all, a susceptible Argentine. Shutting his eyes, waiting for a thunderbolt to descend, he blew a foul on Miguel for wasting time. When all the O'Briens closed in on him he appealed to the third man, who woke up with a start. Deciding that the O'Briens were getting above themselves, he upheld Jaime's decision. Giving the O'Briens no time to reassemble themselves, Luke lofted the ball over their heads, slap between the posts.

With a minute to go the score was tied. The throw-in was murder, sticks going everywhere. Luke felt Fantasma wince as the ball hit her smack on the knee, but such was her courage that she limped for only a few paces, then set out again, vroom, vroom, vroom, to defend her own goal.

The clock showed only twenty seconds left as Luke saved the Mendozas from certain defeat with another backshot. Swinging round, he streaked up the field like a man on a motor bike, outrunning Juan's black thoroughbred, passing the two O'Brien cousins. What a glorious horse! Any minute he expected her to take off like Pegasus.

Leering like some terrible shark, Miguel was now coming towards Luke and Fantasma at right-angles. Luke waited until the last moment to pass to Patricio who passed to Perdita.

I'm going to score at last, she thought joyfully, then groaned in horror as she hit wide. They were all in the goal-mouth now, raising such a dust with their flailing sticks that no-one could see. Five seconds to go. Then, miraculously, Perdita saw the ball six feet in front of her. One of the O'Brien cousins was looming in through the smokescreen on her right. Clambering halfway up Cuchilla's neck, only just managing to stay on by clinging on to the martingale with her left hand, she lunged forward and, with a one-handed billiard-cue shot, ignoring the pony crashing in on her left, she shunted the ball between the posts. She would have fallen under the pounding hooves if someone hadn't grabbed her primrose jersey, ripping it apart in the process so her slim brown shoulder was laid bare, and tugged her back into the saddle.

Coughing and spluttering, she swung round, reluctant to take her eyes off the jubilantly waving red flag, then realized in amazement that it had been Angel. For a second they glared at each other, then yelling, 'We've beaten the O'Briens,' they fell into each other's arms.

29

Having drunk a great deal of champagne, they drove home in a manic mood, yelling, 'Juan O'Brien's body lies a-mouldering in the grave, but his cock goes pumping on,' and howling with laughter. It was a beautiful evening, a great stretch of brown-flecked cloud lay like a turned-down sheet over an endless blue blanket. They had each been given a little silver cup. Perdita's lay between her thighs, clinking against Luke's. Angel clutched his and in its reflection he occasionally examined an eye that was turning purple where Miguel's elbow had caught him. Luke drove, his heart simultaneously bursting with pride and heavy with foreboding. Hanging from the windscreen was the red, white and blue rosette Fantasma had won as Best Playing Pony. Even though she'd nearly savaged the VIP presenting the awards when he tried to pin it on her headcollar, everyone wanted to buy her now. Alejandro might even overcome his greed and hang on to her himself. Worse still, Angel's arm lay along the back of the seat, grazing Perdita's hair. Was he going to lose her *and* Fantasma, wondered Luke. Then he told himself not to be absurd. Neither was his to lose. As he listened to Angel and Perdita re-living every stroke of the game, it never occurred to him to mind that it had not occurred to either of them that he had set up every goal they scored.

'Juan asked me for my card,' said Angel.

'He asked me for other things,' said Perdita. 'Stupid prat. I don't like used men. I wouldn't touch him with a pitchfork.'

'Don't talk to me of peetchforks,' shuddered Angel. Then, waving airily at the pampas, 'My great-grandfather used to own all this land. We was in charge of the frontier. To the North to Buenos Aires it was civilized, to the

285

South it was Indian. My great-grandfather and the Army destroyed the Indians. They were 'orrible – very non-U.'

Perdita giggled. 'You make Margaret Thatcher sound like Karl Marx. How long did it take to tattoo that heart on your arm?'

'About a bottle of wheesky,' said Angel.

Perdita screamed with laughter.

Oh Christ, thought Luke, I meant to bring them together, but not that much.

'Give us a poem, Luke,' said Perdita. 'Something to cool us down.'

Luke thought for a minute.

'*Whose woods these are I think I know*,' he began. His voice was hoarse from the dust and shouting.

'*His house is in the village though:*
He will not see me stopping here
To watch his woods fill up with snow.'

Listening, Perdita thought about snow in Rutshire and battling through the drifts to take hay to Ricky's ponies.

'*The woods are lovely, dark and deep*,' went on Luke with a slight break in his voice,

'*But I have promises to keep,*
And miles to go before I sleep,
And miles to go before I sleep.'

I've got miles to go before I sleep, thought Angel, until I get to England and avenge Pedro's death.

'Eagle,' said Luke, pointing to a quivering dot in the sky.

'There are three good things about the Argentines,' said Angel, 'their nature: birds, flowers and theengs; their women, and their individuality. But they are very ghastly in a crisis.'

'You were pretty good today,' said Perdita. 'I think the Argentines are the loveliest, funniest people in the world.'

Later they went to a local night-club to celebrate. Sharon Kaputnik, regal in midnight blue with her red hair piled up on top, was practically held together by sapphires.

'If you threw her into the river,' murmured Luke, 'she'd sink like Virginia Woolf.'

'Alejandro's the wolf,' said Perdita. 'He's had his hand up her skirt all dinner. I don't know if it's a compliment to Alejandro's right-arm muscles or the beef that he can cut it up with a fork.'

Victor, as usual adoring the sound of his own voice, was slagging off the O'Briens.

'All Argentines are crooks.'

'Alejandro's not laike that,' said Sharon, whose eyes were getting rather glazed.

'Nevair,' said Alejandro, whose hand was still burrowing.

'Miguel boasted they'd win easy today,' went on Victor.

'Easily, Victor, easily,' corrected Sharon. 'You ought to learn to talk proper, laike what I do.'

'She very beautiful,' whispered Angel.

'She's hell,' hissed Perdita. 'All you Argentines are too stupid to see how naff she is – and someone should get Alejandro a finger bowl.'

'All ay'm interested in is buyin' that lovely waite pony, Fandango,' said Sharon.

Luke, aching all over from bangs and bumps, was overwhelmed with tiredness. The strain of captaining the team was now telling on him. A bang on the ankle, which was now so swollen he couldn't get a shoe on, ruled out any dancing, so he was forced to watch Perdita and Angel joyfully celebrating their armistice on the dance floor. Perdita's arctic blond hair flew loose and newly washed (as usual Luke had boiled up the water for the shower). Her body was starkly but seductively clad in an elongated black T-shirt. Angel's khaki face was dead-pan. His eyes never moved from Perdita's, as his body writhed like a snake.

Sharon gazed at Angel greedily.

'Who does that young man play for in Palm Beach?' she asked Luke.

'No one at the moment.'

'Ay'll have a word with Victor.'

An hour later, Perdita having bopped also with Alejandro and Victor, came back and threw herself on Luke's knee like a child.

'Oh, Luke, darling, I'm having so much fun, it's all due to you. Without you Alejandro would never have let me play and he's just been really complimentary, and you'll never guess . . . ' She put her mouth to Luke's ear. As her hair tickled his cheek and he smelt her scent and felt the excited heat of her body, his senses reeled.

'Sharon,' whispered Perdita, 'is going to put a Mogadon in Victor's brandy so she can spend the whole night with Angel. That'll be three men in one day. She *is* a whore. D'you think Angel will shout Port Stanley at the moment of orgasm and stick a blue-and-white flag on her bum?'

So Perdita wasn't falling for Angel. Luke felt almost giddy with relief. Then reality reasserted itself.

'And Alejandro says I can ring Ricky when I get home,' went on Perdita joyfully. 'Aren't the Argentines the most adorable people in the world?'

Perdita's euphoria was tempered the next morning. While Sharon enjoyed her beauty sleep and possibly Alejandro as well, Victor played in a practice game with Alejandro's young sons, and Angel, Perdita and Patricio, who all had fearful hangovers. Determined to try out Fantasma, Victor had only been deterred because Alejandro lied that she'd come up slightly lame from her bang on the knee yesterday.

'You see how good she was. No need to try 'er.'

Victor's game had not improved since 1981. He slumped around on other horses like a sack of pony nuts, crossing everyone. As the sun grew hotter, and her headache worse, his uselessness began to irritate Perdita. The others were letting him get away with murder. They couldn't be that hungover. As he teetered towards her, she rode him off so viciously he nearly fell off.

'Come 'ere,' yelled Alejandro who'd just arrived. Then, dropping his voice as she drew near, 'Lay off, you stupid beetch.'

His conniving little eyes were vicious with fury at the prospect of losing a good deal. 'Your job ees to make Veector look breeliant, and for 'im to score as many goals as possible.'

So, for the next half-hour, they all cantered round, tipping the ball on to the end of Victor's stick, greeting every goal with roars of applause.

'Your horses are much better schooled than the O'Briens',' said Victor as he rode off the field, flushed with triumph.

He proceeded to buy twenty horses and said that after lunch he would haggle with Alejandro over a price for Fantasma.

Luke, whose ankle was murder, had spent a frustrating
morning in the village telephone-exchange tracking down
his patron Hal Peters, the automobile billionaire. He finally
located him in the Four Seasons in New York, closing a
mega-deal with some Italians.

'Fantasma's a dream,' shouted Luke. 'Lines me up for
every shot, changes legs at a gallop, got acceleration that
brings tears to your eyes. She outran all the O'Briens'
ponies yesterday and she's only four.'

'You talking about a woman?' said Hal Peters, who
wanted to show off to the Italians and their bimbos.
'Is she pretty?'

'Prettiest horse you ever saw, silver as a unicorn and all
the grace. If we have her on the team, everyone'll talk about
her. Best publicity you could have, but we've gotta move
fast. People are after her.'

'Pay what you like,' said Hal.

Luke belted back to the house to tell Alejandro he
could top any bid of Victor's and the haggling started in
earnest.

'I buy her for $7,000 as a two year old,' said Alejandro.

'Bullshit!' said Luke. 'She only came into the yard
two months ago and you told me Patricio only paid
$700 for her.'

Alejandro gave a great roar of laughter. 'That was when
he bought her. Now I am selling her.'

They settled for $12,000.

In the afternoon Luke had a telephone call at Alejandro's
from his father, also in New York. Off the drink and
living on shrimp and diet Coke in order to shed ten
pounds before the Palm Beach season, Bart was not
in a good mood. He did, however, congratulate Luke
on going up to seven in the latest handicap listings
and asked him to join him, Bibi and Red in the
Fathers and Sons Tournament which began in the middle
of December.

'I've got to fly a lot of horses back for myself and
Hal,' said Luke, 'but if you can put in a substitute
for the first two games, I should make the semi-final.
How's Red?'

'Lousy,' said Bart. 'Got himself involved with some actress called Auriel Kingham.'

'Christ!' Luke tried not to laugh. 'Wasn't she at college with Grace?'

'Almost,' said Bart. 'She's junked her husband who's citing Red, so we've got reporters staking out the house night and day.'

Bart, however, was much more furious because the underhandicapped player, known in the game as a ringer, whom he'd signed up to play with him, Juan and Miguel in Palm Beach, had been put up two places in the November handicaps, which put the aggregate of the team's handicap over the required twenty-six.

'I called the American Polo Association,' snarled Bart, 'I said, "We've paid him money and he signed the contract eight months ago and we'll pull out altogether because it wrecks our team", but the assholes wouldn't budge.'

Luke privately thought that the APA, having been pushed around once too often by Bart, had probably decided to take a stand.

'I've gotta find another ringer at once,' said Bart. 'You got any ideas? I'm pissed off with Juan's and Miguel's cousins.'

'Sure,' said Luke. 'Guy called Angel. Plays like one too. He's rated one here, but he's at least four. Got class too. I'll bring him back with me.'

It touched Luke that, despite their differences, his father trusted him more than the O'Briens when it came to finding players. Having told Angel, he limped outside. Christ, his ankle hurt. He saw that Perdita was cantering Tero round the corral. The change in the little mare was amazing. She had filled out, her iron-grey coat gleamed like stainless steel, her long silver-blond mane, still unclipped to indicate she was a novice, fell coquettishly over her eyelashes. Her brown nose looked as if it had been dipped in paprika.

She no longer trembled or flinched away when Perdita touched her, and this morning, a huge victory, she had accepted a Polo from Perdita's hand. Schooling and stick and balling her mostly behind Alejandro's back, Perdita had fallen totally in love with the pony and was desperate to buy her for Apocalypse next summer. But Ricky hadn't answered any of her letters and he'd been out when she'd rung him last night.

Now Tero was executing a perfect figure of eight, not flinching at all at the stick Perdita was swinging around to get her used to it.

Oh, happy horse to bear the weight of Perdita, thought Luke.

Instead he said, 'Angel's gonna play on my father's team in Palm Beach next season.'

'That's great,' said Perdita, battling with jealousy. 'What did Angel say?'

'He's so fired up that he galloped three times round the stick-and-ball field yelling: "Sheet, sheet, I'm going to play for the Flyers." I warned him he'd have to play with the O'Briens, and that my father isn't easy, but at least it's a polo boot in the door.'

'Lucky thing,' said Perdita fretfully. 'I'd love to play in Palm Beach.'

As Luke stroked Tero's satin neck, it was difficult to tell if his hand was shaking the mare, or the mare shaking him. Not looking up, he drawled, 'Why don't you come and spend Christmas with us? It's kinda wild. And we can certainly arrange some polo.'

'*Dear Mum,*' wrote Perdita that evening, '*I'm having such a fantastic time. I hate, hate, hate the way the Argentines treat their horses, but I adore them as people. They're so larky and funny. Yesterday we beat the O'Briens, an incredible turnaround. I got a cup, so at least I'm bringing home some silver from Argentina. And since the match, the Argies have been so nice and are taking me seriously as a player at last. There's an American here called Luke Alderton. He's seriously nice too. He's going back to Palm Beach next week after the Open and has asked me to go with him and spend Christmas there. It's a fantastic offer, as their high goal season starts in January. And as Ricky's not coming back to England until March, there's nothing for me to come home to. Hope you don't mind. Violet and Eddie'll be home, and I'd only disrupt things.*

Love, Perdita.
PS Hugs and kisses to Ethel and Gainsborough.'

'That's the first letter I've ever seen you write to your mother,' said Luke when she gave it to him to post.

Perdita's face shut down. 'I keep telling you, we don't get on.'

Luke still had eight more horses to buy for Hal Peters, so the haggling went on amicable but deadly, for the next four days. Going out into the yard the day before they were due to leave, Perdita was staggered when Raimundo asked her into his little wooden house for some *maté*, a herbal tea which gauchos drink out of a silver cup from a communal straw. Although Perdita thought it tasted like grass mowings peed on by a dog, she'd learnt enough tact in the last months to say it was delicious and to thank Raimundo for the honour.

As she left his house, she stroked his lurchers who jostled against her, desperate to be petted, and looked at the ponies wandering loose under the gum trees in the twilight. She couldn't see Tero anywhere.

'Has she been turned out in one of the paddocks?' she asked.

'Alejandro sell her.'

'To Victor?' asked Perdita, aghast. 'She'll hate it. We must get her back.'

'Is all right,' said Raimundo soothingly. 'Señor Gracias got her very cheap as Alejandro theenk her hopeless. It was the only one 'e did. Alejandro overcharge him for the rest.'

Hurtling off to find Luke, Perdita threw her arms round his neck. 'Oh, thank you, thank you. I'll persuade Ricky to buy her. Promise you won't sell her on. Oh, can I ride her in Palm Beach?'

On their last night there was a massive barbecue called an *asado* under the stars. Luke pointed out the Southern Cross. Guitars strummed in the background. Everything was already packed as they were driving the horses to the airport first thing in the morning. In thirty-six hours, thought Perdita, I'll be in Palm Beach. She was so nervous and excited she fed all her dinner to the lurchers.

292

'Those dogs will go into mourning when you leave,' said Alejandro. 'Try this.' He put some stringy-looking white meat on her plate.

'Ugh!' said Perdita. 'Tastes like chewing gum without any flavour. What is it?'

'Intestine,' said Alejandro. 'No worse than 'aggis. I had 'aggis once in England. It looked like sheet. When I eat it, I wish it was.'

Perdita laughed. 'My stepfather was Scottish. He used to recite poems to haggises, stupid dickhead.'

'We will all mees you,' said Claudia sadly to Luke.

'You'll see us in Palm Beach in less than a month,' said Luke.

'It won't be the same. We will not be together every day. Who will mend my washing machine and the children's bicycles? Who will tell them stories at night?'

As pudding arrived, a beautiful cake of meringues, peaches and cream, Perdita's mind started to wander. Was she doing the right thing staying with Luke in Palm Beach and obviously sooner or later bumping into Chessie and Bart? Would Ricky ever forgive her for fraternizing with the enemy? Would Chessie still be as ravishing? Perdita was worried, too, because her image of Ricky was becoming increasingly remote. She kissed his photograph every night, but often panicked because she couldn't remember what he was like. Her heartache had certainly lessened. Would seeing Chessie trigger off all this hurt again? Absent-mindedly she fed a piece of meringue to a hovering lurcher.

'The Eenglish are a strange people,' said Alejandro. 'They love their dogs more than their 'usbands. We Argentines are more romantic. Love is for always.'

Having seen that Claudia was deep in conversation with Luke, Perdita cracked back, 'But not necessarily with the same woman.'

'In Argentina,' went on Alejandro, the firelight flickering on his swarthy, wrinkled face, 'we 'ave a saying. "With you, bread and onions". It mean eef you really love someone, money doesn't matter. Just being with them, even if you only have bread and onions to eat, is enough.'

'Sure,' said Luke, who'd been listening with half an ear, 'I'd go along with that.'

'Crap,' and 'Bullshit!' howled Angel and Perdita simultaneously. 'Money ees essential,' said Angel emphatically. 'Particularly eef you've once 'ad it. I go to Palm Beach to find very rich, beautiful woman.'

Perdita grinned. 'I'm going to marry the richest man I can stand.'

Luke's face was in darkness. He turned back to Claudia.

Later, fuelled by Bourbon, Alejandro became very sentimental.

'I haf to tell you, Luke, Angel, even Perdita eef she learn to control the temper, you are the three best pupil I ever have. But Luke,' his voice softened, 'will always be my *amigo* and special friend. One day Señor Gracias, you step into my boots as the greatest back in zee world.'

Luke was touched, but not too carried away the following morning not to check the horses they were taking with them. Alejandro tried to distract him by merrily checking and re-checking the bill.

'Wiz inflation at one hundred per cent, eet's probably gone up in the last five minutes,' he kept saying, as he fingered his calculator like a lute player.

But Luke was not to be deflected. At the back of the lorry he discovered that Alejandro had substituted a donkey of an old mare for Fantasma. Only after much Argy-bargy and histrionic protestation that Luke was utterly 'meestaken', Fantasma was located, muzzled, hobbled, but still trying to kick out, in an old pigsty at the bottom of the garden, with grey dapples ringing her white coat.

Unfortunately, as Luke led her out the heavens opened, as though the River Plate had been diverted on to the yard, and all the dapples ran.

Alejandro was philosophical. 'I cannot 'elp it eef my grooms want me to 'ang on to a good horse,' he said as he waved them off.

Angel shook his head. 'The Argentines are a people very *simpaticos*, but utterly irresponsible.'

30

The flight was a nightmare of delays, misroutings and arguments with officials over the authenticity of papers and Fantasma's irritable inability to keep her hooves to herself. Then, on the way to Miami, Tero went berserk and nearly kicked the plane out. She would have had to be put down if Luke hadn't calmed her with a shot and, almost more, with his solid, inevitably reassuring presence.

Having groggily settled the horses when they arrived, Perdita fell into bed and slept for twenty-four hours. Waking alone in a very comfortable double bed, she had no idea where she was. Groping for a light switch, she realized she was in Luke's bedroom. The only furniture apart from the bed was a chest of drawers and a record player. The colour in the room was provided by the books, which covered the walls and much of the carpetless floor, but in orderly piles. Four whole shelves were devoted to tapes and records, mostly classical, and Luke must have bought every book on polo, albeit second-hand. The rest of the books seemed to be poetry and novels, American, English and translations from every European language, including Latin and Greek.

Opening the curtains, Perdita was almost blinded by sunshine. Blinking, she realized she'd been sleeping in the attic of an L-shaped barn. To the right she could see a row of loose boxes and behind them a stick-and-ball field with floodlighting so horses could be worked after dark. Beyond were paddocks dotted with pines, gums and palm trees. She could see Tero and Fantasma grazing contentedly. They'd become even more inseparable after the ordeal of their first flight.

Below her in the yard, Luke, stripped to the waist in a pair of faded Bermudas, was talking nonsense to a pony as he hosed the soap suds off her dark brown coat. A Siamese cat with blue eyes and a blue collar weaved voluptuously between his legs, watched jealously by a ferocious-looking black mongrel who had gone berserk when Luke got home yesterday.

'Who's that pony?' Perdita shouted down.

Luke glanced up and smiled. 'Ophelia – came from Miguel O'Brien just a year ago. When I first walked into her stable she used to turn her back on me, put her head down in the corner and shake. You couldn't put a halter on her.'

'How d'you sort her out?'

'Handled her very gently. Let her get away with a few things. All she needed was a little TLC.'

Perdita remembered how all the ponies had come racing in from the paddocks and nearly sent Luke flying yesterday. She'd never seen horses so affectionate and so relaxed. The mare was flattening her ears now as Luke hosed under her headcollar. Then, unbuckling it, he gave her a gentle pat on the rump and sent her trotting off into the paddock to join the others.

'What time is it?' she asked.

'About half-eleven.' Luke squinted up at her. 'If you can get your ass into gear, we've been invited to lunch by my father.'

'I've gotta wash my hair,' squeaked Perdita, feeling quite unable to face Chessie. 'And all my clothes are dirty. I suppose I could wear my new leather trousers.'

'I wouldn't, you'll be far too hot,' said Luke. 'Borrow one of my shirts, second drawer down. You'll find coffee next door, orange juice in the ice box, and, after Argentina, the shower's like Niagara.'

'My father wants to discuss the Fathers and Sons final tomorrow,' said Luke as he drove into Palm Beach. 'The beauty of this tournament is that families are forced to bury the hatchet once a year in order to play in it.'

After the poverty and primitive barbarity of the pampas, Perdita couldn't believe Palm Beach. On either side of the road reared up vast ficus hedges like ramparts of green fudge. Occasionally, through towering electric gates, she caught a glimpse of pastel palaces so like blocks of ice-cream that she expected them to melt in the burning sun. Occasionally down a side road she caught a glimpse of the ocean. Apart from the odd security guard, no-one was around in the streets. Limousines, stealthily overtaking, made Luke's dusty pick-up truck look very shabby. In the back, a security guard in himself, sat Luke's ferocious mongrel, who growled every time an increasingly nervous Perdita leant towards Luke to check her reflection in the driving mirror.

'He's worse than Fantasma,' she grumbled.

'Let him get used to you,' said Luke. 'He's kinda over protective where I'm concerned. He came from Juan's yard. When the Argies go home, they often abandon a dog.'

'Bastards,' said Perdita. 'What's his name?'

'Leroy, because he's big and black and from the South.'

'Is Red coming to lunch?' asked Perdita.

'I guess not. He got his picture on the cover of *People* magazine this week as polo's bad guy and Auriel Kingham's toyboy. The piece inside was less pretty. A charitable interpretation would be that the reporter stitched him up, but I recognize Red's style in most of the snide quotes.'

'Like what?'

Luke shook his head ruefully. 'Describing Chessie as an ageing bimbo and as shallow as a paddling pool, saying she was such a gold digger she must have majored in opencast mining, and that Dad has to employ all his security guards ready gelded.'

'Golly,' said Perdita in awe, 'I adore him already.'

'Chessie is OK,' said Luke firmly.

Oh, please make her have gone off, prayed Perdita.

As Luke swung round the corner, on the right, towering above the ficus battlement was the biggest palest pink house in the road.

'There you are, Alderton Towers,' said Luke. 'It used to be eight houses. Dad knocked down three to extend the garden. This one belongs to him and Chessie, the one beyond's kept for servants and guards, another's for guests, and the other two for Red and Bibi.'

'What about you?' asked Perdita, thinking indignantly about the tiny kitchen and the bedroom overcrowded with books.

'I make my own way,' said Luke.

Bart's gates were swarming with press who were being almost kept at bay by two large guards.

'Go round to the back,' snapped the larger one when he saw the pick-up truck. Then, recognizing Luke, 'Oh sorry, Mr Alderton. Welcome home.'

The reporters surged forward in excitement. 'It's Luke, the brother. You got anything to say about Red and Auriel Kingham, Mr Alderton?'

'Don't know anything,' said Luke grinning.

'Knock it off, you guys,' said the guard, punching them back as his mate pressed the remote control to open the gates.

Oh, my God, thought Perdita, I'm not ready for this.

Instead of a lawn, the front garden was covered in periwinkle-blue slats like the deck of a ship which only stopped to take in the occasional massive mast-like tree. The lack of foliage outside, however, was more than compensated by the tropical plants inside. A drawing room, almost as big as a hockey pitch, was overflowing with scented orchids of all colours. Jungle flora rioted also over the wallpaper and the chintz on two vast sofas, thirty feet apart on either side of the green marble fireplace. Did Bart and Chessie occupy one each on cosy winter evenings, wondered Perdita. Like at Robinsgrove, the grand piano was covered with silver-framed photographs of members of the Alderton family, mostly on polo ponies. But Perdita only took in the one at the front, of an adorable blond, brown-eyed small boy, who was so like Ricky he could only be Will. She had never seen a picture of him before. No wonder losing him had broken Ricky's heart.

Tearing her eyes away she was staggered by the paintings, including a Gauguin, two Dalis, a Jackson Pollock and three Andy Warhols, which covered two walls. Spotlit polo trophies like a great leaping silver shoal of fish covered a third. The fourth, all window and now open, looked on to a beautiful swimming-pool, flanked by high walls, entirely smothered in bougainvillaea, honeysuckle, stephanotis, jasmine and pale pink roses. Through a wrought-iron gate on the other side the ocean flashed as peacock-blue as Angel's eyes.

'That's the best painting in the room,' said Luke, pointing to some massed pink water-lilies above the fireplace.

'Everyone says I married Bart for his Monet,' drawled a voice.

Perdita swung round. Hell, she thought, she's more stunning than ever. Even ferocious Leroy thumped his stubby black tail.

'Luke, darling,' murmured Chessie, wafting the scent of

298

lily of the valley into the room. Giving him the benefit of her body in a sopping-wet lime-green bikini, she weaved into Luke's embrace as voluptuously as the Siamese stable cat had earlier:

'Thank God you've come home to bring some sanity to this dump.'

'You look incredible, as usual,' said Luke, kissing her on both cheeks. 'This is Perdita.'

'Hi,' said Chessie. 'I hear you've been in Argentina. Isn't it bliss, but aren't they lecherous? Juan and Miguel would have gang-banged me years ago if they weren't so terrified of losing Bart's custom.'

Chessie must have lost a stone since Perdita last saw her, and was on the borderline that appears exquisite in clothes, but rather too thin uncovered. With her very short streaked hair, flawless golden skin, and shadowed eyes she now looked more like the new boy every prefect wants to take behind the squash court than a rather too-knowing Botticelli angel.

You stupid cow, Perdita told herself. Her own hair hadn't been cut for four months. Not used to the heat, her face was still flushed from the hair dryer. Luke's red and white striped shirt belted with one of his few ties, which had looked so sexy and original when she had teetered on his bed to see into the tiny mirror, now just looked silly and her bloody brown leather trousers were too tight and punishingly hot. It was entirely Luke's fault for not being insistent enough that she shouldn't wear them. Beside Chessie, she felt like a carthorse let loose in the paddock at Ascot.

Despite her cool exterior, Chessie was plainly in a foul mood. 'I was going to make Bloodies, but the colour reminds me too much of your unspeakable brother, so I thought we'd have margueritas instead.'

Pressing a bell, she led them out to the swimming-pool, where she and Luke sat in the sun, and Perdita took refuge under a blue and white striped umbrella.

'All because of him,' rattled on Chessie, 'we've been bombarded by the *paparazzi*. One of the guards found a photographer up in that traveller's palm yesterday afternoon. Bart's had to double the security. It's like Colditz! "Ready gelded" indeed!'

Auriel Kingham was such a big star that Perdita couldn't resist asking, 'Is she as beautiful in the flesh?'

'What flesh?' said Chess scornfully. 'There isn't an inch of cellulite that hasn't been sucked out. She's so lifted she could wear her pubes as a moustache.'

'Ouch,' said Luke, half-laughing. 'Where's Dad?'

'Talking on four telephones, reading faxes, dictating letters, playing with his computer, thinking about polo. Why do I always end up with obsessives? He'll be out soon to give you his divided attention. What took you so long?' she snapped as a maid came out with the margueritas.

Grabbing one, she drained half in one gulp.

'Hi, Conchita,' Luke smiled up at the maid. 'I'd honestly rather have a beer, please.'

'I'll have yours as well then.' Chessie grabbed Luke's marguerita. 'And hurry up with that beer,' she shouted at the maid's retreating back, then, turning to Luke, 'Have you seen that piece in *People*?'

Luke nodded.

'How dare he call me a bimbo? He's the bloody bimbo selling himself to any man, woman or Rottweiler as long as they pick up his bills.'

'Oh, c'mon,' said Luke. 'He was probably looped when he gave the interview. He doesn't mean it.'

'Course he does.' Chessie lit a cigarette with a shaking hand. 'Your kid brother was born with a wooden spoon in his mouth for stirring things.'

'He's only jealous because you're prettier than him,' said Luke, feeding potato chips to a slavering Leroy.

'Well, he shouldn't expose his jealousy in public along with everything else. And how your bloody father can play with him in the Fathers and Sons tomorrow after all those things he's said about me?'

Luke shrugged. 'That's polo. I know it hurts. I'm sorry.'

Having finished her marguerita, Chessie reached for the second one.

'Bart's secretly delighted,' she said bitterly, 'because *People* said he ran the best barn in Palm Beach, and was the only high-goal patron who fully carried his weight on the team. He'll need to be tomorrow. Red'll be coked up to the eyeballs, and Bibi's so busy working all hours she's completely out of practice – and out of shape,' she added maliciously, as a girl wandered out of the sitting room.

'Unlike you,' said the girl furiously, 'I don't spend all day having my body and my ego massaged. Hi, Lukie,' she added, kissing him. 'You look great.'

'This is my sister Bibi,' Luke said to Perdita.

Amid all this paradise and effortless access to wealth, Perdita was amazed how aggressively plain Bibi was. Admittedly her face wasn't helped by Bart's heavy jaw and a sallow skin. But her hair, the colour of marmalade and scraped back in a bun, and huge horn-rimmed spectacles only emphasized a big nose and hazel eyes that were unmade-up and bloodshot from the overnight flight from LA. Her figure was also totally disguised by a severely cut, lightweight, pin-striped suit. The only thing she couldn't hide were long, beautiful, coltish legs. She was obviously trying to look much older than her twenty-two years.

Totally ignoring Chessie, she accepted a glass of Perrier from the maid and, sharing the shade of another blue and white striped umbrella with a panting Leroy, started questioning Luke about Argentina.

Perdita was getting sauna-ed in her leather trousers. She must make some contribution to the conversation, but a mixture of jet lag and Chessie's utterly haunting beauty had knocked her for six. Bart, joining them a few minutes later, made her feel even more shy. A few more grey hairs had been added to his wolf's pelt and a few more crows' feet to his angry aggressive eyes, but he was suntanned and lean from frantic dieting and had kept his movie-star looks.

Putting a brief hand on Luke's arm but ignoring Perdita, he turned to Bibi. 'Hi, sweetheart, what did the Saudis say?'

'If they don't get those twenty Lightnings before Christmas they're going to cancel the order. I've shouted myself hoarse at the factory, but they won't take any notice,' said Bibi furiously.

Bart turned back towards the house. 'I'll talk to them.'

'*After* lunch,' said Chessie, so icily that Bart stopped in his tracks. 'This is Perdita,' she added.

Bart nodded unenthusiastically in Perdita's direction, then, anxious to conciliate Chessie: 'New bikini? Nice, suits you.'

'Cost enough,' said Bibi spitefully. 'I saw the bill. If

Red moves in with Auriel, you can fill his house with all your clothes.'

They had lunch by the pool. Tuna-fish open sandwiches and a taco salad, so delicious that despite the heat Perdita wanted to wolf the lot. Chessie, who hardly ate anything, moved on to white wine. When Bart wasn't obsessively taking telephone calls, he and Luke and Bibi discussed tactics and what ponies they would ride tomorrow. Bart would mount Red and Bibi; Luke would bring his own. Every time Luke tried to draw Perdita into the conversation, Bart rode her off.

He looked really cheerful, however, when he heard that Victor had been fleeced by Alejandro.

'I saw Lando Medici at the Players Club last night,' he told Luke. 'He was boasting about this wonder pony he bought from Alejandro, Fanfare or something, the grey responsible for the Mendozas taking out the O'Briens in the Copa de Republic. I told Miguel he was slipping to let her go.'

'Is that a fact?' Luke grinned. 'That's three people Alejandro's sold Fantasma to,' he murmured to Perdita.

'I really liked that piece in *People*,' said Bibi loudly.

'Shut up,' Luke said to her softly. 'Is it serious, him and Auriel?'

'With her it is. I cannot understand how Red can fall for such an awful polo player,' said Bibi. 'I played against her in a charity match in Palm Springs. She simply cannot control her horses.'

'What's in it for Red?'

Bibi shrugged. 'He just says, "I want that", and she buys it for him.'

'Like what?'

'Four ponies last week.'

'Shit,' said Luke.

Chessie was so fed up with Bibi and Bart that she suddenly rolled over to brown her back and started asking Perdita all about Argentina.

'You're probably too jet lagged today, but next week I'll show you Worth Avenue and we can go shopping.'

'I'd love a haircut,' said Perdita ruefully.

'I'll take you to Xavier's. He won't chop it all off. It's gorgeous hair.'

She's my rival, thought Perdita in confusion, and suddenly she's being so nice to me. If Ricky saw her again now, how could he possibly fail to be a million times more in love with her?

Luke, who was acquiring even more freckles in the sunshine, was having his work cut out trying to persuade Bart to give Angel a year's contract.

'Is he as idle and conniving as the rest of them?' asked Bart.

'He's lovely,' butted in Perdita. 'You'll really like him.'

'I'm not gonna socialize with him,' said Bart rudely. 'I just want to know if the guy's any good.'

'My husband has so much charm,' said Chessie lightly.

Having refused the fruit salad, she lit a cigarette and, as Bart was now jabbering on the telephone to some Jap, turned to Bibi: 'How's your love life?'

'Fine,' said Bibi, picking only lychees and guavas out of the fruit salad, then adding to Luke, 'I sure appreciate you telling Ricky to look me up in LA.'

Then, smiling evilly, almost toadlike, she turned back to Chessie, 'I know Dad's cute, but how could you dump Ricky? He is to die for. We spent a lot of time together.'

'Really?' Chessie drew slightly faster on her cigarette.

'He's being such a wow with all the movie stars he's coaching,' went on Bibi, slowly pouring too much cream over her fruit salad. 'Being Ricky, he hasn't a clue who any of them are and keeps yelling "Come here, you" to Stacy Keach and Pamela Sue Martin and Stefanie Powers. They just adore him.'

Luke put a hand over Perdita's.

'Don't rise,' he murmured. 'She's only winding Chessie up.'

'Of course the women are spectacular in LA,' went on Bibi. 'Everyone's beautiful there.'

'You must be the exception,' said Chessie sweetly, but she was balling her napkin.

'How's Ricky's elbow?' asked Luke.

'Holding up pretty good,' said Bibi. 'In fact he seems to be spending a lot of time on both elbows, screwing his brains out. There are women coming out of his ears.'

'Oh, c'mon,' said Luke sharply.

Chessie didn't react. Perdita had less restraint.

'I don't believe it,' she stormed. 'Ricky's not like that.'

'How d'you know?' said Chessie sharply.

'I'm his protégée,' said Perdita simply. 'I've been working in his yard for the last two and a half years. He fixed up for me to stay with Alejandro, and I'm going back to England to play with him in Dancer Maitland's team next year. We've already met,' she added to Chessie. 'You gave me a lift home from David Waterlane's party the night you got off with Bart.'

There was a stunned pause. Both Bibi and Chessie were looking at her as though she were a maggot who'd strayed into their raddichio.

'You'll never guess,' drawled Chessie as Bart came off the telephone. 'Your son's brought a little Trojan polo pony into the house. Perdita works for Ricky and she's going to be playing for him when we're in England next year. You could be marking each other.'

'She'll give you a hard time,' said Luke evenly. 'She's pretty good. Come on, baby.' Taking Perdita's hand, he pulled her to his feet. 'I've got work to do. Thanks for a great lunch.' Briefly he kissed Chessie's rigid cheek. 'See you tomorrow, Dad.'

31

Bart Alderton was an indelibly competitive man, but not altogether a bad one. To spite Grace and Ricky, who had both patronized him, he had stolen Ricky's wife. Will's death, however, had shaken him to his working-class roots. Afterwards he had been magic to Chessie, displaying uncharacteristic gentleness and patience, not only wheeling in an army of bereavement counsellors, but also listening endlessly and comforting her himself. He had also been jolted by how much his defection had destroyed Grace and the animosity this had aroused in Bibi and particularly Red.

Until Bart met Chessie, driven on by Grace, he had been a total workaholic, who only played polo so hard because he liked the snob element and was addicted to winning. But in Chessie he had acquired the perfect accessory to flaunt on the sidelines. Having fallen in love with her as well, he was so frantic to stop her ever going back to Ricky that becoming a better polo player and annihilating Ricky on the field had become his ultimate fix.

He was faced, therefore, with the conflict of winning on all fronts. It was hard satisfying Chessie in bed if his elbow had been hit by a ball the day before, his right shin was black and blue from a pulverizing ride-off and he had to fly off to New York first thing in the morning. How, too, could he concentrate on a board meeting, if he felt as though he'd been hit by a truck, or when half his mind was on whether he could dump the sales seminar in Detroit and the speech to the LA Chamber of Commerce in order to make tomorrow's final?

That afternoon when Luke and Perdita came to lunch in Palm Beach he was desperate to stick and ball, but he was supposed to fly to Washington immediately to meet the Saudi Minister of Defence to clinch an order for 100 helicopters. Picking up his briefcase, he went out to the pool to find Chessie doing backstroke with absolutely no clothes on at all, surreptitiously being watched through the wrought-iron gates by two security guards, whose crotches were bulging as much as their side pockets.

'Chessie!' he snarled.

Christ, she was beautiful, with her breasts so small and firm they hardly splayed to the sides at all and her curling waist, and the red jewels of her painted toenails. Smiling sleepily and lasciviously up at him, she deliberately opened her legs, so he could see the pink, shining coral of her labia.

'Come out of that pool,' he said hoarsely. 'Fuck off, you two sons of bitches!' he roared at the security men.

'Dad, are you coming?' Clutching a burgundy briefcase, Bibi appeared impatiently at the drawing-room window.

'Jolly nearly,' mocked Chessie, not closing her legs.

'Christ, you slut,' said Bibi in disgust.

'You handle the Defence Minister,' said Bart, not looking round. 'Iranians like women.'

'They don't listen to them,' raged Bibi. 'You oughta be there, Dad.'

'Give me twenty minutes,' said Bart.

'Five's quite enough for your father,' said Chessie.

'You bitch,' said Bart a minute later, as he slammed the bedroom door. 'Why d'you keep winding Bibi up, for Chrissake?'

'Why does your bloody son wind me up?' screamed Chessie. 'Why d'you have to play with him tomorrow?'

'We've been through all that,' said Bart roughly. Then drawing her to him, 'You'll have to pay for it, you know.'

He felt her breath quicken.

'Punish me then,' whispered Chessie.

He left her after half an hour, sated, sore but satisfied. She hated him, but he had totally cracked her sexually. She wouldn't be swimming in the nude for a few days.

Perdita was in a far worse mood than Chessie.

'I do not believe it,' she stormed, too angry to cry as they drove back to Luke's barn in Wellington. 'Ricky is not promiscuous.'

'Sure he isn't,' said Luke. 'Bibi was just paying Chessie back for asking about her love life. Bibi's boyfriend Skipper's what we call a Trust Fund Baby. He lives off his father and does damn all, and now he's playing her up. He's an asshole. But it always hurts.'

'I can't see Ricky fancying her,' said Perdita. 'She's not remotely glamorous.'

'Can be,' said Luke as they drove past scummy canals full of condoms and Coke tins. 'When she's dressed up for the evening with her hair loose and her jewels on and her contact lenses in, she looks fantastic. She's tired too. Grace knew all the polo schedules well in advance so everything ran smoothly. Chessie's not interested, so Bibi has to do all that as well as running the LA office. She's got a terrific body.'

'Pity about the face. And that Chessie's a bitch,' said Perdita, gazing moodily out at an airport, where hundreds of private planes – mostly Alderton Lightnings – flocked like seagulls. 'And she's so bloody beautiful. Mind you, it's easy if you're that rich. Christ, I'd like to spend a million pounds on clothes and a hundred years in a beauty parlour. If only I wasn't so broke! How can I compete with that sort of thing?'

Luke touched her cheek with his hand.

'You're beautiful. No one holds a candle to you.'

He ought to go home and tune up the horses for to-morrow. He also had a mass of paperwork to go through, having been away so long, but to cheer Perdita up he took her to Palm Beach Polo Club, which was only a mile from his barn.

Entering the gates, they passed incredibly manicured land, flawless lawns, tennis courts and swimming-pools. On the left were khaki lakes and polo pitches, flanked by mushroom-coloured houses with wonderful gardens overflowing with hibiscus, oleander and bougainvillaea. Fountains and sprinklers sparkled in the brilliant sunlight. Only the palm trees, lurching lanky and gawky with their scruffy mopheads, seemed out of place.

'Six years ago there was nothing here,' said Luke. 'Cattle grazed and most of it was swamp. That house belongs to an oil heiress. She's twenty-three. That house cost fifteen million. The husband bought it for his wife because she likes to watch polo. They spend two weeks a year here, and that's Polo Island, and there's the house Auriel's rented.'

'They look like upmarket mud huts,' said Perdita sourly. 'Fancy paying fifteen million for one of those.'

'There's the Players Club. I'll take you there tomorrow after the match, and there's Field One. Doesn't that give you a *frisson*?'

Driving on, Luke pointed out the most amazing barns, each one painted in a different colour, pale pink, sky-blue, black and white, all open-plan and with the sort of gardens you could open to the public.

'You'd expect the ponies to spend all day painting their toenails and reading *Vanity Fair*,' said Luke. 'Instead they come out on to the pitches and get bashed and yanked to pieces in the roughest polo in the world. It all looks so perfect, but up in those palm trees live rattlesnakes, and in those smooth brown pools lurk alligators. They symbolize the play. A handful of the richest men in the world converge on Palm Beach every January, merely for the buzz of taking each other out. My father rolls up like Genghis Khan with seventy horses. He's run out of challenges in the boardroom. Screwing a billion out of the government, raking up another billion in the portfolio, stripping assets, stripping girls, is nothing to being within an inch of death while you kick the shit out of Victor Kaputnik, or Lando

Medici, or even Hal Peters, on the field. Over in the UK you don't get the thrust of the patron. They don't play to win here, but to annihilate.'

'Wow,' said Perdita, startled out of her sulks. 'You do sound disapproving – talk about the Sermon on the Mounted.'

Luke grinned. 'Sorry, I was getting heavy. It's taken the fun out of polo, but I guess I'll exploit it until I make enough dough not to have to sell on ponies I like. Come and see the best-run barn in Palm Beach.'

As he swung the truck to the right Leroy jumped across Perdita's legs, scrabbling at her leather trousers – not that it mattered, beastly hot things – and started barking provocatively out of the window at a couple of Rottweilers who nearly broke their chains barking back.

Bart's barn, *El Paradiso*, was built in the middle of an orange grove. A colonnade of white pillars, smothered in white roses and jasmine led up to where loose boxes, painted duck-egg blue, the Alderton Flyers' colours, contained the sleekest, fittest thoroughbred ponies Perdita had ever seen. An amazing tack room housed a computer giving print-outs of every chukka every pony had ever played. On the end was built an apartment with a bar, a kitchen, a shower room, a massive jacuzzi to soothe aching polo bones, and a living room with a vast portrait of Bart on a pony, as well as a Stubbs, a Herring, and two Munnings on the walls. How extraordinary, thought Perdita, to have two such lavish establishments within half an hour of each other and no wonder they needed all those security guards and Rottweilers on the gates.

Outside, white geraniums and impatiens grew in blue tubs and hanging baskets, and a fountain fell as regularly as a transparent comb into a pond edged with white irises. Everywhere the orange blossom wafted suffocatingly sweet.

Luke whistled at Leroy who, at a safe distance, was still winding up the Rottweilers.

'Come and meet Red,' he said.

Overwhelmed by such blatant perfection, Perdita snapped back sulkily that she absolutely loathed men with red hair.

'Oh well, perhaps I don't,' she admitted in a small voice

a second later. For there, cantering round a jade-green paddock with a cordless telephone in one hand and a polo stick in the other, his reddy-brown boots the same colour as his sleek sorrel pony and his gleaming chestnut hair, was Red Alderton. But there was no red in his deep, smooth mahogany suntan, which was enhanced by onyx-brown eyes with thick very dark lashes, a short straight nose and a wonderfully passionate, smiling mouth.

For three and a half years Perdita hadn't been remotely sexually attracted to anyone but Ricky, but Red jolted her. Not only was he the best-looking man she had ever seen, but from the way he had knotted the reins on his pony's neck, and was guiding her round the paddock with his thighs and his lean, supple, whipcord body, he was also the most effortlessly gifted polo player.

'Hi, you guys,' he said, waving his stick at them, and still giving himself time to execute another perfect shot, 'be with you in a second. Lucy, baby, I gotta go. He'll be home tomorrow, won't he, so I'd better not call. Who did you say Chuck had run off with?'

A typical Gemini, Red lived on the telephone, adored gossip and had an increasingly low threshold of boredom. People were invariably pleased to see him because he made them laugh and had so much charm. Despite his languid insouciance, however, he had Bart's killer instinct and, although he adored Luke, had to beat him at everything. Normally he never bothered to stick and ball. He was only doing so today because Luke, by sheer grind, had gone above him in the November handicap ratings.

He was now winding up his conversation.

'Look, meet me at Cobblestones at six tomorrow. Love you too, baby.'

'Cobblestones is the bar where all the players and grooms hang out,' explained Luke.

And that's not Auriel Kingham he's talking to, thought Perdita.

As Red switched off the telephone, Luke introduced Perdita. 'She's from England. She's going to play with Ricky and Dancer Maitland next year.'

'I met Dancer at a Band-Aid concert in New York last week,' said Red. 'Christ, I wish I didn't know it was Christmas. Nice guy, though, kinda fun to play with. I

309

figured my stepmother had put me off English women for good, but,' he smiled at Perdita, who blushed to the roots of her hair, 'I guess you could convert me. How are you enjoying this hot, swampy, mosquito-infested paradise?'

Realizing Perdita was too jolted to speak, Luke said: 'We only arrived yesterday.'

'Bring any good ponies?'

'One genius,' said Luke, 'and I'm not selling her on. Where did you get that one?'

'Miguel bought her,' said Red. 'Got the speed, but still a bit green. Thank Christ you've come back to help us clinch the match tomorrow. Before the semi-finals Auriel and I had our own private party and I went on to the pitch absolutely looped. All I could see was two balls, two mallets, eight goal posts, four pony's ears in front of me, sixteen players, four screaming umpires and after the match my father twice over chasing me round two polo fields, out to bury me. Jesus!'

Throughout this languid patter, dispatched with the broadest of grins, Red's eyes roved over Perdita in a way that made her feel edgy and hopelessly excited at the same time.

The telephone rang, making the sorrel mare jump.

'Hi, Lorna, sweetheart, how ya been? Sorry I didn't call, I've been up to here.' Then, suddenly flaring up, 'Oh, for Chrissake, get off my case.' Red switched off the telephone so she couldn't ring back.

Then, as Leroy bounced up and nipped the sorrel on her pink nose, making her jump more than ever, he added, 'And keep that brute away from me. He was so pissed off waiting for you to come home, he bit me last week. He'll bite a patron one of these days.'

'How's Auriel?' said Luke, calling an unrepentant Leroy to heel.

'Pretty good,' said Red blandly. 'I'm teaching her to play polo. She's teaching me other things. She's in LA making a movie about the corrupting effect of money. As she's making five million bucks out of it, I guess she's being corrupted all the way to the bank.'

'D'you want to play in a charity match next Sunday?' asked Luke.

Red looked wary. 'Not a lot.'

'It's for Ethiopia. Bob Geldof's flying down.'

'Auriel better throw-in,' said Red. 'She adores publicity. Who else is playing?'

'Victor, Shark Nelligan, Bobby Ferraro and Alejandro, against Hal, me, Jesus and, hopefully, you.'

'How much?'

'We're playing for free.'

'Bullshit. Shark and Alejandro won't even tack up for free. Nor am I going to be bashed around by all those thugs for nothing.'

'Three thousand,' said Luke.

'I'll think about it,' said Red. 'What colour's Hal Peters on?'

'Purple.'

'Doesn't suit me,' grumbled Red. 'Drains all my colour. Make it four. I've got to buy Auriel a Christmas present. I've had three offers for the World Cup and two for the Open, by the way.'

At that moment a car drew up in front of the barn and a man in a crumpled dark blue suit got out.

'Mr Alderton? I'm from the *Daily News*.'

'How the hell did you get in here?' snapped Red. 'Those Rottweilers oughta be fired.'

'We had an appointment.'

'Well, we don't any more, right?'

'Could you just tell me about your relationship with Miss Kingham?'

'I could,' said Red amiably, watching the reporter brighten at the possibility of a scoop, 'but I'm not going to.'

He glanced at his watch.

'I must fly – literally. I've gotta party in LA this evening. Christ, I better call the airport.'

The minute he switched on the telephone it rang. Red listened for five seconds, and then said, 'Aw, fuck off, Lorna.'

As he held the telephone at arm's length, Perdita could hear the stream of abuse. Cantering back to the stable, he calmly lobbed the telephone into the pond.

'My brother's allergic to commitment,' sighed Luke. 'He suffers from the seven-minute itch.'

'That's why he took up polo,' said Perdita. 'At least his

attention span lasts a chukka. He's not a bit like you,' she went on as they drove back to Luke's barn, 'not a millionth as nice.'

'He's OK,' said Luke. 'He just can't handle people getting heavy.'

'But screwing $4,000 out of you.'

'He's always broke,' countered Luke, 'because he's so generous, not just with himself, but to everyone else. He could make a fortune playing polo. Patrons adore having him on their teams because he's so glamorous, but they're cautious. Players these days tend not to party till three o'clock in the morning before a final. There's too much at stake. Red's a party animal. He's likely to turn up looped or not at all.'

'You love him, don't you?'

'Sure, he's my kid brother. But I hope to Christ he gets back in time tomorrow.'

32

Red, however, did not get back in time. Perdita came in from stick and balling at midday the following morning to find Chessie had telephoned to ask her to lunch at the Players Club and then to watch the match. Perdita was livid.

'I haven't got anything to wear. I can't wear shorts or a dress because my legs are so pale and I haven't had time to shave them. And she only wants to pump me about Ricky, and I want to help you on the pony lines.'

'I'd keep out of the way,' advised Luke. 'You'll enjoy Chessie, and she needs some friends.'

Reluctantly Perdita did find herself liking Chessie. She was so unrepentantly bitchy, and even more ravishing today in pale pink Bermudas and a T-shirt to match her pale pink and perfect mouth. Perdita absolutely adored the Players Club, with its yellow and white striped awning and dark forest-green walls inside, which were covered with photographs of famous players. There were the Napiers looking thuggish, and Jesus very unholy, and Miguel and Alejandro conniving, and Juan younger before he grew his celebrated black moustache,

312

and Bobby Ferraro and Shark Nelligan, the two great American players.

I'll be up there one day, vowed Perdita.

'They took Ricky's picture down,' said Chessie drily. 'Probably because Bart offered them so much money.'

'He'll be back,' said Perdita quickly. 'Oh, there's Luke.'

'Made it for the first time this year,' said Chessie.

They stopped in front of Luke's photograph. He was so brown his freckles had almost joined up, and he was smiling so broadly his eyes had almost disappeared.

'Lovely open face,' mused Chessie. 'And, goodness, he deserves to be up there. He works so hard, making those ponies night after night until he falls off with exhaustion. And Red just swans in and takes his pick of Bart's ponies. I long to slip Luke the odd billion in his tea. Bart'd never notice. He spends that in a year on vets' bills and Mrs Juan's electrolysis.'

Perdita giggled. 'She's a horror, isn't she? The umpires are more scared of her than Miguel.'

Chessie also showed Perdita the glass case full of trophies – the World Cup a towering three-foot samovar and the gold Jaipur horse on an ebony stand. Missing from its space on the green baize was the Fathers and Sons Cup to be contested in a couple of hours. Perdita wondered if Luke was getting nervous.

'Where's the Westchester?' asked Perdita, without thinking.

'Incarcerated in New York,' said Chessie mockingly. 'And I imagine it's going to stay there.'

They lunched on Sancerre and lobster salad, served by beautiful blonde waitresses in dark green shirts the colour of the walls, and white shorts showing off their long, smooth, brown legs.

'Red's had most of them,' said Chessie dismissively.

'He'll get some competition when he meets Angel,' said Perdita. 'Gosh, this lobster is wonderful. And the orange juice here is the best I've ever tasted. I had four glasses for breakfast. I went into a supermarket with Luke last night, and they were offering a free bottle of champagne for every bottle you bought.'

'That's Palm Beach,' said Chessie bitterly. 'When men get married, they offer them a free bimbo as well.'

313

'Is Red really keen on Auriel?' asked Perdita, forking up raw spinach.

'Likes the publicity,' said Chessie, 'although he won't admit it, and adores annoying his father. It's also a wonderful coup for her. She may be the most famous forty-five year old in the world, but heterosexual men are like gold dust in America, and in Palm Beach non-existent. I promise you, the women round here are carnivorous. If I left Bart for a weekend some frisky bit of crumpet would snap him up, and it's not just the bimbos. Every time he goes out to dinner he feels some crone's claw on his thigh.'

'Does Red really go through lots of women?'

Chessie nodded. 'This afternoon at the match you'll see legions of amazing girls enjoying the sunshine and loathing each other. They're known as the Red Army. They turn up in droves to watch him play.'

'Like Rupert Campbell-Black,' said Perdita.

Chessie perked up. 'He adored Ricky so much he bypassed me. I was very disappointed. They say there isn't a marriage he can't crack. Now he really *is* attractive. I can't see what the girls see in Red. He's so narcissistic. I mean he dyes his eyelashes. They aren't that colour at all, and in the evening he wears eyeliner. And just you watch the way he takes off his knee pads and smooths down his breeches before the presentation.'

As they drove over to Field Two Perdita felt despondent. Chessie was right; she'd never seen so many beautiful girls, mostly blondes with hair that looked as though it had been tossed in the tumble dryer. No one seemed to be looking at her. Perhaps it was because she'd come from Argentina, where men stared and whistled at anything remotely passable, that she felt so invisible in her old jeans and grey shirt.

'Dearie me,' said Chessie happily as they drove past the pony lines and heard shouting, 'I suspect Ethel-Red the unready hasn't turned up.'

She was right. Bart, Luke and Bibi and their opponents the Van Dorens – the father, once a great player and still with a nine-goal mind, and his three sons – were all waiting to play. Red's pony for the first chukka was tacked up in his duck-egg-blue bandages and saddle blanket. The umpires were looking at their watches – but there was no sign of Red.

The Aldertons had won the Fathers and Sons match for the last three years, and with Bart on five, Red and Luke on six and seven respectively, and Bibi now a useful one, they should have walked it today. But without Red they were stymied. The *paparazzi*, out in force for Red, were enjoying listening to an apopleptic Bart yelling at Luke and Bibi.

'I don't know the shorthand for asshole or son of a bitch,' grumbled a girl reporter. 'I wonder if they're grammalogues.'

The Van Dorens, who were cool and WASP, with very long arms to hook their opponents' sticks, were much amused that Red hadn't arrived. Like every other player in Palm Beach, they were fed up with Bart bringing in ringers and spending so much on ponies that he priced everyone else out of existence. Chessie, sitting in the aluminium stands with Perdita, was most amused of all.

'The little shit,' she remarked, not lowering her voice at all. 'I warned Bart not to rely on him. And best of all his ghastly mother is sitting down below us: *"Take my napkin, rub thy brow, Hamlet"*. The silly old bag rolls up at every match, the spectre at the feast to drool over her baby. I'm afraid she's going to be disappointed yet again.'

Having only seen Grace once a long time ago, Perdita couldn't identify her at first.

'The one in the scrambled-egg-yellow dress,' said Chessie.

Perdita was shocked. It was though Medusa and Jack Frost had ganged up on Grace in a single night, turning her face to stone and her dark hair hoarfrost-white. She had aged twenty years. She looked grief-eroded and quite out of place on such a lovely day.

Rain all morning had given way to brilliant sunshine. Every leaf and grass blade glistened. Palm trees like unkempt, emaciated drunks lurched above the flawless, green field and the mushroom-brown houses. A large crowd had assembled on both sides behind the boards. The true polo addicts watched with the sun behind them. Those more interested in getting a tan, principally the Red

Army, faced the sun. Pitch and ponies beckoned. Oh, I wish I could play, thought Perdita.

'Bart will murder Red when he arrives,' said Chessie with satisfaction. 'Last year Red got so fed up with Bart shouting that he hit a ball straight into his ribs. The year before Bibi got knocked unconscious in a ride-off. Bart just bundled her into an ambulance and went on playing. Blood certainly isn't thicker than polo.'

'Why've they got three ambulances?'

'One's Bart's, another's the Van Dorens', the third belongs to the club. Good thing they've brought two fire-engines to put out the blaze when Red finally turns up. Look, Gracie is twisting her Hermes scarf to shreds,' said Chessie gleefully. 'Talk about Grace under pressure. We are not amused.'

Poor Grace was even less amused a second later, when a passing cameraman yelled up into the stands for Mrs Alderton.

'Yes,' called back Grace, rising regally to her feet.

But the cameraman was looking at Chessie. 'Mrs Alderton?'

'Yes,' said Chessie silkily.

'Can I get a picture of you on the pitch at divot-stomping time?'

'Sure,' said Chessie, 'if there is one. Doesn't look as though this match is going to get started.' She added in an undertone to Perdita. 'That will really wind up the old bag.'

Looking at Grace's stricken face, Perdita totally understood why Red and Bibi loathed Chessie.

The crowd was getting restless. Down on the pony lines Bart and Luke were still arguing about a substitute. Luke had tried to ring Angel, but he'd pushed off to spend the day with some Argentine players and couldn't be traced, which did not endear him to Bart. He wanted a six-goal substitute, which would enable Red to play if he turned up. Luke, who wanted Perdita, was arguing that they'd never find a six as good as Red, and with a lower handicapped substitute at least they'd get a four- or five-goal start, which they'd be more likely to hold on to because the Van Dorens were chiefly strong on defence. Bibi was backing up Luke. Leroy, who disliked rows because they reminded him of his former home in Miguel's yard, came to his master's aid by biting Bart sharply on his booted ankle, causing Bart's security guards to reach for their guns. Luke called Leroy off. The row escalated.

Up came the umpire, Shark Nelligan, a rough-tough cowboy with crooked teeth, who repeatedly claimed he was not going to kiss anyone's butt. Shark hated Luke because Hal Peters had been Shark's patron in medium-goal matches last summer, but, fed up with being ripped off and bawled out, Hal had switched to Luke for the high-goal Palm Beach season.

'You'll have to forfeit, Bart,' said Shark with some relish, 'if you're not on the pitch in five minutes.'

'You can hear the Aldertons rowing three continents away,' said Chessie. 'At least you're sitting in the best part of Palm Beach to hear all the latest scandal – whose horses are unsound, whose are for sale, which pros are about to be dropped, who's made the latest hot-horse deal.' Chessie's eyes sparkled wickedly. 'Who's screwing who. You're the *latest* gossip.'

'Me?' gasped Perdita.

Chessie lowered her voice only a fraction.

'Luke bringing you back from Argentina. Cassandra Murdoch, his girlfriend, is shattered.'

'But I'm not his . . . ' began Perdita aghast.

'That's her down there.' Chessie pointed out a tall brunette in a rust-coloured shirt and white sawn-off jeans. 'Luke's levelled with her, wrote to her some weeks ago, saying it was over and how desperately sorry he was. They've been together for three years. She's wiped out, even more cut-up than the pitch is going to be if they ever start playing.'

'But Luke and I aren't having an affair,' said Perdita, deeply shocked. 'He's my friend.'

'Faithful and just to me,' mocked Chessie. 'Rumour has it you're sharing his bed.'

'I am *not*. I may be sleeping in his bed, but he's sleeping in one of the grooms' caravans.'

Chessie shrugged. 'I'm only passing on what's being said.'

Perdita was so shaken it was a few seconds before she

317

realized Luke was yelling at her. 'Perdita, move your ass. You've gotta play.'

Frantic desire to escape from Chessie's interrogation overcame any nerves Perdita might have had. She shot down the steps and, only for a second as she raced along the boards, was she aware of the hollow-eyed anguished face of Cassandra Murdoch.

One of the grooms had picked up her knee pads, gloves, boots and stick from the back of Luke's car. Keeping on her jeans, she dived behind a trailer and swapped her grey T-shirt for the Alderton Flyer's duck-egg blue with the streak of dark blue lightning down the front and back, and borrowed a band from a groom to tie back her hair. There was no time to discuss tactics.

'With a weak Number Four, you could leave him,' advised Luke, 'but Chuck Van Doren's very solid, so stick around.'

'We're going to be a fucking laughing stock,' snarled Bart, glaring at Perdita. 'Two broads for Chrissake.'

'Knock it off, Dad,' said Luke curtly, zipping up Perdita's boots. 'We've gotta five-goal lead. Let's bloody well hang on to it.'

Next moment he had shoved Perdita up on to Red's pony for the first chukka, a skewbald with a broad white face and a jaunty walled eye.

'This horse is called Spotty,' said Luke, adjusting her stirrups. 'He couldn't outrun a fat man, but he gets everything done, because he's so handy, and he never runs out of gas. He also counts the crowd and shows off accordingly. Today he'll shift faster than the lightning down your back.'

Vaulting on to the dark brown Ophelia, he cantered beside her on to the field where the Van Dorens, Bart and Bibi were waiting. News sizzled round the pitch that this was the English girl Luke had brought back from Alejandro's. The crowd relaxed happily in anticipation of slaughter. At last Bart was going to be taken out.

Tempers tend to get up a lot on the polo field – but never as much as when the most united families play together. Bart, determined to play better than both Luke and Bruce Van Doren, swore at his team non-stop.

'How dare you call me an asshole, you stupid dickhead,'

screamed back Bibi as she missed an easy under-the-neck shot at goal. 'I've never been so insulted in my life. I'm not a fucking board meeting, Dad, do not address me as a board meeting.'

'Leave her alone,' Luke shouted at his father. 'Can't you see she plays doubly horrible when you yell at her all the time?'

At first Luke refused to be rattled, which annoyed Bart even more.

'I don't know why the fuck I asked you to come back from Argentina,' he howled.

'Can't you be more constructive in your criticism?' said Luke sarcastically.

'Don't give me that lip,' yelled Bart. 'Leave it, leave it,' he added, thundering down the pitch, and, seeing Perdita in front of him about to attempt a nearside forehand, 'for Christ's sake, leave it to me, you stupid bitch.'

'Don't call her a bitch, you evil fucker,' roared Luke.

The crowd, straining to hear every expletive, were highly edified. The Van Dorens were so amused they failed to stop Bart from scoring. Six-love to the Aldertons.

Perdita, used to playing with Ricky, was unfazed by the abuse, but was amazed, on the other hand, by how much Bart had improved. Having been coached regularly by Miguel, he now played well up to his five handicap, a far cry from the ball-chasing traffic hazard of three and a half years ago. And with a polo helmet covering his greying hair and lined forehead and softening the crows' feet round his sexy, slanting eyes, he looked virile, handsome and much younger than his forty-seven years. Perhaps Chessie might have trouble holding him.

After a dicey start herself, as she frantically adjusted to the vastly superior acceleration and handiness of Red's ponies, Perdita played gloriously. Spoon-fed by Luke, who was desperate for her to do well, and used to playing with him anyway, she scored three goals.

Finding themselves playing against two women and expecting a walk-over anyway, the Van Dorens initially behaved like gentlemen. When they came in for a ride-off against Bibi or Perdita, they just brushed them. But after Bibi and Perdita had crashed back into them like a flying ton of bricks several times, they sharpened up.

Perdita, too, loving every moment of riding these wonderful ponies and turned on by the crowd who whooped at every good shot or goal scored and groaned at every miss, had never enjoyed a game more in her life.

Gradually, however, the Van Dorens, the better side on paper, gained the ascendancy. At half-time, when Chessie was photographed pretending to tread in divots, the score was tied at seven all. By the middle of the sixth chukka the Van Dorens were running out the winners at 11-9 and the heavens opened. Up went the tailgates, like seats after a ball game. Off along the boards drove the Lincolns, the Bentleys and the Cadillacs of spectators anxious to get away before the mass exodus and assuming the Van Dorens had won. Bart had yelled himself almost hoarse when Perdita lost her temper.

'Stop screaming and muddling us all,' she screeched at him, and, crashing off like a dodgem car with a Ferrari engine, sent the youngest Van Doren flying and scorched off to score a goal. Then, almost before they'd changed ends and thrown in, Luke had got the ball out and handed it to her. Picking up her whip, Perdita belted down the field and scored again, tying the score.

Despite the downpour, the Lincolns, Bentleys and Cadillacs stopped in their tracks and started hooting encouragement. Spurred on by Perdita, Bibi scored as well. 12-11 to the Flyers.

A minute to go, Chuck Van Doren got the ball out this time and, leaving his back door open, raced down the boards looking dangerous. One glorious offside forehand took the ball well within striking distance, another would find the flags.

Luke, pounding back to defend his goal, desperately attempted to hook Chuck. The sight of the ball bouncing past, however, was too much for Leroy. Barking joyfully, he shot on to the pitch, and, just avoiding being trampled to death by Chuck's pony, bore the ball triumphantly off into the pony lines.

The crowd whooped and screamed with laughter. Up went the Van Dorens' sticks. It had, after all, been an Alderton dog who had crossed Chuck. Shark Nelligan, who in the past had been bitten several times by Leroy, awarded a penalty three to the Van Dorens.

Make him miss, please make him miss, prayed Perdita, unable to look. Fortunately the strain was too much for Chuck who hit wide. As play began the final bell went.

'Well played, congratulations,' said the Van Dorens, smiling and gracious in defeat as they shook Perdita's hand.

Bart, grinning from ear to ear and extraordinarily ungracious in victory, dropped his pony's reins and, taking his whip and his stick in his left hand, put his right arm round Perdita's shoulders, yelling hoarsely. 'We beat those preppy fuckers, we pussy-whipped them. That'll teach them to patronize Bart Alderton. You played real super, baby.'

A square was roped off and, despite the heavy drizzle, a lot of people gathered round, mostly to get a look at Luke's latest acquisition who had played so well and who got the loudest cheer as she went up to get her little silver statue of a father with his hand on his young son's shoulder. Although she could see her reflection all pink, hot, sweaty and damp-haired in the great silver cup from which the Van Dorens, being the losers, had the first swig, she felt terrific, particularly because Luke was so delighted.

Just then the heavens opened again and, across the cut-up pitch wearing dark glasses, cream Chinos, a cream silk shirt, a pale blue blazer braided with jade-green silk and carrying a black umbrella across the front of which was written 'Shit, it's raining', sauntered Red Alderton.

'Sorry, Dad,' he said, without a trace of contrition. 'I got held up. Lucky you had Perdita to fill in. I'd never have played so good, and this hangover would not have fitted under my helmet. No, fuck off, I've got nothing to say to you,' he snapped, as the *paparazzi* swooped.

'I'd have disinherited you if we'd lost,' said Bart furiously.

'I guess you would.' Red put his head on one side. 'And Mom will probably disinherit me anyway, so I better go make my peace. Well done,' he added to Perdita. 'You're definitely not just a pretty ass.'

After Luke had checked his horses he took Perdita for a drink at the Players Club. She was no longer invisible now. Everyone congratulated her. Immediately Bart drew her aside and, without even consulting Chessie or Luke, invited her to stay at Alderton Towers.

'You can't stop in Luke's pokey rathole any more.'

'I like it,' protested Perdita.

'Well, Luke can't like sleeping in a mobile home.'

'Sure I do,' said Luke.

'Well, come for Christmas dinner. We have it at *El Paradiso.*'

Luke raised an eyebrow in the direction of Leroy who was looking up, showing the whites of his eyes like two sickled slices of boiled egg, his legs splayed out behind like a frog. He was still carrying his polo ball and thumping his tail.

'Oh, bring the goddam dog too if you must,' said Bart irritably, 'but I'm not having him terrorizing my Rottweilers.'

Infuriated with Red, Bart was doubly anxious to bring Luke back into the fold. Like many men whose business enemies were legion, he valued family ties very highly, even while constantly abusing them. His aim was to have Luke financially dependent on him like the other two so he could manipulate him. The neatest thing he could do would be to buy Perdita. Half an hour later he and Chessie had to leave to change for some silver wedding party. Perdita sensed that Bart would rather have stayed and gone through every play of the match. Chessie was equally reluctant.

'Just another lot of geriatrics whinnying at Bart and thinking what an unsuitable marriage he's made,' she said bitterly as she drained her glass of champagne.

She's far too young for that kind of evening, thought Perdita. Just before he left, Bart thrust something into Perdita's hand.

'Go buy yourself something nice,' he said. 'Chessie'll take you to Worth Avenue.'

Glancing down, Perdita saw it was a wad of $1,000 bills.

'I can't,' she said, trying to sound shocked.

'Sure you can. You'd get a fee as a pro. You sure played a pro's game this afternoon.'

Perdita waltzed back to Luke. 'Look what your father's given me.'

Jesus, I could do with that right now, thought Luke. Perdita'd played so well, he wanted to take her to Chez Colbert and pour Moët down her all night, but he simply couldn't afford it. He'd been financially crippled buying and flying back four horses of his own from Alejandro's who might take weeks to adjust to the Palm Beach climate. He still had to pay grain bills and the grooms' salaries. Nor had the fat cheque promised by Hal Peters arrived yet, and he felt it was uncool to hassle.

He tried to persuade Bibi to come out with them, but she said she had too much work and had to fly straight back to LA.

'You played super,' she said to an amazed Perdita. 'You must be floating on air.'

Perdita giggled. 'I'm floating on hairs. The first thing I'm doing tomorrow is get my legs waxed.'

'Very painful, worse than childbirth,' warned Bibi.

'I'll hold your hand,' said Luke. 'No one shall accuse me of not being present at the waxing.'

33

The rain had stopped, giving way to a glorious evening with a huge apricot-pink moon and clouds rising like an indigo tidal wave on the horizon. Orion was lying on his back with the Dog Star above him. It was hard to tell the other stars from the lights of the incoming planes. The air was as soft as a shawl round Perdita's shoulders.

'Isn't Palm Beach the most heavenly place in the world?' she said, taking Luke's hand.

Red was waiting for them at Cobblestones, the famous polo bar. Early diners were devouring huge steaks, veal and french fries, or mountaineering through vast salads in the front room, which was very light, decorated in ice-cream colours with some rather crude paintings of polo games on the walls.

'Don't think my father would fork out two million for any of those,' said Red, sweeping them into the darker bar at the back. He was already very high and giggly, drinking green devils, a lethal concoction which included vodka, *crème de menthe* and cointreau. Immediately he ordered a bottle of Dom Perignon for Perdita and Luke. Luke bought a packet of crisps for Leroy, who sat on a bar stool as close to his master as possible.

'You'll have to drop that ball now,' said Luke, 'if you want a potato chip.'

'I gotta job for that brute,' said Red. 'I'll buy him a dozen polo balls if he eats Auriel's Yorkshire terriers. She ordered them tuna-fish sandwiches on the airplane and they threw them up just as we were landing.'

Then, taking Perdita's arm, he spun her round towards a square doorway concealed in the back of the bar.

'That, my darling, is the famous disappearing door. When husbands barge in here looking for their errant wives, the lovers nip out through that door. And that's the phone where all the players make assignations with people they shouldn't. I don't know why they don't install a second booth for Juan O'Brien and Jesus.'

A crowd had soon gathered round them, congratulating Perdita, admiring Red's blue blazer with the green silk braiding, and asking him what the hell had happened.

'Auriel gave me a Ferrari today in the colour of my choice. I chose red to match my hair and my bank balance. I couldn't just leave her and fly back.'

'What we all want to know,' asked Bobby Ferraro, the great American player who was so strong no horse ever answered back and who was playing for the Kaputnik Tigers in Luke's charity match, 'is what's she like?'

'OK,' said Red. 'Got more stitches in her face than I have in this coat, but OK.'

Over the laughter, Bobby Ferraro insisted: 'No, what's she like in the sack?'

'Pretty good,' said Red, grinning. 'Takes some getting used to. First time she gave me a blow job, her wig came off in my hands. I haven't been so embarrassed since they repossessed my helicopter.'

Everyone yelled with laughter.

'You're a shit, Red,' said Luke, shaking his head.

He had tried to call Angel to get him to join them, but Angel was still out carousing.

'Miguel and Juan are hopping you've brought this greaseball over,' said Red. 'They wanted another cousin they could manipulate. They'll give him a hard time. So will Bibi. She's got awful bossy.'

'Not when she sees Angel,' said Perdita.

Luke turned to talk to Bobby Ferraro, who was handsome in a chunky Neanderthal way.

'Bobby's known as All-Brawn because he's so thick,' Red told Perdita. 'Comes from Montana. They turn the ponies out at night there. If the wolves don't catch them, they know they're fast enough to play polo.'

He yawned; his fingers drummed on the bar. He was getting restless.

Unnerved, Perdita blurted out: 'What did you read at university?'

'Dirty books mostly.'

'Sorry – what did you major in?'

'Underwater basketweaving.'

'Oh, stop taking the piss.'

'Howdya like my ponies?'

'Fantastic!' Perdita's face brightened. 'I've never ridden anything like them. Spotty was terrific and that bay mare with the four white socks in the last chukka was like a Porsche with four legs, she came round so fast. I nearly came off her each time. What's her name?'

'Haven't a clue,' said Red. 'My father owns them. Juan and Miguel school them. I just sit on their backs.'

'Aren't you interested in horses?'

'Not particularly. A polo pony isn't an animal, it's a means to an end.'

'I disagree,' said Perdita coldly. 'So does Luke.'

'Luke loves them too much for his own good,' said Red dismissively. 'Eats his heart out when he sells them on.'

He ordered another green devil.

'I wouldn't,' said Luke. 'And will you please lay off on Saturday night.'

'Christ, it's only a charity match,' snapped Red.

'But it's my first game with Hal, OK? And I want to win.'

'I hear Hal's found God,' said Red. 'That's one helluva pass.'

Luke grinned. 'Is Auriel coming to watch you on Sunday?'

'I guess so,' said Red. He seemed abstracted. 'Where are we going to eat – Charlie's Crab?'

Luke yawned. He'd been up at five and jet lag had finally caught up with him. The adrenalin pumping in the match had given way to aches and pains. All he wanted to do was to go home, talk to his horses and fall into bed, but Perdita was obviously dying to go out on the town.

'I'll pay,' said Red. 'As long as you pay for the drinks here. I owe them so much, they won't give me any credit. Let's go.' He got off his bar stool, and then got back on again. 'Second thoughts, let's not.'

Following his gaze, Perdita noticed a girl with tousled dark hair in a flame-red dress, telephoning with her back to the room. Although she had picked up the receiver, it was plain she was only pretending to telephone. After a few minutes she looked round and gave a start of surprise.

'Hi, Lucy,' said Red softly. 'Long time no see.'

'Hi, Red. Where have you been hiding?'

She had big brown eyes, a face and body so olive-skinned, soft and supple that they looked as though they'd spent their life in linseed oil and she smelt of dollars and Diorella.

'This is Perdita,' said Red. 'My brother Luke's just brought her back from Argentina. She played a blinder this afternoon. Stood in for me and scored four goals.'

'That's great,' said Lucy, who seemed to be laughing at some private joke and not remotely interested in goals.

Suddenly Perdita felt *de trop*. She had a feeling Lucy had something to do with Red not getting back for the match. She turned back to Luke who was being chatted up.

'My Daddy owns a chunk of Florida,' a stunning red-head was telling him. 'You're a seriously good polo player. Are you as good in bed?' Luke was just laughing.

Perdita was furious. 'Don't be fatuous,' she said to the redhead. 'Just bugger off.'

'I was only asking.' The redhead flounced off.

'Silly cow,' said Perdita crossly, then added to Luke, 'Chessie was telling me about Cassandra Murdoch.'

Luke looked at her steadily. 'So?'

326

'That you went out with her for a long time and she's absolutely heart-broken.'

'She doesn't deserve that. She's beautiful,' said Luke.

'Why did you dump her then?'

Luke's gaze was unflinching. 'Because I met you, I guess.'

Perdita felt herself blushing. 'But there isn't . . . ' she began.

'I know, but it wasn't fair to Cass.'

At that moment a waiter sidled up and whispered something to Red and Lucy.

'Oh Christ,' gasped Lucy, the colour draining from her face, 'my husband's just come in. See you, darling,' and, pecking Red on the cheek, she shot out of the famous disappearing door. Instantly Red shot round the bar to the darkest corner and engaged an eager brunette and her disgruntled boyfriend in conversation.

'I guess my brother's been playing fast and Lucy,' said Luke.

A second later a man with a blazing red face and upturned white hair stormed into the back bar, flanked by two enormous heavies.

'Jesus,' muttered Luke, putting three fingers through Leroy's collar. 'Red shouldn't tangle with that.'

'Who's he?'

'Winston Chalmers,' said Luke. 'Best lawyer in town; on his fourth wife; specializes in getting off very rich, very guilty people.'

'I'm sure there's some mistake, Mr Chalmers,' said the manager, who was trying to block his advance. 'Mrs Chalmers hasn't been in for days.'

Winston Chalmers pushed him away as easily as a bamboo curtain. 'Luke Alderton,' he bellowed. 'I want to see Luke Alderton. I know the fucker's here.'

'Sure I am,' said Luke.

'You know my wife, Lucy.'

'Never met her. First time I clapped eyes on her was this evening,' said Luke, getting to his feet and towering over Winston Chalmers. 'Seems a nice lady.'

'That's bullshit,' said Chalmers. 'Get him,' he ordered the heavies.

The next minute one of the heavies had hit Luke

across the room. Then, as he struggled to his feet, the second heavy helped him up and hit him again in the stomach. Then the first heavy came in with a punishing right to the side of the head, knocking Luke to the floor again. Then he gave a yell as Leroy buried his teeth in his arm. No one moved in the bar except Perdita.

'Stop it, you bastards,' she screamed, snatching up a bar stool.

'Don't be silly, honey,' said the second heavy, trying to wrench the stool from her. 'We're bigger than you.'

'And call off this fucking dog,' screamed the first heavy, reaching for his gun.

Perdita put down the stool and grabbed Leroy's collar. 'Drop,' she screamed, '*drop*.'

'Drop,' mumbled Luke, raising himself a couple of inches.

Leroy dropped. Luke collapsed back on to the floor.

Winston Chalmers stepped over him, kicking him in the ribs. 'Tell your friend,' he said to Perdita, 'to stay away from my wife. If he contacts her again, he'll get acid in that ugly mug of his.'

'He is not ugly,' screamed Perdita, running after them out into the parking lot with Leroy barking at her side. But they had jumped into their big Cadillac and were screaming off past a bank at the end of the road, inappropriately named Fidelity Federal.

Going back into the bar, Perdita found Red chucking a bucket of water over Luke.

'What the hell's going on?' she screamed. 'Didn't you hear Luke saying he'd never met her before this evening? And now he's out cold and he's got to play on Sunday.'

She knelt down beside Luke.

'Luke, lovie, are you OK? Call an ambulance,' she shouted at Red.

'I'm OK,' groaned Luke, feeling his jaw, 'but I swear I've never met that woman before in my life.'

'I know you haven't,' said Red, starting to laugh as he pulled Luke to his feet. 'Whenever I call her up, I keep getting Winston, so I say I'm Luke Alderton.'

34

Three days later Perdita saw her first big Sunday match and was staggered by the razzmatazz. It had poured with rain all night, so four helicopters were brought in to blow-dry the field. After a lunch of lobster, chicken, bilberries and champagne, which cost each guest $200 a head, there was an auction for Band Aid, and, so that no-one could avoid coughing up, silver buckets were passed round the tables which were soon filled up with $100 and $1,000 bills. Each woman, as she left, was presented with a toy model of Hal Peters' Cheetah convertible, and, as she reached her allotted seat, waitresses rushed forward to wipe off the rain with towels. Favoured clients of Hal Peters found glasses and bottles of champagne in ice awaiting them.

On the field before the match, two pop groups belted out: 'Do they know it's Christmas any more?', and as both Bob Geldof and Auriel Kingham were alleged to be putting in an appearance during the game, the media were out in force.

Even with the temperature in the high sixties, the huge grandstand was filled with women smothered in jewels and huge hats as if they were going to a wedding. Some of them were young and very beautiful, but many were old. Perdita noticed some disgusting old crones looking like Egyptian mummies who'd spent the afternoon at Estée Lauder. Almost more gaudily dressed were the men who rolled up in jackets and trousers in an amazing variety of lime greens, terracottas and crocus yellows, and panamas with coloured ribbons. Bart, who'd paid for Perdita's lunch, and her stand ticket, was wearing an extraordinary petrol-blue silk coat woven with yellow snaffles.

The teams had been expected to attend the lunch. Luke, looking very pale, had eaten nothing. He had refused to see a doctor, but Perdita was sure he was still slightly concussed and his right shoulder was giving him such hell that he had to resort to repeated shots of Novocaine. His amusement on Thursday night, which had been aided by alcohol, had given way to dread that he might be seriously injured. He could only feed his ponies and pay his grooms if he were able to make and sell on horses from dawn to midnight and play high goal for Hal Peters. It was crucial they won their first match this afternoon. Even Leroy kept a respectful six-foot distance from his master that morning.

As the teams lined up in front of the grandstand Luke was further irritated by Red, who couldn't stop laughing at Hal Peters, who was so fat that you could hardly see his pony beneath him. Hal, however, who was an even worse rider than Victor Kaputnik, was loving every minute. Grinning from very clean ear to ear, his face aglow like a Dutch cheese, he waved to all his friends in the crowd. The commentator announced each player and they then had to canter forward, to loud cheers, taking off their hats while hanging on to their whips and sticks and controlling their ponies. Hal's horse, an opinionated piebald called Horace, nearly carted him back to the pony lines, much to the joy of the crowd.

Victor's canter forward was even more hazardous as he had to hang on to a new, and rather startling, ginger toupee as well as removing his hat.

'Ay encouraged Victor to wear his toupee,' announced Sharon in the stands. 'Ay think one is as young as one looks.'

There was another dicey moment when a vicar took the microphone and exhorted the crowd to 'pray for these brave players', and begged God to look after them all and save the President.

'Ay-men,' said Sharon bowing her head.

Hal, being a born-again Christian, insisted on putting his gloved hands together and closing his eyes during the prayer. Horace would have taken off again if Luke hadn't grabbed his reins.

'Hal is about to be borne away again,' said Red, wiping his eyes.

'Pack it in,' snarled Luke. 'And where the hell's Auriel?'

Auriel, who had promised to ride on to the pitch in a Cheetah convertible and throw-in, had not turned up.

'Oh, she'll show,' said Red arrogantly. 'She likes making an entrance.'

Luke's reply was drowned by a rock star in a maroon shirt slashed to the waist inviting the crowd to sing along to the Star Spangled Banner.

Among the two teams there was great potential for

aggro. The thuggish Shark Nelligan was determined to take Luke out for pinching his patron. Alejandro and Shark, both backs, hated each other anyway, and Shark was particularly irritated today because Alejandro, being the higher-rated player, had retained the Number Four spot, forcing Shark to play at Number Three. Shark also hated Bobby Ferraro because he was younger and better looking. Jesus, the Chilean, hated Alejandro because they'd tangled over a Cuban beauty last year, and Jesus had a long-standing grudge against Victor because Victor had sacked him after finding him on the floor of a trailer with Sharon. All of them except Luke mistrusted Red because he was conceited and unpredictable.

After ten minutes, when Auriel still hadn't shown up and the pop groups had played 'Do they know it's Christmas?' twice more, her place was taken by Hal's wife, Myrtle, who was even fatter and jollier than Hal, and who whooped and thrust up her arms to the crowd as the purple Cheetah convertible cruised to mid-field.

Chessie, who was sitting in the stands with Perdita, looked at Mrs Peters in horror. 'Is Hal advertising spare tyres as well as cars?' she said. 'If he gets seriously caught up in polo, he'll certainly dump Mrs Peters in a year or two for a Mark-II model with bum-length hair and a *café au lait* spray-on tan.'

'Luke says they adore each other,' said Perdita, 'and pray by the bed every night.'

'Mrs Peters ought to pray for a fifty-pound weight-loss,' said Chessie. She was looking particularly beautiful in beige bermudas, a white cricket shirt with the sleeves rolled up and a straw hat trimmed with pale pink roses.

Perdita, who'd had her hair cut and thinned and was wearing a kingfisher-blue suit which had given absolutely no change from one of Bart's $1,000 bills, was also feeling pretty good. Chessie had taken her to Worth Avenue on Friday and increased Perdita's conviction that if she couldn't have Ricky she'd only settle for a seriously rich man.

Huge thunderclouds were now gathering on the horizon. With all the delays, Mrs Peters didn't throw-in until a quarter to four which wasn't much fun for the ponies who'd been eaten alive by flies for two hours. As the players waded in as though they were killing rattlesnakes a huge illuminated scoreboard, like a Blackpool illumination, flashed up the name of the player hitting the ball and, later, whether he'd hit a safety or a penalty or scored, and how many seconds were left in the chukka.

'Ay hear Angel, that charmin' Argentine boy, is playing for Bart this season,' Sharon said to Perdita. 'Victor was most impressed by him. Do give him our number. That player is *most* attractive.' She adjusted her binoculars. 'Bay Jove, who's he?'

'My stepson,' said Chessie drily.

'He's very appealing,' said Sharon.

'He never stops appealing,' snapped Chessie. 'He's the bane of every umpire in Palm Beach.'

Sharon was bubbling with happiness and hardly able to keep secret the fact that Victor had poured so much money into the Tory party that he was to be knighted in the New Year's Honour's List.

'Lady Sharon, Lady Kaputnik,' she kept murmuring to herself. What a shame Victor hadn't changed his name to something like Cavendish Whapshott.

'Oh, there's Hoo-arn arraiving,' she squeaked in excitement. 'Hello, Hoo-arn.'

'Not a panti-girdle untwanged,' said Chessie as Juan in a black bomber jacket, teeth flashing, progressed along the crones to sit beside Sharon.

'Mrs Juan's obviously been left in Argentina,' murmured Chessie.

The commentator, meanwhile, was filling every second with chatter.

'The leather contraption these brave ponies wear on their heads, ladies and gentlemen,' he was telling the crowd, 'is called a bridle.'

Perdita giggled. But she soon forgot the commentary and the crowd, unable to believe the ferocity and the gladiatorial splendour of the game, nor the crookedness of the umpiring as egos and mallets clashed below her.

'Why doesn't the Argentine umpire ever blow a foul on Alejandro,' she asked Bart, who had just joined them, after yet another piece of deliberate obstruction.

'Because he's playing with him in the Rolex Challenge Cup,' said Bart. 'You'll also notice a tremendous dimension of intimidation not picked up. In Palm Beach you don't make fouls anyone sees.'

Bart was furious that Peters' Cheetahs, despite the collective weight of Jesus, Luke and Red, were losing badly against his detested rival Victor Kaputnik. The large crowd, always interested in a new patron, watched Hal Peters charging round like a baby elephant crossing every player in sight, so the umpire kept awarding penalties to the other side, which Alejandro effortlessly converted. Jesus was playing beautifully when Alejandro allowed him to, but Red was simply not trying, all his energy going into arguing with the umpire. Luke had to cover up for him again and again. Luke's Novocaine was also wearing off. His head was muzzy and he really had to concentrate to see the ball.

Red, in fact, was sulking. He had boasted that the notoriously unpunctual Auriel would, for once, be on time because she was so crazy about him. Now she had made a fool of him by not turning up. Perhaps she'd got wind of the fight.

At the end of the chukka the sun came out. Cautiously coats were being shed and crepey elbows and arms, hanging in festoons, emerged from wildly expensive little-girl jerseys.

'They've even got designer liver spots in Palm Beach,' said Chessie.

Why does she bitch about everything, wondered Perdita.

On the field, matters were getting serious. The orange and black shirted Tigers were leading the Lenten-purple Cheetahs 8-0 when Luke came out in the third chukka on Fantasma who, throwing off any jet lag, showed staggering bursts of speed, enabling Luke to scorch down the length of the pitch and score two goals. Her action was so smooth and graceful that she jarred his damaged shoulder far less than his other ponies. Her coat was as dazzling white in the sunshine as the thunderclouds. As usual her beauty caught everyone's eye.

'That's a good pony,' said Bart. 'Runs to a stop. So many horses stop on their back legs and take so much more effort to get started.'

Victor, however, was absolutely outraged.

'That was the mare I bought in Argentina,' he bellowed at Alejandro. 'You told me it had broken its leg. I paid for that mare.'

333

'Eees different mare,' protested Alejandro innocently. 'Would I cheat you, Veector?'

'Yes,' said Victor.

Hal wasn't very pleased either. It was his first Palm Beach match and all his clients had flown down to watch him.

'I thought you said your brother was a six. He's playing like minus six. And where's his famous woman-friend you promised?' he grumbled at Luke.

A minute later Luke picked up the ball – God, his shoulder was agony now – and, giving Fantasma her lovely head, he took it upfield again. Carefully he placed it five yards in front of goal on the end of Hal Peters' stick.

'Now's the chance for Hal to be a hero for his team,' said the commentator.

Hal took an almighty swipe and missed.

Half-time – and the crones took out their compacts and fluffed powder on their faces. People poured on to the pitch to tread in and play some sponsored game in which they wriggled along a rolling poll and tried to hit a ball between two posts. A helicopter dropped $100 and $10 bills on to the pitch and people scurried hysterically after them. Heart-shaped gas balloons floated into the air, trailing red ribbons.

Down in the pony lines Victor, in between threatening to sue Alejandro and Luke for diddling him over Fantasma, was on his car telephone to Hong Kong trying to close a deal.

Half-time – ten minutes in England and normally fifteen in America – stretched out to forty-five minutes. The game was losing all momentum. They were just throwing-in when another helicopter landed on the pitch bringing Bob Geldof. Cheering hysterically, the crowd rose to their feet.

Gaunt, white-faced, unshaven, totally unsmiling and all in black, he was driven round the edge of the field in an open Peters Cheetah, looking as though he'd been to hell and caught it on an off-day.

'That's an attractive man,' said Chessie. 'Takes suffering head on.'

'He reminds me of Ricky,' said Perdita, unthinking.

Chessie glanced at her. For a second her eyes filled with tears. 'Yes, he does,' she said.

Bob Geldof then picked up the microphone, thanked the crowd for raising the incredible sum of $250,000 and said he was sorry he couldn't stop but he had other engagements in New York and LA.

As he left the wind got up and the rain came down and all the crones dived for cover under the roof at the top of the stand. Hanging baskets rocked hazardously in the wind, men watched golf on tiny portable televisions. Perdita looked over a sea of coloured umbrellas as the players came back on to the field. Peters' Cheetahs were still 2-8 down and Luke was the colour of the pitch.

The fourth chukka was characterized by Jesus having a shouting match with Shark Nelligan.

'You should have checked,' he screamed at Shark. 'You don't 'ave to 'eet me so hard.'

'You came in front of me, you greaseball,' bellowed Shark. 'You always do.'

'For Chrissake shut up, fucking eedioto,' screamed Jesus.

'If you take the name of Our Lord in vain once more, young man, you will not play for me again,' Hal sternly chided Jesus, who thundered off in a frenzy of Latin shrugs.

Alejandro smote the resulting free hit yards down the pitch bang in front of Victor and the goal.

'Leave the fucking thing, Victor, you'll only miss it,' yelled Shark, thundering down the pitch.

'Now Victor Kaputnik has the chance to be a hero for his team,' said the commentator.

Victor took a great swipe and missed. Luke rode him off and backed the ball up the field to Jesus, who dummied round Alejandro and passed to Red, who hit the ball once, then took an idle shot at goal and missed. Luke rode up to him.

'For fuck's sake,' he hissed, 'those heavies have totally buggered my shoulder. Get your finger out. All you're doing is riding up and down breaking up the divots.'

'I can't pull rabbits out of the hat every time,' said Red sulkily. 'It's only a fucking charity match.'

'I'll murder that boy,' said Bart furiously. 'I'm going to chew him out.'

He had just reached the pony lines at the beginning of the

fifth chukka when a figure entered the stands smothered in a mink-lined Barbour, a fur hat, dark glasses and several silk scarves. She was so surrounded by minders that a rumour went round that it was Princess Diana or the President's wife.

'I want absolutely no publicity,' she was saying in a loud, deep, throaty voice to the bowing and scraping club secretary. 'I've just come to watch a friend play polo.'

'Miss Kingham is here on a private visit,' said her publicity manager to the press.

A chukka's anonymity, however, was more than enough for Auriel. As Red rode back to the pony lines after failing to score once again, Auriel called out to him. Instantly a smile illuminated his scowling face and he cantered towards her. Immediately she whipped off her fur hat, her dark glasses, her silk scarves and her Barbour; everyone recognized her and screamed with delight, and the press swarmed on to the field, lighting up the gloom with a firework display of flash bulbs. Auriel then insisted on going down to the pony lines and massaging Red's shoulders and running her hands through his damp hair.

'This is a fucking circus,' said Luke, on whose shoulder the latest shot of Novocaine had totally failed to work.

Hal Peters, in the meantime, was kneeling down in the pony lines: 'Dear Lord Jesus, if you think it's right make Hal Peters and his team win this match . . . ' and was nearly run over by Shark Nelligan returning on his fastest pony for the last chukka.

'Now will you start playing properly?' begged Luke as he and Red rode back on to the pitch.

'Don't worry, I'll win this match for you,' said Red.

'What a beautiful woman,' said Hal Peters, gazing so hard at Auriel that he bumped into the umpire.

Red, who always got a charge from holding back and lulling the opposition into a feeling of false security, now proceeded to storm through with a volley of goals all in front of the press and the television cameras.

'Red, Red, Red,' was suddenly the only word on the commentator's lips. Despite disapproving strongly of Red, Perdita couldn't help melting. As he hit the ball on the ground, in the air, to the left, to the right, underneath, over, behind and in front of his matching sorrel pony, she realized that he was so supremely gifted he could win a match off his own stick.

'If he played like that all the time,' said Bart in an I-told-you-so voice to Chessie, 'he'd go straight to ten.'

Red also had Ricky's ability to get the last ounce out of his pony. As he felt her tiring, he picked up his whip. Hal Peters was in ecstasy.

'The Lord has answered my prayer,' he told Luke.

The Tigers were only one goal ahead now, with two minutes to go. Victor, at this point, decided to fall off and lie on the ground. Sharon, busy making an assignation with Juan, looked without interest at the pitch. Then the horrid possibility dawned on her that if Victor passed away she'd never be Lady Kaputnik.

'Oh, Victor, oh, may husband,' she screeched.

'He's done it on purpose,' muttered Chessie to Perdita. 'Then they'll put in a ringer instead to win the match.'

'Water, water,' moaned Victor.

On ran an official with a silver tray, a jug and a glass. Picking up the jug, Shark emptied it over Victor, dislodging his ginger toupee.

'Get up, Victor,' he said brusquely. 'You're not hurt.'

'Don't speak to me like that,' squealed Victor. 'You haven't had your cheque yet.'

From the ground he could also see the freckling of rust spots on Fantasma's belly.

'It *is* that mare, Alejandro, I remember the marking.'

Spitting with fury, he laboriously climbed on to his pony. The umpire chucked in the ball.

'Come on, you guys,' said Luke faintly. All he could see was a swirling mist in front of his eyes; it was like riding through a snow storm. Next moment Victor had crossed Red and the Argentine umpire, suddenly taking against Alejandro, awarded a rightful penalty three to the Cheetahs.

'Now is Luke Alderton's chance to be a hero for his team and level the score for another chukka,' said the commentator.

'I can't take it, my shoulder's fucked,' gasped Luke. 'You take it, Jesus.'

Down came Jesus in a slow theatrical canter. Alejandro,

cantering across goal, blocked the shot for the Tigers. Jesus pounded down to score, but the next moment Alejandro, with a ten-goal swing, had hit the ball again, lofting it halfway upfield into the stands, only just missing Sharon, as the whistle went.

As the players surged together to shake hands, Fantasma, showing a responsibility belying her four years, swung round and gently bore Luke back to the pony lines as though she were carrying a tray of Waterford glass.

'Luke's hurt,' cried Perdita, fighting her way through the crowds. She found Luke slumped on an upturned bucket, with Fantasma and Leroy ferociously but misguidedly protecting him from two of Bart's paramedics.

Mrs Peters sportingly stood down so that Auriel could present the prizes. The crowd surged forward to get a closer look. Auriel had reached an age when people wanted to see how many times her face had been lifted, if it was all make-up, or whether the cracks were showing. In fact she was an astonishingly beautiful woman. She wore a smoke-blue chiffon dress to match her smoke-blue eyes, and her wafting dark hair certainly wasn't a wig and she had a good enough pink-and-white skin not to need much make-up. With her full bosom and hips emphasizing her incredibly slender waist, wrists and ankles, she made the lean, blond, suntanned polo beauties look slightly commonplace by comparison.

Up came the players. Victor, his toupee firmly in place, was vulgarly delighted to win the cup.

'It takes two teams to make a game,' droned on the commentator, 'and they need two towels and a mirror to wipe away the perspiration. Each player gets something to take home, I expect most of them would like to take home Miss Kingham.'

Red, however, was the only player Auriel kissed and the crowd and the photographers went crazy.

Despite his totally non-contributory first five chukkas, Red also won the Most Valuable Player award to Auriel's somewhat exaggerated ecstasy. He's stolen Luke's thunder and probably his patron, thought Perdita furiously. Fantasma, who won Best Playing Pony, came on muzzled and gazing fretfully back for Luke. A shimmer of silver white in the sun that had just returned, she disappeared under a royal-blue rug which stretched from her flattened ears to her newly brushed-out but angrily whisking tail.

'These horses are thoroughbred and specially trained,' chipped in the commentator. 'We honour these brave animals which are seventy-five per cent of the game. The Blanket of Honour is just our way of saying thank you to the ponies.'

'That's my pony,' yelled Victor, clutching his cup. 'I'm getting Winston Chalmers on to you and Luke, Alejandro.'

'If I'd known how good she was,' said Alejandro to the Argentine umpire, 'I'd have keep her myself.'

Any disappointment Hal might have felt at not winning was dispelled when he was photographed arm in arm with Auriel by the entire press corps.

'You smell wonderful, Miss Kingham,' he said, his Dutch cheese face redder than ever.

'It's my own fragrance,' said Auriel, who had a heavily mascared eye for publicity. 'It's going to be called "Auriel". I'll send your wife a presentation pack. I just adore your Cheetah Convertibles.'

In the Players Club Hal, who was teetotal, bought everyone else champagne.

'Where's Luke?' he asked.

'Gone to hospital,' said Perdita, who'd arrived with Leroy on a lead. 'He's dislocated his shoulder. He was in agony even before the match started. Bart clobbered him by the pony lines and threw him into an ambulance. I'm going to see him in a minute. He asked me to make his apologies.'

'Oh, poor Luke, wish him our best,' said Mrs Peters. 'How brave of him to play with a dislocated arm.'

'When did he do it?' asked Hal.

Red suddenly looked wary.

'On Thursday night,' said Shark Nelligan evilly. 'Luke's been knocking off a married woman. Her husband stormed into Cobblestones with half-a-dozen heavies and took him out.'

Both Hal and Mrs Peters looked extremely disapproving.

'Who was the woman?' asked Sharon.

'Winston Chalmers's wife, Lucy,' said Shark, who was really enjoying himself.

'Pretty woman,' sighed Bobby Ferraro.

'Winston Chalmers is handling my divorce!' said Auriel in amazement. Then, turning to Red: 'You didn't tell me Lucy was having an affair with your brother.'

'Didn't think it was any concern of mine,' said Red, going dead-eyed. 'That was a barnstorming game you played, Hal.'

'I'd never have guessed it of Luke,' said Mrs Peters, really shocked.

'Nor would I,' said Red, shaking his head.

'Thou shalt not commit adultery,' said Hal sanctimoniously.

Perdita looked out at the evening sunlight slanting across the pitch. The thunderclouds had retreated and were turning coral pink. In the Players Club garden begonias and impatiens glowed like jewels after the rain. Horses were being ridden home three abreast to their barns.

'I wouldn't put anything past Luke Alderton,' Shark was saying. 'People who steal patrons steal other people's wives.'

'And their horses,' chipped in Victor.

'Bullshit,' said Perdita, draining her glass of champagne. 'It isn't Luke who's having an affair with Lucy Chalmers, it's Red. Every time he gets Winston on the telephone he pretends to be Luke. I'd stick to someone your own age in future,' she added to a furiously mouthing Auriel, 'and always remember to put your toyboys away before you go to bed.'

35

'The moment I divorce you,' Chessie screamed at Bart over the buzz of his electric razor, 'you'll be cut out of the Forbes four hundred richest people list, and I'll be in it.'

Christmas had got to Chessie as it had always got to her when, married to Ricky, she'd had to look after Will as well as having Ricky's father and her parents to stay. This year, when she had nothing to do except instruct a fleet of servants, she'd decided she missed feeling sweaty, exhausted and put upon like 99 per cent of the world's married women.

Watching his wife rearing out of the bath, her maenad's face sullen as the water slid off her golden boy's body, Bart tried to be conciliatory.

'I know you miss Will worst at Christmas, honey, but there's a perfectly simple remedy. Have some more kids with me. Give you something to do and fill the gap.'

'Any child I had with you could never mean as much as Will,' yelled Chessie.

Bart had walked out after that. It was the pattern of their relationship that she would play him up and he would punish her if she went too far. But this time she knew she had overdone it and when she called his office, on the flimsy excuse of asking him to find out if Red was coming, his secretary, Miss Leditsky, who was mean, lean and sexy, said he had meetings all day and had asked not to be disturbed.

Feeling like a row, Chessie rang Red.

'The number you have called is being checked for trouble,' said the operator's recorded message.

'You bet it is!' Chessie slammed down the receiver. The little beast must have had his telephone cut off again.

The post didn't improve her temper. The first Christmas card she opened was postmarked Australia and addressed to Bart and Grace, the second to Bart and Chrissie.

'I saw three yachts come sailing by,' said Chessie gazing moodily out on to an ocean as blue as Mary's robes.

Then, with a stab, she remembered Will tunelessly singing: 'Little Lord Jesus, asleep in the hedge.' It had been one of hers and Ricky's few shared jokes. No-one came to sing carols at Alderton Towers. They'd be too terrified of the Rottweilers and the security guards and the *paparazzi* still hanging around for the latest news on Red's break-up with Auriel.

She'd go crackers if she didn't do something. Grace was in Uruguay with a woman friend, so tomorrow, for the first time, Bibi, and supposedly Red, as well as Luke and Perdita, were coming to Christmas dinner with her and Bart, who was cock-a-hoop at having all his family under one roof.

They're bloody well going to have a better dinner than

341

ever they had with Grace, thought Chessie, suddenly excited at the challenge.

The telephone rang. 'Mr Alderton for you, Mrs Alderton,'
said Conchita.

Chessie's heart eased. Bart had forgiven her. 'Mr Luke
Alderton,' added Conchita.

Yet Luke calmed her more than Bart would have done,
as he said, in his deep, slow, sleepy voice, that he and
Perdita would be there at eight tomorrow, and would
Chessie mind if they asked Angel who was on his own
and might cheer up Bibi, whose boyfriend, Skipper, had
begged off again at the last moment.

'Anything to put her in a better mood,' said Chessie. 'Is
he presentable?'

'Christmas present-able,' said Luke. 'Wouldn't even
need gift-wrapping. He's very glamorous.'

'Good,' said Chessie. 'Might put your rotten brother's
perfectly straight nose out of all those joints he smokes. Is
he coming?'

'Haven't seen him.'

'How's your shoulder?'

'So, so,' – which means bloody painful, thought Chessie
– 'I'll be off games till mid-January at least. I'll miss the
Challenge and the January cups and have to put in a
substitute for the Sunshine League.'

'Christ,' said Chessie, appalled. 'That's losing serious
money. Let Bart help out. You know he's dying to.'

'Nope,' said Luke firmly.

'And is it true you're squeezing into one of those grooms'
caravans while Perdita hogs your bed? I can't believe you
haven't bonked her yet.'

Luke laughed. 'Making ponies taught me one thing –
to be patient. If you bump young horses too early they'll
throw in the towel.'

Chessie sighed. 'You love her, don't you? She's a lucky
girl.'

Luke, in fact, was fighting depression. A caravan was
indeed not the ideal place for a shoulder injury or for lying
awake night after night wracked by desire. Out of the
tack-room window he'd just seen Perdita flying off to the
mail box, desperate for a word from Ricky. She pretended
it was because she was frantic for him to buy Tero who

was improving by the day, but Luke understood that all the loving kindness of Christmas and pop songs singing 'I just called to say I love you' every five minutes on the radio made her miss Ricky more than ever.

Luke's heart was even heavier because he'd had to sell a favourite pony that morning. It was the only way he could feed his other ponies and pay the grooms' wages and give them Christmas presents and take Perdita out in the evening, which was what she expected after long days schooling all his ponies.

In addition, Perdita, having screwed up Red and Auriel by spilling the beans about Lucy Chalmers, was getting increasingly uptight about meeting Red tomorrow at Christmas dinner. Finally Luke had spent an agonizing two hours yesterday trying to comfort his ex-girlfriend, Cassandra Murdoch, who was coming apart at the seams.

Chessie spent a fraught and joyful Christmas Day doing what she did best in the world after sex – cooking, keeping the kitchen staff in a flurry, stuffing a fresh goose with truffles, creating an exquisitely delicate smoked salmon mousse in the shape of fishes, one for each person, and finally, as it was Christmas, making a surprise pudding which she knew Red adored.

By seven-thirty she was really pleased with herself. The ten-foot Christmas tree which grazed the top of the *El Paradiso* living room was covered with tinsel and glass balls the exact duck-egg blue of the Alderton Flyers' shirts. Holly, with the berries painted blue, decorated every priceless painting, blue paperchains criss-crossed the room and three huge vases were filled with sky-blue delphiniums. In the dining room the dark crimson tablecloth was laid with a new blue-and-gold dinner service, decorated by blue candles and crackers, with a centrepiece of gentians, forget-me-nots, scabious, dyed-blue carnations and Father Christmas in a blue polo shirt and white breeches driving a sledge pulled by four model polo ponies. The whole effect was gloriously vulgar.

Bart, who'd spent the day working and stick and balling, absolutely adored it, principally because of the tremendous effort the chronically lazy Chessie had made to please him.

She was wearing a duck-egg-blue watered-silk dress,

very clinging to emphasize the fragility of her body and leaving one arm and shoulder bare to show off the flawless tawny-gold skin. The colour, which exquisitely enhanced her bruised-blue eyes and her greenish-gold curls, had never suited any of his players, even Red, so well.

'Christ, you look miraculous.' Bart put his hands under the diagonal of duck-egg-blue silk to stroke a small pointed breast which seemed to leap upward at his touch. He noticed that the scheming minx had left her neck and wrists bare in anticipation of his present and he loved her for it.

'Open it before the others arrive,' he said roughly, taking a blue velvet box out of his white dinner-jacket pocket.

Even Chessie gasped. It contained a pendant, bracelet and earrings of emeralds as big as wrens' eggs.

'Oh, Bartholomew,' breathed Chessie. 'They *will* make everyone green-eyed!'

'Very old,' Bart couldn't resist boasting. 'The stone of the pendant comes from Louis XIV's sword.'

They had drinks outside. Now that the blazing heat of the day had given way to a suavely cool, beautiful evening, Christmas didn't seem so impossible. A pale, luminous, prairie sky arched overhead, the palm trees rattled and on the velvet air drifted a heady scent of orange blossom, Chessie's Diorissimo and merrily roasting goose stuffed with truffles, which was driving the lean, stable cat crazy as he weaved himself around Chessie's bare brown legs. The frogs and crickets croaked to a counterpoint of contented snorts from Bart's ponies who'd had an extra Christmas helping of carrots and molasses.

Chessie put a hand, cold from clutching her vodka and tonic, in Bart's.

'I love you,' she said softly. 'I've started my New Year's resolution a week early. I won't bitch all evening.'

Bibi arrived first and dropped a pile of presents unceremoniously under the tree to stress the insignificance of the occasion. With her frumpy black dress which bypassed every curve, her lack of jewellery and make-up, and her hair scraped back, she looked like a minor character in a sixth-form production of Lorca. What was the point of dressing up for her father and two brothers, when Skipper, her boyfriend, had stood her up yet again? Getting into the office at 4.30 a.m. every day for the last year so that she could handle the 7.30 a.m. calls coming from New York had drained her emotionally and physically. Even the knowledge that, against all the odds as a woman, she'd managed to settle a strike of 650 mechanics this week didn't lift her spirits.

She made no comment on Chessie's decorations beyond remarking acidly there had certainly been some changes, and why didn't they stick up the blue Argentine flag to match. Then, as she kissed her father, she caught sight of Chessie's emeralds.

'Emptying Cartiers *again*, Daddy?' she said even more acidly. Then, still speaking directly to Bart: 'One thing to cheer you up. Red and Auriel are definitely off. It was on the car radio. Auriel is quoted as making no comment, which must be unique for her; Red as saying it wasn't the difference in age that screwed them up, but Auriel being such a famous woman that the press wouldn't leave them alone.'

'That's the best Christmas present I'm gonna get,' said Bart delightedly. Then, as Bibi asked for a Perrier: 'This is a celebration, for Chrissake,' and he filled her glass with champagne.

Again to exclude Chessie, Bibi started discussing a fax that had just come in from Hong Kong. She would reserve the heavy sniping for later when Red arrived. The growing tension was broken by the arrival of Perdita, Luke and Leroy, who had a red bow round his thick neck and who promptly chased the stable cat up a palm tree and collapsed panting on the floor. Luke, as black as his dinner jacket under the eyes, still had his arm in a sling.

'Just a formality,' he explained as he kissed Chessie. 'Stops people clutching it.'

His bottle-brush hair, slicked back in the shower, was beginning to stick up. Spiky hair, unspiky personality, thought Chessie. 'Those are lovely cufflinks,' she added.

'Perdita bought them for me – and a shirt,' said Luke, not adding that he'd given her money to buy them, and all the other presents she was happily putting under the tree.

Having made no comment about Chessie's duck-egg-blue dress, Bibi went into ecstasies over Perdita's cream silk trouser suit.

'You look sensational. You must have been jet lagged last time we met. And you have terrific dress sense.'

'Not me – Chessie,' said Perdita simply. 'She took me to Worth Avenue and pointed me at the right shops. I'm sorry about wearing trousers, but my legs are so bruised from practice chukkas.'

'You've heard Red and Auriel are officially kaput?' Bibi asked Luke.

'Can't say I'm not pleased,' admitted Bart, 'and Grace was going bananas.'

'Shall we call and tell her?' Bibi picked up one of the portable telephones.

Chessie bit her lip.

'I think you're a shade premature,' said Luke, trying not to laugh as Leroy went into a frenzy of barking as the most stretched limo in the world drew up and out jumped an Indian chauffeur in a turban to open the doors for Auriel, Red and two Yorkshire terriers. Luke only just grabbed Leroy's collar in time.

'I am not ready for this. I am truly not ready for this,' screeched Auriel. 'Don't forget to get all those gifts out of the car, Raschid. This must be the most glorious barn ever, and the perfume of the orange blossom is just like my own fragrance.'

Orange blossom! Glancing at Auriel's left hand, Bart was at least relieved to see no engagement ring, despite jewellery everywhere else, including a diamond bracelet on her perfect ankle.

Grinning insolently, Red dropped the Yorkshire terriers in front of Luke.

'I told you I'd bring a Christmas take-out for Leroy. Merry Christmas, Dad,' he added to Bart.

'Merry Christmas, my ass,' snapped Bart.

'So glad to know you, Mr Alderton,' said Auriel, taking Bart's hand. Then, turning to Bibi in her frumpy black dress, 'And you, Mrs Alderton.'

Chessie gave a gasp of laughter.

'I'm afraid I'm Mrs Alderton.'

'But you look sixteen.'

'For that you may call me Chessie.'

'I prefer Francesca,' said Auriel. 'It's more gracious and I can see, Francesca, you are a very gracious lady.'

'Gee, thanks,' said Chessie.

'I hope you don't mind my gatecrashing your Christmas festivities,' went on Auriel. 'Red assured me you wouldn't mind.'

'Red is so generous,' murmured Chessie, wondering how the hell she was going to divide seven smoked salmon fishes between eight. She supposed it was better than five thousand.

'And I've brought you all gifts from my new range,' went on Auriel. 'It's called "Auriel" and it is glorious. Fragrance for you, Francesca. Fragrance for you, Bibi. Antiseptic cream for you,' she couldn't bring herself to use Perdita's name, 'and aftershave and cologne for you, Bart, and you must be Luke. If you like it, I know you'll tell all your friends.'

'I'd better organize another place,' said Chessie, pressing a bell.

Bart was absolutely furious.

'What the fuck d'you think you're doing?' he hissed, taking Red aside.

'Following yonder star,' said Red, nodding in Auriel's direction. 'Oh, star of wonder, star of light, Star of World Class Bank account.'

'Shut up,' snarled Bart. 'How dare you barge in here with her! It's goddam rude to Chessie and she's too goddam old for you.'

'You can give Chessie a good twenty-two years,' said Red coolly. 'Perhaps we ought to swap. Christ!' He looked round the living room. 'What have we he-ah – Conchita's blue period, or blue collar period? Why are you kicking my ankle, Luke? Chessie did it all? Oh, right. That explains it.'

'Mom liked things simple,' said Bibi. 'She always had red roses, and she always wore her rubies at Christmas dinner. D'you remember, Red?'

'I'm starving,' said Luke evenly, smiling at Chessie. 'It smells incredible.'

'I thought we'd dine in half an hour, after we've opened our presents,' Chessie told him gratefully.

'Mom believed in self-control,' taunted Bibi. 'She always made us wait to open our presents till after dinner. Have you heard from her, Red?'

'We called her this evening,' said Auriel, accepting a glass of champagne from Conchita. 'What a gracious lady. Now Grace truly is a gracious lady.'

'Crack!' murmured Chessie to Bart. 'Can you hear the breaking of New Year's Resolutions? You were at school with Grace, weren't you, Auriel? Why don't you have a Very Old Girl's Reunion.'

But Auriel had drawn Bart down beside her on the sofa.

'Red's been showing me videos,' she purred. 'My, you're a fine player. I hope to join Red in England this summer when he plays on your team.'

Auriel and Red, Luke reflected five minutes later, got away with murder because people were so anxious to go to bed with them – Red in terms of behaviour, Auriel in terms of conversation.

'I never have time to practise,' she was now telling a glazed Bart. 'That's why my handicap's only minus one.'

'I wish we were minus her,' Luke murmured to Chessie. 'Her ego's even bigger than her boobs.'

'Not a lot,' said Chessie drily. 'Bart's going to fall down her cleavage if she gets any nearer. It's so embarrassing we haven't got her any presents.'

'Just giftwrap Red. That's all she wants, judging by the number she's doing on Dad.'

Red turned to Perdita, who'd been increasingly edgy all evening about seeing him again.

'Hi, Judas,' he said coldly; then, grinning and lowering his voice, 'You did me a good turn tipping Auriel off about Lucy Chalmers. After a lot of foot-stamping she admitted she really cares,' he dropped his voice an octave, aping sincerity, 'which means I get all my bills picked up.'

'Red bought me a Sheraton sideboard from Christie's for Christmas. Isn't that darling?' Auriel was now telling a blanching Bart.

'She paid for it,' Red murmured to Perdita.

'Didn't you give her anything?'

Red smiled. He had a trick of letting those amazing, kholed eyes suddenly gaze deep into yours, so for a second you thought he was being serious.

'She's had her labia pierced, so I gave her a couple of

348

diamond studs. Makes it hard, eating her out. Like getting bits of grit in one's oyster.'

Perdita gave a scream of shocked amusement.

'I want you personally to design me my own airplane. The Alderton Auriel, I can just picture it – flamingo pink,' Auriel was now saying as though she was bestowing a great favour on Bart, who was desperately trying to prevent a Yorkshire terrier fornicating with his left leg without actually kicking it.

'I think we'd better open our presents,' said Chessie.

'Good idea,' said Luke. 'I'm sorry about Angel. He's not usually as late as this.'

'Who?' said Bibi sharply.

'Your father's new ringer,' said Chessie. 'Luke thought he might be lonely away from home.'

'For Chrissake,' snapped Bibi.

'He's lovely,' chipped in Perdita. 'Luke rang to ask the name of his street. He said: "I look out of the weendow," then came back and said it is called "One Way".'

'Christmas is for the family,' Bibi glared at Luke. 'Why d'you want to ask some hick Argy who'll be completely out of his depth?'

'Lame ducks are better than lame dicks,' said Red, draining and refilling his glass.

On cue Leroy barked, the Rottweilers bayed, the York-shire terriers yapped and Bibi's heavy jaw dropped as Angel came through the door. For the last fortnight he'd been enjoying the sun and the girls of Palm Beach. He was tanned a smooth milk-chocolate brown, his bronzed curls were bleached and streaked. White jeans and a blue, sleeveless T-shirt covered with car oil and black, rubber tyre marks clung to his wonderfully elongated, elegant body. He looked a hundred million dollars and was carry-ing a rose pink poinsettia. Going up to Chessie, he said, 'For you. I am very unwise man bearing gifts. I am sorry I am late. I 'ad flat tyre and got 'opelessly lost.'

'How lovely, thank you,' said Chessie taking the plant, then, adding to Luke, 'you were quite right, he's so beauti-ful I think we'll keep him just for stud purposes. Now, let me introduce everyone. You know Bart,' Bart and Angel nodded at each other without friendliness. 'And Bart's beloved son, Red, by whom he has been well fleeced.'

'Very funny,' said Red, shooting his stepmother a look of pure hatred.

'I watch the match against the Kaputnik Tigers,' Angel told Red. 'Zat last chukka, you play like an Argentine. I nevair realize you zat good.'

'Well, thank you,' said Red, mollified. 'Luke says you're pretty sharp too. How are those bastards Juan and Miguel treating you?'

'Terrible,' began Angel, then seeing Bart's look of disapproval, 'terribly nicely.'

'And this is Bart's daughter, Bibi,' went on Chessie.

'Hi,' said Angel, thinking what a pity Bibi didn't have Red's looks.

'And Auriel, who needs no introduction.'

Angel kissed Auriel's hand.

'How darling,' sighed Auriel, 'and what a glorious poinsettia.'

'We've got an English setta at home,' said Perdita idly.

'I am sorry I'm not properly dressed,' said Angel, who was utterly unfazed. 'Luke say dinner at the barn, I thought we would be 'aving pony nuts. It smell wonderful.' He smiled at Bibi, who didn't smile back. Inside she was seething. How could she possibly keep Angel in order and at a distance if Luke included him on a social footing? Now he'd never get up in the morning.

She was even crosser because Angel was so utterly devastating and she hadn't bothered to tart up, and everyone else looked so stunning. She loathed her black dress, which was one of Grace's cast-offs. Tomorrow she'd go out and buy a new wardrobe.

Just as they were about to open their presents Grace rang to wish Red and Bibi a prolonged Merry Christmas.

Listening to Bibi's cries of 'I miss you, Mom, nothing's the same without you,' Angel thought how beautiful, fragile and vulnerable Chessie looked and decided which side he was on.

The second telephone rang – it was Tokyo for Bart.

'The Japs obviously don't know it's Christmas either,' said Chessie savagely, sloshing two inches of vodka into her glass.

36

Perdita had never seen such presents, and was amazed how everyone took them for granted. Bibi, however, was delighted to open an envelope containing a set of keys for an Alderton Skylark.

'Oh, Daddy, thank you,' she gasped, kissing him.

'Reckon if you're going to be my new polo manager you'd need a helicopter.'

'What!' exploded Red and Angel.

Bart smiled malevolently. 'Bibi's worked her ass off this year. I'm fed up with having her so far from home, so I've put her on the board, and made her my new polo manager. She'll operate out of Florida and New York from now on.'

'Sheet,' whispered Angel to Perdita. 'Think of working for zat ugly cow.'

Red wasn't even remotely appeased when Bart gave him a Stubbs.

'If you hock it,' said Bart, 'I'll disinherit you.'

And what about Luke? thought Perdita in outrage. Bart had only given him a disgusting, monogrammed gold pen-and-pencil set.

Luke, however, was knocked out when Chessie gave him a signed first edition of his bible: *Marco on Polo*, and also first editions of Longfellow and Emerson.

'My wicked stepmother,' he said, hugging her.

Chessie flushed, but made no comment when she tore open some red paper containing a cushion embroidered with the words: 'Eat, drink and re-marry' which was a joint present from Bibi and Red.

Perdita felt a bit despondent. Chessie had given her a Gucci bag and Bibi a very pretty white-and-yellow dressing gown, but she had had nothing from Red, Bart or Luke. Luke had buggered off in fact. She took a slug of champagne. God, she wanted to be rich.

Then, suddenly clattering along the floodlit rose-festooned colonnade and through the french windows came little Tero. Her dark eyes darting with panic, she was all done up in a scarlet headcollar, scarlet bandages and with pieces of holly and mistletoe braided into her tail and still unhogged mane.

'Tero,' gasped Perdita so loudly that only Luke's strength stopped the pony bolting. Then she recognized Perdita and gave a deep, throaty whicker of joy.

'Sure knows her new mistress,' said Luke, putting the lead rope in Perdita's hand.

'I don't believe it,' whispered Perdita. Bursting into tears, she flung her arms round Luke's and Tero's necks. 'Oh, you're so kind, I so dreaded leaving her. Oh, darling, darling Luke, thank you,' and she kissed Luke just under the left jaw bone, breathing in his strength and goodness.

For a second Luke felt dizzy with relief. Perdita would have to stay in Palm Beach another three weeks while Tero went through quarantine.

No-one, however, upstaged Bart Alderton. Two minutes later he returned from the stables leading Spotty, the skewbald Perdita had ridden in the first chukka of the Fathers and Sons. Spotty's wall eye gave him a very old-fashioned look and his skewbald markings included white quarters and brown back legs, so he looked as though he was wearing stockings kept up by garters. A brilliant, wilful, merry, courageous pony who could keep going for ever and who refused to be intimidated even by Juan or Miguel, he caused cheers and yells of laughter when-ever he played.

'Here's a good old boy,' said Bart, handing a second lead rope to Perdita. 'Merry Christmas, and thanks for clinching the Fathers and Sons. Spotty and you should get along.'

'Oh,' breathed Perdita, handing Tero's rope to Luke, 'I love this pony. He's a dream to ride. You *are* so, so kind,' and, flinging her arms round Bart, she covered his face with kisses like a child.

Red was seething. First Bibi on the board and Bart's polo manager, and now Spotty.

'That's a good horse, Dad,' he and Bibi said simul-taneously.

'Who was only saying last week that Spotty looked as though the milkman's horse got his mother?' said Bart smugly.

'That sort of horse is only conceived,' said Auriel dreamily, 'when the stallion jumps over the fence and couples with a mare at the moment of the eclipse.'

Well, he's certainly eclipsed Tero, thought Chessie furiously. 'Why didn't you give Spotty to Luke?' she hissed, drawing Bart aside. 'He's the one who needs him.'

Bart smiled chillingly. 'I want Luke so short of dough he has to come to me and beg.'

'Stupid idiot,' said Chessie. 'Don't you realize when that horse goes to England Ricky'll be playing it in matches against you all summer?'

Looking at the enraged faces, Perdita didn't care. She was used to being the centre of a family row. Two really good ponies could turn her career around. It never entered her head, as she left Luke to take both ponies back to their stables, how she would pay for flying them back to England.

'You'd better come and play on my team, and bring Spotty with you,' Bart told her, thinking how amusing it would be to take Perdita off Ricky as he picked up one of the telephones to take a call from Australia.

'Dinner is served,' announced Conchita.

Almost on cue, the second telephone rang. Bibi picked it up. Suddenly her eyes gleamed and her sallow face lit up. She looked almost pretty.

'Ricky,' she cried joyfully. 'How *are* you? Who'd you want to talk to? Oh, right. I *am* flattered. I'll take it next door. I've been missing you too, darling.'

Perdita turned grey as reality reasserted itself like a stubbed toe. Here she was in Palm Beach, spending Christmas with the sworn enemy of the man she loved, taking his ponies and accepting his hospitality and money. Bibi had probably told Ricky everything, rubbing it in like washing-up machine powder into a cut. No wonder he hadn't answered her calls. Seeing her look of utter desolation, a returning Luke put his good arm round her shoulders. Somehow Chessie managed to stay cool.

'Let's go and dine,' she said to Auriel, adding maliciously, 'I know Bart will enjoy having you on his right.'

'May I be allowed to say Grace?' asked Auriel, dropping her voice dramatically.

'I wouldn't,' said Chessie. 'It's not an awfully popular word round here.'

Dinner was out of this world. Chessie had retained all her old skills. Not feeling hungry herself, she was only too happy to give up her smoked salmon to Auriel, but incensed that Red took one bite, and, dropping his fork, promptly lit a yellow Sobranie.

Bibi was still on the telephone, the bitch. If she was trying to get off with Ricky, there was no way Chessie was going to allow her to get off with Angel too. Turning her languorous, blue eyes towards him, she asked if he'd telephoned his family today.

'I did,' said Angel, who had finished his smoked salmon and was looking at Red's discarded helping as longingly as the orange stable cat who had jumped on to the table.

'That cat's been trying to get at the goose all day,' said Chessie, putting it back on the floor.

'Cat?' said Angel, clutching his smooth brown forehead. 'That is "cat" in American?' Then he started to laugh. 'Zat is why I am so late. Of course it is gatto too. In Argentina we have the same word *gatto* for a jack. I 'ave my flat tyre on the freeway, I look up *gatto* in the dictionary, it say "cat". I keep stopping drivers, and ask them if they have a cat in their car. They drive on as eef I am crazy man. My English is not very well, but I am learning it more better by Phoney-Lingus.'

'That's my husband's perversion,' said Chessie.

She is beautiful, thought Angel, and so sweet.

'What part of America you come from?' he asked.

'I'm English.'

Suddenly wild-eyed and distraught, Angel rose to his feet: 'Luke didn't tell me.'

Chessie put a hand on his arm. 'You've forgiven Perdita. Can't you forgive me? I'm sorry about your brother. You must miss him dreadfully, particularly at Christmas. It was a horrible war.'

She was so beautiful, thought Angel, sitting down again, he could forgive her anything.

'This is wonderful food,' he said as Bibi floated back into the room, oblivious of black glances from Perdita and Chessie.

'Who she talking to?' asked Angel.

'My ex,' said Chessie bitterly.

'*El Orgulloso*?' said Angel in disbelief. 'He not interested in ugly cow like that. She look like an 'orse, and not a very pretty one.'

'Ricky likes horses better than anything else. Perhaps that's the attraction.'

Looking down the table, seeing his dramatically under-handicapped ringer mauling his wife, Bart toyed with the idea of sacking Angel on the spot, but, having played practice chukkas with him yesterday, decided he was too good to kick out so early in the season. Used to calling the conversational shots, he had to confess himself beaten by Auriel as she regaled him with stories of famous movie stars she knew – namely, herself.

Bibi, having also left her mousse, was bitching to Red in French about the dishonesty of Miguel and Juan. 'They'd installed four boarders at the barn and were charging them $800 each a month – straight into their own pockets.'

'And the reason Juan came back for the Geldof match was to charge Dad expenses for screwing Sharon Kaputnik,' answered Red, also in French.

'This one doesn't seem much better,' added Bibi dismissively. 'The way he's mauling Chessie, he's just another jumped-up gigolo.'

Whereupon Angel butted in in perfect French.

'I have never asked money for my sexual services,' he told Bibi coldly and turned back to Chessie.

Red was highly amused; Bibi went scarlet. Angel needed putting down, but not like that.

The goose was even better than the smoked salmon.

'This turkey is simply delicious, Francesca,' said Auriel, feeding large slices to the slavering Yorkshire terriers. 'The white meat is so subtly flavoured.'

'I used truffles under the skin,' said Chessie, grateful for any praise. 'Ricky's father used to pronounce it Truefles,' she added idly.

'True was the one thing you weren't to Ricky,' said Red nastily.

'It's all awesome, Chessie,' said Luke, who was eating a lot, despite not being hungry.

Bart was off the telephone to Sydney at last.

'To my beautiful and gifted wife,' he said raising his glass.

'To the second Mrs Alderton,' said Red, draining his glass.

'Yes – to Mom,' agreed Bibi.

They had a pause before pudding.

'I'm gonna make a full-scale assault on American Airlines,' Bart told Auriel.

'My agent says I'm his favourite client,' said Auriel. 'He's closing a deal with a really good author to write a book on the Auriel Kingham Phenomenon.'

'Seeking control of the company,' went on Bart.

'I'd like to write my own autobiography, but I don't have the time,' went on Auriel.

'By November I'd purchased nearly five per cent of American Airplanes. Do I hold on to the stock as investment, do I go for control of the company?' went on Bart.

'Dustin says he can't wait to make a movie with me,' confided Auriel, 'about a beautiful sophisticated woman whose son's college friend falls madly in love with her.'

'Or do I sell out for a nice profit?' asked Bart.

'Traditionally, older men have always married younger women, right, like you and Francesca. But getting it on with younger guys is definitely a thing of the future,' said Auriel.

Bart forgot about American Airplanes. 'Red needs sons,' he said brusquely.

Auriel smiled warmly into Bart's eyes. 'That's ungallant, Mr Alderton. What makes you think I couldn't give them to him? Why, the bellboy in the elevator this very morning was saying, "You don't look a day over twenty-five, Miss Kingham."'

'I wonder if I ought to get my face elevated,' said Chessie, examining herself in her spoon.

Angel, who normally hardly drank, got very giggly. 'Just looking at you geeves me zee duck bumps,' he told Chessie.

How dare he flirt so blatantly in front of Dad, thought Bibi. Looking at her stepmother, luminous skin like ivory in the candlelight, one beautiful bare shoulder so close to Angel's lips, her hatred bubbled over. Look at those emeralds glittering like drops of *crème de menthe*. The new dinner service must have cost a fortune not to mention the blue silk dress. She was sure it was Ungaro. Chessie was fleecing Bart as she had fleeced Ricky. She was like bindweed that delicately but lethally winds itself round a delphinium until it snaps.

'This Barsac is truly amazing,' said Auriel, assuming Bart had chosen it. 'You have as much a taste for fine wines as fine pictures.'

'It is good,' said Bart. 'Ninety-four years old in fact.'

'Older than both your ages put together, fancy that,' said Chessie from the other end of the table.

Red's eyes slid towards Perdita. 'Nice, isn't she?'

Perdita shrugged. 'Auriel's jolly boring. What d'you see in her?'

'Very good in bed,' said Red, picking up one of the polo ponies pulling Father Christmas's sleigh and mounting it on the pony in front. 'I'm learning a lot. You can never be too good in bed.' He let his eyes run over her body. 'The better you are the more you can manipulate people and I'm very expensive.'

'But you're rich,' said Perdita, admiring his flawless cheekbones.

'Ten million? That's just a piece of chicken shit.'

Perdita giggled in disbelief.

'To exist here you need at least a hundred million,' said Red.

'You're quite different from Luke.'

'Sure,' said Red. 'I have no principles at all.'

Bart came off the telephone from Tokyo again.

'Now we can have pudding,' said Chessie coldly.

'Sorry, honey. You can keep the phone.' Bart put the receiver down on the table beside her. Immediately the other telephone rang.

'Sydney again, Dad,' said Bibi.

'Jesus Christ,' said Chessie. 'Shut up, you utterly bloody thing,' she added hysterically as the first telephone started to ring again. Furiously she snatched it up.

'Go away!' Then, suddenly, in the candlelight her face lost all its expression.

'Hi,' she drawled. 'Did you ring here about two hours ago?' It was as though a huge thorn had been tugged out of her side. 'I thought not,' she smiled luxuriously at Bibi who had turned an ugly maroon.

Ricky, having mindlessly sat through *Down and Out in Beverly Hills* three times surrounded by other lonely people, was now at a party in Beverly Hills surrounded by blondes, but lonely as one can only be at Christmas. Ringing on the flimsy pretext of finding out how Perdita was getting on, ready to hang up if he got Bart, he had come through to the only blonde he had ever loved.

'How are you?' asked Chessie.

'OK,' said Ricky flatly. Then he was almost sobbing, 'No, I'm f-f-f-ucking not. I m-miss you.'

'Me too.'

'Are you coming to England this summer?'

'Yes.'

'Can I see you?'

'Of course, whenever.'

Then, aware Luke and Bibi were listening: 'She's fine. I'll pass you on to her. Perdita – it's Ricky.'

Perdita turned away from Red like a dog who hears the crunch of his master's car on the drive. 'He's rung to talk to me?' she stammered.

'No-one but you,' lied Chessie.

Shooting round the table, Perdita picked up the cordless telephone like a baton in a relay race and hurtled into the night.

Outside the frogs stepped up their croaking.

'What a pity you can't kiss one of those frogs and turn it into a prince, Bibi,' drawled Chessie. 'It might make you less bad-tempered. Ricky said he definitely didn't ring earlier.'

Perdita came back ten minutes later so insulated with happiness she put the glittering blue Christmas tree in the shade.

'Ricky was on terrific form, really, really cheerful. Palm Springs must have done him so much good, he can't wait till next season, nor can I. I can't wait to get Spotty and Tero home.'

Luke suddenly looked grey and exhausted.

'Don't worry,' said Chessie softly, running a hand down his cheek. 'You're much nicer than any of them. Perdita'll realize it one day.'

With everyone on diets for the polo season, Chessie had decided against Christmas pudding or hard sauce or pecan pie, and then irrationally settled for something far more fattening: sweetened whipped cream shaped like a polo ball, rolled in melted chocolate, and then coated in coconut.

'Oh, how darling,' said Auriel. 'Chessie must have known it was your favourite dessert, Red. They always make it for him at the club.'

'No, it isn't,' snapped Red. 'Suddenly I feel sick.'

'Oh, poor baby,' Auriel was all concern. 'I better take you home.'

The smaller of the Yorkshire terriers was sick.

Chessie flushed. 'I should have forgotten you weren't on solid foods yet, Red, and provided you with a bottle of Cow and Gate.' Then turning, spitting with rage, to Auriel: 'It must be such a drag picking him up from play-group every day. Don't forget to put the baby alarm on when he goes to sleep tonight. Revolting little toyboy.'

Auriel, however, oblivious of the sniping and able to forgive a potential customer, was telling a deliriously happy Perdita about her new range.

'You were saying you couldn't wear a dress because of the bruises. In my range we've invented a cream which completely disguises them. I'll mail you some.'

'You ought to send some to Chessie,' drawled Red. 'Then she could use it on her ass – Mrs Regularly Beaten.'

There was a shocked pause.

'Pack it in,' snapped Luke.

'What are you talking about?' stammered Chessie.

'Your little hang-up,' said Red, 'about having pain before pleasure. We've all heard smacks and screams coming from your bedroom.'

He got no further. Seizing him by the collar, Bart had hauled him to his feet.

'Don't you speak to Chessie like that,' he bellowed. 'I won't KO you, I'd probably kill you. But you get out of my house – now.'

The glasses jangled, the rafters shook. Leroy shot trembling under the table. The second Yorkshire terrier was sick.

'Don't touch him,' screamed Auriel.

'I'm only stating facts,' said Red laughing as he drifted towards the door. 'Truth shouldn't hurt – anyway I thought that was what turned Chessie on.'

'Get out,' yelled Bart, 'and you can forget about playing on my team in England this summer until you learn some manners.'

37

Back in Rutshire, Daisy was dreading Christmas all on her own. Eddie and Violet were flying off to LA to spend a week with Hamish, Wendy, little Bridget and a two-month-old addition to the family called Fergus.

'I must keep cheerful until they go,' Daisy kept telling herself as she took the bus into Cheltenham to buy them Christmas presents. 'I mustn't cling. I must stay jolly for Ethel and Gainsborough.'

Her boss, the Caring Chauvinist, had sourly given her the afternoon off. After all, Christmas was his busiest time, but Daisy had managed to escape from the office party before he started chasing her round the desks. An added grievance was that she'd already had an afternoon off early in the month to show her paintings to a London gallery.

'I really like your work,' the owner had told her. 'I could easily sell your paintings if you used brighter colours.'

Daisy gazed dolefully out of the bus on frost-bleached fields, bare trees, khaki stubble, beige houses and grey woolly sheep all blending in. She thought how hard it was to paint brightly in winter, particularly when all the money she'd saved to buy a car had been spent on mending the washing machine, and her hair needed cutting and she was seven pounds overweight. Even three years after Hamish had left her she still suffered from wildly ricocheting moods. Only that morning she'd wept to find a list – 'Toads, Eddie's tooth, Gainsborough's mouse, sunset' – which she'd once scribbled down as topics to keep the conversation going with Hamish at dinner. She had forgotten how demanding, bad-tempered, and intolerant Hamish had been. The breakdown of the marriage she now felt had been all her fault.

Suddenly, out of a ploughed field, rose four magpies.

One for sorrow, two for joy, three for a girl, four for a toyboy, thought Daisy longingly.

'What d'you want for Christmas?' her mother had asked the day before, and Daisy's mind had gone completely blank, because all she wanted was a man. She'd tried going into pubs, but she always drank too fast out of nerves, then had to hide her empty glass in her skirt, so men didn't feel they had to buy her a drink. There were a few party invitations, but without a car she had to rely on lifts. She'd even been to a Gingerbread meeting for single parents last month, but all the men had beards and kept insisting they weren't remotely chauvinistic, but very caring. Daisy had got off with the only attractive man, who'd afterwards turned out to be married and only posing as single to take advantage of lonely women.

Cheltenham was hell – absolutely packed with people grumbling about the difficulty of parking their expensive cars and spending fortunes. The post-Christmas sales were already on. I'm a marked-down dress no one wants, thought Daisy.

She passed the record shop. She'd get the Wham record for Eddie and Beethoven's fourth piano concerto for Violet on the way back. Out of the loudspeakers belched 'Last Christmas'. The hopes and fears of all the years are met in Thee tonight, she thought to herself. So many fears, so few hopes. Daisy bit back the tears and nearly got run over crossing George Street before plunging into the supermarket to buy a tiny turkey for Christmas dinner for her, Ethel and Gainsborough.

'Fresh luxury bird,' said a large sign of a fat turkey holding a piece of mistletoe, 'with wishbone removed for luxury carving.'

How awful, thought Daisy, when she'd got so much to wish for: Perdita forgiving her, Eddie and Violet wanting to spend Christmas with her one day, money getting all right, her paintings being good enough for an exhibition, Eddie and Violet passing their exams, Perdita not getting pregnant in Palm Beach.

Would she ever have a man in her life to carve the turkey? Rubbing her eyes, she ran out of the supermarket. She was getting nowhere, Eddie wanted the new Adrian Mole book, Violet was taking *Emma* for A levels and wanted the complete Jane Austen, the Caring Chauvinist wanted the latest Jeffrey Archer.

In the corner of Hammicks a beauty wafting a cloud of Jolie Madame was thumbing mindlessly through a biography of Wellington, constantly looking at her watch and checking her face in the mirror. She wore a wedding ring. Lucky thing, thought Daisy wistfully, to have a lover *and* a husband.

Handing over the books to the assistant, she burrowed in her bag. It was only after the till had been rung up that she realized she'd left both her cheque book and her cheque card behind. She wished that the carpet would swallow her up, but it was such a hideous green it had probably swallowed several people before that day and was suffering from frightful indigestion.

Her account was in Stroud and overdrawn, so there was no possibility they'd guarantee a blank cheque at a Cheltenham branch. There was no way she could buy anything now for Eddie and Violet, which Hamish and Wendy would construe as a further example of parental neglect and a reason to assume custody.

Running sobbing out of the shop, she collapsed on one of the octagonal benches in front of the clock at the north end of the arcade. A drunk reeled up to her and offered her the remains of his whisky bottle.

'Go away,' howled Daisy. Then, conscious of being ungrateful, howled even louder.

'Mrs Macleod,' said a soft voice.

Frantically wiping away the tears and the mascara, Daisy looked up. It was Drew Benedict, who seemed to have arrived from a different planet. He'd obviously been playing polo somewhere hot and he handed her his green-and-red Paisley silk handkerchief which smelt faintly of French Fern.

'I got an afternoon off for Christmas shopping' – Daisy blew her reddened nose noisily – 'and I left my cheque book behind.'

Taking her arm, Drew pulled her to her feet.

'I'll get you some money.'

Waving aside her frantic apologies, he took her to his bank and drew out £150.

'I've got to see my lawyer about a contract, have a pair

of boots fitted, buy something for Sukey and some arsenic for her ghastly mother, who's staying with us. I'll give you a lift home in a couple of hours.'

Embarrassed but cheered up, Daisy scurried around, managing to get everything done in time, and even buying a bottle of Polo aftershave for Drew because she felt so guilty dragging him out of his way when he must be so busy. She was also shocked to find herself going into the Ladies at Cavendish House to clean her teeth, redo her face and retie her hair back in its elastic band. It was too dirty to wear loose. As she went past the scent counter she sprayed herself with Jolie Madame. Outside the beauty who'd been reading Wellington was sobbing uncontrollably as an embarrassed but very good-looking man ushered her into a taxi.

'Don't cry, darling,' he was saying, 'I'll ring you every day when Emma goes out to walk the dogs. If Patrick answers I'll hang up. It's only nine days.'

'Oh, come all ye faithful,' sang the loud speaker.

'Daisy,' yelled a voice. It was Drew in a dark green Mini. Between them they managed to fill up the back seat with their purchases. The temperature had dropped. The sun was setting in nougat colours, pale purple and cyclamen-pink.

'Where have you been to get so brown?' asked Daisy.

'Middle East with the Carlisle twins, playing for Victor Kaputnik against the Sultan of Araby. Contrary to what people say, the country is not dry. Everyone was so drunk on Sunday afternoon that the ball stayed in the same place while everyone swiped at it.'

'How lovely,' said Daisy.

'Pay was good,' went on Drew cheerfully. 'The twins have gone to Italy so they can ski into Switzerland next door and put all their loot into a Swiss bank. I'll bank mine when I play snow polo at St Moritz in January. How the hell d'you manage without a car?'

'Very badly,' said Daisy gloomily.

Drew had removed his coat and was wearing a light blue cashmere jersey, so new it still had the creases in and which matched his eyes. Rutshire, Cirencester and Guards polo stickers curled on the windscreen.

'How did Perdita get on in Argentina?'

'She adored it,' said Daisy on the evidence of one letter, 'but she found the Argentines a bit cruel.'

'They train the best polo ponies in the world.'

'And she's spending Christmas in Palm Beach with Bart Alderton's son, Luke.'

'Bloody nice,' said Drew approvingly. 'She couldn't be in better hands, and a very good polo player. Might get her over Ricky.'

'D'you think Ricky'll mind her spending Christmas so near Bart Alderton?'

Drew shook his head. 'Ricky's not small-minded. Bart's the only person he's got any fight with.'

Like all polo players, Drew drove very quickly, overtaking much faster cars on bends with a centimetre to spare. He was so nice to talk to, Daisy wished he would slow down She longed to ask him in, and tried to remember if she'd drunk all that bottle of cheap white last night, and if she'd put it back in the fridge. It was only drinkable if it were cold.

'That's Declan O'Hara's house – he's just moved in,' said Daisy, pointing to towers and battlements hidden by yew trees and huge Wellingtonias. 'I think his telly interviews are so wonderful. Everyone's going to Midnight Mass at Cotchester Cathedral to gawp at him.'

'We're going to a party there on New Year's Eve,' said Drew. 'Promises to be the thrash of the decade. Rupert's got a terrific yen for Declan's daughter, Taggie. He's coming back specially from Gstaad to have a crack at her.'

'What's she like?' asked Daisy wistfully.

'Ravishing, but too tall for me. I don't like standing on tiptoe to kiss girls.'

The setting sun was firing the windows of Snow Cottage as they bumped along the dirt track.

'Ricky ought to do something about this road, it's terrible,' said Drew disapprovingly. 'You need a snow plough rather than a car.'

Weaving, singing, her eyes screwed up with sleep, Ethel temporarily distracted them from the mess left by the children. All the kitchen chairs had been pulled out. Orange juice cartons, bowls barnacled with muesli, overflowing ashtrays littered the kitchen table.

'Thank you so much,' said Daisy, writing out a cheque at once, then blushing furiously, 'but would you possibly mind not cashing it until the New Year.'

'Won't be going near a bank before then,' said Drew, getting a bottle of Moët out of a Cavendish House bag. 'Let's have a drink.'

Daisy, having extracted two clean glasses from the washing-up machine, hastily cleared the kitchen table. As the cork flew out of the bottle, Ethel fled out of the room.

'Not much use for shooting,' said Drew as Daisy put some anemones she'd bought in water.

'Beautiful, aren't they?' she said, fingering the scarlet-and-violet petals. 'They're for Will's grave.' Then, blushing and wishing she hadn't said that, she added, 'Ricky asked me to keep an eye on it while he was away.'

Drew eyed her speculatively. 'D'you find him attractive?'

'Yes,' confessed Daisy, taking a huge gulp of champagne. 'One couldn't not, but he's only interested in Chessie, and I'm too old for him. I was six when he was born.'

'And seven when I was born,' said Drew.

'I might have been allowed to give you your bottle.'

'I can give you mine now,' said Drew, topping up her glass.

Idly he picked up her sketch pad, immediately becoming transfixed with interest.

'There's Hermia and there's Wayne! You've got his wicked eye to a T. Christ, they're good, and recognizable even in their winter coats.' Taking the sketch book to the light, he looked at it more closely. 'And that's marvellous of Little Chef.'

He gazed at Daisy with new respect. Drew had bought a lot of paintings since he married Sukey, because he liked them and expected them to shoot up in value. If Daisy could catch such vivid likenesses without being chocolate-boxy, she might well be worth investing in.

'That's good. That's Kinta, dangerous brute. When's Perdita coming home?'

'Sometime in the New Year.'

Drew looked up sharply. 'And the other children?'

'They're going to LA to my ex.'

'You can't stay here on your own.'

'I've got Ethel,' mumbled Daisy.

'Not much of a guard dog.' Drew filled up her glass again. 'Don't you get frightened by yourself?'

'No,' lied Daisy. 'Anyway, I usually wear so many jerseys against the cold, any rapist would get dead bored before he managed to undress me. Lots of people asked me to stay, but Ethel's a bit of a liability. She broke three Christopher Wray lamps and got into a chicken coop last time we went away.'

'It's all wrong. Come to us for Christmas dinner.'

Daisy's eyes filled with tears.

'You're so kind, but honestly, I've got to paint.'

Putting a hand on her shoulder, Drew felt it trembling. 'You're not OK.'

Daisy gazed at the bubbles rising in her glass.

'I'm getting better at being single,' she mumbled, pleating her dark red skirt, 'but my heart isn't really in it. I'd love to find a man, but you never find mushrooms when you're looking for them, do you? Anyway at my age you'd have to break a marriage up to get married yourself and I couldn't do that, knowing how awful it was for me.'

Daisy's cheeks were bright pink, but she was deathly white under her eyes, which were still red-rimmed from crying outside the bookshop. Her lovely soft mouth had nearly disappeared in her desperate attempt not to cry again.

Drew, who said nothing and went on stroking Ethel, had a reputation for coolness because he had an analytical mind and always thought before he spoke. Being in the Army for nine years had also given him a certain fixity of outlook, but he was extremely kind in a detached way, never took himself very seriously and was an excellent listener.

'I bet you haven't had any lunch,' said Daisy leaping to her feet. 'I'll make us some scrambled eggs. Lots of people are like me,' she rattled on. 'There's a frightfully pompous piece in the paper today saying the New Singleton is the emblematic, contemporary figure.'

Her hands shook so much she spilt most of the eggs as she cracked them on the edge of the bowl. Her co-ordination was so jiggered she could hardly manage to watch the toast and cook the eggs at the same time.

'This piece rabbited on about always looking your best in case Mr Right Mark II came along, but I don't see anyone except my awful boss and it seems silly looking smart while I'm painting or walking Ethel. D'you think the badgers would appreciate bright red lipstick to match a red scarf and taupe eyeshadow? Besides I don't think anyone would put up with me now.' She scraped the wooden spoon frantically against the bottom of the pan. 'You get into such awful habits living alone. Talking to yourself, wiping your hands on your trousers. Oh, bugger, I've turned off the grill.'

'I turned it off,' said Drew. 'I adore the way your bum judders when you stir those eggs,' he added, turning off the gas as well, 'and I like cold scrambled eggs.'

Next moment he had taken her in his arms.

'Oh no,' squeaked Daisy. 'What about Sukey?'

'Shut up,' said Drew gently. 'She's at home making lists for Easter. I have a marriage of convenience. It was the only way I could play polo.'

The arctic-blue eyes which turned down at the corners were suddenly anything but cold. Daisy's resolve weakened. 'It's still wrong.'

'Hush, two wrongs make a Mr Right,' said Drew and kissed her. Daisy was utterly lost. Until one kisses a man, one cannot tell if one truly desires him, and something melted inside Daisy and as Drew's tongue coolly and languorously explored her mouth, her hands shot upwards to tangle in his fine silky hair, and then to feel the wonderful muscular strength of his shoulders. She was so taken by surprise that next moment she found herself upstairs. Thank goodness she'd changed the sheets that morning, Ethel hadn't shredded a bone in her bed and there were more clothes on the chair than the floor.

'Lovely room,' said Drew, admiring the huge roses, peonies and delphiniums which Daisy had painted growing out of the skirting board. 'It'll be like screwing on the lawn on a summer evening.'

'I haven't slept with anyone for three years,' mumbled Daisy in panic, as Drew slowly undid the buttons of her black cardigan, until he could drop an infinitely leisured kiss on her bare shoulder.

367

'It'll come back. It's like riding a bicycle,' whispered Drew as his hand slid round to the back to unhook her bra.

'I'll need stabilizers to start off with,' said Daisy feeling wildly unstable.

'Christ,' said Drew lifting one heavy breast after another in delight, 'they *are* beautiful.'

And he really admired them from all angles before bending his head and kissing each nipple. As he slowly removed her skirt, her laddered tights, and her pants, grey as a dishcloth which ought to have been retired years ago, Daisy curled up with embarrassment.

'I haven't shaved my legs or anywhere else. I'm like an old ewe.'

'The Welsh Guards were always known as the sheep shaggers. That's better,' he went on as Daisy laughed and as his warm hands moved over her body, just grazing the hairs, he had her leaping with desire. Still dressed, he sat beside her on the bed and stroked down her belly.

'This is the only bit that needs cutting back,' he said, parting her pubic hair and gently fingering. 'All you need is a bit of spit and polish. Don't hurry, my darling. I've no desire to get back to my mother-in-law.'

Daisy giggled, shuddered, tensed, came and then burst into tears. Appalled, Drew pulled her into his arms.

'Darling, what's the matter?'

'I never came with Hamish,' sobbed Daisy, 'never in fifteen years, I never believed anything could be so lovely.'

'Then we'd better make up for lost orgasms. It's my turn next.'

Dreamily Daisy watched him undress. Apart from slightly bow legs and a shrapnel scar from the Falklands, he was wonderfully built – stocky and muscular without being fat. Even his cock seemed to have biceps as, with the ball of his thumb seldom far away from her clitoris, he drove her to extremes of joy. She was amazed anyone so phlegmatic could be such a sensitive, imaginative lover. He didn't even mind when Ethel, unaccustomed to sex, and stumbling upon an unbelievably jolly romp, decided to join in with a great leap on the bed.

Afterwards, as she sat wrapped in a scratchy, dark blue

towel watching Drew have a bath, Daisy said again that she felt quite awful about Sukey.

'Don't,' said Drew, who certainly scrubbed himself very vigorously. 'As long as she doesn't find out, it won't hurt her. Anyway, I've always had a crush on you.'

'Me?' said Daisy incredulously.

'Ever since you got rained on the first time we met at the Pony Club, and I could have hung my polo hat on your nipples.'

'A crush helmet,' giggled Daisy.

'I've been wondering,' went on Drew, 'what you'd look like without your clothes on.'

'Hairy,' said Daisy.

Drew shook his head as he reared out of the bath. 'Absolutely gorgeous.'

Pulling off her towel, he gently squeezed her right breast. 'Promise never to lose any weight.'

He glanced at the watch that he'd left on the edge of the basin. 'Christ, I must go.' Then, seeing the shadow of desolation flicker across Daisy's face, 'I'll ring you tomorrow morning.'

'How?' asked Daisy.

'When Sukey rides out with my mother-in-law.'

Outside, Ricky's ash trees, like a clump of swaying broomsticks, were trying to sweep the stars out of a pearly grey sky. Drew kissed her again. 'Merry Christmas, Mrs Macleod, I'm afraid you've got yourself a toyboy.'

Daisy felt it was all dreadfully immoral, but she couldn't help being hugely cheered up, particularly when Drew rang her as promised next day saying how much he wanted to see her again. Going into the garden, she found midges dancing and crab apples glittering crimson against a bright ultramarine sky. Breathing in the wild-rose scent of a pale pink rambler called The New Dawn, which clambered up to the cottage eaves, and always seemed to be in flower, Daisy hoped it would be a new dawn for her and she might do some brighter paintings.

On Christmas Day she had another surprise. Ricky rang up stammering badly and thanked her for the drawing of Little Chef she'd sent him as a Christmas present.

'It's f-f-fantastic. How is he?'

'Fine, but missing you.'

'And Perdita?'

'Fine – in Palm Beach staying with the Aldertons.'

Oh God, why had she blurted that out? She must have wrecked his Christmas.

But, after a long pause, Ricky asked, 'You're not by yourself?'

'Yes, but I've got a lot of friends dropping in' (well, one friend).

'Good.' Then, after a really long pause: 'Have you got Perdita's number?'

Perhaps he was keen on Perdita after all, thought Daisy after he'd rung off. If she hadn't met Drew again, she might have been very jealous.

Later on Violet rang from LA.

'Daddy and Wendy have gone out. Eddie and I spend our time baby-sitting. Oh, Mummy, it's awful. Daddy was present at the birth, and Wendy insisted we watched the video last night. It was disgusting. Eddie nearly fainted. And they've got a white album of even more disgusting photographs – even of the afterbirth, and they show it to everyone, and Wendy breastfeeds in public, in the shops and at parties. And she's gone completely Californian, no salt in food, no getting brown, no drink, no fags. I wish we could come home. I love you, Mum. You're not too lonely on your own?'

Daisy put down the telephone feeling so happy.

Drew seemed to have ignited some creative spark. Daisy painted and painted late into the night, listening to the foxes barking, and singing 'I just called to say I love you' that she slept until she was woken by Drew's telephone call in the morning.

On Boxing Day it turned bitterly cold. In the west a band of crocus-yellow was fading into daffodil below a dark purple cloud. Having shaved her legs and her armpits, Daisy rigged up a mirror in the drawing room, lit the fire and did a series of sketches of herself in the nude. If Drew liked her body maybe it wasn't that bad. She mustn't be too obvious, she mustn't glamorize herself. Completely absorbed, she didn't hear the door bell at first. Wrapping herself in a rose-pink shawl she'd draped over the sofa to hide two large cigarette burns, she opened the front door and gave a gasp. For there was Drew in a red coat, white breeches and brown-topped boots.

'I decided to change the quarry,' he said, shoving her back into the house and slamming the door.

'How lovely. Where's your horse?'

'Gone home. Sukey thinks I'm having a drink with Rupert.'

'Does he know you aren't?'

'Yes, I've covered up enough for him over the years.'

Imagine Rupert being used as an alibi for me, thought Daisy amazed.

'You been down a mine?' asked Drew, taking in her charcoal smudged face and hands.

'D'you want a drink?' asked Daisy.

'No, I want you.' Drew ripped off her shawl.

As he took her in his arms the taut athletic muscular hardness of his body evoked some distant memory, something familiar yet incredibly disturbing, stirring like a hibernating butterfly at the back of her consciousness.

His face was ice-cold against hers, so were his hands as they moved over her body. There was nothing measured or leisurely about his approach today. Whisking her into the drawing room, he laid her down on the threadbare carpet, unzipped his flies and, forcing his way into her, came almost immediately.

'Sorry, darling,' he murmured into her shoulder, 'that was bloody selfish, but I couldn't help myself – pleasured my lady with my boots on. Stay there. I don't want to ruin your carpet.'

Easing himself out, he returned with some kitchen roll.

'That was lovely,' sighed Daisy truthfully. After years of indifference from Hamish, the greatest aphrodisiac for her was that Drew wanted her so much.

'How was your party at lunchtime?' he asked.

'Undemanding,' said Daisy, flattered that he'd remembered. 'Mawled wine and retired colonels rabbiting on about wind breaks and frost pockets. I still feel awful about Sukey. The same thing happened to me at Christmas. I remember the telephone always smelling of Paco Rabanne when I came back from being out and not understanding why when Hamish claimed no one had rung. Then there were all the dropped telephone calls.'

'Don't torture yourself,' said Drew, leaning up on his elbow and stroking her belly. 'Every situation is different. Ricky married for love, and look where that got him. I didn't. I'm not attracted to Sukey. We never sleep together, but I love Jamie and I'm fond of the old thing. This isn't doing her any harm, and it's doing me so much good,' he slid his fingers inside her, 'and this is definitely not a frost pocket.'

Catching sight of them both in the mirror, he reached over and adjusted the angle so they could both watch.

'Hamish never did that either,' said Daisy afterwards.

'Sounds a prat.' Then, out of the blue: 'If you didn't come with him, what about Perdita's father?'

Burying her face in his chest, Daisy decided to tell the truth and the circumstances because she trusted Drew to keep his trap shut.

'So it might have been some handsome rock star or polo player,' said Drew afterwards. 'Could have been me. I was eleven and *very* precocious.'

'Don't think there were any children present. Jackie wasn't into paedophilia.'

Making a joke of it suddenly made the whole thing less awful.

'You're not shocked?' asked Daisy.

'Having been a friend of Rupert's for fifteen years, nothing shocks me. Anyway, you were a baby.'

Daisy felt weak with gratitude.

'My parents were dreadfully upset. They tried to sweep it under the carpet, but as they had fitted carpets at home it was rather hard.'

'I'm getting rather hard too,' said Drew, pulling her on top of him.

'Oh, I love you,' said Daisy covering him with kisses, then added hastily, 'but don't worry, I say "I love you", all the time to Ethel and Gainsborough and the children. I'm honestly not getting heavy.'

'I know you're not,' said Drew, guiding his cock inside her. 'I told you I didn't want you to lose weight.'

'Can I draw you before you get dressed?' said Daisy later.

'If you want to,' said Drew, sitting down on the sofa. 'As long as you hide it from Perdita. She'd be bound to sneak to Sukey.'

Oh, his face is so lovely when he smiles, thought Daisy, pinning a fresh piece of paper on the board.

'You'll have to draw an erection in in a minute,' said Drew.

They were on the carpet in each other's arms when Drew looked at his watch. 'Jesus, it's nearly eight o'clock. D'you mind running me over to Rupert's?'

'I haven't got a car,' said Daisy miserably. 'I'll try to ring for a taxi, or borrow Philippa's.'

Drew brushed her hair back from her forehead and kissed it.

'The car I came here in is your Christmas present. It's only an old banger, but it'll get you about. It's all right. Sukey didn't pay for it, I bought it with my Sultan of Araby money.'

'An old banger for an old bang-ee,' said Daisy, 'but I really can't take it.'

Drew stopped her protests with a kiss.

After she'd dropped him off and bumped back home, grinding gears and singing at the top of her voice, Daisy hid the drawing of Drew in the potting shed. But she soon retrieved it and put it in her bedroom. After all, the children weren't coming back until the New Year and Drew was without doubt the nicest thing that had happened in all her life.

38

'Quarantine,' as Luke's comely headgroom, Lizzie, was fond of pointing out, 'is a real ass-kicker.'

But, predictably, Perdita left all the hassle of scrubbing out the boxes with disinfectant, isolating Spotty and Tero, and dealing with the interminable inspections by vets and government officials to Luke and his grooms. Luke even arranged for Spotty and Tero to be flown to Heathrow cheap, as part of a twenty-pony job lot which Victor Kaputnik was smuggling in from Argentina via

Palm Beach. Aware that Perdita had no money, Luke picked up the bill for that, too.

He refused to hear a word against her, but it would be fair to say that his grooms regarded Perdita with a dislike bordering on hatred. They worked for the best boss in Palm Beach, but now this spoilt little bitch had swanned in, ordering him around, squandering his money and dragging him out to the high spots every night. Lizzie had even made a day chart until Perdita went back to England and the barn returned to normal.

Having spent her last day stick and balling in the tiniest bikini to top up her tan for Ricky, Perdita popped in on Chessie to say goodbye on her way to the airport. Luke was delayed at the barn because Ophelia was tied up with colic, but said he would catch up with her.

Perdita found Chessie by the pool in the same lime-green bikini she'd worn the day after Perdita had flown in from Argentina and which was now much too big for her. Nor did Chessie hitch it up in time to hide a dark bruise on her left hip.

'Gosh, what have you done?' asked Perdita without thinking.

'Been gored on the horns of a dilemma,' said Chessie bitterly. 'Oh, for Christ's sake, put on a bikini and come into the pool with me, I'm sure this umbrella is bugged, and probably the ice in your glass.'

Perdita didn't want to swim. It would crinkle her newly washed hair and she wanted to look her best in case by some miracle Ricky met the plane. But such was the force of Chessie's discontent that five minutes later she was dog-paddling into the centre of the pool.

'Every time I go shopping Bart insists that two guards accompany me,' rattled Chessie, who'd lost all her normal laid-back cool and whose jaw above the blue water was rigid with tension.

'I daren't ring England, I know the telephone's bugged. Look, can you give Ricky a message? Tell him not to risk getting in touch with me. Security's too tight, but tell him I'll ring him somehow the minute I get to London.'

For a stunned second Perdita disappeared beneath the water, then she emerged spluttering and had to paddle backwards until her feet touched the bottom.

'I d-d-don't understand.'

'The reason Ricky rang at Christmas,' said Chessie hysterically, 'was to tell me in those few desperate seconds that he's still absolutely mad about me – only me. Talking to you later was just a smokescreen.'

'But he seemed so happy to hear my voice.'

'That's because he'd just heard mine. Can't you understand? All Ricky wants is to have me back. I'd love to go, but I'm not sure if one should turn back the clock, and would I be constantly reminded of Will again, and Ricky hasn't got any money, and would I hate being poor again?'

Despite the warmth of the pool and the day, Perdita suddenly felt icy cold and dizzy. Her mouth had gone dry and acid. She wanted to scream at Chessie not to be so bloody selfish, screwing up Ricky's life again. Then Chessie disarmed her by bursting into tears.

'I'm dying of homesickness. I haven't been back to England since Will died, and now Bart's bought Rutminster Abbey so we can spend the summer there, and think of all the memories. I can't face it, and I know I can't *not* face it.'

Perdita wanted to plunge into the soft silky water, which was the same duck-egg blue as the Alderton Flyer shirt Ricky had been wearing the first day she'd fallen in love with him, and never come up again. Involuntarily her thoughts strayed to Red, the only other man who'd seriously jolted her, but Red was a playboy. As if in answer to her prayer the Rottweilers started barking furiously and there, chatting to one of the guards and stroking the head of the no-longer snarling dog, stood Luke.

'That's the one,' said Chessie reading her thoughts. 'He's the nicest, strongest man you'll ever meet.'

Luke has no money, thought Perdita, and, after the glitz of Palm Beach, she was never, never, going to be poor again.

The divide between rich and poor was further intensified when they got to Miami Airport, which was its usual shambles of bewildered passengers and despairing hair-tearing insolent porters. Luke hadn't even had time to change his shirt which was soaked with sweat. His white jeans were filthy, and dust streaked one side of his face. Ophelia was still fighting colic. He ought to drop Perdita off and go straight back to her, but he couldn't tear himself away. She'd been so manic when she'd set off to see Chessie; now her eyes were glittering with unshed tears and her mouth trembling. Perhaps miraculously, she'd suddenly realized she was going to miss him. He bought her a vodka and tonic and they sat in the bar. Perdita, in whom deep unhappiness invariably manifested itself as bad temper, stared moodily at the other passengers; Luke stared at Perdita. Frantic excitement was generated because Paul Newman and Joanne Woodward were on the same flight and immediately wafted through to the VIP lounge.

'Christ, he's attractive,' grumbled Perdita. 'Why the hell can't I travel First?'

Luke was tired and had to resist snapping at her that she was bloody lucky to have her return ticket paid for at all. Committed to play for Hal in Chicago, Houston, Detroit, and then Greenwich in the Fall, there was no way he'd get to England to see her this year.

He took her hand. 'I'm gonna miss you. Will you write?'

Perdita shrugged. 'I'm a stinking correspondent.'

Not to Ricky you weren't, thought Luke, remembering the dozens of unanswered letters.

'At least you'll have your own bed back,' Perdita tried to pull herself together, adding listlessly, 'Thanks for everything. It's been great.'

'What did Chessie say to you?' asked Luke.

'Nothing,' said Perdita, about to blurt the whole thing out. 'Oh, hell, that's all I need.'

Coming towards her was her old Pony Club enemy, Trace Coley, clanking duty free and looking a million dollars.

'Last time we met,' Perdita muttered to Luke, 'I tried to drown her mother.'

Trace, however, was prepared to suspend hostilities in order to swank.

'Hello, Perdita, long time no see. What are you doing here, buying ponies?'

'I'm bringing back two,' said Perdita defiantly.

'Daddy bought me seven,' said Trace. 'I'm playing medium goal with him and Drew Benedict and the most heavenly Mexican out of Cowdray next season. I must check in. Let's gossip on the flight.' Then, glancing down at the label on Perdita's handluggage: 'Oh, poor you. Economy gets so hot and smelly on this flight. What a pity you're not travelling First.'

'She is, she is,' said a voice.

Perdita gave a start. For there, lean as a spear in black jeans and a shirt the pale scarlet of a runner bean flower, stood Red. He was as high as a kite, his tiger eyes glittering, and absolutely reeking of Auriel's new scent.

'Perdita, baby, I had to come and say goodbye. Hi, Luke.'

'Do introduce me, Perdita,' shrieked Trace Coley whose eyes were popping like a squeezed peke. 'You're Red Alderton, and you're having a walk-out with Auriel Kingham, and you're an absolutely brilliant polo player.'

'I wouldn't argue with any of that,' said Red.

He turned reproachfully to Luke. 'How can you let this poor baby travel Economy?'

Then he smiled wickedly at Perdita. 'I never gave you a Christmas present, so I've upgraded you instead. Paul and Joanne are in the VIP lounge and are dying to meet you. Let's go and say hello.'

Luke looked at his brother, his face expressionless. 'You are an absolute shit, Red.'

Whatever his feelings about Chessie, Ricky returned brown and incredibly chipper from Palm Springs. He was delighted that Perdita had improved so dramatically and that she had brought home two such good ponies.

Tero, having driven Victor's grooms crackers on the journey calling piteously for Fantasma, had now chummed up with Spotty and the two were inseparable. Spotty, wearing three extra rugs and an expression of outrage on his red-and-white face at the arctic conditions that greeted him, was soon bickering with Wayne over who should be boss of the yard.

The first time he and Tero were turned out, Kinta, who was a thug and a bully, went for the timid little mare, shoving her into the water trough and laying into her with teeth and feet. Immediately, Spotty bustled round the corner to Tero's rescue, and Kinta, who'd never come across a skewbald in polo or in her previous racing career, spooked and ran away in horror. After that, Ricky moved Spotty and Tero to another paddock, where, slavish with gratitude, Tero followed Spotty everywhere, but still had to be given a nose bag every day to stop Spotty and all the other ponies pinching her food.

The Argentine ponies Ricky had smuggled in, through France in the end, arrived looking very poor and miserable, but soon picked up as the winter turned mild.

The best tonic of all was that Ricky's elbow had recovered. Having played every day in the warmth of Palm Springs, he was back to his old dazzling form. This summer he would play high goal with Bas, Mike Waterlane and Dancer, and medium goal with Bas, Dancer and Perdita. At the beginning of March they started getting the ponies ready for the new season, walking them out, then trotting them, then riding them up and down the steep Rutshire hills to harden up their muscles. Ricky also applied for membership for Dancer and himself at the Rutshire Polo Club, and was stunned to receive a letter from Brigadier Hughie saying they would be unwelcome. Going straight to the top, Ricky rang David Waterlane, the Club President, who, after some huffing and puffing, admitted that Bart Alderton was behind the blackballing.

'Chap's poured a lot of money into the club's diminishing funds over the past three years. Got Hughie eating out of the palm of his hand. Bart says Rutshire's reputation shouldn't be tarnished by allowing in two players with police records, one an ex-junkie, and,' David Waterlane added heavily, 'a queer.'

'Polo's accommodated plenty of those in the past,' said Ricky, 'and bad hats too. Can't be the real reason.'

'Bart's bought Rutminster Abbey,' admitted David. 'Due to move in with Chessie in April. Doesn't want you bumping into Chessie week in week out at the club. See his point. Wouldn't like to spend every weekend avoiding Clemency. Put me off my game.'

What did Fatty Harris think about all this? demanded Ricky.

'Oh, his palm's been so liberally greased by Bart, he'll be able to bath in Margaux for the rest of his life. He's quite happy to send you and Dancer to perdition. And

Miss Lodsworth's on his side. She's never really forgiven you for your disgusting language, or Dancer for his burst water-main. 'Fraid there's not much I can do about it.'

Ricky was absolutely furious. Cirencester was a much better club than Rutshire, but it was twenty-five miles away instead of four, which was too far to hack to, and anyway his family had always played at Rutshire.

Bas Baddingham, who'd been skiing when the black-balling took place, came roaring to Ricky's rescue. 'Don't worry. We'll marshal support at the next AGM and get you reinstated.'

The AGM was held on the third Sunday in March at the Dog and Trumpet in Rutminster High Street. Excitement that spring had arrived and a new polo season was on the way was slightly doused by an overnight blizzard. Perdita, who'd just passed her driving test, pinched Daisy's car to drive into Rutminster. The roads were very icy, and she enjoyed skidding all over them. She couldn't understand why her mother was so protective about a clapped-out Volkswagen and had even burst into tears when Perdita backed it into a wall the other day.

And if she can afford a car, thought Perdita, pulling up with a jerk beside Brigadier Hughie's Rover, she can jolly well buy me a new pair of boots.

The meeting was already packed. Brigadier Hughie waved Perdita to a lone empty seat in the second row on the left by the window. In front of her sat Sharon Kaputnik smothered in mink and Victor smothered in smugness over his recent knighthood. On the right sat a solid phalanx of players in tweed coats and check shirts, their heavily muscled arms and shoulders overflowing on either side of the back of their narrow gold chairs and making the rows look even fuller. The more highly handicapped players had suntans from playing abroad. The left side seemed to be largely inhabited by non-playing members, including Miss Lodsworth and her cronies, their capaciously drooping cashmere bosoms resting on their tweed-skirted bellies, their feet sensibly clad in brogues and coloured wool stockings. Miss Lodsworth, who was wearing burgundy-red tights to match her face, was making lists.

'Bad language, five ponies abreast in Eldercombe High

Street, loose grooms' dogs in Rutminster Park, cruelty, excessive use of whip,' wrote Miss Lodsworth in her masculine hand and glared at Perdita, who, having been guilty of at least three of these sins, glared back.

At a table facing the room sat Brigadier Hughie, Fatty Harris and Basil Baddingham. On the end sat Posy Jones, the pretty club secretary, who was already getting too hot in her Prussian-blue jersey.

He looks like a nineteenth-century French cavalry officer, thought Posy, gazing surreptitiously at Bas. There was something exotic and un-English about the highly polished gold buttons on his blazer, the beautifully manicured hands, and the uniformly dark gold suntan. His glossy, patent-leather hair was exactly the same Vandyke brown as his moustache and his wickedly roving eyes. He's really attractive, decided Posy, then flushed as Bas shot her a look of unashamed lust. The reason the minutes were not recorded as accurately that year was because Bas's long fingers kept idly caressing the back of Posy's navy-blue stockinged legs, as he gazed equally idly at Perdita. Perdita was seriously worried. The purpose of the meeting for her was to get Ricky reinstated and Bas seemed to be the only one of Ricky's supporters to have turned up. The twins and Jesus were playing in the Cartier Open and Handicap in Palm Beach. Mike Waterlane was too terrified of his father to be any use, and Drew hadn't arrived yet.

'I can't think what's happened to Drew,' said Sukey, who was planning the menu for a dinner party on Tuesday. 'He went to look at a pony outside Cotchester and was meeting me here.'

As Rutminster Cathedral struck the half-hour Brigadier Hughie rose to his feet.

'Better get started. Our President, Sir David Waterlane, has been delayed by a puncture and is about to come through the door. I expect that's him now, so I'll shut up.'

Instead, in wandered Seb Carlisle, blond hair ruffled, tie over one collar, yawning widely and holding a treble whisky in one hand. A ripple of laughter went round the room.

'We thought you were in Palm Beach,' said Brigadier Hughie disapprovingly.

'Cartilage playing up,' murmured Seb. 'Sorry I'm late.'
Then, noticing Perdita on the end of the row, he made
a furiously chuntering Miss Lodsworth and her cronies
budge up so he could slide along and sit next to her.

'How the hell did you get that whisky?' whispered
Perdita.

'Booked a room on Victor and ordered room service,'
whispered Sebbie, giving her a smacking kiss. 'We can try
out the bed if this meeting gets too boring.'

Perdita shook her head. 'We've got to get Ricky reinstated.'

'That's why I came back,' said Seb. 'I've brought you
this.'

It was a feature from the American magazine *Polo* saying
that Luke had recovered from his shoulder injury and was
playing gloriously again. The accompanying photograph
showed Luke in the barn with Leroy bristling at his feet
and an adoring Fantasma resting her pink nose on his
shoulder with her top lip curled upwards.

'Oh, how sweet,' murmured Perdita.

'That's a dream horse when she's not savaging patrons
and biting other ponies in the line out,' said Seb. 'Luke
ought to rename her Fang-tasma.'

'How's Luke's spoilt brat of a brother?' asked Perdita
ultracasually.

'Spoilt,' said Seb. 'Fancy Red, do you?'

'Don't be so fucking stupid,' snarled Perdita, going
absolutely crimson.

'Be the only one who doesn't,' said Seb grinning.
'Victor's frightfully excited,' he added, lowering his voice,
'because his company's just discovered a cure for piles.'

'I know a cure for piles of money – it's called polo,'
said Perdita.

'Can we get started?' said Brigadier Hughie sternly.

Apologies for absence were received and minutes of the
previous meeting passed before they moved on to last year's
accounts, which had been disastrous owing to the weather.
Attendance and bar takings were right down.

'Not surprising,' interrupted Seb, taking a slug of
whisky, 'when it takes the barmaid five minutes to chop
the cucumber for each Pimm's.'

'Matters are not helped,' Brigadier Hughie glared at Seb,
'by far too many players not settling their bar bills.'

They were lucky, he went on, that Basil Baddingham, who ran a most successful wine bar in Cotchester High Street, had joined the committee and agreed to act in an advisory capacity.

'To keep an eye on Fatty,' muttered Seb.

Fatty Harris, feeling curiously naked without a panama or a flat cap from under which to crinkle his bloodshot eyes, was livid that Bas had been brought in, and even more so because the bounder was fingering Posy Jones, which Fatty felt was strictly his prerogative.

'Another more serious problem,' went on the Brigadier sternly, 'is that far too many players have been using Commander Harris's mobile telephone without paying. There were calls recorded to Paris, Florida, Chile, Tokyo, Palm Beach and Sydney. The bill for the two summer quarters came to well over £2,000. In future a lock will be put on the telephone.'

'There have also been complaints,' the Brigadier peered over his bifocals, 'from several local restaurants that certain players, after winning matches, haven't behaved as well as they might. There was the case of the Star of India in Rutminster High Street.'

'That was my brother, Dommie,' said Seb tipping his ash on Sharon's mink which was now hanging over the back of her chair, 'and he had extreme provocation. He mistook the kitchen door for the Gents and found the Chef piling Pedigree Chum into the Chicken Vindaloo pan, so he landed him one.'

The room rocked with laughter.

'That's quite enough, Seb,' snapped David Waterlane, who'd just arrived with snowflakes melting in his hair. 'We don't want post mortems, we want better behaviour.'

'Curried unanimously,' murmured Perdita.

'Where is Drew?' said Sukey, glancing at her watch. 'The roads are awfully icy. I hope he hasn't had a shunt.'

The meeting droned on. The news wasn't all bad, announced Brigadier Hughie. They had Bart Alderton to thank for the magnificent new pavilion, new stands and excellent new changing rooms. Then, seeing Victor turn puce at such preferential treatment of his hated rival: 'And of course we must thank Victor Kaputnik . . . '

'*Sir* Victor, if you please,' reproved Sharon.

'I beg your pardon, *Sir* Victor, for providing us with a splendid first-aid hut and a year's supply of his excellent medical products and for a new marquee for sponsors' lunches. We must also thank him for boarding our third and fourth pitches, and for giving us a new commentary box to replace the one that blew away and is probably someone's garden shed now.'

Moving on to the Social Calendar, Brigadier Hughie praised Miss Lodsworth for her excellent floral arrangements in the tea room and announced dates for several barbecues and cocktail parties. The highlight of the season, however, would be in June, when Lady Kaputnik had very kindly offered her home for a ball, but felt 350 was the limit she could accommodate at one time.

'Three fifty would be stretching it even for Sharon,' said Seb, grinning broadly as he returned with his second glass of whisky.

The meeting switched to the perils of ringworm. Brigadier Hughie remembered ringworm in Singapore. Perdita fought sleep and looked out of the window. The blizzard had come from the west, so the trees in the hotel garden resembled a Head and Shoulders ad with their east sides black and bare and the west sides powdered with snow. Pigeons drifted disconsolately round a blanked-out bird table. Yellow-and-purple crocus tips rose like flood victims out of an ocean of white snow. It was hard to believe she'd be playing chukkas again in a month.

If Seb and I and Perdita can get here, thought Bas, as his fingers moved upwards to caress the softness of Posy Jones' thighs, why can't the others.

He had a lunch date, but he wondered if it was worth booking Posy into a room upstairs for a quickie. He liked the way her bosom rose and fell as she wrote the shorthand outline for wrongworm rather than ringworm.

'Which brings us to the matter of dogs,' said Brigadier Hughie. 'I cannot reiterate too strongly that they should be kept on leads during matches.'

'Here, here,' Miss Lodsworth rose to her feet, 'I for one . . . '

David Waterlane pointedly unfolded the *Sunday Express*. 'What's all this about Rupert Campbell-Black and Declan O'Hara getting drunk together, and your brother firing

Declan from Corinium Television?' he asked Bas in a very audible whisper.

Sharon Kaputnik discreetly unfolded the *News of the World* to read the same story.

It was nearly midday. Brigadier Hughie was rabbiting on about the necessity for a decent walkie-talkie system.

'Drew Benedict must have plenty of experience of walkie-talkies, having recently left the Army. Where are you, Drew?'

'Not here,' said Fatty Harris thankfully. He feared Drew's exacting standards far more than Bas's.

'Yes, I am. Sorry I'm late, Hughie,' said Drew, walking in. 'There was a pile-up on the Cotchester bypass. My experience of walkie-talkies was they never worked.'

Coming back to earth, warm from Daisy's arms, he sat down beside Sukey and took off his jacket.

'It wasn't ponies he was trying out,' whispered Seb, nudging Perdita. 'He's got his jersey on inside out.'

Catching Drew's eye behind Sukey's back, Seb pointed frantically to his own sweater and then at Drew's. Drew looked down and hastily put his jacket on again.

'I warmly recommend Drew Benedict for the committee,' said Brigadier Hughie smiling at Drew. 'I can't think of anyone who shoulders responsibility more willingly and I know his wife, Sukey, will be a tower of strength.'

'Has Drew got someone else?' whispered Perdita, utterly riveted.

'So Rupert says,' whispered back Seb, 'but Drew won't say who she is.'

'Hush,' thundered Miss Lodsworth down the row.

'Any other business?' said Brigadier Hughie, looking at his watch and gathering up his papers.

'I have,' said Miss Lodsworth, rising to her feet again. 'First, I would like to deplore the repeated use of bad language on the field.'

'Hear, hear,' chorused the old trout quintet who flanked her.

Fatty Harris heaved a sigh of relief. Miss Lodsworth would bang on until twelve, when they had to vacate the room anyway, so no one would have time to bring up the matter of Ricky and Dancer. Bart had already lined Fatty's pockets liberally, but there was much more

384

to come if the blackballing survived the AGM. Perdita looked despairingly at Bas, who grinned and squared his shoulders to interrupt Miss Lodsworth's invective. But as the Cathedral clock struck twelve, distraction from bad language and ponies thundering five abreast was provided by a government helicopter landing on the lawn outside, blowing snow off the trees and sending it up in swirling, white fountains, as if the blizzard had started again. Then, out of the door, spilled Dommie Carlisle and Jesus, followed by a brunette and a blonde, who ran shrieking across the lawn in their high heels, and finally the Minister for Sport, Rupert Campbell-Black. Bas heaved a sigh of relief. Posy blushed and pulled down her jersey. The last time she'd seen Rupert she'd been wearing no clothes at all. Miss Lodsworth inflated like a bullfrog. The press woke up and started scribbling.

Leaving the girls by the fire in the bar, the three men came straight into the meeting.

'This is an honour, Minister,' lied Brigadier Hughie. Rupert always spelt trouble. 'I thought you were in Florida.'

'We were eight hours ago,' said Rupert.

'He hasn't been near an AGM in twenty years,' hissed Fatty Harris.

'I didn't know Rupert played polo,' whispered Perdita.

'Only as a hobby between show-jumping,' said Seb, 'but he's bloody good. Christ knows how far he'd have got if he'd taken it up seriously.'

'Come and have a drink, Rupert,' said the Brigadier, getting to his feet. 'We've just finished.'

'No, we haven't,' said Bas amiably. 'Item eleven – any other business.'

'They want to lay the room for a luncheon party,' said Brigadier Hughie fussily. 'No time for that now.'

'Oh yes there is,' said Rupert.

As he reached the top of the aisle the dull winter light fell on his blond hair and the crows' feet round his hard, dissipated, blue eyes. He's divine, thought Perdita wistfully. No one could resist him.

'As a member of this club for many years,' drawled Rupert, 'I want to oppose the blackballing of Ricky France-Lynch and Dancer Maitland.'

'Not a matter for an AGM,' snapped David Waterlane, putting down the *Sunday Express*. 'These things should be discussed in camera.'

'Oh dear!' Brigadier Hughie mopped his forehead with a red spotted handkerchief, 'Oh dear, oh dear.'

The press scribbled more feverishly. Miss Lodsworth, dammed up in mid-flow, turned puce.

'Hardly the time,' said Fatty Harris.

'When better?' Rupert was speaking very distinctly as though he was dictating to some idiot typist. 'I think the press might be interested to know that Ricky France-Lynch, the best player Rutshire has ever had, having survived a horrific car crash and six even more horrific operations, is anxious to return and bring back some glory to this clapped-out club.'

'This is disgraceful. How dare you?' spluttered Brigadier Hughie.

'Dancer Maitland may have been a junkie once,' went on Rupert, 'but has since raised millions for charity this winter, offering his services free to Band Aid. If you want crowds at Rutshire, Ricky and Dancer will pack them in.

'Bart Alderton,' Rupert was speaking even slower now, so even the reporters doing longhand got everything down, 'not only stole Ricky's wife, but now wants to rob him of the chance to return to the club he loves and for which his family has played for generations. Bart has therefore poured fortunes into the club and certain club secretaries' pockets' – Rupert smiled coldly at Fatty Harris – 'on condition that Ricky and Dancer are kept out. Pretty shabby behaviour.'

'Hear, hear,' said Victor. 'Bart's walked off with Ricky's wife. He's the one who ought to be blackballed.'

'Hey, steady on,' said David Waterlane. 'That's going a bit far. If we stuck to that rule we wouldn't have any members left.'

Rupert turned to the players. 'D'you lot want to play for a club as bent as it is lacking in compassion?'

'I resent that, sir,' said Fatty Harris.

'No,' shouted Dommie from the back of the hall. 'If you don't reinstate Ricky – and allow Dancer in – I'm off down the road to Cirencester.'

'So am I,' said Seb, draining his whisky and raising Perdita's hand, 'and so's she.'

'And so am I,' said Bas.

'And I,' said Drew, ignoring Sukey's look of disapproval.

'And me,' brayed Mike Waterlane, ignoring his father's even blacker look of disapproval.

'And I,' said Jesus, who'd been nudged in the ribs by Dommie.

'And I,' said Victor.

'Don't be silly, Victor,' said Sharon, seeing her ball for 350 fast rolling away.

'Anyone else?' said Rupert.

Every player and most of the non-playing members, except Miss Lodsworth and her satellite crones, got to their feet.

'This is most irregular,' spluttered Brigadier Hughie.

'But conclusive,' said Rupert briskly.

'I agree,' said David Waterlane, turning to Fatty Harris, whose pockets were suddenly feeling very unlined. 'You'll have to accept a majority vote, Stanley. I declare the meeting closed, and now you can buy me a glass of beer, Rupert, and tell me what really happened with you and Declan O'Hara.'

'I would,' said Rupert, as the press swarmed round and the waitresses surged in to clear the room, 'but we've got to go straight back to Florida. Dommie and Jesus are playing in the finals.'

Dommie, Jesus and the girls could now be seen running across the white lawn to the helicopter, as the blades blew the rest of the snow off the trees.

'D'you mean you flew all the way from Florida just to vote, Minister?' asked the *Rutshire Echo*.

'Ricky's a very old friend,' said Rupert.

39

Bart Alderton was so incensed at the result of the AGM that he promptly put Rutchester Abbey back on the market and cancelled his trip to England, preferring to spend the summer playing polo on the American circuit. This meant that, although Ricky was reinstated at Rutshire Polo Club, he was deprived of Chessie's return.

'Why d'you all have to interfere in my life?' he shouted at Rupert.

'Of all the ungrateful sods,' complained Rupert furiously to Bas.

All this was extremely bad news for Angel who, banned as an Argentine from playing in England, had hoped for a restful summer, retained by Bart, but spared his company.

After a brilliant season in which he had contributed in no small way to the Alderton Flyers sweeping the board, Angel was tipped to go to four or even five in the November handicap listings. But this was no compensation for living in a horrible little bedsitter with no curtains nor air-conditioning and only a trickle of cold water which stopped altogether when the meter ran out; nor for being bullied by Miguel, who, operating his own mafia, bitterly resented Angel constantly seeking Alejandro's advice, nor being bitched at by Juan, who equally resented Angel being as good-looking as he was and much better bred.

Angel detested Bart and dreamed of cuckolding him with the exquisite and discontented Chessie. His worst cross, however, was Bibi, who had taken on the job as Bart's polo manager with all the fervour of a neophyte. Finding Angel surly and temperamental, she was constantly pulling him up for never getting up in the morning and letting down the Flyers by slopping round in sleeveless T-shirts, designer stubble, and too long hair flapping under his polo helmet.

In return, Angel had not revised his opinion at Christmas that Bibi was a spoilt, uptight, ugly bitch. He was fed up with her recording his botched shots in her little red book, and noisily remonstrating with him between chukkas. Argentine women were beautiful, submissive, admiring and not like this.

Angel had been often tempted to walk out, but swallowed his pride and clung on because he was desperate for a green card which would establish him as a registered alien and enable him to work anywhere in America. Half the foreign grooms and low-goal Argentine players were, like him, in the States illegally and, although they didn't pay tax, they could be arrested, fined and immediately sent home if they were rumbled – which made Angel feel very insecure.

*

The day before the first round of the World Cup, Angel
was taking six ponies round the vast, oval, sandy exercise ring at Palm Beach Polo Club. Persistent drizzle and
lowering dark grey clouds reflected his mood. Refusing
him player status, the infernal Bibi insisted that he do
grooms' work when he should be stick and balling. The
sole compensation was that ahead, above the rump of
a sleek, sorrel pony, bounced the even sleeker rump of
Samantha, Shark Nelligan's blonde and beautiful groom.
Working for Shark for four years had bashed any as-
sertiveness out of Samantha, and she thought Angel was
absolutely wonderful. As Angel squeezed his pony and
dragged the other five into a gallop to catch her up the
April drizzle suddenly became a deluge. A second later
Angel was overtaken by Jesus's Chilean groom who, like
a cat, loathed getting wet and was thundering his six
ponies home as fast as possible. Next minute Angel was
into a horse race.

'Wanker,' he screamed at the Chilean as his own six
ponies fanned out, nearly pulling his arms off. He managed
to stay put until he caught up with Samantha. Then one
of her six horses kicked up a clod of sand into his face,
and he had to let go of three of the lead ropes for fear of
garrotting Samantha from the back. In the stampede that
followed he was bucked off and, letting forth a stream of
expletives, he watched the rest of his ponies disappearing
into the Everglades.

Bibi, who'd just arrived by helicopter totally drained
after filling in for Bart and having to address the Boston
Chamber of Commerce last night, was absolutely furious. A mocking bird perched on the fence laughing at
her and now Angel hobbled into the yard minus six of
the horses who should have been playing in the World
Cup tomorrow.

Nor would she listen to any excuses that Jesus's groom
had triggered off the cavalry charge. It was all Angel's fault
for trying to cut corners, ponying too many horses at once,
who were now no doubt stuffing themselves with scrub,
drinking contaminated swamp water and being threatened
by alligators and rattlesnakes.

A prolonged search rounded up four of the ponies, two

in Victor's garden where they disturbed Lady Kaputnik sunbathing in the nude, one trying to enter the Players Club without membership and the fourth outside the local hypermarket.

'Probably knew they were offering half-price carrots this week for the Easter Bunny,' said Angel.

Bibi's lips tightened. Miguel's best pony, Maria, and Glitz, the black gelding Juan always saved for the vital fifth chukka, were still missing.

'I'll look for them in the Skylark. You'd better come with me,' she ordered Angel, 'and bring some headcollars.'

Angel growled histrionically. He hated woman drivers, particularly in helicopters, and Bibi had only just passed her test.

'Why d'you need a helicopter?' he hissed as he climbed into the passenger seat. 'I thought you flew everywhere on your broomstick.'

Bibi's bloodshot eyes glared at him over her huge horn-rimmed spectacles. 'If you want to go on working for my father don't give me any more lip, OK?'

The control stick had been taken out on the passenger side, but Angel still had pedals and a collective lever in front of him. A groom locked the doors and gave Bibi a thumbs up. Satisfied everything was in order, she started the two engines. With a last look round to see everything was clear, she pulled on the power with the collective lever, and with a shudder the Skylark lifted off the apron scattering orange blossom, putting up the mocking bird and sending the ponies galloping around the paddock.

Making a slow turn through 360 degrees to make sure no other machine was coming in behind her, she called the control tower who asked her her destination.

'Local flying along the coast and around the Everglades and Palm Beach not above a thousand feet,' replied Bibi, trying to appear wildly confident. She'd only done a few hours without an instructor, but she was damned if she'd betray any nerves.

'Too much engine,' said Angel idly.

'Concentrate on the job,' said Bibi curtly. 'There are some binoculars behind you.'

Peering down, Angel saw scummy canals, swamp, olive-green scrub, ribbons of grey road and emerald-green polo pitches. There was the big stand, the aquamarine flash of a swimming-pool, and the white-and-yellow awnings of the Players Club – but no sorrel or black ponies. As they flew towards the ocean, sighting shrimp-pink swimmers and a few small boats on the azure water, the sun beat down on the glass bubble and the weather seemed perfect.

'Nice piece of real estate,' said Angel, squinting down at Donald Trump's house.

'You're looking for forty thousand bucks' worth of horses,' reproved Bibi. 'I'm going to switch on to automatic pilot.'

Angel watched her set the white balls on the auto-pilot indicator and, when she was satisfied they were stable, click on the switch. Hesitantly she took her hands off the controls, but the Skylark held its course and height. Bibi snatched the binoculars. She'd show this Latin creep how to search.

There's Victor's barn, thought Angel, leaning over to see if he could see a naked Sharon. The Everglades seemed to stretch out for ever, the canals glinting dully like crocodiles' eyes in the baking sun. In the distance was a line of hills where, as usual, hung a bank of elephant-grey cloud. As they drew nearer, Angel disliked the look of the rain that hung like a dingy lace curtain between the swamps and the clouds. Bibi had not noticed any storm and was still busy scouring the scrub for ponies.

Then suddenly they were into rain. Bibi, who'd never faced a downpour before, hadn't realized that the clear glass of the bubble would immediately lose its transparency like the frosted glass in a bathroom, making visibility impossible. Instinctively she reduced the power and the Skylark immediately slowed, making it even harder to see out without forward speed to clear the glass of rain. Next moment one of the engines had stalled. Seeing Bibi's white knuckles on the controls, Angel realized she was absolutely terrified.

'Christ, the altimeter doesn't seem to be working!'

The rain became denser, a white snake of lightning unzipped the sky.

'What am I going to do?' screamed Bibi.

'I can fly 'elicopters,' Angel said. 'Let me take over.'

'Don't be stupid,' said Bibi hysterically.

Ignoring her, totally in control, Angel reached across and turned off the auto-pilot. He had the pedals and the collective lever on his side, but no control stick. Gently, but firmly, he tried to remove her hands. The Skylark was loosing height fast now and they were encased in lashing rain.

'D'you want to get us both keeled? Let go. Leave it to me.'

Bibi was too frightened to resist. Flying a helicopter from the left-hand seat is not recommended in the flight manual, but somehow Angel managed to turn the machine round so they were flying out of the deluge and into the sunshine. To steady his hand, Angel rested his elbow on Bibi's knee. Now he could feel the heat of her body, her T-shirt drenched with sweat, her heart hammering her ribs and the surprisingly full firmness of her left breast. Instinctively he moved his elbow up until it was resting in her groin.

Glancing down, Bibi saw Angel's grooved, brown arm with its down of dark blond hairs lying along her thigh. Suddenly her legs seemed to have a mind of their own and closed to increase the pressure on his arm. As the Skylark shrugged off the rain and emerged into bright blue sky, she found herself wildly excited by such physical contact which was heightened by terror and a feeling half of resentment, half of slavish gratitude towards this handsome boy, who had so effortlessly taken over and probably saved her life.

She was in no hurry for him to remove his arm as they cruised slowly back to the polo club. But as Bart's barn came into view, Angel handed back the control stick.

'You breeng us down, I think.'

'Shall I?' she asked tentatively.

'Is OK. I am here.'

Overwhelmed with relief that she wasn't going to be shown up in front of the grooms, Bibi asked somewhat ungraciously where he'd learnt to fly.

'In the Argentine Air Force – four years,' said Angel simply. 'Four months in zee Malvinas.'

'Helicopters?' whispered Bibi disbelievingly.

'No, Mirages,' said Angel.

When they got back to the barn, both ponies had been caught and were no worse for their joy ride. Bibi rang

Luke the moment she got home. 'Why didn't you tell me Angel flew Mirages in the Falklands?'

'You didn't ask,' said Luke flatly. 'He and his brother Pedro brought down more Brit planes than any other pilots. Angel crashed behind enemy lines, and was interrogated by the Brits. Pedro was killed. Angel doesn't like to talk about it.'

Bibi told Luke about the storm and Angel saving her life.

'I guess you'll have to be a bit nicer to him in future,' said Luke curtly. 'I gotta go. You might tell Dad what Angel did, then he might be a bit nicer to him too.'

Bibi felt rebuked. Red claimed that Luke hadn't even been sleeping with Perdita, but he'd certainly been in a vile mood since she'd gone back.

Bibi, despite her cranky exterior, had a very big heart. She had never really got on with Grace, who quite blatantly preferred Red. Jealous of Red's dazzling looks and charm, Bibi had nevertheless been conscious that Bart preferred her to Red, of whom Bart was also wildly jealous. But then Bart had fallen for Chessie and for months on end had had no time for Bibi at all, and Bibi had felt as though she'd lost a lover. Being so rich, she couldn't comprehend any man loving her except for her money. Being Bart's daughter, she worked triply hard in the hope people would think she'd got to the top by her own abilities rather than by nepotism.

Perversely, in the same way that an actress lets herself put on weight or is habitually late for auditions so she can blame her fatness or the lateness and not herself for not getting the part, Bibi wore huge spectacles and ugly baggy clothes and scraped back her hair, so she could attribute this to her not having a steady boyfriend. Anything rather than the agony of being hunted for her fortune. What she really wanted was an old-fashioned billionaire and loads of children, but felt that this was as against her feminist principles as it would have been to have a nose job in order to attract men.

Ahead lay one of the busiest weeks of Bibi's life. Frantic at the office, she was also organizing a large charity ball for Cancer Relief in Palm Beach.

After a panic on Friday afternoon, because one couldn't serve non-vintage champagne if one was charging $600 a ticket, Bibi got home to a smirking Chessie and a thunderous Bart. Her Trust Fund Baby boyfriend Skipper, who was supposed to be taking her to the ball, had begged off again saying his stepmother was dying.

'The rat,' said Bibi furiously. 'Skipper loathes his stepmother.'

'Perhaps he's planning to hold a dance on her grave,' said Chessie, who was having a manicure.

'And it's too late to get someone else.' Bibi crashed down a large, white jasmine someone had sent for the tombola.

'Take a shower, honey,' said Bart. 'I'll find you a partner.'

The moment she was out of earshot, he dialled the barn.

'I guess I've gotta thank you for saving Bibi's life,' he said to Angel.

'Is nothing.'

'For a start, I want you to have dinner with us tonight.'

Angel said he had a previous engagement.

'Cancel it.'

'Mrs Miguel ask me to deener.'

'I'll square Mrs Miguel. She'll understand.'

Angel was outraged, particularly as Mrs Miguel had also asked Shark Nelligan's groom, Samantha, and Angel would have had Samantha on a plate as well as the *asada* Mrs Miguel must be already cooking.

Having dressed for dinner frequently at home, Angel was further incensed when Bart ordered him to wear a tuxedo.

'The hire-shop's open on Worth Avenue, and for Chrissake don't get a coloured shirt or a made-up tie, and see you shave properly, and don't be late. Bibi'll expect you around half seven. You're going to the ball, Cinderella.'

Bart summoned Bibi out of the shower. She was wrapped in a pink towel, her soapy hair rising in a unicorn horn above her head. She had a glorious body and wonderful shoulders, reflected Bart. Such a pity she covered them up with all those butch suits and baggy dresses.

'I've found you a guy – Angel. Luke tells me he saved your life.'

'Did he tell you why he saved my life?' said Bibi, suddenly hysterical. 'Because he was ponying five horses and they carted him and we nearly lost the lot. I'd rather have *no* partner than him. Anyway, I'll be too busy organizing things. And he's a hick. He may have flown Mirages, but he's got no savvy. He'll probably roll up in jeans.'

'I sent him to Worth Avenue,' said Bart, 'and I called them to make sure he hires the right gear.'

Bibi was thrown into a turmoil. I hate him, she thought furiously, he's my social and professional inferior. I must not let myself be fazed.

But instead of the black-and-white sack-dress, which made her look like an overweight zebra, she picked from her wardrobe a clinging, coral-pink dress which had a short skirt and was cut low back and front. She'd bought it to wow Ricky in LA, but had never had the guts to wear it. Chessie and Bart had gone off to a drinks party and, in a rare act of charity, Chessie had sent her maid, Esmeralda, who used to be a beautician, to help Bibi dress.

'Oh, Miss Bibi, just let me make you look gorgeous.'

By half past seven Bibi was ready. Her mane of hair flopped dark red and curly round her face and down her back. Replacing her heavy spectacles with contact lenses, she had allowed Esmeralda to draw kohl round her big, brown eyes and apply three layers of black mascara. She'd always been embarrassed by the size of her mouth and painted well inside it as Grace had taught her, but tonight Esmeralda took the lipbrush round the full outline and filled it in with bright coral.

The voluptuousness of Esmeralda rubbing moisturiser and brown make-up into her back and shoulders, with those magic fingers that daily massaged Chessie, had made Bibi realize with a pang how much she craved the caress of another human being.

Her red shoes had spike heels which she would plunge into Angel's feet if he started cheeking her. Then she put on her diamonds, chandeliers at each ear, stones as big as marbles round her neck and left wrist. Inherited from Grace's mother, they lit up her sallow skin, which the coral dress had already warmed.

'You look beautiful, Miss Bibi,' cried Esmeralda in ecstasy. She'd always felt Bibi got a raw deal.

'If only my nose weren't so big.'

'You crazy?' said Esmeralda. 'No one worries about a Borzoi having too big a nose.'

Bibi was so excited she thought she'd faint. I am waiting for a man I really really want, she thought. Then Angel ruined it by arriving an hour late, by which time Bibi had drunk three-quarters of a bottle of champagne to steady her nerves. She needed it. Angel, with his bronze curls slicked back to show off the exquisite bone structure of his forehead, temple and cheek bones, his beautifully planed cheeks and jaw denuded of stubble and his eyes flashing like an angry Siamese cat, completely took her Gold-Spotted breath away. How could such angelic features conceal such a black heart?

With one of those diamonds I could buy half a dozen ponies, thought Angel sourly, as he paused to admire the beautiful pale pink house, the pale turquoise sweep of swimming-pool, the tree house in the multi-branched grasp of the ficus, the blue-decked lawn going into the ocean and the other wonderful houses peeping out of the trees on the opposite bank. Bad luck to live in Fairyland, reflected Angel, when you didn't look like a princess. All the same Bibi looked much better than he expected, and her breasts were amazing; tawny smooth and full in that tight coral dress and he'd never dreamt the rest of her was so slim.

'We're not going in that,' she said in horror, as Angel opened the door of his filthy Mini. 'We go in mine.'

'No, in mine.' Angel took her arm firmly.

Bibi was about to jump away, but the sureness of his touch made her feel very unsteady on her red heels. For a second they glared at each other. Bibi dropped her eyes first and, getting meekly into his car, threw a wicked-looking pair of spurs he'd left on the passenger seat into the back.

'You going to use those on me?' she spat, trying to control the hopeless thumping of her heart.

'Not unless I 'ave to.' Leaning across her to lock the door, Angel deliberately brushed her breast with his arm. 'I only keep them for big matches.'

'And I'm only a low-goal friendly?'

Angel switched on the ignition. 'Nothing friendly about you,' he said.

It was a hot, muggy evening. The ball was held in the garden of a house which reared up ghostly white in the moonlight like the Taj Mahal. Faint stars dotted a gleaming grey sky like children kept up too late. Vast oblong cars dropped off their passengers outside a big blue and white striped marquee. One of the men valet-parking looked at Angel's Mini in disdain and took the keys from him by the tag, as though they were some particularly mangled shrew the cat had brought in. Lurking *paparazzi* went beserk when they saw Bibi with such a handsome stranger.

'Look this way, Miss Alderton. Smile, Miss Alderton. Who's your escort, Miss Alderton? What's he been in, Miss Alderton?'

Angel looked as though he was going to smash all their cameras, so Bibi hustled him into the marquee.

'He's called Angel,' she shouted over her shoulder.

'Can you spell that, Miss Alderton?'

Bibi had worked hard. The marquee looked enchanting. Palms were banked at each end. Round the edge were tables draped in long, pale pink tablecloths, topped with pink roses, pale blue delphiniums and white freesias. A pale pink balloon rose from each da-glo pink number. The floor was covered in green astra-turf, which kept catching the high heels of the women, so their swooping progress towards one another was not unlike that of mechanical dolls. Their faces were doll-like too, thought Angel, beautiful, tremendously overmade-up, and unsmiling because smiles betrayed lines round the eyes. Their jewels glittered in the candlelight, but although they made a lot of noise as they chattered away, like the Everglades outside, there was no real communication between them. And their eyes swivelled continually and rapaciously to see if anyone over their partners' shoulder was richer, more famous or more interesting.

Bibi, used to attending parties like this with Trust Fund Babies who were perfectly at ease and tended to know everyone, was worried Angel would be gauche and out of place. But although she was kept frantically busy, organizing the tombola, finding people's seats, seeing the waitresses kept the Moët circulating, and working the room herself because half the people in the room hadn't yet bought Alderton airplanes, every time she glanced across at Angel he had been collared by another predatory lady and was looking quite at ease.

Fighting her way to his side, she introduced him to a Master of Foxhounds from Virginia in a red coat, who announced that the hunting season went from September to December.

'Pity it's over,' said his mettlesome wife, gazing hungrily at Angel. 'We must have a dance later. Argentines have such a wonderful sense of rhythm. I've got a big, big, day tomorrow,' she went on. 'I'm organizing Adopt a Handicapped Animal Day.'

'Does that include Lame Ducks?' drawled Chessie, ravishing in black lace, who had popped up on Angel's other side.

'You OK?' Bibi asked Angel.

'Don't be unflattering,' said Chessie. 'I'll look after him. Your father wants you to go and chat up George Ricardo, Bibi. He's not struck by Alderton Lightnings enough yet. She looks quite good tonight,' she admitted, as Bibi sulkily retreated into the centre of the room.

Angel shrugged. 'OK eef you cut off her head.'

Chessie laughed. 'Not very kind.'

'I 'ate leetle Hitlers,' said Angel moodily.

'It's in the blood,' sighed Chessie. 'Bart is the biggest bully, and Grace is appallingly bossy, never stops trying to improve people. It's rubbed off on Bibi. She always goes out with such wimps, they never answer back. Oh God, Bart's glowering at me. He's wildly jealous of you. Hasn't forgiven me for chatting you up on Christmas Day.'

Angel flushed slightly. 'It was best part of dinner.'

Looking across, Bibi went cold. Not content with enslaving Ricky and her father, Chessie was out to catch Angel as well. By a hasty shifting of place cards, Bibi made sure she and Angel were nowhere near her and Bart.

Unfortunately, when they sat down she discovered that on Angel's right was a beautiful, very tarty woman, with tanned shoulders rising out of a turquoise taffeta, strapless dress, turquoise toe and finger nails, and turquoise pearls to match.

'My husband's thinking of sponsoring a polo team,' she said, squeezing Angel's arm. 'How would you like to come and play for us?'

'He plays for my father,' snapped Bibi. Champagne and longing had made her more aggressive.

Angel had been drinking Perrier. Starving, he wolfed his own egg mayonnaise and ring of caviar, and then Bibi's.

Continuing to drink, Bibi tried to pump him about Miguel and Juan.

'I don't want to talk about them,' said Angel. 'Eef I tell you, you will run to your father, and why you interrupt when ozzer people,' he nodded at the tarty woman in turquoise, 'want me to play for them?'

'She says that to all good-looking players. She hasn't got a husband.'

'What prospect do I 'ave wiz you? Your father say to me, eef you stick at one, you go on playing wiz me, eef you go up, you're fired. If I play well, I lose my job; eef I don't, I get fired anyway.' He gazed moodily at a quivering pink balloon, 'Full of 'ot air, like everyone in Palm Beach.'

Angel had such a big mouth, thought Bibi, that when he yawned he looked really bored.

Stuffed breast of chicken followed and every time she tried to engage him in conversation, a new vegetable was plonked between them. Once again Angel wolfed everything on his plate, and Bibi ate nothing.

'Are you sleeming? You don't need to.' Angel looked her up and down. 'You look good tonight. Why don't you look like that all the time?'

'I could hardly wear this dress to the office.'

'You'd get better results,' said Angel, forking up her chicken.

'I want to be taken seriously as a woman.'

'No-one know you're a woman in those 'orrible suits. Why you deliberately make youself look awful with those beeg glasses and your hair scraped back? I nevair knew you had a body before this evening. Why you 'ide it?'

'I don't know,' mumbled Bibi.

'Because you're frightened of sex. You don't think anyone will love you except for zee money.'

'And would they?' asked Bibi with a sob.

'Of course, if you stop hurling zee weight around.' Leaning across, Angel pinched the turquoise woman's roll, spread it thickly with butter and tipped salt over it.

'That's *so* bad for you,' reproached Bibi.

'Zere you go again. Stop trying to improve people.'

Across the room Bart was singularly unamused to see his grossly underhandicapped ringer getting on far too well with his daughter. He should never have let them sit by themselves. Detesting small talk, he'd intended spending dinner talking polo with Angel.

'What's a toyboy?' boomed the Queen of England's second cousin who was sitting on Bart's right. 'You Americans, Mr Aldgate, are so good at remembering names.'

Bibi felt as though for twenty-two years she'd been a ship wrecked at the bottom of the ocean which is suddenly aware far above of a sun warming the surface.

'What kind of woman are you looking for?' she asked Angel.

'Like my mother, but with none of her defects.' He took Bibi's wrist, examining each diamond. 'I want a woman who is sexually liberated with a mind of her own,' then, looking straight into Bibi's eyes, 'that I can dominate utterly.'

Bibi felt her entrails go liquid. 'That is obnoxious,' she said furiously. Out of the corner of her eye she could see her father bearing down on them, looking boot-faced. He was going to order her to work the room again. The band were playing.

'Shall we dance?' she asked Angel.

'No,' said Angel. Then, seeing her face fall, 'Let's start wiz the first lesson. I do zee asking. Will you dance wiz me?'

'Oh, yes, please,' breathed Bibi, leaping to her feet.

And her fate was sealed, because Angel was the best dancer she'd ever met. As he instantly became one with every horse he rode, he now became part of the music.

'Wow,' said Chessie enviously, watching Angel's gyrating pelvis and flying feet, and his utterly still face, 'talk about Travoltage.'

Gradually the room cleared. To keep up, Bibi kicked off her red shoes. Her scarlet toenails flashed like swarming ladybirds, her dark red hair flowed like seaweed and her lovely body writhed like a flame. Then the band switched to 'Rock Around the Clock', and each time Angel took her hand and put his other hand on her waist to swing her around, it was as though he was giving her an electric shock. Finally, such was the violence of her turning that he had to catch her as she fell.

'Don't move,' he hissed as she tried to wriggle free. 'That's zee second lesson, don't move until I say.'

Meekly Bibi rested in his arms, luxuriating in the heat of his body and the strength of his arms.

'We go now,' said Angel.

'We can't,' said Bibi aghast. 'They haven't even drawn the raffle yet.'

Returning to their table, Angel took a sheaf of pink tickets from her bag and, tearing them into tiny pieces, dropped them on the floor.

'You win me. I am first prize.'

Bibi's jaw dropped. Her heart was pounding so hard she could hardly whisper. 'Your place or mine?'

'Mine,' said Angel. 'I want you to see my 'ovel, and I don't want your father barging in in zee middle.'

Ignoring a furiously waving Bart, they slid out of the french windows. Picking a gardenia whiter than the moon, Angel put it behind Bibi's ear.

40

Angel lived in a rundown housing estate near the airport. Bibi was appalled by his room which was tiny, airless and impossibly hot, with only a minute chest of drawers, a narrow bed little wider than an ironing board, no carpets and no curtains.

'This is awful. Why didn't you tell me?'

'Would you have listened?'

'Why've you put tin foil on the windows?'

'Zee sun gets up earlier than I like to do.'

Down the landing was a grimy bathroom, with a john, a cracked basin and a creaking inadequate shower.

'Miguel found this room,' said Angel. 'He theenk eet five star for spy of Alejandro.'

'We'll move you tomorrow, right. I'm so sorry. I feel terrible.'

Bibi moved to the chest of drawers, admiring first the photograph of Pedro. 'He's like you, and so handsome.'

'He's dead,' snapped Angel.

'That's a purple heart,' said Bibi in surprise. 'Dad got one in Korea.'

'Eet was sent me by American pilot.' Removing his dinner jacket and black tie, Angel threw them in the corner. 'He won eet in Vietnam. He say it was the most important of his medal, and he wish to present it as a token of respect to the professionalism and unbreakable courage of Argentine pilots.'

'But that's wonderful,' sighed Bibi.

'The Eenglish say we were kamikaze, but a fighter pilot 'as to be in complete control. We were fighting for something that was ours. We knew it was dangerous, but we 'ad to go on.'

Slightly frightened by the fanaticism in his eyes, Bibi picked up the jar of earth. 'What's this?'

'Malvinas earth. I brung it back. One day it will be Argentine earth.'

Tears triggered off by champagne filled Bibi's eyes. 'I'm so sorry.'

'I don't need peety,' snarled Angel. 'I need vengeance.'

A Simenon paperback lay face down by the bed. Bibi blushed as she remembered how she and Red had bitched in French about Angel at Christmas. As he pulled his shirt out of his trousers, she went over and put her arms round his neck. For a second Angel went rigid. 'I thought I was the one calling the shoots.'

'I'm just checking the monitors,' whispered Bibi.

Looking down, he could see between her breasts to her scarlet pants and breathed in the remains of Giorgio and the acid reek of hot, hopelessly excited woman. Her nose might be like Concorde, but her eyes were dark, long, loving and glazed with desire. She was Bart's daughter, rich as an Arab sheik and the key to worldly goods.

Angel laid a warm, steady hand on the back of her neck, then stretched his long fingers round to the front to gently stroke her cheek. Bibi gave a moan as he spat on the thumb of his other hand and smoothed away the mascara that had streaked under her eyes. Her mouth, huge, red and smudged, was trembling as Angel ran a lazy tongue along her upper lip then back along the lower one, then, slowly, as his hand slid down her neck to caress her collar bone, he kissed her properly. Simultaneously he turned her sideways, so his left hand could slide into her coral dress to stroke her breasts. The bra was built in. His right hand reached for the zip, and she was naked except for her red pants and her diamonds.

God, thought Angel, what a glorious undreamt-of body. He could have rewritten the Song of Solomon just for her. Comparisons with pomegranates, twin roes and sheafs of corn were totally inadequate. Her hands were shaking so much a pearl button flew off as she undid his shirt. His jockey shorts were made up of two pieces of blue-and-white Argentine flag.

'You're so beautiful,' muttered Bibi burying her face in the silken softness of his chest, 'I've never met anyone as beautiful as you.'

'Flattery will get you a preek as hard as a truncheon,' said Angel with a slight smirk.

Dropping to her knees, Bibi very gently put her lips round it, her tongue flickering like a captured moth. Just managing to control himself, Angel drew her to her feet and laid her back on the narrow bed. Running his tongue up the smooth hillock of her breast, he fastened on her nipple and slid two fingers between her legs. Christ, he could restore polo sticks in the slippery linseed oiliness. Rubbing expertly until she was moaning with ecstasy, anxious not to lose the momentum, only when he was sure she was on the brink did he open her mouth with his tongue and drive his cock deep inside her. As his hips had undulated on the dance floor, so they writhed on top of her now, his pelvic bone driving her towards pleasure.

'Omigod, I'm coming,' gasped Bibi, bucking as joyously as a pony.

Angel gave a groan that turned into a sob and came too.

'You are old phoney,' he whispered in her ear a minute later. 'All that macho talk and you are soft as marsh-mallow inside.'

And, despite the repeated roar of landing and departing aircraft which shook the little room as a terrier shakes a rat, he immediately fell asleep.

Bibi lay on her side reliving every moment of the last half-hour, which would spoil her for the fumblings of Trust Fund Babies for ever. As she waited for stubble to darken his cheek, and admired the long lashes sweeping the scattering of freckles like the inside of a tiger lily on his cheekbones, she also counted his ribs, and, remembering how he wolfed his food at dinner, wondered how many meals he'd been skipping. Perhaps he was sending money home to his peasant mother. Bibi imagined her, black-eyed in her black dress, a black scarf over her greying hair, with a certain dignity in her prune-wrinkled face despite her desperate poverty in the slums of Buenos Aires.

She would rescue Angel. She would give him a massive pay rise Bart would never know about. Then she would buy him the best ponies in the world and he would lovingly consult her on every move. Light was creeping along the edges of the tinfoil. Every lining has a window of silver, thought Bibi, gazing down at this glorious animal lying beside her so much in need of her protection.

'This is adopt-an-underhandicapped-animal day,' she said out loud, and had to stuff her face into the pillow to stop herself laughing.

Bart was outraged when Bibi drifted into the office at eleven in the morning, still in her coral dress, absol-utely bowlegged from screwing, with stars in her eyes far brighter than the diamonds still in her ears. Having languorously closed a deal with a Japanese for twenty-five Skylarks, she went home to bed.

'You ordered Angel to take good care of me,' was her only explanation, 'and, oh boy, he obeyed you almost to the french letter.'

She woke early in the evening adrift with love and, having showered and washed her hair, drove down to Worth Avenue where she bought a wildly expensive, skin-tight, rust-red cotton sweater and tight, off-white jeans.

Putting them on, she dropped her $2,000 pin-striped suit in the waste basket and set off for the barn.

As she drove up the colonnade of Iceberg roses, the ground was littered with white petals. Bart liked them swept up on the hour and Bibi was about to give the grooms a rocket, then thought what the hell – it was roses, roses all the way.

Rounding the corner, she found ponies running all round the orange grove and stick-and-ball field and the barn deserted except for two lugubrious-looking men in shiny dark suits.

'How in hell did you get in here?' she snapped, trying to catch the $30,000 Glitz who clattered past her covered in drying suds, tail still wet whisking water everywhere, with his duck-egg-blue lead rope flying.

'We're from Immigration,' said the taller and seedier of the men. 'We've got occasion to believe,' he consulted his notebook, 'one Rafael Solis de Gonzales is working here without a work permit.'

Bibi's heart plummeted. She had a sick feeling her father must have tipped them off.

'Not here,' she said firmly. 'I know all the grooms – only by their given names admittedly, but we don't have a Rafael.'

'Answers to the name of "Angel".'

'No way,' gasped Bibi, hoping she wasn't going scarlet.

Out of the corner of her eye she saw a trainer on the end of a slim brown ankle hanging down from one of the rafters of the nearest box. All the grooms must be hiding up there.

'Everyone's out in the exercise ring with the ponies,' said Bibi, quickly walking away from the stables. 'I'll make enquiries and call you tomorrow.'

'Seems weird having horses of this quality running loose,' queried the taller Immigration Officer.

Fortunately the second, less repulsive, Immigration Officer had a date with his wife's best friend in half an hour.

'Right,' he said shutting his notebook. 'But you better getcha act together by tomorrow.'

'You can come down now,' Bibi shouted up into the rafters as soon as they'd gone. Tentatively, grooms and low-goal foreign players clambered down.

'Where's Angel?' asked Bibi sharply.

'Gone,' said Juan's cousin, rubbing his back where a rafter had dug into him. 'He caught the six o'clock flight out of Miami.'

Bibi clutched on to one of the white pillars.

'What did you say?'

'Herbie from the polo office called at lunchtime, saying Emigration 'ad been tipped off, and were after him, and on their way down.'

'They search his room,' said Miguel's cousin, 'and found one thousand buck cheque from Mr Alderton.'

'Shit,' said Bibi. 'Did he leave a forwarding address?'

''E didn't have time. But Alejandro know where he live.'

'Who tipped off Immigration?'

'Herbie say it was Mr Alderton's secretary.'

Bibi was devastated. Going home, she cried herself into total insomnia and by dawn had decided to fly to Buenos Aires. Angel hadn't been paid for the first fortnight of April. He'd left clothes behind at the barn, and she wanted to apologize for Bart shopping him – but these were excuses. She knew she couldn't live without him.

Miami Airport had been reduced to even worse chaos than usual by polo players who'd been knocked out of the World Cup returning home to Argentina. It was hard to tell if the airport officials were more bemused by the amount of luggage Alejandro and his family had accumulated (which included two vast van loads of prams, toys, furniture, polo sticks, and Worth Avenue clothes which would be flogged for five times their value), or by the bullying of Alejandro's mistress.

'Mr Mendoza and his sons must each have five seats to sleep in,' she was yelling. 'They're international polo players who need their sleep.'

Having acquired Angel's address already from Alejandro, Bibi sauntered into First Class. Wrapped in her own thoughts, she was oblivious of the everflowing champagne, the caviar, the poached salmon, the free scent, the washing kit, the rests for head and feet, the interested glances of businessmen across the gangway.

But when she went to the john she peered round the

iron social curtain which divided First from Economy and for the first time saw the red-faced mothers trying to quieten fractious children and puking babies, the men leaning snoring into the gangways, all packed together like sardines, and breathed in the hot foetid air with a shudder. She thought of Angel sitting there last night and vowed he would never go Economy again.

Back in her seat, deeply apprehensive about the morrow, Bibi concentrated on the guidebook, which was so badly translated that she nodded off until six thirty. That was the longest sleep she'd had in months. Waking she felt more cheerful and able to cope.

Reaching Buenos Aires, she booked into the Plaza Hotel, showered and washed her hair, and put on a new, short and clinging, shocking-pink cotton jersey dress. It was the beginning of autumn and the great dark green trees outside were beginning to turn. As she bowled along in a taxi, the wide roads, heroic statues and bosky parkland reminded her of a lusher Paris. The taxi driver didn't freak out when she told him her destination; perhaps he was used to driving into the slums.

'This can't be right,' she said five minutes later as he drew up outside a row of beautiful mid-nineteenth-century houses with exquisite wrought-iron balconies on the edge of a park.

'Sí,' he pointed to the name and number. 'They are apartments.'

Uncharacteristically overtipping, heart hammering, Bibi went to the door. There beside the bell was the name Solis de Gonzales in copperplate. Perhaps Angel's mother worked as a maid. Bibi rearranged her mental picture to an ancient retainer, still in black and wrinkled like a prune, but with a white apron and depended upon by all the family.

She pressed the bell.

'Sí,' said a voice.

'Is Angel – I mean Rafael there?'

'You are not tax inspector?' said a female voice in fluent, but husky, broken English.

Bibi felt sick. Perhaps Angel lived with a rich mistress. But the woman who answered the door of the private lift, although a charming blonde in a cashmere grey twin-set

407

which matched her eyes, was well into her fifties. The pearls at her neck, and the rings flashing on the hand she extended, were not those of a poor retainer.

'Come in,' she smiled at Bibi. 'Angel go out. He'll be back soon. Would you like some coffee?' She tugged a black embroidered bell pull.

'Please,' said Bibi, who was gaping at the apartment. At a glance she noticed a Sisley, a Pissarro and a Utrillo of a mackerelled sky, as well as marvellous eighteenth-century oils of dogs, horses and hunting scenes. Making up three sides of a square with the fireplace were white sofas with grass-green and violet cushions to match a beautiful black, violet and green carpet which covered most of the polished floor. On a big, polished table in front of a huge mauve vase of michaelmas daisies were silver-framed photographs of beautiful people playing polo or leading in racehorses. There was Angel as a solemn little boy. There were Pedro and Angel together, arms round each other's shoulders. Beyond the park outside, which was criss-crossed with rust-pink paths and dotted with trees smothered in shocking pink blossom, huge flat-roofed buildings rose like liners out of an ocean of dark green.

'It is so beautiful here,' stammered Bibi. 'Are you Angel's mother?'

'No, I am his Aunt Betty. His mother is in Rio, I theenk, or perhaps Paris. She marry an Italian. Where you stay?'

'The Plaza.'

'Angel's grandmother, my mother, live there. You will perhaps have tea together.'

Bibi's mind was reeling. 'Is Angel OK?'

'He arrive very mad,' said Aunt Betty, rolling her big grey eyes. 'He say his boss reported him to Immigration, so he catch next plane. Angel is very impulsive. He regret it, I think. He play polo well?'

'He plays wonderfully,' said Bibi. 'On my father's team. There was some misunderstanding. I've come to beg him to come back.'

This girl is not so plain after all, thought Aunt Betty as the maid came in with coffee, and a plate of croissants and greengage jam. She has good clothes and she love Angel.

Bibi's eyes returned to the paintings. That was definitely a little Watteau in the corner. Her father would go berserk.

Not having eaten for forty-eight hours, and suddenly feeling dizzy, she sat down and took a croissant.

'But I don't understand. Angel's so poor.'

'Angel have very extravagant family. He had to sell family land to pay his father's debts after the Malvinas war. The family has not forgiven him. I would help heem out, but my husband, the brother of Angel's father, is very tight,' she rubbed her thumb and forefinger together like a cicada, 'he go through all my cheques. He would keel me if I gave Angel money but he is away in Europe, so Angel can stay 'ere till he get back.'

'This is delicious coffee,' said Bibi gazing into its sable depths. 'Angel could be a great polo player – but he is so proud.'

Aunt Betty shrugged. 'We are the eighth-generation Spanish-Irish. Angel have all zee aristocratic insteencts of his father and grandfather, but no money to back it up. It's difficult for him to, how you say, lick the bottom. When he was eighteen, his mother was so worried about him, she sent heem to a psychiatrist. After two sessions, the shreenk say there is nuzzing I can do: Angel have indelible superiority complex.'

Bibi started to laugh, then jumped out of her skin-tight dress as the lift clanged outside the door.

Reaching for her bag, she frantically fluffed her hair and daubed blusher on her blanched cheeks.

'I leave you,' said Aunt Betty.

'Please don't,' said Bibi in panic. 'He may still be mad at me.'

Angel looked pale and desperately tired, and went paler still when he saw Bibi.

'Why you 'ere?'

'To say I'm sorry – to ask you to come back.'

'Nevair. Your father, he betray me.'

'Why don't you both go for a walk in the park? Take the Mercedes, Angel,' said Betty.

Angel gazed moodily at the maniacal traffic which roared and raced round them and said nothing until they passed a vast heroic statue of a field marshal in a Napoleonic hat astride a prancing horse with a woman with flowing hair in a long dress leaning against the plinth.

'That is one of my relations on my mother's side,' said Angel.

'Trust an Argentine to ride while the woman walked. I expect she was searching for his fifty-two,' said Bibi.

'Don't be stupid,' snapped Angel.

Grudgingly he showed her the airport which the anti-pollution lobby were clamouring to close down, and the great Hippodrome at Palermo, where the greatest polo tournament in the world, the Argentine Open, took place, and then down the Avenida del Libertador, full of embassies and softened by huge trees.

'My cousin Sylvestre lives there.'

'How beautiful,' said Bibi, impressed.

'Not beautiful,' growled Angel, 'just beeg. I show you better house.'

Five minutes later he drew up outside some huge iron gates, flanked by a high spiked fence. Inside loomed a truly beautiful house built at the turn of the century and influenced by the *petits hôtels* of France. The gravel path up to the peeling, dark green front door was choked with weeds. Two lichened urns spilled over with pale pink geraniums. A lawn on the right grew three feet tall and was filled with nettles and willow herb. Angel opened the front door with a latch key.

'I lived here as a boy,' said Angel as they wandered from room to vast room. 'In the holidays we went to the country. This was the Chinese room where the tradesman come and my grandmother pay the bills. This was the drawing room where Pedro and I were allowed down for tea with my parents.'

On the walls was a sepia mural of gods and goddesses. The frame of a vast mirror was covered in gold leaf. The glass itself was so coated with dust that Bibi's reflection gazed back at her softened, huge-eyed and strangely beautiful. Workmen had left beer cans on the marble fireplace.

'Who does it belong to now?'

'It has been bought by a foundation,' said Angel bitterly. 'Different designers will decorate each room free to show off their skills, a landscape gardener will redesign the garden to suit the time the 'ouse was built. The public will pay to see over it. The money will go to open a clinic. I wish they give it to me to buy ponies.'

'You must have been so happy here,' said Bibi humbly.

'I didn't appreciate it then. When the sun shone we were always trying to get to the camp to play polo. My grandmother's 'ouse down the road has been turned into a school.'

In the garden, two huge trees were covered in the same shocking pink blossom.

'What's that tree?'

'Jacaranda,' said Angel. 'No, zat's blue. It's called *pala borracho*, that is drunken stick. It means the end of the summer.' Standing behind her, he could feel her legs quivering and see the languorous curve of her waist into her hips. What a backview! If she never turned round he could love her. There was an old mattress in the corner. Angel turned her round to face him. Her breasts were pretty lovable too.

'Why you come here?'

'To see you.'

'Where you stay?'

'The Plaza.'

'Ouf, don't tell my grandmother. She'll try and borrow money off you.'

He examined her face. She wasn't beautiful, and Argentine men want to feel proud of their wives, and he was reluctant to admit how much he'd enjoyed making love to her and how he now longed to throw her down on the dusty mattress in the corner and set her alight again. He knew she was crazy about him and he could manipulate her like a bendy toy. Her vast income could buy him the best horses and if he took American citizenship he could beat the Argentine ban and play in England. Suddenly he had a vision of the languid British officer with the cold Falklands light falling on his even colder face with the butt of jaw and the turned-down, curiously unemotional, blue eyes. He also remembered the voice which grew softer as it became more brutal: 'You do want to play polo again, don't you, Rafael? The sooner they operate on that knee of yours the better. Just give me a few details.'

They hadn't tortured him except to allow him no morphine and to make him stand on his damaged knee hour after hour. Then, after he'd fainted and come round, the

411

British officer had continued talking: 'There's no way Argentina can beat the Brits. No-one will know what you tell us. It'll just end the war quicker and fewer of your mates will get killed. I play polo too. My handicap would probably have gone up to seven if it hadn't been for this bloody war. Polo's an addictive game.'

'Angel, are you OK?' Bibi was suddenly terrified of the expression on his face. 'You're miles away.'

'About 1,800 miles,' said Angel tonelessly.

Bibi took a deep breath. 'D'you think it's possible to fall in love in forty-eight hours?'

'Is possible in forty-eight seconds,' said Angel and pulled her into his arms.

Under the dusty chandelier, her hair was a light bay.

'I want to marry you,' mumbled Bibi into his bomber jacket which said World Cup 1985 on the back. 'If it didn't work out, we could always get divorced, but at least you could stay in the States. We could find a home and a barn of our own, away from my father, and you wouldn't have to work for him any more.'

Angel put up his hand to still her trembling lips.

'I don't want to be keeped.'

'You wouldn't be,' sobbed Bibi. 'It'd be your money too. I've got loads for both of us.'

Angel felt quite choked himself. 'You're so sweet. You won't boss me around? I can wear the trousers?'

'Sure you can.'

Angel looked at her watch. 'We have time.'

'All the time in the world,' whispered Bibi, unhooking her pearl earrings and putting them on the mantelpiece.

'I am playing in the Mundialito this afternoon,' said Angel, hooking them on again. 'There's a horse in Pilar Chico I very much want to try before. If we 'urry we 'ave time.'

Then, seeing the outrage on Bibi's face, 'On zee way we look for a ring, I buy it,' he added hastily. 'I sell my watch this morning, and tonight after zee match, I make love to you so you won't get up for three days.'

Despite such promises, Bibi managed to gird her ransacked loins and meet Angel's grandmother at the Plaza the next day.

'But who is she?' Angel's grandmother kept saying to Betty beforehand.

'She's very rich, Mama. You know Angel hasn't got any money.'

'But who are they?'

'Aeroplanes,' explained Betty.

'Better than cars, not as good as railroads. Not a great beauty, is she?' added Angel's grandmother loudly as Bibi approached. 'She'll never hold him.'

'My dear,' she advised Bibi later, 'you must remember that in Argentina flattering the husband's ego is of supreme importance. You must constantly demonstrate how much you love him.'

'Oh, I do,' sighed Bibi.

'But I 'ave to warn you, Jean-Baptiste, my 'usband, was constantly unfaithful to me, my son Pierre was constantly unfaithful to his wife. That's why she run away with this Italian. Rafael will be unfaithful to you. American women who marry Argentines are always shocked by their promiscuity, but you mustn't take it personally. They just have to demonstrate their virility.'

41

Despite being the long-distance target of Angel's obsessive loathing, Drew Benedict had an excellent season in England. Not only were he and Bas on the Rutshire committee, where they made themselves very unpopular with Fatty Harris by putting the club on a sounder commercial footing, but Drew had also been elected to the handicap committee of the British Polo Association, polo's governing body. This meant players and patrons alike courted him for inside information, the latter even offering him large backhanders to keep the handicaps of their team members down. Drew never accepted cash, but several extremely nice ponies found their way into his yard which Sukey, who handled Drew's tax returns, was amazed he had acquired so cheaply.

One of Drew's first tasks was to handicap Ricky and Dancer. Turning up at the Rutshire at the beginning of the season, Drew noticed with a stab of envy that Ricky was back to his old form; hitting the ball with relentless accuracy, getting the last panting ounce out of his ponies, but still hogging the play, too often roaring at Perdita, Dancer, and even Bas, to leave the ball. On Drew's recommendation, Ricky was rated at seven, two places lower than his handicap before he smashed his elbow. He could always be put up in July. Perdita, riding Spotty and Tero, was so improved that, to Ricky's intense irritation, Drew put her up to two. He was even crosser when Dancer, whom Ricky wanted rated as minus one to keep the team's collective handicap down, was, after a freak forty-yard forehand slap between the goal posts, rated by Drew at nought.

'The bugger barely watched two chukkas,' exploded Ricky in the bar afterwards. 'How can he assess anyone on that?'

'Drew,' said Bas philosophically, removing a sprig of mint from his Pimm's, 'has other fish to fry. He only spent ten minutes at a Rutshire committee meeting the other night before beetling off. Must be establishing alibis. Any idea who she might be?'

'Haven't a clue,' snapped Ricky, who didn't want to hear about other people's extramarital rompings.

With Bas on six, the collective handicap of the team was fifteen, which meant they could play together in medium-goal tournaments. Thus Apocalypse was born. Looking it up, they found that the four horsemen of the Apocalypse, Famine, Justice, Pestilence and Death, had stalked through the land on white, black, red and pale horses so the beautiful jet-black shirts designed by Dancer's marketing department each had a different coloured horse on the front and a number in the same colour on the back. The helmets were also black, giving the entire team a sinister air. Bas was Justice, Perdita Pestilence, the lean, emaciated Dancer appropriately Famine and Ricky the pale rider on the pale horse – the custard-yellow Wayne filled the bill perfectly – was Death. As a team their first problem was that they were all attacking players and Bas, as the second-best player in the team, was reduced to playing back which didn't suit him at all.

The second problem was organizing their schedules. Dancer had endless concert, recording and television commitments. Bas, as well as running the Bar Sinister in

Cotchester High Street and pulling off numerous property deals, was always sloping off to Paris or the South of France or even the Seychelles to appease one of his demanding mistresses.

Even worse, in May, just before the season proper began, Bas joined forces with Rupert, Declan O'Hara and various businessmen and local worthies and set up a consortium called Venturer. Venturer's aim was to oust the local ITV station, Corinium, which was run by Bas's corrupt and machiavellian brother, Anthony, second Baron Baddingham. This meant that Bas had to spend much of the summer in secret meetings or canvassing round the area which drove Ricky mad because Bas kept missing matches or having to switch dates.

'It just takes a lot of spade work,' explained Bas soothingly. 'Impressing the right people that we're the right people to run a television station.'

'I can't see you are at all,' snapped Ricky. 'You can't even organize yourself to play in a polo team.'

'When Venturer get the franchise, Rupert and I are determined to get polo, particularly the Rutshire, regularly on television. It's the ideal television sport – brave and incredibly charismatic men.'

'Speak for yourself.'

'And ravishing women. It just needs promoting. You'll be grateful next year.'

'I am not interested in next year, we've got a Merrill Lynch match tomorrow and we've already changed the date three times to fit in with you. Anyway, what makes you so sure you'll get the franchise?'

'Because my brother is such a shit,' said Bas. 'And Corinium's programmes are so frightful and all the staff are in such a state of anarchy since Declan left, we can't not.'

Despite Bas's frequent absences, Apocalypse had a wonderful first season, with Ricky's handicap going up to eight, Perdita's to three and Dancer's to one in the July ratings. Venturer's publicity, on the other hand, got worse and worse and, as autumn gave way to winter, it looked less and less likely that they would wrest the franchise from Corinium.

For a start the press got wind of the story that Rupert was running after Declan's teenage daughter Taggie, then that he had seduced Cameron Cook, Anthony Baddingham's mistress and Corinium's star producer, into his bed and on to Venturer's side. This was followed by endless leaks about other staff Venturer had poached. It was also rumoured that Bas was having an affair with Declan's wife, Maud, and was also keen on Taggie.

With Rupert and Bas behaving so irresponsibly, Drew didn't see why he should behave any better. Having played one season with the repulsive and demanding Kevin Coley and his dreadful wife, Enid, whom he frequently wished Perdita had drowned in the swimming-pool, Drew was looking for another patron. He found being dependent on Sukey more and more irksome, but if he left her he would be solely dependent on patrons like Kevin. He had also become accustomed to having money, which enabled him to spend a lot of time with Daisy Macleod. His endless committee meetings in fact gave him the perfect alibi. He also established a commendable reputation for uxoriousness. Leaving long before the end of the meeting, never staying for drinks afterwards, he pretended he must rush home to Sukey, then beetled off to bed with Daisy.

As a loving wife, Sukey accompanied him to most matches, so Daisy avoided these except when Perdita was playing. On these occasions Drew would invariably manage to touch Daisy's hand in the pony lines or murmur some endearment as he passed her at treading-in time.

Sometimes when he rode out Daisy would meet him in her car and when autumn came it was extraordinary how frequently the East Cotchester foxes ran in the direction of Snow Cottage. Often they met in London in the Great Western Hotel or at Sukey's house off Kensington Church Street. At first Daisy was appalled that Drew could make love in his and Sukey's ancient four-poster, but as he was fond of pointing out, 'A standing prick has no conscience'. Love, too, made Daisy worry less and less about morality. Her gratitude to Drew was unbounded because he had completely transformed her life. He had given her comfort and endless advice on bringing

416

up her children and animals. Even Ethel didn't take flying troilistic leaps into Daisy's bed at the wrong moment any more.

Drew had also persuaded her to give up her job and trebled her income by finding her commissions. She was now not only painting people's dogs and horses, but also their wives, children and houses, and everyone seemed delighted. He had even asked an utterly unsuspecting Sukey to show Daisy how to do invoices and tax returns and introduced her to several galleries who showed interest in putting on exhibitions. But as she tended to sell whatever she did, it was difficult to get enough paintings together.

Termtime gave Daisy a great deal of freedom. Eddie and Violet were still at boarding school. Perdita spent every day until long after dusk up at Ricky's. Whenever Drew was able to see her, therefore, Daisy downed brushes and instead painted all night and most of the weekend.

The holidays, however, were a nightmare, because Violet and Eddie, having taken against Hamish and Wendy, refused to go to LA any more, insisting on staying at home and hogging the telephone. Drew was used to ringing Daisy three times a day: in the morning when Sukey walked the dogs, from his car telephone and then, just to say he missed her, last thing at night while Sukey was having her bath. All this was pegged when the children came home. And now Christmas was approaching and Daisy was ashamed that she was dreading it more than ever.

Towards the end of November, on the eve of Venturer's crucial interview with the Independent Broadcasting Authority in London, all the papers were seething with speculation as to whether they'd win the franchise. Daisy, however, was only concerned that Drew, after a week playing polo in Dubai with Prince Charles, was flying home a day early, unknown to Sukey, in order to spend a whole night with her. This was a rare treat they had only managed twice since the affair had started.

Daisy had done no painting for twenty-four hours, she was so frantic polishing the house, putting flowers in every alcove, making the most succulent scallop, prawn and lobster pie, and lighting a fire of apple logs in the sitting room.

She'd just got out of her bath and was painting her nipples rose-madder when she heard a car door slam outside. Goodness, Drew was early. Tearing off her bath cap, shaking out her very clean hair, she dived into the clinging bottle-green wool dress she'd bought specially, dragged on the fantastically expensive brown boots Drew had brought her back from Deauville and, squirting Je Reviens behind each ear, charged downstairs. Drew was pounding on the door. He must have left his key behind.

'Darling, how heavenly!'

'Yes, I thought you'd be pleased to see me,' said Violet, standing pink-faced on the doorstep in her navy-blue school uniform. 'We spent the afternoon inspecting some ghastly Roman fortifications at Cotchester. They said we could have the night off yesterday but I thought I'd surprise you. Have you got a tenner for the taxi?'

As Daisy scrabbled up a shoal of coins from her bag, her mind was racing. She daren't ring Drew on his car telephone in case he was giving someone a lift. Besides, if she warned him, he might not come and after a week's absence she couldn't bear it.

'That's nine-fifty,' said Violet.

'There might be a pound in the lining of my dark blue coat,' said Daisy.

As Violet went out to pay the driver Daisy tugged the blue bow off Ethel. She'd just have to brazen it out. Mercifully Violet seemed far more interested in Rupert Campbell-Black's memoirs, which were plastered all over *The Scorpion* and in abridged form in the late editions of every national newspaper. Daisy had been too preoccupied with Drew's visit to turn on the wireless or read a paper all day.

'Absolutely riveting stuff, Mum,' said Violet in excitement. 'Rupert had an affair with this journalist, Beattie Johnson, who was supposed to be writing his memoirs, then he ditched her and she's had her revenge by telling everything about Rupert and his women in *The Scorpion*. The *Daily Express* said it would have brought the Government down if the Tories were still in power.'

There was a hiss as the potatoes boiled over on to the gas flame.

'We were all reading it on the coach,' said Violet, turning down the gas, 'until bloody Miss Lovett-Standing confiscated it. All about kinky foursomes and Rupert's ex-wife being frigid and even implying Rupert might be a bit gay. Tomorrow it's going to be all about under-age schoolgirls, lucky things, and how Rupert got into politics by sleeping with the Foreign Minister's wife, who loves being spanked.'

Violet giggled and blushed, which clashed with her red hair. She was nearly very pretty now.

'Oh, poor Rupert,' said Daisy, for a moment distracted from her panic over Drew. 'I didn't know anything about it.'

'You *are* out of touch,' said Violet fondly. 'You must have been painting all day. Gosh, I'm starving. Something smells delicious. What are we having for supper?'

'Fish pie,' said Daisy faintly. 'I haven't mashed the potatoes yet.'

'I'll mash them.' Violet prodded the potatoes with a fork.

Then, to Daisy's horror, she opened the fridge and discovered passion and kiwi fruit salad, two bottles of champagne and a large plate of smoked salmon.

'Yum,' said Violet, peeling off a slice of salmon, 'who's coming round?'

Suddenly she took in the huge bunch of freesias on the table, the pink candles, the two laid places and the bowl of chocolates.

'Mum, you've got a lover!'

'Of course not.' To hide her blushes Daisy grabbed the salt and added more to the potatoes.

'Drew Benedict's coming round. Sukey's away and he's been so good to Perdita, I invited him to take pot luck.'

'Luck's the word,' said Violet. 'Christ, this smoked salmon's good. Drew's a great friend of Rupert's, isn't he? He'll be able to give us all the lowdown.'

Grabbing pieces of iceberg lettuce with the avidity of a starved rabbit, Violet suddenly noticed a painting of a springer spaniel emerging from the reddening bracken which was propped up against one of the kitchen chairs.

'That's lovely. Bit like Ethel. Who's it for?'

'Drew and Sukey,' mumbled Daisy.

She was doing it for Drew, then, as a way of getting it into the house, he could give it to Sukey. The subterfuges they resorted to were quite awful.

'Drew – er – commissioned it,' lied Daisy. 'It's a surprise present for Sukey. Drew's coming round to fetch it this evening.'

'That's nice,' said Violet. 'I love it when husbands love their wives enough to surprise them like that. You haven't painted in its left ear.'

'So I haven't,' said Daisy, then jumped as Ethel's great bass-baritone bark rang out. She must warn Drew before he let himself in with a latch key.

Skidding down the frozen garden path, the night air hitting her burning face like a cold shower, she crashed into Drew who was getting carrier-bags full of drink and duty-free scent out of the car.

'Hello, darling, lovely welcome. That's a nice dress.'

'Violet's here,' gasped Daisy.

'Christ!' Suddenly, as cold and distant as the stars above, Drew reversed back into his car. Daisy couldn't bear it.

'She knows you're coming,' she gabbled. 'She hasn't turned a hair. I told her you were picking up Flash's picture, and I'd asked you to supper because Sukey was away.'

Drew havered. He'd been looking forward to getting mildly pissed and screwing Daisy all night for the past week. A stilted dinner with a beady schoolgirl, who might easily sneak to Perdita, and limited booze because he had to drive home was no substitute.

'Please stay. I've missed you.'

'OK.' Drew chucked the carrier bags back into the car. 'But we must be careful.'

'Hi,' said Violet, who was emptying the cream intended for the passion fruit salad into the potatoes and reading about Rupert in the *Daily Mail*, which had extensive extra coverage on all his exes. 'Isn't it awful? The *Mail* says Venturer'll never get the franchise now.'

'They won't,' said Drew. 'Rupert was always the wild card in that consortium. The IBA won't like his escapades one bit. I spoke to Bas before I left Dubai this morning.

Rupert's in a frightful stew, tried to resign from Venturer, but Declan and Bas won't let him, saying they've got to stick together, but I reckon he's cooked their goose. Poor Rupert.'

Drew expressed sympathy but didn't feel it. Rupert, arrogant enough to think himself above the law, had always been flagrantly indiscreet because he'd never cared what people thought. Drew believed that discretion was much the better part of valour and the only way of having your cake and eating it.

'Rupert's dead attractive.' Violet added half a pound of unsalted butter to the potatoes. 'And it's not as though he's married now. I think it's disgusting married men playing around, but Rupert's been single for ages.'

She turned to Daisy who hadn't had time to put on any make-up. 'You look exhausted, Mum. I'll put the potato on top of the fish pie. You go and have a drink with Drew.'

Taking the bottle of Moët from Daisy, Drew followed her into the sitting room where Daisy's apple logs had nearly gone out.

'I'm so sorry,' she moaned, noticing that Drew, after a week in temperatures of more than 100°, was shivering like a whippet.

Crouching down in front of the fireplace she pulled four more firelighters out of their packet and, shoving them under the logs, started frantically to puff.

'What a stupid mess, I couldn't get in touch with you. Did you win?'

'Lost one, won two,' said Drew, filling up three glasses and taking one into Violet. Returning, he waited until he could hear the crash of the potato masher on the bottom of the pan, then said, 'Let me help you.'

Kneeling down, he put his hands under Daisy's skirt and encountered bare Daisy. 'Jesus Christ!'

Daisy gave a muffled squawk. 'I didn't have time to put any pants on. Violet arrived as I was getting out of the bath.'

Slowly Drew ran his hand over her generous buttocks, then slid it between them to her still damp bush.

'No! Violet! We mustn't,' gasped Daisy.

'She's only got to page two of the memoirs,' murmured Drew. 'Three to go. Shut up and enjoy it.'

Daisy could feel his breath on the back of her neck, as gently, assuredly, his fingering continued.

'All right, Violet?' gasped Daisy a minute later.

'Fine, thanks.'

Drew propped the drawing-room door shut with his back as, with trembling hands, Daisy unzipped his flies and slid her mouth over the rampant red fireman's helmet. It was over in ten seconds.

'Oh, goodness, your cock'll smell of firelighters,' said Daisy collapsing on to the sofa.

'Come on baby, light my fire,' said Drew, handing her her glass.

'That was crazy,' mumbled Daisy as the apple logs sprung into merry flame.

'But incredibly nice,' said Drew, sitting down close to her. 'Very Rupert sort of behaviour.'

'Is he OK?'

'Not at all. Crucified he's let Venturer down and worried sick about the effect the memoirs are going to have on the children. Worst of all he's now decided he's madly in love with Declan's daughter, Taggie, and there's no way now Declan'll ever let him marry her.' He put a hand on Daisy's thigh. 'When's Violet going?'

'Tomorrow early.'

'I'll pop back mid-morning. Sukey's not back till the afternoon. Christ, that fish pie smells good. I didn't have any lunch.' He kicked open the door slightly. 'You OK, Violet?'

Violet came in hanging her head.

'Oh, Mum, I was so busy reading about Rupert I've eaten all the mashed potato and all the scallops out of the fish pie.'

'Oh, darling,' wailed Daisy. 'Never mind, there's a packet of Smash in the cupboard.'

'There was,' admitted Violet, 'but two moths and a bluebottle flew out so I threw it away.'

Drew fortunately thought it was funny. 'I'll take you both out to dinner.'

I love him, thought Daisy, in passionate gratitude, imagining the scene Hamish would have made. She knew Drew had said he couldn't leave Sukey, but she could still hope.

*

422

Contrary to every expectation Venturer won the franchise.

'And you'll never guess what,' said Drew when he rang to tell Daisy. 'Rupert's getting married to Taggie O'Hara. I'm going to be an usher and I've persuaded her to commission you to paint Rupert's old Olympic horse Rocky as a wedding present. Can you do it in a week?'

'I'll try,' said Daisy. 'You *are* wonderful.'

'I'll smuggle you into the house while Rupert's in London and there are masses of photographs. And I've got you an invite to the wedding. It'll be the thrash of the century. Cotchester Cathedral first, then back to Rupert's. He'll pay for everything because Declan's flat broke, but he's so happy he'd buy Taggie the sun and the moon.'

'D'you like her?'

'Adorable and virtually untouched by human hand. She must be nearly twenty years younger than Rupert, lucky sod.'

Then, realizing what he'd said, 'And you look about twelve, my darling. Anyway I've always been attracted to older women.'

'I love you,' sighed Daisy gratefully. 'Can I really come to the wedding? What ought I to wear?'

'I'll take you into Bath and buy you something. The crumpet will be astonishing so you've got to look stunning.'

As Sukey had been nagging him about over-spending all week, he would take perverse pleasure in blueing her money on Daisy.

42

Not since the Civil War when it had been a Royalist stronghold, which only yielded to the Roundheads after a long and bloody battle, had the sleepy market town of Cotchester witnessed such scenes of mayhem. Police had been bused in from all over the West of England to control the crowds who, despite driving snow and bitter East winds, had turned up to catch a glimpse of Rupert and his bride. The media, who almost outnumbered the crowd, were going berserk because Rupert had banned them from the cathedral and refused, to the rage of his mother and his mother-in-law, even to allow the wedding service to be privately videoed. 'We are not fucking film stars and the only record we need of this marriage is Tag's wedding ring.'

Dusk had fallen and the snow turned to sleet as Daisy arrived. There were such traffic jams in the High Street that she was frightened she might be late. She was also slightly apprehensive about the clothes Drew had bought her which consisted of a black velvet blazer printed with big pale pink roses, black velvet knickerbockers, a white frilled shirt and black buckled shoes. She had added a bright pink cummerbund and tied her hair back with a black satin bow.

But all her nerves disappeared when the first person she saw was Drew holding a vast blue-and-green umbrella over the Tory Leader and her husband as they progressed to loud cheers and the popping of hundreds of flashbulbs through the great doors of the cathedral. Next minute Basil Baddingham, a wonderfully elongated figure with his red-and-yellow umbrella bucking in the wind like a spinnaker sail, dived forward to shield Daisy from the blizzard. 'Darling, you look so sexy, just like Dick Turpin. Bags I be Black Bess.'

Daisy giggled. The flash bulbs popped.

'There's that Koo Stark,' yelled a fat flushed woman, pointing at Daisy.

'Well done getting the franchise,' said Daisy, breathing in the heady scent of Givenchy for Men and Bas's gardenia.

'Marvellous, isn't it. About time my awful brother got his come-uppance. When can I come and see your etchings?' Gazing down, Bas massaged the inside of her rose-patterned arm with his thumb.

'Any time.' Daisy was anxious to spin out the conversation as long as possible so she might grab a word with Drew on his return journey.

'How was Rupert's stag party?'

'Hell.' Bas put down his umbrella as they entered the cathedral. 'Rupert wouldn't drink, wouldn't chat up any of the stunning crumpet we'd provided, just banged on and on that he wasn't good enough for Taggie, with which I entirely agree, and how he wasn't going to see her until this evening and how he was suffering from the most godawful withdrawal symptoms, which is not something that'll happen in their nuptial bed this evening.'

Inside the cathedral to the smell of musk, incense and antiquity were added wafts of a hundred scents and after-shaves and of huge banks of white roses, lilies and freesias. The women's jewellery, much of it paid for in the past by Rupert, and their excited painted faces were lit up by thousands of white flickering candles. And the clothes they wore were also in jewel colours, sapphire, ruby, garnet-pink, emerald and amethyst; satins, silks and taffetas all rustling and gleaming. Daisy thanked God she'd taken so much trouble with her appearance.

'We could fill the bridegroom's side alone with Rupert's step-parents and his exes,' murmured Bas. 'Now, where can we find a space to squeeze you in?'

'For Christ's sake stop gassing, Bas,' snapped Drew. 'Hello, Daisy, you look pretty.'

'Just finding a glamorous, unattached man for her to sit next to,' said Bas maliciously, 'No, let's make it two,' and he swept Daisy off to a pew ten rows in front, which was already noisily inhabited by the Carlisle twins, mahogany-tanned from playing in the Mexican and Argentine Opens, and Janey Lloyd-Foxe, an incredibly glamorous journalist, married to Billy Lloyd-Foxe, Rupert's best man and old show-jumping crony.

'They'll tell you who everyone is,' said Bas, massaging Janey's collarbone, and sliding his hand down the front of her bright blue suit.

'Mrs Macleod, you look stunning,' said Seb, patting the space between him and Dommie. 'How's that sexy, toffee-nosed daughter of yours? Janey's just telling us how furious the Bishop is.'

'The Bishop's got a thumping crush on Taggie,' Janey smiled wickedly at Daisy, 'so he agreed to marry her in Christmas week, which is quite unprecedented, before he realized she was marrying his *bête noire*, or rather bête-Campbell-Black. And Declan told the Bishop it was going to be the tiniest wedding, and now look at this circus.' She waved a gold-braceleted hand at the packed pews who were yelling away like a vast drinks party. 'And someone's lit all the candles which were meant for Midnight Mass. God, look at that.' Janey paused in her lecture as a Brazilian polo player with blackcurrant ripple hair and an amazing brunette on his arm, shimmered past. 'And the Bishop's even more miffed because Rupert's mother – that's her up the front with her fifth husband and roulette chips rattling round in the bottom of her bag – insisted on inviting an outside priest to help. That's him in the red cassock. I'm sure he's got breeches and boots underneath like Richard Chamberlain in *The Thorn Birds*.'

'Here comes the bride's mother,' said Dommie, as Declan O'Hara's wife Maud swept by in a fuschia-pink suit, clashing dazzlingly with her piled-up red hair.

'That suit cost more than the wedding put together,' said Janey scribbling frantically. 'Balmain, I think. She's determined to upstage the bride.'

'And that's Rupert's immediate ex-mistress, Cameron Cook, even more determined to upstage the bride,' said Seb, as a furious-looking girl in a clinging, leopard-skin dress and no hat on her short, sleeked-back hair stalked by.

'Cameron's taken up with Declan's son, Patrick,' explained Janey to Daisy. 'He's the beauty following her. Isn't he amazing looking? But it must be hell for Cameron handing the torch over to Taggie so publicly. My God, there's Victor and Sharon Kaputnik. How the hell did they get invited?'

'Victor paid me £5,000,' said Seb simply, 'half of which I split with Rupert.'

'You never told me. I should get a cut,' protested Dommie as Victor, carrying his telephone, and Sharon all in white like a great swan, filled up almost an entire pew.

'That's Declan's other daughter, Caitlin,' went on Janey, as a pretty teenager with grass-green hair clumped by in a black cloak and Doc Marten boots. 'She refused to be a bridesmaid unless she could wear jeans,' she added, as Caitlin slid into a pew two rows in front, already inhabited by her brother and Cameron Cook, and promptly lit a cigarette.

Daisy was aware of Drew going steadily back and forth bringing in different people, smiling slightly in her direction. He made so much less din and worked twice as efficiently as the other ushers, particularly Bas, who couldn't resist squeezing and joking with every girl he accompanied. I love Drew, thought Daisy, I love his dependability and sense of responsibility.

'Interesting, she's turned up,' said Dommie, offering Daisy a swig of brandy, as the arrival of Rupert's ex-wife Helen caused a ripple of interest. She was wearing a dark grey suit with a white, puritan collar and a tiny grey hat with a veil over her huge, yellow eyes.

'She's stunning,' sighed Daisy.

'Bit earnest,' said Janey. 'Beattie Johnson was dead right describing her as a lead balloon at an orgy. That's their son, Marcus, sweet boy, never got on with Rupert. Taggie might bring them together.'

A colossal cheer went up from outside the cathedral as Dancer came in, glamorously emaciated in a light grey morning coat, his glittering, grey eyes emphasized by kohl, his streaked, tousled mane coaxed forward to hide the Mantan join on the hairline.

'He's going to sing the anthem,' said Dommie.

'And I'm the only member of the press Rupert's allowed in to witness it,' said Janey smugly, 'although that acolyte who's just whisked by in that white laundry bag looks suspiciously like Nigel Dempster. I'll kill Nigel if . . . That's the one I want,' went on Janey lowering her voice and her neckline by a button.

'Who?' asked Daisy.

'*El Orgulloso*,' murmured Janey, pointing at Ricky who'd just sat down beside Dancer. 'Look at that duelling scar and those hard, hard cheekbones beneath those dark, dark eyes, and all that sadness waiting to be comforted. And he still never takes off that black tie in mourning for Will.'

'He is lovely,' agreed Daisy.

'I could cheer him up. In fact I'm going to have a crack at him this evening.' Janey had to raise her voice above another even more deafening burst of cheering, accompanied by pealing bells. 'Oh look, here comes my husband and the bridegroom.'

Having not seen Rupert for eighteen months, when he'd been chatting up pretty mothers and cheering on his daughter Tabitha at the Pony Club Championships, Daisy was shocked by his appearance. He must have lost a stone and a half, and was as white as his carnation.

As he stalked up the aisle, he was followed by Janey's husband, Billy, whose top shirt button was missing and whose morning coat had split on the left seam. Running to keep up with Rupert, smiling and waving at everyone, he paused to kiss Janey.

'Rupert's in the most frightful tiz. I've been trying to force-feed him quadruple brandies, but he won't drink because he's got to fly the helicopter afterwards. See you later,' and he was off to the front pew, simultaneously trying to calm Rupert down and turning round to chatter to Rupert's score of stepparents in the rows behind.

'What a lovely man,' said Daisy.

'Isn't he?' said Janey, who was, however, looking at the bridegroom's cold, unsmiling face. 'Perhaps Rupert's having second thoughts. I never thought Taggie was very pretty.'

'That's because you're not a man,' said Dommie, offering Daisy another swig. 'We're awfully late starting. Oh, do look.' He started to laugh. The next moment Janey, Daisy and Seb had joined in. For on Caitlin O'Hara's heavily laddered black knees sat a little black-and-white mongrel Gertrude, with a pink bow round her neck bristling with disapproval and shutting her eyes to avoid Caitlin's cigarette smoke.

'I do think you ought to take that dog out,' said her mother petulantly. 'It's so selfish of Rupert not to allow the television cameras in.'

Rupert looked at his watch.

'Go and ring and see what's happened,' he snapped at Billy.

'Do use Sir Victor's phone,' said Sharon Kaputnik, graciously waylaying Billy on the way down the aisle and cutting off a furious Victor in mid-call to New York.

'Oh, look,' whispered Janey to Daisy. 'Here comes Sukey Benedict. Silly old fossil always doing up other people's buttons. That's a nice suit, Sukey,' she called out as Bas maliciously showed Sukey into the pew in front.

'Drew chose it,' said Sukey, lowering her voice in deference to her surroundings. 'Hello, twins, hello, Daisy. I absolutely adore the picture of Flash. Drew couldn't resist giving it to me before Christmas. Such a good likeness.'

Drew, on his way back from delivering yet another of Rupert's stepmothers, froze in his tracks when he saw where Sukey was sitting. Bloody Bas stirring it again.

'Hello, darling,' stage-whispered Sukey. 'Just telling Daisy how much we love Flash.'

Drew's eyes flickered. 'It's very good.'

A great party of show-jumpers and their wives, who'd obviously just finished a good lunch, were ushered into a side aisle as a returning Billy sat down beside Rupert whispering that Taggie was on her way.

With stately dignity the Bishop mounted the steps to the pulpit, which was topped with pink-and-white carnations, leaning out for a first glimpse of the bride. He looked thunderous. The heathen had invaded his church.

'I should like everyone to spend the next five minutes before the bride arrives,' he announced heavily over the microphone, 'in silence, praying for the happiness of Rupert and Agatha and examining their own marriages.'

Everyone's jaw dropped in amazement. Then, because none of them wanted to think about their marriages, they all started yakking again, ignoring the Bishop stomping furiously back down the aisle.

'Rather suspect vowel sounds,' said Rupert's mother.

'Who on earth's Agatha?' grumbled Rupert's father. 'Thought Rupert was marrying someone called Taggie.'

'D'you think Rupert's got AIDS?' murmured Sharon Kaputnik nervously. 'He looks so thin. Oh, do stop phoning for a second, Victor.'

'Where the fuck is she?' snarled Rupert. 'I bet Declan's had a shunt. I should never have let her out of my sight.'

His knuckles were white where he gripped the edge of the pew. A muscle flickered non-stop in his cheek.

Just a simple service, thought the Bishop, inflating like a bullfrog as he began the long procession up the church, followed by choirboys and acolytes.

'I'm sure that's Nigel Dempster,' said Janey. 'Nigel . . .' she hissed.

The passing acolyte flicked his censer in her direction, winked and moved on.

I want to marry Drew, thought Daisy, as Handel's *Water Music* petered out and the organ swelled to the soaring yellow roof with 'Here comes the Bride'. Rupert, who was tone deaf, didn't recognize the tune, but the congregation stumbled to their feet.

'It's OK. It's your opening number,' said Billy soothingly.

And slowly up the long, long aisle came Declan O'Hara. His hair was almost all silver now, the worry of the fight for the franchise had dug great trenches on his forehead and on either side of his mouth. His morning coat was crumpled, he was wearing odd socks, tears poured down his cheeks, but Daisy, glancing round, thought his face should have been hewn out of rock on Mount Vernon. Surreptitiously taking a pencil out of her bag, she started to draw him on the back of her service sheet.

Beside him, almost as tall but half the breadth and shivering frantically like a young poplar in a force-ten gale, walked the bride. She wore Rupert's mother's tiara, shaped like the new moon, in her cloudy dark hair, now covered by the slightly yellowing Campbell-Black family veil. Her dress of heavy, ivory silk, only finished two days ago, was already too big for her. The train glittered in the candlelight like a dragonfly's wing and seemed to have a life all its own as it slithered, iridescent, over the faded flagstones.

'Look at that body,' sighed Seb. 'Oh lucky, lucky Rupert.'

The Bishop of Cotchester waited in his gold robes on the red-carpeted steps. Rupert glanced round. For a second he gazed unbelievingly at the trembling white figure, then the tension seemed to drain out of him. Walking straight down the aisle with his arms out, a huge smile suddenly transformed his face, the handsomest man in England once again. Meeting Taggie just level with Daisy's row, he drew her against him, shutting his eyes for a second, stilling her trembling, checking she was real. Then he looked down at her and mouthed, 'I love you.'

'Hello, Daddy,' interrupted the shrill voice of Tabitha Campbell-Black, angelic in light and dark pink striped taffeta with a coronet of pink-and-white freesias over her nose. 'D'you like my dress?'

A rumble of laughter went through the cathedral.

'You look gorgeous,' said Rupert, taking her hand, then, turning back to Taggie and putting his arm round her shoulder: 'Let's get this over with.'

'Oh, how sweet,' mumbled Daisy, wiping her eyes. Glancing round, Drew smiled at her fleetingly.

'Dearly Beloved,' intoned the Bishop, who managed to conduct the entire service without once looking at Rupert. It was disgraceful that such an utter bounder should have captured such a beautiful, innocent child.

'I, Agatha Maud,' stammered Taggie gazing in wonder at Rupert, 'take thee, R-r-rupert Edward Algernon.'

'Forsaking all others,' said the Bishop.

'Forsaking *all* others,' repeated Rupert squeezing Taggie's hand.

'That'll be the day,' said Janey still scribbling.

Everyone jumped out of their skins as Victor's telephone rang.

The Bishop's temper was further taxed when Gertrude, the mongrel, who'd been held up to watch, unable to bear being put asunder from her mistress a moment longer, wriggled out of Caitlin's arms. Again the congregation rocked with laughter as she scampered along the pew, up the aisle, her claws clattering on the flagstones and stationed herself firmly between Rupert and Taggie, who both had to exert the utmost self-control not to laugh as well.

'I would like to take as my text the words: Forsaking all Others,' began the Bishop heavily, and launched into a long rant about AIDS, the perils of infidelity and the low morals of his congregation. Gertrude the mongrel, listening intently, started to pant.

'*Let flesh retire, speak through the earthquake, wind and fire, oh, still small voice of calm,*' bellowed the congregation.

'I wish my flesh would retire,' whispered Janey, fingering the beginning of a spare tyre. 'I find weddings frightfully unsettling, don't you? Particularly when the couple are so madly in love. One starts looking at one's own marriage, or lack of marriage in your case, Daisy, and saying why aren't I as happy as them. Oh look, they're going to sign the register and here comes Dancer to sing the anthem.'

Lucky Rupert, lucky Taggie, thought Dancer as he adjusted the microphone and gazed out over the sea of cynical, mocking faces, waiting for him to make a cockup. As the lovely strains of Gluck's *Orpheus* swept over the cathedral like a river of sunlight, Dancer's eyes were automatically drawn to Ricky's face, as pale and frozen as Rupert's had been a quarter of an hour before. Dancer had given his heart irrevocably to Ricky three years ago in prison, but Ricky would never have any idea.

'*What is life to me without you*,' sang Dancer in his haunting light tenor. He played it absolutely straight – no frenziedly flying blond mane, no jabbing fingers, no juddering pelvis, just a slight smile lifting his sad clown's face. A shiver of amazed joy ran through the congregation. Daisy's cheeks were not the only ones to be soaked with tears.

'I like that crooner,' said Rupert's father loudly. 'Didyer say he'd made a record or he had one?'

'What a pity he didn't take up opera,' whispered Sukey.

'Don't think he'd have made so much money,' said Seb, 'and he certainly wouldn't have been able to support a polo team.'

Nudging Daisy, he pointed to Sukey's fingers which were tangling with Drew's, paddling the centre of his palm and caressing the inside of his powerful wrist.

'Captain Benedict's going to get it tonight,' whispered Seb in Daisy's ear. Then, seeing her look of anguish, squeezed her hand. ' 'Spect all this reminds you of your own marriage. Don't cry. Everyone thinks you're stunning.'

At last the organ broke into the Wedding March and down they came, Taggie and Rupert glued together. Taggie, with her veil back, dark tendrils escaping on to her forehead, eyes huge with love, all her lipstick kissed off in the vestry, kept breaking into laughter at Rupert's outrageous asides.

'You'd think Rupert had won a gold and the World Championships all in one,' said Janey, opening another notebook. 'I must say she is pretty now.'

'He absolutely adores her,' said the Leader of the Opposition, checking her mascara in a powder compact, 'and she's so enchantingly unsmug about getting him.'

Out into the snow went Rupert and his bride and the cheers and the bells rang out as the flashes of a thousand photographers lit up the High Street.

'I mustn't cry,' Daisy told herself, as she followed the twins out.

'Must just go and have a word with the horse physiotherapist,' said Sukey, bolting off down a side aisle.

Then, so quickly Daisy couldn't believe it was happening, a *warm* hand slid into her frozen one and Drew's voice whispered, 'Wow! I want to worship you with my body.'

43

Daisy had always longed to see inside Rupert's house, which she'd admired so often from the Penscombe-Chalford Road, lying serene and golden against its pillow of beech woods, now thickly counterpaned with snow. Inside Dom Perignon flowed faster than the Frogsmore after a rainstorm as a wildly yelling party spread through the ground floor out into a large marquee where a band was playing 'You'd be so easy to love'.

The line-up took less time than usual because Rupert was more interested in talking to Taggie than any of the guests, and Rupert's father, Eddie, was busy chatting up Maud O'Hara and sniping at his first wife, Rupert's mother.

Daisy wandered from room to beautiful pastel room, absolutely knocked out by the pictures – two Gainsboroughs, a Van Eyck, a Manet, several Stubbs, a Rembrandt and a Cotman for starters – and listening to the comments of Rupert's army of exes.

'Hasn't let go of her hand for one moment, has he?'

'Terrified of someone telling stories out of school.'

'Good thing she was too dyslexic to read the memoirs.'

'She'll never hold him.'

'I just cannot believe Rupert's ability to bounce back. Those memoirs must be *the* most damaging publicity anyone's *ever* had, but now he's hitched to this sweet young thing all the press and the shadow cabinet are clamouring for him to stay.'

'He's told the Leader of the Opposition he's not even going to stay on as an MP because it involves too many late nights.'

'Ah well, we'll all have to find someone else. That Dancer's dead sexy, isn't he?'

'Darling, he's gay.'

'I heard he goes both ways, and he *is* Ricky's patron, *and* the way into Ricky, and you know how much we all want that.'

'I think Ricky's more attractive than Rupert.'

'More unobtainable – up until now – you mean.'

Wandering on, Daisy heard desperate weeping. Peering into Rupert's dark green study, she saw Rupert's ex-mistress, Cameron Cook, slumped over the desk.

'I can't help it. I know Rupert wouldn't have made me happy, but I'd rather be miserable with him than happy with anyone else,' she sobbed.

'No, you wouldn't,' said Declan's son, Patrick, gently stroking the back of her neck. 'We both knew today would be a nightmare for you, right. You just hang in with me.' He was so young and handsome and certain.

Lucky Cameron, thought Daisy. She wondered where Drew was. There were so many beautiful women around. She felt a wave of relief that she wasn't married to Hamish any more. He'd have been belting round, kilt aswirl, attempting to get off with all of them.

The Irish contingent were already dancing. In one corner the twins were having a fight, scuffling like bear cubs.

'You bloody well could have given me a cut of that five grand,' Dommie was saying. 'I gave you half the money from that pony of his I sold back to Victor.'

Sitting under a mournful Landseer bloodhound, Daisy found Tabitha Campbell-Black drinking champagne and feeding profiteroles to Rupert's pack of slavering dogs.

'I've had eight profiteroles,' she informed Daisy. 'D'you think Daddy's fertilized Taggie yet?'

'I wouldn't think so,' said Daisy. 'D'you like her?'

'Yes, but Daddy won't let me go on the honeymoon.'

'Shall I draw a picture of you?' asked Daisy.

'Yes, please,' said Tabitha.

Later, having danced with the twins and Bas and several foreign showjumpers, and rocked and rolled for an amazingly sexy, energetic ten minutes with Dancer, Daisy wandered upstairs to repair her face.

Going through a door, she found a bathroom. The wall was covered with photographs of Rupert in his show-jumping days. In one he was riding a splendid chestnut mare and being presented with a cup by a famous middle-aged beauty. Underneath she had scrawled: 'So happy to mount you – Grania.' How would Taggie cope with that every time she had a pee, wondered Daisy. Hamish had never really coped with her past.

Opening the door on the other side, Daisy found herself in a bedroom with old rose walls, pink-and-yellow silk curtains and a great Jacobean four-poster which was so smothered in fur coats that it seemed to have a slumbering animal life of its own. Perched on a yellow *chaise-longue*, in an olive green overcoat, was Sukey Benedict talking to Mrs Hughie.

'Hello, Daisy,' said Sukey. 'Love your outfit. So original, don't you think, Edwina? How are you getting on in Snow Cottage? Not too lonely?' Then, before Daisy had time to answer, 'Drew and I were just saying we must find you a super chap. Drew's brother's home on leave soon. Perhaps you'll come and have kitchen sups when he's staying?

As Daisy sat down at the dressing-room table, Sukey turned back to Mrs Hughie. Having mouthed, 'Bit of a Bohemian,' pointing in Daisy's direction, she continued, 'We're off to St Moritz to play snow polo after Christmas. It's going to be just like a second honeymoon.'

With trembling hands, Daisy got a tube of base foundation out of her bag.

'I won't be able to ski, of course. My gynie said it wasn't wise, as I lost the last one at three months.' Sukey's voice was as insistent as Philippa's burglar alarm. 'It's funny we had no difficulty getting Jamie, but we've been trying and trying for this one. I had my tubes blown and Drew was about to have a sperm test when I found I was pregnant.'

Is that really Drew's mistress looking back at me? thought Daisy numbly as she gazed at her ashen face. Drew had never mentioned the miscarriage and swore he never slept with Sukey.

'Drew's over the moon, because he's always wanted a huge family,' Sukey was off again. 'He's being so caring at the moment. He gave me the most gorgeous recording of *Cosi Fan Tutte* – our favourite opera – as a celebration present. We've been playing it all week. He says at least if I'm listening, I'm not scurrying about.'

That's what I gave Drew for Christmas. It's *our* favourite opera, thought Daisy.

Looking down, she saw she'd spilled base all over her new velvet knickerbockers. Frantically rubbing it away with a Kleenex, she fled downstairs, slap into Drew.

'I've been looking for you everywhere,' he said, putting his hands round her pink cummerbund.

'Sukey's leaving,' said Daisy with a sob. 'She's just told me the good news that you're having another baby, and you've both been trying for ages, and you're going to find me a "super chap" and you gave her *Cosi* for Christmas.'

'It was the tape you gave me,' explained Drew, taking her hands. 'It was the only way I could get it into the house and play it non-stop. Look, I'll come and see you tomorrow. Meet me on the north side of Eldercombe woods at ten thirty.'

Daisy glanced into the study which now contained the bride and bridegroom locked in each other's arms.

'No, it's no good. I can't cope with half measures any more,' she sobbed.

Fighting her way through a hall full of people eating plates of chicken, she passed Janey Lloyd-Foxe telephoning through her copy: 'Rupert said: Open quotes: bugger off; close quotes.'

Daisy opened a side door and went out on to the terrace. It was bitterly cold and snowing steadily. The magnolia on the lawn buckled under its weight of whiteness. The valley stretched out through the blizzard, shadowed electric blue and darkly furred with woods. Daisy gave a gasp as a ghostly figure rose up from a bench. His face was deathly pale, his hair, his eyebrows and the shoulders of his morning coat were covered in snowflakes. Only his hollowed eyes were as black as whirlpools. He was like some doomed figure in a black-and-white Russian film.

'I hate weddings,' wept Daisy.

'So do I,' said Ricky.

'You must be frozen.' Daisy dabbed her eyes with the base-smeared Kleenex. 'What are you doing out here?'

'Trying not to be a spectre at the feast. Thought I'd try out a wedding to see if I was cured. Now I know I'm not. I should be over her. It's three and a half years.'

'Not at times like this,' comforted Daisy. 'Weddings are killers. Christmas is a killer, not being able to drink doesn't help, and seeing people as blissful as Rupert and Taggie is worst of all. You've got all four.'

'Chessie looked like an angel as a bride,' said Ricky. 'Her hair was filled with spring flowers. I thought I'd arrived in heaven. I loved her so much, but I couldn't show it. She found me utterly uncommunicative.'

'I showed it too much,' said Daisy sadly. 'Hamish found me utterly claustrophobic. You can't win really.'

'You don't want me, but you want me to go on wanting you,' sang the bandleader.

'I wish I wasn't so attractive to birds,' sighed Dancer, seeking refuge in the pantry.

'You wouldn't be so rich if you weren't,' said Bas, who was already very drunk.

Dancer had seen Ricky go on to the terrace. It broke his heart to see him so miserable. 'We've got to do somefink positive about Ricky.'

'You've done a helluva lot,' protested Bas. 'You've financed the bugger and put up with his moods. But I tell you he'll never win his beloved Gold Cup or get to ten with the present team.'

'You think I ought to stand down and be a non-playing patron?' said Dancer stoically. 'You gotta level with me.'

'Christ, no. It's me who should,' said Bas. 'I've got far too many business commitments to play high goal, and next year I'm going to be run off my feet with Venturer. We start transmitting at the beginning of the following year, and Rupert and I are planning to revive the Westchester in the States in September.'

Dancer, who'd been arranging his tangled curls in the reflection of the window, swung round.

'But the Westchester's Ricky's Holy Grail,' he said excitedly. 'You're not having me on? You fink you could?'

'Sure,' said Bas, topping up both their glasses. 'There's been such a polo explosion, particularly in America. Rupert's mad about the idea, and he never gets involved with anything that doesn't mean big bucks.'

Dancer shook his head. 'We'll miss you on the team. You give us class.'

'And a lot of headaches. You need a seriously good defensive back.'

'Who d'you suggest? Money no object.'

'Alejandro Mendoza's the best,' said Bas, 'but he'd rip you off and he's not allowed in. Ben Napier's a bastard, and wouldn't even charm you while he ripped you off. Shark Nelligan's an animal.'

'You know anything about Luke Alderton?'

'That's an idea,' admitted Bas. 'You'd like him. He's playing brilliantly at the moment – scored two penalties from beyond the half-way line in the American Open – and he's got this amazing grey – Fantasma. He's rock solid and he'd be brilliant at de-fusing Perdita and Ricky.'

'I'll ring him tomorrow.' Dancer was really happy now. 'And I'm knocked out about the Westchester. Is there anyfing I can do for Venturer?'

'I expect so,' said Bas. 'Hullo, Janey darling.' Slowly he undid the buttons of her bright blue suit and did them up again correctly.

'Where's Ricky? I can't find him anywhere,' said Janey fretfully. 'It's absolutely infuriating. I've just filed copy only to find Rupert's father has suddenly proposed again to Rupert's mother with nine other wives and husbands to be taken into consideration. I wonder if the *Daily Mail* diary page has gone to bed. I could flog it to Nigel.'

'Anyone seen Rupert and Taggie?' Patrick O'Hara put his head round the door. 'We must get them to cut the cake or my father'll be too drunk to make his speech. He's been rehearsing snatches of Yeats all week.'

'So many loved Rupert's moments of glad disgrace,' said Janey drily. 'I hope Declan's not going to quote Yeats at those Philistines. They know far more about snatches.'

'Not the Irish,' said Patrick.

Rupert and Taggie, who'd escaped upstairs, gazed over the white valley.

'It's all yours now,' he murmured, removing her veil and her tiara and ruffling her long, dark hair. 'If I really told you how much I loved you, you'd be still here gathering dust and cobwebs in a hundred years. D'you know, I feel faint.'

'Oh, darling,' interrupted Taggie, all concern. 'I bet you haven't eaten since yesterday.'

'Faint with longing,' went on Rupert. 'I'm fed up with all these people.'

'Shall we go?'

'But we haven't cut the cake,' said Rupert, shocked. 'And I'm supposed to thank your parents.'

'For letting you pay for the entire wedding?'

'Declan wants to make his speech.'

'He'll make it whether we're here or not.'

'We ought to stay,' said Rupert doubtfully. 'It's your big day.'

'Only because I married you. I'd much rather we were alone.'

'What is life to me without you?' said Rupert, dropping a kiss on her forehead. 'Go and change.'

Declan quite understood their leaving early. Maud, who was pathologically jealous of her daughter, chuntered with disapproval, but was secretly relieved. Only a few guests, realizing they were going, fought their way through the snowstorm like arctic explorers to wave them off.

'No, you can't go too,' Caitlin O'Hara told Gertrude who was whining irritably, 'or you'd have to spend six months in quarantine on the way home.'

As Rupert, now in a dark suit, did a last-minute check of the helicopter, Taggie came out of a side door. Wearing a scarlet wool coat over shiny black boots, with her long hair lifting in the wind, she made a brilliant splash of colour.

'Have my bouquet,' she said shyly, throwing it to Daisy. 'Rupert's so thrilled with your painting of Rocky. It's his best present.'

As Rupert was about to help Taggie into the helicopter, Tabitha hurled herself on her new stepmother.

'I want to go on the honeymoon,' she sobbed.

'She could really,' said Taggie, looking up at Rupert, 'You both could,' she added taking Marcus's hand.

'No, they bloody couldn't,' said Rupert.

'Throw some confetti,' said Billy Lloyd-Foxe, giving Tabitha a huge handful to distract her. But as she flung it, most of the pink-and-blue circles were caught up in the whirling blizzard and swept away.

'Where are Taggie and Rupert?' demanded Rupert's mother, from the warmth of the drawing room.

'Gorn,' said Rupert's father, looking out of the window on what used to be his valley.

'Strrordinary behaviour in the middle of one's own wedding. Damn rude I call it,' grumbled Rupert's mother. 'Anyway, as I was saying, my darling old cook dropped dead this morning.'

'Before lunch?' said Rupert's father, shocked. 'How frightfully selfish.'

'So I've no one to cook for me.'

'Come and live with me in the Ritz.'

'I don't think Rudolpho would like it.'

'Who's he?'

'My husband.'

'Thought you were married to someone called Luigi.'

'That was the one before.'

Declan waved as the helicopter soared into the white night, lighting up the swirling snowflakes and the igloos that had formed over yew tree and rose bush.

'*And they are gone, ay ages long ago,*' he said huskily, '*These lovers fled away into the storm.* God bless them both.'

As Daisy handed him her last Kleenex, he turned to her, smiling through his tears. 'And you got the bride's flowers, darling,' he touched her cheek. 'You're so pretty. You deserve a decent husband.'

'Thank you,' said Daisy.

'Even if he is somebody else's,' whispered a voice behind her.

Leaping round, Daisy found Drew with the brown velvet collar of his coat turned up, and his blond eyelashes thick with snow.

'I thought you'd gone.'

'I dropped Sukey and came straight back. I'm sorry about what she said, but it is you that I love.'

44

In March Luke flew through similar snowstorms over white-capped peaks to Denver, Colorado. He had arranged to meet Dancer who was in the middle of a punishing, but wildly successful, forty-five-concert tour across America to coincide with the launch of his new album: *Four Horsemen*. Dancer's noisy entourage had taken over the Warwick Hotel, which was barricaded up like Fort Knox. Four security men, screaming 'He's gonna bed, for Chrissake,' to the hordes of fans stamping their feet in the snow outside, smuggled Luke in.

After two hours on stage, during which he reckoned to run six miles and lose as many pounds to the accompaniment of rockets, squibs, flame throwers, videos and millions of watts of flashing lights, Dancer was slumped on a sofa, eating doughnuts and unenthusiastically sipping herbal tea sweetened with honey to protect his voice.

He had kicked off his shoes and undone the top buttons of the crumpled, white, Regency shirt he'd worn on stage. His streaked mane, now dark with sweat, was drawn into a pony tail. The famous face was tanned and flushed with colour, and with the light behind him it was hard to tell how much of this was stage make-up. The demoniacally glittering eyes were hollowed and bloodshot. He looks more like Mephistopheles than a fallen angel, thought Luke.

'Christ, I could murder a bottle of Bourbon.' Dancer winced slightly as Luke's powerful handshake pressed a plethora of heavy metal rings into his hand. 'Wiv sixty-thousand people screamin' at you, it takes about three hours to come down off the high. Sit down. What can I get you?'

'Bourbon'd be great,' said Luke.

Dancer nodded curtly to a minion with strawberry-pink hair who was eyeing Luke with considerable excitement.

'I just love the album,' said Luke. 'The whole of Palm Beach Polo Club is thrumming to the beat of the "Four Horsemen". Blacksmiths shoe to it, grooms strap to it, every car stereo booms it across the pitches. It's the best tune since "High Noon". Thanks,' Luke grinned lazily up at the minion who went as pink as his hair.

'How many more weeks have you got to do?' he went on, even making an armchair look tiny as he sat down.

'Abart a month and ten cities,' sighed Dancer. 'God, I wish it was over.'

'*I have promises to keep and miles to go before I sleep,*' murmured Luke.

'Nice,' said Dancer, selecting another doughnut. 'About 10,000 miles in my case. What d'you want to eat? The T-bones come off dinosaurs here.'

Luke shook his head.

'Well, perhaps later,' said Dancer. 'I wish we could go to a restaurant, but we'd only get 'assled. Leave the Bourbon out and 'op it, you lot,' he added to the entourage.

'We oughta stay. You're going to talk terms,' insisted the lawyers in their pin-striped suits.

'We oughta stay,' said the minders, eyeing the breadth of Luke's shoulders.

'You oughta get out of that shirt, Dancer. It's sopping,' said his dresser.

'Piss off,' snapped Dancer.

'Trust you to keep all the nice ones to yourself, Dancer. Ouch!' squealed the pink-haired minion as a doughnut hit him on the forehead. 'Bye, bye, Luke. So nice not to be allowed to meet you.'

Reluctantly, grumbling, the entourage dispersed.

Luke picked up a photograph on the side table of a jubilant Apocalypse team winning the Royal Windsor Cup. The print had obviously been chosen because, for once, Ricky was looking relaxed and smiling. Perdita, flushed and sweaty, didn't look her best. But Luke's heart still jumped in pain.

'How is she?' he asked, his face impassive.

'Tricky,' said Dancer. 'Bitching at that lovely mother, rowing with Ricky, screaming at umpires, believing the world owes her £50,000 a year after tax. Little Miss McEnroe, in fact. But rewarding.'

'Situation normal,' said Luke.

'Every bit of affection going on the animals,' went on Dancer, fishing, 'but I reckon she's still a virgin.'

Luke drained half his Bourbon. 'I wouldn't know.'

'She the only reason you're taking the job?' asked Dancer, gouging the jammy centre out of another doughnut and chucking the rest away.

'Yes and no. I guess your album's great, and you could play real good polo if you spent more time, and Ricky's potentially the best player in the world, and I've always wanted to visit Stratford.' Sweating from the central heating, Luke took off his US Open bomber jacket. Underneath he wore the much-patched blue-and-green check shirt Perdita had given him the Christmas before last. It was the nearest he could get to her.

Ugly, but seriously attractive, decided Dancer, as he admired the generous friendly face and the marvellous body. But Luke looked weary beneath the freckles, like some young Civil War general who's been fighting without sleep for too many days in the burning sun, but still has to radiate calmness and confidence to the troops.

'We gotta win the Gold Cup this year,' said Dancer flatly.

'You're the boss,' said Luke, 'but you've all gotta get your act together. You never fielded the same team twice last year and I know it's hard when you're working, but you've gotta make time to practise.'

Dancer smiled. 'I'll make twelve million on this tour. I guess I could take May, June and July off. I can write the odd song in the mornings.'

'You'll be stick and balling every morning.'

Dancer shuddered. 'Fucking hell. The nick cured me of getting up early. Ricky's been abroad buying ponies. D'you need any?'

'I'll bring ma own,' said Luke.

Oh, that straightforwardness and that deep, husky, Florida drawl, thought Dancer. It conjured up images of orange juice, sunshine, blond beaches and all the time in the world to train ponies and make love. Perdita needed her swollen head examined.

'I'm looking forward to meeting your dream machine,' he said.

'Fantasma?' Luke's face softened. 'She's a once-in-a-lifetime mare. I'm two goals better when I ride her, and she's so clever. If I play her in jeans, she'll buck me off, but if I put on boots and whites and a polo shirt, she knows she's going to a match and becomes the soul of responsibility.' He blushed slightly. 'I guess I just adore her.'

Having heard from Ricky how pushed Luke always was for cash, Dancer started picking polish off his nails.

'Now about dosh, I was finking . . . ' After all, he had sent the lawyers and the accountants packing and it was his money ' . . . about $100,000, plus all expenses, airfare for you and the 'orses, and of course a car, and you'll stay with Ricky.'

'That sounds just about OK,' said Luke, trying to be cool. Then he laughed a slow, rumbling, infectious laugh. 'Jesus, man, it's fantastic, beyond my wildest dreams, and they're pretty wild sometimes. You sure?'

'Course,' said Dancer. 'Fuck the lawyers! And it's a grand every time we win.'

For a second Luke frowned. 'My father does that. Makes players super-aggressive.'

'Your father wins a lot of matches,' pointed out Dancer, 'and he's coming to England this year. What's he going to say about you playing for the enemy?'

'That's my problem,' said Luke.

45

The weeks until Luke left for England were the longest of his life. He made a day chart and through sleepless nights read a lot of poetry, and for the first time stick and balled in jeans in the hope of getting a decent tan, but merely ended up with more freckles. He had, however, played more magnificent polo, managing with Angel's and Fantasma's help to power Hal Peters' Cheetahs to the Finals of the Rolex and the World Cup. Here he was only beaten by the O'Briens and his father, who was predictably foaming at the goal-mouth that Luke was off to play for Ricky. Hal Peters, who had very reluctantly released Luke for the summer, said he would be praying daily that Luke would not succumb to Dancer's wicked ways.

Sitting on Concorde, being plied with champagne and caviar which he was too excited to eat, Luke wasn't sure he hadn't already succumbed. His only sadness was that Leroy wasn't sitting beside him in a collar and tie. The hulking black dog had seemed to shrink to pug-size as he crept into Luke's suitcase, burrowing frantically under the new sweaters bought for an English summer, gazing up at Luke with despairing eyes. Luckier were Fantasma and the rest of Luke's ponies, who, having completed quarantine, would be over with the grooms in a fortnight.

Normally Luke would have insisted on travelling with them, but fortunately Fantasma had at last suspended hostilities with Lizzie, Luke's comely head groom, and grudgingly allowed her to look after her when Luke wasn't around. His longing to see Perdita again and Dancer's increasingly frantic pleas to come and sort out Apocalypse had also sent him on ahead.

Luke was so nervous and excited at the thought of Perdita coming to meet him that he had drenched one shirt with sweat. He took another from his overnight bag. Yellow and white striped, it came from Worth Avenue and had been given him with a honey-coloured silk tie 'to match his eyes' by Lizzie and the other grooms for his birthday, the previous day.

It had never occurred to Luke to match something to his eyes. He considered his mug too ugly to be enhanced by anything he wore. At least the Concorde Johns were big. Usually he could hardly get his shoulders through those buckling doors. It was a beautiful shirt, but his hands were shaking so much he couldn't do up the cufflinks, so he rolled up the sleeves and left off the honey-coloured tie.

It seemed strange to leave New York in blazing lunch-time sunshine and arrive three hours later in the middle of the English night – like plunging into Hades. He antici-pated a long wait at customs. Seeing polo sticks, officials invariably imagined drugs or illegal currency and tended to disembowel everything. But under Dancer's aegis he was whizzed straight out into the airport, his knees hardly able to carry him, his crashing heart bruising his ribs, walking past the eager faces, searching everywhere for Perdita. But she wasn't there. It was as though Miguel O'Brien had clouted a penalty two slap into his belly. Twenty minutes later the crowd had dispersed. Fighting despair, exhaustion and post-champagne depression, Luke mindlessly gazed at *The New York Times* crossword. If he nipped off to call Ricky's, he'd be bound to miss her. Give it five more minutes.

Then he caught his breath, for, pummelling her way through the crowd forming to meet the next plane, scowling with fury like a winning yachtsman pegged by a sudden squall, came Perdita. There was a smudge on her cheek, her hair was escaping from its plait, she still wore breeches, boots and a ripped polo shirt, but, as choirs instinctively turn eastwards in the Creed, everyone swivelled round to gaze at her.

'Bloody, bloody traffic,' she screamed. 'I've been in a traffic jam on the M4 for over an hour, and when I parked the car outside some dickhead in a peaked cap rushes up and tells me I can't, so I left it. I expect it's been towed away by now with Wayne's bridle just back from the menders in it. Christ, I hate this country.'

'Hush, sweetheart. I've come 3,000 miles and I'd like to say hello.' Luke held out his arms and she went into them. For a second she was rigid with rage, then she relaxed against him. Her hair smelt of sweat, the stables and cigarette smoke, but her clear, white forehead glowed like the moon. Then she looked up and grinned.

'I am really pleased to see you. I need you so badly.'

'You do?' asked Luke, madly encouraged.

'To sort out my game,' said Perdita. 'I'm playing like shit, and that asshole Ricky won't let me near the ball.'

Not knowing whether to laugh or cry, Luke laughed.

'You haven't changed.'

'I didn't have time. I came straight from the yard. D'you know, the Kaputnik Tigers thrashed us 8–0 yesterday, and Victor didn't do a bloody thing all the match. Oh yes he did, he fell off.'

Luke went to bed deeply depressed. Ricky had welcomed him guardedly and without any friendliness, making it clear he was the boss of Apocalypse and would only seek Luke's advice if he needed it.

After Florida in the nineties, Robinsgrove seemed bitterly cold. As a polo player, Luke was used to lousy accommodation, but there was something particularly chilling about Ricky's spare room, with the heavy, dark furniture, bare floors, apple-green walls and a royal-blue Best Playing Pony blanket instead of a counterpane. There were no flowers, and a pile of yellowing 1981 *Tatlers* and *Harpers and Queens* indicated that no one had used the room since Chessie left.

Woken next morning by the cuckoo, however, he looked down Eldercombe Valley and freaked. Below him lawns, dotted with daisies, flowed into an orchard foaming with coral-pink apple blossom, then into paddocks full of buttercups and sleek, grazing ponies, then falling into the jade-green ride which fell three-quarters of a mile down between wooded cliff walls to the little cottage where Perdita lived. The sweet scent of the montana clambering round his window and the primulas and dark red wallflowers below were fighting a losing battle with the rampant reek of the wild garlic which was sweeping the woods in an emerald-green tidal wave.

And whoever wakes in England,
Sees some morning unaware, thought Luke.

Wandering downstairs in search of breakfast, he paused to examine the photographs in the hall. Christ, that was a Westchester team beside the grandfather clock. He found Ricky drinking black coffee, feeding pieces of sausage to Little Chef and making lists matching ponies to players for the medium-goal match at the Rutshire Polo Club that afternoon.

'This house is incredible,' said Luke. 'And the view from my room is to die for, and who are all those guys in the photographs in the hall?'

'Oh, various relations,' said Ricky, uninterested.

Luke admired the drawings of ponies crowding the kitchen walls. 'Those are neat. Who did them?'

'Perdita's mother. Not bad, is she? She's just painted Rupert Campbell-Black's wife, Taggie. Even Rupert liked it after the hundredth sitting.'

'Paint must never hope to reproduce that faint half-flush that dies along her throat,' murmured Luke. 'What's she like – Perdita's mother?'

Ricky looked up from his lists and frowned. 'Sweet, like a hot bath after hunting. I wonder if Wayne's fit enough to play two chukkas.'

To Ricky's and Perdita's irritated envy, Dancer had provided Luke with a brand-new, dark green Mercedes, stuffed full of classical tapes. As *Don Giovanni* serenaded nesting birds on the way to the match, Luke was so knocked out by the beauty of the Rutshire countryside that he kept forgetting to drive on the left side of the road. Like sleeping, yellow, Labrador puppies, the ancient Cotswold

447

villages seemed to sprawl across the wooded valleys. The fierce sapphire of the bluebells had been faded by a hot April to pale periwinkle-blue, but the verges frothed with cow parsley, the fields were full of cowslips, silver cuckoo flower and leaping lambs, and many of the trees were putting out acid-green leaves against a threatening navy-blue sky.

To the right Perdita pointed out David Waterlane's splendid Queen Anne house, peeping over its dark fan of yew hedge, and the sweep of land Rupert and Bas had snapped up on which to build polo yards.

Then, driving through large, lichened gates up a long drive of beech trees, passing little gazebos and towers on the edge of grassy rides or adding lustre to a view, they finally reached the clubhouse and the fields with their ring of splendid trees and the magnificent stands donated by Bart.

The presence of both the Prince of Wales and Dancer Maitland in the same match had attracted a much larger crowd than usual for a Thursday afternoon. Perdita, who had changed into her black shirt with the red horse on the front, and who was more nervous than she cared to admit of playing in front of Luke again, shot off to the pony lines. She was enraged to go slap into Daisy.

'What are you doing here?'

'Cheering you on,' said Daisy, not altogether truthfully. Drew was playing for opposing Rutminster Hall with David Waterlane, the Prince and an underhandicapped Chilean called José.

'Is Luke playing?' asked Daisy.

'How many times do I have to tell you fifteen's the limit for medium goal? Luke and Ricky add up to sixteen between them. We're playing with Dancer and Mike Waterlane, who'll be useless because his father's playing for the other side.'

'Is Luke here?'

'Over there, listening to some stupid Mozart tape,' and she raced off to find Ricky yelling at Louisa, who'd replaced Frances as head groom and who'd put in the wrong bridle for Tero.

Fischer-Dieskau finished the aria. Coming down to earth, wishing he was as successful with women as Don

Giovanni, Luke discovered an adorable brunette tapping on his window. Unable to find the button to lower it, he opened the door and the next moment was being licked all over by a large, scruffy English setter.

'I'm desperately sorry,' gasped the brunette, ineffectually trying to tug the dog off.

'It's OK. I like dogs, particularly when they come on the end of such pretty ladies.'

The brunette blushed. 'I'm sorry to bother you, but I'm Daisy Macleod. I wanted to thank you for being so kind to Perdita.'

Luke's jaw dropped. From Perdita's chronically unflattering descriptions he'd expected some bushy-haired middle-aged weirdo with vinaigrette stains all over her caftan. Christ, she's not much older than me, he thought.

'It was so wonderful of you to give her Tero last Christmas,' went on Daisy. 'She's so adorable. She used to be petrified of me, but she wintered in the field near our, or rather Ricky's, cottage. I used to feed the ponies carrots and Tero'd always lurk at the back, never barging like the others. Then I discovered she adored toast and Marmite, and we used to have secret trysts behind hawthorn bushes so I could feed her when the others weren't looking. She's got such a sweet way of coming up and giving you a little nudge in the back. She got so tame, she came into the kitchen while we were having Christmas dinner. She adores Spotty; they lie down side by side. Perdita says ponies never normally do that in case their legs get entangled. I'm sorry,' she flushed again, 'I didn't mean to bore you.'

'Bore me?' said Luke. 'I'm just blown away how young you are. You haven't got a portrait getting all wrinkled in the attic?'

'Only ones painted by me,' giggled Daisy.

'I saw your drawings in Ricky's kitchen. If I save up, will you do Fantasma when she comes over?'

'I'll do her for nothing after all you did for Perdita. She'd never have survived Argentina without you.'

Goodness, he's tall, thought Daisy, as Luke got out of the car. And what a friendly, charming and amiable face – you felt you could tell him anything.

Daisy shivered in the sharp east wind which whistled across the field. She'd been baking when she'd left the shelter of Snow Cottage, particularly as she'd just blow-dried her hair for Drew. Not wanting to waste a chance to get brown she had unearthed an ancient, blue sun-dress with lacing across the front, which was now strained horizontally across her breasts. Duo-tanned legs on their fifth day were turning purple. Taking off his US Open jacket, Luke put it round her shoulders.

'You'll need it, coming from Florida,' stammered Daisy.

Luke grinned. 'I'm tough.'

What a lovely man, thought Daisy.

'Will you come to dinner tonight?' she blurted out.

But before Luke had time to answer, Perdita had thundered up on Spotty.

'What a cock-up! Neither Dancer nor Mike has arrived. The Prince has got to be in London to unveil some plaque by seven and Ricky's having a blazing row with that prat Harris who says we've got to forfeit if the match doesn't start on time.'

'Your mother's just asked me to dinner,' said Luke. 'I don't know what Ricky's plans are. Why don't we eat out?'

'Bloody stupid idea,' snapped Perdita. 'Ricky'll be in no mood to go anywhere if we have to play two against four,' and she stormed off.

Luke grinned at Daisy. 'Let's go find a seat.'

On the way they passed Ricky shouting in the pony lines. Kinta's bandages were too tight. Spotty had the wrong martingale, Tero the wrong bit. Luke hoped Ricky was just psyching himself up.

It was so nice to have someone to sit with, thought Daisy. As they climbed to the top of the stands, Luke was greeted from all sides by players who knew him from Palm Beach.

'Trust you to pick up the best piece of crumpet in Rutshire. I've been trying to become Mrs Macleod's toyboy for years,' yelled Dommie, patting the seats beside him, and offering a bite of his Mars Bar to Daisy. 'Go on, you might burst even more out of that exciting dress. Welcome to Rutshire,' he added, extending a hand to Luke.

'Nice dog,' said Luke as Decorum, the bull terrier, greeted his friend Ethel so delightedly that his tail dislodged the tweed cap of Brigadier Hughie in front.

'Lovely,' agreed Dommie. 'Apocalypse certainly needs you, Luke. We lynched them two days ago. Ricky's absolutely livid you're here. Worried you're going to queer his pitch, or,' Dommie giggled at his own joke, 'pitch for his queer. I see Dancer's given you a new Merc. What'd you have to do for that? Bend over?'

'That's not funny,' rumbled Brigadier Hughie disapprovingly.

'Should think not,' said Dommie. 'More likely bloody painful.'

Totally unfazed, Luke grinned broadly.

'Oh, here come the Prince and Drew,' said Daisy excitedly, as Rutminster Hall rode on in their cherry-red shirts and security men with expressionless faces and walkie-talkies spread out round the field.

Luke admired the upright figure of the Prince of Wales. 'He's a good back,' he told Daisy. 'Always takes his man out. It's incredibly difficult to get past him.'

'Have you ever played against Drew?' Daisy couldn't resist asking.

Luke nodded. 'He's pretty good. Gets all his team working for him. Never has any passengers.'

'Captain Benedict's having an affair with someone,' said Dommie, unwrapping another Mars Bar. 'We tried to tail him the other night, but he really shifts that BMW. I'm surprised Sukey hasn't put a combination lock on his flies.'

Feeling her leap beside him as though the dentist had hit a nerve, Luke decided that Daisy, in addition to being terrified of Perdita, was also in love with the handsome Captain who was now tapping the ball around the field with incredible assurance.

'Here's José the Mexican, Sharon's latest, and here's Seb,' cried Dommie gleefully. 'Green as the field! People are going to tread him in at half-time. Forgot he was umpiring today when he got pissed last night. Ben Napier's the other umpire. He hates Ricky so much, he'll give goal after open goal to Rutminster Hall.'

Aware that he'd got the attention of the entire stand, Dommie opened a can of Coke with a hiss, and asked loudly, 'What we're all riveted to know is what will happen when your fiendish father meets Ricky on the field this summer? Will we have the first polo murder, sticks flying, duel in the sun, Bart coming at Ricky at 100 m.p.h? And isn't Chessie going to love it – two knights jousting for her favours? Well?'

Luke shrugged and grinned back at him. 'You expect me to answer all that?'

'I'll give you time to think,' said Dommie. 'Oh, look here comes the Puffatrain.'

Since she had acquired a title, Sharon had been slowly modelling herself on Sukey. Today they were both wearing blue Puffas, blue Guernseys, striped shirts with turned-up collars, navy-blue skirts and stockings, and Gucci shoes.

'Good afternoon, Dominic,' said Sharon graciously. 'Good afternoon, Luke. When did you arrive?' Not waiting for an answer, she sat down and gathered up her binoculars, 'Now, where's the Prince? Oh, doesn't cerise suit his Hay-ness. Hullo, hullo, your Hay-ness.'

The Prince of Wales turned, nodding rather vaguely towards the stand.

'We've met him several taimes,' Sharon told Luke, 'and of course we 'ad cocktails with his mother when Sir Victor got his knaighthood.'

'Drew's known him for years,' said Sukey slightly acidly.

'Look at the love bites on José's neck. I thought you'd gone vegetarian, Sharon,' chided Dommie.

'Don't be cheeky, Dominic,' said Sharon icily.

Ponies, neighing like mad, were already arriving for the second match. Fatty Harris, on his third whisky, was shouting in the warm-up area.

'The throw-in will be in five minutes, Ricky, or you'll forfeit; you've had half an hour to get ready. You just delay and delay.'

'Oh, fuck off,' snarled Ricky.

Rutminster Hall had dismounted to rest their horses, except for David Waterlane, who rode over to the stands to cadge a cigarette. Seeing Luke, he yelled, 'That black mare you sold me in Palm Beach, why does she drop her head all the time?'

'I guess she's bashful she hasn't been paid for,' drawled Luke.

The stand collapsed with laughter. David Waterlane rode off discomfited.

'He owes Ladbrokes half a million,' said Dommie. 'You may be rather low down the list.'

Ricky was in despair. There was bloody Luke Alderton grinning up in the stands and he couldn't even get a polo side together.

As if in answer to his prayer, Dancer's black helicopter soared over the trees and landed behind the clubhouse. Mercifully Dancer was already changed. Racing towards the pitch, telling the autograph hunters he'd see them after the game and trailing security men, he jumped on to the pony Louisa was holding.

'Terribly sorry, Rick,' he said, quailing at Ricky's stony face. 'I overslept. I was recording till four o'clock this morning.'

'I hope you're going to get a chance to see England, Luke,' said Sharon, pressing her knees against his back. 'Ay'd love to show you round.'

'I hope Perdita's going to take me,' said Luke, 'but thanks all the same.'

'Dancer's security guards are going to have a punch-up with the Prince's in a minute,' said Dommie happily.

'Oh, thank goodness,' said Daisy. 'Here comes Mike Waterlane.'

Driving his Golf GTI to a screeching halt at the side of the pitch, a sweating Mike leapt out and, to the disapproval of Miss Lodsworth and her satellite trouts, continued to bray into his portable telephone as he did a one-handed strip out of his pin-stripe suit down to his Dennis the Menace boxer shorts.

'If you can go to five million, I think I've got just the job,' he went on, as he wriggled into his breeches and his black, Apocalypse shirt, 'but if you want much more land, you might have to go higher.'

As he zipped up his boots, Louisa fastened his knee pads and plonked his hat on his head.

'I'll get back to you later this afternoon,' he added, hoarse with excitement and, handing Louisa the telephone in exchange for his stick and whip, jumped on to his old pony, Dopey, and thundered off on to the field.

'What the fuck d'you think you're playing at?' howled Ricky and David Waterlane in unison.

'Mick Jagger had a house under survey,' mumbled Mike. 'Discovered it's got dry rot; wants us to find him another one.'

'Mike Waterlane is so thick,' announced Dommie, 'that he started cheering for Reading University during the Boat Race last week.'

Luke laughed. Oh, to be in England now that April was there.

46

Luke wasn't laughing half an hour later. Apocalypse was a complete shambles. Ricky, as usual, was over-extending himself and his horses, doing everything including all the shouting, never giving Perdita or Dancer a chance to score, or Mike, whose head was full of dry rot, a chance to defend.

Ricky was a brilliant player, but he couldn't take on Rutminster Hall, all good players who knew what each other were doing, single-handed. And whenever he wasn't blasting his own side, he was shouting at the umpire, Ben Napier, who as Dommie predicted gave penalties at every opportunity to Rutminster Hall. While Drew was taking one of these in the third chukka, Ricky whizzed off to change ponies, only to find Wayne had slipped his bridle and gone trot-about in the direction of the tea-tent.

'Get me a fucking horse,' he screamed, to the edification of the entire crowd.

By the time another pony had been saddled, Rutminster Hall had scored again, bringing the score to 11-4. The Prince's security men sneered discreetly at Dancer's minders.

Drew, by contrast, was playing beautifully. For Daisy the supreme pleasure, after sleeping with him, was watching him on the field. She longed to cheer, her fingers itched to draw him on her score sheet, but Sukey was all too noisily just behind.

'Oh, well done, Drew, well played. Oh look, we're going through. Oh dear, it's gone over. No, it hasn't. Oh, well stopped Drew. I must put my glass down to clap.'

Fatty Harris, who'd slipped in a fourth whisky while waiting for the off, was providing the official commentary:

'The Wince of Prales takes the backhand. Oh, well hit, Your Majeshty.'

At half-time, profoundly depressed, frozen without his jacket, Luke went out to stomp in the divots. Dogs whisking everywhere made him long for Leroy. Daisy had drifted to the right, and Luke noticed that the first player back, on a dapple-grey with black points, was Drew Benedict. Luke watched him ride past her, masking her for a second from the stands and Sukey.

'I'll ring you this evening,' said Drew softly, and rode on. Perdita, next back, charged up to Luke.

'I haven't had the fucking ball all afternoon. I'm really pissed off.'

'Take out the Prince. He was loose most of the first half, then at least Ricky can come through.'

Luke's advice worked. With the Prince pegged, Ricky took the game by the throat and in a flurry of breathtaking goals, had pulled back the score to 10–11 by the end of the fifth chukka. The crowd forgot the icy wind.

'Ner, ner, ner-ner, ner,' Dancer's minders taunted the Prince's boot-faced guards.

It's the last chukka and I've done nothing, thought Perdita furiously. Spotty, a fearful exhibitionist who only caught fire when applauded, was also sulking. Then, miraculously, Mike hit a lovely backhand in Perdita's direction. There was no one between her and the goal posts.

'Leave it,' bellowed Ricky.

Ignoring him, Perdita put her reins in her stick hand and gave Spotty a couple of whacks with her whip. Spotty bridled in outrage, then shot forward. Perdita's first forehand put the ball ten yards in front of goal.

'Man coming,' yelled Ricky.

Heedless, Perdita careered after it. She was going to tie up the score on Luke's first day. Almost nonchalantly, oblivious of the shouting behind her, she lifted her stick, then howled with exasperation as she was hooked.

'You fucking bastard!' she screeched. Then turning round, she gave a gasp of horror: 'Gosh, I'm *terribly* sorry, Sir.'

'Off,' thundered Ben Napier.

'Don't be fucking stupid!' In a second Perdita switched from abject contrition to outrage.

'There's nuffink in the rule book abart swearin' at Royalty,' said Dancer, galloping up.

'Off,' insisted Ben Napier, pointing towards the pony lines.

'You asshole,' shouted Perdita. 'Why don't you get out the fucking rule book and learn to read?'

'Off,' said Ben Napier, triumphantly. 'Abuse of umpire.'

'For Chrissake, help me,' Perdita pleaded to Seb, the second umpire.

But Seb, terrified of opening his mouth in case he was sick, merely shook his head.

In a blind fury Perdita lifted her stick and hit the ball straight into the bonnet of a nearby Bentley. Choking on his cucumber sandwich, the owner leapt out, waving his fist. Miss Lodsworth turned puce and everyone else looked very excited as Perdita galloped off.

'Straight to the Tower of London,' said Dommie.

Luke gave a highly embarrassed Daisy a reassuring smile. Three against four is no contest. Rutminster Hall ran out the winners by 13-10.

Luke found Perdita sobbing into Spotty's shoulder.

'We could have won, we could have bloody won.'

He took her in his arms. 'It's OK, sweetheart.' Over her shuddering shoulder he saw an utterly dejected Dancer riding up.

'You coming back to Robinsgrove?' he asked.

'I played like a pig wiv the trots; fink I'll go home,' said Dancer.

'You did pretty good, except for being late,' said Luke. 'I'll call you tomorrow.'

Back at Robinsgrove, having dropped Perdita off at Snow Cottage, Luke put on two sweaters and went into the yard, where all was activity. Louisa trundled by with a wheelbarrow loaded up with tack to be hung up. Kinta had a cut mouth which one of the younger grooms was rinsing out with salt and water. Another groom was sweeping up the yard and swearing at Little Chef as he chased the stable cat through a pile of straw and shavings, while yet another was being greeted with a thunder of whickering and whinnying as she raced round lobbing wodges of hay into racks. Later most of the ponies would be turned out. Luke felt a wave of longing for Fantasma.

'Is there an axe round here?' he asked Louisa.

'You going to chop off Perdita's head for treason?' Louisa tried to make a joke, but she was depressed about losing and having wolfed two KitKats to cheer herself up on the way home.

'I'm going to light a fire,' said Luke. 'I don't want to die of pneumonia.'

The logs were wet and took a long time to kindle. Like Perdita, thought Luke wryly. He noticed the yellowing cups and the gap still over the fireplace where the Munnings had been. He had just retrieved his duty-free Bourbon from the kitchen and was pouring himself three fingers when Ricky stalked in, glaring disapprovingly at the greeny-blue flames and the acrid smoke that was drifting out into the room.

'Bit late for a fire,' he snapped. 'Daisy's just rung. Says you're welcome to supper any time after eight.'

'You coming too?' asked Luke.

'Christ, no.'

He was about to stalk out again, when Luke said, 'We oughta talk.'

'We?' Ricky raised his eyebrows. 'There's nothing to talk about.'

Luke poured a second large Bourbon and handed it to Ricky.

'I don't drink.'

'You better start,' said Luke gently. 'You gotta loosen up.'

Hearing the crackling from a painted stick, Little Chef trotted in and, seeing the fire, stretched out blissfully. Sitting down, Luke took a slug of his whisky and a deep breath. 'You should've walked it today.'

'With three fucking incompetents?'

'It was your fault,' said Luke steadily. 'Entirely your fault. You've totally demoralized Perdita and Dancer for a start. Perdita's dying of hypothermia and loneliness out there waiting for a pass, and when she gets one she's so uptight she goofs. Dancer's the same. He's worried the whole time, not where to hit the ball, but whether he's going to hit it at all. And Mike Waterlane's out to lunch. He was just cantering about not marking anyone.'

Then, when Ricky opened his mouth in outrage, Luke went on. 'No, I haven't finished. No one knows what they're meant to be doing, there's no game plan. You just fluster them by shouting, right, and at the same time you're telegraphing every punch to the opposition. You're always going to be the most marked man on the team. If you give the others the ball, they can take it away.'

The logs, suddenly deciding to be co-operative, burst into flames. Flickering over Ricky's set, frozen face, they gave it a rare illusion of mobility. Luke got up and threw on another log. 'Forget the Gold Cup,' he said brutally. 'If you're not careful you'll lose every game this season.'

'Have you flown three thousand m-m-miles to give me this crap?' said Ricky softly. 'I was playing for England when you were still in High School. *I'm* captain of Apocalypse.'

'Sure you are,' said Luke, 'and you've got unique charisma, right, that'll make guys go over the top into the face of hell for you, and make horses run till they drop, but you're abusing it. You're too fucking arrogant. I know you're sore Dancer hired me without asking you. I don't want to steal your thunder. I wanna learn all I can from you, and I wanna give something back. Potentially, we've got a brilliant side. And you're so goddam lucky you've got a patron who's a saint – a patron saint, he pays you a fucking fortune and all you do is give him earache.'

Little Chef jumped on to Ricky's knee and started to growl at Luke. Ricky's face was grey, his eyes black whirlpools of fury, his long fingers curled round his glass. For a second Luke thought he was going to hurl it in his face.

'My horses haven't left,' he said slowly. 'I'd rather get on the next plane home than spend summer watching you self-destruct.'

'Get out,' hissed Ricky.

In the kitchen Luke found that his legs were shaking violently. Outside, the wind was systematically stripping the cherry trees and the montana. Out in the yard Wayne, confined to barracks with a puffy hock, and suffering mild indigestion from wolfing too many cucumber sandwiches, cream cakes and a clubhouse tablecloth, hung out of his specially bolted door like a burglar about to crack a safe.

He'd hoped the footstep would be Ricky's, but Luke would do. Unable to stop shaking, Luke clung on to the ugly, yellow, lop-eared head.

'I've blown it,' he groaned.

He'd been so excited this time yesterday, flying over the Atlantic dreaming of Perdita, of the Gold Cup, of shaking hands with the Queen and going to Stratford and Tintern Abbey. He'd have to pay back Dancer's fee, and holding a sobbing Perdita in his arms earlier had made him realize once again how hopelessly he was still in love with her.

He jumped as the stable cat weaved her way round his trembling legs. Picked up, she purred against him for a second, then, jumping on to Wayne's withers, settled down happily on his quarters.

Christ, thought Luke in horror, that poor guy killed his kid when he was looped and I force liquor on him.

'Look, I'm sorry,' he said, going back into the drawing room. 'I came on too strong.'

Ricky looked up, then suddenly smiled. 'No, you didn't. Everything you said was right. I know it in my head, but the moment I get on the field I tense up, and ever since Chessie buggered off and Will died I've never trusted anyone, least of all myself.' Picking up his glass, he examined it for a second, then drained it. 'Let's get plastered.'

Reluctant to break the mood, Luke waited until an hour later, when Ricky went off to have a pee, to call Perdita. He got an earful.

'Tell your mother I'm really sorry,' he said, when he could get a word in, 'but Ricky and I've got a lot of things to work through. I'll take you both out tomorrow.'

'What makes you think I'd want to come?' snapped Perdita. Even though she knew there was no hope with Ricky, she was furiously jealous of Luke spending an evening alone with him.

'I'll take your mother then,' said Luke, hanging up.

After midnight, when they'd moved four white and four black horses round the green baize board until they could see sixteen of them, they tottered out to the stables. The ponies, surprised to be roused, blinked sleepily. Tero's feed was still in her manger and she shrank to the back of her box as they approached.

'Get's so uptight she won't eat for forty-eight hours after a game,' said Ricky, clumsily putting another rug on her and having great difficulty doing it up.

'She will when we start winning,' said Luke. 'You wait till you see Fantasma – sweeps down the field like a yacht in full sail.'

'I had a horse called Mattie once,' said Ricky, stumbling off towards the forage room. 'Best pair of legs I ever saw on a pony, or a woman. Christ, she was beautiful. Faster than Kinta, cannier than Wayne, turned quicker than Spotty. You always have one you love best, don't you?'

Absolutely plastered, he tripped over an upturned bucket and, just managing to right himself, sat down very suddenly on a bale of hay. His black curls were ruffled, his black eyes crossing. 'You know Ch-Ch-Chessie, don't you?'

'Sure,' said Luke, leaning against the door.

'Beautiful, isn't she?'

'Incredible.'

'She happy with your father?'

Luke shrugged. 'I don't know. I guess all marriages are Africa. They did an autopsy on one of Shark Nelligan's ponies the other day, the hide looked fine, but inside where the spurs had gone in, the scar tissue, the tearing, and the bruising were appalling. That's marriage. Same way, I gotta horse, cut to pieces outside, scars everywhere; inside, she's one of the best mares ever. Hard to generalize.'

Ricky felt pole-axed with misery. Even talking about Chessie crucified him, and with performances as lousy as today's, how could he ever win the Gold Cup, let alone get to ten or bring the Westchester back to England?

'I can't stand other people being happy,' he mumbled shame-facedly. 'It makes me s-s-such a shit. D'you think I'll ever get over her?'

'Sure you will,' said Luke, thinking that he hadn't remotely got over Perdita. 'You need some fun.'

Stretching out a hand, he found Ricky had collapsed on his hay bale, nudged asleep perhaps by the velvet muzzle of Mattie's ghost. Little Chef curled into the hollow of his back with a martyred sigh. Fetching a couple of rugs, Luke covered both of them.

God, he was handsome, even with that wicked scar running livid down the side of his face. No wonder Perdita loved him. Giving a wide-awake Wayne a handful of pony nuts, Luke wandered off to Ricky's library to find something to read. Tomorrow they'd get down to work.

A fortnight later Luke went into Rutminster with Ricky to look for a new bit for Kinta. Returning home, he found his grooms and ponies had caught an earlier flight and were already installed. Racing round to the yard, he called Fantasma's name. Recognizing his voice, she promptly tried to bash her way out of her box, and, finding that impossible, stood back on her hocks and cleared the dark blue half-door, clattering up to her master, whickering in ecstasy, nudging him all over, searching his pockets for Polo mints.

'Christ, what a beautiful horse,' said Ricky who wasn't given to superlatives. 'I never expected her to be so big.'

'I can't believe she's grown so much,' said Perdita in amazement.

'Nearly a hand,' said Luke proudly.

'And she's filled out everywhere,' went on Perdita.

'When you see the girth on her,' said Luke, his voice breaking slightly as he buried his face in Fantasma's neck, 'you realize why she's got so much heart. It's a real privilege to own a horse like this. Ouch,' he yelled, as Fantasma, resentful of being abandoned for a fortnight, took a sharp bite out of his arm, then nudged him apologetically.

'Bitch,' said Luke, grinning and getting out a packet of Polos. 'That's because I didn't take her with me on Concorde.'

He also found it faintly embarrassing, having insisted that all the Apocalypse team get up early and work all their ponies every day, that he waived the rules with Fantasma. Instead he hacked her gently round the Rutshire countryside.

'She gets awful bored if I stick and ball her,' he told Ricky apologetically, 'and only just tolerates practice chukkas. I guess she saves herself for the real thing.'

'If she takes out your bloody father, I'll forgive her,' said Ricky grimly.

47

If Ricky's hatred for Bart grew deep inside him like a beast, then Bart was equally obsessed with Ricky. The prospect of coming to England with enough ponies for a cavalry regiment and publicly showing the world who was the better man gave him an unbelievable sexual *frisson*. He was therefore outraged by a piece in the April issue of *Polo* magazine questioning the future invincibility of the Flyers.

'Hitherto Bart Alderton has been shored up by the mighty ten goalers, Juan and Miguel O'Brien, and wildly underhandicapped ringers. Allied to the volatile and extremely vocal Napier brothers and an unknown Mexican this summer in England, will Bart be able to retain the Flyers' supremacy?'

Having fired off a solicitor's letter to *Polo* magazine Bart went into an orgy of pony-buying. Nor could the pleadings of Bibi that Alderton Airlines had recorded their first loss in twenty years, that 500 blue-collar and 400 white-collar workers had to be laid off and Bart ought to be there to fire them personally, that the vice-presidents of the various sections of the Alderton empire were at each others' throats, stop him spending May, June and July in England.

The lay-offs and losses were just symptoms of a worldwide malaise, Bart told Bibi airily. Business would pick up in the fall. Anyway he was always at the end of the telephone or a fax machine. He couldn't understand either why Bibi, as his polo manager, couldn't accompany him and Chessie to England. Things wouldn't run nearly as smoothly without her. But Bibi insisted that one member of the Alderton family must stay home to mind the shop. Nor was she prepared to leave Angel, who was still banned from playing in England, loose on his own on the US circuit for two and a half months. The punishing hours she worked for Bart had already put a great strain on her marriage.

'Surely Angel could spare you for the big matches? Marriages need ventilating,' grumbled Bart, totally forgetting that he wasn't prepared to leave Chessie on her own for a second in England. As it was, he already had security guards following her twenty-four hours a day and had bugged the telephones and rooms both at the huge house he had just bought near Cowdray and at the flat in Knightsbridge. Chessie got her revenge by spending a fortune on clothes and enlisting the help of the guards even to choosing the colour and shape of her lingerie. If the world's press was clamouring to witness her first meeting with her ex-husband in four and half years, Chessie reasoned, she better look good.

To the press's disappointment this meeting didn't occur until the final of the Queen's Cup. Apocalypse, who, under Luke's crash course, had finally got their act together, stormed through their side of the draw, taking huge delight in thrashing the Kaputnik Tigers, consisting of Victor, the twins and the great American Number Three, Bobby Ferraro, in the semi-finals, before meeting Bart, the Napiers and an unknown Mexican in the final.

Luke's greatest headache on the day was keeping Apocalypse calm. It was like ponying three wild mustangs along a freeway. Perdita, suffering from appalling stage fright, became more histrionic and picky than ever. Ricky, whose stomach had been churning all summer at the prospect of bumping into Chessie, had been throwing up all night. Dancer, the most frightened of the three, hid it the best and consequently became the recipient of a lot of flak from Perdita and Ricky, particularly during practice chukkas and while they were watching videos of earlier Alderton Flyer matches.

'It's only because you take criticism so well that we can tell you things,' Luke kept comforting Dancer.

Most patrons worried more about the bank manager than playing badly. Dancer, acutely aware he was the weak link in the team, was terrified of letting Apocalypse down. He had to mark Ben Napier, who was twice his size and four times his strength. He hardly slept the night before and in his fitful dreams was ridden off by the whole world.

As none of the three could keep anything down, there was no question of a team lunch to create solidarity before the match. Dancer, because he liked to get up slowly, cope with his nerves on his own and arrive as late as possible to avoid being mobbed, flew to the Guards Club by helicopter. The others went by car. Ricky drove with Perdita in front because she felt sick and Luke and Little Chef, dancing across Luke's knees to bark at every dog they passed, in the back. As he was the team mascot, Dancer had given him a collar of jet from which dangled a tiny ivory horse.

'That dog is so spoilt,' grumbled Perdita, 'he even gets the gardeners to bury his bones for him.'

Luke had done his homework on the Alderton Flyers. He had watched every match they played in England and, by judicious chatting up of grooms and other players, had familiarized himself with every pony they'd be riding and had briefed Apocalypse accordingly.

'Team's top-heavy, with my father and the Napiers yelling their heads off and all wanting their own way. The only person they've got to boss around is this Mexican guy called José, who can't understand a word of English, which may enhance his peace of mind, but doesn't make for cohesion. We'll flatten them.'

On paper the Flyers were much stronger. The game plan was to harass the hell out of them until they fouled out of exasperation. Then, against long, accurate penalties from Luke, there would be no defence. If the match went Apocalypse's way, the others would leave Luke as a rock-solid wall of defence and concentrate on attack.

Luke wished he felt more cheerful. As Ricky overtook everyone on the M4, the damp patches under his arms joined across his back until his whole shirt was soaked in sweat and Luke could see his shoulder muscles as rigid as petrified snakes.

It was a close, punishingly hot day. Thunder grumbled on the horizon. The heatwave was in its third week. Wild roses and the creamy discs of elderflowers draped over the hedgerows shrivelled in a day. A heat haze undulated on the tarmac ahead. It was a relief to come off the motorway into the dark green oak and chestnut tunnels on the road to Windsor. Behind fern-filled verges and ramparts of purple rhododendrons, Luke caught glimpses of large pink-and-white houses which reminded him of Palm Beach, lawns yellow from the hosepipe ban and paddocks full of jumps and ponies whisking unpulled tails across glossy rumps.

Men in shirtsleeves and girls in sundresses were drinking outside pubs.

'Christ, I'd like to spend the afternoon knocking back Pimm's and watching someone else make a fool of themselves,' said Perdita in a hollow voice. Luke felt as if an ice-cube had been slipped into his hand. Glancing down he saw it was Perdita's hand reaching back to him. Although the nails were bitten and dirty and the palm calloused, he had to resist lifting it to his lips. Instead he squeezed it gently.

'Give us a poem, Luke,' she asked.

'*Once more unto the breach, dear friends, once more,*' began Luke, his deep voice slightly croaky from dust.

They were passing Windsor Castle now and Luke thought ruefully of the sightseeing he had hoped to do. He hadn't been to London yet, let alone Stratford.

'*Or close the wall up with our English dead!*' he went on.

'*In peace there's nothing so becomes a man*
As modest stillness and humility;
But when the blast of war blows in our ears,
Then imitate the action of the tiger.'

'Not the Kaputnik Tigers I hope,' said Perdita. 'I'm so scared I'll probably play like Victor. Christ – look at those crowds and those tents.'

From the car-park came a humming like a vast swarm of bees, as chauffeurs, not wanting to melt away, kept on the air-conditioning of their limos. No wind displaced the wilting flags along the pitch, but inside the hospitality tents electric fans could be seen ruffling vast clumps of pink peonies and pale blue delphiniums as men, wishing they'd worn striped shirts which didn't show the sweat, and beautiful women refusing red wine because it would make their faces even pinker, toyed with lobster, cold beef and strawberries and cream.

Ricky, aware that the Alderton Flyers and their wives were lunching in the tent of Alfred Dunhill, the sponsors, suddenly thought he saw Chessie and nearly ran over a programme seller.

'Oh, look,' said a fat waitress, chucking leftovers into a grey, plastic dustbin, 'there's that Perdita, the one that said "eff off" to Prince Charles.'

'Ow, yes,' said her friend excitedly. 'Hello, Perdy, can

465

we have your autograph? Thought you was in the Tower. Stuck up little madam,' she added, as Perdita gazed stonily ahead.

Down by the pony lines crowds surged forward to admire Apocalypse's equine stars. Wayne appeared to be sleeping peacefully but was actually wondering how to bite his way through his new reinforced lead rope. They did awfully good teas at the Guards Club. Spotty, the show-off, was thrilled to see so many people. Fantasma, as usual, was standing on her front legs lashing out simultaneously with both back barrels.

'Thank God you've arrived,' said Luke's groom, Lizzie, despairingly. 'I've got one more stud to screw into her hoof and I can't get near her in this mood.'

Next door to Fantasma, Perdita was trying to calm down a frantically trembling, sweating Tero.

'God, the Flyers' horses look well,' she said gloomily. 'There's Glitz, and that chestnut Andromeda's even faster than Fantasma.'

'That's because the Napiers cut their horses up before a match,' said Luke, taking the spanner from Lizzie and picking up a now comparatively docile Fantasma's nearside hoof. 'One touch of their spurs and they fly.'

'Bastards, I hate them,' stormed Perdita.

'That's the right attitude,' said Luke. 'Napiers keep their horses in all the time. They're not so relaxed as ours.'

'Could have fooled me,' said Lizzie, rubbing a large purpling bruise on her arm.

'I'm sorry, honey.' Luke patted her cheek as he handed her back the spanner. 'Thirty minutes to the parade. We'd better get changed,' he added, propelling Ricky, who, despite the heat, was shivering even worse than Tero, towards the players' changing room.

'And where am I supposed to change?' demanded Perdita.

'In the Ladies,' said Ricky curtly.

'And get gawped at? I'd rather use the lorry, but you can all flaming well stand guard, or Guards, while I have a shower later.'

Ricky sat in a dark corner of the changing room taking ages to zip up his boots, buckle his knee pads and his lucky belt, and button up his lucky gloves which had almost fallen to pieces. He must get a grip on himself. He'd only get Chessie back by hammering Bart. At the moment he wouldn't know where to stand to hit a sixty-yard penalty.

Suddenly he froze as Bart came in and dived for the nearest loo. Prolonged peeing followed by a volley of farts and a vile smell told him Bart was as nervous as he was. Ricky felt slightly better, and better still when Bart came out and spent several minutes combing his wolf's pelt forward to cover a receding hairline and re-smoothing his shirt into his belt and his breeches into his knee pads and boots. He then dived into his locker and produced some bronzing gel called 'Indela', newly launched by Victor's pharmaceutical empire, which didn't run when you sweated.

Outside, a band, redder than their tunics, were playing the British Grenadiers as clouds, blacker than their bearskins, marshalled on the horizon. A curious light had turned the field viridian as military men with lean figures strode around barking instructions into walkie-talkies.

Ricky, who was madly superstitious, was slightly cheered as the band, bored with military marches, launched, to the ecstasy of the crowd, into 'Four Horsemen'.

'Four Hor-*ses*, white horse, black horse, red horse, pale horse, plague, famine, justice, death, riding, riding, riding,' roared the crowd stamping their feet in time on the wooden boards, as the menacing music swept through the ground.

'Isn't that marvellous!' cried Perdita.

'Unfair bloody advantage, hyping up Apocalypse,' snarled Bart to the Napiers and the uncomprehending Mexican.

'Let's object,' said Ben Napier, two spots of colour staining his cadaverous cheeks as, exactly on cue, a vast, black helicopter cast its shadow over the pitch.

With great difficulty and the help of a dozen security guards Dancer fought his way through to the pony lines.

'Fuckin' 'ell, don't it sound grite?' he grinned at his team-mates. 'I might go out and give them an encore. I love the Guards Club,' he went on, lowering his voice. 'They can't believe anyfink as cockney as me can play polo. Colonels keep comin' up and saying " 'Ullo, Dancer, you over from New Zealand again?" '

Perdita giggled; even Ricky smiled slightly. But he was

watching Bart who'd cut all the Apocalypse team, even Luke, stone dead and was now shouting at the Napiers and into a telephone at the same time. How could Chessie be married to that, he thought with a shudder. Luke edged closer to his father.

'I don't give a shit if it has crashed,' Bart was saying. 'I can't bring them back to life. Put Winston Chalmers on to it at once. I'll call you later.'

'What's happened?' Luke asked one of Bart's grooms whom he knew from Palm Beach. The groom pulled a long face.

'Alderton Pegasus totalled in the desert with no survivors.'

'Shit,' said Luke. 'Dad should fly home.'

'And miss a final? Pigs would fly,' said the groom.

The Queen had arrived. State trumpeters and drum horses from the Household Cavalry in their gold uniforms, followed by the band, were lining up between the goal posts to lead the two teams, with the two umpires as a bolster between them, ten abreast on to the field. Players tend to ride their oldest, quietest horses in the parade in case the bands and the crowd overexcite them. Apocalypse, however, stuck to their theme. Ricky rode the pale yellow Wayne, Perdita was on Hermia, her red-chestnut friend from Pony Club days who leapt all over the place snatching excitedly at her bit. Dancer had a safer passage on black Geoffrey, the hangover horse. Luke had reluctantly agreed to ride Fantasma, the only white horse in the yard, and had great difficulty controlling her. A natural loner, she longed to be out in front leading the parade. When she wasn't humping her back in temper, she was taking bites out of poor, kind Geoffrey on her right, and, less advisedly, out of umpire Shark Nelligan's horse on her left. Despite this, Apocalypse, in their black shirts with their black hats over their noses, looked both sinister and threatening.

Ricky had just galloped Wayne back after the parade and was mounting a hopelessly over-excited Sinatra when he heard a frantic clicking of cameras as journalists and photographers broke through the ropes. Then he heard a soft voice saying, 'Hello, Luke darling.'

Catching a great waft of Diorissimo, Ricky swung round as though a rattlesnake had bitten him, colour draining from his face. The heat had made everyone appear as though they'd been boiled alive. Chessie, by comparison, looked like a lily of the valley just picked from some cool, shady dell. She wore a pale green linen suit, exquisitely cut to show off the fragility of her body, and flat green pumps on her feet. Her face, faintly flushed from champagne in the Dunhill tent, was tanned to a smooth *café au lait*, the eyes were turned to aquamarine by the green suit and her full, pouting lips were as palely pink as the wild roses dying in the hedgerows.

Hugging Luke, but gazing over his shoulder at Ricky, she murmured, 'How exciting you're in the final and how ironic you're playing against your father. What *embarras de* Aldertons. The commentator's going to get so muddled.'

Then, wriggling out of Luke's grasp, like a sleepwalker she moved over to Ricky. Gazing up, she took in the hollowed cheeks with their suspicion of black stubble and the grim intransigent mouth which was belied by the fierce, yet desperately wounded, dark eyes beneath the black polo hat.

'Hello, Ricky,' she said mockingly. 'How's our bet going? Still a long way to go. No Gold Cup yet, no ten goal, no Westchester. You'll have to do better than that.'

Oblivious of the photographers going crazy all round them, Ricky stared down at her. He simply couldn't get a word out as she gently caressed Sinatra's silky shoulder. Sinatra had been known to take people's hands off, but now relaxed almost ecstatically under Chessie's touch.

'Four and a half years is a long time,' she whispered. 'Haven't you missed me?'

Seeing her wanton, taunting little face, flawless except for the velvet smudges under the eyes, and her caressing suntanned hand inching towards his thigh, Ricky wanted to gather her up on Sinatra, gallop all the way back to Robinsgrove, ram every bolt and never let her go again.

They were interrupted by Luke, now mounted on Ophelia and looking more thunderous than the cloud now hanging above the pitch.

'Back off, Chessie,' he said roughly. 'I don't know if Dad put you up to this, but it is definitely out of order.'

Perdita was less reticent. 'Fuck off, you bitch,' she screamed. 'What a bloody awful time to stage a comeback.'

The reporters scribbled avidly.

'Any chance of a reconciliation, Mrs Alderton?' asked *The Scorpion*, wrestling with one of Dancer's security men.

Chessie gave a sob. 'You'll have to ask my ex-husband,' she said.

'For God's sake get on, Ricky,' snapped Major Ferguson, who masterminded every move at the Guards Club.

The Flyers were already on the field.

'Here come the undertakers,' sneered Charles Napier, deliberately barging his big brown mare into Spotty whom Perdita had just changed on to. 'Black's the right colour for you lot. You'll certainly be flying that fag,' he nodded at Dancer, 'at half-mast by the end of this match.'

Ricky had gone to pieces. White, sweating, shaking violently, he hardly seemed to know where he was.

'Take it easy,' said Luke, putting an arm round his shoulders.

'Thought Dancer was the fag,' taunted Ben Napier. 'Didn't know you and Ricky were having it off. I hear you had to buy the Rutshire, Dancer, to get your handicap up to one.'

'Knock it off,' ordered Shark Nelligan who was umpiring and wanted to throw-in.

'That was definitely below the belt, Dad,' said Luke as he lined up beside Bart. 'If you want Chessie to be a widow before the end of the match you're going about it in the right way.'

'Whaddya talking about?' Bart spat out his gum.

'Sending her out to the pony lines to screw up Ricky.'

For a second Bart was roused out of his obsessive pre-throw-in catatonia.

'Nothing to do with me,' he said in outrage. 'She must have got looped at lunchtime.'

As the ball thumped into the forest of legs and sticks the first three pairs missed it. Luke and Bart clashed mallets for a couple of seconds, then Luke got the ball out, immediately whacking it up towards the enemy goal posts, then, following his right of way, hit it again. But he wasn't on his fastest pony. At the touch of spurs on her desperately cut-up flesh, Charles Napier's big brown mare bounded forward like a cheetah. Luke could hear the thunder of her hooves on the dry ground behind him. Then suddenly, to his left, Spotty, electrified by a large cheering crowd, was streaking down the field with Perdita's arms, legs and whip going like a jockey's.

Aware that Charles was about to hook him, Luke swung Ophelia to the right and cut the ball to Perdita on the nearside. Fleetingly he felt Charles's knee under his but managed to stay put.

'Take your time,' he yelled to Perdita.

Conscious of the cheers of the crowd, Perdita stroked the ball upfield. Then, out of nowhere, Ben Napier was hurtling towards her at ninety degrees like a boulder in an avalanche.

Oh my God, thought Perdita.

Oh my God, thought Spotty, who didn't like the look of Ben Napier's big bay gelding any better.

Rolling his white eye, he put on another amazing burst of acceleration, whisking his brown-and-white rump forward so Ben Napier bumped the burning air instead. Then, bearing Perdita on as proudly as a gun dog with his master's newspaper, Spotty positioned her to meet the ball exactly right and flick it between the posts.

Grinning from ear to ear and unashamedly raising her stick to the cheers of the crowd, she cantered back to the halfway line, patting Spotty over and over again. Apocalypse, who had received two goals on handicap, were now 3-0 up.

'You doll,' breathed Luke, hugging her.

Ricky said nothing. He was plainly still suffering from shock. Bart just scowled.

'Aren't you sorry you gave me Spotty for Christmas?' Perdita taunted him.

Euphoria, however, was shortlived. Ricky simply wasn't connecting with the ball. It was as if he was wearing a pair of reading glasses to run down a steep flight of steps and such, eventually, was his frustration and rage and the ferocity of his ride-offs that he finally sent Bart and black Glitz flying five feet through the air so that even the Queen in the Royal Box could hear the bump.

Next moment the Napiers were twirling their sticks in the air and Shark Nelligan had blown a foul on Ricky. Contemptuously, Charles Napier converted. Soon it became plain to everyone that Ricky was out to bury Bart. By half-time he had given away three penalties and

Ben Napier, whom Ricky was supposed to be marking, had scored three goals.

As the crowd surged on to the field to tread in, Luke rode Fantasma back to the pony lines in a towering rage. The mare was panting desperately, her bottom lip flapping, her nostrils dark red, her tail thrashing at her sweating dock, the blood pumping visibly through her enlarged veins like some biology experiment. Luke had never known her so exhausted. Handing her to Lizzie to cool down, he dragged Ricky aside.

'What the fuck are you playing at?' he hissed. 'I've just ridden the duck soup out of Fantasma covering up for you. This final is between Apocalypse and the Flyers not you and my father. It's goddam selfish to take your personal vendetta on to the field.'

Luke had sweat in his eyes, dust in his throat, his ribs ached from a foul hook no-one had seen, he'd had to change ponies twice in the first two chukkas because two had gone lame and he could see his dreams going up in smoke. Nor could he bear to see Dancer and Perdita's dejected faces. They deserved better.

'This match is dirtier than a coal hole,' said Seb Carlisle as he bought Chessie a Pimm's up in the stands during the second half, 'and you ought to be wearing a duck-egg-blue shirt with five stamped on the back, you've contributed so much to Ricky's disintegration and Apocalypse's certain defeat.'

'Oh, shut up,' said Chessie. 'I had to talk to him. With two bloody bodyguards tailing me all the time I may not get another chance this season.'

'Why don't you lure them both into your bedroom?' suggested Seb, 'then rush out and lock the door on them. Oh, lovely pass, Perdita. Luke Alderton has certainly worked miracles with her and Dancer. They're hassling the shit out of your husband and Ben Napier and, Christ, look at that.' He waved his programme disapprovingly at Charles Napier's pony who was bleeding both from her mouth and her lacerated sides. 'I have nightmares that I'm going to come back in another life as one of Charles's horses.'

Charles Napier was also famous for using his elbows during ride-offs and at the throw-in, and he was using them with increasing ferocity in the fifth chukka when he was riding the lightning Andromeda and the Flyers had failed to increase their lead. Fed up with Perdita giving him the slip as they were fighting for the ball on the boards, he deliberately rammed an elbow so hard into her left breast that she gave a shriek.

'Why don't you go back to the kitchen where you belong?' he hissed.

'Why don't you go back to the gorilla house?' screamed Perdita, so doubled up with pain she could hardly lift her stick.

Next minute Luke had thundered up.

'You OK, baby?'

Perdita bit her lip and nodded.

'Well, belt up and leave this to me.'

At the beginning of the last chukka Charles galloped towards goal. As Luke, back on Fantasma again, rode him off, out came Charles's elbows.

'Get out of my way, you goddam prick,' bellowed Charles.

'Takes a prick to know a prick,' said Luke, putting his arm through Charles's. And such was his massive strength that he lifted him off his horse as easily as if he was pulling the plug out of the bath. Charles crashed to the ground.

'Man down,' said Luke, grinning.

'Foul,' yelled Charles furiously.

'No foul,' said Shark and Dommie Carlisle, the other umpire, in unison. Both had been the recipients of Charles Napier's elbows far too often.

The sun behind the stands lit up the thundery indigo clouds, the acid-yellow fir trees, the jade-green statue of Prince Albert on his horse, the yellow-and-white goal posts and the tiring ponies. It was stiflingly hot and stuffy.

'Luke must be very much in love with Perdita to risk a foul like that,' said Seb to Chessie.

No one quite knew how it happened, but in the following frantic mêlée in front of the Apocalypse goal, Charles Napier took a mighty swipe at the ball and instead hit Luke on the head with his stick. As Luke slumped in his saddle, Fantasma pulled up with a jerk and the pitted field came up to meet him.

Perdita was off Tero in a trice, begging Luke frantically

to be all right. Beside her Fantasma gazed down at her master with huge, dark, worried eyes, nudging him impatiently in the ribs to get up, then raking his shoulder gently with her hoof.

'Out cold,' said the doctor, who'd arrived with the ambulance, bending over Luke. 'Ouch,' he howled a second later as Fantasma bit him jealously on the bottom.

Bart and the Napiers belted off to change ponies.

'I'll get another player,' said Ricky, at long last coming out of his coma. But as he galloped towards the stands, the heavens opened, lightning ripped the inky clouds apart and rain, coming down in torrents, bounced eighteen inches off the dry ground. In the stands, spectators huddled under coloured umbrellas. Others fled for the hospitality tents or their cars. The deluge almost halted the windscreen wipers of the ambulance as it ploughed off to hospital.

As the substitute calmly changed into a spare black shirt and borrowed Luke's helmet which was too big and fell over his handsome nose, a demented Perdita kept demanding if Luke would be OK.

'I 'ope so,' said Dancer who was looking very shaken himself. Without Luke, he felt as though his rudder had been taken away.

'You don't look very happy, Dancer,' sneered Bart.

'I'm *not* very 'appy, Bart,' replied Dancer. 'We've just lost our best player, we're 3-6 down wiv five minutes to go and it's pouring with fucking rain. No, I'm not very 'appy, Bart.'

After ten drenching minutes the rain let up and play started again. It had always been arguable that Fantasma was wasted on a Number Four player, who is mostly occupied with defence. With her handiness and dazzling turn of speed, she was more suited to a Number Three. The substitute was a brilliant rider. Everyone noticed how wonderfully Fantasma went with him. Luke had been so busy covering up for Ricky earlier, the mare had had no chance to show off her paces. Although she now swished her tail furiously and rolled her eyes when the substitute gave her half a dozen whacks, she set off towards goal like a Derby winner.

What a horse, thought the substitute, as ghostly white Fantasma streaked through the gloom. And what smooth action – he could have carried a glass of champagne without spilling it. Then, as Bart raced to cut off the ball and back it up the field, Fantasma swung round like a weathercock when the wind changes.

I want this horse, decided the substitute as the gallant mare reached the ball, waited while he backed it once more towards the Flyer's goal, then instantly turned. This time he scored, and a minute later he had scored again.

Then the Flyers' poor Mexican ringer crossed Dancer out of nerves. His face expressionless, all the joy and power in his stick, Ricky drove home a miraculous sixty-yard penalty, making it six all as the bell went. Emerging from under their coloured umbrellas into the diminishing drizzle, the crowd went berserk, overjoyed that such a thrilling match would go to an extra chukka.

Through dense fog Luke heard voices, shouts of laughter and some singing and slowly opened his eyes. The room seemed to blaze with gleaming cups. Then he heard Perdita's shrill voice.

'Luke darling, please come round.'

He could feel her hand and, laboriously, he tried to focus finally identifying Perdita and Dancer, drunk as skunks and brandishing a huge gilt cup.

'We won,' cried Perdita, overjoyed.

'What happened?' asked Luke.

'We went into extra time.' Dancer took Luke's other hand. 'I tell you I was shaking like a leaf. Wiv you gone I had to play back and Ricky and Perdita and the sub was up the other end going towards goal, and next moment Charles Napier's thundering towards me yelling, "Leave it, leave it", and Bart yells, "I'm not going to fuckin' leave it," and hits the ball straight at me. Thank Christ, it hits my pony who gives a fuckin' groan and somehow I hits it back past Charles and next moment the boy's waving the flag up the other end. "Fuckin' ell," I yelled, "We've won."'

'And Spotty kicked the ball in,' crowed Perdita.

'Riding back past your Dad,' went on Dancer, 'I said, "You don't look very 'appy, Bart," and he was so angry he bundled his wife into 'is helicopter and flew straight back to 'is new 'ouse at Cowdray.'

'That's terrific,' said Luke, wondering why they were now disappearing in a whirling snowstorm.

'And Fantasma won Best Playing Pony yet again,' said Perdita, laying a royal-blue blanket edged with scarlet over the bed. 'There's the most terrific party going on at the Star of India in Windsor. The twins started a food fight and hit Mrs Hughie on the nose with an onion bargie. Victor's so pissed Dommie's sold another of his horses back to him and Sharon is comforting the Mexican José who speaks no English.'

Sitting down on Fantasma's prize-winning blanket, they started going through every play.

'What did the Queen say to you, Dancer?' Luke asked wistfully.

'That she was very pleased. She's met me before at the Royal Variety Performance, but she was less shy this time.'

Perdita giggled. 'She said she was sorry you were out cold and hoped you'd be better soon.'

Luke had never known her so happy.

'Who was the guy who stood in for me?' he asked. 'Pretty good scoring two goals right away.'

'Oh, didn't we tell you?' said Dancer in surprise. 'It was your bruvver, Red.'

'What's he doing over here?'

'Victor's so furious at being beaten by your father that he's dropped poor Bobby Ferraro for the rest of the season and flown Red over at vast expense to play for him instead.'

48

Next day Red's name dominated the headlines. '*Auriel's toyboy turns game around*', screamed the *Sun*; '*Bart sees Red*', said *The Scorpion* with a splendid picture of Bart having a shouting match with Red and Major Ferguson. The *Telegraph* warmly praised Red's polo skills: he could hit a ball through the eye of a needle. *The Times* concentrated on his horsemanship and how the great grey mare Fantasma rose like Pegasus to the challenge.

Not content with bringing a sparkle to Perdita's eyes,

Red had seduced his beloved Fantasma as well. Luke was ashamed how jealous he felt. He loved his brother but Red always spelt trouble and at the moment Luke felt incapable of getting him out of any more scrapes. Yesterday's feeling of floating detachment had given way to sickness and a blinding headache. He felt dizzy if he sat up; if he lay down his bed pitched like a raft in a force-ten gale; any sudden movement of the head made him leap with pain. The X-ray showed no fractures, but nurses were taking his pulse and blood pressure on the hour. He definitely wouldn't be fit for the Royal Windsor in which he was playing with Kevin Coley next week. Despite heavy sedation, Luke was desperately worried. Injury was the professional's worst nightmare. Just when Apocalypse was coming good he had to desert them.

Ricky, looking very pale, had dropped in first thing in the morning. He obviously hadn't slept and, stammering badly, apologized for playing so hopelessly yesterday. He never dreamed he'd be so pole-axed by seeing Chessie, but that was no excuse.

Knowing how much it must have cost the great *El Orgulloso* to admit such a thing, Luke was touched.

'No sweat,' he said. 'We won anyway. How's Fantasma?'

'Got a bang on the nearside cannon bone.' Then, seeing Luke's face: 'No, she's OK. We poulticed her and she was almost sound when we walked her out this morning.'

After Ricky had gone, Luke fretted. Tempted to discharge himself to check that Fantasma was all right, he was slightly cheered around lunchtime when an Irish nurse with eyes greener than a Granny Smith and a white cap riding on her lustrous piled-up black hair, like a paper boat on stormy rapids, came in to check his blood pressure.

'Why are you doing that?'

'A sudden drop might indicate bleeding in the skull.' Her voice was like a furry bell.

'No-one's blood pressure could drop with you around,' said Luke as she checked his pulse.

Looking at the badge on her starched apron he saw her name was Rosie O'Grady, and couldn't remotely imagine her being a sister under the skin to Mrs Hughie.

'Who's Perdita?' she asked slyly. 'Your wife? A girlfriend?'

'Just a friend,' said Luke carefully. 'Why d'you ask?'

'I was on when you came in yesterday. You never stopped babbling about her. She's a lucky girl,' she added softly. 'I had to undress you. I never knew polo players were,' she smiled sleepily, 'so . . . er . . . well-hung.'

Luke blushed beneath his red-gold stubble. 'And I was out cold. Jesus, what a waste!'

'There'll be other opportunities. We're not letting you out yet.'

She handed him some blue pills and a glass of water which he had difficulty in keeping down.

'What are they?'

'Analgesic and sedatives.'

'I don't want to feel sedated,' said Luke, taking her hand. Perhaps he was still concussed. 'Please stay with me.'

They both jumped as the door flew open and Perdita stormed in. She was wearing dark glasses, which emphasized her long nose, jeans and a torn, grey T-shirt of Daisy's. Her hair was scraped back with a mauve plastic clip. She didn't look her best.

'What's she doing?' she snapped as Nurse O'Grady melted away. 'Giving you intensive care? Thought she'd have better things to do. How are you feeling?'

'Pretty good,' lied Luke.

'That's more than I am. I've got such a bloody awful hangover and there was a four-mile tailback on the motorway with the sun pounding down on the roof of the car. Christ, look at all your flowers. I've brought you grapes and some Lucozade. Luke-ozade, it's a joke!'

'Very funny, thanks a lot,' said Luke who'd heard it often before.

'This is a jolly nice room.' Perdita switched on the racing on television. The horses' hooves seemed to be pounding through Luke's skull. 'Ricky's thinking of buying that grey.'

It came fourth. Perdita switched it off.

'I see you got the papers. Your bloody brother stole all our thunder. No-one even mentioned Dancer or me or Ricky and Chessie. The press were clinging to Red like burrs all last night. He got plastered and Seb and Dommie had a fight in the Taj Mahal because Seb was winding Dommie up saying Decorum loved him more

478

than Dommie. I had a good morning though.' She started eating the grapes she'd brought. '*Horse and Hound* want to put me on the cover. The *Daily Mail* want me to do a fashion feature. Best of all, Rupert Campbell-Black rang. Venturer are keen on making a documentary, or it might be a series of six half-hour programmes, taking me through the Gold Cup, Deauville, possibly Argentina and then Palm Beach next spring. I'm lunching with him and Bas later this week.'

'That's terrific,' said Luke, wishing he felt more enthusiastic. She seemed to be slipping away from him. Christ, he mustn't be possessive. He took her hand. 'It's really great.'

There was a hammering on the door and the twins and Red burst in all wearing dark glasses.

'Hi, baby boy,' said Seb.

'We are *so* ill,' announced Red putting a hand on Luke's shoulder.

But even Red's hangover and no sleep couldn't dim his beauty. Luke noticed how Perdita had whipped away her hand when he came in. Now she was surreptitiously removing the mauve plastic clip from her hair and raking it out with her fingers.

'We brought you some booze,' said Seb, plonking three bottles of Moët and one of Lucozade down on Luke's bedside table. 'We didn't think you'd have time to get any in.'

'How're you feeling?' asked Dommie. 'It was your fault, you know. You mustn't go round pulling Charles Napier off his horses. If I hadn't loathed him so much I'd have blown a foul on you.'

'He's a bastard. Have you seen my bruises?' Perdita lifted her T-shirt to show ribs dappled black and blue.

'Higher,' clamoured Dommie. 'But we've brought you some porn mags to cheer you up, Luke.'

'Thanks, and congratulations.' Luke turned to Red, who was opening a bottle. 'I hear you played great.'

Red laughed. 'I intend to make headlines with my mallet rather than my cock from now on.'

As usual he was miraculously dressed in off-white trousers, a cream shirt and a yellow blazer braided with pale grey silk to out-fox the young bloods in Palm Beach who were all now wearing pale blue blazers with green silk braiding. Luke winced as the champagne cork flew out.

'Blimey,' said Dommie, who was deep in a porn mag. 'It's wicked the things that girl's doing to that horse.'

'Horse seems to be rather enjoying it,' drawled Red, peering over Dommie's shoulder and handing him a glass.

'Better than being ridden by Charles Napier,' said Sebbie, holding out toothmugs for himself and Perdita. 'All his ponies will be queueing up for auditions.'

'When are they letting you out of here?' asked Red, sitting down on Luke's bed.

'I won't make the Royal Windsor on Thursday,' said Luke, taking a sip of champagne and nearly throwing up.

'Don't give it a thought,' said Red. 'Kevin already knows. He left a message on my machine asking me to stand in for you until you're OK.'

'I'm not OK,' said Dommie, fretfully putting down the porn mag and pressing the bell beside Luke's head. 'I feel awful.'

'How's Auriel?' asked Luke. The cigarette smoke clouding the room was making him feel even sicker.

'Making a movie near Deauville,' said Red. 'She gave me a lift over here. How about that stupid bitch Chessie marching up to Ricky just before the game?'

'Didn't help,' said Luke.

'I wish she'd stop spending Dad's money and I wish he'd go back to work. They had to close another plant last week. And he's going to get a lot of flak over the Pegasus. That's the third crash in three months.'

'How's Bibi?' asked Luke, who was watching Perdita watching Red, frightened yet excited by him like a mare with a stallion.

Red shrugged. 'Spending too much time covering up for Dad, which pisses Angel off. Like all Argies he expects her to wait on him hand and clay foot.'

'You wanted something, Mr Alderton?' It was Nurse O'Grady answering the bell.

'I'd like some Fernet-Brancat,' said Dommie, then, taking in her charms, 'and a large, secluded, pay bed for two if you've got a tea-break coming up.'

'I'll get you some Alka-Seltzer, but you ought to put

480

those cigarettes out,' said Nurse O'Grady and, turning to Luke with gentle reproof, 'and you oughtn't to be drinking.'

'He's not,' said Red, draining Luke's glass. 'Christ, you're good-looking. Come and take my pulse.'

Grinning, he, Seb and Dommie all held out their hands like dogs' paws.

'I'll go and get you some Alka-Seltzer,' said Nurse O'Grady, backing hastily out of the room.

'I'll help you carry it,' said Dommie, belting after her.

'Talk about Florence Night-in-the-Sack,' said Seb. Having eaten all the grapes Perdita had brought, he started on his own.

Red was opening the second bottle of Moët when the door opened and Daisy walked in. She was looking incredibly pretty, thought Luke, with her dark hair shiny and loose, her rosy cheeks just beginning to break through the layers of Clinique's Basic Beige and her mascara smudged under her eyes. She was wearing jeans and a man's blue and white striped shirt and reeked of Je Reviens.

'That's all I bloody need,' snarled Perdita.

Daisy blushed. 'I'm sorry to barge in,' she faltered. 'I just came to see how Luke was. How are you?' She handed him a bunch of roses as pink as her face. 'They don't smell much, I'm afraid. Violet's doing her A levels, but she's sent you a card and some poems by Kingsley Amis, and some Lucozade as a joke.' She plonked them down on the bed.

'Wow, that's kind,' said Luke, taking her hand and kissing her cheek. 'You are an incredibly nice lady.'

My mother, thought Perdita furiously, has a thumping great crush on Luke.

'What the fuck are you doing here anyway?' she asked Daisy.

'I went to London to see the Annual Exhibition of the Royal Society of Portrait Painters. Marvellous stuff,' mumbled Daisy, then, changing the subject, she turned to Luke. 'We were all so worried about you. Have you got a ghastly headache?'

'Not nearly as bad as ours,' said Seb, putting down the porn mag and pouring Daisy a glass of champagne. 'You look stunning today, Mrs Macleod.'

481

'This is my brother Red,' said Luke.

Oh, what a beauty, thought Daisy in wonder – that staggering perfection of feature allied to that rain-soaked red setter colouring.

'This is Perdita's mother,' added Luke.

'Jesus!' Red was shaken out of his habitual cool. 'You kidding? She must be Perdita's daughter.'

Strolling over to Daisy he idly zipped up her jeans and removed a buttercup petal from her hair. Then, grinning down at her, he murmured, 'I always figure the best way to see paintings is lying down,' as he poured her a toothmug of champagne.

'I shouldn't,' said Daisy, who'd gone absolutely scarlet. 'I'm driving.'

'Why don't you come to Paris with us?' said Red, realizing in a trice that Perdita was wildly jealous of her mother and such an invitation would irritate the hell out of her. 'If we leave in twenty minutes we can have an hour at the Louvre before it closes. My father's lent a painting to the Renoir exhibition. We can book in to the Ritz, dine at Maxim's and I'll take you to Montmartre tomorrow.'

'Come on, Mrs Macleod,' urged Seb. 'If we can't show you a good time, no-one can. We're coming back tomorrow lunchtime. We've got a four-thirty match at Cowdray.'

Seeing the two of them so brown, carefree and handsome, Daisy suddenly thought how heavenly it would be to take off.

'I can't leave Ethel and Gainsborough,' she stammered.

'Course you can,' said Seb. 'Perdita'll look after them. Haven't I been trying to seduce your mother for ages?' he added over his shoulder to an absolutely spitting Perdita. 'Dommie's been a long time with that nurse. This must be him.'

But instead Drew walked in. Taking in the number of bottles and people, he went straight up to Luke's bed.

'You poor sod, how you feeling? Besieged, I should think. You don't want this mob here, do you?'

'They're OK,' Luke grinned weakly.

'I'll get rid of them in a minute. I've just spoken to Ricky. He's had another look at Fantasma. She'll be fine. If it's any comfort, we had five ponies lame after the

482

second match. We're all going to be out of horses by the Gold Cup.'

Putting more grapes and a new book on polo pony management down on the bed, he nodded to the others.

Daisy, who'd gone as red as a peony, again pretended to gaze out of the window. She'd popped in on Luke to establish an alibi and her blood froze at the thought that Perdita might have decided to go for a walk in Windsor Park and disturbed Drew and her in the bracken.

Drew, following her, removed more buttercup petals from her hair.

'That was heavenly,' said Daisy faintly.

'It always is with you, my love,' whispered Drew. Then, more loudly: 'D'you need a lift back to Rutshire?'

'No, I've got the car,' said Daisy, which Drew already knew.

'Oh my God,' howled Red as Chessie swanned in carrying two bottles of Dom Perignon, a vast box of chocolates and a new translation of Dante's *Inferno*. 'How you've got the gall to barge in here, having nearly screwed Luke's match yesterday?'

'Good girl,' said Seb, relieving her of the bottles. 'We've just run out of drink.'

Having nodded fairly coolly to everyone else, Chessie kissed Luke. 'So sorry you had a shunt, angel, bloody bad luck.' Then, lowering her voice: 'Has Ricky been in?'

'First thing this morning,' said Luke.

'Hell, I missed him,' said Chessie furiously. 'How was he?'

'Tired,' said Luke, lying back on his pillows. The snowstorm was whirling in front of his eyes again. He couldn't handle all the cross-currents.

Chessie departed almost immediately but no-one else showed any signs of shifting.

'Your taxi's arrived, Red,' announced Seb, who'd started on Luke's chocolates as Auriel's pink helicopter landed on the lawn outside, sending patients on crutches and in wheelchairs leaping for safety.

As everyone crossed the room to have a look, Daisy noticed how green Luke had gone. Getting an envelope out of a carrier bag she timidly handed it to him.

'I thought you might like this.'

Opening it, Luke had great difficulty in not breaking down.

'Wow, it's terrific, beautiful!' he said finally in a choked voice. 'Thanks a million.'

It was a miniature of Fantasma standing fetlock deep in Ricky's watermeadows, faintly rose-pink in the rising sun, ears pricked, lovely eyes slightly suspicious and with ash woods soaring up like organ pipes behind her.

'It is good, isn't it?' said Drew, who'd already seen it in several stages, trying to subdue the pride in his voice as he ran a hand up the back of Daisy's jeaned thigh.

'It's *very* good,' said Red, topping up Daisy's glass. 'How much d'you want for that pony?'

'She's not for sale.' Luke was still gazing in wonder at the painting.

'She will be,' said Red arrogantly. 'Everyone'll be after her after yesterday.'

'They already are,' snapped Drew, who didn't like Red, 'and we ought to leave Luke alone.' Then, as a couple of nurses staggered in buckling under more bunches of flowers, 'Christ, you're popular.'

Just for a second Red's face tightened. Then he turned to Daisy: 'Did you say you'd just been to an Exhibition of the Royal Society of Portrait Painters?' he asked softly. 'What did you think of Auriel's portrait?'

'I'm afraid there was so much to look at I didn't get round to it,' said Daisy, going crimson again. Mercifully Perdita was nose to nose with Seb on the other side of the room.

'Hardly surprising,' drawled Red, just above a whisper. 'The exhibition closed yesterday. Nice one, Mrs Macleod!' Then, laughing at her discomfort, added, 'What's it worth not to tell your cantankerous daughter?'

'Oh, *please* don't,' begged Daisy.

She was saved by the arrival of José the Mexican brandishing a huge bunch of clashing mauve and salmon-pink gladioli, and by the return of Dommie and Nurse O'Grady with more flowers and her white cap on back to front.

'Rosie's coming to Paris with us,' said Dommie joyfully. 'She's off duty in ten minutes.'

'That's great,' said Seb. 'You can tell us apart, Rosie,

because I've got a scar on the inside of my right knee and I'm the one Decorum loves best.'

'He bloody doesn't,' howled Dommie, brandishing an empty bottle.

'I very sorry.' José the Mexican handed Luke the gladioli and accepted some champagne in a teacup. 'I hop you very better now.'

'Thanks a lot,' said Luke, trying to sound really grateful. The snowstorm had become a blizzard. For a second he closed his eyes.

'Hello, Luke. Ayve brought you some Lucozade and some Penhaligon's Bluebell to remaind you of Rutshire.' It was Sharon Kaputnik wafting graciousness and Jolie Madame. 'Hello, boys, hello, Red. Victor's absolutely delaighted you're goin' to be on our team. He's convinced he's got a winning formula at last.'

'Not if he's part of it,' murmured Red.

But Sharon had turned to the Mexican, feigning amazement, 'Well, hello, Hosé. Fancy seein' you here.'

Dommie giggled. 'We've got a hosé-pipe ban in Rutshire. You better keep your willy under wraps when you play down there, José.'

'Have a look at *Tatler*,' said Seb, handing Sharon a porn mag. 'I'm sure you'll find yourself in it.' But Sharon was gazing deep into José's black eyes.

Drew was talking in an undertone to Daisy. Seb and Dommie were making plans with Nurse O'Grady.

'We'll buy you something to wear,' Dommie was saying.

I want to go to Paris, thought Perdita furiously. I want to go to Maxim's and the Ritz and the Faubourg St Germain. I want to deplete some man's cheque-book.

Red was getting restless. 'We oughta go. Are you coming with us, Daisy?'

'Don't be fatuous,' said Drew sharply. 'Daisy's got a family to look after and all her painting commitments.'

'Let Daisy answer for herself,' said Seb, dabbing Penhaligon's Bluebell behind his ears.

'I really can't,' giggled Daisy.

She was saved this time by the arrival of Matron, six foot high and breathing fire. 'A pink helicopter has just landed on the lawn seriously jeopardizing the lives of the patients,' she thundered. 'I assume it belongs to one of you.'

'You suspected right, Lofty,' said Red, gathering up Daisy's roses. 'These are nice. They'll do for Auriel.'

'They're Luke's,' protested Daisy.

'Any more flowers and he'll get hay-fever. Come on, you guys.'

Matron, who'd been mouthing ineffectually, found her voice.

'Where are you taking that nurse?' she demanded.

'To Paris.' Dommie handed Matron two empties as he sauntered out.

'She's off duty,' said Seb, handing her two more.

'See you,' they chorused to Luke.

'Where are you living?' he called after Red.

'With Seb and Dommie. I'll call you, and I'll certainly call *you*.' Blowing a kiss at Daisy, Red vanished, grinning like the Cheshire cat.

Daisy was not sure who was angrier – Perdita, Matron or Drew.

Perdita disapproved of everything about Red. He shouldn't have stolen the job of his friend and fellow American, Bobby Ferraro. He shouldn't keep trying out horses, laming them, playing the hell out of them in a couple of chukkas, then handing them back saying they were no good. His grooms worked for him for next to nothing because he was so handsome, and, even worse, on the field he was the soul of dishonesty, endlessly manufacturing fouls, and avoiding a sixty, if a ball crossed the line, by tapping it back and claiming it hadn't gone over.

The twins were wild enough, but in the company of Red they became impossible, whooping it up all night, with groupies coming out of their ears.

In the weeks running up to the Gold Cup one prank followed another. The twins, for example, pinched Victor's helicopter just as he was about to fly to Frankfurt for a Board Meeting in order to scour the countryside for a missing Decorum whom they were convinced had been stolen for pit-bull fighting.

Then there was the Saturday afternoon they all got drunk round the pool and set off in Victor's open Bentley with Red lolling naked between the twins and using a road map as a figleaf. Stopping an old lady by a T-junction they asked her to show them the way to Rutminster on the map, which she did until the map slipped upwards and she ran shrieking into the nearest beechwood. Next they passed a deaf old man on a bike and asked *him* the way to Rutminster. When the old man, who was deaf, didn't answer immediately Red shot him with a starting pistol, whereupon the old man had a mini-heart attack and fell off his bike. A yokel taking Victor's car number reported the incident to the police, who needed a lot of hush money. Victor was absolutely furious.

Even worse, Red held his birthday party in Victor's house. Victor had expected two dozen people. Nearly two hundred turned up and all treated Red as the host. Decorum ate one of Victor's toupées, mistaking it for a hamster.

'This is a genuine surprise party,' Red kept saying, 'because I asked everyone when I was looped and I have no idea who's coming.'

Apocalypse boycotted the party and went to bed early. Perdita, who longed to go, felt incredibly cheated. She was fed up with working long hours for a measly salary. At nineteen she wasn't getting any younger and she wanted some fun. It further irked her that she must be the only girl in the South of England whom Red hadn't made the slightest pass at.

The afternoon after the party Apocalypse met the Tigers in the opening match of the Warwickshire Cup which was played at Cirencester and was, after the Queen's Cup and the Gold Cup, the most prestigious tournament of the year. It was Luke's first match back and he was still feeling groggy. Ricky, laid low by a vicious bout of flu, was also very weak and a lot more of their horses had fallen by the wayside in the Royal Windsor.

But, as Victor was the only member of the Tigers' team who wasn't still plastered from the night before, Apocalypse had no difficulty thrashing them 12-1 and going on to win the entire tournament. As the three-week-long toil of Gold Cup matches started at the end of June, at last giving Ricky a chance to win the first leg of his bet with Chessie, he grew increasingly remote. Perdita had abdicated any hope of his love, but it still hurt that he might be seeing Chessie on the sly. He had certainly hit miraculous form.

49

And so Apocalypse – the hottest favourites for years – came to play the Tigers in the finals of the Gold Cup. The Alderton Flyers, who'd never reconciled their differences since the Queen's Cup, were playing Kevin Coley's Doggie Dins in the second match for third place.

The long, hot summer had taken its toll. With pitches burnt brown from the hose-pipe ban and harder than the M4, a pony with four sound legs was as rare as an icicle in the tropics. Kinta was lame, Ophelia was lame, so were Tero, Willis, Sinatra, Hermia and Portia. Of the equine stars, only Spotty, Wayne and Fantasma soldiered on. Apocalypse were down to stick-and-ball horses; even fat Nigger, Ricky's oldest pony, would have to be loaded up and taken to Cowdray.

The day before the match Ricky grew increasingly picky and bloody-minded. At sunset, to avoid coming to blows, Luke took Fantasma for a gentle ride round Ricky's estate, admiring the red-gold barley and the sudden, bright mauve flash of willow herb against the darkening trees. He also noticed conkers on the horse chestnuts as big as golf balls, and realized with a shiver that the season was nearly over. After Deauville he'd have to leave Perdita and return to Florida. Earlier in the week, having a drink with Daisy, he'd asked her idly if she knew whether he was going up.

Daisy had blushed and said that on the grapevine (which, translated, meant on the pillow beside Drew) she'd heard that all the Apocalypse team were going up: Luke and Ricky to nine, Dancer to two and Perdita in a great leap to four. This meant their aggregate would be twenty-four, too high to play together any more in England. He would have to declare himself in Deauville. He and Perdita seemed to be growing further and further apart. She was very abstracted. He dared not think with whom.

Inattentive, he was nearly unseated as Fantasma gave a shrill, alarmed whinny like a skirl of bagpipes and went up on her hind legs. Luke saw nothing in the grassy ride to frighten her except an old disused tractor. She was obviously picking up Ricky's pre-match nerves. But by the time he got back to Robinsgrove her fetlock had swollen to three times its size like a vast white beachball.

Phil Bagley, summoned immediately, was totally flummoxed until he shaved away some of the hair, saw small fang marks and diagnosed adder bite.

'She won't die,' he reassured a demented Luke, 'but she certainly can't play tomorrow. I'm terribly sorry. You've lost your lethal weapon.'

'At last she's met something that bites worse than herself,' snarled Ricky.

He couldn't actually blame Luke for Fantasma not being sound, but he had to kick out at someone. Emerging trembling with rage from her box, he saw the young girl groom, who'd only started that week, gingerly trying to pick out one of Spotty's hind hooves.

'For Christ's sake,' he roared at her, 'you're supposed to lift the hoof with your left hand, and just lay it along your thigh – like this.' He picked up Spotty's foot.

Giving Ricky a reproving look for shouting, Spotty calmly removed his hoof from Ricky's thigh and placing it in the small of his back, gave a brisk shove, catching Ricky off-guard and spreadeagling him on the ground. Perdita made the mistake of screaming with laughter.

His dignity bruised more than anything else, Ricky picked himself up. 'You bloody animal.' He raised his fist at Spotty.

'Don't you touch my pony,' screamed Perdita, seizing the yard broom.

'Knock it off both of you,' yelled Luke.

'This is *my* yard.'

'And you're not fit to run it!' Luke lowered his voice. 'Jesus, man, simmer down. God knows where your head was in the final of the Queen's Cup, but we don't want a repeat performance tomorrow. Perdita's got *Champions* and *International Velvet* out of the video shop to keep you quiet. Just fuck off and watch them and give us all a break.'

For a moment Luke expected Ricky to land him one, then he swung round and stalked into the house.

Gazing mindlessly at *International Velvet* ten minutes later, Ricky felt bitterly ashamed of himself and wished he had as nice a nature as Nanette Newman. What a fucking awful example to set to Perdita and the grooms. Sitting grimly through both films, he was continually distracted by visions of Chessie, exquisite in her pale green suit, taunting him that he hadn't even won the first leg of his bet.

He woke in tears to find himself gazing at a black leaping screen. It was dark outside. He'd better go and apologize yet again. But he found Luke slumped at the kitchen table, fallen asleep over *The Maltese Cat*, a hardly touched ham sandwich on a plate beside him.

It was still impossibly hot as Ricky wandered out into the yard. The air was heavy with meadowsweet and the night-scented stock Louisa had planted in the stable tubs this summer around the geraniums. Overhead the sky was crowded with stars. There was the Swan, winging out of the Milky Way, and Pegasus soaring above the clock tower and Boötes, the Shepherd, going gently home in the west. Then Ricky caught his breath, for striding jauntily above him was the constellation Hercules. That must be a sign. Hercules had won immortality and his heart's desire by accomplishing all ten labours. Ricky had only three to achieve and the first leg, the Gold Cup, must surely be within his grasp tomorrow. Fantasma might have dropped out this evening, but the Kaputnik Tigers, after Red and the twins' roughriding, had even more horses unsound.

A whicker of affection startled him out of his trance. Wayne, as usual avid for distraction, was hanging out of his box.

'You've got a lot of work to do tomorrow.' Ricky scratched him along his bristly mane. 'We don't have Fantasma to get us out of trouble any more. You've got to outrun and ride off everyone, and forget about the Cowdray tea tent.'

Wayne's lop ears flickered as he listened to every word.

'If we win tomorrow,' went on Ricky, burying his face in the pony's silky, yellow neck, 'you can have every cucumber sandwich in the world.' Then, his voice becoming a sob, 'Oh, Wayne, just help me get my wife back.'

Next morning, after three months of drought except for the thunderstorm on the afternoon of the Queen's Cup, the temperature plummeted and torrential rain and vicious east winds stripped the roses of their petals and blew straw all round the yard. At the last moment Perdita had another screaming match with Ricky and opted to go in the helicopter with Dancer. The drive from Robinsgrove was long and dogged by roadworks. At each sign pointing to 'Polo' Ricky felt sicker.

As they passed the greying blond ruins of Cowdray Castle, with the cows and horses grazing around the battlements, he had to leap out of the car and throw up behind an oak tree.

Down by the pony lines everyone was uptight. Grooms bumped into each other and cursed as tails refused to go up and bandages wouldn't go on smoothly. Ponies were flattening their ears and lashing out at each other. At Thursday's semi-final the problem had been flies; now it was keeping them warm.

'Golly, I wish Dancer hadn't chosen black rugs; every hair shows up,' moaned Louisa.

'I scored with Red Alderton last night,' said Victor's prettiest groom. 'Fucking marvellous, marvellous fucking, but the moment it was over he looked at his watch and said, "Christ, I'm dining at Windsor Castle in half an hour!" and was out of bed like a rocket.'

Which means Red'll be hung over today, thought Louisa with satisfaction. What on earth was that din coming from the direction of Dancer's helicopter?

The row had blown up because a distracted Perdita had not only forgotten to get the second set of Apocalypse shirts out of the cleaners, but, far worse, hadn't shut the hatch of the helicopter properly so the first set of lucky shirts which had been worn in every final this season had all fallen out and were now probably being worn by rabbits and squirrels all over the Savernake Forest. Ricky was yelling at Perdita, who was half-yelling, half-crying back.

'It's no big deal,' Luke was shouting at Ricky. 'It was us won the matches, not the goddam shirts.'

Apocalypse were therefore forced to play in white shirts which matched their complexions but considerably reduced their air of menace.

'We'll all be pale riders,' said Dancer, trying to make a joke.

Sobbing, Perdita rushed off to change in the Ladies' loo.

Venturer Television, on their first day of making a documentary about Perdita, were out in force. Directed by Cameron Cook, Rupert's ex-mistress and a virago with short spiky hair and a rapacious body, they had gleefully filmed the entire row. Now they were filming another one. Perdita, because she wanted to compete with Red's army of groupies, had bought a new pair of breeches for the final.

'Oh my God, can they go any tighter?' whooped Dommie Carlisle, clapping his hands over his eyes as she came out of the Ladies. Then, peering through splayed fingers: 'And you're not wearing any pants. How wildly exciting.'

'Go and put some on,' snarled Ricky.

'It'll ruin the line,' shrieked Perdita.

'It'll ruin your reputation if they split, for Chrissake,' yelled Luke. 'Go back and change.'

The Gold Cup had been sponsored by Davidoff who'd laid on a splendid lunch in their marquee. Drew, who was umpiring and playing for Kevin Coley in the second match, had wangled Daisy a ticket. He'd also seen Sukey into hospital that morning to have her baby, ringing on the hour to see how she was. As Daisy ate lobster, prawns and ratatouille, followed by strawberries and cream, and drank a great deal of Pouilly Fumé and admired Drew's handsome profile and enjoyed his left hand on her thigh as he forked up strawberries with his right, she was desperately ashamed to find herself praying that Sukey might die in childbirth.

'My father was an MFH,' said Brigadier Hughie, who was sitting opposite. 'When I was a baby I was knocked out of my pram and nearly eaten by two hound puppies. My father said it would have been a glorious death.'

Daisy was acutely conscious of Chessie at the next table, who ate nothing but drank a great deal of excellent burgundy which matched her ravishing, red wool Yves St Laurent suit. Hardly addressing a word to Bart, she seemed wildly elated at the possibility of Ricky winning the first leg of his bet within the next two hours.

As everyone poured out to watch the final, wincing at the cold, Chessie wrapped a pale grey, fringed shawl round her shoulders. Despite a plethora of gorgeous girls yearning after Red, she was easily the most glamorous woman in the stands. What a prize for Ricky to win back, thought Daisy.

Down by the warm-up area Apocalypse, looking curiously vulnerable in their white shirts, were being geed up by Ricky. Stammering and swearing, he ran for the twentieth time through the game plan, urging on them the need to win, win, win.

'The Tigers are brilliant in attack, but they have no defence. We must attack. Your job, Dancer, is to make Victor foul.'

'He's foul enough already,' said Perdita through chattering teeth.

'Don't be fatuous,' snapped Ricky. 'And then Luke can convert the penalty. At least he will if the wind's behind him. All I want you to do for the first two chukkas, Perdita, is stick to Red till he loses his temper. He's hellishly quick, too, in the line-out. He scored two goals from there in the Warwickshire, so watch him.' Suddenly he paused in horror. 'What the fuck's Miguel O'Brien doing here?'

No-one could fail to recognize the hulking shoulders and the crinkly, greasy mop of black hair. Miguel, looking like a Mafia hood in a belted fur coat and dark glasses, was hissing instructions at Victor, Red and the twins. Bart was hovering in the background.

'I guess Bart isn't too keen on you winning the Gold Cup,' said Dancer.

'He's probably just advising Dad in the second match,' said Luke. 'Let's go and bury them.'

From the start both teams played with colossal driven intensity. Apocalypse's greatest fear was letting the twins and Red, all dazzlingly aggressive players, get loose, knowing they'd go straight down and score. But between them, Luke and Ricky managed to hold the twins, while Perdita shadowed Red the whole time, until he was screaming with rage. Then, suddenly, at the end of the second chukka Ricky hit a miraculous nearside forehand from the halfway line and the wind carried it through the goal. In the next chukka Victor, on his favourite pony, Tiger Lily, showing profound contempt for his enemy's right of way, gave away two penalties which Luke converted despite the wind. In the third chukka, after a pep-talk from Miguel, Red pulled himself together and scored twice, but was countered by Ricky picking up a short pass from Perdita and sinking a big nearside neck shot. 4-2 to Apocalypse at half-time.

'You're doing great,' Luke told his huddled team-mates. 'You're doing terrific. Just don't let up. Red's greatest buzz is to lull us into a state of false security and then pow, he'll zap us, the later the better. If we're gonna win, we've got to attack.'

Treading in the divots, running to get warm, Daisy was towed straight up to Drew by Ethel, who started singing with delight to see such a familiar friend umpiring.

'Stop sneaking, Ethel,' said Drew, who was shivering from the cold. 'Perdita's playing brilliantly. Looks as though Ricky's going to clinch the first leg of his bet.' Then, dropping his voice: 'I rang the hospital. Sukey's just had a daughter.'

'Oh, I'm so thrilled for you.'

'So am I. You and I can spend the night together. I'll go and see her straight after our match and be with you about nine.'

Chessie, who had just applied lipstick to match her red suit and who didn't seem to go blue like everyone else, drifted towards Ricky as he rode back on to the field. For a second they stared at each other, then Chessie smiled.

'Good luck, my darling, you can do it,' she murmured, pretending to tread in a divot. Then breaking off a long pale-grey strand of wool from her fringed shawl, she handed it quickly up to him. 'Wear it on your lance.'

'I love you,' Ricky called after her as he rode on. He was about to knot the wool round his stick, then realized he would be changing it and tied it to his whip. They would win now, he knew it.

Early in the fourth chukka, Red narrowed the gap with a penalty, but a second later Ricky widened it again. Galloping down the field with love in his heart, he skedaddled like a child in a bending race round Dommie, then Red, dummied passed Seb and with two magical offside forehands found the flags: 5-3. The stand went crazy. As if Chessie's favour had put a spell on him, he went on to score three more goals.

'Ricky France-Lynch has a secret weapon there,' explained Terry Hanlon, the Cowdray commentator, 'and it's called practice. There he goes – eight goals of Rutshire dynamite – soon to be nine, if my spies are telling me right.

Good to see you back on form, Ricky, oh, what a lovely shot, but it's hit the posts. And Luke Alderton gives him back the sort of pass all players dream about, and Ricky slams it in. Apocalypse lead 9-3.'

In the fifth chukka, the Flyers tried repeatedly to score, but were foiled by the dogged bloody-minded courage of Apocalypse.

On its green baize table the Gold Cup, which had been reflecting the desperate struggle on the field, seemed to be waiting to be carried home in triumph to Robinsgrove. Surely even Red couldn't score eight goals in one chukka.

But now Apocalypse changed on to stick-and-ball horses, which were all they had left. Luke, getting on to Geoffrey, the hangover horse, kept up the pressure.

'Cool it, you guys. Don't get over-confident. Red's scored seven goals in a chukka before now and his blood's up. Just keep rattling them, stop them scoring, above all stick to Red, Perdita, and we can do it,' he exhorted, clamping a great hand on Dancer and then on Perdita's back.

Without Fantasma he felt like a mercenary who's run out of ammo in enemy territory, but he kept his fears to himself. Silently Ricky mounted Wayne. He was seven minutes away from his first leg and he didn't dare to hope. As they rode out for the last chukka their shirts were no longer white but black with mud – Apocalypse again. Already they could hear the Midhurst town band warming up for the presentation; 'Four horsemen, riding, riding, riding'.

'Come on, Nigger,' said Perdita clamping her legs round her fat black pony. 'Why are you so fucking slow?'

'You better rename him Snowflake if he wins Best Playing Pony,' said Luke with a grin. 'It's being presented by some African prince. Oh, Jesus! No!'

The others followed his gaze.

'Shit,' whispered Ricky.

'Oh, my God,' gasped Perdita in horror, for the Tigers were riding towards them on four of the most beautiful, glossy, well-muscled thoroughbred ponies she had ever seen. 'Who the hell are they?'

'Inecita, Cecilia, Leila and Carmen – in a word,' said Luke bleakly. 'I don't believe it, I simply do not believe it. Miguel must have flown them over.'

He cantered up to Red. 'What the fuck are you doing on those ponies?'

Red grinned, white teeth flashing in a mud-caked face. 'Dad was worried we were out of horses so he lent us four of his.'

'Why isn't he playing them in his own match?'

Red laughed. 'He's so unselfish he thought our need was greater. After all, he really doesn't want Ricky to win the Gold Cup.'

'And how does Victor feel riding his worst enemy's horses?'

'I guess he hasn't noticed and he won't care as long as he wins.'

The sixth chukka was crucifixion. On four matchless horses, who had each won Best Playing Pony in the Argentine Open, there was no defence. It was like putting three-legged bulldogs against greyhounds. And from the way Red and the twins were riding them, it was obvious they'd tried them out several times before. From the first throw-in Red scored goal after goal until the crowd, most of whom had no idea what had happened, were yelling on their feet. A wide-angled shot from Seb thirty seconds from the end of the match had the Tigers in front and now they had the wind behind them. Ricky was near suicide.

'There's still time,' beseeched Luke. 'For Christ's sake, settle down, you guys.'

Then Victor, failing to control Inecita, barged across Dancer's line. Whoever converted would tie up the score and take the match into extra time.

'I'll take it,' said Ricky.

'You sure?' asked Luke.

Dancer opened his mouth to protest, then realizing Ricky needed the ultimate responsibility, shut it again.

Ricky turned, and for a moment stared at Chessie, who pointedly held up two crossed fingers; then he cantered Wayne round in a perfect arc before a totally silent crowd. Forward went his stick then back, then down it swooped like an eagle, meeting the ball perfectly so it flew straight and true between the posts. Then at the last moment a gust of wind tossed it against the right goal post and it bounced back. Apocalypse lunged forward, but the bell had gone.

Perdita burst into floods of tears. 'We've been robbed! We've been bloody robbed!'

Luke cantered over and pulled her against his chest. Geoffrey and Nigger were so exhausted they just stood still, leaning against each other.

The twins, looking very sheepish, rode up to shake hands, followed by an openly laughing Red.

'Fuck off, the lot of you,' said Luke.

With his arm round Perdita's shoulders he rode back to the pony lines where all the Apocalypse grooms were in tears and Ricky was sitting in the boot of his car, head in his hands, absolutely stunned.

Perdita threw her arms round him. 'They stabbed us in the back,' she sobbed frantically. 'Oh, poor, poor Ricky.'

'Why don't you bugger off?' snapped Luke to Cameron Cook and Venturer who were still avidly filming.

Putting a coat round Perdita's shoulders and leaving her with Dancer and Daisy, who'd just arrived, Luke went off in search of his father whom he found putting on his knee pads for the second match.

'You son-of-a-bitch,' he roared. 'We had it in the bag and we were robbed. I've always stuck up for you, but, by God, I'm well and truly in the enemy camp now.'

Bart looked up, as coldly angry as Luke was inflamed. 'I know how to guard my own,' he said softly. 'It's my marriage I'm fighting for. You're the one who betrayed me, right? Publicly helping Ricky to win his bet.'

'What bet?' demanded Luke. 'I don't know anything about a bet.'

'You'd better ask your friend Dancer.'

50

That night Luke had a blazing row with Dancer.

'I've been working my ass off all summer trying to help Ricky win a bet everyone seems to have known about but me. Dad said I was being treacherous coming over here. I'd no idea how treacherous, and that son-of-a-bitch Ricky was in on it too.'

Dancer shook his head vehemently. 'It weren't Ricky's fault. You know how pissed off he was when I hired you.

He wanted to win the Gold Cup without any help from the Aldertons. An' anyway your Dad started it by nicking Ricky's wife in the first place.'

'Why the fuck didn't you level with me?'

'You wouldn't have come,' said Dancer disarmingly. 'I knew you was too effical. But I also knew you was the only guy who could sort out Ricky's game, and Perdita's too, for that matter. I knew how you felt about her, so I was doin' you a favour.'

'Bullshit,' howled Luke. 'You had no idea how I felt about her. I've been bloody conned.'

But such is the nature of polo that all the players in the Gold Cup drama had to meet in the Cowdray Park Challenge Cup next week when the Tigers triumphed yet again. Luke, who didn't believe in prolonging rows, was speaking to his father again. On a totally recovered Fantasma, he was also big-hearted enough to set up all five goals scored by Red in the International at the end of July when America beat England 8–3, mostly because Ricky had lost so much form.

Luke was worried about Ricky, who'd sunk into the deepest depression, but even more so about Perdita, who was very distant and most uncharacteristically subdued. She wasn't even excited when the whole Apocalypse team swanned off to Deauville for three weeks in August for the French and then the World Championships. Dancer had put them up in the five-star Hotel Normandie and as they wouldn't have to belt back to Robinsgrove after every match, they would have time to gamble at the casino, swim in the sea and enjoy race meetings, barbecues and endless parties. Deauville was polo at its most ritzy and glamorous. Luke hoped he would have a chance to get Perdita on his own, but he was filled with unease.

And so everyone crossed the Channel to Deauville. In one of the first matches of the French Championships the Tigers were drawn against a local team whom they were expected to thrash.

Polo in Deauville tends to take twice as long and start twice as late. The two grounds are situated inside the racecourse and accessible only between races. Nor can a chukka be started or a penalty taken while a race is going on. And, if French chic is achieved, like genius, by a supreme capacity for taking pains, the French players certainly took even longer than Red Alderton to smooth down their skin-tight breeches and tuck in their exquisitely cut polo shirts before taking the field.

As usual therefore, the Tigers' match started late. Victor was champing at the delay because he had to fly to Geneva straight afterwards for a business meeting. Red was cold and wanted to go back to bed. It was a raw August day with a vicious breeze coming off the sea. Luke was still down at the stables waiting for the vet. As one of the French umpires had failed to turn up, Perdita was summoned down from the stands to take his place. She was very nervous because her French was extremely limited and she'd never umpired a match that big. Fortunately Jesus, the other umpire, was highly experienced.

Because of the continued heavy rain in the past week, which had nearly washed the sponsor's tent into the sea, the smooth green pitch was churned up in an instant. Language grew worse as ponies slid all over the place and the ball hit divots and bounced awkwardly.

Red promptly started playing dirty. No-one was better at pulling up in mock horror and pretending an opposition player had crossed his right of way. Marking him was a charming French boy who had bought Perdita a drink at the Hotel Normandie the previous night. He couldn't be a day over eighteen. Red rode him off so fiercely that he was almost sitting on the French boy's saddle.

'Do that again,' said Perdita sharply, 'and I'll blow a foul on you.'

Ignoring her, Red increased the angle.

Perdita blew her whistle and looked at Jesus, who disliked Red and had once been sacked by Victor; he nodded in agreement. Pointing to the sixty-yard mark Perdita awarded the French side a penalty, a free hit sixty yards from the goal line.

Red promptly launched into such a storm of abuse that Perdita upped the penalty to forty yards.

'Don't give me that shit,' yelled Red. 'Bloody woman umpire.'

Jesus nodded at Perdita, who upped the penalty to

thirty, and left her, Jesus and Red all screaming at each other.

Although a race had just started, racegoers in the stands had their binoculars firmly focused on the far more interesting row in the middle of the polo field. As Perdita awarded a goal to the other side, Red let rip.

'You fucking bitch, don't you land that number on me.'

'Off,' screamed Perdita, forgetting to consult Jesus.

'You've got to be joking,' snarled Red. 'When you look at the video, you'll see it wasn't a foul.'

'When *you* look at the video,' shouted Perdita, 'you'll see me sending you off!'

'Off,' agreed Jesus happily.

'Oh, c'mon, don't be silly, Perdita,' said the twins. Next moment the whole side, including Victor on his beloved Tiger Lily, were circling her like the tigers in Little Black Sambo. Any minute they'd turn into melted butter. Not even when all the Tigers' grooms in their black jeans and orange and black striped shirts threatened to pull Perdita off her pony would she give in.

'You can't do this to your old friends,' pleaded Dommie. 'Victor's paying us two grand a win. If we get knocked out now we lose a fortune. I won't be able to buy Rosie an engagement ring.'

'You're over-reacting,' Seb told her, furiously.

'I am not,' screamed Perdita. 'Dommie and Ben Napier sent me off when I swore at the Prince of Wales. Alejandro's elder son in Argentina was suspended for four months for arguing. Count yourself bloody lucky,' she added to Red. 'Off! *Vamos*! *Va't'en*, go on! Scram!'

The French side took advantage of playing four against three to clinch the match. Soon word was sizzling round the polo community that not only had Red been sent off but the Mighty Tigers, winners of the Gold Cup, had been knocked out in the first round. The Tigers stormed off to the French polo authorities who, after a good deal of Gallic shrugging, said there was nothing they could do.

Red was so angry he would have flown straight back to Paris to join Auriel, but he was committed to play in a charity match with the Prince of Wales the following afternoon which Auriel was flying down to watch.

That afternoon was another bitterly cold day. Perdita, who'd squandered the entire grand Luke had given her to buy clothes on bikinis, shorts and sundresses before she left England, was glad she had pinched two cashmere jerseys which had recently found their way into Daisy's wardrobe. Her need was much greater than her mother's. She couldn't think why Daisy was always moaning about money if she could afford expensive clothes like these.

Drew Benedict, freezing in the stands, was absolutely livid when Perdita rolled up wearing the dark brown cashmere polo neck he'd given Daisy last week, but he couldn't say anything, particularly as Sukey was breast-feeding little Charlotte under a Puffa beside him. He wished Sukey'd do it in the hotel. He was finding her presence at Deauville and the crying of little Charlotte increasingly irksome.

Dommie Carlisle, scuttling into the stands just before the 4.15 race, had to forgive Perdita for putting the Tigers out of the Cup because he wanted to show her the huge emerald engagement ring he'd just bought for Rosie, the Irish nurse.

'Lovely. Match her eyes,' said Perdita, relieved to be forgiven.

'Where's Luke?' asked Dommie.

'Gone to look at his great uncle's grave or something boring. Where's Rosie?'

'Having a kip. We didn't get in till six o'clock this morning. Seb's gone to a bloodstock sale. I've had a bet on this race.' Dommie trained his binoculars on the race track.

'I say,' he said, lowering his voice, 'Seb and I found the spitting image of Tayger Lily pulling a milk cart in Le Havre. We tidied him up and sold him to Victor for £10,000 as Tayger Lily's half-brother. He's as quiet as a riding-school horse – perfect for Victor. That's how I afforded Rosie's ring.'

'You *are* awful,' said Perdita, giggling. 'You'll get caught one day. Christ, they start late here.'

Dommie moved on to the subject of the Fancy Dress birthday party Victor was giving for Sharon at the Casino that night. The theme was Medieval and Mystery.

'Rosie's going as Robert the Bruce's spider,' he said.

'Luke won't like that,' said Perdita. 'He's terrified of spiders. I thought I'd mug an onion man and go as the Lady of Shallot. I bet Chessie and Auriel and Sharon will spend fortunes on their costumes. Here they come at last,' she added, trying to sound detached as Red led the players on to the field.

In the first chukka, Sharon's handsome Mexican, José, had a fall and lay flat on his back in the middle of the field. A second later his great black-clad whale of a wife had floundered on to the pitch shrieking and moaning and followed by six children and a nanny. By the time they had reached him, however, José had jumped up, dusted himself down and remounted, which meant the poor wife, nanny and children had to flounder desperately back to avoid getting run over by Red.

'So uncool to behave like that,' said Perdita scornfully.

'Christ, Red's playing badly,' said Dommie.

'How good d'you reckon he really is?' asked Perdita.

'If he's on form we win, it's as simple as that.'

I loathe and detest Red, thought Perdita, but he was the only player she watched on the field.

In the next chukka Red bore down on José, attempting to hook him and getting his pony's legs entangled with the back legs of José's bay pony. Red was so far out of his saddle that he couldn't save himself or his pony and crashed to the ground with both ponies on top of him. There was a horrible pause as the ponies struggled to their feet.

'He's moving. He's OK,' said Dommie.

'He's not,' whispered Perdita.

Auriel, who'd just rolled up flanked by minders, ran gracefully on to the field as though she was doing classical ballet, throwing her arms round Red, begging him in her deep throaty tenor to be all right, and crying loudly, but not enough to make her mascara run: 'Oh, Reddie, my darling. Oh, Reddie.'

'Steady, go,' giggled Dommie, pretending to play a violin. 'Stupid old ham.'

'We must ambulance him to hospital at once,' moaned Auriel.

Both Venturer and the *paparazzi*, out in force for the

Prince of Wales, were capturing the full tragic scene when, like an unleashed Dobermann, Perdita erupted on to the pitch.

'Back off, you fucking geriatrics, he belongs to me,' she screamed, sending two French doctors, two umpires and Auriel flying.

With absolutely no thought for her mascara, she flung her arms round Red sobbing unrestrainedly. 'Please, please don't die. I love you so much.'

'Can I have that in writing?' said a muffled voice.

Leaping away, Perdita realized that Red was quite all right and shaking with unrepentant laughter. Despite her frantic struggles, his hand clamped over the back of her neck and he pulled her down with all the muscle in his forearm and carried on kissing her until an enraged David Waterlane, who was umpiring, ordered him to stop fooling around and get on with the game.

'Oh dear, oh dear,' murmured Dommie to a boot-faced Drew. 'I wondered when that was going to happen. It was only a matter of time. Shits rush in where angels fear to tread. What the hell is Luke going to say?'

Wriggling out of Red's embrace Perdita fled across the pitch with Venturer's film crew pounding after her.

'Hang on a second,' yelled Cameron Cook.

'If you think you're going to re-shoot that . . . ' howled Perdita. 'Oh no!' The little bridge over the race track had just closed and she wouldn't be able to get across until after the next race.

Ignoring the shifting rainbow of jockeys' silks in the distance and the announcement that they were under starter's orders, she scrambled over the five-foot railing, tore across the track and only just missed being trampled to death by the 4.45.

Several apoplectic race officials now joined in the chase as well as Venturer and the *paparazzi*. But Perdita was too swift for them. Shopkeepers, raising their blinds after the long afternoon siesta, paused in amazement as this fierce Valkyrie with wild eyes, inflamed cheeks and flying hair pounded past sending holiday makers for six, running until she reached the Hotel Normandie with its hundreds of white balconies, fretting flags and brilliantly coloured flowerbeds. She had just locked herself into her

503

room with a 'Do Not Disturb' sign on the door when the telephone rang.

'Hi, Perdita,' said the *Sun*. 'You taken Auriel's place?'

'Fuck off!' Perdita slammed the receiver down, took it off the hook and threw herself down on her bed in utter confusion.

Red had kissed her as though he meant it. She could still feel the burning heat of his lean, far from languid, body and smell the heady mix of horses' sweat and Givenchy for Men, and see the thick, dark eyelashes fanning the flawless cheekbones when for a terrible moment she'd thought he was dead. Then, when she had finally opened her eyes, his had been already open and full of amusement and devilry at the shattering effect he was having on her. The earth had moved so far she'd need a Pickford's van to bring it back.

Impossibly restless, she paced the room. In the mirror she looked deranged and feverish. Tearing off her clothes she clutched her breasts, fingering her nipples, as hard as biro tops, wondering what they would feel like to Red, running her hands over her waist and hips, holding back her head until her white-gold hair cascaded down to caress the cleft of her bottom. What the hell could she wear at the fancy dress party tonight? Everyone else would be so glamorous and expensively dressed. Draping herself with onions as the Lady of Shalott seemed not only tame but malodorous. Suddenly she had a brainwave. It was certainly medieval. It would infuriate Auriel, shock Sukey, enrage Luke, Drew and Ricky, if he arrived in time, and certainly require the kind of daring Red would admire. Dialling room service, she ordered a bottle of champagne.

Luke, feeling he needed a day on his own, had gone to visit the Normandy beachheads. He went first to St Laurent-sur-Mer and stood by the plaque that marked the spot where the first wave of US troops had fought their way doggedly up the sandbanks. Below him lay Omaha Beach, platinum-blond as Perdita's hair, the stormy, grey waters of the Channel the same colour as her eyes. Then he wandered round the beautiful, American graveyard, admiring the tidy, white crosses and the lawns as greenly immaculate as the Deauville polo fields. Passing the graves of two Roosevelts, he put a bunch of red-and-mauve asters on the grave of his mother's eldest brother.

Afterwards he drove to Point du Hoc, where his grandfather had been one of Colonel Rudder's American Rangers who had stormed its perilously steep cliffs and seized and held its German fortifications under terrible bombardment. Out of forty-eight, fourteen had survived intact. His grandfather had been killed – only for his family to learn later that the Rangers had attacked the wrong promontory. Was he, like them, barking up the wrong tree?

I'm alive, they're dead, thought Luke. He had hoped that seeing the setting for so much greater a tragedy than his might diminish his heartache, but tears kept embarrassingly filling his eyes. Facts had to be faced. He loved Perdita hopelessly. Even the brief few hours away from her today had been an agony. Her tantrums and indifference were better than being without her.

He bought a salami roll and a beer, sat on the front and wrote postcards to his mother and his grandmother telling them what he had seen. A big, black, stray dog wandered up, reminding him painfully of Leroy and he gave it most of his roll. If Leroy was in Europe he might miss Perdita less. At least he wouldn't have to sleep alone every night.

He wished there was another war he could fight in, or that he could run away and lose himself visiting Chateaubriand's house and Proust's birthplace, then drive to Paris and on to the South of France and Italy. But his heartache would follow him.

He knew with a terrible foreboding, as the French must have waited for the Germans to sweep across Europe, that Red was going to sweep Perdita off her feet at any minute. He'd seen many, many girls fall in love with Red before and recover, but Perdita was so vulnerable because she was so passionate and uncompromising and he knew in the end it would destroy her.

As he walked to the edge of the cliffs the waters swirled below him. It would be so easy to jump. Would anyone really mind? Christ, he must get a grip on himself. There were grooms to be paid, horses to be fed, Leroy waiting patiently and probably with ebbing hope in Florida and there was Apocalypse to be steered to victory in the French

505

Championships. He had promises to keep and miles to go before he slept.

Returning to the Normandie he felt that sick churning in the belly that was chronic these days. Perdita's key wasn't hanging downstairs and she wouldn't answer her telephone. Ignoring the 'Do Not Disturb' notice, he banged on the door.

'You OK? It's Luke.'

'Piss off. I'm trying to get some sleep.'

'Let me in.'

'I'll see you at the party.'

'How are you getting there?'

'I'll make my own way. For God's sake, leave me alone.'

51

Two hours later Sharon Kaputnik's Medieval and Mystery party, held in one of the big rooms of the casino, was well under way. The clatter of roulette chips and the cries of the croupiers could be heard from the gambling tables next door. Rich red velvet curtains blotted out an angry grey sea. Huge chandeliers lit up knights, kings, Black Princes, Robin Hoods, crusaders, wizards, friars and abbesses. Shrieks of delight greeted each new costume. Dommie Carlisle, with his blond hair brushed down into a pudding basin and a card round his neck saying 'We thrashed the fuckers at Agincourt', had come as Henry V. Seb, daggers sticking out of him like a hedgehog, was supposed to be Thomas à Becket. Ben Napier was wildly miscast as a jester. David Waterlane, too unimaginative to invent a costume and too mean to hire one, clanked round in one of his own suits of armour flown over from Rutminster Park. Luke, stripped to the waist, his face and massive torso streaked with grey paint and splodges of green for lichen, his hair turned metallic grey by spray, had come as a gargoyle.

'Rather sexy,' drawled Chessie, 'but you ought to be spouting water rather than wisdom.' For once free of Bart's chaperonage, she was looking sensational in clinging dampened see-through green as Queen Guinevere.

'I hardly think Bart has the moral rectitude necessary for

Arthur,' giggled Seb, bouncing up and grabbing Chessie's waist from behind, 'but bags I be Lancelot. My brother is so thick with that nurse I've got no-one to hunt with any more.'

Sukey, who had good legs, broad shoulders and not much waist, was looking unusually good as Joan of Arc.

'Can I come and burn my cakes at your stake?' said Bas who was dressed as Alfred the Great.

Juan O'Brien, who had misunderstood the word Mystery, had turned up as Miss Marple in a pull-on felt hat, a beige coat and skirt and a spy glass with which he was examining Chessie's nipples.

With shrieks of restrained excitement, wearing a long blue dress and a wimple like an upended ice-cream cornet, Sharon was opening her presents.

'What's she supposed to be: Self-made Marion?' Chessie asked Sebbie.

'A damsel in distress.'

'Not much to be distressed about with all those presents,' added Chessie enviously, as Sharon drew a diamond necklace glittering like the Pleiades out of a red leather box. 'Victor's already given her an Ingres.'

'She's distressed,' said Seb, 'because Perdita has pipped her to the post with Red.'

'Shut up,' said Dommie, filling up their glasses. 'Luke's coming. And I don't like the way our patron's fratting with the enemy.'

Victor, encased in a scarlet dragon's costume which showed off his pot belly, was talking to Drew who, in black tights and a white tunic with a red cross painted on the front and back, had come as St George.

'Perhaps St George will wrest Lady Sharon from Victor's clutches,' said Chessie.

Victor, very smug because his pharmaceutical empire had found a cure for scurf, was slagging off Bart.

'Two more plants closed this week,' he was saying gleefully, 'and the families of the Pegasus crash victims are suing Alderton Airlines for reckless homicide. Bart's in Frankfurt to effect a merger with Marcos, who must be the biggest aeroplane company in the world. Once they get a look at Bart's balance sheets, they'll pull out.'

'He'll recover,' said Drew. It seemed ridiculous discussing

high finance with a dragon, particularly as Victor's breath from gazpacho at lunchtime was as fiery as any flames.

'You can't pour every penny into polo and stay on course,' gloated Victor. 'He's ripe for take-over. Have you seen my new pony, Tiger Lily's half-brother?'

'Drew's so fucking oily with patrons, I'm sure he's going to pinch Victor,' said Seb, grabbing an angel-on-horseback and hurling it at Drew. Drew, wishing Daisy were there, ducked to avoid it. That afternoon Victor had offered him serious money, three times what he was earning with David Waterlane, for a three-year contract to play in Palm Beach and England. He was very tempted. David was mean and capricious and wouldn't commit himself beyond next year.

'You'd enjoy Palm Beach, Drew,' said Sharon, joining them. 'You wouldn't have to bring your waife and kiddies if you didn't want to.'

Drew ignored the innuendo. He wished he could take Daisy. In a minute he'd make some excuse and go and ring her, but as he'd promised to keep an eye on Perdita, he'd better wait until she arrived. He didn't trust Red an inch. The bastard had just rolled up looking very pleased with himself in a floppy white silk shirt, brown tights to emphasize his long legs, and brown suede thigh boots.

'Who are you supposed to be, Doublet and Pantihose?' Chessie, suddenly rigid with hostility, asked him.

'Iago, I thought.'

Chessie shivered. 'Inspired casting. Just keep away from me.'

'Try and keep me near!' Red drifted off towards the gambling tables. He had just bought $100,000 worth of chips and was planning to put the lot on *noire deux*, which was Perdita's normal place in the Apocalypse team. If it came up he would make a play for her. It would irritate so many people: Ricky, Luke, his mother, his father, Auriel. He watched the colours merging as the wheel spun round. He'd always been turned on by stiff opposition, he'd make a play for her anyway.

'*Rien ne va plus*,' said the croupier.

Looking at his watch for the hundredth time, Luke was distracted by a spectacularly good-looking man, who'd just come in wearing a dark suit, and was talking to Cameron Cook, who was hovering with a film crew.

It had to be Rupert Campbell-Black. Luke, in his humility, was a passionate admirer of beauty, particularly in humans. Looking at Red had always given him intense pleasure, but there was something about the angles of Rupert's face, the long, dark blue eyes, the casual elegance of the body, the exquisite shape of the sleek, blond head and wide, smooth forehead, that set him apart from everyone else. Unlike Red, he was also totally unselfconscious. Luke felt his eyes drawn like a magnet.

'How's it going?' Rupert asked Cameron.

'Hairy. Sending Red off yesterday, getting into a clinch with him this afternoon. Christ knows what she'll do next. The material's god-given, but the press are getting all of it. She is under contract. We need something exclusive. I'm supposed to be interviewing her at dawn tomorrow.'

'I'll speak to her,' said Rupert. 'We're not standing any shit.'

'Having said that,' admitted Cameron, 'she does look superb in the rushes, and so natural, particularly when she's mad.'

'What about Red? Is he going to ditch Auriel for Perdita? He's such a little shit.'

Cameron laughed. 'He rather reminds me of you.'

'Don't be ridiculous,' said Rupert coldly.

'I'd better go and see what's happened to her,' said Cameron, going towards the door.

Immediately her place was taken by Chessie, but as she kissed Rupert, his face was even colder and he almost flinched away.

'It's been so long,' Chessie flushed slightly. 'I never see any of Ricky's old friends these days. Drew, Bas, you, Billy, Ronnie Ferguson. None of you ask us to dinner any more. You might have asked us to your wedding. I haven't even met Taggie yet. No-one could be as divine as everyone says she is. Bart's due tomorrow. Why don't you and Taggie have dinner with us?'

'No, thanks,' said Rupert curtly. Then, lowering his voice: 'Chessie darling, have you no idea of the animosity you aroused when you ran out on Ricky?'

'For Christ's sake,' hissed Chessie, 'you ran out on enough people.'

'Not wives I didn't. Helen walked out on me.'

'Aren't you glad she did?'

'Of course. I never dreamed such happiness existed. But you've totally fucked Ricky up. You never wrote to him when Will died, never forgave him.'

'Why should I? It was all his fault.' Chessie was getting hysterical. 'He was dead drunk.'

'Having been deliberately wound up by you. Then you abandon him to the most ghastly prison sentence, then to coming back to the loneliness of Robinsgrove. I was there when he came out. It was crucifixion. I know what it was like being on my own at Penscombe.'

'You had women coming out of your ears.'

'I hadn't met Taggie then. Ricky's a one-woman man, and did you know he's never worn anything but a black tie since Will died? Not a week passes without him putting flowers on Will's grave, or getting Daisy Macleod to do it.'

'That frump,' said Chessie sharply.

'She's sweet,' said Rupert, 'and that's a typical reaction. Bloody bitch in the manger. You want to carry on shored up by Bart's billions and at the same time dangle Ricky on a string. All this stupid business about the Gold Cup and winning the Westchester is carving him up. Let him go. He'll never be rich enough for you.'

'You've never been poor,' said Chessie furiously. 'You get used to living in a gilded cage.'

'You could fly out, but you're too fucking spoilt, so you go on prick-teasing.'

Chessie burst into tears. Suddenly realizing that everyone was listening to them, Rupert put an arm round her shoulder.

'Ha, I like that,' said Red, who'd just come out of the roulette room. Tapping the *Sunday Mirror* photographer on the shoulder, he whispered, 'Get some close-ups of Rupert and my stepmother.'

But even as the photographer sidled up and surreptitiously started snapping away, some sixth sense made Rupert turn and reach out a long arm. Practically garrotting the photographer, he removed the film from the camera and pocketed it.

The photographer was livid.

'I 'ad some nice pix of Lady Shar and Pouf the Magic Dragon on that roll. Give it back. He put me up to it,' he added sulkily, nodding at Red.

'I'm sure,' said Rupert. 'You can still fuck off.'

Wiping her eyes on her flowing green sleeves, Chessie pulled herself together.

'This is my stepson, Red,' she said bleakly.

'A step in the wrong direction,' said Rupert witheringly. 'What were you going to do with that film?' he asked Red. 'Brandish it in front of your father or my wife? With stepchildren that evil, Chessie, I'm even more amazed you stay with Bart. This one's more anxious to make a fast buck than a gay rabbit. I'm staggered he's allowed himself to be prised away from Auriel's bank balance for a second.'

Red, who was seldom lost for words, was frantically thinking up a devastating reply when suddenly Rupert's face lost all its animosity and contempt. In the doorway, moving from foot to foot with shy pleasure like an Irish wolfhound, stood a very tall, slim girl with dark hair and huge, grey eyes.

'Taggie – I must go,' said Rupert, dropping a kiss on Chessie's cheek. 'Sorry I gave you a hard time, angel. I just don't want Ricky screwed up any more.'

Leaving a spitting Red, desperate for reassurance Chessie sought out Luke.

'You OK?' he asked.

'Yes, no. Where the hell's Ricky? Isn't he coming?'

'I guess not. Chessie, Dancer didn't tell me about your bet with Ricky. I'd never have played for him, if I'd known. I wouldn't do that to Dad.'

'I know you wouldn't,' said Chessie softly. 'Doesn't your arm ache from holding a torch for Perdita?'

'I guess I've got strong arms.'

Chessie smoothed a blob of grey-green paint on his chest. 'You're strong everywhere. Has anyone ever told you quite how attractive you are? I could get you over Perdita.'

Luke laughed. 'That would really complicate things. But thanks for the offer.'

'I love complications,' sighed Chessie. 'They make everything so much more exciting.'

*

The party roared on. A huge amount of champagne was drunk. Soon the best costume would be judged and it would be time for dinner.

Sharon, having got no change out of Drew, was nose to nose on a window seat with José the Mexican, whose whale of a wife had been left at his hotel and whose English had improved dramatically in the last month.

Seb Carlisle, high as a kite now, was also sitting on the window seat, pretending to read *Horse and Hound*, but actually translating for Dommie and Rosie everything Sharon was saying.

'Ay'm not prepared to be serious, Hosé,' he mouthed to his audience. 'Ay'm so muddled, you must gave me tame. Yes, I would adore to live in Mehico.' Seb grinned wickedly, 'But not all the year round.'

The others were in hysterics. Rosie, as Robert the Bruce's spider, was wearing a black body stocking and hood. Out of her blacked-up face, her white teeth sparkled and her green eyes gleamed.

'I love you,' she told Dommie softly.

'I love you,' said Dommie fingering the square box with the emerald, which had cost every penny from the sale of Tiger Lily's putative half-brother.

'I don't know what got into you this afternoon.' Rosie ran her hand over his chest. 'It must have been because I was half-asleep and not expecting you that I was so relaxed. Being a good Catholic girl, I suppose I've always felt guilty about sex before marriage. But I never dreamed it could be as wonderful as it was this afternoon.' Lifting his hand, she kissed all Dommie's fake rings. 'I have to confess, I lied to you about coming before, just hoped it would get all right. I'm so glad you missed me, and couldn't keep away. You were so in control and yet so sensitive, and your cock.'

But she didn't get any further. Dommie had pulled Seb off the bench beside Sharon and José and hit him across the room.

'You bastard,' he yelled. 'You didn't go near any blood-stock sale this afternoon.'

'I bloody did, too,' yelled back Seb. 'I bought a grey three year old.'

'You bloody didn't. You went to bed with Rosie and pretended to be me.'

'Ouch,' yelled Seb, stubbing his toe on David Water-lane's armoured foot, as he scrambled to his feet. 'I'm not dancing with him later.'

'Don't send me up,' roared Dommie. 'She's the only girl I've ever loved.'

'I can understand why,' said Seb.

Dommie was about to hit him again, when suddenly Seb said, 'Kerist, look at that.'

'Don't change the subject, bloody John Thomas à Becket.' Dommie grabbed Seb's cassock.

'No really, it's worth a break,' protested Seb.

For a second Dommie swung round.

'Jesus.' He let go of Seb.

A clatter of hooves was greeted with whoops of excitement, laughter and shrieks of joy and horror as, ducking her head to avoid the top of the door, Perdita rode side-saddle into the room on Spotty. Dressed – or rather undressed – as Lady Godiva, her flowing blond hair concealed very little.

'Christ, what a body,' said Bas in wonder. 'No wonder Ricky kept it under wraps.'

'Disgraceful,' spluttered Sukey.

'I always suspected she was a natural blonde,' said Seb, sidling away from Dommie.

Miss Marple, eyes on stalks, stalked across the room, spyglass poised.

'I think Lady Godiva was a relation of mine,' said David Waterlane.

'The dollar has absolutely no defence against the controlled yen,' said Victor, still encased inside his dragon's head.

I have an uncontrolled yen for that girl, thought Red.

'Thank you,' said Perdita, accepting a glass of champagne from a drooling waiter.

Spotty, incurably greedy, buried his red-and-white nose in a large plate of sausage rolls, raising his upper lip like a camel when he encountered the sausage. The photographers were going berserk.

'Whatever you do, keep them rolling,' screamed Cameron Cook to the Venturer cameramen.

Fighting his way through the screaming overexcited crowd, Drew pulled off his white tunic to display a splendidly muscular torso.

'Get off that pony, Perdita,' he said softly.

'Put her in the stocks,' shouted Seb.

But Luke was too quick for any of them. Stripped to the waist, unable to give her his shirt, he snatched up a primrose-yellow shawl which had been left hanging over a chair and threw it round Perdita's shoulders.

'Take Spotty back to the stables,' he ordered Red and, dragging Perdita off, carried her screaming, kicking and struggling back to the Normandie, followed by a pack of reporters baying as joyfully as bloodhounds.

Up in her room he threw her on to the bed, chucked a towel at her and leant against the door, not trusting himself to speak. Perdita had never seen him so angry. It was as though the door to a blast furnace had suddenly been wrenched open. Paint was streaked across his chest, arms and face, where it had settled grimly in grooves on either side of his mouth, darkened his eyelashes and smudged even blacker rings under his eyes. His spiky, gold hair was beginning to escape the silver spray. He looked like the only miner to escape alive after some prolonged and terrible pit disaster.

'You drink all this?' he roared, picking up the empty bottle of Moët on the dressing-table.

Perdita nodded.

'What the hell for? Are you crazy?'

'I was making a fucking statement. I came as Lady Godiva because I can't afford a costume. The only way I can compete with all those rich bitches is when I'm naked. Half of them wouldn't dare show off their bodies. They need all those three thousand pound dresses to hide the bulges.'

'What about that grand I gave you last week?'

'Wouldn't buy a bra top round here. I'm fed up with being the best woman player in the world, and so fucking poor. It's no fun gambling in the playground of the rich when you haven't got a bean. I've never had any help from my bloody family.'

'Bullshit,' yelled Luke. 'Daisy never stops making sacrifices for you.'

'She's a whore,' said Perdita tonelessly. 'You don't know what it's like being illegitimate, with no father to relate to.'

The next moment Luke had yanked her to her feet and swung her round to look into the mirror. Grabbing her face, he pulled down her eyes so the blood-red sockets showed, then with the other huge hand pulled her mouth upwards at the corner and squashed her cheeks together, like some hideously deformed cretin.

'Howdya like to be born like that?'

'Well, I wasn't,' said Perdita, wriggling so frantically the shawl slid to the floor.

'Lots of people fucking were,' Luke held her steady. 'You, on the other hand, were given everything: spellbinding talent, charm if you'd bother to use it, a beautiful face, a body like an angel.'

Below the hideously deformed face, the flowing curves of her breasts, belly and thighs showed up even more perfectly, as though some wood nymph had donned a mask of chaos.

'You're eaten up with self-pity,' went on Luke accusingly. 'Millions of people would give their eye teeth to be illegitimate if they had your advantages. You've just got the wrong values. Money doesn't buy happiness unless you know how to use it. You'll be a great polo player. Just give it time.'

Coated now by grey-and-green paint, Perdita tried to wriggle free.

'You're supposed to be strong and silent,' she screamed, 'so shut up. You're not interested in living. All you care about is ponies and working your ass off. With you, bread and onions, for Chrissake. All onions give you is stinking breath.'

For a second they glared at each other's reflections. Her face was streaked with grey now, her eyes glittered. Her breasts were high enough to rest her chin on, her waist as narrow as the width of her face. Luke could feel the white cushion of her bottom against his cock, and in the mirror he saw the soft insides of her thighs just purpled by fading bruises from a match more than a week ago.

Luke was not a heavy drinker, but he had drunk a great deal that evening. Ignorant of what had happened between her and Red on the pitch earlier, he was only aware that he'd never seen anything so beautiful nor so

515

achingly desirable. Dammed too long, passion burst the lid off his normal self-control and reticence.

Swinging her round, he pulled her into his arms.

'I can't pretend any longer, right. I love you, more than anything else in the world. From the moment you came off that plane at Buenos Aires airport two years ago. I'm sorry I chewed you out. I just wanna protect you.'

Her smudged urchin face reminded him of one of those children they sent up chimneys in the old days. Overwhelmed with compassion and love, he bent his head and kissed her. Just for a second Perdita kissed him back, arching her naked body against him, abandoning herself, overwhelmed by rightness, letting her instincts take over. Then the warning bells started. What the hell was she playing at? It was as if her old teddy bear, or Ethel or Spotty had jumped on her, all of whom would be just as useless at giving her the riches she wanted.

Punching herself free, utterly shocked, she slapped his face as hard as she could.

'Fucking hypocrite,' she screamed. 'You just don't want anyone else to have me.'

'No, I bloody don't.'

'Well, get this straight,' Perdita snatched up the shawl. 'With all this sentimental crap about the right values and bread and onions, you'd never give me the things in life I want. I want security and stability, and I don't think I'd find it living in a rathole over a stable for the rest of my life. So you better piss off and stop wasting my time. Now!' she screamed, as Luke hesitated.

His lips were deathly pale, his eyes haunted and staring. For a moment the streaked, gargoyle face looked as though it had been turned to stone. Then he was gone.

Sobbing, Perdita collapsed on the bed. Her dear, dear friend, her bloody prudish friend, her rock turned to sifting sands beneath her feet. How *could* he pounce on her like that and spoil everything?

'I can't bear it,' she sobbed dementedly into the counterpane.

There was a knock on the door. Frantically hopeful, Perdita looked up. It was a bad dream, they were still friends. But it was Red – not Luke – who stood in the doorway, grinning from earring to earring.

'Hi, Godiva,' he said softly. 'Peeping Tom at the gate and no-one's gonna blind me. I bet you don't know why Godiva rode through the streets of Coventry. To save the peasants being taxed out of existence by her lousy husband. From now on, right, every time I don't want to pay a tax bill, you can strip off in front of the tax inspectors. And I have to admit you are worth inspecting.'

'Where's Spotty?' asked Perdita.

'Back in his box. Talk about riding bareback. Jesus!'

Perdita was so distraught that she forgot she was still furious with Red and told him about the row with Luke. Whereupon Red went through to the bathroom, soaked a flannel and taking her face in his hands started to wipe away the green-and-grey smears.

'Sweetheart, Luke's always been dumb about money. He thinks everyone can live on snowballs like himself. If he'd just brown-nosed an iota to my father he could have inherited the earth like the rest of us. Not that it's nearly enough. Lick.' Like a child, Perdita dampened the flannel with her tongue so that he could remove a smear running from her left collarbone down to her breast.

There was just a primrose-yellow silk shawl between Red and gratification. In her present state of shock, he knew he could take her, but he preferred to wait.

'Let's not lose any sleep over Luke.' He produced wads of francs out of his floppy shirt pocket. 'I've had a windfall at the casino. Let's go buy you some clothes.'

'The shops'll be shut,' protested Perdita.

'It's only half-past nine.' It seemed like midnight. 'We'll just catch them.'

52

They got to Yves St Laurent just as they were closing. Grace, Auriel and Chessie had all been excellent customers over the years so the manageress was quite prepared to stay open and even produced a bottle of champagne. Red lounged like some sultan on a white sofa smoking a long cigar, drinking very slowly and totally dominating Perdita's choice.

With that waterfall of hair and strange unicorn looks

and body undulating like an ox-bow river, he wanted her starkly plain, mostly in blacks, navy blues and bottle greens, with the occasional brilliant cyclamen, purple or kingfisher-blue. Everything had to fit perfectly and if it didn't it was kept back to be taken in or up. Perdita, who always wanted everything at once, grumbled like hell. But she was in a state of frantic excitement and arousal.

Red, used to accompanying Grace and Auriel to fashion shows, was an expert on line and cut. He enjoyed watching Perdita's voluptuous pleasure as she swayed and preened in front of him. He liked the way she quivered as he slowly ran his hand over her breasts or her belly, testing the smoothness of the fit.

After an hour and a half, when they'd bought almost the entire shop, he told her to put on a pair of black high heels and an ivy-green taffeta dress, clinging and high-necked at the front, plunging to the base of her spine at the back.

As she came out, having piled up her hair with a dark green sequinned comb given her by the manageress, she found Red examining the contents of some little boxes a jeweller had rushed in from next door. From one he drew out a necklace and drop-earrings in huge, very dark sapphires. 'These'll do. Come here,' he ordered Perdita.

Very slowly he put them round her neck and hooked them on to her ears. All trace of her tears had gone now. The sapphires and the ivy-green taffeta heightened her white skin and made her strange eyes so dark that they seemed all pupil.

'You'll do,' he said.

'You can't give me all this,' said Perdita. 'I hate you.'

Red laughed. 'With enemies like me, who needs friends? One must sapphire to be beautiful.' Then, when she tried to protest, murmured: 'Don't spoil it.'

He paid for the lot out of his casino winnings. He'd call tomorrow and tell the manageress where the rest had to be sent.

Red had kept Auriel's driver waiting. As they drove past the casino they could hear shrieks and yells. A carrot flew out of the window followed by several chicken drumsticks. Next moment, Sharon, her ice-cream cone flopping, erupted into the street squealing, followed by a furious dragon, followed by Seb Carlisle laughing uproariously trying to hold back the dragon by its tail.

Red took Perdita to a very dark night-club where they kept on drinking. When he heard she hadn't eaten all day he ordered some utterly delectable salmon and scallop fishcakes and fed her bite by bite.

'They're soft inside, just like you. What did you think the first time you saw me?'

'That you were the handsomest man I'd ever seen.'

'Better looking than Rupert Campbell-Black?'

'Much. I'm not really attracted to blonds.'

'What about Luke?'

'Luke's more red-gold.'

Red ran an idle finger down her spine, making it almost impossible for her to concentrate.

'He's going to be mad at us.'

'He won't,' said Perdita, not wanting to think about Luke. 'He's such a good loser.'

'No such thing,' said Red brutally, 'There are losers and idiots who pretend they enjoy it.'

'What did you think when you first saw me?' asked Perdita.

Red put his head on one side. 'When was it?'

Christ, it's tattooed on my memory, thought Perdita. Then she said, 'When Luke brought me to *El Paradiso*. You were stick and balling.'

'Oh yes, I remember,' said Red. 'It was the only time I stick and balled in the last two years. Did you arrive that day? Oh, that's right. I thought you were kinda plain and needed a nose job, and you should lose ten pounds and about two feet of hair.'

'Bastard!' Perdita choked on her fishcake.

'But you had promise.' He patted her briskly on the back. 'I always thought you'd be a tiger in the sack.'

'Better than a Tayger,' said Perdita.

She longed and longed for him to kiss her again. But whenever he took her to dance he merely let his hands travel over her back, fingering, stroking, caressing, creeping round almost to her breasts, then almost to her bottom, teasing until she was leaping like a salmon with hopeless, hopeless desire.

Dawn had broken as they left the night-club, but a thick

mist lay over the sea and the beach like a curtain. There was a clatter as grooms rode past leading ponies through the narrow streets down for exercise on the sands.

'The Normandie's only a hundred yards away. Let's walk.' Red turned to Auriel's yawning exhausted driver, who must have been waiting for six hours, and said casually, 'You can push off now. I'll call when I need you.'

As they passed the Metropole, Dommie came running out. He was wearing the top half of his Henry V costume above boxer shorts covered in Father Christmases and swinging Victor's forked dragon's tail.

'Crisis, crisis, we've just been fired! Rosie got so fed up because we wouldn't stop fighting that she went home, so we had to resort to Lady Shar and Victor caught us.' Dommie giggled. 'I told him he was seeing double after all that drink, and it was just Seb bonking, but he wouldn't believe me. So it's just you and Victor playing together now, Red. I wish you luck.' And he ran off down the street, swinging his dragon's tail.

Perdita giggled. 'They are awful.'

Red took her chin and turned her face towards him.

'Your eyes are the eyes of a woman in love,' he sang softly, 'and, oh, how they give you away.'

'They do not,' protested Perdita.

Ahead loomed the Normandie rising out of the mists like Mount Blanc, with the drying bathing suits all damp again on the balconies. As they mounted the steps Perdita's eyes somewhat hazily fell on a pair of brown boots coming down. Slowly, slowly, she looked upwards to jeans with the belt done up on a third extra notch. It was Luke going out to practise. One look at his face told Perdita of his utter crucifixion.

'I'll leave you both to it,' murmured Red, disappearing through the doors.

Desolate but totally unable to give comfort, Perdita gazed at him.

'I'm sorry,' she whispered. 'You put me on a pedestal and I haven't got a head for heights.'

'Be careful,' said Luke wearily. 'You've "fallen among those who are careless with other people's lives".'

An American journalist who'd been at the party lurched up to him, not recognizing Perdita.

'Mr Alderton, we spoke briefly yesterday. I wonder if I could have a few words now.'

Luke shrugged. 'I suppose.'

'Have you had any really serious breaks since you began playing polo?'

Luke looked at him steadily. 'Only my heart,' he said.

With a sob, Perdita fled into the hotel. How *could* she have done that to Luke? But what had she done? Just been vile to him, which she'd often been before, and gone out dancing with Red. Red's door was open. As she went inside all thoughts of Luke were forgotten. Red was packing.

'What are you doing?'

'As you've knocked out my team and ostensibly my mistress, I'm not hanging around here any more.'

Hearing her gasp of horror, he laughed. 'You'd better come with me. The press are going to annihilate you, Lady Godiva.'

'Where to?' whispered Perdita.

'How about Singapore? I need a vacation. And then we could go to Thailand and perhaps to Kenya, and then perhaps to Boston to play a few games at the Myopia Club.'

'But what about Tero and Spotty?'

'My grooms are flying my ponies home. They can take yours at the same time.'

'But I can't just walk out on Ricky and Dancer,' wailed Perdita. 'I'm committed to play for them for the rest of the season, and what about Venturer? Omigod, I'm supposed to meet Cameron Cook in the lobby at seven.'

As if on cue the telephone rang. Red picked it up and held it away from his ear for ten seconds.

'Miss Cook for you,' he told Perdita with a grin. 'She heard we came in together and she doesn't like being kept waiting. Oh, shut up!' he slammed down the receiver.

Perdita gazed out of the window. The mist had rolled back and the rising sun was polishing the white horses and the glassy depths of the Channel. The energetic were already pounding back and forth in the hotel swimming-pool, early riders were bouncing round a little riding-school ring.

Red crossed the room and kissed her properly for the first time.

'Are you sure you've got your priorities right?'

'I'll come with you,' said Perdita helplessly.

The telephone rang. It was Cameron Cook again.

'Go screw yourself,' said Red. Then, cutting her off, immediately started to dial out. 'I'll call Orly and get us on the afternoon flight. You can get on with my packing.'

53

From that moment Perdita was a leaf, ripped untimely and whipped hither and thither by the whirlwind. Within quarter of an hour they were out of the back door of the hotel and flying to Paris in Auriel's helicopter. Perdita was now wearing a scarlet cashmere jersey of Red's over the ivy-green dress and, because her feet were killing her, had swapped last night's new black, spike heels for flat, black pumps. Except for her polo gear, Red insisted she left her other clothes behind, claiming they were all gross.

'But what about the stuff we bought last night?' wailed Perdita.

'They'll send it on to Palm Beach. You won't need wool suits where we're going.' He glanced sideways at her. 'You won't need any clothes at all.'

Nor would he let her leave a note for Luke or for Ricky. 'Never explain, never apologize.'

Landing in Paris, he had whipped her into the smartest hairdresser in the Faubourg St Germain and handed her over to George the boss, who flexed his gold razor in glee at such a challenge.

'I want the whole lot off and the colour changed,' said Red. Then, when Perdita grew hysterical: 'Pack it in. D'you want the press off our backs or not?'

'I'll be like Samson. I'll lose all my strength and probably you.'

Returning three hours later, even Red was jolted by an almost unrecognizable Perdita. Her hair, short as a schoolboy's, thick and darkest Prussian blue as a magpie's stripe, clung sleek to her exquisitely shaped head, emphasizing the long neck, the curling mouth, the long, Greek nose, the smooth, white forehead and the blue-black, blazingly angry, wide-apart eyes. And as her face looked more fierce,

522

more vulnerable, more like a Picasso, more boyish, by contrast her body looked more feminine and voluptuous.

'Omigod!' Red prowled round her. 'What a piece of work! Christ, you look as sexy as hell.'

'I look like hell,' snarled Perdita. 'I hate it, I hate it.'

'Don't be silly. Before you were just any old blowzy blonde. Now you look like no-one else on earth. No, leave it,' he said sharply as she frantically tried to pull some tendrils over her forehead.

'I loathe short hair.'

'Well, I like it, and after two years of Bore-iel I'm not taking up with another woman who spends all day clutching a blow dryer. I've got better things for you to blow.'

'I'll have to spend all day washing my neck and ears now.'

'Stop beefing.' Red slotted the arms of a huge pair of dark glasses behind her ears. 'We've got a plane to catch.'

An hour later they were in the front First-Class seats of an Air France flight to Singapore, drinking champagne and eating caviar. Red's only concession to disguise was dark glasses and a dark blue baseball cap pulled down over his nose hiding most of his hair.

'I'm sorry,' said Perdita. 'I only bitch when I'm rattled.'

'Don't worry on my account. I like rows.'

'Last time I travelled First Class was because you upgraded me.'

Red took her hand and kissed it. 'You're upgraded for good now,' he said softly. Then, as Perdita's heart lurched, longing to ask what he meant, he started examining her hands. 'We'll have to get you a manicure in Singapore. You must've been skipping out the entire Apocalypse barn without a pitchfork. Christ, look at that.'

Two English businessmen across the gangway were drooling over a double-page coloured photograph of a naked Perdita riding Spotty into the Casino with Victor in his dragon's head gazing up at her.

'They've airbrushed your boobs to make them twice as big,' said Red, 'and blackened your bush.'

'And my character,' hissed Perdita.

'Nice tits,' said the nearest businessman thickly, putting on his bifocals to examine them more closely.

'Lucky horse,' said the other. 'Bet he's enjoying it. She's

a raver that Perdita; told Prince Charles to eff off. They say all that stimulation between their legs all day makes ladies really randy.'

'I'm thinking of taking up polo,' said his companion, drawing frantically on his cigar, 'or at least sponsoring a polo function next year. Crumpet's fantastic.'

Perdita was about to erupt. Shaking with laughter Red put a hand on her arm. 'Now aren't you glad you've changed your hair? Flattering picture of Victor though. He should use it in his annual report.'

Spotty's wall eye, caught in the flash, looked both alarmed and disapproving.

'He will be OK, won't he, and Tero too?' pleaded Perdita, taking a slug of champagne. 'I've never been parted from them for a day since I came back from Palm Beach. Tero's petrified of strangers.'

Still drunk when she had walked out on them that morning, she was trying not to sober up.

'I rang Manuel while you were in the hairdressers,' said Red. 'He's going to fly them straight to Boston. We'll stay at the Ritz-Carlton. You'll like that.'

Perdita couldn't eat much dinner, but she kept on drinking. She was also incensed after the lights had been dimmed and the screen pulled down to discover the flight movie was *Treadmill*, Auriel's latest *tour de force*, in which she played a stunning middle-aged woman rediscovering passion and sexuality with a young boy.

'That's good. Won't need a Mogadon,' said Red, pushing back his chair and putting the navy-blue blindfold over his eyes.

'Aren't you going to watch?'

'Why should I? I've had the real thing. Good-night, sweetheart. See you in the morning.' And immediately he fell asleep.

Perdita was outraged. It had been just the same on that long flight to Argentina with Ricky when she'd lain writhing with desire under two blankets and Ricky hadn't lain a finger on her.

What the hell was Red playing at? Having not slept for two days, she had been feeling drowsy and sexy. Now she was wide awake, and however hard she tried not to watch, her eyes seemed to force themselves open as, with horrified fascination, she watched Auriel, big-bosomed, mature, her long, dark hair spilling over pillows, being let down, taken up, tumbling over her shoulders in the shower, as she murmured endearments in her throaty voice, and exuded Experience with a capital E.

'Fucking gorgeous tits,' leered the businessman across the way, whose hand seemed to be revoltingly active beneath his blanket, 'and lovely hair. You can't beat a really attractive mature lady.'

'I wouldn't mind beating her,' said his friend.

Perdita clutched her head. God – her hair was short! It suddenly occurred to her that the only time she'd slept on a plane was when she'd been with Luke.

Three performances of *Carmen* on the headphones, a second film mercifully starring Charles Bronson, and three meals later, during which time Red woke up and read an entire Wilbur Smith, hardly pausing to speak to her, Perdita found herself staggering out into the stifling Singapore dusk.

After that things became a little hazy. The drive from the airport was even more terrifying than Argentina, with people crouching in the back of lorries wearing crash helmets over their coolie hats. A hot breeze wafted a voluptuous smell of soy and frangipani. Little clouds, turned pink by the setting sun, rose like puffs of smoke from the tops of soaring skyscrapers. Fortunately Red had booked them into the most charming hotel, the legendary Goodwood Park. Amid all the modern buildings it looked like a little Persil-white castle, complete with turrets, plucked from the Black Forest and plonked down on a green hill and wrapped in a muffler of jungle greenery.

Even more excitingly, they were staying in the Brunei Suite normally inhabited by kings, princes, prime ministers, and the Sultan of Brunei when he was in town.

'I played for him once,' said Red, propping his polo sticks against the bedroom wall. 'Every time he changed ponies all the crowd stood up and weren't allowed to sit down until the royal ass was back in a different saddle.'

'This place is incredible,' said Perdita, padding from room to room over the thick golden carpet. 'We can have a sauna, give dinner parties in the dining room and play hide and seek.'

'Hyde and Jekyll, if you play with me,' said Red. 'Geminis are totally schizophrenic.'

'What an incredibly comfortable bed,' said Perdita, collapsing on to the golden counterpane. 'Wish I had one as big as this at home. Is this what they call king-size?'

'Depends on the king,' said Red, who had poured himself a huge Scotch on the rocks. 'George VI of England was quite small. Henry VIII bloody large. Edward VII even larger. What d'you want to drink? Shall we eat out or in?'

But Perdita was asleep. In the impossibly crumpled ivy-green taffeta dress she looked like some fourteen-year-old schoolboy playing Amanda in the house production of *Private Lives*. Gripped with lust, Red wondered why he wanted her so much – because she was different, or because she was Luke's, and he had to beat Luke in everything? He toyed with the idea of waking her up, but, as he removed her dress, she didn't stir. Folding the counterpane round her, he left her to sleep.

Waking, Perdita had no idea where she was. Fumbling for the light switch, she saw Red's polo sticks had gone. Perhaps he'd done a bunk. She was just opening the french windows on to a roof garden, filled with tropical plants and blazing sunlight, when there was a knock on the door. Three gently smiling waiters had arrived bearing, first, breakfast of coffee, orange juice, scrambled eggs and croissants, then a vast bunch of incredibly scented yellow orchids, and finally a cardboard box tied with pink ribbon. Inside the box was a pair of black and grey striped silk pyjamas, and a note.

'Darling Perdita, I'm playing polo. Back at sundown, prepare yourself for a Gaudy night. Love Red.'

Looking at the drawing-room clock, she saw it was 5.30 and was so overwhelmed with terror that she forgot to tip the waiters.

By running away with Red, and leaving a trail of broken hearts and contracts, she had totally burnt her junks. What happened if she couldn't deliver the goods tonight? There wasn't a woman Red couldn't have. How could she not be a terrible letdown? And what would happen when he discovered her fearful secret? Skin had formed on the hot milk, the scrambled eggs had congealed and the croissants cooled before she pulled herself together.

Her legs, shaved for Godiva, were already slightly bristly. Using Red's razor, she was shaking so much she cut herself twice. Anyone would think she'd slaughtered a pig. She had a shower and scrubbed every centimetre of her body, and between her legs about twenty times, then rubbed scented body lotion all over herself, particularly into her calloused Brillo-pad hands. Then she rubbed Red's Givenchy for Men into her hair and slicked it back like Lord Snooty. The silk pyjamas were incredibly seductive but too hot, so she folded them on the side of her bed and instead put on a grey and white striped shirt of Red's. The twins and Chessie had often intimated that Red was bisexual. If she looked like a boy, perhaps he would fancy her more.

At seven, by which time two unobtrusive maids had tidied the room and put her flowers in water, a bottle of champagne arrived on ice. Champagne reminded her of walking out on Luke, so she settled for two miniature bottles of vodka and topped them up with lime juice and ice. Sitting out on the roof garden with a guide book of Singapore, she watched a pallid half-moon grow gradually more luminous and Venus quivering golden between the skyscrapers, as the sun went down in a bonfire of orange. Red should have a shirt in that orange. Then, because her stomach was rumbling, she got a packet of peanuts from the fridge, and was so nervous she cleaned her teeth between peanuts. Night had fallen and a slight breeze was lifting the coloured mantillas of the bougainvillaea when Red returned.

He was still wearing boots and breeches. His dark blue polo shirt was dripping, his hair almost black with sweat. 'Christ, it's hot!' He threw his whip on the bed. 'Like playing in a Turkish bath.'

'Good game?' asked Perdita. He looked so glamorous she wanted to run into his arms, but she must play it cool.

'Great. I played nine chukkas. There was a tropical storm after lunch, but the pitch dried out half an hour later.'

'What was the standard like?'

'Pretty average, but there was a wild guy playing for

the other side called Barry Bartlett, just flown in from Australia with half-a-dozen Walers. He's a six, so we spent our time hitting the ball to each other like a Wimbledon final. And those Walers are as tough as shit, legs like iron and wonderful mouths. I'm gonna offer for the lot.'

'Did anyone recognize you?'

'Sure. They all did, but I said we were avoiding the press, so they'll keep their traps suit. They'd also heard about the twins being fired. The story's escalated. Not only were they caught in bed with Sharon but also a pony. How've you been?'

'Fine,' lied Perdita. As she came back into the lit-up bedroom a slow smile spread across Red's face.

'My shirt.'

'Your haircut.'

'My schoolboy,' said Red, running his hand over the slicked hair. 'Fix me a Scotch on the rocks. I'm going to have a shower.'

He was back in five minutes, just wearing a white towel slung round his hips, which emphasized the satin-brown smoothness of his chest. Compared with Luke he was willowy and elongated, a greyhound beside a mastiff. She didn't want to think about Luke. It hurt too much, *and* made her feel too guilty, and she knew if it had been him instead of Red who had been about to take her to bed she wouldn't have been so terrified.

'Thank you for the orchids, they were lovely.' Desperately she tried to stem the rattle of ice. 'They've got lower lips like Juan O'Brien, and the pyjamas are gorgeous.'

'Why didn't you wear them?'

'I thought you might not want to go to bed.'

'You thought wrong, and you've put them on the wrong side.' He picked up the pyjamas and threw them to the left side of the bed. 'Your pal Ricky France-Lynch may be ambidextrous enough to make women come with his left hand, but I only score with my right.'

Turning away to hide her frantic blushes, Perdita drained her vodka.

'It's the most beautiful suite,' she gushed. 'With all those Grecian pillars and chandeliers and alcoves and you coming in all handsome in breeches and boots, it's like the cover of a Barbara Cartland novel.'

'Good,' said Red, who was fiddling around with the mirrors on the dressing table, pulling them in front of the bed to reflect any forthcoming action. He looked up and smiled, revelling in her embarrassment.

Sweat was cascading down her body, her pounding heart made her totally breathless.

'R-red, there's something I've got to tell you.'

'Oh dear,' sighed Red, sitting down in a gold satin armchair and lighting a yellow Sobranie. 'Don't tell me you've got your period. Some guys don't mind, but I've never enjoyed the flavour of the monthly.' Then, when she didn't laugh, 'It's a joke.'

Perdita gazed miserably down at her painted toenails.

'I know I come on blasé,' she muttered, 'but I've never been to bed with anyone in my life.'

Red choked on his whisky. 'You what?'

'I'm a virgin.'

'You've gotta be joking,' he said incredulously. 'What the hell's Ricky been doing all these years?'

'Not me,' whispered Perdita.

'Well, Luke then?'

'Luke didn't because he thought I was in love with Ricky. Anyway, he's such a gentleman.'

'Unlike me,' said Red icily. 'Are you having me on? I figured virgins were extinct.'

'I'm sorry.' Perdita hung her head dejectedly. 'You were expecting nights and days of sophisticated passion. After Auriel, I'm going to be such an anti-climax.'

Standing there in a shirt much too big for her, a tear stealing down her pale cheek, like a raindrop on a magnolia petal, bruises still faintly violet on her long legs, she looked so unbelievably touching that Red's face softened.

'I'm not anti climaxes,' he said. 'I'm rather good at giving them to people. We took your L-plates off when we clipped your mane. Come here.'

Violently trembling, Perdita walked forward until she was almost touching his knees.

'Take off that shirt.'

Each button seemed suddenly far too big for its button-hole. Red's cock's going to be far too big for me, she thought in panic.

'Hurry up,' he said sharply, then as the shirt slid to the

529

carpet: 'Now fold it up. I'll pick up your bills, but not your clothes.'

'Bastard,' said Perdita, as she picked up the shirt.

Red tipped up one of the white lampshades, so her body was flooded with light. Her hands fluttered to cover as much as they could.

'Look at me,' he snapped.

Dragging her eyes upwards as if they were ten-pound weights, she was amazed that he was laughing and his eyes were full of affection.

'I like being the first. I can break you exactly the way I want.'

Stubbing out his cigarette, he took her waist in both hands to still the trembling, and pulled her down on to his knee.

Then he kissed her with incredible gentleness, his mouth cold but tasting slightly ashy from whisky and cigarettes, on and on as his fingers crept up her thighs till he found the damp, blond, pubic hair.

'You're sweet,' he murmured, examining her. 'All pink, tender and glistening, like the inside of a guava.'

As he inserted a finger, she jumped like a branded filly.

'It's OK, darling, you're tight, but not that tight. I'll get you so sopping beforehand, I'll slide in like a cartridge into a twelve bore.'

Perdita had no-one else to judge him by, but had no doubt as he got to work she was in the hands of an expert. For a start he was so detached, and for another he was determined to excise the word 'no' from her vocabulary.

'Red, you can't lick me there, truly you can't, or there, and Christ almighty, certainly not there.'

'Shut up and enjoy it.'

Ten minutes later his tongue was circling her clitoris like an electric eel, his thumb was sliding relentlessly but slowly in and out of her vagina and his middle finger was stabbing in and out of her anus, and it was so excruciatingly shaming and enjoyable she found she was shrieking her head off.

'Hush, my angel, you'll frighten the monkeys.'

And as he promised when he finally drove his cock into her, she was so sodden and slippery with desire she hardly felt anything beyond a brief, excruciating pain. Then, as he moved in and out of her, his hand delicately caressed her clitoris, sideways, up and down, round and round driving her in to a no man's land of pleasure.

'I love you, I love you,' she moaned. 'I know I've never loved anyone else in my life.'

'Not even Luke?' His face over hers was almost satanic. 'Go on say it.'

'Not even Luke. Oh please, please go on.'

'D'you know who's responsible for my being so good in bed?' he asked her as they had a very late breakfast next morning.

'Bloody Auriel, I suppose.'

'My mother.'

'Grace,' said Perdita in amazement. 'She told you how to do all that?'

'No, no, but being a goddam intellectual snob, she insisted I learn the violin and the flute, and locked me into the playroom to practise. Little did I think, as I double-stopped and double-tongued how useful it would be later. I was also underwater swimming champion at school which is why I can go down for so long without taking a breath.'

Perdita giggled and spread apricot jam on a second croissant.

'You are appallingly conceited,' she said, kissing his shoulder, 'and totally accurate. Do you think the maids will mind there being blood all over the sheets?'

'We're paying them fifteen hundred dollars a night not to,' said Red, pulling her into his arms. He knew exactly the spot just an inch below her nipples where her breasts were most responsive. Was it his expertise or her desire that made it so unbelievably pleasurable?

'I can't think why I've done without sex for so long,' she said, arching against him, desperate for him to go on.

'There's only one thing better than pussy in the world,' said Red looking at his watch.

'What's that?'

'Polo. Go and run me a bath.'

Red and Perdita had only one cataclysmic row during

their first week. They had been driving round the island congratulating themselves on avoiding the press for so long. Looking at the monkeys swaying and chattering in the trees and the brilliantly coloured birds and flowers, and the hedges alight with fireflies and huge moths as big as bats, Perdita thought how much Luke would have loved it. She hoped one day they could be friends and perhaps, fingers crossed, he would become her brother-in-law.

They stopped for dinner at Pongool on the North Coast, and sat gazing over the Straits at the lights of Johore. Near by a boy calmly dismembered crabs for their dinner. Ten minutes later they were eating them.

'God, they're delicious,' said Perdita guiltily. 'I'm getting awfully hardened. I couldn't have eaten them a week ago, having seen them killed like that.'

'You need toughening up. You're far too emotional.'

They ate with their fingers off banana leaves instead of plates. From all directions came dollops of rice, beans, squid, giant prawns, lobster and the recently dismembered crabs.

'Christ, you need a fire extinguisher to eat the chillies,' gasped Perdita, taking a huge slug of white wine. 'No, thank you,' she shuddered as the waiter offered her a large fish's head.

'Gourmets suck the eyeballs,' said Red, lighting a cigarette.

'Ugh,' said Perdita.

'It's an acquired taste. You mustn't be so squeamish.'

'Beautiful stars,' said Perdita dreamily. She longed to stroke his thighs, but he'd go berserk if she spread chilli sauce all over his white trousers.

'Stars much bigger in Kenya,' said Red, tipping his head back. 'I'll take you there one day.'

Perdita thought she'd never been happier in her life.

'Can I have some brandy?'

'You've had enough.' Red beckoned for the bill. 'Don't want to dull your reflexes. I've got some amylnitrate and a couple of incredibly blue movies back at the hotel. They'll blow your mind.'

The moment they were back in the Brunei Suite, however, the telephone rang.

'OK, terrific, come on up,' said Red. Then, turning

to Perdita, 'Go and have a shower, darling. I've got a surprise for you.'

Perdita was wary of Red's surprises. It might be the twins, or even the *News of the World*. Anything for novelty.

But when she wandered into the drawing room ten minutes later in a pale pink silk kimono, she found sitting in one of the pale armchairs one of the prettiest Chinese girls she had ever seen.

'This is Doris Chow,' said Red.

Perdita giggled and wondered if Doris had a black tongue.

'Hi,' she said. 'I'm mad about Singapore. Have you lived here long?'

'All my life,' said Doris.

'Doris is a teacher,' drawled Red.

'Oh really. What d'you teach?'

'Sex,' said Red softly; then, to Perdita's utter horror, he put out a hand and started to caress the Chinese girl's neck just above her jade-green cheongsam. 'Isn't she beautiful?' With the other hand he started pulling pins out of her black hair.

'What the hell are you playing at?' whispered Perdita.

'She's going to give you a few lessons,' said Red as though he was explaining fractions to a seven year old. 'You're coming along nicely, but your technique lacks finesse. Wild Barry Bartlett says Doris gives head better than anyone else in Singapore.'

The next minute Perdita had picked up a vase and thrown it at Red.

'You perverted bloody bastard.'

Maddeningly, Red caught it, putting it down on the glass table in the middle of the room.

'Don't be silly,' he said sharply as Perdita reached for an ashtray.

Bursting into tears, she fled to the bedroom.

'I won't do it, I won't. D'you want to turn me into a fucking dyke? Don't make me, please, please, Red. I'm sorry I'm not good enough. I'll read sex books, I'll watch blue movies. Can't *you* tell me where I'm going wrong, not her?'

Most hearts would have melted, not Red's.

'Why are you making such a stupid fuss over something

that'll turn out so nice later? You'd think nothing of going to Hugh Dawnay or Peter Grace to learn polo. What's so different about sex? A few practicals with Doris, and you'll be almost up to Auriel's standards.'

Wham, Perdita had slapped him across the face.

Wham, he slapped her back much harder.

'I can't, Red, truly I can't.'

'You will if you want to stay with me. If not, there's a plane back to England leaving first thing in the morning.'

After Doris had gone hours later, Perdita cried herself to sleep on the sofa in the drawing room. Sometime towards dawn she woke to find Red standing by the window. He was smoking, with an untouched glass of whisky beside him on the table. In the pale light filtering through the net curtains, he looked ghastly, his shoulders hunched, his eyeliner smudged beneath sad, despairing eyes – the picture of desolation.

'Red,' she called out, forgetting the desperate humiliation through which he'd put her, 'are you OK?'

As though he were continents away he looked at her for a second in bewilderment. They met halfway across the room, collapsing into each other's arms.

'I'm sorry.' His lips were against her forehead. 'I'll never put you through anything like that again. I'll make you happy, I promise. I don't know what gets into me.'

'I love you,' mumbled Perdita, who only felt passionate relief he'd forgiven her. 'I thought I'd lost you.'

'I've got problems,' said Red wearily. 'I'll tell you one day.'

'Tell me now.' They both jumped as the telephone rang.

'You get it,' said Red.

'It's *The Scorpion*,' said Perdita in panic a second later. 'They know we're here.'

'Give it to me.' Red took the receiver. 'OK, you bastards,' he said coolly, 'I've only got one thing to say to you and the rest of the world, right. Perdita and I are getting married. We haven't fixed a date yet, but it won't be long. Now, fuck off and leave us alone.' Slamming down the receiver he took it off the hook, and added, turning to a gaping Perdita, 'That should shut them up.'

534

'But you didn't mean it?'

Red laughed. Suddenly he was all sparkle and high spirits at the novelty of the whole thing.

'Yes, I did. I've always been turned on by the idea of arranged marriages, so I arranged this one. Let's go and consummate the engagement.'

54

'*Red to wed*' screamed worldwide headlines. '*Perdita steals Auriel's toyboy*.' '*Chukked her*', said the *Sun* in a huge front-page headline. Every member of the Red Army seemed only too happy to tell all about Red in bed. The press besieged the Goodwood Park Hotel. There were widespread rumours that James Whitaker, dressed as a monkey, had tried to climb into the roof garden of the Brunei Suite. But the tigerishly vigilant hotel staff only let in one person, the most expensive jeweller in Singapore, from whom Red bought an engagement ring for Perdita, containing a sapphire as big as a Victoria plum.

After a couple more days in Singapore they moved on to Thailand, by which time press interest had been considerably distracted by the wedding of another beautiful redhead to the Duke of York in Westminster Abbey. From Thailand they went to Hong Kong, India, then on to Kenya, and everywhere they were pestered.

Perdita secretly enjoyed the publicity. It excited her to be the other half of a beautiful couple with packs of reporters hanging on her every expletive and her photograph in every newspaper, sleek, exotic and shining with love. Lady Godivine, the press had nicknamed her. At last she had become a superstar.

Conversely, for the first time in her life, she was forced to be unselfish. Like a prince, Red expected her to do everything. Mix his drinks, tidy up after him, ring up the Singapore tailor, who arrived in a quarter of an hour quivering with excitement to receive an order for twenty suits and twice as many shirts, jackets and trousers. And Red gave the fitting of the suits – the slant of a pocket, the position of a button – the same total concentration he'd given Wilbur Smith on the plane or to a game of polo when he'd suddenly decided to win it.

He had incredible stamina. When they moved to India and Africa she found it difficult to keep up with the endless round of night-clubs and parties. And, like all wildly unpunctual people, he hated to be kept waiting because he wasn't used to it. If Perdita wasn't ready, he left without her.

Often sadistic, keeping her for ages on the brink of orgasm until she was screaming for it, he was in fact very like a tiger who'd been reared by humans, beautiful, playful, purring, rubbing against you, falling asleep in your arms, but liable at any moment to turn savage and wounding.

But if he had a wicked temper, he didn't bear grudges, even after the most violent rows. Apart from the occasional sniping at Ricky, the only person he hated was Chessie. 'The moment Dad dies of a coronary, there'll be a taxi outside Alderton Towers to take her to the airport.'

Best of all, like a plant brought out of the winter frosts into a warm greenhouse, Perdita adored being rich, having fistfuls of notes to buy what she liked, ordering whatever she wanted to eat. One evening she ate so much caviar she was sick. The same tailor making suits for Red plucked the most amazing silks and cottons out of the rainbow and, strictly supervised by Red, transformed them overnight into a wildly flattering wardrobe.

'I'm going to turn you into a great beauty,' said Red, taking endless photographs of her both dressed and nude. 'Within six months every girl in the world is going to want to look like you.'

Having refused to speak to any of her family or fellow polo players because she was frightened of getting an earful, Perdita finally rang Seb Carlisle to test the water and found it extremely icy.

'Christ, you bitch, Perdita. Have you any idea how many people you fucked up?'

'Who?'

'Your sainted mother for a start.'

'Let her sweat.'

'Don't be a cow. She's sweet. And you've completely screwed up Apocalypse and Venturer. And poor Auriel actually cried in public last week. And your future mother-in-law is tearing her snow-white hair at the thought of Red chucking himself away on a nobody.'

'Bitch,' screamed Perdita.

'Dancer and Ricky will certainly never speak to you again.'

'I don't care. I've never been so happy in my life.'

'It won't last. Red sheds women like cardigans in summer.'

'You're a fine one to talk, pinching your brother's girlfriend.'

'Dommie's dyed his hair black, so she won't mistake us in the future.'

'All twins look grey in the dark,' snarled Perdita. 'And what about both of you going to bed with Sharon?'

'That was the best thing we ever did. Hearing Victor'd fired us, Dancer's hired us to play for Apocalypse next year.'

Perdita felt an appalling stab of jealousy, then steeled herself to ask the most difficult question of all.

'How's Luke?'

'Very unallright,' said Seb bleakly. 'That's why everyone really hates you. You've broken Luke's heart.'

Ecstasy at an autumn spent playing not very serious polo in Zimbabwe was tempered by the prospect of returning to Palm Beach in the middle of November and facing Luke. Perdita didn't know if she was relieved or disappointed on getting back to Red's house to learn that Luke had taken all his ponies and Leroy off to Argentina, wouldn't be back until after Christmas, and by then would be playing out of Boca Raton, so they'd be far less likely to bump into each other.

Any worries next morning that Red might have forgotten her birthday were dispelled when he told her to look out of the window. On the lawn below were three of Red's grooms, each holding two of the most beautiful ponies Perdita had ever seen.

'Happy birthday, darling,' said Red, amused at her speechlessness. 'When you shacked up with me, I told you there'd be strings attached.'

Breaking the rule that one should always approach

horses quietly, Perdita flew downstairs in her pale pink silk kimono and, screaming with delight, flitted from pony to pony, two chestnuts, a couple of Barry Bartlett's tough little Walers from Singapore, and a bay and a dark brown from Argentina, who were head-shy when she tried to hug them.

Then, leaping on to one of the chestnuts, Perdita cantered her through the dew, executing such a perfect figure of eight in and out of two orange trees that she earned herself a round of applause from the grooms.

'Thank you,' she screamed up at Red. 'It's the most wonderful, wonderful present I'll ever have.'

He must love her to spoil her like this, and it meant that now, with Spotty and Tero, she'd have eight ponies. She gave a start of horror. She'd come back so late last night and been so knocked out by the splendour of Red's house that she hadn't even asked after them.

'Spotty and Tero are OK, aren't they?' she asked the grooms, who all looked shifty.

When they had driven down to *El Paradiso* she understood why. Spotty had dropped a lot of weight, but actually looked splendidly fit and well muscled.

'You spoilt him. He was always much too fat,' said Red in answer to Perdita's furious complaints.

Spotty was sulking so much that Perdita had deserted him that for the first few days he stoutly refused to acknowledge her presence, even spurning Polos.

Tero was a different matter. Perdita found her standing alone in one of the paddocks – a caricature of her former, sleek self. Her lustreless coat hung from her jagged backbone. You could have stacked plates between her ribs.

Her two-inch-long mane and tail were sparse and motheaten, her once tender, glowing eyes now sunken and dull, as she shivered in the burning sunlight, unsteady on her legs, the picture of despair. But at the sound of Perdita's wail of horror the little mare pricked up her ears, stared for a second, whickered incredulously and then went as crazy with delight as her desperately weak condition would allow. Perdita was motionless and speechless with shame as Tero staggered forward. Then, as she frantically cuddled the pony, Tero proceeded to nudge her feebly in the ribs trying to comfort her.

'What happened to her?' Perdita screamed later at Manuel, Red's headgroom.

'She pine. She wouldn't eat nothing. Eef anyone ride 'er, she shake, then bolt. So we let 'er out, no good. We keep 'er in, no good. So we geeve up.'

'Fucking useless idiots. Why didn't you ring me?'

Manuel shrugged. 'You didn't leave a number.'

And would she have listened, wondered Perdita, appalled. Red had bewitched her. She was humiliated, shattered at what she had done. Sobbing, she vowed never to leave Tero again, not to rest until the pony was better.

Red thought Perdita was making a most awful fuss. It was only a pony. Even a letter and a birthday present from Bart, waiting when they had driven back from the barn, didn't cheer her up.

'Dear Perdita,' he had written, 'Glad you're back in time for the season. I've fired the Napiers, and I can't play with Miguel and Juan any more because the sonofabitch APA have put me up to six. The good news is that Angel's about to get US citizenship, so with him, you and Red, we've got a world-class team to play in the States and the UK next year. First date: Fathers and Sons next month. Happy Birthday. Yours, Bart.'

The present was a diamond necklace.

'We'll have to hock that for a start,' said Red.

Having ignored a mountain of fan mail, final reminders and unopened bills, and remarked how quiet it was for Palm Beach, Red checked his three telephones and found they'd all been cut off. When he sent Perdita into the kitchen to make him a cup of coffee, she found the gas and electricity had been cut off too. The maid, when she came in, announced she would give Red notice unless he paid her for the last five months. Red gave her a wad of notes and told Perdita they'd better go and tap Grace.

'Mom always chews me out, but she coughs up in the end.'

And puts her hand over her mouth while she's coughing, thought Perdita remembering Grace's obsession with good behaviour.

'I can't leave Tero. I've got to get back to the barn,' she snapped.

'We'll only be gone half a day.'

'And I can't meet her with roots like this.' Mutinously Perdita examined her piebald hair. The white-blonde now growing half an inch into the jet-black looked deliberately aggressive and punk.

'Mom's interested in different kinds of roots. She's a godawful snob.'

'What shall I wear?'

'The Crown Jewels. She'd only be happy if I was marrying the Queen of England, so you might as well settle for disapproval.'

Red borrowed a company jet to fly up to New York that afternoon. Grace was waiting for them in her apartment overlooking a now leafless Central Park. The sitting room was enchanting with rose-red lacquered walls and paintwork, sofas and chairs covered in white chintz splodged with huge, dark pink roses and embroidered cushions. There were dark red and pink roses in vases everywhere. Pictures included a Fragonard and a Watteau of charming lovers sitting on swings.

Leather-bound books rose to the ceiling on either side of the mantelpiece, which could hardly be seen for invitations. Below in the grate apple logs burned merrily. Nothing could have been prettier or more welcoming. But Grace, who had an impeccable clippings service and had familiarized herself with Perdita's every misdemeanour from playing Lady Godiva to dunking Enid Coley and swearing at the future King of England, radiated disapproval. Perdita felt as though she'd come out of the bitter November cold and climbed into the deep freeze.

'It's Perdita's birthday,' said Red, kissing Grace on her rigidly unyielding cheek, 'so she's brought you a present.'

Acquired with one of Red's cheques which would certainly bounce later, it was a red-and-white Staffordshire cow, so adorable Perdita could hardly dare to pack it up.

'Thank you,' said Grace, not deigning to open it. 'How old are you, Perdita?'

'Twenty.'

'And what did Red give you?'

Red shot Perdita a look of warning, but it was too late.

'Six ponies,' sighed Perdita happily. 'They're amazing. One dark brown mare. Manuel says she's a bit green, but she's got a tremendous amount of speed, and a chestnut who evidently turns like a ballerina, and a bay who's so pretty she must be clean bred, and two little Walers who are as tough as shit.' She blushed. 'I mean awfully tough.'

'May I see your engagement ring?'

Perdita held out her hand. The sapphire trembled like a great blob of ink.

'Pretty,' said Grace. 'Red has very good taste. I hope you don't play polo in it.'

'Good for blacking Shark Nelligan's eye,' said Perdita.

'I'm drafting an announcement of the engagement for *The New York Times*,' said Grace frostily, 'and I need to know a little more about you, Perdita. I gather you started as a groom. I so admire people who work their way up. What part of England are you from?'

'Eldercombe in Rutshire.'

If this was not a place that held very happy memories for Grace, she didn't show it.

'And what does your father do?' Grace was writing in a rose-patterned notebook now. Perdita was beginning to sweat. She detested using Hamish, but Grace was looking at her as though she were a large dollop of French dressing that had fallen on a new silk dress.

'He's a lawyer, but now he works as a producer in Hollywood.'

Rackety, she could see Grace thinking.

'I'm flying to Beverly Hills next week,' Grace went on. 'Perhaps I could meet him and your mother.'

Perdita went green.

'My parents are divorced. My mother paints.'

'And your grandparents?'

'Mum's father's dead. My grandmother's a lush.'

'And where did the Macleods come from?' asked Grace. 'I know some Perthshire Macleods. There was a title somewhere.'

'Not us.' Perdita was fed up with being interrogated. 'Grandpa was a hen-pecked old wimp, but good-hearted. Granny Macleod is a bitch. You wouldn't need to be very tall to reach the drawer she came out of.'

Grace's lips tightened. Her silver pen quivered. She expected humility from lesser mortals.

'Which school did you go to?'

'About eight, and I was chucked out of seven of them.'

'You'll certainly find Perdita's name in the Rutshire Anti-Social Register,' said Red, who was laughing himself sick.

'Now you're engaged to Red, I assume you'll give up playing polo professionally.'

'Certainly not,' boasted Perdita. 'I'm going to play for your ex-husband next season.'

Red was still laughing on the way home.

'I'm sorry, I'm sorry, I'm sorry,' moaned Perdita. 'Go to Yale, do not pass go, do not collect two hundred pounds.'

'I'm certainly not going to collect the half million I needed from her to settle a few bills. We're going to have to put you to work, baby.'

Three days later Perdita came back from the barn at lunchtime, passionately relieved after an all-night session that Tero was at last eating and responding to treatment. Making herself a Hellman's and Philadelphia sandwich, Perdita settled down to read an interview with Red in *Esquire* magazine.

Was he going to stop oversleeping and get to matches on time? asked the interviewer.

'I don't need an alarm clock,' Red had replied. 'Who'd want to stay asleep in the morning if they had Perdita beside them?'

Perdita clutched herself with joy. Red really did love her.

Accompanying the piece was an incredibly violent photograph of Red riding off Shark Nelligan. His body bent at the waist, like the head of an arrow, swung two feet out of the saddle, hitting exactly the right pressure points as he drove Shark off the line. Red was smiling, Shark was scowling.

'Lovely piece,' she said, as Red walked in, 'and a heavenly photograph.'

'These are better,' said Red, throwing a hard-backed envelope down on the kitchen table.

Inside were some black-and-white prints he'd taken of

her in Kenya and had blown up. She was wearing a black polo shirt, breeches and boots. Her face was slightly shiny and her hair hanging in damp tendrils.

'Wow! I look OK,' said Perdita in amazement. 'Perhaps you should give up polo and take up photography.'

Red ruffled her hair, which was now all black again.

'You're gonna take up modelling, angel, and start earning your keep. I spent the morning with Ferranti's.'

'Dino Ferranti?' said Perdita in excitement. 'The show-jumper? I had such a crush on him.' Then, seeing Red's face, 'But that was yonks ago.'

'Ferranti's Inc. They're a multi-national,' said Red. 'One of their big moneyspinners is cosmetics and perfume. Dino's on the main board. We had lunch today. They're launching a new perfume next year and thinking of calling it "Perdita".'

'After me?' asked Perdita, delighted.

'After you. I hope it's better than "Auriel". If it takes on, they're thinking of sponsoring a polo team. Dino's always wanted to play polo. It'll be fun playing with Dad and Angel this season, but it might pall. We should keep our options open.'

Perdita always felt dizzy with happiness when he talked in terms of their future.

'All they want you to do,' went on Red, 'if they choose you, is have your picture taken looking unbelievably glamorous and make a few personal appearances when they launch it in the spring. And they're talking megabucks.'

A week later, when Perdita was practising cut shots into goal on Spotty and totally concentrating on the job in hand, Red, without warning, brought Dino Ferranti and two of his brothers to watch her. Next day she and Red lunched with the Ferranti Board in New York.

'We better Scotchtape your mouth,' said Red. 'Don't call anyone an asshole.'

Ferranti's, however, were enchanted and promptly signed her up. Red said he'd handle the money side.

'Dino is kind of attractive,' said Perdita as they flew home.

'Don't be deceived. He's very tough.'

Perdita looked down at the pastel houses and the yachts

543

that dotted the hyacinth-blue ocean as the plane began its descent to Palm Beach Airport.

'What about Venturer?' she asked. 'Aren't I under contract to them?'

'Winston Chalmers'll get you out of that. No sweat,' said Red.

'Hum,' said Perdita.

'Dino doesn't like Rupert Campbell-Black by the way, so he'll be delighted to take Venturer out,' said Red. 'Dino once made a pass at Rupert's first wife. And Rupert was very close to Dino's wife, Fen, before she married Dino, so it makes both guys edgy. Rupert is convinced Dino slept with Helen. Dino swears he didn't, but Rupert can never forgive a right.'

55

Back in Rutshire on an October afternoon, Ricky, having worked young ponies all day, by way of light relief was hacking Wayne through the Eldercombe woods. Little Chef, riding pillion on the pony's plump quarters, bristled at rabbits and occasionally leapt down to chase them through leaves still starched by the morning's frost. A sinking sun, like a day-glo grapefruit, caught the shaggy silver pelts of the traveller's joy and gingered the last leaves of the turkey oaks.

In the distance Ricky could hear the mournful pa, pa, pa of the horn. The hunt must be on their last run of the day. He passed Daisy's cottage. A few pale pink roses still clambered up the walls. Fuchsias drooped in tubs, clashing with the scarlet nasturtiums which splayed across the path. The lights were on in the sitting room and the first flickerings of a fire in the grate. Gainsborough, perched on the wall washing his orange fur, crashed fatly through the cat door at the sight of Little Chef. Ricky suddenly thought how comforting it would be to follow Gainsborough in for tea, crumpets and fruitcake. But he didn't want to inflict his black gloom on poor Daisy who was unhappy enough over Perdita's defection.

So, opening the gate, he turned right up the long, green ride to Robinsgrove. Bracken the colour of Red Alderton's hair singed the sides of the valley, yellow ash wands clogged the stream and Ricky's muddy, unrecognizable ponies, whisking their burr-filled tails, stood head to tail gently gnawing at each other's withers. As he reached the top of the hill a sycamore was systematically shedding shoals of amber leaves, as if slithering out of a silk dress and, in the sunfired waters of the lake, the beeches rinsed their last red leaves.

The most beautiful autumn he could remember was coming to an end, and he was no nearer winning his bet and getting Chessie back. He had two painful cracked ribs from the hoof of a recalcitrant pony. He was worried about Dancer who had a cough that wouldn't go away. He missed Luke's endless good humour and reassuring solidarity since he had returned to America, and, although he wouldn't admit it to anyone, he missed Perdita horribly – and so did Little Chef and the ponies, who had all responded to her passionate attentions. All the fun seemed to have gone out of the yard. And now he had to start welding a new team with the twins, who were charming but foxily unreliable, and the *on dit* was that Bart was spending so much on ponies that next year he really would be unbeatable. Ricky felt like Sisyphus whose boulder had not only rolled down the hill but squashed him flat as well.

As he rode into the yard, Louisa, having taken the geraniums out of the tubs, was planting wallflowers and forget-me-nots instead. He had not forgotten Chessie, but she had not left Bart.

The other grooms raced round the boxes of the ponies that were still inside, chucking wodges of hay into their mangers, anxious to get off and dolled up for Saturday night jaunts.

'Don't forget the clocks go back,' said Louisa to Ricky as she took Wayne from him. 'Heaven to have an extra hour's sleep.'

Or an extra hour's insomnia, thought Ricky wearily.

A second later a dark blue Ferrari roared up the drive scattering an appropriately red carpet of beech leaves and screeched to a halt. It was Bas and Rupert on their way home from hunting, their white breeches spattered with mud, jerseys over their shirts, red coats chucked in the back. Both were in tearing spirits. Ricky thought for the hundredth time how well being happily married suited Rupert. Suddenly the grooms seemed in not nearly such a hurry to slope off.

After a quick whirl round the yard to look at Ricky's new ponies, they went into the house. Ricky, still not drinking, got a bottle out of the cellar.

'Christ, this is priceless,' said Bas, rubbing the dust off the label. 'You sure you want to waste it on us? Why not flog it and buy a pony?'

Ricky shrugged and got two glasses out of the cupboard.

'Black dog?' asked Bas, handing Ricky a corkscrew from the knife drawer. Then, as Ricky nodded, he added: 'You should have come out today. The last fox would have cheered anyone up.'

'I seem to have gone off hunting.'

'You ought to be hunting for a new wife,' said Rupert.

'If I could guarantee getting one like yours,' admitted Ricky. 'And why are you looking so bloody pleased with yourself?'

'Taggie's having a baby,' said Rupert triumphantly. 'I am absolutely knocked out, and I've never known anyone so delighted as she is. She's adorable with children anyway. She's so excited she keeps waking me up in the night.'

As the setting sun, now a blazing blood orange, lit up the long scar down the side of Ricky's face, the corkscrew came out of the bottle with only half the cork.

'Oh, Christ, I'm sorry,' said Rupert. 'I forgot about Will. Bloody tactless of me.'

'It's all right,' said Ricky as Bas took the bottle from him. 'I'm very pleased for you. Is Taggie feeling OK?'

'Wonderful,' said Rupert. 'It's me who had the morning sickness today. I got such a hangover celebrating.'

'Now you're forty, d'you think you'll be able to cope with all those interrupted nights?' said Bas slyly.

'I'm not forty yet,' said Rupert coldly.

To the left in the faded blue sky hung a slim, new moon like a ballerina on her points, so sweet, innocent and virginal beside the blazing orange sun in the west. Taggie and Chessie, thought Ricky. How much happier he'd be with someone like Taggie.

'How's Venturer?' he asked as Bas extracted tiny bits of cork from the two glasses of wine.

'Fantastic. Advertising's terrific. We've flogged loads of programmes to the network and abroad. Cameron Cook may be a bit vocal, but she's bloody good at her job. The only problem with Rupert's new fidelity kick is that the most influential programme buyers in America are women. Once Rupert could have screwed them into submission. Now he has to use his powers of persuasion and he gets frightfully bored.'

Rupert grinned. 'Tell it not in Gath, but I have actually been faithful to Tag for a whole year, and I want to get home to her,' he glanced at his watch, 'but first – Christ, this claret is good – we've got a proposition to make to you. We're definitely going to revive the Westchester in America next year. We want you to act as consultant.'

Ricky went very still; the colour drained from his face.

'The plan,' added Rupert, 'is to transmit it in America, the UK, Europe, certainly Australia and the Argentine, and God knows where else in October. The English team would have to rest their horses after the Gold Cup, then fly them out in September to acclimatize them. You'll captain the English team.'

'American sponsors are crazy about the idea,' chipped in Bas. 'Revlon, BMW, Cartier, Cadillac, Michelob, Peters Cars, they'll all take air time. The network's mad about it, too, and are talking about prime time if we get the Prince and Princess of Wales to present the cup.'

'Polo doesn't work on television,' said Ricky flatly.

'We'll have to edit,' said Rupert. 'The plan is not to change ends until half-time, shorten the pitch a little, play with a yellow ball and have cameras overhead. We've got to capture the excitement and the glamour and the snob element. It'll be like a walking *Tatler* crossed with *Chariots of Fire*.'

'Sounds hell,' said Ricky.

'If properly promoted,' went on Rupert, ignoring the jibe, 'it'll create as much interest as the Ryder Cup or even the America's Cup.'

Ricky's hand shook as he put two heaped spoonfuls of coffee in a mug and filled it up with cold water from the tap.

'That won't taste very nice,' said Bas, removing the cup, throwing the contents away and starting all over again.

'We are utterly pissed off with Perdita for buggering off,' said Rupert, 'but Cameron's got some incredible footage already.'

'She's a disgrace,' snapped Ricky, 'and should be left to stew.'

'She's still under contract,' said Rupert, who liked making money. 'Now she's living with Little Red Riding Hood, she's an even hotter property. Cameron's going to follow her in Palm Beach when she comes up against some really tough opposition, then transmit the film as a teaser just before the Westchester.'

'She'll never hold Red,' said Ricky, sitting down on the window seat with his cup of coffee and patting his knee for Little Chef to jump up.

'Bart's signed up both of them to play with him and Angel Solis de Gonzales in Palm Beach and England,' said Bas.

Now Bart's got Chessie *and* Perdita, thought Ricky savagely.

The whole west had turned a brilliant rippling vermilion. Silhouetted black against it, a poplar copse looked like Daisy's paintbrushes neatly stacked in a jamjar after a day's work. The little moon had turned gold.

'Well,' said Bas, 'are you going to come in with us or not?'

If Chessie had really loved him, reasoned Ricky, she would have come back by now. Rivers of blood had flowed under the bridge since she had left him. On the other hand he could go to ten, he could win the Gold Cup, and now there was a possibility to win the Westchester. He was still utterly obsessed with burying Bart. It was worth a try.

'All right,' he said. 'But Venturer putting so much money in scares the shit out of me. You sure you can afford it? The Americans are virtually unbeatable on their own territory.'

'Well, that should please the Americans if they're putting up most of the money,' said Rupert sensibly.

'Well, I wouldn't waste money on Perdita,' said Ricky harshly. 'Her form's going to plummet once she starts playing with Bart and Red. They're both so hooked on winning, they'll gee her up rather than calm her down, and she'll get more and more explosive.'

'Great,' said Rupert rubbing his hands. 'Tantrums fill stadiums. Look at Nastase. Look at McEnroe and Botham.'

'Look at you,' said Bas. 'You were the biggest crowd-puller of all times.'

'I don't pull crowds any more,' said Rupert, gathering up his car keys. 'I only pull Tag.'

56

Palm Beach was staggered by the change in Red. The ultimate party animal was in bed by midnight and up at seven, and for the first time in his life really working at his polo. As barns filled up with grooms and horses, and patrons went on crash diets getting ready for the season proper which began in January, it was noted that Red and Perdita were spending six or seven hours a day stick and balling, concocting devilish strategies to fox the opposition and working on Perdita's new ponies and the whole Alderton Flyer string.

'Must be even more desperate to bury the opposition than his father,' said Shark Nelligan cynically. 'Just to prove the Alderton Flyers can manage without the O'Briens.'

Perdita, vastly cheered that Tero had made a miraculous recovery and would be able to play again later in the season, was less happy when she had to spend hours being photographed for Ferranti's by the exceedingly famous but equally temperamental photographer they'd employed.

'God, they ought to give the VC to models,' she stormed. 'It's so bloody boring – and the lies! "Last roll" indeed. The fucker only takes so long because he's getting a thousand dollars an hour.'

The results of such conflict, however, were hauntingly beautiful.

'Everyone will be dabbing Perdita on their pulse spots come February,' crowed Red.

As a reward, the weekend before the Fathers and Sons match Red took Perdita to stay at Bart's house in Colorado. Falling over and into Red's arms, Perdita took to skiing as enthusiastically as she had to sex.

The Tuesday after they returned home, Perdita was easing her aching bones in the jacuzzi after a long day in the saddle when Red walked in. Instantly she felt her exhaustion vanish and her stomach churning like the warm waters around her. She never stopped wanting him.

Sitting on the edge of the jacuzzi, he soaked the arm of his shirt as his fingers crept downwards, light and expert as a pastry cook.

'I'm gonna screw you,' he whispered in her ear, 'and then we're going out. Bibi and Angel are back from Argentina. I called Bibi and said we'd drop by for a drink, and then all go out to dinner.'

Bibi's and Angel's barn was grudgingly agreed by the polo community to be the most beautiful in Palm Beach. Built and perfected over the past eighteen months, it consisted of a charming, white, Regency-style house with a grey roof, a garden full of sweet-scented flowers, a walled swimming-pool kept permanently at 100°F, tennis courts, squash courts, a helicopter pad, and a hundred yards away at the end of a perfect lawn, a lemon-and-orange grove ringing stables for thirty horses. Beyond were paddocks, stick-and-ball fields and a complete polo pitch, surrounded by gums and palm trees.

'Must have cost Bibi an arm and a legacy,' said Red, as the blaring din of Status Quo from his car clashed and collided with Phil Collins pouring out of Bibi's and Angel's house. A pungent mix of jasmine, orange blossom and philadelphus mingled with a delicious smell of beef, herbs, wine and garlic.

'Perhaps we're eating in after all,' said Red.

'I haven't seen Angel in two years.' Perdita checked her reflection in the driving mirror.

Ferranti's had taught her to make up her eyes and she was drenched in the scent which had been named after her. Her hair, which had nearly grown back to her collar bones, was streaked blond and black, her face was smooth and brown as treacle toffee from skiing. She was wearing a clinging, elongated, orange T-shirt. She hoped Angel would think she had grown beautiful.

Angel, however, opened the door in a pair of jeans and a white hot rage, his bronze curls tousled, his peacock-blue eyes blazing. She had forgotten his capacity for implacable loathing.

'What zee fuck you doing he-ar?' he spat at them. 'You fucking 'orrible beetch, Perdita. I never want to see you again. Don't darken my doormat, none of you.'

And he launched into a torrent of French, Spanish and English, telling Perdita exactly what he thought of her for running out on his beloved *amigo*, Luke. He was about to slam the door in their faces, when Red put his shoulder against it. For a moment the two men pushed with all their might. But not for nothing could Red ride off Shark Nelligan. The door remained six inches open.

'For Chrissake, Angel, there wasn't anything between Perdita and Luke. It was totally one-sided. He was mad about her, not her about him.'

'It's true, Angel,' stammered a shaken Perdita. 'I knew Luke liked me, but I had no idea how much until Deauville, and by that time I was in love with Red.'

'You take everything from heem, his money, his horses, his time, his heart.'

'I suppose he's been dumping,' said Red. 'There are two sides.'

'Luke never dumps,' snarled Angel. 'He never says one word against you, Perdita. It's everyone else.'

'Oh, don't be an asshole, Angel,' said Red in a bored voice. 'Cut out the macho-Latin crap. Luke's not complaining: why should you? Where's Bibi?'

'Working late,' said Angel bleakly. 'Where else?'

'Well, let us in. I want a drink. Perdita's going to be your sister-in-law. There's enough feuding in our family as it is and we've all got to play together on Thursday.'

Angel was gazing at Perdita, at the long, dark eyes, liquid with tears, the trembling coral-pink mouth. He could see the curve of her breasts and the tuffet of her bush in that clinging orange dress. He detested her, but she had grown incredibly beautiful, and Angel was, after all, an Argentine.

'OK, come in.' Totally unsmiling, he stood back.

Inside were scenes of Petronian debauchery. In a room to the left Jesus lay on the patchwork quilt of a huge double bed with a sleeping, naked blonde beside him. Dropping cigarette ash into Bibi's pot-pourri bowl, he was ringing up different parts of the world on Bibi's three telephones in several languages and trying to organize next season's matches.

'Treble-dating, as usual,' said Red.

Through the french windows they could see a couple of Alejandro's sons and their girlfriends cavorting in the swimming-pool. In the sitting room Juan O'Brien, with one hand inside the dress of a brunette who was certainly not his wife, and several more of Alejandro's sons and their cousins were sitting round on Bibi's flowered chintz sofas, drinking wine, eating a very late lunch of boeuf Provençale and watching the video of the Argentine Open, which once again the O'Briens had won by a narrow margin. The air was blue with cigarette smoke.

Next minute, a ravishingly pretty girl came out of the kitchen in skin-tight jeans, a skimpy pink top to show off a midriff browner than Perdita's face and a long blonde plait falling through the hole in the back of her baseball cap. She had an incredible air of self-importance, was wearing a badge which said: 'Is that a banana in your pocket or are you just pleased to see me?' and was carrying a tray of baked potatoes.

'Ees good?' she asked the catatonically watching men.

'Ees excellent,' said Juan, reaching out for a baked potato with the hand that had been fondling the brunette, but not taking his eyes off the screen.

In the corner two lurcher puppies were having a tug of war with a silk cushion embroidered with the words: 'It's hard being a Princess'.

'Oh, how adorable,' said Perdita. 'Let's get a dog.'

'No,' said Red sharply. 'Dogs get too dependent.'

He was fixing a whisky and soda for himself and a vodka and tonic for Perdita. Suddenly noticing him, the blonde stopped in her tracks.

'Ay, yay, yay,' she said in wonder, 'I am Innocenta.'

'And I am usually guilty,' grinned Red. 'Red Alderton,' he introduced himself, 'and this is Perdita.'

'Oof,' cried the blonde in amazement. 'Bibi's brozzer, you are not like 'er.'

Once the video was finished the Argentines came back to earth, shook Red by the hand and embraced Perdita and congratulated her on her new beauty.

'What's the gossip?' said Red.

'Your father is spending twice as much on 'orses,' said Juan, 'because he's not spending so much on me and Miguel.'

'Jesus is playing for Cartier, BMW and Revlon all at zee same time.'

'Juan's now wearing a face guard on and off the field, so he doesn't have to kees ees wife.'

Juan grinned and all the others screamed with laughter and helped themselves to more wine. They were all so merry, flip and funny that, after a couple of drinks, Perdita recovered from the shock of Angel's disapproval and showed everyone her ring.

Only Angel, who was smoking and not eating or drinking, was still in a black mood. He filled the house with Argentines because he was fed up with being married to a wife who was never at home before nine, then worked long into the night on reports, and was taking telephone calls at five in the morning from all over the world. In the three months he'd just spent in Argentina Bibi had only flown down to join him for a couple of weekends. His resentment was fuelled by his friends who all pointed out that Angel was *numero uno* in the marriage and Bibi was neglecting him. Argentine wives looked beautiful and after their husbands.

His temper had not been improved that morning by an advance issue of *Chief Executive* magazine which had just voted Bibi businesswoman of the year. Inside was a full-page picture of his wife showing off her long, long legs and with her auburn hair spilling over the shoulders of her pin-stripe suit. A paragraph towards the end of the copy claimed that Bibi had 'every designer toy in her Palm Beach mansion, including a devastatingly handsome Argentine polo player husband'.

'Nice picture,' said Red, throwing the magazine down on the table. 'I dropped by the Palm Beach office this afternoon. Two of Dad's secretaries were still at lunch, and Miss Leditsky was painting her toenails, and making long-distance personal calls about the long weekend she was about to take. When secretaries start goofing off, you're in the shit.'

Then, to cheer Angel up, he persuaded him to play the best of three at backgammon to see which of them was going to ride Glitz – Bart's legendary black pony on which Juan had scored so many goals – next season.

'Things seem to be getting a bit out of hand,' said Red about nine-thirty, when no Bibi had turned up and he and Perdita had admired all Angel's new ponies and a new forty-thousand-dollar aluminium trailer, and all the other Argentines were either drunk or shacked up. 'Let's go and eat, and leave a note to Bibi to join us later.'

Charley's Crab, the best fish and shellfood restaurant in Wellington, was much frequented by the polo community. With each new arrival the waiters pinned sheets of clean white paper over the table tops so polo plays and tactics could be drawn on them.

'How's Tero?' asked Angel, relenting slightly.

'Getting better,' said Perdita. 'I don't have to feed everything to her by hand now, and I rode her for a quarter of an hour yesterday, admittedly only walking.'

'How is Luke?' Perdita was unable to resist asking, although she knew it would irritate Red.

'Who can tell?' said Angel. 'Always he smile, always he listen to zee moans of zee other players. But last week his groom tell me he was so drunk he miss zee toll bucket three times.'

Oh God, thought Perdita miserably. She wanted to ask more but the waiter came over for their order.

'For Chrissake, don't spend all night making up your mind,' snapped Red.

Flustered, Perdita chose Cajun prawns, which were delicious but took the roof off her mouth. As they talked polo, Angel noticed she knew everything about Red's ponies and was passionately interested in his game. She was also quite unable to keep her hands off Red. Angel thought darkly of Bibi's distancing. They hadn't slept together for a week because she was always so tired. She arrived as they were having coffee, white with anger and exhaustion.

'I've just had to throw a dozen Argies out of the house, Angel, and only just dissuaded Jaime and Carmen from giving in their notice,' she said furiously. 'Carmen says she can't call her kitchen her own. You know how hard it is to get help. And why the hell was Innocenta hosting the party?'

'Because you weren't there,' snarled Angel.

554

'Someone's got to earn the fucking money,' hissed Bibi. Then, seeing Angel's face, regretted it. 'I'm sorry, darling. It's been a hell of a day.'

'And a night,' said Angel, pointedly looking at his watch.

Bibi visibly pulled herself together and turned to Red and Perdita.

'Hi, congratulations. How are you?'

'Distract Angel for a second,' Red whispered to Perdita.

'Things bad?' he murmured to Bibi, pouring her a glass of Sancerre. 'We must get you something to eat.'

'I'm not hungry.' Bibi was shaking.

'What's up now?'

'This,' said Bibi, producing a cutting from the *Daily News* out of her bag.

It was a piece about Chessie flying Bart's private jet to Paris and spending half a million on clothes for the forthcoming Palm Beach season, not to mention buying one of the Duchess of Windsor's favourite brooches for £50,000 and a Poussin at Sotheby's.

'So what else is new?' said Red coolly, although his eyes were narrowed with rage and his fingers drummed on the white paper tablecloth. 'No wonder Dad wouldn't advance me any money last week.'

'She's done all that,' said Bibi despairingly, 'when Dad's had to lay off seven hundred people this week because he can't pay their wages. The guys are putting her photograph on the factory walls instead of pin-ups so they can throw darts at it.'

'Chessie-Antoinette,' said Red. 'Can't someone assassinate her?'

'Hardly,' said Bibi with a hollow laugh. 'The same piece reports her as attending a fashion show for bullet-proof clothes last week. Red, we are running out of money.'

'I know,' said Red. 'Can't Dad talk to her?'

'Not when he's spending so much on ponies. They're as bad as each other. I don't know who's spending the most – Dad, Chessie or Angel,' Bibi added bitterly. Then, lowering her voice, 'Angel just adores the grand gesture. He gave a friend of his a $20,000 pony last week because his wife had just quit.'

'Shit!' Red shook his head. 'What triggered off Chessie's recent spate of extravagance?'

'You did,' said Bibi. 'You know how she hates Mom ringing Dad, but Mom's been in such a state about you and Perdita, she's been calling him a lot lately. She was bad enough about me and Angel.'

Angel looked round. 'Grace put a private detective on to my family,' he said haughtily. 'All she found was that my side of the family were poor, but not at all non-U.'

'And anyway, you're her ewe lamb, the light of her life,' said Bibi bitterly to Red, then added to Perdita, 'I don't mean it personally. It's nothing to do with you. Mom'd be the same whoever Red married; she's positively oedipal about him. And even when Dad and Chessie are fighting like cats Chessie can't stand him having any communication with Mom.'

'Bibi is going to lose that good-looking boy if she's not careful,' said Red as they drove home. 'He's already catting around with that blonde cook who looks as though cocks wouldn't melt in her mouth.'

But Perdita wasn't listening. Sick with churning fear, she was thinking that if Grace put a private detective on to her, in no time he'd find out about her being illegitimate or worse.

Next week the Aldertons won the Fathers and Sons match, annihilating the Van Dorens by forty goals to five, which presaged well for the coming season.

Christmas in Palm Beach was extremely fraught. Everyone missed Luke. Easy-going, imperturbable, prepared to see the funny side of practically anything, he had been a genius at defusing rows. Red and Perdita being so extravagantly in love seemed to unhinge Chessie. Her temper was not improved on Christmas Day when a vast JCB, wrapped in red ribbon and decorated with holly, was delivered to Alderton Towers.

'Dear Chessie, to help you with your gold digging,' said the note inside, 'Yours never, Red.'

Nor was Angel particularly amused when Bibi gave him a green Lamborghini. She kept him short, humiliated him by refusing to pay his gambling debts, and then expected him to be grateful for a bloody car.

His best present in fact was a small oblong envelope from

Bart. Inside was a US passport. A senator friend of Bart's had pulled strings. This meant that at last Angel could circumnavigate the ban on Argentines and play in England.

'Thank you,' Angel embraced a father-in-law he normally detested. 'I am damn Yanqui now.'

'You're gonna help me bury Apocalypse,' said Bart in an undertone.

'You can play for America in the International,' said Chessie in delight.

'You could even play for them in the Westchester if Bas and Rupert do really revive it in the autumn,' said Perdita.

But Angel was miles away, thinking of Pedro at the bottom of the icy South Atlantic. The fish would have picked his bones clean by now and Angel had another bone to pick with a poker-faced British officer. At last he was going to England to take out Drew Benedict.

57

Daisy Macleod, on the other hand, longed and longed to be taken out by Drew Benedict. Now he was earning serious money playing polo he was spending more time abroad and Daisy saw far less of him. But he assured her good times lay ahead once he was financially independent of Sukey.

Daisy was also low because she blamed herself entirely for Perdita's defection. If only she hadn't conceived Perdita at Jackie's orgy, if she'd been a more forceful mother and hadn't let Perdita run wild, if she'd told Perdita the truth earlier and been able to hold on to Hamish, if she hadn't been distracted by falling in love with Drew.

Since Perdita had run off with Red she had rung her mother twice, the first time from Kenya to say she was deliriously happy, the second to boast about the Fathers and Sons match and Ferranti's paying her a fortune. But when Daisy had reproached her gently for hurting Luke and walking out on Venturer and Apocalypse, Perdita had hung up and cut off all lines of communication.

One of the highlights for Daisy, therefore, of a long, cold winter was a surprise party for Ricky's thirty-second birthday in the middle of February. Louisa had lured him away to look at a pony which turned out to be an absolute dog. Returning irritably home to Robinsgrove, he found a rip-roaring party in full swing with every light blazing, drink from Bas's wine bar flowing and live music provided by Dancer and Apocalypse pounding down the valley. Taggie Campbell-Black had produced the most succulent home-made ravioli stuffed with lobster purée and braised quails, served with fresh mangoes flown specially down from Harrods. To hide how touched he was, Ricky was absolutely furious. But gradually he and the great gloomy house he inhabited responded almost joyously to the intrusion.

Daisy was bitterly disappointed that Drew couldn't make it and very embarrassed about her present; everyone else's were so much more exciting. Only after several drinks did she drag Seb Carlisle, who'd been bopping with a six-foot inflatable rubber doll he'd had gift-wrapped for Ricky, into the study.

'Alone at last,' whooped Seb, grabbing her. 'You and I and Dolly can have a threesome.'

Giggling, Daisy wriggled free. 'I've done a portrait for Ricky. Will you look at it and promise to tell me if you think he'll be upset?'

'I'm the one who's upset, you keep spurning me,' grumbled Seb, unwrapping the red crêpe paper. 'Christ! that is absolutely stunning. How the hell did you get such a likeness? It's Will to a T.'

He traced the thick flaxen hair and the dark slanting eyes with one finger. 'He was such a gorgeous child. Ricky will go apeshit.'

'Are you sure he won't be hurt by it?'

'*Au contraire!* He's never had any decent photographs of Will. Chessie swiped the lot. I'll get him.'

Shaking, Daisy took a great gulp of champagne. Rutshire Polo Club's fixture list for next year was already up on the wall. Ricky came in looking boot-faced. He detested people invading his private sanctum.

'I don't want presents. I can't think why everyone's bothered.' The words died on his lips as he picked up the picture.

'I'll quite understand if you want to throw it on the fire,' gabbled Daisy.

Ricky just gazed and gazed at it and said nothing, then he shook his head in disbelief, tried to speak and found he was quite unable.

'I'm sorry,' mumbled Daisy. 'Give it back to me.'

'No, no, it's beautiful, w-w-wonderful, so like him. I can't begin to tell you what it mm-m-means. I had no record. I've b-b-been haunted by not remembering what he looked like.'

Daisy, in her delighted confusion, frantically stroked Little Chef who'd bounded in after Ricky, wearing a red, white and blue bow. Glancing up, she was amazed to see Ricky's eyes wet with tears.

'How the hell did you do it?'

'I was leafing through those old polo books you lent me for a picture of the Rutshire before the war, and Will's photo fell out. I've got it for you at home.'

'I don't know how to b-b-begin to thank you.'

'Or us you,' mumbled Daisy, 'for letting us stay on at Snow Cottage.'

Later in the evening Rupert took Daisy aside.

'That's a bloody good picture of Will. Ricky is beside himself. Now all we've got to do is persuade Victor Kaputnik to invent a cure for Chessie.'

Daisy found Rupert so incredibly glamorous and shy-making that she always talked rubbish in his presence.

'Wonderful food,' she mumbled. 'Taggie is *so* clever. They always say the way to a man's heart is through his stomach.'

'It's through his heart,' said Rupert quite sharply.

There was a pause, then he said, 'Cameron Cook's flying out to Palm Beach with a crew next week to film Perdita in the Rolex Cup. I hope she's not going to be bolshy. You heard from her?'

Daisy shook her head miserably. 'She doesn't answer letters, and hangs up if I try and ring her.'

'I was just as impossible at her age,' said Rupert more gently. 'She'll come round.'

All the time Daisy was aware of him watching Taggie who was now rather tentatively asking people if they'd like chocolate roulade or raspberry bombe.

'She's so beautiful,' sighed Daisy.

Rupert's face softened. 'She is, isn't she? The nightmare

is trying to stop her doing too much. Look,' he lowered his voice, 'Helen, my first wife, painted the nursery the most appalling jaundice-yellow. It's just been repainted. If I manage to lure Tag away for a long weekend, would you be able to slap on some flowers and birds and butterflies and perhaps the odd horse and dog for a surprise when she comes back?'

'What a gorgeous idea,' said Daisy.

'Hush, she's coming,' said Rupert. 'I'll let you know when we're going, and arrange for you to have a set of keys.'

Next day it snowed and Ricky gave Eddie a virtually new red-and-silver sledge he'd bought for Will one year there had been no snow.

'Pointless it eating its head off in the attic.'

'It's Mum's birthday next week,' confided Eddie. 'What d'you think she'd like?'

The day before Daisy's birthday Drew arrived bearing flowers, champagne, a side of smoked salmon and a great deal of silk underwear.

Later, pretending she'd bought it all herself as a birthday treat, she couldn't resist showing the underwear to Eddie and to Violet, who'd come home for the weekend.

'You goofed there, Mum,' said Eddie, disapprovingly. 'Why waste a fortune on stuff no-one's going to see?'

Next day they brought her breakfast in bed. Violet gave her a black polo neck, Eddie, having borrowed a fiver off his mother, gave her some fishnet tights. Around twelve Violet said, 'Ricky's asked us for a drink.'

'We can't,' said Daisy. 'We've imposed on him enough. He doesn't know it's my birthday, does he?' Thirty-nine seemed horribly old.

'Of course he doesn't,' said Violet.

'Happy birthday,' said Ricky as she walked through the front door.

'Pigs,' hissed Daisy to the grinning Violet and Eddie.

'Happy birthday,' chorused all Ricky's grooms and Joel, the farm manager.

After a glass of red wine, incapable of keeping a secret, Eddie told his mother that Ricky had a present for her.

'Shut your eyes,' he added, at a nod from Ricky.

Taking her hands, the children led her up flight after flight of stairs. Acutely aware of fishnet tights wrinkling around her ankles, Daisy wondered if Ricky was following behind. She was walking on bare boards now. Then she heard a door being opened and felt warmth.

'OK, you can look now,' said Eddie.

She was in a large attic room, with a window stretching the length of the far wall looking over the Eldercombe Valley to the Bristol Channel. A low winter sun was pouring in. By the window was an easel complete with canvas covered in white drawing paper. On a side table were sketch pads, more rolls of paper, a complete set of new paints, rubbers, pencils, brushes in a jar and a huge bowl of snowdrops.

'The smock's from Ethel, so you won't get paint on your clothes any more,' said Violet.

'I don't understand,' muttered Daisy.

Ricky's face was expressionless. 'It's your new studio. I'm f-f-fed up with you covering my cottage with paint.'

'Oh,' gasped Daisy. 'The view, the light, the peace. It's incredible!'

'There's no excuse for you to be sidetracked now, Mum,' said Violet.

'Here are the keys to the front door.' Ricky dropped them into her hand. 'Come and go as you like.'

'But I'll be in your way.'

'I'm out most of the time. Seems a shame to waste such a nice room.'

'I must be dreaming.' Daisy wandered towards the window.

On the horizon was a streak of palest turquoise below a lavender sky. Opal-blue smoke rose straight up from chimneys and bonfires. The woods looked soft and fluffy like the stretched belly of a tabby kitten. Turning, she went up to Ricky and quickly kissed him on the side of his face where there was no scar.

'Ricky can be your toyboy, Mum,' said Eddie.

'It was all Ricky's idea,' said Violet as they floated home an hour later. 'He's so knocked out with Will's portrait.'

'He's a good bloke,' said Eddie. 'We're going to shoot clays this afternoon.'

'And he says I can practise driving on one of his flat fields,' said Violet.

The only person not pleased with the arrangement was Drew.

'How can I possibly get in touch with you if you're up at Ricky's all the time?'

A week later Rupert flew into Palm Beach in a furious temper. Overdoing things, Taggie had nearly lost the baby. James Benson, Rupert's doctor, had ordered her to rest for the next month and had flatly refused to let her travel with Rupert when he was forced to fly over and sort out the ghastly row that had blown up over the documentary on Perdita Macleod.

Venturer had already sunk a great deal of money in the project. Cameron Cook and a very expensive crew were out there filming, and now the mighty Ferranti's had come down like a ton of bricks, saying that their exclusive contract with Perdita precluded her from taking part in anything else.

Cameron Cook had then waved Venturer's contract at Ferranti and was defiantly filming Perdita in an early Rolex Gold Cup match when a posse of Ferranti heavies, secretly alerted by Red, rolled up and frightened Cameron off. Knowing how much it took to frighten Cameron, who'd made programmes in Beirut and Grenada, Rupert realized that the heavies must have been very heavy indeed.

Cameron's temper had not been improved by Perdita turning on the crew, whose presence had made her miss two easy passes, and screaming at them to eff off and make their piss-pot film somewhere else. It was then that the lawyers moved in.

They had now reached a stalemate with neither side prepared to budge an inch, but Ferranti's were infinitely richer than Venturer and had, furthermore, employed Winston – 'If you're innocent, you don't need me' – Chalmers, Florida's toughest lawyer, to act for them. Dino Ferranti, the sales director, who was an old enemy of Rupert's and disliked him intensely, was intending to take no prisoners in the ensuing battle. At this stage Cameron had reluctantly begged Rupert to fly out. It was the sort of tussle he would have relished in the old days, but not since he married Taggie. Under her gentle influence he had shed much of his aggression and he detested letting her out of his sight for a second – particularly now she was having a baby.

They had been married fourteen months now, during which time Rupert had never dreamed he would suffer such extremes of happiness and misery. There was the miracle of her love, not just for him but for his children. Every day he expected some flaw in her character to be revealed, some pettiness or bloody-mindedness, but she had not revealed even a toenail of clay. There had been the unbelievable joys of initiating her sexually, slowly, slowly breaking down her shyness and inhibitions, until he was rewarded a thousand-fold by the passion and enthusiasm of her response.

But this wonderful happiness had a flipside. Rupert was absolutely terrified of losing her. With his track record, Taggie was the one who should have been jealous, but she trusted him implicitly and felt so blessed that he had married her rather than any of the legions of others that she had no right to question her exclusivity. It was Rupert who suffered hell-pains. He was jealous of every man she talked to, of her prodigal, importunate family who were always dropping in to borrow money and enjoy Taggie's cooking, of people she met in the street, even of his own children, dogs and horses. And now she was having his child and he was scared he might be jealous of that too. Although he made heroic attempts to curb this jealousy, every so often it overwhelmed him and he found himself biting her utterly innocent head off. Then, crucified when he saw the bewilderment in her big eyes, he pulled her into his arms frantic with remorse.

As the months passed things had got better, as Taggie, who originally had such a low opinion of herself she couldn't imagine anyone being miserable when denied her company, gradually realized how passionately Rupert loved her, and that these outbursts of rage were merely expressions of his love. As Rupert became more sure of her, the outbursts became fewer.

And, although she still slipped the odd hundred to her family, she had persuaded them to telephone before they dropped in. It had helped, too, that Rupert had installed electric gates after her mother, Maud, had arrived unannounced after a row with Declan to find Rupert in the sitting room using a pastry brush to paint Taggie's labia with olive oil before photographing her in the nude.

They had not spent a night apart since they were married, and now Rupert had to leave her at the Priory in the somewhat dubious care of Maud and Declan. But at least it gave Daisy a chance to paint flowers and animals all over the nursery walls and, flying overnight, he hoped he would be able to sort out Ferranti's in a day and fly back that evening.

He checked into his favourite hotel in Palm Beach, the charmingly old-fashioned Faversham, where he had been given the Kennedy Suite overlooking the ocean. Showering, then changing his shirt, he found a note in his suitcase from Taggie.

'Darling Rupert, I love you dessparately and miss you, pleese come home quickly, I promiss not too do too much. All my love, Taggie.'

It was not Eloise and Abelard standard, but to Rupert it was immeasurably more precious. Taggie had tried so hard to conquer her dyslexia. He was tempted to ring her, but hoped she would be having an afternoon sleep. He was unable, however, to resist getting out of a secret pocket in the lid of his briefcase three nude photographs he'd taken of her last week. One from the waist up showed off her glorious breasts, the second three-quarters turned away from him and smiling shyly over her shoulder displayed her narrow waist, high bottom and endless legs; in the third, she was sitting in an arm chair with her legs apart, showing a muff Rupert had shaved down to a small goatee. Rupert felt himself go hard. God, she was beautiful and all his. Bugger Venturer and Ferranti. He swore as the telephone went. It was Cameron ringing from the lobby.

'Thank Christ you're here. I've got a car waiting downstairs.'

Nine hours later they were still deadlocked – both sides refusing to give an inch. It was immaterial that Ferranti's contract was for a thousand times as much money. Venturer had signed Perdita up first.

'But not exclusively,' drawled Dino Ferranti, his beautiful, blue silk shirt creased, his Siamese cat's eyes squinting with tiredness and irritation. He and Rupert had exchanged very sharp words. But Rupert's real animosity was reserved for Red Alderton, who, in his promiscuity, viciousness, arrogance and total lack of repentance, reminded Rupert of everything he wanted to forget about his own past. He was also allergic to red hair because it reminded him of his first wife and his appallingly grasping mother-in-law. Red, absolutely terrified of losing the $2,000,000 Ferranti's were contracted to pay Perdita, much of which had already been spent, kept butting in, until Rupert lost his temper.

'Just fuck off, Maureen O'Hara and curl your eyelashes,' he yelled. 'You knew all about the Venturer contract when you set up the Ferranti deal, you little pimp. Fucking leech! You'd make Dracula look like a blood donor.'

'You're a fine one,' screamed Perdita, leaping to Red's defence. 'What about those memoirs? Talk about a cock in every porthole. You could bore out the Channel Tunnel solo.'

Dino Ferranti suppressed a smile. Then, as Red weighed in, a fearful slanging match ensued and the lawyers banished both Red and Perdita from the building.

Back at Red's house Perdita lounged on his dark blue silk counterpane drinking Green Devils and watching Red pacing up and down, ranting on and on about Rupert.

'Arrogant shit, who the hell does he think he is?' Then he paused, face lit up with satanic excitement. 'I've got it! I know how we can make him back off.'

'We can't,' breathed Perdita in appalled wonder two minutes later.

At three o'clock in the morning the lawyers decided to adjourn. Rupert rang Taggie, who was still staying at Declan's, to say he definitely wouldn't be home next day. Taggie tried not to sound disappointed, saying she was fine and it had frozen last night and now it was snowing and she missed him dreadfully. Rupert said it was a nightmare and the only person going to make any money were the lawyers, and that he loved her indescribably and would ring her in the morning.

Letting himself into his suite half an hour later Rupert longed to ring her again, but felt he shouldn't crowd her. The quickest undresser in the world, he stepped out of his clothes in the sitting room and wandered into the bathroom to clean his teeth. He'd have a shower when he got up – he glanced wearily at his watch – in about three hours' time. Thinking it would make Taggie seem nearer, he decided to have another look at her photographs, then panicked when he couldn't find them. He was sure he'd left them under his shirts. Checking the bedroom he froze.

'Hello, Rupert,' said Perdita softly. 'I'm sorry I shouted at you earlier. I thought you might be lonely.'

The sheet was drawn up to her chin, but she let it fall, swinging her feet off the bed.

'You shabby little bitch,' whispered Rupert. 'Get out of here.'

'Don't be like that.' Perdita's eyes were as shiny as black olives drenched in oil and, as she stood up, her slender naked body seemed almost incandescent with heat and excitement.

'You must know I've always fancied you.' It was like a child actress trying to play Delilah.

'How did you get in here?' hissed Rupert.

'Easy. I just told them you'd asked me round. The hall porter even winked at me. You must have had loads of girls here in the past.'

In the past Rupert certainly had. Now his mind was racing. If he rang Security, they'd be here in an instant, but with his track record someone would be bound to leak it to the press. The same went for the police. And if anyone saw Perdita leaving his suite, he was also in trouble. She was slowly advancing towards him.

'Get your clothes on.' He tried to sound calm.

'Not so fast,' drawled a voice and Red came out of the wardrobe. Before Rupert could stop him he'd taken half a dozen photographs of both of them naked and dived for the door. But Rupert was too quick for him. Giving a great cat jump, he caught Red by the ankles and brought them both crashing to the ground.

'You little shit,' he howled, grabbing the camera.

Next second Red had tried to knee him in the balls and Rupert had smashed his fist into Red's face. Then, picking him up by his shirt, he smashed him to the floor again.

'Don't kill him,' screamed Perdita.

While Red was lurching to his feet, Rupert grabbed a towel and wrapped it round his waist. Hurling the contents

566

of a vase of flowers on the floor, he smashed the vase on a low glass table and brandished the jagged edge at Red with one hand, reaching for the telephone with the other. 'D'you want me to call the police?'

Red deliberated. 'I guess not.'

'Then give me back Tag's pictures.'

Very slowly Red removed them from his inside pocket and threw them down on the glass table. 'Very pretty. You must introduce me some time.'

'Shut up!' Rupert gave such a howl that the windows rattled and the glasses rang. 'If you ever come within a million miles of her . . . Get dressed.' Picking up Perdita's pink dress, he hurled it at her. 'You cheap little blackmailing whore. I wouldn't put anything past the Scarlet Pimp here, but I thought a bit of Luke or Ricky might have rubbed off on you.'

'We wouldn't have gone to the press,' stammered Perdita. 'We just wanted you to back off.'

Still drunk from the Green Devils, she put her legs into one of the arm holes of her dress and nearly fell over when the telephone rang. Rupert was ashen when he put the receiver down.

'What's the matter?' whispered Perdita.

'Taggie. She was worried no-one would feed the birds and sneaked over to Penscombe and slipped on the ice. Declan thinks she's miscarrying. I've got to go back.'

The events of the last ten minutes might never have happened.

'Borrow one of Dad's jets,' offered Red.

'Thanks,' said Rupert. All that mattered was getting home as fast as possible.

The truce was fleeting. Rupert got back to England to find Taggie had not only lost the baby, but nearly her life as well. She would get better, said James Benson reassuringly, who had never expected to see Rupert so devastated, but she'd never be able to have children. This seemed irrelevant to Rupert at the time, compared with the frantic relief that he wouldn't lose her. Only when she began to recover did he appreciate how shattered she was not to be able to have his children. As she sobbed helplessly in his arms, he looked out at a robin pecking at the bird table, like a drop of blood against the snow which had already blotted out all the skid marks of her fall.

The same afternoon he discovered her weeping just as hopelessly in the nursery that Daisy had covered so riotously with butterflies and birds, and even Gertrude the mongrel, and his heart had blackened against Perdita. If he hadn't had to go to America none of this would have happened. The only time he left Taggie's bedside the next week was to ring Dino Ferranti and tell him they were dropping the case, and to call Cameron Cook home because Venturer had no more interest in making a film about Perdita.

58

Perdita was absolutely appalled that Taggie had lost the baby, but, secretly, what upset her most was that Rupert, whom she had always hero-worshipped, had rejected her sexually and, because of this, she had lost points with Red. But she tucked it under the mattress of her mind alongside her treatment of Luke and her running out on Ricky and tried to forget it. She had much to occupy her. Obsessive, power-driven, the Alderton Flyers swept through the Palm Beach season unbeaten. Many people thought Red and Angel played better together than the O'Briens. They were less powerful physically, but younger and took more risks. Red, riding the legendary Glitz, won Most Valuable Player and Best Playing Pony in every match. Angel, getting $10,000 a win from Bart, which helped pay his gambling debts, had turned himself into a lean, mean, killing machine. The games were fantastically violent. All the other teams, furious that Bart had spent so much on ponies, were determined to beat them. In retaliation, Red and Angel had taught Perdita every dirty trick in the book. She got so terrified before matches that she grew more and more histrionic, while the media gleefully followed every tantrum.

Red egged her on. Nocturnal, sybaritic, self-indulgent, he could sleep anywhere, and, if he'd gone to bed late, could sleep in before a big match until lunchtime, have a huge steak or a toot of cocaine for breakfast and go on and play with no nerves. Perdita, on the other hand, went crazy with stage-fright.

In the past, too, Luke had always listened if she had a problem with a pony or was worried about her game. Red wasn't interested. He wanted to do all the talking. Then, when she wanted to have her say, he was off out of the room.

Nor were matters helped by Grace rolling up at every game and going into ecstasies every time Red touched the ball, but wincing at Perdita's expletives and her botched shots, which made her miss the ball more than ever. Chessie, furious at Grace's presence, stayed at home sulking, spending money and playing tinker, tailor with the caviar. Angel, sulking because Bibi wasn't there, or because she was there and criticizing him, stepped up his flirtation with Innocenta, all of which went down in Grace's little book.

Miraculously, because Luke was playing for Hal Peters at the Royal Polo Club at Boco Raton Perdita didn't bump into him.

Few people realized quite how much Luke suffered. He went on buying runts off the race track and making them under the arc lights until he was so tired he fell off them. He played polo with the same attack and won matches for Hal Peters. He joked with the other players and grooms and listened to their problems. He never talked about himself and appeared outwardly unchanged, except for a twenty-five-pound weight-loss, which hardly showed on his massive frame. Because he was unhappy, he didn't see why the rest of the world should suffer.

Alas, music and reading, his great loves, no longer comforted him. Mozart and Mahler were impossibly painful. Biography and history were bearable, except that he read the same page over again, but poetry tore his guts out. Unable to sleep, tormented by visions of Perdita in Red's arms, he slumped in front of the television, but if any love story or programme about animals or children came on, he found himself racked with tears and had to switch off. Repeatedly he chided himself with Emily Brontë's lines that *'existence could be cherished, strengthened and fed without the aid of joy'*. There was certainly satisfaction in his life when he won a match or mastered a tricky pony, but no joy. For not only had he lost Perdita, but also Red, whom he had loved very deeply. He tried not to hate his brother, and late one night after a quadruple bourbon on no lunch, had called up determined to make it up: 'Red Alderton and Perdita Macleod are having a bang at the moment,' mocked Red's voice on the recording machine, and Luke had hung up and got so drunk he fell off the wooden horse.

And it was difficult to forget Perdita when every newspaper carried pictures of her and Red entwined and laughing: 'The golden couple so in lerve'. Once the Ferranti campaign started in March, her fleshless diamond-hard face with its streaked boy's hair, Greek nose and passionate, arrogant, curling mouth was everywhere. If the press couldn't get hold of her or Red for a quote, they invariably rang Luke.

The two things that saved Luke were Fantasma and Leroy, who had become inseparable. The ugly black mongrel slept in the beautiful grey pony's box, leaping in and out of her half-door, never being savaged or kicked by her, never in return nipping her nose or her fetlocks, proudly leading her out to the paddock with her rope between his snapping, long, white teeth.

Both of them wandered round the yard after Luke, both ganging up if any invader threatened him. Fantasma, given the chance, would have clambered up the narrow stairs into his bed. Sensing Luke was miserable, Leroy would rush in rattling a box of Bonios to make him laugh, or scrape his arm with his paw, gazing up with the crescents of white beneath his big brown eyes, as if to say, 'You still have me.' Often Luke woke from bad dreams to find Leroy licking away his tears.

He knew it was childish, but since Perdita had left him he couldn't bear to be parted from Leroy. So he only went to places that allowed dogs, turning down all invitations to work abroad, which would have helped him to forget, going everywhere by lorry, instead of flying, so Leroy could sit barking beside him.

It was the last tournament of the Palm Beach season with six crack teams playing each other over ten days for a huge silver cup topped with rearing silver horses. On the hottest Sunday of the year the Alderton Flyers were only leading the O'Briens by two goals at half-time. After weeks of no rain, the ground was as hard and dusty as a volcanic crater. The only liquid came from the sweat which poured off pony and player, and from the diet Coke with which the teams slaked their parched throats. Huge white clouds gathering on the horizon suggested a storm to come.

Perdita had had a lousy first half, not helped by a ball on her arm in the second chukka which was now agony. No-one had noticed, but she wasn't going to complain in case the others dismissed her as a whinging female. As she cantered back to the little tent where the other Flyers were taking a break, she saw them standing in a huddle outside looking deadly serious, except Red, who was sitting down wiping his face with a yellow towel, while the ever-adoring Grace massaged his shoulders. Bibi, in a check suit, had obviously just come from the office. Perdita hugged and gave Spotty a Polo before handing him over to a groom. Aware she was tomato-red in the face and dripping like a defrosting fridge, and not wanting Red to see her like that or be subjected to a pep-talk from Grace, she seized some anti-bruise cream from the first-aid box to rub into her arm and lay down on the unyielding ground, using her hat as a pillow.

Then she heard Bart say, 'Well, for Chrissake, don't tell Perdita.'

'Tell Perdita what?' The dust made her hoarse.

'Nothing,' snapped Red, not glancing round.

'What?' Perdita jumped to her feet and saw that Bibi was crying.

'Nothing.' Grace had all the charm of a steam-roller with brake failure. 'We were saying you're not on your man, and please centre the ball when you back it, and you're tapping it too much. It's meant to be hit.'

They were looking at her as if she was a lunatic that needed humouring.

'Oh, piss off,' snarled Perdita. Then, seeing Grace's face: 'I'm sorry, Mrs Alderton, but what mustn't I be told?'

'It's Luke,' sobbed Bibi, whose mascara was streaked by sweat and tears.

'There's been a slight accident,' said Grace coolly.

Suddenly the rock-hard ground had no substance beneath Perdita's feet.

'He's OK,' said Bart, who was thinking only of his polo match.

'He hasn't tried to k-kill himself?' whispered Perdita.

'Don't give yourself the bloody air,' snarled Angel.

Red, who'd gone very pale, was lighting a Black Sobranie with a trembling hand.

'Bobby Ferraro hit him with a ball yesterday,' he said. 'Broke his hand in three places. Bobby's new patron, Pip Gilson, had Luke flown to New York. They've just operated and taken fifty chips of bone out of his hand.'

Perdita flinched, then thinking she was going to black out, sat down, nearly missing the edge of one of the duck-egg-blue canvas chairs.

'Will he be able to play again?'

'Too early to say,' said Bart.

'I must go to him,' said Perdita desperately, peeling off her gloves. 'Why weren't we told yesterday?'

'Luke didn't want anyone to know,' said Red tonelessly. 'It was Bobby who felt he ought to tell us and called Bibi just now.'

The white clouds had turned a dark sullen grey. Alderton Flyer horses that had played in the first half were being walked home. Rising to the canter to rest their horses, the O'Briens were riding back on to the field.

'Luke didn't want to worry us into blowing the semi-final, and we're not going to. Move it, you guys,' said Bart, slotting in his gum shield and putting on his hat. Then, having mounted a leaping sorrel mare whose coat gleamed like cornelian, he asked the groom what sort of mood she was in.

'You can't play knowing this,' said Perdita, aghast.

Bart adjusted his reins. 'If he's just had a three-hour op, he'll be out for hours.'

One of Bart's grooms led up Tero. It was only her third match since she'd recovered.

'She's a bit edgy. Knows it's a key match.'

Tero was already lathered up like a white poodle, her eyes popping, diarrhoea running down her back legs in a thin trickle.

'I'm not playing,' said Perdita.

'Sure you bloody are,' ordered Red. 'Get on that pony.'

For a second they glared at each other. Perdita dropped her eyes first.

'Luke would 'ave expected eet,' said Angel. 'Don't be a dreep, Perdita.'

'Move your ass,' bellowed Shark Nelligan who was umpiring.

Perdita vaulted on to Tero.

'Don't forget to hit not tap,' called Grace.

Perdita had to clench her first and second fingers not to give Grace a V sign.

'I'm bloody well flying up to see him immediately after the match.'

'I wouldn't,' said Red icily, 'if you want him to get better.'

It was a good thing Perdita was only marking the O'Brien's new patron, who had a one handicap and only that because he'd bunged the APA so heavily, because in the next three chukkas he went virtually unmarked. Perdita hardly connected with the ball and missed several easy shots at goal. It was purely Red's and Angel's flamboyant courage and Bart's Exocet penalties that kept the Flyers just ahead.

'Are you still in love with Luke?' hissed Red, as they lined up for the presentation.

'Course I'm bloody not. You're the only person I'm crazy about. But Luke's been a really good friend to me, and I don't know how you could play so well after what's happened,' Perdita hissed back.

'It's the mark of the great player to rise above adversity,' said Red. 'The second-rate go to pieces in a crisis.'

'He's your brother, and Bart's son,' whispered Perdita furiously. 'Thank you very much,' she smiled briefly as the President of Cadillac gave her a silver ashtray in the shape of a car.

'Thank you very much, sir.' Red accepted his silver ashtray. Then, out of the corner of his mouth, 'Never noticed blood was thicker than water in your family.'

'We *must* go and see him,' said Perdita hysterically.

'Perdita,' said Red softly, 'he needs to be kept quiet.'

'If Luke's sidelined for the summer we might be able

573

to get our hands on Fantasma and take her to England,'
chipped in Bart.

'I don't understand any of you,' screamed Perdita. 'Luke
may have been put out of polo for ever, and all you can
think about is your own fucking game.'

Four days later Perdita disobeyed everyone's advice and,
cutting a Ferranti's promotional lunch for all their buyers,
flew up to see Luke. She didn't tell Red she was going.
He'd been determined to punish her since they'd heard
the news, even insisting on her watching a video of him
and Auriel making love, which revolted her, particularly
when she saw how skilled and beautiful Auriel was and
how she and Red seemed to be enjoying themselves. She
needed Luke's advice on how to handle Red and about
her fast-deteriorating game.

After Palm Beach in the nineties, New York was
freezing. Perdita, hopelessly under-dressed in white jeans
and a black sleeveless T-shirt, shivered as much from
nerves as the cold. The hospital, which had Impressionist
reproductions on the walls and banks of flowers and floodlit
fountains on every floor, was more plush than most hotels
and must have been costing Hal Peters a fortune.

'Luke Alderton?' said the nurse on the fourth floor
reception desk excitedly. 'Third on the right. I hope you'll
be able to get in for the flowers. Dancer Maitland dropped
by this morning and Auriel Kingham last night.'

'How is he?' snapped Perdita, who didn't want to hear
about Auriel.

'Well, he's still in some discomfort,' (bloody silly word,
thought Perdita) 'but he's a very brave guy.'

'I know that. Will he be able to play again?'

'Early days,' said the nurse. 'Don't stay long. Aren't you
the Ferranti girl?'

But Perdita had gone, amazed how much her heart was
hammering as she threw open the door.

'It's the prodigal,' she announced. 'Darling Luke, have
you forgiven me?'

Then she dropped her parcels all over the floor, for,
sitting on Luke's bed, holding his hand, was an incredibly
attractive girl. Her second, almost more agonizing, impression was how desperately ill Luke looked. His brown,

574

freckled face was tinged lurid green, and darkly shadowed, the bottle-brush hair dank with sweat, the big generous mouth practically disappearing in the attempt not to cry out, the honey-coloured eyes no longer amused and sleepy. His shoulders were still huge, but everywhere else the weight had dropped off. He reminded Perdita of a Great Dane who'd fallen into the hands of the vivisectionists and was bewildered why it should undergo such horrific pain without an anaesthetic.

She wanted to rush over and hug him, but there was the impediment of this girl in the wonderfully understated coral-pink suit, with a pale clever face and shiny dark hair and wonderful long legs. Her grey eyes were looking at Luke with tenderness and her coral-tipped fingers were gently stroking his forehead.

Bristling with hostility, Perdita picked up her parcels. Relinquishing Luke's hand, the girl rose to her feet.

'You must be Perdita,' she said coolly. 'I recognize you from the posters. Luke's told me a lot about you.'

'Funny, he's told me absolutely nothing about you,' said Perdita furiously. She turned to Luke: 'Christ, I'm sorry! You poor thing! What the hell happened? Bloody Bobby.'

'Wasn't his fault.' Even the deep, slow, husky drawl was weakened. 'It was an airshot. I blocked it.'

'The blow knocked Luke off his horse,' said the girl. 'When he didn't get up the players formed a circle round him, but I could see he wasn't moving. I was shaking and shaking. Alejandro, who was watching with me, put his arm round me. I sat beside Luke in the ambulance crying all the way, because I figured he was unconscious, but in fact he was in such agony he couldn't talk. Then we had to wait three hours in casualty, because they had to look after some people who'd been in a car crash.'

Perdita looked at this cool girl, who'd suddenly gone as white as Luke's sheets. What right had she got to cry over Luke and be comforted by Alejandro?

'Who's she?' she asked Luke, nodding rudely in the girl's direction.

'Margie Bridgwater.' Luke made no attempt at explanation. His hand swathed in bandages strapped up in the air didn't seem part of him.

'D'you want a drink? Vodka, white wine?' he asked. 'Margie'll get it.'

Perdita shook her head. 'Is it absolute agony?'

Luke shrugged. 'The first night was the worst, all night on the hour, I was woken by a vast black lady, saying, "Roll over, Mr Alderton", and then shoving a thermometer up my ass.'

Just for a second, he grinned and was the old Luke again.

'I've bought you a biography of Robert Lowell.' Perdita put it on the bed. 'The one you were always quoting about the woods being snowy, dark and deep.'

'*Lovely, dark and deep,*' corrected Margie. '*And I have promises to keep, and miles to go before I sleep.* That's Robert Frost not Robert Lowell.' Then, catching a warning look from Luke, added more gently, 'But *The New York Times* said the Lowell biography was terrific.'

'I wouldn't know, I'm not an intellectual,' spat back Perdita. 'And some freesias and a tape of *Crocodile Dundee*.'

'Thanks,' said Luke. 'That's really neat. How's Spotty?'

'Feeling his feet. Bute doesn't seem to be working.'

'Give him some stuff called Arkell,' said Luke. 'Makes the blood flow. And Tero?'

'Bloody Miguel gave her such a bump last week, she's lost her nerve. She won't bump any more. She still gets the runs twenty-four hours before a big match and won't eat for days afterwards. I can't afford to let her lose weight. I ought to turn her away for the summer, but if I don't take her to England she'll pine, and so will I, I love her so much.'

She was so shocked by Luke's appearance that she hardly listened to his answers. It was as though Big Ben or Westminster Abbey had suddenly been bombed. And, to cap it all, here was this bloody girl guarding him like a lioness.

Interrupting him, she said, 'For the first time I can see how like Red you are.'

Luke smiled ruefully. 'I guess there must be some plusses about getting sidelined. My brother's an Adonis,' he added to Margie.

'I've seen pictures.' Margie put her hand over his. 'I like my guys more rugged.'

'Red is the handsomest man in the world,' exploded Perdita.

'Not as good-looking as Rupert Campbell-Black,' said Margie. 'Wow! He came to see Luke this morning.'

Perdita felt sick. 'Did he mention me?'

'Only to say Venturer weren't making a movie about you any more,' said Luke. 'He was over to finalize American sponsors for the Westchester.'

'And you're going to play in it,' said Margie warmly.

Perdita clenched her fists.

'Shame they lost the baby,' went on Margie. 'He and Taggie are going to adopt one, but they're having problems in England. Rupert's forty in the fall and the adoption societies don't see him as ideal father material, so they're putting feelers out in the States.'

'He's *rich*,' said Perdita, who didn't want to talk about Rupert. 'If you're rich you can buy anything. Who's playing for Hal now?'

'Alejandro.'

'For ten times more than Luke was getting,' said Margie bitterly.

'The receptionist told me Dancer was here,' said Perdita.

'He is so charming,' said Margie. 'He wants Luke to see Seth Newcombe, the guy who sorted out Ricky's hand.'

'I know,' snapped Perdita. 'I was at the hospital when Seth operated. Of course Luke should see him.'

Seeing Luke absolutely wiped out, Perdita added to Margie, 'Look, Luke and I go back a long way. Would you like to piss off and leave us alone for five minutes?'

Margie raised a thick dark eyebrow at Luke, who nodded.

'Well, only five minutes. I'll be outside if you need me.'

Bloody cow, thought Perdita, but she did have wonderful legs. She moved round to see the framed photographs on Luke's bedside table, disappointed to see they were of Leroy and Fantasma and not of herself.

'It was nice of you to come,' he said.

'I would have come sooner. The others were convinced I'd do more harm than good.'

Luke gazed at her steadily for a second. There was exhaustion but no reproach in his eyes, but he didn't contradict her.

Lowering herself gingerly on to the bed, so as not to jolt him, she started pleating the white counterpane.

'I'm sorry I buggered off at Deauville. I didn't know how you felt.'

'That's OK.'

'You all right?'

'Yeah, I'm fine now.'

'I just fell madly in love with Red. I couldn't help myself.'

'Sure. How is he?'

'Doesn't know I'm here. I hope it might make him a bit jealous. He's wildly jealous of you, because everyone loves you so much, I guess. They fancy Red, but they don't seem to like him, but then they don't know him. Tell me, what's the best way to hold him?'

'Don't get heavy,' said Luke, then, on reflection, '*He who bends to himself a joy doth the winged life destroy.*'

'I miss your poems,' said Perdita. 'Red's almost illiterate. You should be nicknamed Well-Read and Ill-Red. Why are you staring at me?'

'Because I've just twigged.'

'W-what?'

They were interrupted by Margie the Martinet coming back with a doctor and a nurse, who asked Perdita to leave as they wanted to look at Luke's hand. Beads of sweat were forming on his forehead at the prospect of more debilitating pain.

'But I've only been here a few minutes,' stormed Perdita.

'Visitation's being restricted to quarter of an hour,' said the doctor.

'Oh, for Christ's sake.'

Once more the doctor, the nurse and Margie were confronting her as though she was a dangerous lunatic.

'All right, I'm going.' Perdita was fighting back the tears. 'I hope you get better soon.'

Margie followed her out into the passage. Forcing her hands furiously into her trouser pocket, Perdita pulled out a bottle.

'Give it to Luke,' she said. 'Morphine from Bart's medicine cupboard in case the pain gets too bad.'

'He needed that in August,' said Margie, 'when you shoved off with Red. Smashing up his hand and probably terminating his career was a day in the country compared with what you put him through last summer.'

As she went back into the room to grip Luke's other hand as the doctor started to undo his bandages, he said through gritted teeth, 'I've just realized who Perdita's father is.'

59

Red's temper was blazing like a forest fire when Perdita got home.

'Where the fuck have you been? You were supposed to be at a Ferranti promotional lunch.'

'I went to see Luke. I rang Dino's secretary and said I couldn't make it.'

'Bullshit. You're under contract. Buyers flew in from all over the world to meet you. Dino went apeshit. What in hell are you playing at? How was Luke anyway?'

'Awful, simply terrible.'

'You can't have helped. I'll go and see him tomorrow and you better call Dino and crawl or they'll slap Winston Chalmers on you.'

Dino Ferranti was icy with rage. 'You step out of line once more, right, and you're fired, *and* we'll sue you for breach of contract.'

All in all Perdita wasn't in a very chipper mood to go to a barbecue that evening, particularly when Red was immediately collared by a comely female feature writer in a groin-level, blue suede skirt from *Vanity Fair*.

The party was held in a copse near one of the polo barns. Coloured lights hung from the trunks of the pine trees, which soared upwards like pillars blotting out the stars. The still air was heavy with the smell of charcoal, pine needles, long-marinaded hunks of lamb, pork and chickens which sizzled and spat as they turned on the barbecue. Rather like me, thought Perdita as she looked across at Red working his magic on the sexy journalist. He'd given up his yellow blazer because all the young bloods in Palm Beach had slavishly copied him. Now he had reverted to his pale blue one braided with emerald

579

green. A lock of hair had fallen over his forehead; his eyes were dreamy; he looked like Rupert Brooke.

'I prefer to ride mares, in and out of bed,' he was saying. 'They're more competitive.'

The girl smiled and arched her lean and hungry blue suede pelvis towards him.

There's no point being jealous, thought Perdita echoing one of Red's commandments, it hurts only yourself.

Away from the fire was a large wheelbarrow, stacked with drink people had brought. Perdita was mixing herself a Green Devil when Angel came up.

'You saw Luke. 'Ow was he?'

'Not brilliant. He looked dreadful.'

'I 'ear Alejandro is being paid $20,000 a match to play for Hal. Is crazy.'

Perdita took a slug of her Green Devil and choked. It was nearly neat vodka. 'He had a girl with him called Margie. Jolly bossy, but horribly attractive.'

'Bibi say she's very nice.'

Perdita leant against a pine tree. 'Is it serious?'

'She looking after Leroy for Luke so it must be.'

Perdita experienced a jab of jealousy so bad it winded her. Some of the younger players had started a food fight. Wham was pounding round the pine trees. Angel ducked to avoid a flying sausage roll.

'You pick the wrong guy,' he said.

'I did *not*,' snapped Perdita. 'Red and I are just like that.' She held up two crossed fingers.

'So it would seem,' said Angel, glancing across at Red who was dancing under a gum tree with the *Vanity Fair* reporter. The same height, they touched in the most interesting places.

'You picked the wrong wife,' said Perdita.

From the nearby barn the occasional stamp or snort of the ponies could be heard. Red-and-silver heart-shaped balloons tied to each box bobbed up to the roof.

'If someone cut the string your heart would float away like one of those balloons.'

'Not yet.' Angel's face was in shadow. '*I 'ave promises to keep and miles to go before I sleep.*'

'Oh, for Chrissake, I'm sick of that bloody poem.'

The inevitable polo dogs wandered around crunching

bones and being tripped over and sworn at. Shark Nelligan's white bull terrier, confined to his master's truck because he tended to kill other dogs, leant genially out of the window, his elbow resting on the ledge, being fed pieces of meat and petted by passers-by.

Mixing herself another drink, Perdita couldn't remember when she had last eaten. She could see Juan coiled round a blonde. To make up his days and avoid paying tax a reluctant Victor had had to leave the party and fly out of Palm Beach before midnight, leaving Sharon to chat up the latest beefcake from Brazil. Jesus was ringing England on Sharon's car telephone. 'I weel play for you, Sir Waterloo, eef you pay me $200,000. Veector already offer me that much money. And pay my airplane fare, and a 'ouse. No, I don't need to breeng my wife − you save on that.'

'Is Bibi coming?' Perdita asked Angel.

'She's working,' said Angel flatly. 'Don't drink too much, Perdita. Go 'ome before you do anything silly.'

'Come and dance with me,' said Perdita.

But at that moment Innocenta emerged from the lilac shadows bringing a plate piled with lamb chops, potato salad and barbecue sauce which she proceeded to share with Angel. Red was necking openly as he danced now. If she hadn't been scared of his temper, Perdita would have hurled the greasiest pork chop she could find at the girl's gyrating blue suede bottom.

'They're called barbecues because you queue up to receive barbs,' she said to no-one in particular as she finished her drink.

'How's Luke?' Shark Nelligan came up to her with a plate piled disgustingly high with food. He was interested because he and Luke both played back and would be competing for the same place in the US team, particularly for the Westchester which would mean serious money.

'I hear his career's washed up and Hal Peters is paying Alejandro $50,000 a match,' he went on. 'I want to get my hands on Fantasma.'

'Luke won't sell and he'll recover,' said Perdita, filling her glass yet again.

Shark grinned evilly. 'I'm not sure Hal will. Myrtle, his ex, is taking him to the cleaners. And his new bimbo's making so free with his Amex he's praying for it to get stolen.

And Luke's medical bills will be even more astronomical if they call in Seth Newcombe.'

'But Hal must be insured?' said Perdita anxiously.

'Sure he is,' said Shark with his mouth full, 'but he's overstretched. He's the best car man in Detroit, but he's so off the wall he exported a thousand Peters' Cheetahs to the UK last week with left-hand drive.'

'But Luke'll be all right, won't he?' persisted Perdita.

'He's got Bart to fall back on.' Shark gave a piece of lamb to his slavering bull terrier.

Perdita shook her head. 'He's too proud.'

'And he's got a pretty sharp new girlfriend,' added Shark spitefully.

'Who?' said Perdita, fishing, though it hurt her.

'Margie someone. She's a lawyer. She won't let him starve.'

As Perdita turned away stricken, Angel emerged from the gloom with Innocenta looking a lot less innocent. Red was still talking to his journalist.

'Lots of guys won't have sex the night before a big game,' Red was saying caressingly, 'but I always do, and the following morning, although I might try less hard.'

One more drink, thought Perdita, and I'll make a scene and separate them. She didn't think she'd ever been more miserable in her life.

'Hi. Aren't you Perdita Macleod?' said a soft voice.

A man with white-blond hair was smiling down at her. He was wearing a cream suit, a buttoned-down, pale blue shirt and a blue spotted tie. He appeared mercifully civilized compared with all these polo hicks, thought Perdita. He was nice-looking rather than handsome and had very light eyes in a beige face like Ricky's pony, Sinatra.

'Who are you?' she asked aggressively.

'Simpson Hastings.'

If Perdita had been less drunk she would have heard warning bells. Simpson Hastings appeared to know a lot about polo and particularly about her.

'They say you're a phenomenon beyond genius.'

'Not to my face they don't,' said Perdita sulkily.

'It's a beautiful face. That's your problem. If you were butch and ugly they could slag you off for being almost a man. They find your sex appeal disturbing.'

'Not tonight, they don't. I've got as much appeal here as a mink coat at an Animal Rights meeting.'

'Where did the skill come from? D'your parents ride?'

'My mother's never been on a horse in her life.'

'And Hamish?'

Simpson Hastings did know a flattering amount about her.

Swaying slightly, Perdita clung on to the truck. 'Hamish wasn't my father.'

'Is that a fact?' Simpson Hastings didn't bat a pale-lashed eyelid. 'He certainly didn't look like you.' Then, with the utmost gentleness, 'Who was?'

'I don't know.' To hell with everyone. Suddenly an Ancient Mariner compulsion to tell all swept over her. 'My mother went to an orgy in the sixties given by her art master. He was called Jackie Cosgrave. Everyone screwed everyone, particularly my sodding mother. She has no idea which one was my father.'

'Difficult for you,' murmured Simpson Hastings without a trace of excitement. 'Hard to know who to relate to. But he must have been a very good rider.'

Back in Rutshire, Daisy had had a long day finishing off a painting, which Ricky said she'd never get paid for, of Billy and Janey Lloyd-Foxe's children. As the two-year-old daughter had nearly smashed up Ricky's house on the first sitting while Janey got happily plastered, Daisy had worked thereafter from photographs and had just painted Billy's late mongrel, Mavis, as a dog cherub up in the sky. As a background she'd used the particularly tranquil view from Ricky's balustrade of perpendicular woods and jade-green fields dotted with ponies grazing westward towards the setting sun. Not wanting to disturb Ricky, she slipped out of Robinsgrove by a side door. There was an air of tremendous bustle and excitement about the yard because practice chukkas were starting at the Rutshire tomorrow. She paused for a second to watch the twins, Mike Waterlane and Ricky working out fiendish strategies to fox the opposition.

The twins, back from Palm Beach, were dazzlingly blond and brown and shouting their heads off as usual. Despite the high spirits, however, they'd been training incredibly hard together. No-one was going to take the Gold Cup away from them this year.

It was a spellbinding evening. Two grey geese and a squad of pale yellow goslings broke the turquoise surface of the lake. Three days of rain after a spate of warm weather had brought out the white cherries and the bluebells in a sapphire mist on either side of the ride. The poplars, shiny, acid-green, were wafting the scent of balsam down the valley. Crows nesting in Ricky's beeches had splattered the wild garlic leaves like milk of magnesia on green hangover tongues. Daisy had heard the cuckoo through the open window of her studio all day. She felt quite faint with happiness. Ricky had become such a friend recently and her painting was going wonderfully. Perdita was due back in three weeks and surely couldn't sustain the feud for ever; and Daisy was expecting Drew that evening. By the law of sod, if ever she glammed herself up and washed her hair Drew had to back down at the last moment. Today she'd chanced it and put on a dark green jersey he'd bought her and her best jeans. She was in luck, for there outside the cottage was Drew's BMW. Splashing through the last twenty yards of watermeadow, she clambered over Ricky's padlocked gate, raced up the path, then gave a gasp of disappointment. For outside the door was not Drew, but a glamorous, if slightly grubby-looking, blonde, wearing rather too much eye make-up for daytime, a creased denim suit and scuffed black shoes with the steel high heels escaping from the leather. With her was a man carrying a camera with the leering face of a drunken vulture and snowdrifts of scurf on the shoulders of his shiny grey suit.

'Mrs Macleod?' said the girl, as though she was about to sell Daisy insurance. Ethel, for once, bristled and started to growl.

'We're from *The Scorpion*,' the girl went on. 'Can we have a word?'

'What about?' stammered Daisy.

'It'd be easier inside.'

Daisy opened the front door.

'Don't you ever lock up?' asked the girl.

'Nothing to steal,' said Daisy. 'Look, if it's about Red and Perdita, I've got nothing to say.'

584

'Well, it is.' The girl dumped her bag on the kitchen table. 'Perdita told Simpson Hastings in Florida yesterday that she'd no idea who her father was.'

'Oh, no,' Daisy licked her lips, eyes darting from the girl to the man. 'Perdita's father was killed in a car crash. He never knew I was pregnant.'

'That's not what Perdita told Simpson,' interrupted the girl cosily.

She opened her notebook but made no notes because a tiny tape recorder was rotating in the breast pocket of her denim suit.

'What a nice kitchen. I love all the flowers. Perdita said you went to a party in 1966 and everyone got stoned and screwed each other and you got pregnant as a result.'

'She couldn't have said that,' mumbled Daisy, groping for the kettle switch.

'D'you want to read the exact words?' The girl produced a rather crumpled newspaper proof from her bag. It smelt of Femme. Daisy was too shocked to take much in. Her legs wouldn't stop trembling.

'*I loathe my mother,*' she read. '*She must have been a tart to sleep with all those men. She claims she was stoned but that's her story. She's lied to me for years that my father was killed in a car crash.*'

Ethel, having climbed heavily on to the kitchen table, was now licking the blonde's face.

'Don't be disloyal, Ethel,' said Daisy in a high, unnatural voice.

'But I love dogs,' protested the blonde.

'Dogs get on with dogs, I suppose,' said Daisy. 'Sorry, that was frightfully rude. I can't read any more.'

Racing upstairs to the loo, she retched and retched until she thought she would bring up her hammering heart. Then she cleaned her teeth and wiped her face, closing her eyes desperately trying to still the trembling. As she returned to the kitchen the blonde said: 'We thought we'd give you a chance to put your point of view.'

'I've nothing to say. Oh, poor Violet and Eddie.'

'Your kids,' said the blonde consulting an earlier page in her notebook. 'They're at boarding school, aren't they? Let's all have that cup of tea.'

Daisy filled the kettle and switched on the gas, but didn't

light it. After a couple of seconds the blonde leapt forward with her lighter.

'Don't want to blow ourselves up. We'd make it very worth your while. You could do with a new washing-up machine and a lovely conservatory out into the garden, and a new car – that Volkswagen is on its last legs and we could help with the school fees and a really nice holiday so you could escape from all this.'

Then, as Daisy looked at her uncomprehendingly: 'We're talking five or six figures.'

'It's a lovely car,' said Daisy, thinking that Drew had given it to her. 'It goes perfectly well.'

'Perdita says a man called Jackie Cosgrave hosted the orgy.' The blonde was getting down mugs and the tea caddy. 'Is he still around?'

'No,' said Daisy in terror. 'I haven't seen him since that winter.'

A flash lit up the room.

'You're awfully young to have a twenty-year-old daughter,' leered the photographer.

'I was only seventeen,' sobbed Daisy. 'Please don't take pictures. I don't remember anyone at the party. I was so drunk, but that doesn't make it any better. Please go away.'

They all jumped as the kettle whistled and the telephone rang.

It was Drew. 'Thank Christ I've got you. I wish you'd stop working up at Ricky's.'

'*The Scorpion* are here,' gasped Daisy. 'Perdita's told them about the orgy and that she hasn't a clue who her father is.'

'Fucking bitch,' said Drew absolutely appalled. 'Oh, my poor darling. Don't say anything to them.'

'They're in the house.'

'I'll come straight over.'

'Oh, please.' Then, after the first blessed relief: 'No, you mustn't. It isn't safe. Sukey, the children . . . ' She stopped, realizing she'd probably said too much.

'I'll ring Ricky,' said Drew. 'Look, I love you. It'll be OK. Don't worry.'

The flash bulbs were going like mad. Gainsborough

crashed fatly in through the cat door, then crashed out again in dismay.

'Have you got any photographs of yourself when you were seventeen?' asked the blonde, opening a drawer.

'Get out,' shrieked Daisy.

'Hard for Perdita, not having a father. No wonder she's screwed up,' said the blonde losing some of her cosiness.

Kinta had never been encouraged to run away before but, as Ricky, alerted by Drew's telephone call, picked up his whip, the mare thundering down the valley, crushing cowslips and cuckoo flowers, jumping the bustling stream as it twisted and turned and sending up twelve feet of spray, frightened even herself.

Hearing a thud of hooves, Daisy glanced out of the window. For a second she thought Ricky was going to jump the gate. The skid marks were six feet long after Kinta jammed on her brakes. Next minute her reins had been knotted to the bars and Ricky had vaulted over the gate. As he came through the door his face, jeans and check shirt were splashed with mud and he was so angry that at first he couldn't get any words out.

Instinctively the blonde's hand rose to lift her tousled hair and wipe away the shine beneath her eyes and on the sides of her nose. Ricky crossed the room and put his arms round Daisy. 'It's all right, pet.'

'Hullo, Ricky,' said the blonde, whose mouth was watering. 'Remember me?' She waved her hand in front of his eyes to break up his blank stare.

With a shudder of disgust, Ricky recognized the author of Rupert's memoirs.

'It's you, Beattie,' he said icily. 'I might have guessed it.'

'Been cheering Daisy up since she became your tenant, have you?' mocked Beattie. 'All the world loves a landlord, and all.'

'No, I have bloody not,' snapped Ricky. 'Now beat it.'

'Perdita worked for you and had a crush on you.' Under Ricky's ferocious glare Beattie started backing towards the door. 'She says all she wants to do is find her real father and experience some real love and understanding.'

'Bullshit,' thundered Ricky. 'She's had a bloody sight

too much love and understanding. Perdita is basically a good child who's fallen among thieves. Do I have to throw you out?'

'You wouldn't dare,' said Beattie in excitement, then screamed as Ricky opened the window, gathered her up and threw her out kicking and struggling into a flowerbed.

'Sorry about your wallflowers,' he added to Daisy as, two seconds later, the photographer and his expensive camera followed suit.

'You bastard,' yelled Beattie, picking herself out of a rose bush. 'These tights are Dior and new on. I'll get you for assault.'

But as Ricky went out of the front door in pursuit they jumped into their BMW and drove furiously away. Ricky turned back to Daisy. Her eyes were huge and staring. She was still shaking uncontrollably.

'I never knew Perdita hated me that much,' she whispered through white lips. 'And what am I going to do about Violet and Eddie?'

Ricky went to the cupboard and, finding an inch of vodka in a half-bottle, tipped it into a glass and topped it up with orange juice.

'Get that down you, then I'll drive you over to tell them.'

'But it's the beginning of the season. You've got so much on. It isn't fair you should be dragged in.'

'I'm in already. Don't imagine Beattie'll forget her hurt pride and her laddered tights in a hurry.'

They didn't talk much as they drove through the emergent spring thirty miles to Violet's school and then another twenty miles on to Eddie's. In her numbed state Daisy wondered if Ricky was working out polo plays. When he met Violet's headmistress his coolness and detachment seemed to diffuse her disapproval. She was obviously captivated by his looks.

Violet went scarlet when Daisy stumbled out with the truth, then she put her arms round her mother. 'Perdita's a bitch, but she's so off the wall at the moment and she'd probably just had a row with Red. You were younger than her when it happened. We'll look after you.'

Eddie's headmaster, a breezy, bearded homosexual, couldn't look Daisy in the eye, but his voice became much warmer when he spoke to Ricky. Eddie seemed outwardly unfazed.

'Perdita's father might be a pop star then. Can I come home with you? We've got a history exam tomorrow and I haven't revised.'

'Come home at the weekend,' said Ricky. 'We'll shoot clays. I'll lend you a rod and you can fish in the lake.'

Drew rang up when they got back to Ricky's house. He was forced to be very matter of fact, but Daisy could tell he was worried sick.

'I'll come over and see Ricky tomorrow,' then with an endearing stab of jealousy, 'it's a good idea for you to stay there tonight. He'll protect you from the press. But don't fall in love with him.'

'Of course I won't,' stammered Daisy.

Never had she missed Drew more. But Ricky was angelic. He gave her two sleeping pills left over from the ones prescribed for him when Will died and had left orders, despite the warmth of the evening, for one of the grooms to light a fire in the spare room.

'You said one very important thing to me about Will's death,' he told her, 'that night we had dinner together, that I'd got to learn to forgive myself. You've got to do the same.'

But, however angelic Ricky was, nothing prepared Daisy for the horror of *The Scorpion* next day.

'*Gang, bang, thank you, Mum,*' said huge front-page headlines. Then beneath a ravishing, tremulously tearful picture of Perdita, a caption: '*Please find my real Dad,*' pleads Perdita, '*everyone had Mum that night.*'

Inside under a headline: '*Red's Raver tells all,*' they had printed the full interview with Perdita, saying how much she detested her mother for cheating her out of a father. Even worse, they had somehow got hold of a ravishing photograph of a seventeen-year-old Daisy, with a sixties fringe, long, straight hair and huge eyes, and superimposed it on an incredibly voluptuous, naked, Page Three body.

'*If you recognize this girl, you may be Perdita's Dad,*' said the caption.

Over the page under another headline: '*Caring Ricky in*

Mercy Dash,' the copy began: '*Fun-loving Daisy was hiding out yesterday with her landlord, ace polo player Ricky France-Lynch (Family Motto: Never Surrender). Caring Ricky left his ten-bedroom Georgian home and galloped through his 400-acre estate on a polo pony to stand by his lovely tenant. Known as* El Orgulloso *for his snooty manner, Ricky once employed Perdita as his groom. "Perdita has got into bad company," claims Ricky, "Daisy has been a very support-ive mother."*'

'Poor old Daisy,' said Bas Baddingham to Rupert. 'Gosh, she was pretty in those days.'

Taking *The Scorpion* from him, Rupert examined the photographs. 'Pretty now. Christ, Beattie's excelled herself this time. At least it might make Ricky finally get his act together where Daisy is concerned.'

'Didn't we used to know a creep called Cosgrave?' asked Bas. 'Used to give wild parties in the sixties?'

'Everyone gave wild parties in the sixties,' said Rupert.

Jackie Cosgrave hadn't prospered in later life. Teaching art bored him, his waist had thickened, his yellow hair turned white, his white teeth yellow, his mouth petulant. Women were no longer so keen to buy his paintings, nor girl students to sleep with him.

'Oh, Mr Cosgrave, it's all about you in *The Scorpion,*' said the art college cleaner as she swept up charcoal, paint-stained rags, old tubes of paint and scraps of newspaper.

Picking up *The Scorpion* Jackie looked long and hard at Daisy. He remembered her and, after wracking his brains, he remembered the party. In those days when he had beauty and could get drugs, the world was his friend. Returning to his flat, he took down his diary for 1966 and turned to February which he'd been wise enough to illustrate with photographs. The central heating had been turned up to tropical that night, he'd taken a lot of photographs and written down the names of all the people who'd been at the orgy. Studying Perdita's face, the answer was cut and dried. Picking up the telephone he rang *The Scorpion* News Desk.

'I'll tell you who Perdita's father is, but it's going to cost you.'

60

Rupert Campbell-Black was so much in love with his wife that he most uncharacteristically agreed to undergo a solo grilling on whether he was a suitable person to adopt a baby.

Mrs Paget, who interviewed him, had already been charmed by Taggie last week. In her thirties with a 'brood', as she called it, of her own, Mrs Paget had the kindly but patronizing air of one who works for nothing for those less fortunate. She reminded Rupert of a more rounded, prettier Sukey Benedict. In the old days for the hell of it he would have made a pass at her, but now he had no need of the divide of the gleaming mahogany table, nor the chaperonage of hundreds of babies who had been successfully adopted into loving homes whose photographs gazed down from the dark red wallpaper. Tabitha, his daughter, was the only baby Rupert had ever liked, but he would have been happy to adopt a chimpanzee for Taggie's sake, and was trying not to lose his temper with this earnest, probing woman.

'When you first saw Mrs Campbell-Black, was it love at first sight?'

'No, lust,' drawled Rupert, then added hastily, 'but it would have been the reaction of any man. She's very pretty but I was involved with someone else at the time.'

'And you lead a full sex life?'

Full of Taggie, thought Rupert. 'I'm afraid I'm not prepared to discuss our sex life with anyone,' he said coldly. 'The reason she can't have children has nothing to do with sex.'

Mrs Paget fingered her pearls. 'You've only been married seventeen months, hardly long enough for us to place one of our very special babies with you. With the pill, the abortion law and girls keeping their babies, children to adopt are like gold dust today. And you are in a catch 22.' She brought out the expression to show she read. 'You're forty at the end of this year, which makes you too old to adopt.'

Rupert gritted his teeth. 'I know that.'

'And we have couples who've been on our waiting-list for years. You wouldn't consider an older child, handicapped perhaps, or coloured? I'm sure Mrs Campbell-Black has the necessary patience and understanding.'

'Well, I don't,' said Rupert truthfully. 'We want a baby.'

'Beggars can't be choosers,' said Mrs Paget almost archly.

The stupid bitch is trying to rile me, thought Rupert. If I lose my temper she'll mark me down as a baby-basher.

'Hardly a beggar,' he snapped.

It was all a ghastly game. In his inside pocket was a cheque for a quarter of a million pounds, which would buy a house in Battersea for the society to house their unmarried mothers. The donation would be anonymous – so the press would never find out – and Rupert and Taggie would jump the queue.

'Are you sure you personally want to adopt, and it wouldn't be better for Mrs Campbell-Black to concentrate on being a mother to your own children? I'm sure they need a stable background.'

'Plenty of stables already at Penscombe,' said Rupert idly.

'There's no need to be flippant. Couples who lose a baby often try to adopt one immediately to fill the aching void, but it's the wrong motive.'

'Works perfectly well with puppies,' said Rupert.

'Mr Campbell-Black,' Mrs Paget's midnight-blue cashmere bosom swelled, 'I don't like your attitude. We have to ensure you'd make a suitable father. Your track record isn't exactly . . .'

'Oh, for Christ's sake, ask my own children!' Getting to his feet, Rupert walked over to the window. Outside, under a colonnade of burgeoning plane trees, a slim girl in jeans was pushing a pram and gabbling happy nonsense to the baby inside. He'd be reduced to kidnapping soon.

'You're supposed to be a Christian organization,' he went on. 'Isn't there something in the Bible about more rejoicing in heaven over one lost sheep?'

'Calm down,' said Mrs Paget, thinking how frightfully attractive he was. She wanted the money for the unmarried mothers' house very badly. The committee would regard it as a tremendous coup and had already earmarked an adorable Irish baby for Rupert and Taggie, but she felt he ought to be made to sweat a little longer.

'I understand,' she went on soothingly. 'You must be feeling very threatened. It happens to lots of middle-aged men who marry very young wives and worry not only about satisfying them sexually, but keeping them amused. A baby seems the perfect answer.'

Rupert's jaw dropped. There was an imperious knock on the door.

'I'm interviewing, Miss Roach,' cried Mrs Paget.

'I think you should see this,' said Miss Roach who looked more like a cod. Barging in, she thrust a copy of *The Evening Scorpion* in front of Mrs Paget, whose pale pink wild-rose complexion slowly turned the dark crimson of an Ena Harkness as she read.

'I'm afraid there's not an adoption society in the country who'll touch you now,' she said, handing Rupert the paper.

On the front page were two huge photographs of Perdita and Rupert at eighteen. Both in profile, they were incriminatingly identical. '*Snap!*' said the huge headline.

Rupert was as pale as the lilies-of-the-valley on the table as he turned to the centre pages where Jackie Cosgrave's statement was quoted in full:

'*There were seven men at the Sidney Street Orgy. They included rock star Bob Riley and his lead guitarist Harry Nelson, actor Johnny Friedlander, the Hon Basil Baddingham, a polo player, show-jumpers Rupert Campbell-Black and Billy Lloyd-Foxe and myself. At eighteen, Rupert was an officer in an exclusive cavalry regiment, the Blues, and was home on leave from Cyprus. He was very brown and so beautiful no-one could take their eyes off him. Being in the forces, he was also the only one with short hair. Rupert was very much taken with Daisy, and being very fit, made love to her most of the night. We all had bets how long he could keep going. The rest of us were too stoned to do very much, though we all had a go at her, I remember, because she was so tasty.*'

Jackie Cosgrave had always been disgusting, thought Rupert irrationally. Like Daisy two days before, he couldn't read any more. Inside were fuzzy blown-up snapshots, including one of Daisy and Rupert both naked. In one he was smiling down at her and stroking her left breast. In another he was kissing her passionately and his left hand had disappeared below the cropping of the photograph. There were also pictures of everyone else at the orgy, and, even more horrible, on the next page of Eddie, Violet, Marcus and Tabitha, with a caption: '*You're half-brothers and sisters now.*'

'Jesus,' exploded Rupert, crumpling up the paper and throwing it in the corner. Then, turning to Mrs Paget, 'And you believe this junk?'

'It seems conclusive,' she stammered. 'You could be twins.'

'I'm going to get the highest damages in history. Can I use your telephone?'

Mrs Paget nodded. After the initial rage, she told Miss Roach later, he was terrifying in his calmness.

It was a good thing the helicopter knew its own way back to Penscombe because Rupert was totally unaware of flying it. As towns, motorways and the winding Thames gave way to acid-green woods, emerald fields and tawny villages, he churned with rage. Perdita was responsible for Taggie losing their own child, and now an adopted baby. And God knows what lasting damage she'd done to his children, just as they were getting over the devastating revelations of his memoirs eighteen months ago.

He couldn't see the gravel outside his house for reporters and cameramen, and took a savage pleasure in sending them scurrying for their lives. As he leapt out, they all swarmed back.

'Hello, Rupe, talk about gaining a daughter,' said the *Sun*.

'She's a chip off the old block where horses are concerned,' said the *Mirror*. 'You going to teach her to show-jump?'

'We heard you were trying to adopt a baby. What chances of that now?' asked *The Scorpion*.

'Are you going to recognize paternity?' asked ITN.

As they ringed him, ravenous for information, there was something of the cornered, maddened bull about Rupert. Then, with his phenomenal strength, he shoved them out of the way and, sending *The Scorpion* and the *Star* flying, charged the front door, which opened like a trap door to admit him, then slammed against their frenzied hammering fists.

Frantically Taggie and Rupert clung to each other. She tried to smile, but she was deathly pale and her eyes were red-rimmed. 'You poor, poor thing, it's so horrible for you.'

'I'm so desperately sorry.' As he held her, Rupert felt comfort flowing back into his body like a transfusion after a massive loss of blood. 'Please don't leave me. I can face anything as long as I've got you.'

'I'd never leave you,' said Taggie, appalled. 'I love you. Anyway, it all happened years ago, long before I met you.'

'It could have been any of the other guys at the party. They can make anyone look like anyone in photographs.'

'Course they can. What did they say at the adoption society?' She was trying to control her longing.

Rupert shook his head. Since they married there had only been truth between them. 'I'm afraid they're not going to give us a baby, but we'll get one from somewhere.'

'It's OK. We've still got Tabitha and Marcus and the dogs,' her voice faltered. 'And Perdita,' she was about to say. Rupert's ability to have children seemed so at odds with her own recently enforced infertility. The reporters stepped up the hammering on the door.

'How could Perdita have done it?' she said in bewilderment. 'To poor Daisy as well.'

'I don't give a fuck about Daisy. You're the only thing I care about.'

Mrs Bodkin, Rupert's ancient housekeeper, who'd seen endless dramas in her time, came into the hall. Thank God he had Miss Taggie. Seeing them in each other's arms, she coughed.

'It's Tabitha on the private line, Mr Campbell-Black.'

Rupert picked up the telephone. 'I was just going to ring you, darling. I'm terribly sorry. D'you want to come over?'

'Yes, please,' said Tabitha. 'Your new intermediate daughter won't take all our money, will she?' Her shrill voice suddenly broke. 'You won't love her more than me, will you?'

'I'm bloody well going to have it out with Daisy,' snarled Rupert as he came off the telephone.

Ten minutes later his helicopter landed on Ricky's front lawn, and this time the press fell back, scalded by the white heat of his rage. He found Daisy in Ricky's kitchen, mindlessly making a shepherd's pie for supper, not because Ricky wanted it, but to give herself something to do. A smell of frying onion, garlic, peppers and minced lamb drifted through the house. Ricky had pulled down the blue and white striped blinds so the hovering press couldn't see in. For a second Rupert and Daisy stared at each other, both unable not to think of the night they had spent together. How could I? thought Rupert. Daisy looked utterly wretched, her red eyes vanished beneath red swollen lids as though they'd been stung by ants, her face blotchy from crying. An old grey sweater of Ricky's couldn't disguise the weight that had dropped off her.

'Oh, Rupert, I'm so sorry.' All Daisy could think of was how incredible that such an attractive man should once have screwed her all those years ago.

'So you fucking should be!' Rupert hurled his fury like acid in her face. 'Why the hell didn't you have an abortion?'

'I didn't have the money.'

'You can't prove Perdita's my child. Bas has got black eyes just like hers. She could have inherited her riding skills from him or Billy. Bob Riley was almost an albino.'

'I'm not going to say she's yours,' whispered Daisy. 'I just said I was drunk, and can't remember anyone there. It's so awful. You and Taggie have been so sweet to me.'

'Perdita's completely fucked up Taggie's chances of having or adopting a baby, and what about the effect on Tab and Marcus? God, I'm going to sue her into the next world. I'll ruin her if it kills me.'

Daisy started to cry and throw whole carrots into the frantically spitting onions and mince.

'It's burning, lovie.' Ricky crossed the room and turned off the gas. 'Let's leave it and have a drink.'

As Daisy collapsed on to a kitchen chair with her face in her hands, the twins bounded in.

'Hello, Daddy,' said Dommie, grinning at Rupert.

'Orgy, porgy, pudding and pie, kissed the girls and made them pregnant,' said Seb. 'Christ, I'm starving.' Grabbing a spoon, he started eating the mince out of the frying pan. 'What I feel most sorry for you about, Rupert, is having that frightful little shit, Red Alderton, as a son-in-law.'

'It's not funny,' shouted Rupert.

'Well, it's not Daisy's fault,' shouted back Ricky, getting a bottle out of the cupboard, splashing whisky into four glasses and giving one to Daisy.

'I don't want a drink,' said Rupert.

'All the more for me,' said Dommie, tipping Rupert's share into his glass. 'Are these for Wayne and Kinta?' He picked the whole carrots out of the frying pan.

'I said it's not Daisy's fault,' repeated Ricky icily.

'Bloody is,' said Rupert. 'Fucking hippie bringing up her fucking children by Dr Spock rules, letting them run wild, and everything hang out. If she hadn't spoilt Perdita rotten, none of this would have happened.'

'Balls,' yelled Ricky. 'Perdita just happens to have inherited your sodding awful nature.'

'Who tried to bail you out of prison, and appealed against your conviction?' demanded Rupert in outrage.

'Below the belt,' said Seb.

'So was Rupert's dick,' giggled Dommie. 'You shouldn't go round screwing girls when they're stoned.'

'This isn't getting anyone anywhere,' said Ricky. 'Are you going to admit paternity or not?'

'Like hell I am. I'd rather father a mamba.'

'With Red geeing her up, she may easily take you to court,' said Seb.

'Let her,' said Rupert flatly. 'After what she's done to my children and Taggie twice, I'll bury her.'

Rupert's children were not the only ones affected. Violet was devastated, particularly when her boyfriend's parents suddenly withdrew a long-standing invitation to spend a weekend at their house. At Eddie's prep school the rest of his form trooped down to the kitchen and read the cook's copy of *The Scorpion*.

'Common Entrance, Common Entrance,' chanted Blair-Harrison, the most evil boy in the class. 'Your mother seems to have a communal entrance.'

And Eddie had hit Blair-Harrison across the classroom breaking two of his flawless front teeth. One of Dancer's minders had brought Eddie back to Robinsgrove where he had fished and shot clays and apparently happily watched television. But after midnight, long after Daisy had been knocked out by one of Ricky's pills, Ricky found Eddie sobbing his heart out.

'How could Mum let all those blokes stick it in her?'

'It wasn't her fault,' said Ricky. 'Someone got her drunk and drugged her.'

Eddie clenched his fists. 'I'm going to kill Perdita.'

'You're not the only one,' said Ricky grimly.

He wanted nothing more than to concentrate on his polo. His house had been besieged by press for forty-eight hours, and when he went to the Rutshire to play practice chukkas the following day they were ten deep round the clubhouse waiting for him.

For once the expletives were worse off the field than on. The twins, losing their tempers, had started hitting balls at the reporters' ankles, and the police had been called. Miss Lodsworth had for once been on Apocalypse's side and had driven *The Times* cameraman off with her shooting stick. Decorum, the bull terrier, had bitten both *The Scorpion* and the *Guardian*.

Ironically Ricky had become the hero of the press. The cameraman with Beattie Johnson had taken a photograph of Ricky throwing Beattie out of the window and sold it to the *Sun* who'd put it on their front page.

Over in Palm Beach Perdita was on the rack. Electric gates and Rottweilers kept out the press, but not the feelings of utter horror at what she'd unearthed. Talk about Pandora's boxing ring.

Still smarting with rejection that Rupert had turned her down so summarily on finding her in his bed, she had been plagued since then by embarrassingly erotic dreams about him. But now the scalding hot lava of humiliation was pouring over her as she realized she'd tried to bed her own father.

Red the unpredictable, however, was absolutely delighted. Any novelty and strangeness excited him.

'What a good thing you didn't get him into bed in

Florida,' he said gleefully. 'He'd probably have negated the pill and impregnated you.'

'Don't be disgusting,' screamed Perdita. 'If it hadn't been for you, I'd never have tried to pull him that night. If you hadn't been getting off with that girl from *Vanity Fair*, I'd never have got pissed and spilled the beans to Simpson Hastings.'

It was a further source of irritation that no-one believed she hadn't taken a massive pay-off from *The Scorpion*. Red caught the short back ends of her hair, yanking her head back, his eyes blazing with desire.

'Rupert's mega-bucks, just think what we can screw him for.'

'We can't prove he's my father.'

'Haven't you ever heard of genetic engineering? I wonder if my mother will feel differently now she knows you've got some good blood.'

Letting go of her hair, he began to stroke the back of her neck. It was hopeless. He just had to touch her to make her dripping.

'Be nice to me, Red. I need you so badly. Don't leave me.'

Red pushed her back on to the press clippings which littered his dark blue triple bed, and with one practised hand undid the top button of her jeans.

'I'm not quitting, baby. You're just getting interesting.'

Afterwards, having plugged her between the legs with a handful of scrumpled press clippings, Red fell asleep. Feeling hopelessly twitchy and in need of comfort, Perdita rang Luke at the hospital only to learn that he had discharged himself that afternoon. So deep was her self-preoccupation that she didn't even question the utter insanity of such an action, and promptly telephoned him at his barn. 'Oh, Luke, I've done such a terrible thing.'

'I guess you have,' said Luke and hung up. Then, turning back to Margie: 'That was Perdita. I can't handle her at the moment.'

Fantasma and Leroy, delirious to have him home, had followed him into the tack room. After the first ecstatic welcome, both seemed to sense how excruciatingly painful his hand was and just wanted to be near him as quietly as possible. Leroy sat on his feet to stop him ever going away again. Fantasma rested her pink nose on his good shoulder, blowing adoringly down his neck. On the tack-room wall was a photograph of her racing round the paddock without saddle or bridle as white and as swift and as beautiful as summer lightning.

Luke took a slug of the quadruple brandy Margie had just given him. 'I gotta sell her,' he said.

He had learnt that afternoon that Hal Peters had been voted off his own board and gone spectacularly belly-up. Not only had he not paid Luke's salary since January or for the last half-dozen horses Luke had bought for him, but far, far worse, he had let Luke's medical insurance lapse, so there would be massive hospital bills to be paid. That was why – despite doctors and sobbing nurses practically restraining him with a strait-jacket – Luke had walked out of hospital that afternoon.

'You've got to sue,' implored Margie. 'I'll defend you for free.'

Luke shook his head. 'He hasn't got any money to pay me.'

'Then go to your father.'

'He's in enough shit as it is,' said Luke wearily.

'You bloody stubborn Taurean,' stormed Margie, 'lend him Fantasma. Lend him all your ponies. If he's that anxious to smash Ricky this summer, he'll pay anything.'

'There's no way I could ever pay my medical bills and pay him back.'

His hand was agonizingly painful and he was slowly coming to terms with the fact that he might never play polo again. The only honourable way he could pay his debts and see the grooms right was to sell the ponies.

61

At the end of April eighty-five suitcases, fifty-five polo ponies, sixteen grooms, a mountain of tack and polo sticks and a fleet of maids and secretaries were flown in a special Alderton Jumbo over to England. A week later, when everything had been unpacked and made ready for them in Bart's ravishing Sussex house, Chessie, Bart, Red, Perdita and Angel flew over in Bart's new private jet – the

Alderton Quicksilver. Specially designed to dispel rumours that Alderton Airways were going belly-up, it crossed the Atlantic in three hours and was as gleamingly silver as its name. Bart was hoping to raise the money in Europe to market it next year.

Inside the Quicksilver the atmosphere was as highly charged as usual. Red, failing to hide his dislike of his stepmother, had taken Perdita into one of the back bedrooms. Chessie drank a whole bottle of champagne, because Grace only drank water on flights and because she was still furious with Ricky for giving such public sanctuary to Perdita's frumpy mother. Bart put aside the balance sheets he ought to be digesting before his meeting with European Electronics tomorrow and read a computer print-out on his ponies.

Perdita, having stuffed her face with caviar, was now lying post-multi-orgasmic in Red's arms and thinking this really was the life. She and Red had just returned from four magic days in Hawaii where his sexual inventiveness had overwhelmed her. On the Rupert front things had gone unnaturally quiet, with the press switching their attention to a Royal scandal and the lawyers locked behind closed doors. Was Rupert going to sue? Was Perdita going to push for recognition and a massive settlement? It was a war of nerves. She was apprehensive about her reception in England. Sooner or later she'd have to bump into Ricky, her mother, and probably Rupert. But she felt insulated by Red's love. If she was going to be the new Mrs Alderton, what did it matter if she was née Campbell-Black?

Angel sat by himself gazing bleakly out of the window at a dazzling dream-topping of cloud. Three hours was too short a time to adjust to entering loathsome British territory. Awaiting him would be a posse of apoplectic colonels and brigadiers utterly incensed that Bart had pulled a fast one and circumnavigated the ban. Angel had also suffered a lot of flak from the other Argentine players, particularly Alejandro, Juan and Miguel, who spoke enviously of the lack of pressure in England, the hospitality, the beautiful, available girls, the freezing-cold swimming-pools they'd been chucked into by fire-breathing fathers, and the utterly revolting food.

'You 'aven't died until you 'ave Eenglish cabbage,' said

Alejandro. 'We'll send you a food parcel every week.'

'And a suitcase full of condoms,' sighed Juan.

'How can I pull girls,' Angel had grumbled, 'when my father-in-law wants me in bed by ten every night? And if Grace comes over I might as well be gelded.'

But all this was irrelevant when Angel's sole reason for going to England was revenge. His temper was not improved by the latest edition of *International Polo*, where, among the glamorous photographs of massive silver cups, grooved muscular arms, flashing teeth beneath ebony moustaches and ponies with glued-down ears and rolling eyes, was a four-page feature on Drew Benedict. The text was printed in four languages, so Angel was able to read in French, Italian, Spanish and English that Drew, hero of the Falklands, was the rock on which both the Kaputnik Tigers and the British team were built. There were photographs of him outside his beautiful house, flanked by a horsey-looking wife, and two expressionless, well-behaved children, and in his library with a Jack Russell on his knee. Shivering with hatred, Angel examined the handsome, belligerent, unsmiling face, a boxer crossed with a Labrador. Even the comparative shortness of Drew's legs didn't comfort him. Angel's grandmother, who lived in the Plaza, had always claimed that men with short legs were brilliant in bed.

Getting out a Pentel, Angel drew in a moustache and some Shirley Temple curls. But the blue eyes were still cool and appraising, so Angel made one of them squint, then cursed himself for his childishness.

Anyway, how could he concentrate on his mission of vengeance when his marriage was in injury time? The publicity hand-out was that Bibi was staying in America to mind the shop while Bart took virtually three months off, and that she would fly over on the Quicksilver at weekends. In fact, Angel was doubtful if she'd turn up at all. The row had started innocently enough. Left on his own so much, Angel had run up more gambling debts. Aware that their anniversary was coming up, strapped for cash, he had taken a modelling job so he could buy her a present with his own money. Bibi, growing increasingly suspicious, had followed him, seen him arrive at a house, kiss a beautiful model who had arrived at the same time and go inside with her. Instead of following him, where she would have found cameras, lights and silver umbrellas, Bibi had gone home in floods. Confronted, Angel had blurted out the truth. After a blazing row, refusing to believe him, Bibi had stormed round to the agency, who confirmed Angel's story. Mortified, Bibi had flown home early from the office in an Alderton helicopter which was an anniversary present for him. As she walked into the house with her arms full of flowers, however, Angel had walked out of the bedroom with a towel wrapped round his waist. A second later he was followed by Innocenta in Bibi's silk dressing gown.

'What's that scrubber got to offer that I haven't?' Bibi screamed later.

'She's got time,' said Angel with chilling accuracy.

In the cold war that ensued, Angel and Bibi had lain as far apart as possible on the cliff edges of their double bed, longing for the other to weaken and stretch out a hand; and a stony-faced monosyllabic Bibi had come home from the office each night and ostentatiously cooked Angel's dinner.

'Bibi only say seven word to me this week,' Angel had grumbled to Red as they boarded the plane, 'dinner, dinner, dinner, dinner, dinner, dinner, dinner.'

'Why doesn't she dispense with all the chitchat,' said Red, grinning, 'and buy a gong?'

As he flipped sullenly through *International Polo*, Angel noticed that all the girls were far more beautiful than Bibi. Why the hell did he feel so miserable?

Three weeks later Daisy Macleod, travelling up to Paddington by train, took the same photograph of Drew out of her bag. Because of the press hanging around, she hadn't seen him since *The Scorpion* revelations, and now they were meeting at Sukey's house off Kensington Church Street. Daisy was incredibly twitchy because Violet was also in London on a school trip visiting the Impressionists at the Tate, and because Eddie had rung up from school that morning. 'First the bad news, Mum, I failed Common Entrance. But now the good news, every single other boy in the school passed.' Daisy was overwhelmed with love for his philosophical stoicism, but she knew he was desperately low and felt even worse because she was sure he'd only ploughed the exam because of *The Scorpion*.

As the train got in at eleven-thirty, and she wasn't meeting Drew until twelve forty-five, she had time to kill. She'd cleaned her teeth on the train, carefully not swallowing the non-drinking water, and then again in the Ladies at Paddington, and again in Harrods, where she'd also covered herself in Je Reviens from the scent counter.

Still with time to kill, she hung around a second-hand book shop near Drew's house and bought him a book called *The Art of Lunging*, then went to an off-licence and bought him a bottle of Möet in return for all the bottles he'd given her.

The man behind the counter, almost asphyxiated by wafts of Je Reviens and Colgate, asked with a leer if Daisy'd like it ready-chilled.

'How lovely,' Daisy blushed. 'I didn't know you could buy it like that.'

'We sell a lot,' said the man, admiring Daisy's bosom in her apple-green T-shirt. 'People like to take a bottle in the park.'

It was still only twelve-forty. Sweating with nerves, Daisy went into a supermarket and checked her face by the dog-food counter. Glancing up, she saw herself on the monitor. She supposed it was one way of getting on television and bought a box of Bonios for Ethel.

Turning into Drew's street, grateful for the shade of the plane trees, Daisy walked down the road until she came to Number Fifteen. Drew's blue BMW wasn't outside. Across the road a pretty girl, holding an estate agent's hand-out, stared at Daisy intently. Perhaps she was Sukey's sister. Walking to the end of the road, Daisy turned round and walked back. Steeling herself, ignoring the girl still waiting opposite, Daisy marched up the path, pausing to powder her nose. But before she could ring the door bell, the door had opened and a voice said, 'You look fine,' and Drew had pulled her in to the hall.

He was wearing a red and white striped shirt which brought out the red of his complexion. He looked less glamorous than his photograph and, as he kissed her, he tasted of fish. Just for a second Daisy wondered why she'd wasted so many sleepless nights on him.

Following him into the kitchen, she saw the remains of a smoked salmon sandwich and a half-drunk glass of champagne. I'm always far too excited to eat anything before he arrives, she thought, as she handed him a carrier bag.

'Bonios. That's very kind,' said Drew, looking inside.

'Oh, help, I've given you the wrong bag,' said Daisy, shoving the bookshop and off-licence bags at him.

'That's sweet, thank you,' said Drew, filling a glass for her from the bottle already opened and taking another bite of his sandwich.

'Do you want anything to eat?'

Daisy shook her head.

'Poor baby, I'm sorry you've had such a bloody time, but you look great. You must have lost ten pounds, but not off your tits, thank God.'

Daisy went to the window and gazed at Sukey's back garden, which was a rather uncharacteristic riot of roses, honeysuckle and jasmine. 'How lovely,' she sighed. 'Sukey is clever.'

'At some things,' said Drew, running a hand up her backbone and unhooking her bra. As his hands gathered up her breasts and she collapsed against him, she could hear the sound of typing next door and a faint hum of traffic.

'Let's go to bed,' said Drew.

'It was lovely you won yesterday,' said Daisy, 'and scored most of the goals.'

As he followed her upstairs, Drew's hands slid slowly up her legs and between her thighs. 'These are the only goal posts I want to get between.'

On the chest of drawers in his dressing room were an engagement photograph of a mistily glamorous Sukey in pearls and a strapless dress, silver-backed brushes, Penhaligon's English Fern and a panama with a Household Division ribbon. Thrown over an armchair were a dinner jacket, a crumpled evening shirt, a black tie and a pile of Kaputnik Tiger shirts – all the detritus of Drew's other life.

Pulling off her T-shirt, bra and pants, but leaving her trailing, turquoise skirt, he pushed her back on the narrow, single bed and, burying his face in her breasts, murmured,

'You are so comfortable, Mrs Macleod, I'm sure someone comes along and plumps up your body like Sukey's cushions every half-hour.'

Soon his tongue was wandering lazily through the heather of her pubic hair to find the cairn of her clitoris.

'Come inside me, please,' said Daisy, worried that she was too tense to come and that he might be bored.

'Don't be silly,' mumbled Drew. 'I've waited five weeks for this. You can wait five minutes longer.'

'Oh, that tongue,' Daisy squirmed in ecstasy. At last the waves were slowly lapping against the shore, then they were inside her, seeping and sweeping over her. She was a mini-Pacific. She gave a gasp, moaned and floated away on a lilo of pleasure. 'Oh, thank you, thank you, I love you, I love you, I can't help it.'

'Now it's my turn,' said Drew. 'I won't be able to last long.'

'That was bliss,' he said as he rolled off her, 'but next time cut your fingernails.'

'I'm sorry,' said Daisy humbly.

'I'm not. It's always magic with you, my love. I've got you a present. I bought it for Easter, but your bloody daughter and *The Scorpion* got in the way.' Daisy opened the red leather box and gave a gasp. On the white satin lay a brooch with a topaz centre, ringed by diamond petals.

'It's a daisy,' cried Daisy ecstatically. 'It's the loveliest thing I've ever seen. Where did you find it?'

'I had it made,' Drew kissed her shoulder, 'as an expression of my great fondness and regard for you. You will notice there are nine petals, so if you ever play "Loves me, loves me not" with it, it'll always come out loves me.'

'But you shouldn't,' gabbled Daisy. 'I mean it's too much, it isn't . . . ?'

'Real?' said Drew. 'Of course it is, I don't like fake jewels or fake orgasms. We are going to get ourselves organized and I'm going to see a lot more of you in the future.'

Daisy had first bath and watched him having the second one.

'Are you coming to Guards on Thursday?' he asked. The Kaputnik Tigers were meeting the Flyers in the semi-final of the Queen's Cup.

'I don't know,' said Daisy, 'I'd love to watch you and Perdita, but Rupert'll probably be there.' Her voice trailed away. 'Have you seen her?'

'No,' said Drew. Gosh, he washed well, really scrubbing his neck, arms and legs, and between his toes, getting rid of every trace of her before he saw Sukey. Weak with love, fingering her brooch which she'd pinned to her T-shirt, she longed to touch his cock and make him come again.

'But I gather she's not playing very well,' Drew went on. 'I'm told Bart gees her up and Red and Angel are far too selfish to give her any passes.'

'Angel's supposed to be terribly good,' said Daisy.

'Bloody prima donna evidently,' said Drew. 'Manages to keep his absolute loathing of the Brits just within legal bounds.'

'I wrote to her,' said Daisy, 'only last week. She hasn't answered.'

'You mustn't,' said Drew, rearing out of the bath and grabbing a towel. 'You must back off. Let her come to you.'

'That's what Ricky says.'

Drew looked up sharply. 'You're seeing too much of Ricky.'

'Only to listen. He's far too preoccupied with bumping into Chessie and burying Bart.'

'Are you going anywhere nice?' she asked, as she watched Drew brushing dog hairs off his dinner jacket. It was so hard to draw a fine balance between probing and sympathetic interest.

'Lady Sharon's giving one of her little dinner parties. You should see their new house in Eaton Square. What a pity you didn't get the commission to paint all Victor's and Sharon's ancestors. Great-great-great Auntie Tracey, who came over with the Vaykings, and huge Tayger heads, shot by Victor's great-grandfather in India, which were bought at Phillips last week, on every wall. And I'll have to sit on Sharon's right.'

'Lucky Sharon,' said Daisy wistfully.

'Unlucky me,' said Drew, then suddenly businesslike, 'You go out first, darling. We don't want anyone seeing us together.'

62

Daisy had no intention of going to the semi-final between the Flyers and the Tigers. She had urgent commissions to finish and had even refused a lift to the Guards Club with Ricky and the twins, who wanted to watch the teams, one of which they'd be playing in Sunday's final. But suddenly a longing to see Drew and Perdita overwhelmed her and she found herself driving her ancient Volkswagen so fast up the M4 that it overheated.

She had purposely not changed out of her torn jeans and old, blue denim shirt and wore dark glasses and her hair tied back in the hope that no-one would recognize *The Scorpion* trollop, also to discourage herself from going anywhere near the pony lines. She couldn't bear Drew to see her looking so scruffy. But again, such was the magnet of her longing that ten minutes before throw-in she found herself passing the hospitality tents going up for Sunday's final, and there were the Tigers' grooms in their black-and-orange shirts frantically tacking up ponies and screwing studs into their shoes.

Then Daisy's heart stopped, for there was Drew looking almost willowy beside the hulking Shark Nelligan, but towering over fat little Victor and the Brazilian ringer. They all had their heads together as Drew, in his soft voice, urged them on to annihilate the Flyers.

And, oh God, there was Ricky. She'd specifically told him she didn't want to come to the match.

Moving past splendidly glossy ponies, who, nervous before a game, were stamping their feet and flattening their ears at one another, Daisy came to even more splendid and glossier ponies and it seemed as though the sky had been pulled down, so many grooms were tearing round in pale blue, Flyers T-shirts. There was Bart leaning against an iron rail yelling into his telephone because he was having trouble getting through to Johannesburg while a groom did up his kneepads. There was Red smoking a Black Sobranie being gazed at by groupies. Heavens, he was beautiful, but Daisy didn't like the way he was idly chatting up a leggy blonde who was clutching a King Charles spaniel puppy whose ears were as red as his hair. By deduction the other player in the sky-blue shirt must be Angel. He was thinner than Daisy expected, and with his weary, haunted, heavy-lidded eyes, hollowed cheeks, damp, tendrilled hair and elegance, reminded her of Mantegna's *John the Baptist*. His hand shook as he lit one cigarette from another, and, although it was a chill, windy day, and, unlike Bart and Red, he wasn't wearing a jersey under his shirt, he was absolutely pouring with sweat. The poor boy obviously suffered from appalling pre-match nerves.

Daisy, who was shaking as much as Angel, couldn't see Perdita anywhere, but suddenly she heard a joyful rumbling whicker and felt a gentle nudge in her back. Jumping round, she discovered little Tero, whom she'd so often plied with toast and Marmite when she'd wintered in Ricky's field. Unbelievably touched to be remembered, Daisy hugged the equally enchanted pony. The Flyer's groom, who was giving Tero's oyster-grey coat a last polish, looked up in amazement.

'That's really weird. She's head-shy with everyone but Perdita.'

'I'm Perdita's mother,' stammered Daisy.

The girl's mouth formed a perfect O. Then there was a frantic clicking of cameras, a surging forward of the crowd and an even deeper whicker of joy from Tero.

'For Christ's sake,' said a familiar voice furiously, 'Red's been chatting up that blonde all lunch. Is he deliberately trying to screw up my game? Those bandages are too tight; do them again. And why the hell have you put Spotty in a pelham? I told you he went better in a Barry gag. Jesus, can't you concentrate for five minutes?'

'Can we have a word, Perdita?' said the *Sun* ingratiatingly.

'No, you fucking can't, and certainly not before a match.'

Daisy's first impression was how like Rupert Perdita had become. The haughty, dead-pan face with its short, streaked hair betrayed none of her rage and panic. Only the quivering tension of her slender, boyish body gave her away. Knowing how nervous she was, Daisy's one thought was to comfort her. 'Darling, I just wanted to wish you luck.'

Perdita swung round, her face ashen, her eyes glittering like tourmalines, her animosity as blasting as nerve gas.

'Luck is the last thing you've ever brought me. Just fuck off.'

'Perdita,' reproved the groom, shocked.

'You keep out of it. What's she done but screw up my life? Back off,' she spat at Daisy. 'Don't come crawling under my feet. You'll get stamped on.'

Stumbling away, tears pouring under her dark glasses, Daisy was nearly run over by Shark Nelligan's groom taking a pony down to the pitch. Ricky, who'd been only half-listening to Bobby Ferraro and Ronnie Ferguson because he was looking all the time for Chessie, suddenly saw Daisy backing away from Perdita as though she'd had acid thrown in her face, and turned to Seb and Dommie, who'd just come back from ringing their bookmaker.

'Look after Daisy, both of you. Take her up in the stands and buy her a bloody big drink. Perdita's just put the boot in.'

In a trice the twins had caught up with her.

'Daisee, Daisee, Give me your answer do,' sang Seb, putting an arm round Daisy's shoulders.

'I'm half crazy, all for the love of you,' sang Dommie, putting an arm round her waist.

'I haven't got a handkerchief,' sobbed Daisy.

Diving into the men's changing room, Seb came out with a roll of blue Andrex.

'Here you are,' he said, pulling out at least eight feet and handing it to Daisy. 'We're going to force-feed you vodka and orange.'

'Don't worry about that poxy daughter of yours,' said Dommie. 'After the number of times she's kicked you in the teeth, you ought to buy a gum shield. She's only in a bait because Red's playing her up. Now, we've all got to cheer for the Tigers, because they'll be so much easier to beat in the final than the Flyers.'

The stands were unusually packed for a weekday, because so many people had turned up to see the Argentine who had broken the ban, and who was alleged to be the handsomest Latin to invade British soil since Juan O'Brien had cut such a swath through everyone's wives before the Falklands War.

'You cannot imagine the bliss,' said Seb, hardly lowering his voice, as they sat down, 'of not playing for Victor any more. Ricky's a tartar – he doesn't regard bonking and bopping all night as keeping fit – but you don't have to brown-nose him all the time. And have you seen Drew's new Lamborghini? I bet that's a reward for services rendered from Lady Sharlady, although Drew's already got some lady. I wish I knew who it was.'

Giggling, Dommie pointed a frantic finger at two rows in front, where Sukey, wearing a khaki shirt, canvas jodhpurs and a pith helmet, had just sat down.

'She looks as though she's been shooting Tayger,' he whispered to a twitching Daisy. 'Can't you see her resting a well-shod foot on Drew's back?'

Next moment Daisy felt even worse, for Bas had come into the stand with Rupert and Taggie. All in dark glasses, they totally ignored the photographers who were going berserk. Rupert was wearing a panama over his nose and holding Taggie, who was looking very pale and thin, tightly by the hand. Daisy hadn't seen him since the awful row when Ricky had thrown him out.

'Here they come,' said Seb, as the players cantered on to the field. 'Have you ever seen ponies like the Flyers? Bart must have bred every single one from Derby winners on both sides.'

But Daisy was watching Drew who, as he rode past, was still issuing last-minute instructions to the Brazilian ringer. She hoped the back of Sukey's very clean white neck wouldn't be scorched by her longing. Red, who was now hitting a ball around near the stands, very pointedly blew a kiss at the leggy blonde with the King Charles spaniel puppy.

'Who's she?' asked Daisy.

'A slag,' said Seb. 'Dommie and I had her last week.'

'Why are you two so addicted to threesomes?' drawled a voice.

'Because Seb's too lazy to get girls for himself,' said Dommie. 'Hello, Mrs Alderton.'

As Chessie, minxy as ever in white jeans and a navy-blue cashmere jersey, but wearing a fraction too much rouge to hide her pallor, sat down beside him, Dommie kissed her on both cheeks.

'Thank God your ex is only umpiring,' he went on, 'so you can't put a hex on his game. We were only just saying how beautifully your husband's mounted his team.'

'Costs him enough!' Chessie helped herself to Dommie's drink. 'Oh, there's Ricky,' she added wistfully. 'You have to admit, he's the best-constructed man in polo. Look at the way those broad shoulders narrow into the hips, and at the length of his thighs. Christ, he's gorgeous.'

As if drawn by her desire, Ricky glanced up, and glanced hastily away.

'We'll have to throw a bucket of water over you in a minute,' said Seb. Then, lowering his voice: 'Do look! Suke's neck's gone bright pink with disapproval.'

'Silly bitch,' said Chessie. 'Bart's livid. Jesus was the first umpire he objected to, because he'd once sacked him. Then they offered him Charles and Ben Napier, and Bart objected again, because he'd sacked them too. Then they came up with Ricky, and Bart said, "My wife sacked him, so *he's* not going to be impartial." After that Ronnie Ferguson stuck his toes in, thank God.'

'Ricky hated doing it,' said Dommie. 'He loathes coming within a million miles of your husband, but he reckoned the best way he'd size up the opposition was to umpire the match.'

'I'm sure we've met,' said Chessie, knowing perfectly well who Daisy was, and that Ricky'd been protecting her. God knows why thought Chessie. Daisy struck her as being extremely plain.

'This is Daisy, Perdita's mother,' said Seb.

'Ah,' said Chessie, 'Perdita wouldn't be my favourite person if I were you.'

'She's none of our favourite person,' said Dommie. 'No, don't cry, sweetheart,' and, unrolling another eight feet of blue Andrex, he proceeded to wipe Daisy's eyes.

'Dommie's madly in love,' announced Seb.

'Do we know her?' asked Chessie, mildly interested.

'It's a "he" and a pony,' said Dommie excitedly. 'No, I know horses bore you rigid, Chessie, but this one's something else. He's a little Australian Waler with legs like crowbars. I saw him at a gymkhana last summer and he was so competitive, he galloped ahead in the sack race and brought the sack back every time in his teeth. His owners wouldn't part with him then, but this summer he started napping badly so they let me have him for meat money.

He is so brilliant and so clever and so gutsy like Fantasma he'll take anything on. And he's got two white stripes on his withers, so I've called him Corporal.'

'Oh, belt up, Dom,' said Seb. 'Go and get us all another drink.'

Down below them on the field, Angel couldn't stop shaking. He could hardly hold the reins, let alone manage his whip and stick. He'd spent an hour at the nearest Catholic church that morning, but how can one ask for absolution for a murder one is about to commit? On the other hand, as Bibi still wouldn't return his calls, his marriage was obviously over, so what did it matter if he spent the next twenty-five years in some British gaol? The Guards Club, with its rain-soaked banks of azaleas, fields stretching out like eternal billiard tables and revolting English ex-army officers in blazers barking instructions into walkie-talkies, made him feel sick. No-one knew that there was a sprinkling of Malvinas earth in the bottom of his polo boots, and no one had noticed the silhouette of the Malvinas stamped on the front of his pale blue helmet. A plane flew over and he wished he was on it.

But there was the loathsome Captain Benedict unconcernedly tapping a ball around a few yards away. Instantly, Angel was back in the Malvinas, with Drew lounging behind a table with a borrowed sheepskin coat round his shoulders against the punishing cold, drinking one cup of coffee after another and not offering anything to Angel, who was standing on his agonizingly smashed-up knee, trying not to sob with pain, as one question relentlessly followed another in Drew's strongly accented but fluent Spanish.

At that moment in Angel's terrifying reverie his dark bay mare, Maria, took advantage of his inattention to give a colossal buck, which sent Angel flying through the air.

'There's Angel Solis de Gonzales, ex-fighter pilot, showing us how well he can fly without a plane,' mocked Terry Hanlon, polo's joker, from the commentary box.

The crowd roared with laughter. Angel ground his teeth. Red, who had caught Maria, brought her back to him. As Angel replaced his hat, Drew noticed the Malvinas silhouette stamped on the front. Taking in the wild, haunted eyes, the deathly pallor, the stubble and the damp, bronze curls escaping from beneath the rim, he knew he'd seen Angel before somewhere and was assailed by a feeling of menace.

Two by two, like animals going into the ark, the teams lined up. Victor beside Perdita, the Brazilian beside Angel, Drew beside the leaping, dancing Red, and hulking Shark beside a constantly shouting Bart. Ricky hurled the ball in with unaccustomed viciousness.

As planned beforehand, Angel and Perdita rode their opposing players off the line to let the ball pound through to Red, who whacked it towards the boards, scorched after it, then stroked a beautiful forehand round to Perdita who had galloped upfield towards the centre. Caught off guard and making gallant attempts to catch up with her, Drew felt as if a truck had hit him as he was ferociously bumped by Angel, who then thundered upfield so that when Perdita, out of nerves, totally missed a long shot at goal, he was able to charge up behind her, pick up the ball and, with a beautiful nearside forehand, pass to a racing-down Red, who effortlessly stroked it between the posts.

'Oh, Christ,' said Seb in awe, 'if those two are going to be the pivot of the Flyers' team, they'll be bloody hard to beat on Sunday. Come on, Tigers, sock it to them.'

Victor took a swipe and missed the ball.

Behind the stands the sun, which had had difficulty getting through, like Bart, at last pierced the grey curtain of cloud, spotlighting the drama on the field. Rupert put his panama on Taggie's head.

'Rupert's alleged daughter has hardly touched the ball at all,' murmured Dommie to Chessie.

Shark was meant to be marking Perdita, but as no-one gave her any passes, he left her and went to Drew's aid. But although he and Drew were both incredibly powerful defensive players, they couldn't contain Red and Angel.

'Red, Red, Red, Gonzales, Gonzales, Gonzales' (he hadn't time for Solis) seemed to be the only words on Terry Hanlon's lips.

Then Angel jumped the boards at mid-off and hit a nearside backshot of forty yards, placing the ball just in front of the opposition posts. Before Shark or Drew could get there, Red had whistled down like a bullet and in it went. The crowd were in ecstasy, bursting over and over again into roars of applause.

At first Drew thought he was imagining things. As his opposing Number Two, Angel was meant to mark him, so initially he dismissed the hurtling kamikaze bumps as Latin exhuberance. Then a pelham bit was jabbed into his kidneys, a pony's head swung into his shoulder so hard that even the pony shook its head for twenty seconds, elbows rammed his ribs and, riding up beside him, Angel got his knee underneath Drew's leg and tried to tip him out of the saddle.

Finally, the ball came out in Drew's direction and he had a lovely open sweep to goal in front of him. As he swung his stick back, he was hooked perilously low, Angel's stick catching his pony's legs and nearly bringing her down.

'What the fuck are you playing at, you bloody wop?' yelled Drew.

Ricky blew his whistle and, having awarded a thirty to the Tigers, took Angel aside.

'You're pushing your luck. Pack it in.'

Drew took the penalty, deliberately spending as long as possible to get his breath back. His ribs were agony. Forward went his stick, then back, then whistling down like Jove releasing his thunderbolt, slap between the posts.

'Well done,' cried Daisy in delight.

Drew looked straight at Angel. 'Well?' he said coolly.

It was a mistake. Thirty seconds later Angel rode him off at ninety degrees, sending his pony flying. As Drew turned in fury, he was suddenly terrified. There was the icy madness of the killer in Angel's eyes.

In the third chukka Drew was riding Malteser, his fastest but most explosively excitable pony. It usually took half a chukka to calm her down. Red was loose again. Giving Malteser her head, Drew galloped over to mark him, but on his way Shark backed the ball somewhat wildly up towards him. Attempting to stop it, Drew leant right out of his saddle. Hearing a pounding of hooves behind him, and feeling Angel's knee under his, he crashed to the ground.

'Oh no,' screamed Daisy, caught off her guard.

Sukey leapt to her feet. 'That Argentine is trying to kill my husband,' she called out in a trembling voice.

Oh God, thought Daisy, feeling an icy hand squeezing her heart. If Angel was a Falklands pilot, perhaps he was taking Drew out for being on the other side.

Numb with horror, she watched Ricky, then Bart, then Red, remonstrating with Angel, as Drew climbed groggily on to his pony to take the penalty. As he hit the ball, Angel bounded forward and blocked the shot, then, as the ball bounced awkwardly in the air, miraculously hit it again twenty yards upfield and was galloping furiously in pursuit. Drew, carried down by the impetus of taking the penalty, swung round to ride Angel off. Together they raced for the ball. Angel, riding Minerva, Bart's fastest pony after Glitz, pulled ahead.

'D'you remember me, handsome *capitán*?' he said, smiling evilly round at Drew. ' " 'Ow many planes 'ave you got? 'Ow many pilots? When is zee next attack planned and where? Eef you wish to play polo again, you better answer my questions.'"

Drew let out a sigh. 'So it *is* you, you fucking dago.'

The next moment Angel had pulled over towards Drew, and his wicked-looking spur had caught the cheek strap of Drew's bridle, narrowly missing Malteser's terrified, rolling eye, and ripped it apart. A second later his stick crashed into Drew's jaw and Drew slumped to the ground like a felled pine. But his foot was caught in the stirrup. Picking up her master's sense of panic, Malteser dragged him for twenty yards before Shark caught up with her and yanked her to a halt.

As the ambulance screamed on, Ricky rode furiously up to Angel. 'Off, you bastard.'

'Don't you send him off,' shouted Bart. 'He's my best player. Fucking biased umpiring.'

'Off,' bellowed Bobby Ferraro, the second umpire, in agreement.

In the stands, Bas had put an arm round a shaking, sobbing Sukey's shoulders.

'It's OK, old duck. He's tough, he'll be OK.'

'Oh no, no, no,' moaned Daisy, gazing in agony and horror at a lifeless Drew.

There was a crack and, looking down, she saw she had broken her dark glasses. She had already nearly bitten her lower lip through trying not to cry out. As she watched Drew being lifted unconscious into the ambulance, she gave a shuddering wail. Glancing round, Dommie suddenly realized everything. 'So you're the one,' he whispered.

Then, pulling her into his arms: 'Hang on to me. For Christ's sake, don't blow it, sweetheart. He'll be all right.'

Dommie was utterly angelic.

'She's upset about Perdita,' he told everyone blandly as he hustled a sobbing Daisy out of the stands. 'Little bitch bit her head off just before the match.'

And when Daisy sobbed even louder in protest, Dommie told her to shut up. 'Perdita's committed enough crimes against humanity for it not to matter if one of them's blamed on her unfairly.'

Although it was only half-time, he insisted on driving Daisy's rickety old Volkswagen faster than it had ever been driven back to Rutshire.

'I'm not letting you near Ricky in this condition. He'd be bound to winkle it out of you and you know how pompous he is about extra-marital frolics – although this was plainly more than a frolic.'

'The awful thing,' said Daisy numbly, 'was that Sukey was so upset. I really did think it was a marriage of convenience.'

'Convenient for Drew. Move over, Granny,' said Dommie, honking furiously as he overtook some Sunday afternoon drivers admiring the Rutshire countryside at twenty mph. 'No wonder he was so ratty when Red and I tried to take you to Paris last summer.'

'He's been so kind to me since Hamish left.'

'Not difficult. I'd be kind to you – and unlike him I've got weekends, Christmas and Easter free.' Dommie put his arm round her shoulders. 'He's a lucky sod.'

'Not if he dies,' sobbed Daisy.

'Course he won't.'

Without a car telephone he was unable to ring the hospital for news until they got home and even then the Intensive Care Ward would only tell him Drew had been admitted.

'But it's his father speaking.' Dommie put on a gruff military voice.

But all he could glean was that Drew had not yet regained consciousness.

Dommie and Daisy were stuck into the vodka and Dommie was trying to distract her by telling her more stories about his new pony, Corporal, when the telephone rang. Daisy jumped out of her skin. Perhaps it was news of Drew. Then she thought how bloody silly; she was only the mistress who had to grin and bear it. Why should anyone tell her anything? Fighting back the tears, she grabbed the receiver.

It was Ricky.

'You OK?' he asked brusquely. 'Sorry about Perdita.'

'She always gets uptight before a game.'

'No bloody excuse.'

'Have you heard anything about Drew?'

'Still out cold, but he hasn't broken anything.'

When he had told her all he knew, Ricky asked Daisy if she'd like him to come over. 'You shouldn't be on your own.'

'Dommie's here.'

There was a pause.

'Be careful,' said Ricky.

'Hospital says Drew's in a stable condition,' Daisy told Dommie as she put down the receiver.

'Fatuous expression. You'd think he was sleeping on wood shavings!' Dommie filled up their glasses. 'Needs a muzzle, too, to stop him babbling on about you in his delirium.'

'Ricky said the only thing he's calling out for is Malteser,' said Daisy sadly.

Eventually she managed to persuade a reluctant Dommie that she was really happier on her own.

'You've been so kind, but I just want to slink into my lair and lick my wounds.'

'I'd lick much more exciting parts of you,' grumbled Dommie as he borrowed her car to drive home.

Only after she'd finished the vodka and sobbed it all out in tears did Daisy rashly ring the hospital.

'It's very late. Are you a relation?' enquired the night sister.

'Yes, I'm Drew's Great-Aunt Araminta,' said Daisy. 'I just want to know he's OK.'

Twenty seconds later she nearly dropped the receiver.

'If that's *The Scorpion* or anyone else pretending to be Drew's father, who incidentally died five years ago' – Sukey's normally brisk no-nonsense voice was cracked with strain – 'you can sugar off.'

618

Hanging up, Daisy slumped wailing over the kitchen table. Nothing – not the secret trysts, nor the ecstatic love-making nor the vats of scent and Moët, not the diamond brooches, cashmere jerseys and the slithering slinky satin underwear – made up for not being able to sit beside Drew's bed, holding his hand and willing him back to consciousness.

63

The inquiry was held the following afternoon in an up-stairs room at the Naval and Military Club in Piccadilly. Stewards from the British Polo Association, including David Waterlane, Charles Napier, Brigadier Hughie and Brigadier Canford from Cowdray, made up the Committee. Evidence was given by the umpires, Bobby Ferraro and Ricky, looking particularly bleak in a dark suit and his habitual black tie, and from the third man. The BPA had tried to get a signed statement from Drew. But, confined to hospital with severe concussion and a cracked jaw, he could remember nothing.

The ramblings of Brigadier Hughie, who'd had two glasses of port at luncheon and who could see parallels for everything in Singapore and India, were mercifully cut short by David Waterlane, who was not drinking because it was the polo season and who wanted to go to a strip club.

Victor Kaputnik had been furious that Drew, his star player, had been taken out. But his fury had been consider-ably assuaged when, with Ben Napier standing in for Drew, the Tigers had smashed the Flyers (down to three men after Angel had been sent off) by 12-8, which put them in the final. To upstage Bart, who'd only brought four lawyers, Victor rolled up with five, whereupon Bart promptly sent out for two more – like a takeaway.

Angel, sullen and shell-shocked from being bawled out by an enraged Bart and an even more hysterically angry Red, had been ordered by Bart's principal lawyer, Winston Chalmers, who'd flown through the night on Concorde at vast expense, to keep his pretty trap shut.

'All you gotta do,' said Winston, 'is to say you're very sorry and admit it was a terrible mistake.'

619

'The only meestake was not to keel him,' snarled Angel.

'D'you want to be sidelined for ten years?'

Angel shrugged sulkily.

'Well, shut up then, and, for Chrissake, take him to Jermyn Street, Red, get him a tie and a haircut.'

Winston Chalmers was a fine lawyer.

'Angel Solis de Gonzales,' he told the stewards, 'comes from one of the oldest families in the Argentine and was one of the most distinguished pilots in the Falklands War. All players get strung up before a match – particularly a semi-final. Suddenly, by extraordinary coincidence, he sees on the opposite side a British officer who interrogated him in the Falklands. A volatile, hot-blooded Latin, he sees red and hits him.'

'No,' piped up Angel, 'I did not heet Red. I saw Drew and heet him.'

'Pack it in,' muttered Winston Chalmers savagely.

'I come to Eengland to avenge my brother, Pedro. We in Argentina honour the family.'

'Your brother was a fine player?' asked Brigadier Hughie, easing a sliver of cutlet *en gelée* out of his teeth.

'Excellent. He make Red Alderton look like Veector Kaputnik.'

The Committee tried not to laugh.

'I must tell zee truth,' continued Angel. 'I know Drew Benedict was polo player. I know everytheenk about 'im. 'E torture me in Falklands.'

'What we want to know,' asked David Waterlane, 'is whether the whole thing was premeditated?'

'I no understand.'

'Did you plan it beforehand?'

Angel glanced out on to the dusty plane trees of Green Park. People were lounging in emerald-green deck chairs, girls were stretched out in bikinis. He felt a great wave of shame as he said, 'No, I did not.'

Everyone left the room except the stewards and the discussion became very acrimonious.

'We've got to suspend him for a year and send him home,' said Brigadier Canford from Cowdray, who wanted to continue the ban. 'Solis de Gonzales's behaviour is utterly indicative of what will happen if we get the Argentines back. If he comes up against Rutminster

620

Hall in the next few weeks he could easily take out the Prince of Wales.'

David Waterlane, however, who hadn't won a major cup nor lost a wife since Miguel and Juan played for him, came down heavily in support of Angel.

'Chap hasn't displayed a trace of aggression in any other game. Played against Brits in Palm Beach. Plays in the same team as Perdita. She's a Brit. Drew's an isolated case. Gave him a hard time in the Falklands, had a rush of blood to the head. Suspend him for a week with a £5,000 fine.'

'I remember a chappie in India,' began Brigadier Hughie, 'furious with another player for walking off with his wife. About to kill him, when a wild pig, wounded by some guns, ran across the pitch, so we all gave chase.'

'Oh, shut up, Hughie,' snapped David Waterlane. 'I know for a fact that if you ban Gonzales, Bart for one will pull out of the Gold Cup altogether and go back to America.'

'We don't want that,' said Brigadier Canford, going pale. Bart had promised to pour a vast amount of money into the club which he'd just joined, but hadn't signed the cheque yet. Brigadier Canford had visions of being landed with a bill for new showers, a new bar and Ladies' loos with a Tampax machine.

'When I was in Singapore,' interrupted Brigadier Hughie, 'chappie got so miffed at being beaten, he hijacked the opposition ponies and syces on the train home.'

'Oh, shut up, Hughie,' said Brigadier Canford.

Angel waited outside in the smoking room. Forgetting its similarity to the Jockey Club in Buenos Aires, he thought how odiously British were the thick red carpet, the ornate plaster ceiling, the heavy, dark furniture, the members silently reading *The Times* and the *Sporting Life*.

He hadn't eaten since yesterday morning and he felt exhausted, miserable and desperately ashamed of himself for having lied to the stewards. Glancing up, he thought he was hallucinating, for there, hovering in the doorway with the club porter, was Bibi, looking adorably fragile and worried.

'I just came from the airport. What's happening?'

'They're still talking,' said Angel.

621

Joyously crossing the room, he was about to take her in his arms when she said coldly, 'What in hell were you doing trying to murder Drew Benedict?'

Angel could lie to the inquiry, but not to Bibi.

'Drew Benedict is complete sheet who torture me in Malvinas. Now his jaw is cracked he won't find it so easy to interrogate people.'

They were out in the passage now, both shaking with animosity and longing.

'How long have you planned this?'

'For ever,' said Angel. 'I had to avenge Pedro.'

Bibi went to the window and gazed past the swooning Union Jack over the windowbox of red geraniums at the lovers in the park. My life is over, she thought. Angel, gazing at her long, beautiful legs, her tousled, red hair and her hunched, padded shoulders in the petrol-blue suit, thought he'd never needed or wanted her so badly.

'So you didn't marry me for my money,' whispered Bibi, turning on him. 'You did it to get American nationality and your revenge on poor Drew.'

'What other reason could there be?' hissed Angel.

He didn't mean it, but he was fed up with being lectured and shouted at, and was aware of newspapers being lowered in the smoking room next door.

'I want a divorce. Winston's over here, so he can handle it right away,' said Bibi, and, sobbing hysterically, she fled down the stairs out into the traffic of Piccadilly. Angel was about to run after her when a voice said, 'Mr Solis de Gonzales, will you come in, please.'

He felt no better when Brigadier Hughie told him that this time he'd get away with a fortnight's suspension and a £5,000 fine.

'And you can fucking well pay it,' roared Bart. 'You only got off because I threatened to pull out of the Gold Cup.'

64

Perdita was in turmoil. There was no doubt Red was playing her up. It was as if, spurred on by the media attention showered on Angel, he wanted to establish himself as the chief headturner, the one the girls flocked round the most.

He was also furious with Perdita for playing so badly in the semi-final of the Queen's Cup. Since then he had hardly touched her, and Perdita, deaf, dumb and blind with love, didn't know how to play it. She should have backed off and flirted with other men. Instead she made scenes, then, overwhelmed with remorse, crawled back again with morale plummeting.

The Polo Ball at Hurlingham the following week didn't help matters. Bart, furious they'd been beaten by the Tigers, who'd in turn been smashed by Apocalypse in the final, insisted that all the Flyers turned up. It was a foul night with torrential rain drumming a million, irritable fingers on the roof of the marquee, flattening the blue hydrangeas and preventing anyone stealing off into the romantically shadowed garden glades.

Perdita, who had a black eye, a tooth knocked out and a swollen purple lip from playing in the Royal Windsor and had to play in an All-Ladies match at the Royal Berkshire the following day, longed to back down.

'If you hadn't made me cut my hair off,' she stormed at Red, 'I could at least have trailed it over my face. Now I just look hideous.'

Red, by contrast, always looked his most desirable in a dinner jacket. He had no truck with white tuxedos, or coloured ties, shirts or cummerbunds. Just black and white, perfected after ten fittings and setting off his beech-leaf colouring.

Bart, having annexed a table for six, promptly disappeared to telephone. Red, who was in a strange, detached mood, took advantage of his father's absence to bitch up Chessie, who was looking heart-breaking in Prussian-blue strapless taffeta with white roses dyed Prussian blue in her hair.

Angel, whose mood was anything but detached, was attaching himself to every blonde he could find. Aware that she had lost him, but unable to tear herself away, Bibi was near to suicide. Looking round at all the smooth brown backs, the shining manes, the jewelled, lit-up, happily chatting faces, she gave a sob.

'I must be the only ugly woman in polo.'

Perdita, who couldn't get drunk because of the All-Ladies match next day, took another slug of Perrier.

'That makes two of us,' she said gloomily.

'But you'll be beautiful when the bruises go,' said Bibi despairingly.

Realizing she should have contradicted Bibi's earlier remark, Perdita said quickly, 'But you're terrific-looking.'

Idly Red turned Bibi's profile to face him.

'I don't know why you don't have a nose job. Then you'd be fine.'

'Then she'd look just like you, you mean,' snapped Chessie. 'If you had a heart job, you'd be fine. Yes, I'd love to come and dance,' she added, grabbing Dommie Carlisle who was sidling past.

'I'm on my way to the Gents,' protested Dommie.

'Well, you won't find any at this table,' said Chessie.

She was undoubtedly the most beautiful woman in the room. Eyes followed her. Men pressed their cheeks against their partners so they could gaze undetected as she passed. The Prussian-blue taffeta seemed part of her body like a fish's tail. The roses in her greeny-gold hair gave her the look of some naiad.

Red, flanked by two girls miserably aware of not feeling beautiful, watched Chessie lazily.

'What's bitten her?' he asked Bibi.

'Dad's been calling Mom about me and Angel. Ricky's been talking to Dancer and Rupert all evening and hasn't asked her to dance. Take your pick,' said Bibi.

'Any news of Luke?' asked Red.

'Good,' said Bibi, cheering up for a second. 'The last op's been a total success. And he's talking about starting a green pony clinic in Palm Beach. You know how he could always sort out anything difficult.'

'Didn't work with Perdita,' drawled Red.

'Don't be bitchy,' said Bibi. 'Oh, Christ.'

Through a gap in the dancers, she could see Angel bopping with Jesus's baby sister, whose sense of rhythm was as good as his. All her seventeen-year-old peanut-butter-coloured body seemed to be bouncing out of her gold dress.

Seeing his worst enemy's wife miserably neglected, Drew Benedict felt it was not only a duty but a pleasure to rescue her.

'May I have this dance?'

Bibi looked up with a start. 'Oh my God, Drew. How are you?'

'OK. Talking's a bit painful. But I've never been into yattering.'

'I'm so sorry about last week.'

'Thank you for the flowers.'

'They were from all of us,' stammered Bibi. 'Angel should never have . . . I guess he was provoked.'

'Get up,' said Drew gently, 'and we'll provoke him some more.' Then, as Bibi slid into his arms: 'Has anyone ever told you you've got the most beautiful body in polo.'

'Prettier than Malteser's?'

'Much,' said Drew.

'Wow!' Perdita turned to Red. '*That* could cause some problems.'

Looking round in mid-gyration, Angel saw Bibi laughing up at Drew. With a growl, he broke away from Jesus's sister. Dommie, returning with Chessie and sizing up the situation, blocked Angel's path by shoving Chessie into his arms.

'Dance with your stepmother-in-law, Angel, I truly must go and have a slash.'

Red and Perdita were left alone. She wanted to dance so desperately, but she was damned if she was going to beg.

'Are you coming to the Ladies' match tomorrow?'

'No,' said Red, filling up his glass.

'Please come.' I go to every match in which he's playing, she thought.

'I don't want to.'

'Auriel's playing.'

'You are totally irrational,' snapped Red. 'You'd raise hell if I came saying it was because I wanted to see her, if I don't come, you'll complain I'm neglecting you.'

'I'm sorry,' said Perdita humbly. 'Christ, talk of the devil.'

'Hi, Red,' said Auriel, 'I've just come from the airport. Victor and Sharon persuaded me to drop by.'

She was looking stunning and, in her starkly simple, black linen suit amidst all the bare shoulders and ball dresses, curiously seductive. Her perfect ankles were not remotely swollen from the flight.

'Shall we have a dance for old time's sake?' she added to Red.

'Old is the operative word,' snarled Perdita.

'Don't be bitchy, Perdita,' said Auriel. 'Under the circumstances I would have thought you could afford to be generous.'

Sitting alone at the table, Perdita was suddenly aware that people didn't like her any more. The twins, who never bore grudges and who'd been buying drinks for Victor, who'd sacked them only last year, were avoiding her. Ricky had cut her dead just now. Bas had nodded unsmiling and walked passed. Her erstwhile great mate, Dancer, couldn't wait to get away from her and now Red was dancing with Auriel, smiling affectionately down at her, holding her tiny waist as though it were the stem of a glass of priceless brandy he was about to drink.

I must not make a scene, I must not make a scene, she told herself. In the looking glass she could see her black eye coming through the make-up. She looked like a battered fiancée.

She was saved by a roll of drums and the bandleader announcing that, as the rain had stopped, the fireworks would take place after all. But as everyone surged outside, her isolation seemed even more apparent. Kicking off her high heels she soothed her aching feet in the drenched grass. Nor did she care that her long white dress trailed along the ground snagging on twigs and rose thorns. Living with Red had accustomed her to throwing clothes out after one wearing if she didn't like them.

Roman candles in silver, pink and yellow were lighting up the night. Spluttering like me, thought Perdita. She hoped there weren't any dogs loose in the nearby streets who might be frightened by the bangs. For a second, after the brilliant light, it seemed almost dark in the dripping garden.

Then almost immediately the big Catherine wheels came alive, slowly at first, then faster and faster, accelerating into fiery revolving chrysanthemums like an affair taking off, like her and Red. Oh God, it hurt to think of that first night in Deauville.

Miserably she watched the Catherine wheels burn out until they were only dim red glows on their posts.

Rockets were now going up in swift succession with a whistling hiss, as though they were vying to touch the stars, then erupting into a cascade of rival stars. One went sideways and lodged in the heart of a huge oak trunk, writhing and jumping abortively. That's even more like me, thought Perdita. Did everything have to burn out?

As rose-red and royal-blue flares exploded into the sky, to the smell of sulphur and brimstone was added an overpowering waft of Diorissimo. Glancing right, Perdita gasped as she saw Ricky and Chessie under a huge livid yellow catalpa, gazing at each other like souls in hell.

Frantically Perdita looked for Bart. He was coming towards her, clutching his telephone.

'Seen Chessie?' he asked curtly. 'We gotta go.'

'Oh look, isn't that beautiful?' Desperate to distract him, Perdita pointed to the word 'Polo' written in red, white and blue shimmering and erupting against the russet night.

'That's neat,' said Bart.

'Chessie was dancing,' said Perdita.

'I'll go find her,' said Bart, plunging back into the house.

The display was ending in a massive explosion of coloured stars. War must sound like this, thought Perdita.

Chessie and Ricky had gone, but in the shade of a large magnolia, Perdita imagined she caught a glimpse of Sharon and David Waterlane. For a second she thought that little Victor was rooted to the spot with wonder at the fireworks until she realized that his high-heeled boots were plugged into the wet lawn.

To her left stood Bibi, her face round with excitement, her lips parted, suddenly pretty. Fascinated, envious, Perdita watched Drew's fingers sliding down the inside of Bibi's arm, pausing to brush her breast with his knuckles, then sliding his fingers into hers as the garden went dark again. He must be doing it deliberately to wind Angel up.

Queuing for her coat five minutes later, Perdita listened to a rapturous Sukey.

'D'you know, we made fifteen thousand on the auction. I was terrified that lovely Zandra Rhodes dress wouldn't reach its reserve. But Dancer Maitland bought it – so sweet.' Then, lowering her voice to Mrs Hughie, she confided, 'He's *frite*-fly nice for a queer.'

'Probably going to wear it himself,' said Chessie.

Bart, who'd sold his London house to realize capital, was flying straight back to New York with Bibi to mastermind some take-over before the Gold Cup. Red, because he couldn't be bothered to drive back to Bart's house in Sussex, had booked himself and Perdita into the Savoy. Chessie had also booked a room there and to Red's absolute fury came along to their suite for a drink.

'I do not want to listen to her bitching all night about my father,' he said, going off to bed and slamming the door behind him. So poor Perdita had to sit up until dawn listening to Chessie sobbing her heart out.

'I can't stand it any more. I know he loves me but he's so appallingly uncompromising. Says I've got to leave Bart or nothing.'

It seemed unfair, too, that Perdita had to leave Red in bed, but she was determined to have her tooth capped before she drove down to meet Auriel.

Outside, London had recovered its youth, the rain had washed the dust off the plane trees and heightened the reticulated giraffe-patterning of their long, lanky trunks. Bronze workmen were stripping off in the sunshine. As Perdita came out of the dentist, however, a cloud blacker than her bruised eye hung over the west. Ringing the Royal Berkshire she discovered the match had been cancelled.

Bliss, thought Perdita, she could go back to the Savoy for a jolly lunch with Red. She hadn't had a day off for ages. It was lovely to be in London. The girls looked so pretty in their summer dresses; people were drinking outside pubs; the flower shops were a riot of colour.

Stopping off at Harvie & Hudson, Perdita bought their latest shirt, lilac and pale blue stripes, as a present for Red. If it clashed with his hair she could always wear it.

Maids were clearing away breakfast as she got back to the Savoy. A 'Do Not Disturb' sign hung on the door of their room. Red would sleep all day given the opportunity, thought Perdita fondly as she let herself in very quietly. Then she heard voices. He must be watching television.

'I'm back,' she barged into the bedroom. 'The match was cancelled and I've bought you the most divine shirt.' The words shrivelled on her lips, for, lying in bed, one light gold, the other darker gold, were Chessie and Red. Chessie

628

was lying on her belly. Red was kissing her shoulders, caressing her bottom with one hand, the other was buried in her pubic hair. For a moment they all stared at each other.

Perdita was so shocked she could only think how beautiful they looked in that huge bed reflected in the mirrored fronts of the cupboards which lined the left side of the room. Then she screamed and was about to run out of the door when, quick as a lurcher on a hare, Red had seized her.

'You're not going anywhere!' He shoved her into the bathroom and slammed the door, clinging on to the gold handle for grim death, as Perdita tugged, screamed and pummelled against the other side, which gave Chessie the chance to put on her pale blue dress and make a bolt for it.

Releasing her, Red expected a monumental scene, curious what she'd throw at him first; but she stumbled out as grey and subdued as a released hostage.

'Why?' she whispered. 'Why her? I don't understand.'

Red never blushed; it didn't go with red hair. Slowly, deliberately, his hands totally steady, he put a yellow Sobranie between his faintly smiling lips.

'I wanted to prove what a little tramp she was.'

'But she spent most of last night telling me how much she loved Ricky.'

'Perhaps she does.' Red's lighter flared. 'Perhaps she wanted to put you off the scent. Did she actually mention Ricky's name? She's such a bitch, she's been trying to get me into bed for years. She may have been uptight because I'd been dancing with Auriel.'

Straightening a magazine that had been knocked crooked, he moved towards the fridge. 'D'you want a drink?'

Perdita shook her head. 'But you must have planned it deliberately, knowing I'd be away?'

'I know.' Red banged the steel ice-tray on the top of the fridge. 'I wish to hell they'd use plastic. I was kinda curious what she'd be like. I guess one occasionally likes variety. It's as simple as that.'

Like a lift whose cable has broken, Perdita sat down suddenly on the sofa.

'Was this the first time?'

Red paused a fraction too long.

'Sure. She called me this morning.'

'Are you going to tell your father?'

Red laughed and emptied the whisky over his ice. 'Not yet. I don't want to be disinherited.'

'How can you do that to him? You bastard!' hissed Perdita. It was her sole outburst of reproof.

'On the contrary,' said Red mockingly. 'Unlike you, I was regularly conceived.' Drifting towards her, he examined her new tooth.

'That's better. D'you want to stay with me?'

Frantic he was going to chuck her, Perdita nodded.

'Well, you better keep your trap shut for a change. No blathering to Simpson Hastings this time. If you tell anyone, in fact, you and I are over – understand?'

'Yes, of course.'

'And since you interrupted what I'd started with Chessie, I'd quite like to finish it.' As he pulled her towards him, his cock jabbed her stomach. Beneath the feline languor, she could sense his frenzied excitement. Never had he made love to her more passionately, and when the manager rang up asking them to check out he booked in for another night.

65

Perdita told no-one about Red and Chessie except Tero into whose sympathetic grey shoulder she sobbed endlessly, trying to make sense out of what had happened. Did Red really loathe Chessie? Had he just pulled her to prove he could and that Chessie was a whore, or was it for the novelty of something as utterly *verboten* as a cream bun in a health farm? Even more confusingly a couple of days after she'd stumbled on them, she had a letter from Chessie:

'*Dear Perdita,*

Sorry about Thursday morning, but please don't blame me. I'd never have gone to bed with Red if he hadn't pestered me ever since I married Bart (that's why he's always been so poisonous to me), so that I finally gave in, because I was flattered, I suppose, and because I was so miserable about Ricky. I'm sorry you're hurt, but if you hadn't come back you'd never have found out. Yours, red-faced and red-handed, Chessie.'

Even when she'd shattered someone's life, Chessie

couldn't avoid being flip. Either she or Red was lying, but Perdita couldn't imagine Red pestering anyone. She knew she should pack her bags, but where could she go? Tero and Spotty could hardly live in a bedsit, and would Red give her custody of the six ponies, and all the jewels and clothes he'd given her? She hadn't saved a penny, relying on the wads of dollars and pound notes he'd thrust so freely into her eager hands. What terrified her most was the total loss of pride and willpower. She loved him too much to walk out, however much he humiliated her. As electrodes of jealousy wracked her body, she realized for the first time how much Luke must have suffered.

Perdita's game disintegrated. If Red and Angel hadn't continued so majestically together, the Flyers would have never reached the final of the Gold Cup. After a very tough draw, in which they beat the Tigers in extra time, Apocalypse also reached the final.

Ricky tried to sleep on the eve of the match but kept listening for the banging of hooves against the stable walls, which would tell him one of his horses had cast itself or was down with colic. When he did drop off, he found he was playing the whole world in his dreams. At three he got up and wandered round the house. It was unbearably hot and stuffy with distant thunder grumbling round the Rutshire hills. Little Chef, who'd trailed his restless master all day and tried to bring a smile to his lips by rushing in with a clothes brush or lying on his back sneezing with his paws over his eyes, followed yawning and blinking. The thunder was getting nearer.

On the drawing-room table lay the endlessly rescribbled and crossed-out lists of tomorrow's playing order. He had spent hours working out which horses would go best in which chukka, so one always had a balance of speed and manoeuvrability. Heavy rain would change all that. He was also in a dilemma about Wayne, who, as an old horse, didn't go well in very hot weather and who'd got crafty recently and, fed up with Ricky making him do sharp turns at a gallop, had started falling over deliberately. Nor was he entirely reliable in ride-offs. Seeing a bump coming, he'd hesitate and take Ricky out of it. Young horses loved to bump. Old horses like Wayne tended to cheat on you.

Like young wives, thought Ricky bitterly, which brought him back to Chessie. If he won tomorrow – what then? It was the first rung reached, but if Chessie came back, would he ever trust her again? He wished Luke were here. Dancer was frozen with panic, unable to eat. Even the twins were subdued, like puppies removed too early from their mother, so Ricky himself had to be the stabilizer. The smell of meadowsweet drifted hot and soapy from the lake. At the bottom of the moonlit valley, like a low, low star, Ricky saw Daisy's light on. He glanced at her painting of Will which had brought him such bitter-sweet pleasure. Suddenly the temptation to dump was too much. If he weren't playing Wayne tomorrow, he could ride him down to see Daisy.

'Hullo.' Daisy answered the telephone on the first ring, her voice tremulous with excitement.

'It's Ricky.'

There was a pause.

'How are you?' said Daisy, trying to keep the desperate disappointment out of her voice.

'Can't sleep. It's so light outside. Can I come over?'

The same moonlight that flooded the Eldercombe Valley silvered Chessie's naked body as she lay in the great, green silk four-poster listening to the crunch of the security guards on the gravel outside. Beside her, Bart churned with demoniacal sexual excitement. Challenges were his fix, and this was the greatest challenge he'd ever faced.

Alderton Airlines was about to merge with Euro-Electronics. Determined to merge with a splurge, Bart was flying in both his own and the German boards who would enjoy a splendid lunch in a duck-egg-blue tent before watching the Flyers retain the Gold Cup.

Bibi had been so incensed by such extravagance that she'd refused to come.

'We can't pay wages or suppliers, Dad.'

'We can after we've closed the deal,' said Bart. Helmut Wallstein, the Chairman of Euro-Electronics, owned race horses and would recognize quality when he saw Bart's ponies.

He longed to screw Chessie to release the tension, but he always avoided sex before a key match. He needed the built-up pressure to zap the other side. Hearing her reach out for a glass of water, he said, 'Remember that red suit you wore at last year's Gold Cup? It brought us luck. Will you wear it again?'

'On one condition,' Chessie wriggled up to him, 'that you fuck me stupid now.'

In contrast to its cool, silver, moonlit appearance, her sweating body gave off a white-hot heat.

'I mustn't,' said Bart regretfully. 'Tomorrow night I'll bang you insensible.'

'Real men screw their wives and win matches,' taunted Chessie, climbing on top of him and taking his cock between her lips.

'With access to this,' mumbled Bart, as the oily, silken warmth tickled his face, 'I must be the luckiest guy in the world. I'd kill to keep you, you know that.'

The thunderstorm broke in the west around breakfast time and reached Cowdray by midday, with lightning unzipping a purply-black sky and deafening claps of thunder unnerving the ponies. The storm passed on, but driving rain birched the faces of the two teams as they cantered a lap of honour and bounced off a pitch which, after weeks of sunshine, was now dangerously slick and greasy on top and as hard as Red Alderton's heart underneath.

But rain had never stopped play at Cowdray. The scarlet ribbons on the hats of the band playing 'Four Horsemen, Riding, Riding, Riding', the umbrellas of the spectators and the duck-egg-blue shirts of the Flyers provided the only colourful notes.

'And they'll be black with mud by treading-in time,' said Dommie through chattering teeth, 'and we'll all be black and blue before it's over.'

Wayne loathed rain and his long, yellow ears never left his ewe neck as Ricky rode him in the parade. But when he was untacked and realized he wouldn't be playing, he put his ugly head down, hunched his shoulders and, ignoring everyone, sulked in the corner.

Angel, who hated rain even more than Wayne, was near suicide. Bibi hadn't come over for the match and the icy west wind whistling across the pitch felt to him as if it was coming directly from her in New York. Perdita felt even worse than Angel. Ricky had cut her dead again, so had

Dancer, and Rupert had just come into the stands.

Yesterday, she'd begged Red to stick and ball with her in a faint attempt to capture her lost form. He had rolled up an hour late.

'You got me out of bed, OK?' he had snapped. 'Whatja want me to tell you?'

Then, at the team meeting in the pony lines, Bart had had such a row with Red and Angel, who'd both refused to lunch in the Alderton tent with all the Krauts, that nothing was discussed at all. Bart, in turn, was enraged because Chessie had turned up late for lunch wearing a brown suede jacket and gauchos tucked into black boots and clinched with a big black leather belt, and making all the other women, who'd expected a heatwave, look silly in their flimsy dresses.

'You promised you'd wear your red suit,' hissed Bart.

'I tried it on,' said Chessie lightly, 'but the skirt was last year's length.'

Bart was a powerful and consistent player, but Chessie's feverish sexual demands last night and again this morning had sapped him and, with all the Krauts and his own board to entertain at lunch, he didn't have a chance to distance himself. He'd also mislaid his lucky belt and had turned the house and the barn upside down looking for it. Grace would have found it, he thought darkly, *and* hosted this lunch *and* made every Kraut and his wife feel special. Why was he blowing his entire livelihood on this exquisite, irresponsible malicious child?

Perdita watched Chessie, who'd now topped the whole outfit with a black sombrero, saunter up the gangway of the stands, swinging her hips like Gary Cooper in *High Noon*. God, I hate her, she thought. Three players, Bart, Red and Ricky, are all obsessed with her, Angel wouldn't say no, and the twins have probably had her in duplicate, which only leaves me and Dancer immune. No wonder she's looking so chipper.

Huddled under their coloured umbrellas, the crowd chattered in an incredible number of languages. Sharon Kaputnik who'd been lunching in the Davidoff tent, it was noticed by the press, was sharing her rose-lined parasol with David Waterlane because Sir Victor, having been knocked out by Apocalypse, refused to come to the match.

'So unsportin',' said Sharon rolling her blue eyes. 'Ay wouldn't refuse to come because I'd been beaten.'

'I'll bet you wouldn't,' murmured Chessie, who, seeing the front rows occupied by Helmut and Gisela Wallstein and the rest of the Euro-Electronics Board, deliberately sat down between Rupert and Sukey Benedict in the row behind.

'Davidoff Waterlane is obviously about to havidoff with Lady Shar,' she said in a stage whisper. 'I do hope Dancer's wearing waterproof mascara in this rain. Oh, stop looking so boot-faced, Rupert. Haven't you forgiven me yet?'

But Rupert had turned his back and was gazing moodily at the huge green field with its egg-yolk goal posts and flags and its panorama of rolling green-and-gold cornfields beneath glowing black-and-grey clouds. The grooves made in the cornfields by the drillers were not much deeper than the lines on either side of Ricky's mouth as he gave last-minute instructions to his team. 'Don't go into a daze, Dancer. For Christ's sake concentrate, and if you're going to change ponies, Dommie, ask first. Last time it cost us a goal.'

'I thought it was a penalty, so I buzzed off,' said Dommie, mounting his pony. 'Christ, my reins are starting to slip already.'

'We're the better side, so we attack,' Bart ordered the Flyers as they rode grimly on to the pitch.

'Solis de Gonzales and Red Alderton have dominated every headline this summer,' said William Loyd of the *Telegraph*, frantically trying to make his biro work on a wet page. 'Nice to get France-Lynch into a headline.'

'France-Lynched is the only headline you're likely to get,' said JNP Watson of *The Times*. 'Case of too many late nights, I'm afraid. Seb, Dommie and Dancer were evidently playing poker till three in the morning last night.'

'Better than boozing,' said William Loyd giving up and resorting to pencil. 'Is Bart going to keep his best pony for the last chukka?' he asked Chessie.

'All my husband's ponies are best,' said Chessie tonelessly.

It was raining even harder now, but nothing doused the loathing between the two teams, which seemed to singe the clouds above and set the drenched cornfields on fire. Drew was waiting to throw-in as they lined up.

'I don't want any aggro,' he said crisply. 'Anyone who

swears or argues with the umpire will be sent off, except any Argentines,' he added with a glint, 'who will be shot.'

Only Bart grabbing Angel's shirt stopped him flying through the air and landing on Drew.

'Pack it in. I'm paying you to bury the opposition not the umpire.'

In the first chukka Angel and Red tried to play at their usual breakneck speed, but it was as if someone had spilt turkey fat all over the kitchen floor, and after both had overturned their ponies and Angel had nearly been trampled to death by a furiously galloping Seb, they slowed down. The Flyers were infinitely superior in pony power, but for once they couldn't take advantage of their fleet, light, thoroughbred horses. The much slower ground played havoc with their timing and the rain not only aquapunctured their faces, drastically reducing visibility, but made reins, gloves and sticks incredibly slippery and almost impossible to hold. Accustomed to such conditions and on much heavier ponies, Apocalypse started winning the ride-offs and, having endlessly practised lofting the ball over a sea of mud, were therefore unfazed when the whole field became black with skidmarks and divots.

Apocalypse had also learnt one vital lesson from Luke. They had practised, played, almost slept together all summer and knew each others' ponies backwards. They wanted not individual glory, but for the team to win. The twins, normally attacking players, were marking the hell out of Angel and Red, driving them crackers.

There were plenty of spats. Angel, thundering down the boards, was being threatened by Ricky.

'Get out of my way, you fucker,' he howled. '*Puniatero, forro*, Eenglish preek!' Then, seeing Drew out of the corner of his eye, added with excessive politeness, 'Excuse me, Meester France-Lynch, my line I theenk,' and clouted the ball straight between Kinta's legs.

Up went Ricky's stick. 'Foul!' he yelled at Drew. 'Dangerous stick work.'

'He crossed me,' protested Angel.

'He pulled up on the ball,' shouted Ricky. 'If Kinta's got any legs left, it's no thanks to him.'

Drew, reluctant to be accused of bias, turned to Shark Nelligan, the other umpire.

636

'Apocalypse foul,' said Shark.

'Thank you, Mr Nelligan,' said Angel making a V-sign on his mud-spattered thigh, but only lifting it an inch in Ricky's direction. He found the flags without difficulty.

'High time the Argies came back,' said David Waterlane, returning the pressure of Sharon's leg.

In the third chukka the score stuck at 3-2 to the Flyers, as ponies and players, all plastered with mud, groped desperately for a foothold, trying to gain the ascendancy as the usual thunderous dry rattle of hooves was replaced by the dull relentless thud of a murderer's cudgel.

Then by some miracle Dancer, who'd been marked by Bart, got the ball.

'And here comes Dancer,' said Terry Hanlon, the Cowdray commentator, 'heading for goal; riding, riding, riding, famine, justice, pestilence, and whoops, oh dear, he didn't connect with that offside forehand and the ball went wide. Got the mud to hide your blushes. Stick to singing in future, Dancer.'

The stands giggled. As Dancer hung his head, Bart picked up the ball and backed it to Red, who missed it completely, then, spinning round, picked it up and came triumphantly down the field, dummying past Seb, then Ricky, then Dommie, whipping and whipping Glitz into a breakneck gallop until the crowd started grumbling with disapproval.

'And here comes Red Alderton,' said Terry Hanlon, dropping his voice an octave, 'who's lived more nights than days. Look at him opening up his shoulders for the big one. And it's a goal, ladies and gentlemen and seahorses, 4-2 to the Flyers.'

Back in the pony lines, grooms had the thankless task of getting the mud off and drying utterly exhausted ponies in torrential rain. The Apocalypse grooms, in their black bomber jackets, had experienced such conditions and were far more cheerful than the Flyers' Argentines who hated rain as much as Angel. Wayne, utterly unplaced by four ounces of barley sugar and a bucket of water, still sulking with his head down, suddenly heard his old friend and last year's team-mate, Spotty, yelling out for Tero, who was still on the field, and started calling back like a lunatic. Ducking out of his headcollar, whickering with delight, he bustled off to join Spotty across a sea of mud and started kissing and nuzzling him all over.

'Get that fucking dog off the pitch,' roared Bart, as his weary pony nearly tripped over Little Chef racing out to welcome Ricky as the players came off at half-time.

Apocalypse had contained the Flyers very well, and Bart, not best pleased, went off to shout at his team. 'We should be at least five goals up by now.'

'Well done,' said Ricky quietly to Dancer and the twins. 'We've rattled them. Now we've got to get some goals.'

Hearing 'Tea for Two' over the tannoy, Wayne bustled off towards the tea tent. Drew, tweed cap resting on his eyelashes, riding round on his drenched pony as the crowd swarmed back to the stands after treading in, thought how amazing it was that the field, which, five minutes ago, had been a black sea of holes and divots, was now a smooth sweep of emerald green again. Like my marriage, he thought wryly, and for a second scoured the stands for Daisy, hoping she might have turned up. He'd promised to ring her during the week, but he'd been too busy to get over to Eldercombe and he hated hearing the disappointment in her voice. He'd try and get her this evening, although he could hardly cheer her up with the news that Perdita was playing well.

Perdita was equally conscious she wasn't pulling her weight. Bart had yelled at her so continually she hardly heard him. Then, in the fourth chukka, Angel gave her a pass, and there was only forty yards between her and goal. Perdita was so surprised she hesitated, but Tero, putting on an amazing turn of speed, took her upfield, placing her beside the ball, so she was able to judge the first shot beautifully. Now the ball was waiting for her, ten feet in front of the goal. Oh, please God. God blocked his ears, and she hit a divot instead of the ball. Frantically she tugged at the sodden reins and, willing Tero, turned on her hocks at full gallop. That's a good pony, thought Red.

But as the little mare floundered to stay upright, she slipped and came down with Perdita beneath her. The crowd gave a gasp of horror and agreed it was not a girl's game. Tero rolled off in a trice. Seeing Perdita was moving, Red belted off to change ponies. When he returned, Perdita was screaming at Bart: 'I can't go on. I've got to change my breeches.'

Glancing down, Red saw blood mingling with the mud. All the trauma over Chessie had made the curse so late Perdita'd forgotten all about it.

'There's only ninety seconds to go,' shouted Bart.

'Everyone'll notice.'

'If you play in a man's game, you play by men's rules,' howled Red. 'Get back on that pony. Pull your shirt outside.'

Angel put an arm round Perdita's shoulder, feeling her shaking with sobs. 'No one can see zee blood for zee mud,' he said comfortingly.

'Your daughter seems to be getting rather a lot of earache from my husband,' said Chessie slyly to Rupert as the clock started again.

Rupert gazed stonily ahead, holding Taggie's hand so tightly that she winced.

'Mr Alderton is a very forceful captain,' said Gisela Wallstein, who was bitterly cold and couldn't understand what was going on at all.

'Oh, Bart always shouts when he's near the stands,' said Chessie lightly. 'The team don't take any notice, but the crowd think *what* a big macho guy.'

Helmut Wallstein looked round at Chessie speculatively. 'I have not often seen such beautiful horses.'

'Subsidized by Alderton Airlines,' said Chessie with a shrug.

Sukey paused in the menus she was writing out for two dinner parties next week. If Drew were just umpiring, she felt it was all right only to keep half an eye on the game.

'How can you be so unsupportive, Chessie?' she murmured.

'Vot is the name of that bay mare he's riding now?' asked Helmut.

'I haven't a clue.'

'You should be able to recognize Bart's ponies,' reproved Sukey. 'That's Marina, a Criolla pony from Argentina,' she told Helmut.

Chessie turned smiling to Sukey. 'Do remind me to take your husband to bed when I get a moment.'

Sukey went magenta, but her reply was drowned by

Terry Hanlon telling them that the head had broken off Ricky's stick in the desperate mêlée in the Apocalypse goal mouth.

'And Ricky France-Lynch is managing to do an amazing amount of damage with his stick alone, but it's looking very dangerous for Apocalypse. Is it going to be 6-2? No, Seb Carlisle's taken the ball upfield.'

Swinging round, Ricky thundered towards the boards where his sticks were leaning against the fence, their handles fretting in the wind.

'Fifty-one,' he bellowed to Louisa. But for once Chessie was too quick. Bounding down the gangway, she snatched the right stick and handed it to Ricky. For a second their eyes met.

'Good luck darling, you're doing brilliantly,' she called out quite audibly.

'And Mrs Alderton is giving her ex-husband stick,' announced Terry Hanlon drily. 'Ex-wives generally do, I expect she was asking for more dosh.' The crowd, despite being drenched, giggled.

Mr and Mrs Wallstein exchanged surprised glances. 'Is it customary in England you support the other side?'

'Only if your name's Oswald Mosley,' snapped Rupert.

Conditions were worsening, the rain coming down in a steady torrent, the wind growing more vicious. Ricky had found Kinta's strength in the third chukka a two-edged sword. She was powerful enough to play two, even three chukkas, but in these conditions she was a liability because she wouldn't stop.

Ricky couldn't afford any more penalties if Kinta cannoned into other ponies or barged across their right of way. As he rode back to the pony lines at the end of the fourth chukka, he shouted to Louisa to tack up Wayne for the last chukka. This was the kind of weather when you needed old friends.

'Oh my God,' muttered Louisa as she handed his new, dark brown pony, Corporal, over to Dommie. 'Wayne's sunk a bucket of water, had half a ton of barley sugar and I've just retrieved him from the Flyer's pony lines with chocolate cake all over his whiskers trying to mount Spotty. Should I tell Ricky?'

'Leave it,' said Dommie. 'If he gives Ricky confidence,

that's what matters.' He looked down at Louisa's plump, freckled, mud-spattered face. Her hair clung to her head like a mermaid.

'Will you sleep with me if we win?'

Louisa's smile suddenly lit up the Cowdray gloom. 'I thought you'd never ask. Yes, please.'

'And if we lose, so I don't shoot myself?'

'Yes, please,' said Louisa.

The mud in fact had been too thick for any of the crowd to notice the blood, but, still numb with embarrassment and misery and shaken by the fall, Perdita felt even more conspicuous riding back on to the field in snow-white breeches.

'You've got two chukkas left to redeem yourself,' said Bart bullyingly. 'You don't want to be the reason we lost the cup.'

The Flyers had a good fifth chukka, dominating the play and pushing the score up to 6-2, then Apocalypse caught fire, and Seb and Ricky both scored in the closing minutes and the stands went wild.

As the players rode out for the last chukka, it was noticed that Red had taken off the white sweater he wore under his blue polo shirt for the first time this season.

'That's ominous,' said Ricky. 'Get your fingers out, Apocalypse.'

After two minutes of frantic barging and bumps-a-daisy, Red took matters into his own hands. Giving Dommie and Seb the slip and Glitz his head, he raced off upfield.

That's it, thought Ricky dully. That'll be 7-4; there's only Dancer anywhere near him.

God had let Dancer down last time, so this time he concentrated on Red, who was messing around in front of goal, insolently positioning himself so he could score the clinching goal. But as he lifted his stick, he found himself nearly pulled off his horse. Dancer had hooked him.

'With pressure it is better,' said Helmut Wallstein. 'He had all zee time in the world, and he relaxed.'

'Well hooked, Dancer. You read the play,' hollered Dommie, grinning out of his round ruffian blackamore face, as he raced Corporal down to bring the ball back to Ricky. Perdita, who was out of position and should have been marking Dancer, raced back towards the Apocalypse

goal. But as all the players converged on Ricky trying to
help or hinder him, a pony kicked a divot up in Perdita's
eyes, totally blinding her, so she crashed across Ricky's
right of way. Up went every Apocalypse stick.

'Foul,' screamed the twins.

Ricky on Wayne took the penalty.

'Pale rider, pale horse,' said William Loyd.

'And his name was death to the Flyers' hopes,' murmured Chessie.

The wind, which had been Ricky's enemy all day, had
moved slightly to the south. Slowly he cantered a circle that
would have won a dressage prize. The picture of control, his
gait as smooth as his yellow face was ugly, Wayne floated
proudly towards the ball. There was a ripple of muscle, the
piston arm hurtled down again, Ricky aimed deliberately
to the left and nudged back by the wind, the ball sailed
high above the leaping Flyers' sticks, slap between the
posts. The crowd, who could hardly see through the rain,
waited on tenterhooks, then, seeing the waving yellow flag,
bellowed their delight.

'The penalty is mightier than the sword,' cried Chessie,
clapping ecstatically.

There were two and a half minutes to go, the score was
6-5 and Dommie, mis-hitting, clouted the ball towards the
Flyers' goal-mouth, but to no-one in particular. Ahead
of everyone, Red scorched after it, flogging Glitz like a
jockey at Tattenham Corner. Glitz, however, was fed up
with the weather and too many hidings. He was used to
cheering crowds under a Palm Beach sun as he shook off
the opposition like a dog a towel. Out of the corner of his
beautiful eye, he saw Wayne hurtling down to ride him
off. Wayne was very ugly and his pale face was fearsome.
Red turned his heel into Glitz's sodden right flank to turn
him left. He had heard that Wayne was spooked about
bumping and anticipated no contest. The next minute Glitz
had ducked out and Ricky had taken the line.

'You fucking son of a bitch,' screamed Red to Glitz, but
it was too late.

'I misjudged you, you old bugger, I'm sorry,' said Ricky
in amazement, as Wayne pulled away from the tiring Glitz.

The buttercup-yellow posts rose out of the gloom to his
left. Master of the cut shot, Ricky sliced the ball, but,

scuppered by nerves, he misjudged and hit the post.

'Oh,' groaned the crowd.

Bart hit in. A minute and a half to go. Seb blocked the shot and passed to Dommie, who tapped it in, screaming with frustration as again it hit the post.

'The afternoon of the woodwork,' said Terry Hanlon sympathetically.

But an instant later Ricky had thundered in and slapped in a tennis shot in the air. Chessie's scream of joy was not the only one. Six all, a minute to go.

Suddenly the rain stopped, every tree and flat cap dripped, water cascaded down spectators' necks as other spectators lowered their umbrellas. The Gold Cup on its green baize table was carried out and glittered like the Holy Grail in a lone shaft of sunlight. As the ball flashed frantically from goal-mouth to goal-mouth and Bart crashed round like a maddened Rottweiler, bumping into everyone, the crowd were on their feet yelling their heads off. Now they were down the Flyers' end and Seb, Dommie, Ricky and Dancer were all taking desperate swipes at the ball until it was buried, trodden deep into the ground, with everyone frantically looking for it until the whistle went.

After a lot of shouting, the ball was dug out and thrown in where it had been buried, twenty yards in front of goal.

'This is very dangerous for the Flyers,' warned Terry Hanlon. 'The fat is in the fire, the chips are in the pan.'

'Get it out,' screamed Red, as the frantically thrashing sticks hit ponies' and players' legs indiscriminately in a churning whirlpool of mud. Then, god-given, the ball rolled out on Perdita's side. At last she had a chance to redeem herself and get the ball back upfield. Throwing herself forward, her fingers in her slippery glove lost control of her stick, which totally mis-hit the ball.

'Oh no, please God, no,' she screamed in horror, as the ball slowly trickled between her own goal posts. For a second the goal judge seemed as stunned as she was, then slowly up went the flag once again. Bart's anguished howl of rage was drowned by the sound of the bell.

And it was all over and Ricky was shaking hands with everyone and thanking Shark and Drew, who, abandoning any attempt at impartiality, put his arm round Ricky's shoulders, yelling: 'Fucking, fucking marvellous.'

Dancer was crying openly.

'You did it, you bleedin' did it,' he shouted at the twins.

'You bleeding did it,' shouted back Seb. 'You hooked Red when he would have scored the winning goal, didn't he, Dommie?' But Dommie was streaking up the field as fast as tired, little Corporal could carry him and was next seen locked in an ecstatic Louisa's arms. Little Chef darting through equine and human legs, as the crowd spilled overjoyed on to the pitch, took a flying leap on to Ricky's saddle, frantically licking away the tears of joy that striped his master's blackened face.

'We won, Cheffie,' Ricky babbled to him incoherently. 'We fucking did it, Cheffie.'

Mishearing him, a maddened Bart stopped in his tracks.

'You may have won the cup, you asshole, but you won't get her. She's fucking mine!'

Bewildered for an instant, Ricky realized that, in the joy of winning, he'd forgotten all about Chessie.

As he rode off the field, shaking hands with everyone, Louisa, extricating herself from Dommie's embrace, ran up to him.

'Oh, it's so lovely, Wayne's won Best Playing Pony.'

Seb, shaking up a magnum of champagne, made everyone even wetter than they were already. Terry Hanlon had to exert all his vocal skills to get things on course for the presentation.

'Put your cigarettes out before you come up,' he chided the teams. 'We'll have the bad boys first.'

As Seb sauntered up, he turned grinning to the jostling reporters and cameramen and made a very pointed V-sign.

'Too many late nights indeed.'

Good-naturedly, they cheered and whooped.

Ricky's face was impassive as he accepted the huge glittering cup from Lord Cowdray, but later, when it was filled with champagne, he grimly raised it to Chessie who was making no attempt to contain her delight.

Bart couldn't make a scene because of the Germans, but the moment he'd seen them into one of his helicopters he unleashed his fury on Perdita. It was entirely her fault for fouling and scoring an own goal at the end.

'Comes of playing with a fucking broad. Of all the fucking stupid things to do,' he yelled, to the edification of the entire pony lines. Red was even more lethally nasty, until Angel put an arm round the hysterically sobbing Perdita.

'Eet could 'appen to anybody,' he protested. 'Eef you hadn't got hooked because you were messing around in front of goal, they'd never 'ave caught up.'

'Shut up,' screamed Red. 'And for Christ's sake, stop blubbing, Perdita.'

'It wasn't her fault,' shouted Angel.

'Piss off,' said Bart. 'I don't pay you to have opinions.' He found Chessie talking to Lord Cowdray, stuck into her third glass of champagne and looking radiant.

'We're leaving,' he snapped.

'How very unsporting,' said Chessie. 'I wanted to watch the second match.'

'Well, you can't.'

Two more teams were doing a lap of honour before playing off for third place, as Perdita raced towards Bart's helicopter. Blinded by tears, she ran slap into a man stalking in the other direction.

'Can't you look where you're fucking going?' she screamed, then gasped and shrank away, for it was Rupert. For a second they gazed at each other, assessing the damage.

'I'm sorry,' sobbed Perdita. 'I didn't mean to screw up your life. I'm sorry Taggie can't have babies, and I'm sorry I played so badly. I can't do anything right any more. When I dumped about Mum, I didn't know I was your child. I'd never have hurt you deliberately. I've just lost the m-match for them. Red'll never talk to me again. Please let me come and explain. Please help me.' Hysterically she clung to him.

'I'm not fucking social security,' said Rupert, his eyes suddenly as cold as an Eskimo's graveyard. 'And there's no way you're my child. No Campbell-Black could ever ride as badly as you just did.'

As the rain came down again, mingling with her tears and running nose, Perdita gave a wail and stumbled away from him. As she clambered into the helicopter, Chessie was saying happily, 'Oh, look, Bart, I've just found your lucky belt under the seat.'

66

Back at Robinsgrove next morning Ricky, still high on euphoria, was the only member of Apocalypse not laid waste by a hangover. Clutching their heads, groaning, some of them still drunk, the grooms leant against the tired ponies as they walked them out for Ricky to inspect. Wayne had an inflamed tendon and had been ordered a few days' box rest. The others – except for a few cuts and bruises – were miraculously free from injury, so Ricky ordered them to be turned out for forty-eight hours. Leaning on the gate, he fondly watched them, revelling in the sunshine, walking poker-legged at first, then, realizing they were free, breaking into a canter, crinkly tails flying and charging down the valley to roll and cool their bruised legs in the stream which raced and hurled itself against the rocks after yesterday's deluge.

Although his ash trees were still a feathery blue-green without a trace of yellow, Ricky could see the slow beginnings of autumn, the toasting of the beeches, the gilding of the poplars, the occasional tree garlanded by acid-green traveller's joy, the barley beyond the stables slowly losing its green flecks. But for once the prospect of winter didn't depress him.

The telephone had rung all morning, patrons suddenly wondering if there was any chance he could play for them next year, friends to congratulate, newspapers wanting quotes – one would have thought the powers of darkness had fallen. The morning papers were equally ecstatic. '*Flyers France-Lynched*,' said *The Times*, which was a slight exaggeration when they had only been beaten by an own goal. '*Flyers Bomb*,' said the *Telegraph*. The tabloids concentrated on Dancer's delight and Perdita's anguish, with variations on Rupert's rejected daughter, Auriel's toyboy, Bart's fury, all reporting the grisly details of the shouting match afterwards.

Looking at the bowed-down heads of the barley still dripping with raindrops, Ricky was reminded of Perdita yesterday, sobbing, bitterly ashamed and desolate. He had talked to Daisy earlier that morning and persuaded her not to weaken. 'Looks as though Red's on the way out, thank God. Let her come back in her own time.'

Returning to the yard, Ricky went into Wayne's box to find him lying down asleep. But as he sat down in the straw, Wayne opened a baleful black-ringed eye, whickered and, accepting several barley sugars, listened attentively as his master took him through every stroke of the chukka in which he had seen off the great Glitz.

'We won, my brave Wayne, we won,' Ricky told him exultantly.

The telephone was ringing again. Remembering the grooms had the day off, Ricky sprinted into the kitchen.

'Hello, Rick,' said *The Scorpion*. 'Congrats on beating your ex-wife's hubby. Your ex seemed over the moon. Any chance of a reconciliation?'

'F-f-fuck off,' said Ricky.

The telephone rang again immediately. Ricky snatched it up. 'F-f-fuck off.'

'Hello, hello.' It was Brigadier Hughie. 'Thought you might like to know that it's rumoured that you're going up to ten.'

Replacing the receiver, Ricky took it off the hook and, picking up the cup, already covered in a thousand ecstatic fingerprints, held it up to the light.

'We won, Cheffie, we won.'

Little Chef thumped his curly tail and sniffed appreciatively at the chicken his master was cooking for him as a celebratory treat. Neither had eaten much yesterday. Then he gave a strangled croak, all he could manage after barking himself hoarse yesterday, and shot off into the yard. Still hugging the cup, Ricky wandered into the hall, holding it up for the photographs of his grandfather, uncles and father to see. 'I did it, you old b-b-buggers.'

'You look like one of the wise men bearing gold. Melchior, was it?'

Ricky almost dropped the cup, for there in the kitchen doorway stood Chessie.

'As I was ripped untimely from yesterday's celebration,' she drawled, 'I thought I'd come and congratulate you personally. I see you haven't painted anything except the stables since I left.'

Wandering back into the kitchen, she noticed that the

shelves, from which she'd swiped all her recipe books, were piled high with old copies of *Horse and Hound* and *Polo* magazine. The spice shelves were down to salt, pepper and mixed herbs. She could smell that there was no tarragon in the chicken Ricky was cooking. A calendar for 1981, the year she'd walked out, still hung on the wall, probably because it bore a photograph of a whippet who looked like Millicent. The washing machine, black inside with Apocalypse shirts, quivered on 'pause'.

She turned to Ricky, who was still holding the cup and staring at her. 'Aren't you pleased to see me?'

'I don't know.'

All he knew was that the sun had gone in and the cup had lost its glitter. Chessie was wearing a clinging black jump suit, sawn off at the knees, with a T-shirt top clinched in with yesterday's leather belt. She appeared to be wearing no make-up at all, but in fact had spent twenty minutes smudging blue-black shadow and a subtle blending of green and beige base to make herself look tired, frail and wildly desirable. Ricky felt himself churning.

'Got a hangover?' she asked.

'I don't drink.'

'I thought you might have made an exception. It is the first rung.'

'I know,' said Ricky flatly.

The Slav face was impassive. Above the high cheek-bones, his eyes were as dark as the rain-soaked cedars in the churchyard.

'Everyone's saying you'll go to ten at the end of the season. All you have to do is win the Westchester.' Her voice was mocking. 'Can I have a look round?'

Sauntering to the window, showing off the slightness of her figure, she caught sight of Wayne, who, having decided to get up, was now leaning nosily out of his box to see what his master was up to. 'Is that Mattie?' How clever of me to remember names, thought Chessie.

'Mattie was put down, if you remember, the day you first slept with Bart.'

Chessie didn't hesitate. 'Oh yes, how stupid of me.'

Putting the cup down, he followed her into the hall.

'You've let the moth get at that tapestry, and look at the damp,' she said reprovingly. 'This place needs a woman's touch. Pity I can't touch Bart for a million to do it up.'

Ricky's cards were still up from his birthday in February, along with an Easter egg Violet had given him for letting her drive in his fields. Absent-mindedly, he started breaking it up and giving pieces to Little Chef.

'What d'you want?' he said bleakly.

'To talk.' She looked him straight in the eyes. 'To find out if you still want me.'

'Don't be bloody silly.'

Her eyes moved to his mouth and back to his eyes again, glancing at him under her lashes, then smiling slowly in a way that had always destroyed him.

'Shall we go to bed?' she whispered. 'Who's up there?'

'The twins and Dancer, all with assorted partners.'

'Christ, the twins are such gossips they'd fax Bart in Dusseldorf with the news in two minutes.'

Fretfully Chessie crossed the room, noticing a Lalique bowl and a Rockingham Dalmatian from her side of the family. If she were coming back to stay, there was no need to take them. The dust was awful. Didn't Ricky have a char any more? Then a shaft of sunlight suddenly illuminated Will's portrait.

'Oh my God, that's beautiful!' Taking it off the wall, she examined it more closely. 'It's stunning. *So* like him. Oh Christ, he was sweet!'

For the first time there was genuine emotion in her voice as she longingly caressed the blond hair, and the round, roguish face. 'It was his birthday last week.'

'I know.' Yet again Ricky felt the whole buckling weight of responsibility for Will's death. 'I'm sorry.'

'I was a good mother, wasn't I?'

'Of course,' lied Ricky.

'God, it's a brilliant likeness.' She looked down at the portrait again. 'Let me have it.'

'I can't.'

Chessie's face hardened. 'You owe it to me.'

'I know.' Ricky had gone yellow, almost parsnip-coloured. 'But it was a present.'

'Who painted it? Perhaps he could do a copy for me?'

'It's a her – Daisy Macleod, Perdita's mother.'

'Ah.' Chessie put the painting down on the piano as though it had suddenly dropped ten thousand pounds in value. 'I've met her, very blowzy . . . the *habituée* of orgies, a bicycle made for six in fact.'

'She's sweet,' said Ricky coldly.

Chessie's eyebrows vanished beneath her fringe.

'How did she get such a good likeness?'

'She found a photograph tucked in an old polo book.'

Chessie went to the drinks' tray, wiped the dust out of the inside of a glass with her sleeve and sloshed in a lot of vodka and very little tonic.

'Did Daisy, Daisy, do all those drawings of the horses in the kitchen?'

'Yes.'

'Making herself very much at home,' said Chessie, downing half her drink.

'Shut up,' said Ricky, losing his temper. 'You know it's only you I love.'

'Well, hold me then.'

Reeling with desire, his heart pounding like a cannon Ricky breathed in the Diorissimo she'd sprayed in her hair, noticed the sweat beading the faint down of blonde hairs on her upper lip. Like a man returning to a once familiar house who half-remembers where the light switches are, he fumbled for one of her hardened nipples, then stretched his hand over the wonderful springiness surrounding it.

'Oh, my d-d-darling.'

Next moment they both jumped out of their quivering skins as the door burst open and in barged Eddie Macleod.

'Oh, there you are, Ricky. Sorry to bother you, but we couldn't get through on the telephone. Ethel had five puppies at five o'clock this morning, three black and two brindle, all with curly tails, so Mum thinks Little Chef must be the father, not Decorum. Would you like to come and see them, and can I get Mum's sketch book from her studio? Ethel's such a good mother, she's licked them all clean, and she's awfully proud. We buried the after-birth and . . . '

'Who's that?' said Chessie when Ricky finally managed to evict Eddie.

'Perdita's brother.'

'And Mum – Daisy, Daisy has a studio here?'

'The attic room,' said Ricky evenly. 'No-one was using it.'

650

'And she uses your library too? Making herself very much at home.'

Ricky glared at Chessie: 'It's my house. Stop being a bitch.'

'I thought Ethel was the bitch. Are you going to be godfather to those puppies?'

Chessie looked through the window at the house-martins catching insects and at the stable cat pretending to sleep on the warm gravel, waiting for birds to swoop down and attack the peas and raspberries no-one had had time to pick.

'I just wondered,' she said softly, 'if you were sucking up to Daisy as a prospective mother-in-law.'

'Don't be fatuous,' exploded Ricky. He had forgotten Chessie's relentless nit-picking jealousy. 'Daisy needed somewhere to paint. Snow Cottage is minute. It must have been like playing polo on a tennis court.'

'I'm sorry.' Examining her reflection in the Queen's Cup, which, having been won only six weeks ago, was still quite shiny, Chessie licked her finger, wiped away a smudge of mascara and smiled – the adorable child again.

'Why don't we go out for a discreet lunch? We could go to L'Aperitif. I haven't been there since we split up.'

'I can't.'

'Can't? Monday's your day off.'

Ricky gritted his teeth. 'I've got to take Violet out to lunch.'

'And who's Violet?' Chessie's fingers were drumming on the top of the piano.

'Daisy's daughter. She passed her driving test first go last week and I said I'd take her out to lunch.'

'Cancel it,' ordered Chessie.

'I promised. Her boyfriend chucked her after all that stuff in *The Scorpion*. She's been terribly low.'

'Jesus,' screamed Chessie. 'Surely us getting it together is more important.'

'Daisy was very good to me,' said Ricky carefully. 'When I was stupid with misery over losing you she listened. She's a friend. We can have dinner this evening. I'll have got rid of Dancer and the twins by then.'

His face was as dead-pan as ever, but there was no

denying the longing and conciliation in his voice. Chessie, however, was miffed.

'I can't. Bart's only gone to Dusseldorf for the day. He's coming back tonight.'

'And we can't rock the Bart.'

'Shut up. I'm the one who makes jokes round here.'

Ricky felt an appalling weariness.

'Let's get one thing clear. I love you, only you. But I've survived without you for six years, Christ knows how, and I'm not prepared for half-measures. You've got to leave B-b-bart and come back for good.'

'How do I know it's for my own good? It wasn't before. We need to get to know each other again.'

Seeing that Ricky'd left the telephone off, she slammed it back on its hook as she charged out of the house, then drove off in such a cloud of dust that the stable cat jumped up from the gravel and Wayne ducked back inside his box.

Slumped in despair against the wall, Ricky reached out to answer the telephone.

It was Violet, whispering ecstatically.

'Oh, Ricky, Julian's just turned up. He says he's so sorry about everything. D'you mind terribly if we have lunch another day?'

Washing up last night's supper and today's breakfast in cold water, because Violet had pinched all the hot, Daisy thought gloomily of the mountain of clothes to be ironed and the children's trunks which she still hadn't tackled and which festered in their rooms full of dirty clothes and, probably in Eddie's case, ancient tuck. She felt absolutely wiped out because she'd been up all night acting as Ethel's midwife. But she knew she'd perk up in an instant, just as Violet had, if Drew rang. He hadn't been in touch for weeks.

She was jolted with hope as the doorbell went. Shaking her hair loose from its elastic band, she opened the door and was astounded to see Chessie.

'Hi!' That wicked sleepy smile was as menacing as it was irresistible. 'I loathe droppers-in myself, but I didn't have your telephone number.'

Conscious of her blood-stained shirt, her straining jeans and her shiny face, Daisy said: 'Come in.'

After Chessie'd showed absolutely no interest in the puppies and Daisy'd opened her last bottle of wine which she was saving for Drew, they went into the garden taking up opposite ends of a peeling bench which Daisy was always meaning to paint.

'I've come for two reasons, three really,' said Chessie. 'I want to thank you for looking after Ricky. He says you've been wonderful.'

'Really?' Daisy perked up.

'Wonderful. I don't think he's ever had a platonic woman friend before.'

Daisy unperked.

'You must have got so bored with him banging on and on about me,' went on Chessie.

Daisy got up and broke off a columbine that was bending double a pale blue delphinium.

'Ricky's not boring. He loves you, but he never bangs on.'

'Does about polo.' Chessie pulled off a piece of paint. 'Anyway I feel I owe you. I've got very fond of Perdita over the years,' she said untruthfully.

'Oh God,' said Daisy miserably, 'I feel so awful.'

'You shouldn't. It wasn't your fault.'

'How is she?'

'Pretty low – particularly after losing us the match yesterday. Needs her Mum actually, but too proud to admit it. I'm going to talk to her tonight and see if I can bring you two together.'

'That's terribly kind,' said Daisy. Perhaps she'd misjudged Chessie. 'It'd be wonderful.'

'And you can do one thing for me in return,' drawled Chessie.

She'll have stripped that bench in a minute, thought Daisy.

'I've just seen your painting of Will,' continued Chessie. 'It's stunning. One day I want you to do me a copy. But what I really want is – it's Bart's fiftieth birthday next week and he's pretty disgruntled about it, particularly after yesterday. Could you possibly paint me in the nude as a surprise for him?'

No, thought Daisy, in horror.

'It's terribly sweet of you,' she said out loud. 'I'm really honoured, but I've got about four commissions I've simply got to finish.'

'Oh, please. It'd be such fun. I'm in such a muddle. I feel I need someone like you to talk to.'

In the end Chessie offered her so much money that Daisy couldn't refuse.

67

Daisy had never disliked a commission so much. Day after day she was taunted by Chessie's naked beauty, as Chessie babbled on as relentlessly as the Frogsmore about how she and Ricky loved each other and how perhaps the portrait would end up as second wedding present for him, and how Bart was so old, and how she didn't want to end up looking after him when he was old and crotchety, and *boy*, he'd be crotchety.

Daisy got lower and lower, particularly when Ricky dropped in to see Ethel's puppies and found Chessie in residence on Daisy's saxe-blue sofa with her body as warm and brown and tempting as new bread from the oven. She had made no attempt to get dressed, and Ricky, shooting Daisy a murderous look as though it was all her fault, had stormed out.

By contrast Little Chef popped down twice a day to kiss, lick and clean Ethel's eyes, ears and nose, to examine his offspring with obvious delight and then to curl up for an hour on the priceless clothes Chessie dropped so casually on the floor. Daisy wished Drew were as attentive. He still hadn't rung. All the telephone calls that week were for Chessie, usually when she wasn't there.

'Say I've just left, whatever time Bart rings,' insisted Chessie or, to explain one day when she wasn't going to turn up at Daisy's at all, 'Just tell him you've reached a really tricky bit and I can't come to the telephone, but I send him a huge kiss, and I'll be home around seven.'

She's seeing Ricky, thought Daisy, and was amazed how desolate she felt. Having now spent some time in Chessie's company, she was now utterly convinced she would only make Ricky miserable if they got together again.

Ashamed of disliking her so much, Daisy also totally

sabotaged any artistic integrity by making Chessie even more beautiful than she was and giving her face a soft wistful sweetness it certainly didn't possess.

Chessie was enchanted and left on the Saturday afternoon giving Daisy a huge hug and a fat cheque, which would at least pay for Eddie's school fees next year, Violet's trip round the world *and* a new dress for Daisy. But what was the point of that if Drew never rang again?

In a furious urge to work off her depression, she painted Chessie again with a glittering rhinestone for a face and a viciously cruel, angular body totally cased in a chain-mail of self-absorption. It was one of the only surrealistic paintings she'd ever done and a much truer likeness.

Exhausted, she took Ethel for a quick walk. Venus was rising to the left as Ethel splashed through the brilliant green watercress and forget-me-nots which clogged Ricky's stream.

I move the sweet forget-me-nots that grow for happy lovers, thought Daisy despairingly.

A vast, black cloud massed threateningly along the horizon like a tidal wave about to engulf her. What worse things could happen in her life? But as she wandered home through the buddleia-scented evening, she saw a dark-green Mini draw up outside her front door with a jerk. Not *more* press? Then she froze – worse than press. Sukey Benedict had got out and was waving like a restrained goal judge.

'I was in the area and thought I'd pop in and say hellair. What a darling cottage, and how charming you've made the garden.'

This was untrue. The lawn, like a hayfield, towered higher than the flower beds, which were a holiday-let to weeds. Even worse the coat rack had collapsed in the hall, so Sukey and Daisy had to mountaineer over a hillock of Barbours and bomber jackets into the kitchen where two days' washing-up jammed the sink.

'I'm sorry,' muttered Daisy. 'I've been finishing a painting.' If Sukey insisted on seeing round, she thought nervously, she might unearth the nude of Drew in the potting shed.

'Would you like a drink?'

Sukey hesitated. 'I'm driving. I'd love a cup of tea.'

Daisy, desperate for vodka, had to winkle two cups out of the sink and wash them in the upstairs bathroom. But Sukey didn't seem to notice anything. She sat down at the kitchen table, playing with one of the yellow roses in a blue vase which promptly collapsed in a shower of petals. She'd always worn her trousers loose to de-emphasize her bottom, but now they were so loose they were almost hipsters, and too loose to contain her striped shirt which was done up on the wrong buttons. A long lock of mousey hair escaped from a most inappropriate Alice band of red velvet dotted with seed pearls. It was like seeing Mrs Thatcher with a punk rocker hairstyle chewing gum, thought Daisy. Despite the muggy warmth of the day, Sukey was shivering uncontrollably.

'Thank you so much.' As she took the cup and saucer it was difficult to tell where Daisy's rattle ended and hers began.

There was a dreadful silence.

'I'm not very good at confiding in people.' Sukey looked down at her big, rubber-glove-cherished hands. 'Daddy was in the Foreign Office and we never talked about feelings. I came to you, Daisy, because you always seem such a sweet person. It's about Drew actually.'

The room darkened. Daisy knew the tidal wave was going to drown her. Never admit to anything, Drew had always insisted, but she was such a dreadful liar.

'I knew Drew married me for my money.' Sukey was busy dismembering another yellow rose. 'He's so frite-fly attractive it couldn't be for any other reason.' Then, when Daisy murmured in protest, 'I've been awfully happy really – even though he's always had other women.'

Drew, the solid, the utterly dependable, thought Daisy aghast. She felt like the conjuror's blonde-haired assistant who hears sawing and realizes she's got into the wrong box.

'Are you sure?'

'Oh, one knows. He's away so much – claiming to stay at his club when I later discovered it was closed down for the summer, meetings he said he'd been to, then finding apologies for his absence in the minutes a month later. Beautiful girls seeking me out at parties, then being particularly nice out of relief that I wasn't pretty. Girl grooms suddenly getting cheeky.'

Daisy could definitely feel the teeth of the magician's saw grazing her side now.

'Didn't you mind?' she asked in a strangled voice.

'Of course, I love him. The worst bit was one *au pair*, very pretty, who left in a hurry to work as a chalet girl. Drew must have met up with her again when he was playing snow polo last Christmas. Afterwards she wrote and gave me all the details of all the other girls he'd slept with. He got eight valentines this year.'

How many times had Drew sworn she was the only other woman he'd ever slept with since he'd been married?

'How horrible!' she moaned, suddenly nauseated by a waft of cat food. Bending down to pick up the plate, she saw it was crawling with maggots. Gagging, she threw it in the bin. Suddenly she remembered Sukey shaking and shaking, the tears pouring down her face, when Angel had knocked Drew off Malteser in the Queen's Cup.

'Did you confront him?' she whispered.

'He denied it,' said Sukey sadly. 'Said the girl was a bit potty, and obsessive, and he adored me and the children and would never leave us. I know it's vulgar to talk about it,' Sukey was frenziedly pleating the tablecloth, 'but he still makes love to me three or four times a week. I never say no to him.'

And Drew had sworn that once the children were born they had had a *mariage blanc*. The tidal wave had passed over, leaving an aeroplane trail across a vermilion sky like a newly stitched scar. Seeing skin had formed on Sukey's tea, Daisy snatched it away.

'Let's have a drink, I'm afraid there's only vodka.' She added diet Coke and ice.

'I could cope with casual flings,' said Sukey, 'but this time I think he's really serious about someone. I was doing his VAT this afternoon. He's gone to America for a couple of days to fix up playing in the US Open and some other tour before the Westchester. I know it's utterly despicable, but I went through his Amex and his cheque stubs. He's been spending a fortune on flowers and hotel bills and restaurants this month, and there's a bill back in May for a diamond and topaz brooch for five thousand pounds.'

That's my daisy brooch, thought Daisy, appalled.

'Perhaps it was for you,' she said quickly.

'I'm Capricorn like Drew,' said Sukey tonelessly.

Daisy suddenly felt bitterly ashamed and utterly suicidal at the same time.

'One doesn't mean to be mean,' continued Sukey. 'I've got a private income, but it's always been a bit of a struggle to make ends meet. Polo's awfully expensive, and the children'll be starting school soon. I never minded going without things, but when I find all his earnings being blued on other women and I'm paying for his ponies and everything else, even his subscription to Boodles, it makes one a bit bitter.'

The magician's saw was definitely deep in Daisy's flesh now, tearing away bone and muscle.

'Who is she?'

'Bibi Alderton. Drew hid some letters under his mattress. They weren't that passionate, just passionately grateful for Drew being so kind to her. And there's been a lot of dropped telephone calls, and he keeps urging me to go out and walk the dogs, and although he claims no-one's rung the telephone reeks of his aftershave when I get home.'

'I had that with Hamish,' said Daisy. She shivered, too, at how often she'd breathed in the tangy, lemony smell on Drew's beautiful strong brown neck and jaw, and felt faint with longing.

'It's awfully easy to imagine these things,' she added helplessly.

Sukey shook her head. 'I was staying with Mummy last week. Drew'd been invited to dinner with Rupert and Taggie. You know what a wonderful cook she is. Drew described every course when I got back. Unfortunately I met Taggie in Sainsbury's the day Drew'd left for America and she said she was so sorry Drew'd only stayed for a quick drink and she hoped the pony with colic was OK. Well, I checked with the grooms, very casually. They said none of the horses had been sick. It's so revolting. One gets just like Miss Marple. There's this ghastly sick exultation in the detective work, then when you stumble on the truth it's the gates of hell. But I always felt Drew wouldn't leave me,' she raised streaming eyes to Daisy, 'because he needs my money to play polo, but Bibi Alderton could buy me out a hundred times over.' Putting her face in her hands, she burst into tears.

Rushing round the table, Daisy put her arms round her.

'Please, please don't cry. He's a bastard. He's not worth it.'

'Why, you're crying too,' said Sukey, as she dried her eyes a couple of minutes later. 'You're so kind, Daisy. You really mind for me, don't you? I shouldn't have dumped on you. All this must remind you of your own marriage breaking up so much. What d'you think I ought to do? I love him so, so, much.'

'I'd sit tight,' said Daisy, then thought what a stupid expression. She'd been tight for days after Hamish left her. 'From what I gather Angel and Bibi are still very snarled up about each other. Angel's gorgeous, but he's been playing Bibi up dreadfully because she's such a workaholic, and she probably wants to make him jealous, and Drew's probably only flirting with Bibi because he wants to get his own back on Angel for jabbing pelhams into his kidneys and trying to break his jaw.'

'It'd be so lovely if you were right,' said Sukey.

'Have another drink.' Daisy felt a ghastly, sick, masochistic craving for more detail.

'No, I *must* go.' Sukey got to her feet, rubbing her eyes like a child. She had no mascara to smear. 'Our Nanny's got a first date with our local bobby: so romantic. He's awfully good-looking with lovely blue eyes – rather like Drew's.' Her voice broke again. 'I love him so much, Daisy.'

With Sukey gone, Daisy wandered distraught into the garden. The sweet tobacco scent of buddleia was cloying, almost overpowering now. She knew she would hate the smell for ever as a reminder of paradise lost.

The owls were hooting from the woods. She had never seen that much of Drew because of the children and because he'd been away so much, but it had been such a heavenly affair; and with his apparent, utter integrity and strength, he had restored her faith in men. In anguish, she realized that dreaming about him and looking forward to seeing him again had been the one thing that had made her life bearable. How stupid not to realize that if a man's capable of being unfaithful to his wife, he's bound to be unfaithful to you. As she sobbed in the darkness, there was no-one to hear her except the hooting owls and the swooping bats.

★

If anyone was more miserable than Daisy that night it was Perdita, wandering barefoot two hundred miles away through an infinitely more beautiful Sussex garden, where totally weedless, herbaceous borders towered above shaven lawns and stone nymphs blanched by the moonlight frolicked at the end of rides battlemented with yews. Floodlighting cast a golden glow on the splendid Georgian house Bart had acquired as his English base. Chessie and Bart inhabited the heart of the house. Angel, without Bibi, smouldered in the West Wing. Perdita and Red appropriately waged cold war in the East Wing. Feeling mossy, stone steps cool beneath her feet, Perdita could see into Bart's and Chessie's jade-green drawing room where the Chippendale table acquired specially to display the Gold Cup had, on Bart's insistence, been left bare to remind and punish Perdita.

Red's definition of a great player was one who raised his game when the chips were down. Luke's, slightly different, was someone who could pick himself off the floor and rise above mistakes that had brought a whole team down.

But Perdita wasn't given the chance because Bart had dropped her from the team after the Gold Cup and, without her, the Flyers had already notched up two dazzling victories in the Cowdray Challenge Cup. She was suffering a total loss of confidence. She was still reeling from Rupert's total rejection, and now at the time of year when patrons were making up their teams for next year, the telephone only rang for Red and Angel. For the first time people were whispering that she was committing that deadliest sin in polo – playing below her handicap.

Even worse, she couldn't stop crying, which drove Red crazy when he was awake. The moment his head hit the pillow he fell asleep, leaving Perdita to toss and turn, tormented by visions of him and Chessie, but not daring to crossquestion him, crawling with frustration, praying that, forgetting the impasse, he would reach out for her when he was half-asleep. But he didn't. They hadn't made love since the marathon at the Savoy.

By day he was frantically busy, playing for Bart, making up his mind whether to play in Saratoga, Deauville, Hawaii or Sotogrande in August, and revving up for the Cartier International on Sunday.

Special tension had been added to this occasion because the first match of the afternoon between England and America would be a trial for the Westchester. An American team consisting of Red, the newly naturalized Angel, Bobby Ferraro and Bart, standing in for Shark who'd been sidelined by a shoulder injury, were to play Ricky, Drew and the repulsive Napiers, which was the squad England planned to field in the Westchester in October.

As the Americans wouldn't have unlimited access to ponies, as they would in a home match, and they weren't fielding their first team, it would bode ill for the Westchester, Venturer and the sponsors if England didn't walk it. Bart, Red and Angel, thirsting to avenge their defeat in the Gold Cup, were determined to rattle the Brits.

Perdita had earlier returned from London, where she'd been seeing a specialist about a sprained wrist, to find the house empty except for servants. Chessie was out somewhere. At least she couldn't be with Red, as he'd gone with Angel and Bart to a dinner and team meeting.

She could no longer read or listen to records or even concentrate on television, Red having rendered her utterly deficient in resources. Anticipating a long wait, she had poured herself a second vodka and tonic and wandered off into the garden. She was wearing the silk pyjamas Red had given her in Singapore. The stars littered the sky like confetti. Oh God, would Red ever marry her now? But to her amazement he was home in tearing spirits just before ten.

'Hi, baby!' He held out his arms.

Perdita bolted into them, frantically covering his face with kisses before finding his mouth.

'I've been so unhappy,' she wailed when he finally let her go. 'I thought you'd never forgive me. I love you. I love you.'

'Good.' Red patted her cheek. 'And I'll love you back if you'll stop throwing wobblies. You know how scenes bore me. Fix me a drink, sweetheart. I've been on diet Coke all evening to impress Brad Dillon.'

Brad Dillon, the American team manager, formerly a Brigadier in the US Marines, a hero both in Korea and

Vietnam, was, despite his macho exterior, a strict tee-totaller and expected similar temperance from his team.

'How was the team meeting?' Joyously Perdita kissed the whisky bottle before splashing it into a glass.

'Acrimonious. Dad's flown in Juan O'Brien to advise the team. He had a row with Angel. The Brits are in a panic. They don't want Angel at Number Three in case he murders Drew Benedict at Number Two so there was talk of him playing Number Two and me going to Number One. Christ, the humiliation. I threatened to quit, so I'm playing Three and Angel One. The Brits have been absolute dickheads and lent us some seriously good ponies. Americans would never do that. It's crazy, like giving the Viet Cong a lot of B52s. I've been trying them out all afternoon.' He half-emptied his glass in one gulp. 'That's better.'

For a second he appraised Perdita's back view as she poured herself a third vodka.

'You're losing too much weight.'

Moving forward, feeling for her breasts, he nuzzled the back of her neck. Perdita felt her stomach curling and missed the glass with the vodka bottle, wiping it off the polished table with her sleeve.

'Your game may be off,' murmured Red into her hair, 'but you're ace at making ponies.'

'What d'you mean?'

'Here's the good news. Brad Dillon and Juan want me to play Tero tomorrow afternoon.'

'Tero!' Utterly outraged, Perdita tried to swing round, but, unwilling to meet her eyes, Red held on to her.

'She's hardly had a man on her back since Argentina. You know how fucked up she was when I went off to Singapore. She'll be terrified.'

'Terofied,' mocked Red. 'She went like a dream. I played a chukka on her this afternoon. Juan reckons she'll do two chukkas. We saw a video of the Gold Cup this afternoon,' he went on, trying to railroad her into submission. 'Juan said I don't mark closely enough. So, I'm not going to let you out of my sight in future.' His hand slid down to her groin. 'Let's go to bed.'

'Don't get off the subject and don't soft-soap me,' stormed Perdita. 'You're *not* riding Tero. I've spent nearly a year getting her confidence back. I'm not letting you fuck her up just for one match.'

'Don't be so unBritish,' teased Red, who was fast losing his conciliatory manner.

'I am not letting you ride her in the *parade*, let alone a single chukka.'

Letting her go, he reached for his drink, then picked up her left hand and examined the huge sapphire.

'After all I've done for you,' he said softly. 'And you deny me seven or at most fifteen minutes, when I'm playing for my country.'

'Tero's different,' stammered Perdita.

'You bet she is. With me on her back she's a good pony.'

'You bastard,' yelled Perdita, drink fuelling her aggression, then jumped at the baying of Bart's Rottweilers. 'Oh, fucking hell, Chessie's back.'

'Look what I've got for your father's big five O,' said Chessie, sauntering into the room. Pulling the portrait out of its wrapping paper, she propped it up on a green and white striped sofa.

Red whistled. 'Talk about a glow job. You look angelic, but kinda overdressed. Why didn't you take off my father's wedding ring while you were about it?'

'Oh, shut up,' said Chessie, but not unamiably.

Perdita's hostility, however, could have frozen bread straight from the oven.

'My mother painted that,' she hissed. 'That's our sitting-room sofa.'

'Needs re-upholstering, like your mother,' said Chessie. 'My cheque should help.'

'It's a bloody conspiracy. How did you get on to her? I bet she wrote smarming to you. What's she been saying about me?'

Chessie looked at her meditatively.

'She misses you,' she said. 'I thought she was rather a nice old thing. Quite charming really.'

'Good at charming snakes like you.'

'Ay, yay, yay.' Chessie's eyes widened. 'What's got into her?' she said, turning to Red. 'Obviously not you, or she wouldn't be so bad-tempered.'

'Red wants to ride Tero in the International. *My*

pony,' she added scornfully, when Chessie looked blank.

'That's great,' said Chessie. 'People fall over themselves to lend ponies for the International. You'll sell her for three times as much afterwards, particularly with Red on her back, and, just think, the whole world will be watching her.'

68

The whole polo world – or rather 27,000 of them – gathered at the Guards Club next day for the Cartier International, the ritziest event in the polo calendar. The blustery weather seemed to be reflecting the tensions of the two teams. Clouds raced across the sky as a warm but frenzied south-west wind whipped off panamas, murdered hairstyles, stripped the petals from the red roses clambering up the clubhouse and fretted the fleet of hospitality tents that lined the pitch like yachts in a regatta. All morning, so their employers could get plastered, chauffeurs, driving everything from Minis to Rollers, edged into the parking lot where picnickers consumed vast quantities of quiche, smoked salmon and chicken drumsticks and drank Pimm's out of paper cups.

Only the jade-green statue of Prince Albert on his splendid charger gazed bleakly northwards, away from such manic guzzling and later from the play, as if he were blocking some distant shot.

Angel escaped into one of the lavatories in the players' changing rooms, so no-one could muddle him with more advice. He was outraged that Guards Club officials, themselves outraged that the Yanks had put him in their team, had insisted on frisking him on arrival. He was livid he was playing Number One. What chance would he have of scoring with the ground drying unevenly and the wind whisking the ball in every direction? His heart blackened in hatred against Drew, the enemy, whom he now suspected of cuckolding him. How could he not kill him? He was about to play for a country belonging to a wife who had deserted him, against a country he loathed. He had spent last night painting a white banner with the words 'The Falklands Belong to Argentina', which he had smuggled in with the tack and intended to brandish during the presentation.

Perdita, even more miserable and isolated, huddled in the stands next to the Royal Box. She wore dark glasses to hide her reddened eyes and the fact that there was no sun in the sky or in her life. After rowing with Red all night, terrified of losing him, she'd let him ride Tero. Now he'd banished her from the pony lines.

'You screwed my sleep. I don't want you hanging around dispensing gratuitous advice.'

The wind was taking everyone's skirts over their heads. Girls with good legs seemed less embarrassed, reflected Perdita. She tipped Angel's sombrero further over her nose for there, arriving with Bas, were Rupert and Taggie. Taggie seemed to have solved the force ten problem by wearing a sand-coloured suit with shorts instead of a skirt, showing off her long, beautiful legs. Over her shoulders was thrown a huge crimson cashmere shawl. From her ears hung long silver earrings, both birthday presents from Rupert. He could give her everything in the world except a baby. With her dark hair lifting and her bright crimson lips as smooth as a tulip, she looked absolutely gorgeous. As usual Rupert never took his arm off her shoulders from the moment they sat down. Perdita's heart twisted with envy and loneliness. Would he never recognize her?

Now the celebrities, who'd come to be looked at, vying to take their seats later than each other, were streaming out of the Cartier tent, replete with champagne, lobster, chicken supreme and peaches poached in Sancerre. As they looked for their seats, they flashed all-embracing smiles at their public.

'I've just seen a Beegee go by,' boomed Miss Lodsworth as Ringo Starr passed by her seat up the gangway.

'Looked like a Monkey to me,' said Mrs Hughie.

'Who are the Monkeys?' asked Brigadier Hughie. 'Those chimps who have tea on television?'

'No, no, a dance band,' said Mrs Hughie. 'You remember the Monkeys when the children were young?'

'We had a monkey in Borneo,' said Brigadier Hughie. 'Dear little chap. Had to leave him behind when I was posted to Malaya.'

'Expect it's Prime Minister now,' muttered Rupert.

A ripple of excitement went through the crowd as Juan O'Brien walked into the stands in a blazer of glory, hailing acquaintances.

'Hoo-arn, Hoo-arn,' cried Lady Sharon. 'Welcome, welcome, or rather *bienvenida*, back to Inglesias. Are you going to be allowed to play next year? Dave's mad about the idea.'

Several members of the Guards Club turned purple and started muttering about Bluff Cove. Rapping out commands on his walkie-talkie, covering a field as flawless and as expectant as a newly laid carpet, strode Major Ferguson. The buttons on his blazer gleamed brighter even than the brass instruments of the band of the Irish Guards in their blood-red tunics.

Suddenly the photographers abandoned the celebrities and shot off to concentrate on the Prince and Princess of Wales, who'd just arrived and were shaking hands in the Royal Box. Only a couple of wagtails looking for worms took no notice.

On came the skewbald drum horse and his Life Guards rider in his gold coat, followed by the American team, the Stars and Stripes streaming out behind them. Angel, his face still as a gold coin, sulked because he'd just been sharply ordered to put out his cigarette. Big Bobby Ferraro, on a wall-eyed sorrel, his hat on the back of his head, had his mouth open at all the pomp. Bart was in a state of ecstasy at achieving two ambitions: to ride for his country and meet the Princess of Wales. Red, aware of the crowd's adulation, was the only one grinning broadly – and he's riding Tero, thought Perdita in fury. How dare he? Tero looked petrified, her pewter coat lathering up like a washing machine primed with too much Daz, big eyes darting, ears disappeared against her pretty head as Red held her in an iron grip. Nor did Perdita know that four grooms, as well as Angel, Bart and Bobby, had had to hold her in the pony lines to enable Red to get on her back.

The British team followed: Ricky very pale, Drew very red from hangover and jet lag, the Napiers very ugly and saturnine. At the clash of cymbals in 'God Save the Queen', the drum horse took off. Only Red sawing savagely at her mouth stopped Tero following suit.

Up in his glass box the commentator, Terry Hanlon,

failed to make the boot-faced English team laugh by pulling faces at them, then thanked Cartier for sponsoring the Coronation Cup. As each member of the teams cantered forward to take a bow, Red got five times as many screams of excitement as all the others. I should never have let him ride Tero, thought Perdita bitterly. Not even Terry Hanlon thanking Sir David Waterlane, Sir Victor Kaputnik, Kevin Coley and Perdita Macleod for lending ponies to the Americans could placate her.

The first chukka went straight into polo history because, at the end of it, the Americans were 7-0 up with six of the goals scored by Red, the contemptuous smile hardly leaving his face. It was as though he'd already seen a video of the match and knew exactly where the ball was going, he and Tero achieving one of those miraculous fusions between rider and pony that happens once in a lifetime. Fear had given wings to Tero's oiled hooves as she streaked after the ball, a blue greyhound chasing an Arctic hare, but at the same time her stopping and turning were so automatic, her positioning near the ball so exact that she seemed hardly to need a rider on her back except as a scoring machine. Perdita was torn between pride and utter humiliation, particularly as the crowd seethed with speculation around her.

'Juan brought that grey over.'

'No, he didn't. Bart brought it for $100,000 from Jesus's brother.'

'She's worth it,' said Bas. 'Christ, look at that acceleration.'

'Isn't that Perdita's pony?' asked Taggie.

'Couldn't be,' said Bas dismissively. 'She was never that good.'

'It is,' said Rupert. 'Just needed a decent rider on her back.'

While America settled into a smooth rhythm, England were in total disarray, a quartet of prima donnas each used to captaining his own side, totally deficient in team spirit, marking badly, never in position. Ricky, in despair, was resorting to his old tricks, doing too much and exhausting his ponies. Drew was just tired. The Napiers barged about, bullies in china shops, bellowing with frustration.

By half-time the score was 12-2 and the crowd were reading their programmes. As the Americans rode back to the pony lines their knees bumped. The Brits rode apart, four thunderclouds symbolizing their alienation.

A square of pitch in front of the Royal Box, where the presentation would later be made, was temporarily roped off so the crowd could close in and gaze at the Prince and Princess of Wales. Babies in prams were wheeled over from the opposite stand. Two Jack Russells, a pug and a cairn in a green scarf were held aloft by their owners to have a good look.

After half-time the English steadied. Red, riding Tero again, stepped up his game and in his enthusiasm had three fouls blown on him. He redeemed himself by galloping across goal and blocking the penalties with a couple of amazing tennis volleys and, finally, with Tero's head, just below the eyes.

'Bastard,' screamed Perdita as, in anguish, she watched Tero shaking her head frantically back and forth.

But her protests were drowned by the roar of the crowd as Angel picked up the ball and took it upfield, riding Drew off with unnecessary violence.

'That'll teach you to seduce my wife,' he hissed.

'Fucking gigolo,' howled Drew, wondering whether Angel's elbow had broken his rib. David Waterlane, who was umpiring, gave England another penalty.

'And what can Red Alderton do this time?' said Terry Hanlon.

Once more Red flew out, blocking the shot with Tero's shoulders and bringing Perdita screaming to her feet.

Rupert and Bas were almost as upset. With England putting up such a pathetic performance, their collossal investment in the Westchester was looking increasingly precarious.

'Come on, England, you're playing like assholes,' yelled Rupert. 'Get your fucking fingers out.'

'Ben and Charles Napier are supposed to be nine,' said Bas, 'but when they play together they're about four. They're not putting their backs into it because you don't get paid for an International.'

'God, he's handsome,' said a beauty behind Perdita, as Red scored again, a lovely sweeping shot under Tero's neck. 'If he's really chucked Perdita Macleod, could you introduce me?'

Perdita gazed across the field to where a shining shingle of parked cars seemed to stretch to infinity. I want to die, she thought. Hell will be as welcoming as a log fire on a cold day compared with this. And now Red and Charles Napier were hurtling towards the boards inside which the ball was nestling. Red must bring Tero down.

'Careful, Red, for God's sake!' she screamed.

But the next second Tero had hopped over the boards at full gallop and somehow, straining every tendon, had turned right in midair, positioning Red perfectly for an offside forehand, enabling him to scoop the ball out and blast it to safety. The crowd gave a sigh of ecstasy as the bell went for the end of the fourth chukka. Tero's part in the match was over. Passionately relieved, shoving protesting onlookers out of the way Perdita raced down to the pony lines by which time Red and Glitz were back on the field.

She found Tero heaving and gasping for breath as she'd only seen ponies doing in the sweltering heat of Palm Beach, with four-inch weals from Red's whip dividing the sweat on her nearside flanks and quarters.

'Oh, my poor baby,' moaned Perdita. 'What has that bastard done to you? And you played so brilliantly, I'll murder him when I catch him.'

But although apparently sound, the little mare seemed utterly shellshocked, not even responding to her mistress when she covered her with kisses. Perhaps it was total exhaustion. Perdita helped dry her off.

'Give her a polish and put on a couple of rugs. She might win Best Playing Pony,' she told Bart's groom, Manuel, before going back to the stands for the last chukka, where America, still leading 12–4, were beginning to get complacent. Red, trying to block another shot, leapt out before Ricky had hit the penalty and a free goal was awarded to England. Ricky then scored two goals and Angel missed an easy one. Furious with himself, he swung his pony's head round inadvertently straight into Drew's face.

Drew, who was far more jet lagged than he had realized, conscious of playing like a geriatric and fed up with Angel histrionically twirling his stick above his head at every real, contrived or imagined foul, lost his temper.

'You fucking grease-ball,' he howled.

'It was a meestake,' howled back Angel, the gold St

Christopher glittering in the damp bronze curls on his chest. 'I teach you to race after my wife,' he hissed, lifting his stick.

'Bad luck for her getting tied up with a gigolo,' snapped Drew, also raising his stick.

'Pack it in,' said David Waterlane, riding between them, 'or I'll send you both off.'

'Tempers getting up on the field,' explained Terry Hanlon. 'Polo's been called a game for gangsters played by gentlemen, or a game for gentlemen played by gangsters. They say you need a cool head and hot blood to play it, and David Waterlane's made the decision. Penalty to England.'

While Ricky converted the penalty Red belted off to change ponies. Looking eastwards Perdita noticed that the frantic activity in the pony lines had subsided and most of the grooms were lined up behind the scoreboard, holding spare ponies and cheering on their respective sides. Then she stiffened. It couldn't be! Snatching Brigadier Hughie's binoculars and nearly strangling him, she saw that Red was actually galloping back on Tero, riding her for the third time which was against the rules. Crashing along the row of protesting spectators, she tore down the steps, sending a returning B. A. Robertson flying.

'Red, you can't! Please not,' she screamed from the second step. 'She's exhausted. You'll kill her.'

But once again, as Red thundered past, her protests were drowned by the ecstatic screams from the crowd.

12–8 to the Americans with four minutes to go. At last England were in with a faint chance. The crowd, catching fire, began to roar. Frantic with worry, Perdita watched only Red. Tero was so game and willing, she'd give him her last ounce. Red picked up his whip. Suddenly the field seemed to stretch from one end of the world to the other as he galloped up and down hooking and fencing with his stick, frantic to gain position. Two minutes to go. Taking advantage of a loose ball, Ricky scored again.

'Come on, England!' shouted Rupert in exultation. 'You can do it.'

At the throw-in, Drew got it out and passed it to Ricky who took off on Kinta towards the posts. Whipped by Red, somehow Tero caught up with them and grimly Red closed in to ride Ricky off. Tero, like the good pony she was, dropped her shoulder and shoved, but Kinta was almost twice the size and strength of her and she took the weight of the bump, flying through the air and nearly going down on her fore-end. As Brigadier Hughie's binoculars shook in Perdita's frantically trembling hands, Tero's head seemed to be all white with lather. Her huge panic-stricken eyes rolled as Red yanked her round with all his strength to pick up the ball which Bart had backed upfield.

'Bastard, stop him,' screamed Perdita from the steps, but her cries were taken by the wind.

'Sit down,' yelled the crowd.

Oblivious, hands to her face, she watched, demented, as Red whipped Tero almost the length of the field, his spurs glinting in the sunshine as they stabbed at the little mare's sides like the needle of a sewing machine. At the last moment he passed to Angel.

Angel, in turn, waited until Drew was almost on him before flicking the ball back to Red who, as Tero strained herself for a final, gallant effort, leaned right out of the saddle, stroking the ball between the posts, almost as an afterthought. 13-9 on the bell.

The cheers ringing out politely for an American victory turned to cries of horror as, like some ghastly *danse macabre*, Tero appeared to lose all co-ordination and Red and she were both down rolling over and over. Red jumped to his feet. Somehow, lurching drunkenly, Tero staggered up, but she was heaving, shuddering and careering round totally disconnected, with all four legs sticking out straight.

'Christ, she's broken something,' said Dommie in horror.

'Heart attack,' snapped Rupert.

In an instant, Ricky and Drew had thrown their horses' reins to the Napiers and were running towards her, followed by David Waterlane, Jesus, the other umpire, and Angel. Reaching her first, Ricky gently pushed Tero to the ground where she quivered convulsively and went still.

Frozen with horror, Perdita at last found her feet and ran down the steps, jumping over the white fence, dropping Brigadier Hughie's binoculars, Angel's sombrero and her bag out of which spilled her passport, diary and all her make-up. With the wind in her screaming mouth, hair ribbing her blanched face, she raced down the pitch, past the stands, past horrified faces in the Royal Box, hurtling towards the little group, outstripping the vet's van bringing the screens, pummelling Ricky and Drew out of the way. 'Lemme get at her.'

Falling to her knees and gathering up the pony's head, which suddenly seemed as heavy as lead, she cradled it in her lap.

'Tero darling, for Christ's sake, you're going to be OK. You're just winded,' she sobbed.

But Tero's once-loving eyes were staring and glassy. 'Tero, Tero, please, please.' Tears ripping her apart, Perdita dropped her head down on the pony's, 'You've got to be all right. You're all I've got. I love you.'

'I'm afraid she's had it.' Desperately trying to keep his voice steady, Ricky put a hand on Perdita's head. She had loved Tero as he had loved Mattie.

Hovering in the background, holding the others' ponies, Bobby Ferraro and Shark instinctively removed their helmets in respect and sympathy. Red seemed quite unmoved, but Angel was less reticent. As the crowd, stunned and silent, watched the screens going round, he crouched down beside Perdita. Taking her in his arms, pulling her head on to his shoulder, crying himself, he gabbled half in Spanish.

'She die playing best game of 'er life. People will always remember her.'

'She can't be dead,' Perdita pleaded with the vet. 'Make her better.'

The vet shook his head. 'Can't, I'm afraid. Absolutely tragic, wonderful pony.'

Perdita went absolutely still. For a second she watched the blood from Red's spurs seeping down Tero's damp, speckled flank, staining the emerald grass.

'C'mon, Perdita,' said Red in a shaken voice, holding out his hand. 'It's only a pony. Could have happened at any time,' he added defensively.

Angel had to hold on to Perdita to stop her clawing Red's face.

'Murderer,' she hissed through white lips. 'You made me let you ride her. You flogged her to death.'

'Oh, pack it in, baby,' said Red, not unkindly.

'It's *you* I'm going to pack in,' sobbed Perdita hysterically, 'and I'm not a baby any more and not your baby ever again. I've grown up in the last five minutes.'

She had become so thin the huge sapphire slid off her finger easily. Flying through the air, the departing bluebird of her happiness, it crashed into Red's chest.

'Let her go. She's outlived her usefulness,' growled Bart, as, leaping to her feet, Perdita fled past the battlements of shocked faces, many of them in tears. Desperately looking for a way out, she paused in front of the Royal Box.

'He killed her,' she screamed. 'Did you see Red kill her?'

Security guards and officials moved forward solicitously, but Taggie Campbell-Black was too quick for them. Stepping over the little white fence, she ran forward, tugging off her crimson shawl, wrapping it round Perdita. 'I'm so sorry. She was such a sweet pony. You poor darling, please don't cry. You're coming home with us.'

'Who? What?' Perdita gazed at Taggie not registering.

'Rupert and I are taking you home,' explained Taggie, putting her arms round Perdita's shoulder.

But the next minute Rupert had joined them. Rage that England had blown the match and Venturer possibly millions, bracketed with an almost pathological loathing of Perdita, made him totally irrational.

'Leave her fucking alone,' he yelled at Taggie. 'She'll bite you like a rabid dog. You don't owe her anything.'

Taggie went very white, but stood her ground.

'Yes, we do,' she pleaded. 'Look what's happened to her. She *needs* you, Rupert.'

'I'll take her,' said Ricky, pushing his way through the fast-gathering photographers. Taking Perdita from Taggie, he turned to Rupert. 'When are you going to stop being so pig-headed and recognize your own child?'

It was part of the meticulous Guards Club organization that within seconds the afternoon was on course again. Ricky caused a few raised eyebrows and several accusations of bad sportsmanship when he missed the presentation. This was probably just as well because a jubilant Bart, making thumbs-up signs to Chessie in the stands, gloated so obscenely to the hovering press, predicting that America would annihilate England in the Westchester.

The object of all this conflict, the Coronation Cup, with

its crown-shaped lid, gold, writhing serpent handles and patterning of laurel leaves and strange faces, rose serenely from its green baize table.

'What a huge pot,' boomed Miss Lodsworth. 'Not Hughie's, that cup!'

Silently the British team lined up, long-faced, eyes cast down, utterly gloomy, a total contrast to the laughing, overjoyed Americans. Out came Princess Diana in a silk dress that seemed woven from light blue and dark blue delphinium petals, her high heels sinking into the grass. Up went Bart to get the Cup, which was so heavy that the Chairman of Cartier had to help the Princess hand it to him. Bart had to wipe away a tear as the band played the Stars and Stripes.

Bobby Ferraro was so overwhelmed to meet the Princess that he seized her hands and kissed them, to the delighted screams of the crowd. Angel followed Red. His Falklands banner was tucked inside his shirt, but he was so appalled by Red's callousness to Perdita and that Red could now joke and smile so devastatingly down at the Princess that he forgot to bring it out. Angel had planned so many gestures of revenge, but all the loathing he felt towards the British seemed to evaporate when he went up to get his clock in its red velvet box and gazed into the kind, blue eyes of the future Queen of England and saw the red roses in her faintly flushed cheeks. Her detective fingered his gun.

'Whaddid she say to you?' whispered Bart furiously when Angel finally floated back to the line-up.

'She say she very sorry my brozzer was keeled in Malvinas,' said Angel. 'She 'ear he was jolly good player like 'er 'usband, and Argentine pilots was very brave, and her brother-in-law had flown 'elicopters in the Malvinas and how worried his mother was about heem and she knew how much I must mees Pedro, and,' Angel added casually, 'you can stuff your bloody job.'

But Bart wasn't listening. 'Shut up,' he snapped. 'I'm going to be photographed with the Princess.'

There was some booing when Angel won the Pegasus Award, a soaring golden horse for the Player of the Match, but deafening cheers when, posthumously, Tero won Best Playing Pony.

'Keep it for Perdita,' said Red when his groom collected

the huge, dark maroon rug. 'It'll cheer her up when she cools down.'

They were outside the bar, surrounded by an admiring crowd, when Bart asked Angel, who was edging the top off a magnum of champagne with his thumbs, what he'd been about to say.

'I say you can stuff your bloody awful job,' said Angel politely. 'You don't treat players or ponies nice enough and you haff as you say outleeve the usefulness,' and he aimed the spurting fountain of champagne straight into Bart's absolutely furious brick-red face.

Back at Snow Cottage Daisy was still numb with misery over Sukey's revelations. She was glad Ricky was at the International. If he'd seen her reddened eyes, he might have got the truth out of her. In the afternoon she tried to pull herself together and clean the house. She even forced herself to go into Perdita's bedroom. The scarlet walls were bare since Perdita'd pulled down all Ricky's photographs. A bluebottle crashed exhausted against the window pane. Perhaps she ought to take a lodger, a nice girl student from the Agricultural College, to keep her company on the long, lone evenings ahead. She mustn't start crying again; there was enough damp in the cottage. It was a while before she heard the telephone. Crashing downstairs to get to it in time, she still prayed it might be Drew. But it was Taggie Campbell-Black. Her soft growling voice was unmistakable and she was stammering badly.

'I'm sorry to bother you, but Tero had a heart attack in the International and died.'

'Oh, God! Darling little Tero and poor, poor Perdita,' whispered Daisy aghast.

'She's broken it off with Red. Ricky's bringing her home to you. We would have brought her, but Rupert wasn't very keen, I do hope . . . ' Taggie was desperate to be fair and not disloyal to Rupert.

'Of course I understand. I'm so sorry. It's so kind of you to ring.'

Utterly desolate, Daisy collapsed on to a kitchen chair. In the middle of the table was a blue jug filled with meadowsweet. Nothing would ever grace a meadow more sweetly than Tero. Remembering the time the little pony had tiptoed into the kitchen during Christmas dinner and the delighted little nudges Tero used to give her in the back to ask for toast and Marmite, Daisy burst into tears.

But after a few minutes she was forced to pull herself together. Perdita was coming home: she must get ready. In panic and trepidation, she scurried round, hoovering frantically, finding hot water-bottles, making up Perdita's bed with clean sheets and all Violet's blankets and putting the jug full of meadowsweet on her bedside table.

There was Ethel barking and the sound of a car drawing up. Steeling herself for Perdita's Force Ten rage, Daisy came slowly downstairs, but all her fears vanished as a thin, grey ghost with anguished funeral-black eyes ran through the door and collapsed, sobbing hysterically, into her arms.

'Oh, Mummy, Mummy, how'll I ever survive without Tero?'

Relief turned to horror as Daisy felt how thin she was. Following her in, still in breeches, boots and his dark blue England shirt came Ricky, who put a reassuring hand to Daisy's cheek.

'She'll be OK. Give her a stiff drink. I'm going to ring the doctor.'

In the sitting room Perdita collapsed on the sofa. 'What'll happen to her now?' she asked wildly.

'She'll go straight to heaven, of course. No pony was gooder,' mumbled Daisy.

'But that's no good for her.' Perdita's sobs redoubled. 'The only heaven for Tero was where I was.'

James Benson, the smooth, private GP from Cheltenham, who'd been Rupert's and Ricky's doctor for years, was just going out to drinks but couldn't resist a chance to look at Rupert's supposedly illegitimate daughter, and her mother as well, and arrived in his Mercedes. She certainly had the Campbell-Black bone structure – rather too near the surface at the moment.

'She's seriously underweight and in shock,' he told Daisy and Ricky as he came downstairs. 'I've given her a shot and something to make her sleep, but I think we should keep her heavily sedated, slowly reducing the dose over the next few days. I should keep these locked up,' he added, as he handed Daisy anti-depressants and sleeping pills. 'One can't be too careful.'

Then, noticing Daisy's own pallor and reddened eyes, 'Are you going to be all right? I don't think you should be alone.'

'I'll look after her,' said Ricky.

'I'll just nip home and check the horses,' he said when James Benson had gone, 'and have a shower. I must smell like a rambler's crotch.'

Daisy flushed. 'You don't *have* to come back. I'll be fine.'

'Don't be silly. Don't do anything. I'll bring a take-away and some drink.'

'I'm honestly not hungry.'

'Don't be even sillier. You can't have two skeletons in one house.' Then, more gently, seeing Daisy's face quivering as she bent over the sink, 'It's all right, lovie, the worst's over. She's home.'

69

It has been said that the real *crime passionnel* occurs when the other woman finds out about the other woman. But Daisy didn't hate Bibi Alderton or any of Drew's alleged legions of girlfriends; she just felt terribly sad. She was also worried sick about Perdita. She had dreaded a return of the old Perdita, denuding her wardrobe and the fridge, pinching all the hot water and drowning the church bells at Eldercombe with her tantrums and her record player. But this new Perdita, who had no desire to eat, or dress up or wash her hair, or play music, worried her far more. She wasn't even interested in Ethel's puppies and just sat gazing at old photographs Daisy had kept of Tero, watching the August sunlight drying the dew on the cobwebs and listening to the urgent bustle of the Frogsmore under the house. Lucky Frogsmore to be so sure where it was going. Perdita had no idea.

Her eyes flickered with hope each time the telephone rang – but it was never Red, only endless press and television people, and all her temporary enemies: Dancer, David Waterlane, Bas, Brigadier and Mrs Hughie, even Miss Lodsworth, all of whom suddenly, after Tero's death, had become friends again. The twins sent a congratulations card from Deauville with the words 'Good Red-dance' inside. Chessie wrote a carefully worded note asking Perdita to tell Ricky to do better in the Westchester than the International. Sharon Kaputnik sent huge mauve chrysanthemums. Taggie, hearing Perdita wasn't eating, arrived with the most delicious smoked salmon quiche. Drew wrote to her from Sotogrande. Feeling awful, Daisy sneaked in when Perdita was asleep to see if she were mentioned in the letter, and felt even worse that she was not.

Realizing Perdita's utter despair, Daisy reproached her with nothing. Ricky had no such reticence. Ten days after Tero's death, he had an extremely humiliating lunch with Rupert and Bas in the Venturer boardroom. Fuelled by Château Lafitte, they had told him exactly what they thought of his performance in the International and that England had better bloody well get their act together before the Westchester. Seeking gentle comfort, Ricky dropped in on Daisy on the way home.

'I've just seen a rabbit in your vegetable patch,' he told her.

'Must have been on a suicide mission,' said Daisy.

Ricky smiled. The crows' feet light up his eyes like rays of the sun, thought Daisy. In an attempt to snap out of her depression, she had bought some very expensive paper and, having spread it out on the hayfield of a lawn, was trying to cut it into pieces. But even when she secured it with two books, it kept rolling up.

'I'll hold it,' said Ricky, taking the other end. Noticing a tawny-orange butterfly landing on the Michaelmas daisies, he added, 'Look, a painted lady.'

'I'm a painting not-quite-a-lady,' sighed Daisy.

The next minute Ethel emerged from the stream and, followed by her puppies, bounced across the paper leaving black footmarks everywhere.

'Oh Ethel, you stupid idiot,' screeched Daisy, then, as Ricky shoved Ethel out of the way, 'I'm sorry, darling. Good dog, I didn't mean to shout at you. I can paint on the other side.'

Amused, Ricky watched her cutting with the scissors. Her hair was piled on top of her head with a green ribbon, but escaping tendrils softened her sweating face. She was wearing red denim shorts, secured with a safety pin, and a purple and white striped bikini top, quite inadequate to contain her big, golden breasts, which, also shining with sweat, were flopping all over the place. She was so busy cutting, her pink tongue clenched between her teeth, that she bumped straight into Ricky.

'Oh, I'm sorry.' She blushed scarlet.

'I'm not complaining . . .'

'For Christ's sake!' It was Perdita at the side door, hysterical with rage. 'There's a note here that Bibi rang. Why the fuck didn't you wake me? You knew I wanted news of Red. How can you be so fucking stupid?'

'That's enough.' Getting to his feet, Ricky seized her by a chunk of her greasy, lifeless hair and, leading her into the sitting room, shut the door and pushed her down on the sofa.

'It's about time the pussy-footing stopped,' he said grimly.

Perdita opened her mouth to scream, her tongue so white, her teeth looked yellow by comparison.

'Shut up,' went on Ricky. 'Have you no idea how many people you've screwed up in the last year?'

'I didn't know Simpson Hastings was a journalist.'

'You could have denied what he wrote, instead of slagging Daisy off to the other papers. You never bothered to apologize afterwards. Daisy is one of the sweetest, kindest most gentle . . .'

'Are you after her then?'

'No, I am bloody not. I just know how different my life would have been if I'd had a mother like her.' For a moment he bleakly remembered childhood at Robinsgrove, alone in a huge, cold house with Herbert, an inconsolable widower, either silent or shouting.

'Have you ever thought what effect it had on Violet and Eddie? All their school chums nudging and giggling. No wonder Eddie ploughed Common Entrance.'

'He'd have ploughed it anyway, he's so thick,' stammered Perdita, fight seeping out of her like air out of a punctured tyre.

'Rubbish, and look how you fucked up Rupert and Taggie. It's not surprising Rupert loathes you. Trying to frame him in bed after he'd only been married for a year to the one true thing in his life. If you hadn't screwed up

Venturer he'd have been in England and never have let Taggie slip on the ice and miscarry, and if you hadn't dumped about the orgy the adoption societies would never have pulled the plug on them.'

Perdita gasped. 'I never knew about that. Taggie's been lovely to me.'

'That's because she's got a sweet, forgiving nature, unlike you, you vengeful bitch. Go away,' he snapped, seeing Daisy's worried, bright pink face appearing at the window.

'Don't kick her when she's down,' pleaded Daisy.

'I haven't finished,' said Ricky, shutting the window on her.

'I'm sorry,' whispered Perdita, who was now haggard and shaking. 'I didn't realize how awful I'd been.'

'And walking out on Apocalypse just as we were getting the team together, and that's nothing to what you did to Luke – short of making a wooden cross and banging the nails into his hands and feet.'

'I don't want to talk about Luke.' She was suddenly hysterical.

'Well, I do. Did you realize that when Hal Peters went bankrupt, he left Luke with all his medical bills and the bills for the yard, so he had to sell all his horses.'

'Even Fantasma?' The tears held back since the night she came home spilled over. 'Oh, no, he loved her as much as I loved Tero.'

'Far more,' said Ricky bleakly. 'He'd never have buggered off to Singapore without seeing she was OK.'

'Where's she gone?'

'Alejandro's.'

'Oh Christ, he's such a bastard to horses. Why didn't anyone tell me?'

'They didn't think you'd be interested.'

Outside they could hear the protests of the mower as Daisy forced it through the hayfield, then the manic rattle as it tried to swallow one of Ethel's shredded bones.

'Did Red know about Luke?'

'Course he did. You must know what a shit he is.'

You'd think he was even more of one, thought Perdita dully, if you'd caught him in bed with Chessie.

'I hate him so much for what he did to Tero,' she whispered, 'but I can't help still wanting him. It's horrible, like being in love with a husband who's battered your child to death. How can I ever get over him?'

'Work,' said Ricky, going towards the door. 'I want you up at the yard by seven o'clock tomorrow.'

'I'm not up to it,' said Perdita in panic.

'Don't be so bloody wet.'

'D'you think Red'll send Spotty back? I asked the twins to ask him. He must be so miserable missing Tero and me.'

'I'll see what I can do,' said Ricky, privately thinking Red was unlikely to relinquish a pony as good as Spotty with the Westchester coming up.

'Ring Chessie, will you?' asked Perdita with a sudden explosion of hostility. 'You expect me to get over Red. You didn't get over her.'

'We're not talking about me,' said Ricky.

Outside, blinking in the low-angled sunshine, Daisy was washing her car. She was straddled, panting, over the bonnet trying to clean the far side of the front window. Her left breast had escaped from her bikini. Moving to the right so as not to embarrass her, Ricky took the cloth from her.

'Shove over. I'll do it.'

The following week brought no news from either Red or Drew. Perdita was getting frantic about Spotty when, at twilight one warm evening, Angel suddenly rolled up in a new Aston Martin with a pig trailer rattling behind, out of which towered an outraged and decidedly car-sick Spotty.

'I keednap heem,' said Angel to an ecstatic Perdita, who instantly revived after a gruelling twelve-hour stint at Ricky's. 'Bart's in New York, Red in Sotogrande. Spotty was being flown back to the States for the Westchester tomorrow, so I steal heem. He not very pleased.'

Spotty, however, was so thrilled to see Perdita that he jumped out of the trailer while he was still tied up, nearly strangling himself. Having thanked Angel incoherently, Perdita leapt on Spotty's red-and-white back and roared him off up the ride to show Ricky.

'Ees better?' Angel asked Daisy.

'Better now she's seen you. She's been desperately down.'

'She can only go up now. Red is a preek,' said Angel.

681

The only time Daisy had seen Angel he'd been trying to murder Drew in the Queen's Cup, scowling under his bright blue hat, with expletives pouring from his pouting lips, and she had thought him the devil incarnate. But this soulful young man with the snake hips, the tumbled curls and the beautiful carved face, waving a bottle of Dom Perignon and a huge bunch of Régale lilies picked from Bart's garden, utterly disarmed her.

'For you,' he said. 'Perdita have enough presents.'

'You really shouldn't,' mumbled Daisy.

'I reech now,' said Angel simply.

As he opened the bottle, he explained that he was going to play for Victor Kaputnik for three times as much as Drew'd been getting and Victor, enraged at not winning any of the major cups in England, had asked Angel to find him twenty horses.

'I shall make ten thousand dollars on each horse.'

'Will you have to ride Sharon as well?' asked Daisy, holding out a glass as the cork flew out.

'No. She about to leave Veector for David Waterlane, so I have not to be service station.'

Daisy giggled. 'Is Veector furious?'

'Not at all. 'E find new bumbo. Ees easy when you're reech.'

'And is Drew upset he's been sacked?' It was like putting a bare foot on broken glass. 'Was he actually sacked?'

' 'E was,' said Angel with satisfaction. 'Slimy bastard.'

'I'll drink to that,' said Daisy, raising her glass. 'Shall we go into the garden?'

Outside it was all blue and misty, with the ravages of the last ten days' heatwave softened by the half-light and the snow-white flowers of the bindweed hanging luminous.

'They're supposed to stay open all night if there's a moon,' said Daisy. 'So life's good?'

'Life is so, so,' said Angel, then, succumbing to Daisy's sweet enquiring gaze, 'No, it's fucking 'orrible. Since Bibi walk out after 'Urlingham Ball, I am totally meeserable. She work too 'ard, I was angry, I play the pitch, so many other women, but it deedn't work and now she's 'aving an affair with Drew Benedict.'

'Oooh,' wailed Daisy. Then, at Angel's look of surprise: 'I'm just so sorry for you.'

'First 'e torture me in the Falklands, then 'e torture me in Eengland, and now in America. Smarmy Eenglish deekhead!' Angel filled up their glasses.

'He is, isn't he?' agreed Daisy. 'Why don't you ring her?'

'It would be weakness.'

'On the contrary, it would be very brave,' urged Daisy, thinking that if the smarmy English dickhead rang her now she would swim straight across the Atlantic to see him. 'I bet she's as miserable as you,' she went on. It wasn't because she wanted to break up Bibi and Drew, but because she couldn't imagine anyone loving Bibi more than this stormy, troubled boy.

They finished the champagne and started on Daisy's Muscadet. Angel, not a heavy drinker, couldn't manage to dial Bibi's number in Florida, so Daisy, who wasn't much soberer, had to do it for him and finally handed him over to Bibi's Filipino maid. Angel launched into a raging torrent of Spanish.

He was sober when he came off the telephone. All the bounce and bubble had gone out of him.

'Bibi 'as gone into the 'ospital for an operation, Carmen won't say what for, so I sack her.'

He tried Red in Sotogrande and Grace in Connecticut; they were both out. He was damned if he was going to ring Bart. The hospital would say nothing except that Mrs Solis de Gonzales had been admitted.

'At least she keep my name. I know eet ees abortion.' He had to count on his fingers three times to work it out. 'Could be my child. Could be Drew's.' His face blackened.

Thrusting a fistful of tenners into Daisy's hands to pay for the telephone calls, he was out of the house in an instant, storming off to Heathrow to catch the next plane to Palm Beach.

Sadly, tearfully, Daisy was finishing off the Muscadet and wishing someone had ever loved her as much as that when the telephone rang. Alas, it was not Drew but Sharon Kaputnik.

'Ay've just seen a fraightfully good paintin' of Chessie Alderton in the Noddy. Dave – we're together now – wants a portrait of me to grace the Long Gallery. Ay wonder if you'd oblaige, Daisy?'

*

Angel took a taxi from Miami Airport. His only luggage was his polo sticks, which he left as security for the driver, as he bounded out of the moving car and dived through a door marked Emergency into the hospital.

The receptionist, who was used to the histrionics and antics of South American polo players, had never seen one so fired up as Angel.

'There were flames coming out of his hair, the glass petition nearly melted,' she told her friend that evening. 'Then I had to explain to him that Mrs Gonzales had gone down to the theatre. Sister Passolini had just stopped by to say "Hi", when this fruitcake falls on her, grabs her by the throat, threatening strangulation if she doesn't take him to the theatre right away. I buzzed a guard, but this Argy KOed him and ran off before we could stop him.'

Loose in the hospital, Angel had raced past rest rooms and elevators and started throwing open doors. In the first room, he found a lot of fat women gazing at a nurse who was drawing a large carrot on the blackboard.

'You can't go in there,' screeched Sister Passolini who, rather taken by Angel, had caught up with him. 'That's Over-Eaters Anonymous. Or in there!' she added in horror, as Angel discovered a lot of sheepish-looking men gazing at another blackboard on which a male nurse with a beard was drawing an even bigger carrot, 'That's the Impotency Support Group. You won't find your wife in there, nor in Freedom from Smoking next door, and beyond that are all the Consultation Rooms. Try the next floor straight on to the end of the passage,' she whispered. 'You better beat it. The heavy brigade has just arrived.'

Chased by two more security guards, Angel sprinted up the stairs past a sign saying, 'Please be quiet, Theatre in Use'. To left and right he was faced with rows of pale grey doors. Seeing a blonde nurse passing by with a syringe in a kidney-shaped bowl, Angel grabbed her. 'My wife, Bibi Gonzales,' he panted. 'Please, she is somewhere in here.'

'Wasn't she Bibi Alderton?' asked the blonde nurse. 'Right? She's in there, first left after the swing doors, but they're operating. You can't go in.'

When the two guards tried to restrain him, Angel fobbed them off with fifty dollars each and started breaking up equipment. A trolley loaded with instruments went flying, a kidney machine crashed to the floor, a cupboard full of medicines was wrenched off the wall and went flying through the window. Angel was just kicking over an X-ray machine when a man in a green overall wearing a mask and rubber gloves backed out through the swing doors, crunching on the glass.

'What the hell's going on? I'm about to operate.'

Angel leapt on him, grabbing him by his gown, shoving him against the wall.

'You not going to abort my child,' he hissed.

'Don't be ridiculous,' squawked the surgeon. 'I don't do terminations.'

Angel's mad eyes were suddenly vast with fear. 'Ees more serious? She 'ave cancer? Oh, my poor Bibi.'

'For goodness sake, cool it,' said the blonde nurse in amusement. Then, ignoring the frantic signals of the surgeon: 'Mrs Gonzales is only having a nose job.'

If she'd hoped to placate Angel, she was quite wrong. Even more incensed, he stormed into the theatre, where Bibi, pale as her white nightgown, like a corpse in a morgue, lay on the operating table, surrounded by people in masks. Woosy from her pre-med, she was not too far gone to whip off the disfiguringly ugly bathcap.

'What zee fuck?' howled Angel. Then, stopped in his tracks: 'What 'ave you done to your beautiful 'air?'

For, spilling over the white pillow, instead of the thick, shaggy, dark red curls was a long, sleek, totally straight, blonde bob.

'Ees thees what Drew Benedict like?' said Angel furiously. 'He may prefer blondes, but 'e is no gentleman.'

Bibi burst into tears. 'I love you so much. I figured if I had long blonde hair and a tiny nose like all the other polo wives, you might love me, too.'

Angel gave a groan. 'I loff you as you are!' Then, running a finger down her nose: 'She is the theeng I like most about you. You are most beautiful girl I haff known. You geeve me the duck bumps. I haff nevair been more meeserable in my life. When you ran away, I theenk I die.'

And, seizing her hands, he covered them with kisses, and then he kissed her lips. There wasn't a dry eye above the masks except for those of the plastic surgeon who was incensed at losing such a rich customer, and who had been intending to remodel Bibi's entire body over the next few years.

'I weel keel Drew Benedict,' said Angel as he paused for breath.

'Oh, please don't,' protested Bibi. 'It was hopeless with him. I thought about you the whole time and how much I loved you.'

'I 'urt you so bad,' moaned Angel. 'I was jealous of your work, I 'ate being a kept boy.'

'You won't be much longer,' said Bibi. 'If Dad goes belly-up, I won't be an heiress any more.'

'You won't be anyway, after paying for all the equipment Rudolph Valentino's just smashed up,' said the plastic surgeon nastily, and he was even crosser when Angel just swept Bibi up and carried her out to the still-waiting taxi, banging on the door of the Impotency Support Group, yelling, 'Keep eet up, two three four,' as he went by.

70

Heeding Ricky's advice, Perdita buried herself in work, standing in for his grooms when they took holidays before the Westchester, playing in low- and medium-goal matches. But she was still desperately pale, thin and unnaturally subdued.

Nor did the situation improve when Violet and Eddie returned from staying with schoolfriends not prepared to be as forgiving as Daisy and stepping warily round their perfidious sister. Soon they were at each other's throats, all three thinking they had exclusive rights to the television, the bathroom and Violet and Perdita the use of Daisy's rickety Volkswagen. Matters grew worse when Violet got straight As in her four A levels, was rewarded with money to buy a car by a delighted Biddy Macleod, and Violet's schoolfriends rang the whole time comparing results and having endless discussions as to what they were going to do in their year out.

Eddie, blissfully unaware that Ricky had pulled strings with the muscular energy of a bell ringer to get him into Bagley Hall, a nearby co-ed, was half-terrified, half-excited at the prospect of boarding with girls in September. He had now reached adolescence, loving and co-operative one moment, moody, withdrawn and resentful the next.

There were compensations. Suddenly the small boy, who Daisy'd had to threaten within an inch of his life to pick up a toothbrush, was cleaning his teeth three times a day and bathing and washing his hair more often than Violet and Perdita. When he wasn't counting his spots and perfecting a sexy pout in the mirror, he poured over *Penthouse* and *The F-Plan Diet*. Soon envelopes addressed to body-building firms were lying around in the hall.

To add to Daisy's problems, the puppies were crapping everywhere and chewing up everything and Sharon Kaputnik had to be painted. Not wanting to trouble Ricky or subject him to constant sexual harassment by painting Sharon in his attic, Daisy used the sitting room at Snow Cottage. This meant that every afternoon Sharon rose like Page Three incarnate from a sofa lined with Jaffacake crumbs, chewed crayon and puppy fur, surrounded by a sea of Coke tins, beer cans, mugs, kicked-off shoes and overflowing ashtrays, while being eyed by Eddie as he pretended to watch programmes on re-upholstering and re-runs of *Falcon Crest*.

Nor was Daisy any longer buoyed up by the prospect of seeing Drew again when the holidays were over. She found her thoughts turning more and more to Ricky, and how awful it would be when he finally went back to Chessie. He'd taken to dropping in late in the evening, often bringing a take-away, and was so wonderful at separating and shutting up the children.

'If you'd ever umpired the Napiers, Bart Alderton and the O'Briens in the same match, you wouldn't have any problems.'

'Unfortunately, one can't send one's children off for arguing,' sighed Daisy.

By the middle of August everyone was revving up for the Westchester, or West-Chessie-ter, as Daisy called it to herself. The English team had been confirmed: Ricky as captain, Drew and the Napiers; the same as the International, with the twins as reserve. Not an exciting team, but a solid one. Ricky detested the Napiers, but they were both nines and, under pressure from the BPA, he couldn't see any way not to select them. He found the prospect deeply depressing, particularly as the very few practice matches they were able to organize were incredibly acrimonious. Rupert, who had high-handedly appointed himself unofficial team manager, because Venturer's stake was so vast and because 'although I don't know that much about polo, I know all about winning', was all too ready to put his show-jumping boot in and tell the players exactly where they were going wrong.

The ponies were due to fly out to California in mid-September to acclimatize them for the match which would begin the first week in October. With an eye to the extra buck, however, the Napiers and Drew had defiantly flown their horses out the third week in August to play in Oakbrook and in the US Open. This, as Ricky furiously pointed out, was the last way to rest them before the Westchester.

A week later Ricky got a telephone call from Charles Napier. His voice had the oily ingratiating timbre of a reporter about to ask a husband what he feels about his wife shoving off.

'Ben and I want to level with you, Ricky. Frankly, we were fucked by the International. Five of our best horses were screwed up, not to mention Ben's cracked collar-bone and my broken finger.'

'So?' said Ricky curtly.

'That's bad enough, but the Westchester's a different ball game.'

'In what way? It involves four people on either s-s-side trying to hit the ball through each other's goal posts. Seems remarkably similar to me.'

Charles wasn't to be deflected. 'There'll be three matches, three times as gruelling and much tougher opposition.'

'It might help,' said Ricky acidly, 'if you rested your horses instead of carting them all over America.'

'If you want the bloody truth,' Charles dropped any attempt at amiability, 'Ben, Drew and I are totally pissed off with putting ourselves and our ponies on the line for the honour of our country. Only women and horses work for nothing. We're professionals.'

'You could have fooled me.'

'Don't be so bloody sarky. We're going on strike. None

of us will play unless we get thirty grand each and a share of the TV action.'

Ricky sighed. Knowing there was absolutely no way Venturer or the big British and US sponsors could pull out at this stage, the Napiers and Drew, feeling they could easily afford the extra cash, were plainly determined to force his hand.

'You still with me, Ricky?'

'I was temporarily speechless. Have you bastards no idea of the honour of playing in the W-w-westchester? Have you no sense of history?'

'Just to bring back some stupid pot your ancestors couldn't manage to hang on to. Ten losses on the trot, wasn't it? Well, we don't want to make it eleven.'

'Look,' Ricky was trying not to lose his temper, 'I'll try and get you ten grand each, but not a cent more. Venturer can't afford it.'

'Surely Rupert could take out a mortgage on his fifth house?'

'Let me talk to Drew,' said Ricky grimly.

There was another long pause. Ricky could almost hear the sweat bubbling on the palm of Charles's great, red, meaty hand as he clapped it over the receiver. After an age Drew came on.

'You've spent nearly thirty grand on this telephone call already,' snapped Ricky. 'I thought you were supposed to be a friend of mine.'

'I am. I also have a living to make.'

'Bullshit. You're just fucking greedy. You wouldn't expect to be paid for the Olympics.'

'I would if I were likely to screw up my best horses.'

Then Ben Napier seized the telephone.

'Thirty grand or no deal,' he said roughly. 'And that'll only replace a couple of ponies.'

'OK,' said Ricky. 'I'm dropping the lot of you.'

'You can't,' said Ben, outraged. 'We've flown our ponies over specially.'

'To play in the Open. Go screw yourselves.'

'The BPA will go apeshit.'

'Good,' said Ricky and hung up. He didn't think he'd ever been so angry in his life.

*

He was unprepared for the storm which broke over his head. Venturer and the BPA went into shock horror to a man and called an emergency meeting in London the next day.

'What the hell are you playing at?' howled Rupert. 'They can't have any television rights, but we could easily have raised another ninety thousand pounds. That's peanuts. We could even stretch to one hundred and fifty thousand.'

'It's immaterial,' said Ricky wearily. 'I was always worried about this team. There were too many chiefs and not an Indian in sight. I could never have made it gel.'

'Remember in Karachi, we had an Indian chappie, brilliant player, but hopeless if you gave him any responsibility,' mumbled Brigadier Hughie. 'Perhaps you'd feel happier if Charles was captain, Ricky.'

'I don't take orders from gorillas,' said Ricky. 'If you don't let me pick my own team, I'll drop out.'

David Waterlane, who had a bad back from an excess of Sharon-shagging, hit the roof. 'Don't be bloody silly. Who the hell did you have in mind?'

'Seb and Dommie.'

'Ludicrously inexperienced,' snapped David, throwing his cigar butt at the half-open window and missing. 'And far too erratic.'

'Mike Waterlane,' added Ricky with the faintest smile.

'Mike!' said David dumbfounded. 'D'you think he's up to it?'

'Easily,' said Ricky. 'I've played all summer with the three of them and,' scowling round the room, defying anyone to challenge him, 'I'm going to take Perdita Macleod as reserve.'

Leaving the meeting in uproar, Ricky drove to Rutshire Polo Club where the last match of the season – always an elegiac occasion – was taking place. It had been raining. As he arrived, the drying boards were shimmering in the sinking sun, which was also warming the feathering willowherb. The huge, domed trees round the pitches were echoed by the grey-blue clouds of a Constable sky as a red tractor chugged back and forth weighed down by bales of straw. Perdita, her hair now shoulder-length and in a net, was watching the second match with Dommie and Mike Waterlane, who had a silver cup under his arm.

Little Chef bounced ahead to greet his friend Decorum, the bull terrier, who grinned down at him, triangular eyes genial, tail going like a *vivace* metronome as he pirouetted on stiff, poker legs.

'How did you do?' asked Ricky.

'Buried them 17-1,' said Dommie.

'Thank Christ for that.'

'Corporal won Best Playing Pony. We're thinking of promoting him,' crowed Dommie.

Seb lay stretched out on the bonnet of his Porsche, his head on the windscreen, his newly washed hair flopping. He had changed into white jeans and a pale blue bomber jacket and had a glass of whisky in one hand and his portable telephone in the other. He opened a bloodshot eye and grinned at Ricky.

'*Ciao*, sweetheart. I'll meet you at Annabel's around ten. I'll book. Hi, where've you been?' he asked Ricky as he switched off the telephone.

'Reselecting the team for the Westchester.'

'Who's in it?'

Ricky told them.

'Yippee,' yelled Dommie, chucking a ball twenty feet in the air.

'Good Lord, I must ring Daddy,' said Mike Waterlane, going as scarlet as the Virginia creeper now smothering the clubhouse.

Perdita, turning to stone, always became most angry when she was frightened. 'I won't go. I can't believe it. I'm not up to it. Whose bloody stupid idea was it to select me?'

'Mine,' said Ricky calmly.

'But I'll have to play against Red.'

'Stop over-reacting,' said Seb. 'You're only reserve. We're much too tough to get injured.'

'Not unless you get a few early nights,' said Ricky, removing Seb's whisky and emptying it on to the grass. 'Annabel's is going to miss you, Seb.'

To the shock horror of Venturer and the BPA were added next day the furious protests of the British and American sponsors and the American Polo Association, who all felt Ricky was making a total mockery of the Westchester. The thirty-five-goal English team had struggled in the

International. How did Ricky imagine he could field a bunch of babies with a team aggregate of twenty-six against the might of the Americans in their own country? The media were equally outraged.

'*Cannon fodder*,' said a huge headline in the *Daily Express*. '*How can David without a sling beat Goliath armed with an exocet? It'll be annihilation*.'

Frantic preparations ensued in the next week. Good horses about to be turned away had to be wheedled out of other owners and flown over to America for Mike and Perdita in case she had to play. Longingly she thought of the six ponies Red had given her. He'd probably be riding them against England. At least she still had Spotty, but he was in a frightful temper, as was Wayne. Announcing that they were both much too fat and that Argentines won matches because their horses carried no spare flesh, Rupert had put both ponies on a rigorous diet. Much to Ricky's irritation, Rupert was in fact supervising the diets of all the ponies. He also insisted that all the team took the equivalent of a Marine's assault course to get fit, but even he couldn't make Ricky go out jogging.

Hell, thought Perdita a day later, as she gritted her teeth to stop herself crying, is being coached by Rupert Campbell-Black. God, he was sarcastic as he rode up and down, blue eyes narrowed, whip tapping his boots, not missing a trick, the nerve-gas hostility in no way abated, the drawling commentary more bitchy than ever.

'I see Ricky's given you a second chance,' had been his first bleak words to her. 'I certainly wouldn't.'

For two chukkas, each time anyone missed a ball or a stab at goal it was greeted with sighs of 'Oh dear, a Perdita pass again'. After shouting at her every time she picked up her stick, he called her over.

'Stylistically you're not bad,' he said softly. 'You've got most of the shots.'

Perdita looked up in amazed relief, a compliment at last.

'It's a pity,' Rupert raised his voice, 'you're so fucking useless at selecting which shot and when.'

Perdita went crimson.

Two minutes later he was yelling, 'For Christ's sake, hook him, Perdita,' as Seb scorched towards goal. Then as Seb scored, 'What's the point of hooking air? Why the fuck didn't you catch up with him?'

'I was twenty yards behind when he started off,' stammered Perdita.

'Then you catch up with him. You're very deceptive. You're even slower than you look.'

Then, after she'd let Seb through a third time, 'Come here, Perdita.' Oh God, how she dreaded that soft, bitchy, upper-class ring. 'This is a pony,' Rupert touched Spotty's neck with his whip. 'Rather an unattractive one, admittedly. These are his legs, these are your legs You're supposed to use them to make him carry you upfield as fast as possible. This is a whip.' For a second he banged his whip against hers like a fencer starting a duel. 'I want you to use it. I want your ponies collapsing when they come off the field.'

For a second Perdita watched a gull drifting across the khaki woods. The Argentine word for gull was *Tero*.

'Like Tero collapsed,' she screamed, suddenly exploding like a pressure cooker.

'If need be, but they won't collapse if you get them fit enough. That pony is still too fat.'

'He is *not*, and he's *not* ugly.'

'Shut up,' said Rupert coldly. 'If you were as quick on the field as you are with your temper, we might get somewhere.'

Perdita burst into tears.

'Oh dear,' sighed Rupert. 'I've always believed a woman's place was in the home, or on her back, or regrettably in the shops, but *not* on the polo field. Ricky's got sprinklers to water this pitch. He doesn't need you.'

Dommie, who had a softer heart than Seb, leapt to Perdita's defence.

'I've known you all my life, Rupert, and I've always liked you, but I never realized you could be quite such a shit.'

'Well, now you know, Sunshine,' snapped Rupert.

The trouble was that Rupert was right. He had a marvellous eye, miraculous anticipation, and saw exactly where they were making mistakes. Every time he picked up a polo stick it looked right. Every time he got on the most refractory pony, it came together.

No-one was spared. He made Ricky cut down drastically on his bad habits, all those accumulated short cuts which great players resort to. Gradually Ricky straightened his swing, found he was hitting the ball twice as far and learnt to use his team again.

71

Feeling a slight chill in the air as the evenings drew in, Daisy brought crumpets, bramble jelly and a large fruitcake from the village shop. To cheer herself up she tried to count all the nice things about winter, but only got as far as roaring fires and being able to cover one's spare tyres with huge jerseys. Then she remembered what a bore it was sweeping out the ashes in the morning!

She was utterly fed up with the constantly ringing telephone. The press were on the whole time trying to get Perdita's reaction to being picked for the Westchester, to seeing Red again and to being coached by Rupert, who still wouldn't admit paternity. Perdita and Violet had had a frightful row that morning because Perdita had pinched Violet's car without asking, smashing a sidelight and leaving hay and sweet-papers all over the floor. Eddie's thumping great crush on Sharon showed no sign of abating and he was not at all pleased to be joined by Violet's friends from the school rugger team, wandering round in boxer shorts showing off Portugal-tanned bodies.

'I could eat them alaive at that age,' said Sharon.

In retaliation, Eddie had borrowed a tenner off Daisy to buy stationery for school and instead came back with a bottle of *crème de menthe* for Sharon which he insisted on serving her *frappé* and sitting chatting to her all afternoon so she never sat still.

'We didn't have girls at my prep school,' he was now telling her, 'as we didn't really need them, but we've got fifty per cent at Bagley Hall, which is OK, as it'd be awful if there weren't enough to go round.'

'Oh look, there's Mrs Thatcher on the telly. What a smart blue costume,' said Sharon. 'She always looks well turned-out, doesn't she?'

'I admire her,' said Eddie reflectively, 'but I wouldn't like her as a mother.'

I suppose that's something, thought Daisy, mixing white with burnt umber to get the colour of Sharon's nipples.

In the corner two puppies were now having a tug of war with a pink-and-black scarf.

'Have some more *crème de menthe*,' said Eddie.

'Ay shall be tiddly,' said Sharon with a giggle as he filled her glass.

'Eddie darling, do rescue that scarf,' said Daisy. 'I'm sure it's Perdita's.'

'I don't care,' said Eddie stonily. 'I hate my sister,' he added to Sharon.

'How's she getting on being coached by Rupert Campbell-Black? There's an attractive man.'

Eddie's face fell. 'He's depressingly sexist,' he said disparagingly. 'Not that I blame him for rubbishing my sister. I would, if she wasn't so strong.'

There was a bang on the door, a bark from Ethel and in came Ricky.

'Christ,' he said taking in the chaos.

'Ricky!' said Sharon excitedly. 'Come in. Don't be shay, although I love shay men. Come and tell us what you think of Daisy's portrait.'

Stepping over several chewing puppies, Ricky looked at the painting.

'It's very good,' he said in surprise. 'Extremely good. Rubens crossed with Renoir.' Then, looking at Daisy's exhausted face: 'Come on, Sharon, Daisy's done enough for one day.'

Sharon leant forward, giving Ricky the benefit of her cleavage to look at her diamond watch: 'Heavens, taime does flay. Can I borrow your bathroom, Daisy? Goodness me,' – swaying as she got up, she deliberately clutched on to Ricky's arm – 'I really do feel a bit tiddly.'

Having toasted some crumpets and put them with the fruitcake and the tea things on a tray, Daisy suggested that they went in the garden as it was the tidiest place.

'You're sweet.' Ricky took the tray from her. 'But I

honestly don't want anything to eat. Have you had a ghastly week?'

'Pretty standard,' said Daisy. 'I really must paint that bench before winter.'

Next minute Violet erupted into the garden in an uncharacteristically bad temper. 'Fucking hell, Mum, you've shrunk my olive-green jersey. Oh hi, Ricky.' She grabbed a crumpet.

She was followed by Eddie in an even worse mood.

'I was cleaning out my fish tank and Perdita's emptied her ashtray into it. I'm leaving home.' He snatched up two crumpets.

A second later Perdita put her head out of her bedroom window. 'Sharon fucking Kaputnik's locked herself in the bathroom, and I've got to go out.'

'I don't want to hear,' said Ricky firmly. 'Go inside all of you, and tidy up the kitchen, and then the sitting room. I've never seen such a tip, and it's all your junk. Go on, bugger off.'

'Ay, ay, sir,' said Eddie, pinching another crumpet.

'Oh, thank you,' sighed Daisy. 'You're so wonderful.'

Blushing, Ricky said he'd found homes for two of the puppies and he'd take one himself.

'Oh, how lovely. That only leaves one. Perhaps we could keep it.' Rubbing buttery fingers on her jeans, Daisy started to sew nametapes on Eddie's school socks. Ricky watched her.

It was a beautiful evening. The sun was setting behind the wood. Arrows of migrating birds, flown in from the sea to scavenge in the newly ploughed fields, were following a hyacinth-blue-and-crimson air balloon drifting across the softest, pink-flecked sky. In the garden red berries glowed on the honeysuckle and sapphire spears of delphiniums, pink Japanese anemones and pale roses crowded the flower-beds, not as vigorous as at their first flowering, but sweeter.

'Is Eddie being a pain too?' asked Ricky.

'Not really. Adolescence is so awful.' Almost as bad as being in one's late thirties, thought Daisy sadly. 'His uniform's being a bit of a bore. In the old days I just went and bought it and the only problem was money. Now he's worse than Beau Brummel about the relative tightness and length of his trousers.' Looking up from her nametapes,

Daisy giggled, 'And having witnessed the rejection of every slip-on shoe in Rutminster, I know exactly how Prince Charming must have despaired at the thought of finding the owner of the glass slipper.'

She broke off the thread and picked up a pair of rugger shorts.

'I'll take him to London tomorrow,' said Ricky, cutting himself a piece of fruitcake. 'I've got to pick up the England shirts from Harrods. I'll get him some trousers and some shoes.'

'Oh no, it'd be such a bore for you,' said Daisy.

'I'd like his company. You know how I loathe London.'

Lucky Eddie, thought Daisy.

'Perdita's not the only one who's lost too much weight around here,' said Ricky, handing Daisy the last crumpet.

Daisy shook her head.

'A handsome husband and a thousand a year,' said a voice. 'Ay'll have it,' and Ricky and Daisy were enveloped in a cloud of Chanel Number 5 as Sharon stretched out a braceleted hand to help herself, pressing her splendid breasts against Ricky's shoulders as she did so.

'You'd certainly make the handsomest husband in the world, Ricky. Do drop in on us sometime.'

'She's definitely having an affair with David Waterlane,' said Ricky after she'd gone. 'He always buys Chanel Number 5 for all his mistresses.'

'She says she's going to marry him,' said Daisy.

In the darkening trees the pigeons were fluttering and cooing. Iceberg roses and white phlox grew more luminous, night-scented stock replaced Chanel Number 5.

'It's so beautiful here,' said Daisy, who was getting cold, but didn't want to break the magic of the moment. 'How's Perdita getting on with Rupert?'

'Not brilliantly,' said Ricky carefully, not wanting to hurt Daisy. 'Rupert's so desperately protective of Taggie, he can't really bring himself to forgive her, even though Taggie has. But he's getting results. He's sharpened up her game two hundred per cent.'

'That's mine,' he added quickly, as one of Ethel's puppies tottered out, speckled as a seal, eyes frowsty with sleep, patrician except for one ear pointing up and an irredeemably curly tail. He picked the puppy up. 'He's just like Little Chef.'

Watching him gently stroking the pink-and-speckled belly, Daisy was appalled to find herself longing to swap places with the puppy. She must get a grip on herself.

'How's the Westchester going?'

Ricky sighed. 'I feel as though the entire contents of your septic tank has been tipped over my head. The BPA and the APA have both been written me threatening letters and ring constantly. The American sponsors are collectively threatening to sue. The Prince rang up and said Hughie had actually had the cheek to ring him and advise him not to fly over to present the cup, as it would be so embarrassing for him to witness a bloodbath. Fortunately the Prince told Hughie to get stuffed, and that if he's said he'll go to something he always goes. Cartier, Asprey, Tiffany and Dunhill have all written complaining. I wrote back saying I would not be dictated to by a bunch of watchmakers in Mayfair.'

'Quite right,' said Daisy indignantly. 'Oh ye of little faith.' She also noticed that he hardly stammered at all now when he talked to her. The moon was rising huge and pink, bats and swallows dived, owls hooted, the sky had darkened to lilac in the west. What Ricky hadn't told Daisy about was the brief bitter note Chessie had sent him: 'I thought you wanted me back. If you insist on playing with schoolboys, I was obviously wrong.'

Realizing Daisy was shivering, he had just taken his coat off and put it round her shoulders when Eddie appeared in the doorway, wiping imaginary sweat from his forehead. 'We've tidied the whole house, Mum. We've even made Ethel's basket.'

'Good boy,' said Ricky.

'Can I have a beer?'

'Later,' said Ricky. 'If you come into Rutminster with me, we'll get an Indian.'

It was the eve of the team's departure. Having finally got Eddie off to school and finished Sharon's portrait, Daisy sent Perdita up to London with money to buy some clothes for America.

Perdita – whose self-confidence seemed to have been finally smashed by Rupert – was in turmoil because she might have to play and would certainly be seeing Red again. Having made heroic attempts to cheer Perdita up, Daisy was overwhelmed with despair. Tomorrow Ricky was off to America, and inevitably out of her life. I must not hate Chessie, she told herself sternly, I am very lucky my children and I are not dying of hunger in Ethiopia, my entire family haven't been wiped out in an earthquake or a volcano and this is the first time I've had access to my own bathroom in nine weeks. God, I look awful.

The only answer, in case Ricky dropped in that evening, was to wash her hair and have a bath. She had just emerged pink and Je Reviens-scented, with legs and armpits shaved and was combing out her wet hair when she heard Ethel barking and a hammering on the front door. Wrapping herself in a big dark-green towel, she ran downstairs and her heart failed. For there, beachboy-blond and absolutely black-brown, stood Drew.

'Darling Daisy!' He put the inevitable bottle of Moët on the kitchen table. 'You've no idea how I've missed you.'

Daisy just stared at him. She'd dreamt of this moment for so long, and she'd planned to be distant and icily disapproving because he'd forced Ricky's hand over the Westchester, but it was hard to be cool when you were hot and lobster-pink from the bath. And Drew looked so handsome and was in such high spirits. Inevitably the conversation turned in moments to polo.

'Boy, am I glad to be out of the Westchester,' he said, tearing the gold paper off the cork. 'It is going to be a ghastly embarrassment to the English. They're having great trouble selling tickets. Americans love American victories, but they like a decent tussle first.'

'Ricky's playing,' said Daisy defensively.

'Maybe, but it'll be like Canute trying to stop the tide and not even bothering to put on gumboots. The twins are wildly erratic and hopeless in defence, which is all they'll have to do. Mike's a dolt.' He paused. 'D'you think Ricky'll ever speak to me again?'

As he went automatically to the right cupboard to get down two glasses, Daisy noticed he had US Open printed on the back of his bomber jacket.

'If he wins, he might,' said Daisy reprovingly. 'He's had so much flak recently.'

'Just because he's got this *idée fixe* about getting Chessie back. Talk about ex-appeal.'

Daisy didn't laugh. 'How's Sukey?'

'Really well. I've got a new American patron for Palm Beach next year, which means mega-bucks.'

'Is he nice?'

'Better than Victor. Christ, I'm relieved to be shot of him.'

At the pop of the champagne cork, Ethel started barking and all the puppies woke up and started wandering round the kitchen.

'Are any of the children at home?' asked Drew casually, as he filled the glasses. Then, glancing through into the sitting room, gave a start as he caught sight of Sharon's finished portrait still on Daisy's easel.

'Christ – that's good. I thought it was the old bat for a second. You really are getting better and better.'

Reluctant to be won over, Daisy followed Drew into the sitting room for a better look and had great difficulty stopping him drawing a moustache on Sharon.

'Well, at least let me draw a tiara on her bush. She's going hammer and hot tongs for David Waterlane at the moment.'

'He kept ringing for her,' said Daisy. 'At first I thought it was you using a false name.'

She shivered and shut the window. 'I must go and get dressed.'

'Why bother?' Drew refilled her glass. 'I'd forgotten how beautiful you are.'

'Evidently,' said Daisy, unable to keep the acid out of her voice. 'Was Sharon amazing in bed?'

Drew shrugged. 'I wouldn't know. You know my heart belongs to you.'

'My true love hath my heart, and I have about one twentieth of his,' said Daisy, and buoyed up by champagne, told him about Sukey's visit.

'That's a pack of lies,' said Drew, gazing into her eyes with that unshiftingly honest look that convinced Daisy he wasn't telling the truth. 'I promise you. I can only assume she got wind of us and decided to spin a story like that to put the boot in.'

'Sukey isn't that subtle or conniving,' said Daisy. 'She

700

was absolutely devastated, and so touchingly grateful that I'd listened to her, I felt an absolute bitch.'

'Honestly, don't,' begged Drew, starting to laugh. 'And as for that ludicrous fantasy about Bibi Alderton. That consisted of one lunch at the Four Seasons in New York. Christ, the food's good! Bibi started crying about Angel. I put my arm round her to comfort her and unfortunately we were seen by Sukey's most indiscreet chum, who leapt for the telephone. The only woman I've ever adored since I was married, probably ever, is you.'

'What about all those valentines?'

'I can't help it if people send me valentines. I bet Red Alderton gets them by the sack. Catch!' He threw the half-full bottle at her. Stretching out both hands, Daisy fumblingly caught it, spilling champagne all over her breasts. The dark green towel slid to the floor.

'God, you're pretty.' Drew moved forward. 'You're the one who should be on Page Three.'

Daisy didn't believe a word Drew had said about Bibi, but she was so suicidal over Ricky, and Drew looked so handsome, and it felt so nice having the champagne licked off her breasts and it was such a relief for a change being caught bathed and shaven and with clean hair that they ended up in bed.

Having supervised the packing of everything for the horses, having started packing for himself, trying to avoid Little Chef's reproachful gaze, and suddenly feeling like a small boy about to go back to prep school, Ricky decided to drop in on Daisy. Ethel didn't even bark because she knew him so well.

Finding Drew's car outside and a three-quarters empty bottle of Moët on the kitchen table and two of Ethel's puppies joyfully demolishing one of Drew's shoes, Ricky drove off in a fury.

An hour later Drew rolled up asking if he could borrow a pair of shoes.

'Talk about being caught on the hop,' he said, hopping after Ricky into the kitchen.

Ricky slammed the kitchen door and shut the window so that the grooms, who had been amazed by the foulness of his temper for the last hour, couldn't listen in.

'How long have you been screwing Daisy?'

'I don't see what the hell it's got to do with you,' said Drew calmly.

'I am her landlord.'

'She's at least six years older than you. She can do what she likes, Dick.'

'Don't call me that,' howled Ricky. 'Daisy had a bloody awful marriage. She's just getting over it and getting her career together. The l-l-last thing she needs is some hole-in-the-corner affair which could easily end in a m-m-messy divorce. She needs a proper relationship.'

'Relationships that pass in the night,' sighed Drew.

'Don't be fucking frivolous. With someone who's free to look after her.'

'Like you I suppose. I've always thought you had the hots for her.'

'I have not,' said Ricky coldly.

'Oh, we all know your heart belongs irrevocably to Chessie, so stop snarling like a guard dog in the manger and give me a drink.'

Little Chef whined querulously, unnerved by the shouting. A new moon the colour of unsalted butter was untangling itself from the racing-fox weathercock over the stables. Furiously clashing decanters, Ricky asked how long it had been going on.

'Nearly three years.'

'Three years,' said Ricky, utterly aghast. 'How often d'you see her?'

'Whenever I can get away from Sukey and Daisy's bloody children aren't hanging around murdering each other. No ice, please.'

'You're a disgrace,' roared Ricky. 'No, not you boy,' he added, gently stooping to stroke Little Chef who was shivering with terror.

'It's absolutely no business of yours,' protested Drew.

'I only happen to be captaining the Westchester team — thank Christ I dropped you. I would now, if I hadn't — in which Daisy's daughter may well have to play. Perdita's impossibly near the edge at the moment. She's never been able to accept Daisy's sexuality. If she finds out about you two, she'll go through the roof.'

'The leaking roof,' corrected Drew. 'You should really

fix that before winter comes, particularly in the bedroom. Talk about raindrops falling on one's cock.'

'Stop taking the piss,' yelled Ricky. 'You ought to pack her in. It can't lead anywhere.'

'It's not meant to. I can't divorce Sukey. That dog must be the father of Ethel's puppies. It just gives Daisy and me an enormous . . . ' he lingered over the word mockingly, 'amount of pleasure, and you've completely drowned that whisky. Christ, it's worse getting a drink here than the bar at the club.'

'What happens if Sukey finds out?'

'She won't if you lend me a pair of shoes.'

'I hope they cripple you,' snarled Ricky.

He was insane with rage, but he decided not to say anything to Daisy, who somehow managed not to cry when she and Little Chef bade him and Perdita goodbye and good luck the following morning. Just as they were leaving, Perdita ran back and hugged her mother tightly.

'I love you, Mum. I'm sorry I've been such a bitch.'

But, as the car crunched away over the conkers and acorns that littered the drive, Daisy didn't think she'd ever been more unhappy.

'I wish we could climb into his suitcase and go too,' she said to a drooping, desolate Little Chef. 'You could nip Chessie's perfect ankles for me.'

Five minutes after they'd gone a truck rolled up and out jumped one of Ricky's gardeners.

'Mr France-Lynch said you were nearly out of logs, so I've brought you another load.'

Then Daisy really did go upstairs and cry. If only it were Ricky not his logs keeping her warm. Please God, she prayed, I'm sorry to be so indecisive. I know I asked you to get me over Drew, and you did. Now could you please get me over Ricky.

72

From the moment she landed in California, Perdita had felt like a patient waiting for the morphine to wear off and the serious, unbearable pain to take over. In England she had been numb with shock. Now the certainty that Red would swan in at any moment had reduced her to crawling, churning, hepped-up, bowel-opening panic.

She found herself leaving half-drunk cups of coffee and glasses of Perrier everywhere, starting sentences, forgetting what she was going to say, asking questions and not being able to take in the answer, putting on deodorant twice or not at all, fussing around trying on a hundred T-shirts before she went out, jumping out of her skin everytime she saw a red-headed man or a red Ferrari.

In fact, she had a three-week wait because the prick-teasing American Polo Association refused to announce the team until the eve of the first match. Their ponies had arrived, however, and were evidence that Bart had snapped up every Best Playing Pony in North and South America. Never had a US team been better mounted.

The English were pleased to find their own ponies in excellent spirits after their rest. Under Rupert's supervision they had been slowly put to work and were now fully acclimatized to the dry, desert heat which soared into the nineties in the afternoon. With the grooms watching like hawks for dehydration, they had also adjusted to different hay, grain and water. Perdita had to hand it to Rupert. Never had England taken the field with a fitter team of ponies.

All the ponies were stabled at Eldorado Polo Club where the Westchester was being staged. It was a friendly, homely place with palms, orange groves and a little wooden club-house where no-one minded you putting your boots on the table. The polo, on the other hand, was so good that members jetted in at weekends from Calgary and New York and movie stars drove down in their hordes from LA. Surrounded by mountains, the Club was set in an oasis of green polo grounds hewn out of the desert.

The American team were booked into La Quinta Hotel which had a golf course and tennis courts, fifteen miles drive from the polo ground. Rupert, insisting on a strict policy of non-fraternization and particularly not wanting Chessie to wind up Ricky, was determined to keep the teams apart and had rented a condominium on the Quinta estate, but well away from the hotel.

A little, pink-roofed, white-walled house, it was called the Villa Victoria, which they all hoped would be symbolic.

Reached through lush avenues of brilliantly coloured hibiscus and bougainvillaea, it had a jacuzzi, a swimming-pool, a garden filled with stephanotis, orange and lemon trees and overlooked a beautifully landscaped golf course, interspersed with palm trees and lakes, which was caressed all day with sprinklers. To Perdita it was beautiful, but as totally unreal as a Hollywood set.

There was plenty to do, though. The fresh, dry, desert air and the mountains were very invigorating and encouraged them to get up at six to jog, play tennis and work the ponies. The twins played endless golf with Ricky and Mike Waterlane to sharpen up their concentration and help them relax. Rupert was frantically dealing with sponsors and television networks. Taggie kept herself amused cooking for everyone. The wonderfully friendly Californians invited them to dinner parties and barbecues and all Ricky's old movie-star pupils, whom he'd coached in Palm Springs the first winter after he'd come out of prison, rang up and invited them to parties in Beverly Hills and took them on trips to Disneyland and round Hollywood. The twins were in their element. Mike Waterlane, on the other hand, who got frightfully excited by all the beautiful girls and then didn't know what to do with them, wasn't sleeping and was getting increasingly terrified about the first match.

Ricky, too, was becoming increasingly edgy. Usually he went into himself twenty-four hours before a game. Twenty-one days to wait was much too long. It all boiled up in a blazing row in which he tried to persuade Rupert to be less bloody to Perdita. Taggie, when Rupert eventually came spitting to bed, had more effect. 'She's so desperate for your approval, Rupert, and trying so hard to behave and be brave about Red. If you could just be a bit gentler with her.'

So Rupert had stopped bitching at Perdita and merely ignored her.

The media, of course, were everywhere – the freedom of the press extended even to the manger. Each time Perdita put a foot outside the door, or ventured down to the stables, a notebook, a camera or a microphone would be stuck into her face. How was she getting on with Rupert? What did she feel about seeing Red? How much more weight was she going to lose? Was she quite sure she wasn't anorexic?

On the eve of the first match she took refuge in Spotty's box. The ponies were restless and excited, knowing something was up after their long, long wait. Poor Spotty so loved showing off to the crowd, but, as Perdita was only reserve, he probably wouldn't get a chance to play at all. Rupert had flown to New York for the day and Perdita was surreptitiously sneaking him a packet of Polos when a car drove up in a cloud of dust. Terrified it might be Rupert, who'd smell peppermint and catch Spotty crunching, Perdita shot out of his box only to find Ricky looking boot-faced.

'The Americans have announced their team.'

'What is it?' croaked Perdita, feeling as if the cloud of dust had blown straight down her throat.

'Ben, Angel, Red,' said Ricky.

Oh, thank God, thought Perdita, I'll see him again.

'But they've dropped Shark and put Luke in instead,' went on Ricky. If Luke had been tuning up all the American ponies, he was thinking bleakly, they'd be unbeatable tomorrow.

'Oh, how wonderful!' Perdita was overjoyed. 'How wonderful for Luke!'

A pungent waft of sweet scent from the nearby orange grove reminded her poignantly of that day at Bart's barn when Luke had first introduced her to Red. How comforting if he were there tomorrow to hold her hand when she saw Red again.

Another perfect afternoon followed next day with a gentian-blue sky arched over a field of bouncy, jade-green Bermuda grass. As the crowd poured into Eldorado Polo Club from all over the world, Perdita had never seen more ravishing sunkissed blondes in shorts and sundresses, or more handsome healthy-looking men. Here was polo at its most relaxed and friendly. Yet beyond the mountains, which ringed the oasis like wrinkled, sleeping elephants, lay the desert where coyotes and rattlesnakes lurked, where dust devils swirled round the creosote bushes and Jacob trees held up their strange, spiky branches like hands praying for an American victory.

In the pony lines Rupert was winding up his final pep-talk. 'All that matters is marking. You've got to unnerve them early on.' Then, turning to Perdita, who was sweating in breeches, boots and her dark blue England shirt, 'Don't think you've got the afternoon off, duckie. Your job is to watch your eyes out, assessing every American pony and player, and I don't just mean Red Alderton.'

Perdita went scarlet.

'Talk of the devil,' said Seb. 'Ouch,' he yelled as Perdita clutched his arm.

For a second she thought she was going to black out. For there, getting out of a brand-new, dark blue Lamborghini to a chorus of female shrieking, was Red wearing the pale amethyst American shirt which went so perfectly with his conker-red hair and his smooth, brown face. Immediately, like cats on raw liver, the press fell on him.

'Whaaddya chances, Red?'

'Pretty good,' drawled Red, then, catching sight of the English team, he started to laugh. 'I guess the Brits aren't exactly weighed down by the responsibility of false expectations. Seeing as how they're fielding a has-been and three new caps, including Mike Waterlane, who's about as thick as a Clydesdale's dick.'

'I say, that's a bit steep,' said Mike, going brick-red.

'Don't rise,' snapped Rupert. 'That's what he wants.'

But Red was still wandering, smiling, towards them, as malicious as he was seductive.

'I cannot imagine there's ever been an English side quite so unfancied by the bookies,' he told the battling, frenzied swarm of reporters. 'Was it necessary to underplay your hand quite so obviously, Ricky? And hi, Rupert.' Another flash of white teeth beneath the coldly calculating, fox-brown eyes. 'I'm surprised you're not wearing your paternity suit. I hope you've got a hot line to the BPA because re-inforcements are sure going to be needed.'

Motionless, the English team watched him. The press were writing avidly, adoring every moment, shoved by television and radio reporters desperate to get their mikes within earshot.

'Any message for Perdita?' yelled the *Sun*.

'Oh, there you are, Perdita darling,' Red's voice softened. 'I couldn't see you for assholes. You're looking good. Your new Daddy must certainly have pulled every string to get *you* on the team.'

Stung and humiliated, Perdita stumbled away, frantically rubbing away the tears.

'I've nothing to say,' she howled to the swarm of reporters. 'Leave me alone.'

Then, suddenly, ahead of her she saw a big, blond man with blacksmith's shoulders and lean, cowboy hips moving down the American pony lines, checking tack and bandages, joking with the grooms, outwardly utterly relaxed, keeping his fears to himself.

'Luke,' called out Perdita desperately.

Swinging round, catching sight of her tearful, anguished face, he was beside her in an instant. His sheer size made the reporters back off.

'I'm really sorry about Tero,' were his first words. 'It blew me away when Red told me.'

She had remembered him slumped with pain, green-faced, pouring with sweat. Now his hair was bleached the colour of faded bracken, and freckles merged in his suntanned face. Pale amethyst wasn't the best colour for him, but he looked great, and Perdita thought once again what a lovely open, generous face he had.

'I'm sorry about Fantasma,' she stammered. 'Have you heard how she is?'

Just for a second the pain flickered in his eyes.

'She's fine,' he said firmly. 'Winning a lot of matches for Alejandro.'

'Luke,' yelled Bart impatiently, 'For Chrissake, stop yakking. Come and take a look at this fetlock.'

'I gotta go,' said Luke.

'Good luck,' whispered Perdita.

The press surged forwards. 'How was Red? Any chance of a reconciliation?'

Perdita had behaved well for too long. 'Why don't all you bastards fuck off?' she screamed.

She was further jolted when she climbed up into the packed stands to the seat Taggie had kept for her and found herself knocked backwards by a huge, juddering, black, rubber bullet. It was Leroy who'd slipped his lead and, bashing his tail back and forth like a hooked salmon, was frantically licking her face.

'Oh, darling,' she moaned, clutching his wonderfully solid body. Then, on his forehead she breathed in a scent, sharp, sophisticated with musky overtones which unsettled her far more than the waft of orange blossom had yesterday. She got a sudden vision of Luke in hospital doubled up with pain.

'Leroy, you're incorrigible,' said a cool voice. 'If you're going to assault the opposition, you'll have to stay in the truck.' Perdita found herself looking up into the lean, olive-skinned face of Margie Bridgwater, the beautiful girl who'd been sitting on Luke's bed in hospital. She was wearing white jeans, loafers and a red shirt and the brilliant sunshine bounced joyfully off her blue-black hair.

'Hi, Perdita,' she said drily. 'Congratulations on making the team.'

'Thanks,' muttered Perdita, collapsing beside Taggie.

'Yes, congratulations, Perdita,' called Chessie and Bibi, who were sitting above Margie, both looking thoroughly over-excited.

'I do hope you win,' added Chessie in a much-too-audible whisper. 'I'm knocked out Luke's been picked,' she added to Margie. 'About bloody time.'

'What's Luke doing now?' asked Bobby Ferraro's wife.

'Running a green pony clinic in Florida,' said Margie proudly. 'He's managed to pay off all his debts. That son-of-a-bitch Hal Peters has run away to Chile so he can't be extradited.'

'I'd have helped Luke out if I'd known,' said Chessie, 'but he's so proud he never told anyone until it was too late. Where are you staying?'

'Luke hates hotels because they won't take Leroy,' said Margie, stroking Leroy's panting shiny head, 'so we've rented a condo.'

'He's so lovely, Luke,' said Chessie.

'Why d'you think I'm with him?' said Margie.

Looking down, Perdita found her nails had drawn blood in the palm of one hand. How dare they discuss Luke as if he was a new biography they were all enjoying?

'Oh, look,' said Taggie, as a burst of band music echoed round the mountains. 'Here come the teams.'

The first match, as Red and the entire polo world had predicted, was a massacre. From the moment Bob Hope threw in the ball from the back of a Cadillac, Ricky knew it would be a tough game and that he, as the most dangerous player in the English team, would take the punishment. For six chukkas it seemed the Americans took positive pleasure in harassing the hell out of him. Particularly violent whenever he got the chance was Red, who seemed less interested in scoring, which he should have been doing from the number two position, than in paralysing Ricky. Time and again Ricky found himself forced off the ball, crushed between the explosive, unpredictable Angel and the sleek, viciously smiling Red, who jabbed his elbows into Ricky's ribs as though he intended to puncture his heart.

On the rare occasions Ricky did get through, like a gundog finally escaping the shackles of a bramble thicket, there was Luke solid as the Rockies backing ball after ball such an incredibly long way that they invariably fell ten yards in front of goal beside the one American player that was loose. And when the English got rattled and started fouling, he hit four glorious penalties from the sixty-yard line.

Luke, whose horses had all been sold to pay his debts, was riding Bart's ponies, which, as Ricky suspected, he had been tuning up for days with all the skill of a Ferrari mechanic. Because of his height and endless legs he still gave the air of a father riding a seaside donkey to amuse his children. But his hands were so light, and so supple was his thirteen-stone bulk that he managed to shift it like a contortionist. For the first time he had the chance to show the world how brilliantly he could ride when given top-class horses. Apart from Fantasma his own ponies had only been good because he'd trained them so well.

But his air of calm was deceptive. A despairing Dommie, who was supposed to be marking him and who had hardly touched the ball at all, saw Luke setting off upfield yet again. Unable to catch him because he was riding one of Bart's fastest ponies, an exquisitely pretty little bay thoroughbred mare, Dommie panicked and ran Corporal into Luke's mare broadside.

There was a sickening thud as the mare hit the ground and lay still. Leaping to his feet, Luke seized a horrified Dommie by his dark blue shirt and pulled him down off a quailing Corporal.

'You goddamm asshole,' he roared, lifting his huge fist.

'Luke, for Chrissake, don't hit him,' howled Red, galloping up. Then, as the bay mare scrambled to her feet: 'Pony's only winded.'

For a second the fist trembled in the air.

'You goddam asshole,' said Luke more gently. Then, seeing how terrified Dommie was looking, he started to laugh and let him go, whereupon Juan O'Brien awarded a free goal to the Americans. Rupert put his head in his hands.

'Unlike Luke to flip his lid,' said Chessie to Bibi. 'Must be more strung up than he looks.'

But Bibi was cocooned in happiness. She was expecting a baby by easily the most dashing man on the field, who, between blowing kisses in her direction, was making Seb Carlisle's life a misery by scoring all the goals. The most miserable man on the field, however, was Mike Waterlane, who'd spent the last twenty-four hours on the loo, whose mallet had developed an allergy to the ball and who, like a policeman on point duty, had waved every American player through. With Ricky pegged like Gulliver, the young English team lost direction and ran out the losers 3-13.

Poor Ricky plunged into another nightmarish week as the clamour of his detractors intensified. Colossal recriminations followed from the sponsors and the two polo associations. Ricky, by his bloody-minded obstinacy, had sabotaged the Westchester. The press carved him up, baying for the return of Drew and the Napiers to prevent the second match being a complete joke.

Drew was quoted as saying he would make himself available but that 'It would be rather like joining the *Titanic* in mid-voyage' which didn't improve Ricky's temper. Rupert stood by him staunchly in public, but, in private, the rows were awful and shook the white walls of the Villa Victoria. If the Americans won the second match the third would be cancelled which meant Venturer would lose a fortune in television rights and sponsorship money. Worse still, David Waterlane insisted on flying over to sort things out. He arrived around midnight on the eve of the second match and was even more incensed to discover that Mike had been out since lunchtime with the twins.

Perdita, who'd valiantly tried to keep everyone's spirits

up during the week, had retreated to her room to avoid the brickbats. She'd been unable to concentrate even on Dick Francis since she'd arrived, but, flipping through the paperbacks she'd scooped up at random before she left, she discovered an old poetry anthology of Luke's. Outside, the delicious spicy smell of Taggie's paella had been overwhelmed by the sweet, voluptuous scent of orange blossom and stephanotis. A shooting star careered across the indigo sky. Croaking tree-frogs harmonized sexily with Bob Marley, throbbing and pounding out of the outside speakers. Perdita started flipping through the anthology. It fell open at Emerson:

'Give all to love,
Obey thy heart,' read Perdita.
'Tis a brave master,
Let it have scope,
Follow it utterly.'

She had difficulty reading the last verse because she was crying and because Luke had written the word 'Perdita' in the margin:

'Though thou loved her as thyself
As a self of purer clay.
Though her parting dims the day
Stealing grace from all alive.
Heartily know
When half-gods go,
The gods arrive.'

Red had been a half-god, she thought bitterly, and he'd gone. And she'd been a half-god and left Luke. That was why he was now with Margie Bridgwater, who was as clever as she was good and beautiful and Perdita absolutely loathed her guts.

Outside, raised voices were definitely winning over Bob Marley and the tree-frogs. Perdita, creeping to the window, noticed Rupert's cigar glowing redly as he increasingly drew on it, trying to keep his temper. His other hand, holding a glass of brandy, rested on Taggie's shoulder. She was shelling peas for tomorrow night's dinner which would either be a celebration or the wake to end all wakes. No one was taking any notice of Sharon, who, rippling the oily, pale turquoise surface of the pool, dog-paddled up and down in the nude, piled-up hair held firmly above the water, diamond earrings upstaging the huge stars.

'Do come in and have a dip, boys. The water's laike satin. Ay'm sure it will cool you down.'

But David was yelling at Ricky. 'I want to know where the hell Mike is. He's not even in bed by midnight on the night' – he looked at his watch – 'or rather the day of the most important match of his life. If I'd been in charge, this would never have happened.'

He was interrupted by the sound of a Mini-Moke roaring up the dust track pouring out Dire Straits, followed by raucous laughter and slamming doors.

'*There is a green hill far away, Without a city wall,*' sang Seb Carlisle in a light tenor, as he pushed his way through the crimson mane of bougainvillaea.

'*Where our dear Lord was crucified.*'

'*Who died to save us all,*' joined in Dommie in harmony.

'*For He's a jolly good fellow,*' brayed Mike coming in on an even lower register, '*For He's a jolly good fellow, for He's a jolly . . .*'

The singing tailed off as the trio encountered a solid phalanx of disapproval lined up round the pool.

'Where have you been?' thundered David Waterlane.

'Hello, David,' said Seb, brushing his blond hair out of his eyes. 'We thought there was no point Mike worrying all evening about you flying over and tomorrow's match so we took him for a jaunt.'

'A seriously good jaunt,' said Mike, swaying towards the swimming-pool and only being saved from falling in by Dommie catching hold of his shirt. Mike's normally slicked-back hair flopped all over his forehead and he was wearing an outsize T-shirt on which was printed the words: 'Fran's Friendly Fornicating Facilities'.

'We took him to a brothel in Nevada,' said Seb who was wearing a T-shirt which said: 'Have a good lay'.

'Pretty sophisticated. Customers landing all the time on the airstrip,' he went on.

Dommie's T-shirt said: 'Support your local hooker'.

'We bought ones for you and Perdita,' he beamed at Ricky. 'You OK, darling?' he shouted up to Perdita, who was by now nearly falling out of the window with laughter. Rupert threw his cigar into the swimming-pool, only just missing Sharon's nose.

'You took Mike to a knocking shop and got him drunk?' he said softly.

'He's not drunk. He smoked a joint on the way home,' said Seb, taking the cigarette from Mike and inhaling deeply. 'You should try this place, Rupert. They've got an orgy room with blue shagpile, leading up to the waterbed and a jacuzzi with red lights under the water and we saw some brilliant blue movies. Much better for Mike's morale than that frightfully depressing video of him letting everyone through in the first match.'

'We nearly tried the dominance dungeon,' added Dommie. 'We thought how much Chessie would have enjoyed it – whoops, sorry,' he added, giggling, as Ricky's face tightened with rage.

'Seriously nice girls,' said Mike, collapsing on to a sunlounger. 'Really seriously friendly.'

'He's had Mona, Lily and Annie,' explained Seb. 'Severally and together, and he's so tired and relaxed he'll sleep like a baby for the first time since he's been out here.'

'Are you crazy?' hissed David. 'You've probably caught AIDS.'

'It's OK, Daddy,' said Mike cheerfully. 'I used a condominium.'

Glancing at Rupert, Perdita saw that he had his head in his hands again, trying to disguise the fact that he was quite hysterical with laughter.

73

The second match was quite different. In losing his virginity Mike seemed to have shed his terrible nerves as well. Primed by Rupert with a vast slug of brandy when his father wasn't looking, he played with unshakeable authority, sledge-hammering the ball upfield, tigerish on any loose balls and twice pounding down like a Panzer division to score splendid goals. Time and again, the US team took the ball right down the field, but the English wouldn't let them score.

Realizing Luke was the most dangerous player on the field, Seb and Dommie weighed in like the two musketeers, duelling with their sticks, hooking, bumping and stabbing the ball away from him, playing a stoically defensive game. With Luke pegged, Red and Angel's life-support machine was cut off and they were unable to score. Ricky, on the other hand, hit form with a knock-out punch. Elusive as the Scarlet Pimpernel, swift as a lurcher, always there to whisk the ball away when Mike or the twins made a frantic last-ditch clear, he played the game of his life.

The crowd, reluctant to witness a second bloodbath, had halved, but now over and over again broke into spontaneous cheers. Umpires Juan and Jesus were so often distracted by Ricky's virtuosity that they missed fouls on other parts of the field. At half-time the English were leading 7-3 and as word flew round the Californian coast that a tussle was in process, spectators started screeching in in their limos and helicopters swooped down out of the sky like gulls on a newly ploughed field.

The temperature had also rocketed. Huge brown-bottomed clouds like dusty meringues gathered menacingly on the horizon beneath a royal-blue sky tinged with purple. But the English players and ponies under Rupert's fitness regime were standing up well. Perdita envied the bikinis and sundresses all round her, as once again she sweated in the stands in her England gear.

In the fifth chukka the English steeled themselves for Red's and Glitz's legendary bombardment. But due to Ricky's sticking to Red like chewing gum to a dog's fur, it never materialized. Bart was gnashing his beautifully capped teeth on the sideline.

'Come on, England,' screamed Chessie. 'Well, I am English,' she added defiantly to a shocked Bibi.

Terry Hanlon, flown specially over from Cowdray to do the commentary, was so petrified of flying that he'd practically had to be doped before he would get on to the plane. But so encouraged was he by his country's gutsy performance that he quite forgot his jet lag.

'And the ball goes out of play. Sorry, Granny,' he added as Red, in a fury of frustration, hit a ball straight into the stands. 'If you watch the ball, you'll never get hit by it. Hit-in to England. And there goes Ricky France-Lynch on his way to ten goals. Did you see the way he just stroked the ball under the nose of Red Alderton, and took it away, sending a lovely lofted pass to Dommie Carlisle? What a chance!

'But here comes Luke Alderton,' he went on, 'steady as the Rockies, thundering down to ride Dommie off, but Dommie flicks the ball back to his captain who powers it between the posts. That's 8-3 to England.' Then, waiting for the cheers to subside, 'You can't fight the entire English side on your own, Luke.'

With a wry grin, Luke lifted his stick in the direction of the commentary box.

In the closing seconds of the chukka, however, the ball was once more bouncing towards the seemingly insatiable American goal-mouth. Frantic to clear, Bobby Ferraro opened his shoulders and let fly. Valiantly Dommie hurled little Corporal forward to block the shot. As if fired by a cannon, it smacked Dommie just below his kneepad as the bell went.

'Oh, shit, shit, shit,' he screamed, slumping over his saddle. To a man, the crowd winced. As the players gathered round and the ambulance roared up, Dommie had gone greener than the inside of an avocado pear.

'I'm sorry, Dommie, I'm real, real, sorry,' said a horrified Bobby Ferraro.

'My fault for riding into it,' mumbled Dommie.

Fortunately he was near the pony lines and, refusing any help from the ambulance, managed to ride Corporal off the field.

'I don't like the look of that,' said the paramedic.

'Give me a bucket of Novocaine,' gasped Dommie, trying not to scream with pain as Ricky, Seb and a demented Louisa lifted him down from Corporal. 'I'll be OK in a minute.'

'You can't go back into that hell-hole,' said Louisa aghast.

Rupert agreed and, sprinting along the edge of the boards, yelled up to Perdita in the stands to get her kneepads on.

The only person, in fact, who was happy when Dommie insisted on playing on was Bart. Slapping a clenched fist into his other palm, he moved round the American team. 'Now we can zap them. Ride into the little bastard's knee as often as possible. Force him to retire and we can get the girl in.'

'Don't be so fucking unsporting, Dad,' said Luke in outrage. 'You could put the guy out of the game for good.'

'Safe journey, my darling.' Louisa's voice broke as Dommie rode back on to the field to deafening applause.

Dommie was as brave as his own bull terrier, but the blow had smashed his left knee and the pain was clearly unhinging him. As Red and Angel unleashed a fusillade of shots, the crowd, who had no idea quite how badly Dommie was hurt, kept up a continuous roar of encouragement. As the score drew level, Dommie, battered by the inevitable rough and tumble, grew greener and greener. Ricky was torn. He ought to protect Dommie but, aware that the Westchester was fast slipping out of his grasp, the only answer was to forget him and plunge into the fray. Thirty seconds later, with a glorious cut shot, he put England ahead. Now it was a question of staying there.

Despite the punishing heat Perdita shivered, encased in an ice-cold sweat. Padded and gloved, with her stick resting against the white fence below the stands, she expected any moment to have to leap on to Dommie's beautiful, fickle pony, Bardot, who was known to be as tricky as she was fast.

'I must read the play,' she kept telling herself grimly.

As poor Dommie came down the field it was like watching a bird trying to fly with two broken wings. But slowly, as she forced herself to concentrate, she became aware that Luke, unlike the rest of the US team, was contradicting Bart's orders and as the man who should have been marking Dommie, and despite the undeniable advantage it would have given him, was deliberately not riding Dommie off on the side of his damaged knee.

There, Dommie had the ball again and Luke, who could have bumped him into the stands, laboriously rode round to hook him on the other side.

Glancing at Perdita, Taggie noticed that tears were pouring down her face. Gently she put her hand over Perdita's.

'Luke's the one, isn't he?'

Perdita nodded. 'I guess he always has been,' she muttered, 'but I've only just realized it, and now it's too late.'

As the teams lined up, jostling and shoving, for the throw-in, Dommie's agony was so blinding he thought he'd faint. Pain was in the mind. He must push himself through the pain barrier and go into mental overdrive.

Bardot, his chestnut mare, fond of batting her long eyelashes and giving a colossal buck when chastised, was for once behaving impeccably and carrying her master as smoothly as a Rolls-Royce. When Mike, menaced by Angel and Red, hit the ball upfield ahead of him, Bardot swung round to follow it. Alas, Red didn't have any of his brother's scruples. Seeing Dommie pounding towards goal looking for an offside drive, Red cannoned into his smashed knee with his pony's right shoulder. Howling with pain, Dommie had to cling on to Bardot's neck to stay on.

'You fucker!' Hysterical with rage, Seb rode straight at Red, slicing the ball away from him towards goal. But Luke was too quick for Seb. Riding him once more off the ball, he turned the play with a staggering sixty-yard backshot.

With ten seconds on the clock, everyone collided in a cloud of dust in front of the British goal, the Americans frantic to whack it home so the game could go to a seventh chukka. Looking for his backhand in a tangle of threshing sticks, Ricky kept his cool. As he cleared for England, saving the game on the bell, everyone crashed over the line, sending a goal post flying in the process and all ending up in a great heap.

'You OK, Dommie?' yelled Seb in anguish through the dust.

'Fine,' said Dommie, who'd dismounted. 'I'm just hanging on to my horse.'

'The only problem,' said Seb as the dust cleared, 'is that it's my horse you're hanging on to.'

'Then where's Corporal?' said Dommie, looking round puzzled.

'Corporal was in the last chukka,' explained Seb, 'and he played so well, he's been promoted to Sergeant.'

Dommie giggled, but as he let go of Seb's pony he collapsed on to the ground like a rag doll. 'I think I've fucked my knee.'

'Don't worry,' said Seb shakily. 'You'll love hospital. The food's terrific.'

'I could murder a T-bone,' said Dommie and passed out.

With Dommie critically ill in a Palm Springs' hospital with

concussion and a splintered knee, Perdita would have to play in the final match. The BPA were singularly unamused and dispatched Brigadier Hughie prematurely to La Quinta to drum some sense into the wayward English squad. Storming into the Villa Victoria at twilight the following evening, sweating in a creased, wool, pin-striped suit, he found them totally euphoric.

Having learnt that the operation had been successful and Dommie would be playing again in a few months, they now felt able to celebrate yesterday's victory properly. Hughie's jaundiced view of Rupert's playboy attitude and Ricky's deviant captaincy were further exacerbated when he found everyone plastered on Harvey Wallbangers, singing rugger songs and resting their aching bones in the swirling waters of the jacuzzi.

'This is worse than an orgy,' spluttered Hughie over the deafening blast of Dancer's latest LP, 'and Sharon Kaputnik ought to put on a bathing dress,' he added as he took Rupert and Ricky into the house.

'Do them good to unwind,' said Rupert. 'They've got four days to sober up.'

'Not how we'd have done it in Singapore,' chuntered Hughie, ducking as a pineapple came flying through the french windows. 'Anyway, it's time you chaps came to your senses. You had a damn good win yesterday, but don't push your luck. The Napiers are playing in Argentina and quite prepared to fly up here if we pay their expenses and give them ten grand each; and Drew'd be an even better bet. He's cooling his heels in Rutshire.'

Ricky, who unlike everyone else, was entirely sober, had had an agonizing twenty-four hours worrying about Dommie. The thought of Drew in Rutshire cooling his heels, and no doubt warming his hands on Daisy's welcoming body, did nothing to improve his temper. 'I'm captaining this team, Hughie, so bugger off.'

'You really prefer a slip of a girl to a fit very experienced nine-goal man?'

'Yes,' said Rupert evenly. 'I've always been heterosexual.'

'What, what! Don't be flippant,' exploded Hughie. 'You can't put in a girl against those thugs.'

'Those thugs might back off a little because she *is* a girl,' went on Rupert reasonably. 'Now, really do bugger off,

719

Hughie, and play Scrabble or have a hot tub with Mrs Hughie, I bet they didn't have those in Singapore.'

Rupert, in fact, was reeling with relief. Assured of a third match, Venturer were likely to make a killing. The British and American sponsors were delighted Perdita was going to play. Such a beautiful, tempestuous, controversial figure would certainly pull in the crowds.

Next day Rupert flew to New York and, after five hours closeted with chief executives and vice presidents, managed to persuade NBS to cancel coverage of an ice hockey match and to transmit the match live instead of recording it for a later date. In England people could watch it if they got up at four o'clock in the morning or see an edited version the following evening. Rupert was considerably aided by the press who pointed out the piquancy of Perdita having to play against her ex-lover and who all showed close-ups of her crying in the stands as she watched the match.

'*Still in love*' wrote *The Scorpion* in delight. '*Rupert's wife comforts grief-stricken Perdita as she sobs for Red the Rat.*'

Bart, on the other hand, was in a towering rage that the Americans had lost the second match. Always on the hunt for a scapegoat, he blamed it entirely on Luke for not riding Dommie off. Red went even further. The morning after the match he rang Brad Dillon, the American team manager.

'Can I speak to you in utter confidence?'

'I guess so.'

'My brother Luke's been crazy about Perdita Macleod for years.'

'I thought he was shacked up with Margie Bridgwater.'

'Maybe he is, but he'll still have to mark Perdita on Sunday. And if he's too much of a wimp to ride off Dommie Carlisle, he'll never carve up Perdita. Why don't you bring back Shark? He's never had a scruple in his life.'

'This is your own brother we're talking about,' said Brad disapprovingly. 'Luke is a very fine player.'

'Sure he is and I just adore him, but he's too soft.'

'Sort of guy who reads poetry in the evening,' mused Brad Dillon. 'Could be you're right, Red. I asked Luke to stick and ball with me in Greenwich early one morning a few weeks ago. He wasn't in the lobby at eight-thirty so I went upstairs and banged on his bedroom door. Can you beat it, Red, he was still in bed, drinking a Bourbon and, even worse, reading a book.'

'What did I tell you?' said Red in triumph. 'He's got a bad attitude.'

Brad Dillon had no difficulty persuading the other selectors. 'Gentlemen, I'm afraid this is no time for gentlemen. Shark's our man.'

At lunchtime the APA issued a press release that Luke would be dropped for the final game.

It was the night before the match. Mike Waterlane, having spent the afternoon in his prospective stepmother's arms while his father played golf, slept like a hound puppy after his first day's hunting.

Seb, on the other hand, had had a very bad four days. Demented when Dommie was injured, he had cried his eyes out when the hospital assured him his brother was out of danger. Always the confident, assertive twin, who'd pinched Dommie's girls and bossed him about for twenty-six years, he now found himself totally lost both on and off the field. How many times before big games had he woken Dommie up to chat and bolster his own confidence? Now, feeling horribly alone, he tried to concentrate on James Herriot. Lucky, lucky Rupert to have Taggie in bed with him. He wished suddenly he was lying in Daisy Macleod's arms, pillowed on her soft breasts. He'd definitely ring her when he got home.

Nor could Ricky get to sleep. He wished he could go down to the stables and discuss tactics for tomorrow's match with Wayne, but security, triggered off by tremendous press interest and the Prince's impending arrival, was incredibly tight and he didn't want to wake the ponies.

At last the Westchester was within his grasp. Under the eye of two security guards the Cup had been on display in the clubhouse yesterday – huge, silver and ungainly with its jug-eared handles and horses rearing out of the side. In his gloomier moments he had to admit that, even if England did their best tomorrow, it wouldn't be enough to beat the Americans. Perdita was simply not as good as Dommie and without Dommie, Seb would be not even half as good as usual. But miracles happen. In moments of true inspiration sides could reach heights never achieved before. It was up to him as captain to instil into them the belief that they could.

And if, by the thousand to one chance, they did win, what then? He still hadn't got to ten. He had seen Chessie at a distance over the last few days, shining more brightly than ever before, silencing rooms and dividing crowds by her beauty. Then, this evening, a florist's van had delivered a single red rose in a Cellophane box.

'*Darling Ricky,*' said the card, '*Carry this red rose of England next to your heart tomorrow. Good luck and my love goes with you, Chessie.*'

The rose was now languishing in a tooth mug, its head drooping in the heat. Nor did it smell. He felt the inevitable sick churning. He mustn't let nerves get to him, he had to calm the others. Switching on the television, he found a weatherman saying that the hurricane that was ravaging Florida, tugging up trees by the roots, ripping off roofs like milk bottle tops, was relentlessly moving towards England. It gave Ricky the excuse to pick up the telephone.

'D-d-daisy, it's Ricky. Sorry to wake you. Yes I'm fine. Perdita's fine too – a bit uptight but that's to be expected. Well, they're not screaming at each other. R-r-rupert's trying to be patient. How's Little Chef?'

When Daisy said he was eating at last – rump steak and chocolate – Ricky laughed and said he'd reimburse her.

'Look,' he went on, 'I rang to say there's a bloody great hurricane on its way to you. I don't want you to walk through the woods. There's a lot of dead trees in there that might get blown down.'

Perdita couldn't sleep either. Frantic excitement that she was going to be the first woman ever to play for England and even better play against Luke, had been utterly doused when she heard he'd been dropped. How could the bastards do that when he'd played so impeccably in the first two matches?

On the chair she'd already laid out her newly washed dark-blue England shirt and white breeches, along with her lucky belt, lucky socks, lucky pants and lucky bra, which

Taggie had mended for her and which had broken once before when she'd been playing with Luke and he'd called out, 'Tack time', and stopped the game, fiddling with his curb chain until she'd managed to fix it. Oh God, why did everything come back to Luke? She must rise above her misery. She fingered the red rose of England on her shirt. Winning tomorrow must be her only thought.

No novel could distract her so she turned again to Luke's poetry book. Emerson made her cry. She certainly hadn't given all to love, only to the pursuit of fame and riches. And there was Robert Frost:

'But I have promises to keep,
And miles to go before I sleep.'

Would she ever sleep peacefully again without Luke? Despairingly she turned back to Shakespeare:

'In peace there's nothing so becomes a man
As modest stillness and humility:
But when the blast of war blows in our ears,
Then imitate the action of a tiger.'

That was Luke to a T. She remembered him declaiming those lines on the way to the Queen's Cup. Again she could hardly read on:

'The game's afoot:
Follow your spirit and upon this charge,
Cry "God for Harry! England and St George!"'

If she learnt it by heart it might send her to sleep. She jumped at a knock on the door. It was Rupert carrying two whiskys.

'Perhaps I better check Red Alderton isn't lurking in the wardrobe,' he said with a faint smile as he sat down on her bed.

For a second they gazed at each other as if into a mirror looking for likenesses. We be of one blood ye and I, thought Perdita.

'You look about twelve,' said Rupert.

Perdita blew her nose noisily on a Kleenex. 'You don't have to be nice to me just because you're going to drop me.'

'I'm going to do no such thing. Taggie's just given me the first bollocking ever, told me to come and say I'm sorry. Actually I was sorry, anyway. I've behaved like a shit.'

'I deserved it,' said Perdita in a choked voice. 'I deserved everything. I've behaved horribly since the day I was born and now I'm paying for it.'

'Your ponies don't think so,' said Rupert gently. 'They absolutely adore you and so would everyone else if you gave them a chance.'

'I've been so awful to Mum and you and Taggie, and, worst of all, to Luke. How could those dickheads drop him?'

'Lucky for us they have,' said Rupert. 'Shark's a killer, but he's nowhere near Luke's class. There's no-one else who can do the things Luke can do under pressure.'

'It makes me so mad.'

'Good,' said Rupert. 'Now listen to me. The Americans dropped Luke because he's too much of a gent to take you out. Your sole task tomorrow is to show the world how stupid they were. Without Luke, we'll bury them.'

'Look at this,' roared Ricky storming into Rupert's bedroom the next morning and thrusting the *Daily News* under his nose.

'You might bloody knock,' grumbled Rupert, hastily drawing the duvet over Taggie's voluptuous naked body.

'*When Francesca Alderton left her husband Ricky France-Lynch, captain of England, six years ago,*' he read, '*and ran off with airline billionaire, Bart Alderton, she taunted her former spouse with a challenge that she would only come back to him on certain conditions: if he won the British Gold Cup, which he did earlier this year, went to ten, the highest rating for a polo player, which he's tipped to do later this year, and won back the Westchester Cup for Britain. Will he achieve this second rung at Eldorado Polo Club this afternoon? Red Alderton must feel he is riding with the responsibility of his father's marriage and happiness in his pocket.*'

Rupert looked up. 'Great stuff,' he said blandly, 'and at the worst it'll ensure that everyone in England and America will tune in to see the result of your marriage. Think of the viewing figures.'

'Who leaked it?' thundered Ricky.

Rupert shrugged. 'How would I know?' His eyes didn't quite meet Ricky's. 'You had any breakfast? You really should eat something, today of all days.'

'Don't get off the subject,' said Ricky furiously. 'What's that piece going to do to Chessie?'

'She'll love it,' said Rupert soothingly. 'You know how she laps up publicity and I'll tell you something else: the New York Over-Eighties Polo Club have invested in a television set for the first time in their history so they can watch the match.'

'Stop taking the piss,' exploded Ricky. Then, turning to Taggie: 'If you don't want to be a widow, you better keep your husband out of my way.'

Despite Rupert's air of insouciance, however, he was worried he might have gone too far. At the team meeting beforehand, Ricky seemed totally out to lunch, his eyes staring, his face dishcloth grey, the lines round his mouth and between his eyebrows so heavy they looked as though they had been etched with a dagger. He seemed to be taking nothing in as Rupert harangued them.

'Go to the man, force every play, make every play a hard one, don't let anyone set up to hit the ball, stop them gaining possession. The Americans are so hot every goal you score'll be a victory. Each time you stop Shark backing the ball you're worth nine goals, Perdita.'

The temperature had soared and it was intensified down at the polo ground by more than five hundred of the world's press, who'd invaded the club in search of a story. Everywhere cine-cameras whirled, tapes rotated, notebooks filled up with superlatives and speculation. Looking up at the mountains as they drove to the game, Perdita had an uneasy feeling that the wrinkled sleeping elephants would wake up and stampede the pitch and that the day would end in terrible disaster.

The press fell on the British team as they got out of their car, but Ricky walked through the lot of them.

'Like trying to interview a rock face,' wrote a girl from the *Mail on Sunday* petulantly. 'I hope *El Orgulloso* comes before a fall.'

An old man on a stick tottered towards him. 'Ricky France-Lynch? Your father lent me a pony for the 1939 Westchester. Damn fine player. Hardest man I ever had to mark. Is he still . . . '

Leaving him in mid-sentence, Ricky walked on down to

725

the pony lines where the horses were tied up in the shade of straw palisades.

'I'm sorry,' Perdita apologized to the old man. 'He gets funny before a big game. I know he'd love to hear about his father afterwards.'

Hollywood was out in force. Once again Perdita thought she'd never seen so many beautiful girls – it must be all that orange juice. But still the brightest star in the firmament was Chessie. She was wearing a scarlet dress and scarlet shoes, but over her slender brown arm she carried a fringed black silk shawl.

'If I'm in mourning at the end of the game,' she told the frantically scribbling reporters with an equivocal smirk, 'I'll put on the black shawl.'

The match kicked off with an amazing show of Holly-wood glitz. Pale mauve and dark blue balloons, the col-ours of the team, were let off in their thousands. Blue-and-mauve hot-air balloons floated overhead, giving great snorts and making any dog that had been brave enough to face the heatwave bristle and cower. Helicopters trailed good luck messages. Vintage cars circled the field bear-ing celebrities. Pop stars, bands and cheerleaders, flashing more flawless golden limbs, entertained the happy, excited crowd. Ferranti's, who'd done an about-turn, handed out free bottles of 'Perdita' in the stands. Revlon countered with red carrier bags containing bottles of shampoo and conditioner. The Americans were way-out favourites, but the odds were shortening on the Brits as the American team led the parade on to the field, following the glittering gold instruments of the band.

Gazing at the lounging, willowy elegance of Red's back, catching frequent glimpses of his perfect profile as he flashed smile after lazy smile at the swooning girls in the crowd, Perdita could only marvel that he'd once had the power to hurt her so much. Then, as they drew up in front of the hastily run-up Royal Box, where the Prince, slightly pink in a lightweight suit, stood smiling down at them, she noticed the size of Shark Nelligan's shoulders, his brawny arms and his walrus torso rolling over his leather belt, and shivered. Soon he'd be waiting for her like his namesake in a still lagoon. For the first time in her career she was terrified, not just that she'd let down her country, but that she might also be killed. If only it were Luke. She couldn't see him or Leroy anywhere in the crowd.

No-one by contrast was happier in the parade than Spotty. Incensed to watch his friends Wayne and Kinta going off to the earlier matches, he now had a chance to show off. Revelling in the laughter and cheers of the crowd, who'd been told by Terry Hanlon he was an all-American pony, he flashed his long brown legs beneath his white rump, rolled his white eyes at the band and deliberately let off a volley of the loudest farts to embarrass his mistress as she circled in front of the Prince after her name was called.

Tero would never have done that to me, thought Perdita with a stab of anguish.

Frank Sinatra and Dancer were to have sung their individual National Anthems, but Dancer's plane had been diverted with engine trouble, to the disappointment of the English team, so Frank Sinatra sung them both, which brought a tingle to everyone's spine.

'Shit, Alejandro's umpiring!' said Seb. 'He's bound to favour Angel.'

'I'm going to be sick,' said Mike in a faint voice.

'Well, be sick in your hat,' said Seb briskly. 'We don't want slippery patches on the grass.'

Still under the careful eyes of the security guards, the Westchester gleamed on its red tablecloth. The television cameras were rolling, a semicircle of cameramen hovered on the edge of the stands solely monitoring Chessie's behaviour.

Back at the pony lines Perdita glanced at Ricky. He looked really ill. Was he that worried about losing Chessie? What a tragedy that Dancer hadn't arrived in time to cheer him up.

'Good luck, you chaps,' said Brigadier Hughie.

'Good luck,' chorused Louisa and the grooms. They had worked so hard and once their precious charges were on the field they could only pray.

'Just rattle them in the first chukka,' said Rupert, then adding to Perdita, as she changed off Spotty on to one of David Waterlane's ponies, a grey mare called Demelza, 'Shark's wildly overweight. He's going to feel the heat.'

It was only as they lined up for Paul Newman to throw in

the first ball from the back of a Cadillac that Ricky realized he'd forgotten to bring Chessie's red rose – not even a petal in the bottom of his boot.

'Come on, you guys,' screamed Perdita, suddenly excited. 'Imitate the action of a tiger.' The next minute the ball – a special bright yellow one to show up on television – crashed into the shifting blockade of ponies and riders and the final of the fourteenth Westchester Cup was off.

74

In fact the Americans played such a dazzlingly aggressive game in the first half that Luke's absence wasn't obvious, and by half-time they were leading 4-0. Taking no prisoners, Shark Nelligan rode Perdita off with such violence that all the breath was knocked out of her body. When she got near the ball his long, beefy arms hooked her stick, and every time she tried to stop him clearing he somehow barged the quarters of one of his huge horses into her. Seb and Mike pressed the battle without let-up, doing their best to stem the American advance, but Ricky's game was definitely off. He had no aggression, his passes didn't connect or went straight to the opposition, and the few stabs he made at goal went wide.

'What the fuck are you playing at?' yelled Rupert as he came off at half-time. 'You select a bunch of kids who are playing like gods. You're meant to lead them over the top and you're being about as uplifting as a five-year-old jock strap.'

The temperature was still rising. Male hands applied oil to vulnerable female shoulders. The crowd was enjoying the sunshine but had lost bounce and were even doing the Spot the Ball competitions in their programmes. The bars were doing a roaring trade. The press wilted in the heat. Their cameras had become very heavy; they'd come all this way and there was no story. Red and Perdita were showing no sign of falling into each other's arms, and Chessie looked stunned rather than stunning at such an English setback. All the animation had drained out of her face and she refused to talk, even to Bibi, who was reeling with joy because Angel had scored three of the goals.

728

Even the arrival of Dancer in Joan Collins's private plane didn't rouse the cameramen. Megastars were two a dime today. Fighting his way to the pony lines, Dancer found the English mounting their ponies for the fourth chukka. 'To fink I've been stuck in an Alderton sardine tin for the last fifteen hours just for your sake, Ricky, only to find you're nil-four down. Get yer fucking finger out.'

Then, seeing how ill Ricky looked: 'It's no big deal, sweetheart. If you lose and Chessie loves you, she'll come back anyway.'

Ricky stared at him bleakly. 'You think so?'

'Course she will. She's looking pretty cheesed off now. Here's somefink to cheer you up,' added Dancer.

It was a photograph of Little Chef in a polo hat and dark glasses.

Ricky laughed and turned it over, where Daisy had written, *'Good luck and love from everyone at Snow Cottage.'*

'When did you see her?'

'Yesterday,' said Dancer.

'Move your ass, Reeky,' yelled Alejandro, 'everyone's waiting.'

Shoving Little Chef's photograph into his breeches' pocket, Ricky vaulted on to Kinta and galloped back on to the field.

At the beginning of the fourth chukka a machiavellian Red pulled up on the ball, convincing Alejandro that Seb had crossed him. Up went the American sticks. Alejandro awarded a penalty from the sixty-yard line, which Shark converted gloriously. The rest of the side crowded round him, their patting hands sinking into his fleshy back. Five–nil.

'Good thing we dropped Luke,' muttered Bart to Brad Dillon. 'Shark's playing great.'

He felt happier than ever before in his life. Red's speciality, the fifth chukka, was coming up. Ricky and the Brits would be utterly humiliated and his beautiful Chessie would stay with him. Earlier he'd seen Grace hanging round the pony lines giving Red advice. She was still a handsome woman, but in the harsh Californian light, she looked sixty. For the millionth time, despite everything, Bart was glad he'd left her for Chessie, whom he adored and understood. She'd be utterly miserable going back to

729

the unimaginative, inhibited Ricky, who was playing like a nought. With any luck, he might be put down. It was a joke he could ever be considered a ten.

As play started again, and they lined up for the throw-in, a bored voice in the crowd called out: 'Oh, come on, England.'

Perdita turned in fury: 'We're doing our best, you fucker,' she screamed. 'You try playing against this ape.'

The crowd shouted with laughter. In the ensuing mêlée Shark swung his pony's head into Perdita's ribs once too often.

'You bastard,' she yelled. Then, to herself: 'Help me, God! We can't let them win so easily!'

And from the spacious royal-blue firmament on high the Almighty seemed to answer by suddenly putting wings on her back and on her pony's heels.

'Cry God for Charlie, England and St George,' she screamed to the others and, cannoning off Shark, then into Red, then stopping short, then wheeling away under their horses' tails, she careered off and put a beautifully angled cutshot from twenty yards into goal. The crowd roared.

'That's better,' pleaded Terry Hanlon. 'Come on, you Brits in the crowd. Give the boys and the girl a chance. They need you.'

Thirty seconds later Perdita came pounding down again, whacking it to Seb, then racing ahead, picking up the ball again and sinking a big nearside neck shot.

'Come on, Ricky,' she yelled as she rode back to the centre, 'we can't do it on our own.'

Every time Red and Shark tried to ride her off now, she was too quick for them and they found they were bumping the breeze. Slowly the English, and particularly Ricky, steadied, and they ended the fourth chukka only 3-6 down.

'Well done! Fucking marvellous,' said an ecstatic Rupert. 'Fantastic play, Perdita! Keep it up all of you. Your job in the next chukka, Seb, is to mark Red mindless. Stop him letting off any fireworks.'

The fifth chukka was uneven. Mike, rather than let Red score, fouled deliberately in the American goal-mouth, so that Shark had to go back to the sixty-yard line to take the penalty. Overcome by nerves, he hit wide.

'Luke wouldn't have missed that,' Perdita taunted him.

Goaded and desperate to make his mark on polo history, Shark was determined to score from the Number Four position, and kept trying to bulldoze the British defence, leaving his own back door wide open and enabling Perdita and Seb to score twice more.

'Corporal's now been promoted to Warrant Officer Two,' whooped Seb, triumphantly patting Dommie's little brown pony as they cantered back for the throw-in.

A second later the play was down near the English goal and an utterly rattled Shark mis-hit so the ball ricocheted off the boards over the back line.

'You stay there, Fatty. I'll be back in a minute,' yelled Perdita at Shark as she belted off to take up her position as Mike hit in. The crowd howled with laughter.

'Wash your mouth out with soap, Perdita,' said Terry Hanlon, 'but isn't she playing well!'

Catching the other side off guard, Mike powered the ball to Ricky who, keeping moving to lure Angel away, broke off to the right to receive the ball, then before Angel could blink, backed it to a hovering Seb, who, swinging Corporal round, scored yet again.

'Corporal's an RSM now,' whooped Seb.

Six-all to England on the bell.

The whole crowd were on their feet yelling their heads off as the teams went into the last chukka, and the Americans steadied and rallied.

'England, England, England,' chanted the galvanized British contingent.

Now they were into a frantic mêlée in front of the American goal. Angel somehow managed to clear and Ricky sent the fleet-footed Wayne after the ball. As he could hear Red thundering down on him, the only answer was to back it. Turning round in his saddle, a miracle of cool, Ricky took a lightning look at the posts, then, picking the left-hand one as a target, keeping his body steady and Wayne moving, leant over to the left until his head was level with Wayne's gallant, pounding heart and raked the ball over the antheap of players slap between the posts. As the flag went up, the crowd gave a collective sigh of horror and ecstasy. Overheard by everyone, Chessie uttered a shriek of joy and raised a clenched fist in a Black Power salute: 'Oh

Ricky, darling, what a wonderful, wonderful goal,' she screamed ecstatically.

The cameramen went berserk. They had a picture at last.

The English were also ahead at last. But with three minutes to go they could feel their ponies wilting. Spotty was panting like an obscene telephone caller and his brown patch foamed, under his breastplate, like an overflowing washing machine. Red and Angel had taken the opportunity when the last goal was scored to change ponies. The English problem was to stop either of them getting the ball. Next minute Mike gave his side a breathing space by clouting the ball firmly into the stands.

'Unsporting but necessary,' said Seb as the players lined up. 'You're learning, Mike.'

In the closing seconds a perfect eighty-yard drive from Red took the ball down to the English end where it was centred by Bobby Ferraro. One after another, yelling with frustration, Angel, Bobby, Shark and a furiously galloping-up Red tried to hammer the ball between the posts. As Mike cleared for England through a thick curtain of dust, a great groan went up from the stands. For once again Shark had left the American posts unattended. Taking the ball up the boards with two mighty driving passes, kicking up a halo of dust as he went, Ricky could feel Wayne struggling to stay ahead and Red on a new pony gaining on him. Just in time he jumped the boards and did a forehand cutshot to Seb, who, hearing Angel's pony behind him and seeing five seconds left on the clock, took a frantic swipe at goal.

Realizing it was going wide, Perdita catapulted forward for the offside forehand.

'Bloody hell,' she screamed as the ball hit a divot and bounced awkwardly to the left. Rupert had permanently taunted her that she had no nearside cut shots. She'd show him.

Dimly she was aware of the great roar of the crowd chorusing: 'Spotty, Spotty, Spotty.'

Triumphant in his moment of glory, revelling in the circus blood which was now pumping on overtime through his veins, Spotty noticed the ball had shifted. Jamming on his brakes, he pirouetted like Nureyev on his conker-brown legs sixty degrees to the left, thrusting Perdita within reach of the ball, but at the same time wrapping her in a cloud of dust.

She couldn't see what she was doing, but, trusting Spotty and her instincts, she leant perilously out to the left and with a flick of her wrist like a tennis backhand stroked the ball where she prayed the posts might be.

Then she dropped her reins and clapped her hands over her eyes, unable to watch as the dust cleared. Slowly opening her fingers, she saw the miracle of the flag going up, then frenziedly joyful waving. The bellow of the crowd was so deafening that no-one heard the final horn. It had been such a wonderful match that the sporting, marvellously good-natured crowd could forgive a British victory and poured on to the pitch to honour all the eight heroes.

Perdita's throat was so dry that she couldn't whoop for joy. Instead she hurled her stick high into the blue and people rushed forward to catch it.

Desperate to get the first quote, a *Scorpion* reporter had pinched one of Bart's ponies and thundered up the field to thrust a tape recorder under Perdita's nose. What with the frantic panting of Spotty and Perdita's delirious croaking, the reply was pretty inaudible.

'Well done, Perdeeta!' It was Angel, reaching out to shake hands and hug her. Next minute Shark was beside her, looking like his namesake deprived of a nice fat human. Then suddenly his ugly face split into a great grin and he clamped a vast sweaty arm round her shoulders.

'Well done, honey. I've gotta admit you outplayed us. I never thought I'd say that to a slip of a girl.'

'Who gave you the slip?' Bouncing through the crowds like a dog through a barley field, Seb hugged Perdita and pumped Shark's hand.

'Jolly big of Shark,' he added in an undertone. 'Evidently Bart offered him a quarter of a million bucks if they won.'

'Christ!' said Perdita in awe, as Spotty nearly disappeared beneath a wave of patting hands.

Refusing to shake hands with anyone, his face a death mask, Red galloped past her.

'Well played,' called out Perdita, amazed that she suddenly felt so sorry for him.

He turned unsmiling. 'Fat lot of good it did me. You did great. Back off, you fuckers,' he snarled at the advancing photographers. Then, seriously endangering their Nikons and their lives, he galloped straight through the lot of them.

It seemed ages before Perdita could wade through the surging ocean of wellwishers back to the pony lines. On the way she lost her hat and her whip and very nearly her shirt. Looking up, she noticed Rupert fighting his way towards her. Seeing the expression of blazing triumph on his face, she glanced wistfully round to see at whom it was directed, but there were only swooning, excited cheering crowds. Slowly it dawned that he was looking just at her. An instant later he'd dragged her off Spotty into his arms.

'I'm all hot and sweaty,' she stammered.

'Well done, my darling! Oh Christ, I'm proud of you!'

As she looked up, bewildered, he put a hand on her soaked head and pulled it against his chest. He could feel the frantic pounding of her heart.

'Come on, Rupe,' shouted the *Sun* as the press closed in.

'You must recognize Perdita as your daughter now.'

Rupert grinned round at them: 'Course I do. Only a Campbell-Black could have played that well.' He looked down at Perdita. 'It's all right, lovie. There's no need to cry. You're mine now. I'll take care of you.' Then, to make her laugh: 'We'd better not hang around or *The Scorpion*'ll accuse you of parent-molesting.'

As the teams lined up, even the normally impassive Ricky was hard put to hide his elation.

'They said we hadn't a fox's chance in a hunt kennel,' he stammered to the grey-mushroom field of microphones, 'but we did it. The boys and Perdita played so well, I just had to follow them round. That's not to say the Americans didn't play brilliantly. But in the end we played better.'

'D'you think all the flak you got from everyone in the last month sharpened up your game?' asked *The Sunday Times*.

Ricky smiled briefly. 'No, I was always good.'

'Oh, isn't he macho?' sighed the girl from the *Mail on Sunday*. 'Talk about a cliff face turning into an avalanche on the field. What are you doing this evening?'

The Westchester Cup had been described by a former

player as a singularly hideous trophy, but nothing had ever looked more beautiful to the English team as Ricky walked up to deafening cheers to accept it from Prince Charles, who was obviously as delighted as he was amazed by the result.

'Well done, Ricky, absolutely marvellous.'

It was hard to curtsy with any grace in boots and breeches, but when Perdita, still red-eyed from dust and her rapprochement with Rupert, approached the Prince, he bent forward and kissed her cheek, and when he pinned a little ruby brooch in the shape of a rose on her dark blue jersey the crowd roared their approval.

To Perdita's amazement Spotty won Best Playing Pony. He was so delighted to be stuffed so full of Polos and the centre of attention that he forgot to fart. There was a brief pause as the Most Valuable Player was announced.

'Must be Red,' whispered Perdita to Seb.

'By general consensus of opinion,' said Brad Dillon rustling his papers, 'because his utter stability held the American team together and because he refused to ride off a seriously injured player in the true tradition of sportmanship, the award for the Most Valuable Player of the series goes to Luke Alderton.'

An amazed hush was followed by the most deafening storm of cheering of the day and it continued long after Luke, in a pair of torn jeans and an old, blue denim shirt, had fought his way up to collect the beautiful, rearing silver pony. Overwhelmed with longing and pride, Perdita wanted to rush forward and hug him, but the whooping, yodelling, ecstatic crowd divided them and the next moment she found herself being swept off by Ricky to ring Daisy before the press conference.

Only Chessie, the ultimate upstager, having ostentatiously flung off her black silk shawl, managed to pummel her way past a clicking frenzy of cameramen and security guards and fling her arms round Ricky's neck in ecstasy.

'You won, my darling, you won! Don't you realize what that means?'

As the photographers swung into action, frantic to capture the moment, Perdita turned away, horror-struck, and found herself looking straight at Bart and Red.

'It was your fucking fault,' Bart was hissing at Red. 'You forced them to drop Luke.'

Red, greyer beneath his suntan than ever Ricky had been, was looking utterly desolate.

After the match there was a celebration dinner at the Quinta Hotel organized by the American Polo Association and the cock-a-hoop sponsors.

'Everyone is expected to get plastered,' Rupert told the England team, 'but there seems to be a general consensus of opinion that the men will wear ties and you will all behave well, at least for the duration of dinner. That means no eloping before the Queen,' he added in an undertone to Ricky.

When they met up in the lobby, Rupert looked disapprovingly at Ricky's black tie. 'At least you might have left that off after winning the Westchester. You can't wallow in misery for ever.' Then, seeing Taggie's face: 'No, I'm sorry, you've won the Westchester. You can do what you bloody well like.'

Perdita, in a black, backless dress which matched her bruises and the dark circles under her eyes, had a feeling of total unreality. The euphoria of winning and of Rupert at last accepting her was fast receding. She was worried about Ricky who seemed unbelievably twitchy and couldn't get plastered like everyone else, but all she could think about was whether or not Luke would turn up.

A louring, glowering Bart arrived with Chessie, who was looking thoroughly over-excited and more minxy than ever in a gold tunic exactly matching her suntan and with a golden rose in her hair.

'Well, thank you, Perdita,' she murmured as she passed. 'You certainly contributed to an English victory this afternoon.'

But before Perdita could answer, there was a burst of cheering as Red walked in with the American team. He had totally regained his composure and was laughing and joking. He was wearing a pink blazer edged with purple, because the entire Polo Youth of America seemed now to have gone back to wearing pale blue blazers braided with emerald green.

There was even more noisy rejoicing when Mike and Seb rolled up, already plastered, with Lily and Annie from the Nevada brothel and a blissful Louisa wheeling a rather pale Dommie, with his knee in plaster, around in a large shopping trolley which they'd pinched from a local hypermarket.

'Haven't you got any dope for Ricky?' whispered Perdita as she hugged Dommie. 'He needs something to cheer him up.'

'He's just won the fucking Westchester,' said Seb. 'Some people are never satisfied.'

'Sharon is,' giggled Dommie. 'She's just seduced Brigadier Hughie.'

'And we've promoted Corporal to General, so he'll be Sharon's next target,' added Seb, chucking a cauliflower floret at Bobby Ferraro.

'She's going to lose David Waterlane at this rate,' said Louisa.

'I think her sights are set somewhat higher than a baronet,' murmured Seb. 'She was last heard remarking, "How naice his hay-ness looked in his off-whaite suit." Oh, come on, Perdita, cheer *up*! We won!'

Taggie, realizing that Perdita's spirits were at rock bottom, took her aside. 'It's so heavenly Rupert's accepted you at last. He's so pleased. He can't wait to get you up on all his ponies. I promise he'll be a marvellous father. Once he's on someone's side, it's one hundred and fifty per cent.'

'You do *love* him,' said Perdita wistfully.

'Oh, more than anything. I still wake up sweating in the middle of the night, and have to reach out and touch him to prove it isn't all a dream.'

'How can you be so nice?' asked Perdita, shaking her head. 'You ought to give lessons.'

After that Perdita got no peace. Everyone wanted to congratulate her and take her through every stroke of the game, until Seb came up grinning wickedly.

'You've drawn the short straw, sweetheart,' he said. 'You've got to sit on Hughie's right. Talk about the price of fame. And watch out now he's in bimbo limbo. He may start touching you up.'

Joining them, Ricky pushed a loose tendril of hair behind Perdita's ear: 'You OK?'

'Of course. I just wish Mummy was here.'

'So do I,' said Seb feelingly.

Ricky frowned: 'Oh, fuck off.'

Then, as Seb sloped off grinning, Ricky added: 'Look, will you give Daisy a message when you get home?'

But Perdita never heard what he was going to say because, as dinner was announced, Luke walked in with Margie Bridgwater who was looking staggering in clinging crimson, slit up the sides to show an eternity of long, brown leg.

I must behave, I must behave, Perdita told herself through gritted teeth. As she fought her way down to her seat at the top table, she had to pass Luke, and almost wrenched her stomach muscles pulling them in, so she needn't touch him.

'Well done,' he said slowly. 'I knew you had mega-star quality, but I never figured you were that good. You pulled them together. You won that game.'

Oh, that deep, slow husky voice. Perdita wanted to collapse into his arms, but Margie was hovering, smiling but tense.

'You taught me everything I know,' stammered Perdita. 'We'd never have won if they hadn't dropped you.'

For a second they gazed at each other, both hollow-eyed, neither able to smile.

'Buck up, Perdita,' said Brigadier Hughie, putting two sweating hands on her bruised arms. 'I'm starving. Too nervous to get any lunch.'

Some joker, to make matters worse, had also put her next to Red. The twins, very drunk now, started bombarding them with rolls, yelling: 'Kiss and make up, kiss and make up.'

Then, as Sharon swept in, somewhat flushed, with a boot-faced David Waterlane, they started singing: 'For she's a jolly good fellater, for she's a jolly good fellater.'

'Shut up, you two,' said Rupert, grinning.

He was trying to listen to the head of Revlon who was forecasting the worst share slide in US history.

'Dollar's sagging, interest rates are soaring.' He lowered his voice. 'I've sold all my capital stock and gone liquid.'

'I'm much more worried about this hurricane reaching England,' said Rupert. 'Christ knows how many trees I'll have down.'

He glanced at his watch – half past ten in the morning in

England. Seeing Taggie was safely sitting down near Bibi and Angel, he nipped out to ring his stockbroker.

Red and Perdita had a perfectly polite conversation as they both failed to touch their pale pink lobster mousse, but there was no longer a flicker of empathy between them. Here is a man who used to have me screaming and begging for more, thought Perdita, as he experimented on my body with all the detachment of a behavioural scientist testing a cageful of rats.

It was like visiting a garden which had seemed vast and mysterious when one was a child, but which now had shrunk to insignificance. Mercifully Luke was at a different table. All she could see was his broad back and his red-gold hair starting to stick upwards despite being slicked down with water. Far too often Margie's laughing, aquiline profile turned towards him. Each time she put a crimson-nailed hand on his arm Perdita felt red-hot pokers stabbing her gut.

Bottles rose green and empty from the table. Courses came and went. A cake with scarlet icing in the shape of the red rose of England was cut by Ricky and passed down the tables and thrown about. The Westchester Cup, brimming with champagne, was passed round and round and each valiant victor and brave loser toasted.

Perdita had no idea what she or Red talked about or what Hughie told her about Singapore, until Brad Dillon, handsome in a sand-coloured suit, rose to propose the toast of the winners to a bombardment of flying grapes.

'We've skunked you in twelve out of fourteen of the series, so I guess we can be generous at this moment in time,' he said expansively, 'but we're coming over to get it back next year. We've only loaned it you.'

I wish Spotty could come in and eat bread dipped in salt like the Maltese Cat, thought Perdita. As Brigadier Hughie, who could never miss an opportunity to yak, lurched to his feet a piece of cake hit him on the shoulder.

'And the Brigadier's blocked the shot,' shouted Seb as the cake was followed by a carrot, a piece of celery and an After Eight which fell out of its paper.

'Shut up, you chaps,' said Hughie. 'I've got a surprise announcement to make.'

'The Japs have invaded Singapore,' shouted Rupert.

Everyone howled with laughter.

'A surprise announcement,' Hughie ploughed on. 'By mutual agreement of the British and American Polo Associations, I should like to announce that Ricky France-Lynch has finally been put up to ten, the first British player since the war to achieve that honour.'

An amazed and delighted storm of cheering followed. People were thumping Ricky on the back and yelling, 'Speech, Speech.'

He's made it, thought Perdita dully, the final rung. How was Chessie taking the news? But, looking across the room, she went cold. Chessie's chair was empty.

75

Back in Eldercombe, Daisy, unable to sleep, stayed up all night putting the finishing touches on a painting of Mrs Hughie's Burmese cats before watching the second half of the match live at five o'clock in the morning. Venturer must be delirious. It was truly gripping television – and Daisy was thrilled Perdita played so brilliantly and didn't seem unduly fazed about Red. She also experienced passionate relief when Perdita rang to say Rupert had at last forgiven her and admitted paternity and how lovely he'd been.

But all this bounty made Daisy even more bitterly ashamed that she should feel so suicidal at a British victory. Throughout the match her eyes had constantly been drawn to Ricky who, despite his suntan, looked incredibly grim and gaunt.

She ought to be pleased for him and managed to congratulate Perdita very convincingly when she rang up, but when Perdita said, 'Talk to Ricky,' Daisy couldn't face it and had hung up and taken the telephone off the hook. Outside the sun was rising and in the hall mirror she saw, wiping away the tears, that she'd streaked burnt sienna all over her face.

Having let the dogs out, she retired to bed, pulling the duvet over her head and falling into a miserable half-sleep. After lunch she took the dogs out for a walk. She noticed next year's sticky buds, the same Mars-red as polo boots, pushing their way through the ragged, orange leaves of the horse chestnuts. She passed a burdock bush, so mildewed, brown and shrivelled among all the ravishing autumnal oranges and golds. It left a cluster of burrs on her coat. Shivering, she thought how it symbolized a desperately clinging, defeated, abandoned woman. Oh, please don't let me get like that, she prayed. A huge, red sun was dropping behind the woods as she crossed Ricky's watermeadows. The dogs were sniffing frantically beside the gate and there was a strong smell of fox. It must have just killed a baby rabbit – soft, grey fur littered the grass.

Daisy started to cry again. Back in the house she put the telephone back on the hook. Immediately the *Daily Star* rang.

'Hi, Daisy, great about Perdita. You must be a very proud Mum.'

'I am.'

'Great about Rupert accepting paternity.'

'It's lovely, but I don't want to talk about it. I won't have any mouth left if I keep shooting it off.'

Slamming down the receiver, Daisy took it off the hook again. She tried and failed to paint and then at eight o'clock took a large vodka and tonic into the sitting room to watch a recording of the match. It was the real thing this time, all six chukkas and Luke winning the MVP award. His freckles were exactly like the puppies, thought Daisy. He'd be lovely to paint. And then she saw Chessie hurtling into Ricky's arms, and, feeling as though someone had dropped a tombstone on her from a great height, turned off the television. All hope gone. She'd never, never, known misery like it.

Outside the wind was rising, so she shut the windows. In the kitchen the puppies were chewing up a dark red book called *The Nude in Painting*. On the table was a thank-you letter Violet had started to the mother of her boyfriend:

'*I had a really good time,*' read Daisy. '*It's lovely to get away from Rutshire. Mum's so depressed at the moment.*'

And I hoped I was putting on a brave face, thought Daisy. Wondering if Red Indians put on brave faces when they got up in the morning, she started to cry again. The only answer was to get drunk. Sobbing unceasingly, she finished the vodka bottle and then passed out.

She woke to find herself on the drawing-room sofa with the dogs crammed into two armchairs gazing at her reproachfully. Outside the Niagara Falls seemed to have been diverted under the house. Whimpering, she opened the curtains and shrieked as a laser beam of light pierced her eyes. There had obviously been a terrific storm in the night. You could have gone white-water rafting on the Frogsmore as it hurtled past. Branches littered the lawn. She could see several trees down in Ricky's woods and the track to Eldercombe was full of puddles turned the colour of strong tea by the disturbed earth.

Incapable of anything else, Daisy carried on crying. As the telephone was off the hook, a succession of reporters were reduced to rolling up at the house to discuss Perdita's great triumph. Unable to face them, Daisy took refuge in the potting shed. Here she discovered the nude she'd done of Drew three years ago and brought it into the kitchen determined to burn it.

At lunchtime, when the whole valley was steaming and a primrose-yellow sun had come through the mist like a halo searching for a saint, a car drew up outside. It was Violet, delighted Perdita had won, but more interested in the weekend she'd just spent in the Lakes with her new boyfriend.

'How d'you tell you're in love, Mum?'

'D'you go weak at the knees when he kisses you?'

'I don't know,' said Violet perplexed, 'because I'm always lying down. Are you all right, Mum? You look awful.'

'I think I'm getting gastric flu,' muttered Daisy.

'Oh, poor you! Go to bed. Why's the telephone off the hook?' asked Violet, putting it back. Immediately it rang.

'It'll be for me.' Violet snatched it up, then, in disappointment as she handed Daisy the receiver, 'It's for you.'

'Where the hell have you been?' howled Ricky.

'Oh, out and about.' Daisy tried desperately to sound bright. 'It's terrific you won. You sound as though you're just next door.'

'I am next door,' said Ricky brusquely. 'We've got to talk. I'll be with you in five minutes.'

Violet picked up her car keys: 'I'm just popping down to the village shop for some cigarettes. D'you want anything?'

But Daisy had bolted upstairs, cleaning her teeth until they bled, scraping the olive-green moss off her tongue. However many vats of eyedrops she poured into her eyes, they still glowed like carbuncles, remaining determinedly piggy and swollen. Sailors could climb the rigging of wrinkles under her eyes, and when she tried desperately to rub them away they wouldn't shift. Frantically she slapped green foundation over her red-veined cheeks, but she still looked like a ghoul, so she rubbed it off, which made her cheeks glow brighter than ever.

Suddenly she remembered the mess in the kitchen and, clutching her pounding skull, stumbled downstairs and started throwing things into the washing-up machine. The puppies were now calmly eviscerating a cushion, scattering feathers all over the hall.

'Oh, oh, oh,' wailed Daisy. It was all hopeless. Slumping down at the kitchen table she started to cry again. Ethel shambled over and put a muddy speckled paw on her knee. Jumping up, Little Chef tried to lick away her tears, but they flowed even faster. Then, through the shaggy curtain of clematis and honeysuckle, she saw Ricky's car draw up and, despite everything, felt her stomach disappear as she watched him get out. He looked shadowed under the eyes and terribly grim. Next minute she winced as Little Chef dug his claws into her jeaned thighs and shot off through the door, screaming with joy to welcome him.

'Oh, please,' pleaded Daisy, clutching her head as Ethel let out her great bass-baritone bark and the puppies took up a yapping chorus.

Ricky looked even grimmer as he came through the door with Little Chef wriggling ecstatically under one arm. Then he caught sight of Daisy and stopped short.

'Jesus! What's up with you?'

'Hangover,' muttered Daisy. 'I feel dreadful.'

'Shouldn't drink so much. Serves you right.'

'I've been under a lot of strain. D'you want a cup of coffee?'

'No. I want you to come outside.' Taking her hand, Ricky dragged her protesting out on to the lawn where everything dripped and sparkled in the sunlight.

'I know the garden's a mess,' groaned Daisy as the two-foot grass drenched her jeans. 'Lend me a combine harvester and I'll make you enough hay to see even Wayne through the winter. I promise I'll tidy up everything, including myself. I know it's awkward with Chessie coming back, but we won't get in your way.' Then, seeing the unrelentingly bleak expression on his face, 'Just let us stay till Christmas.'

'No, I w-w-want you out of here t-t-tonight.'

Daisy's lip started to tremble: 'But you're supposed to give us a month's notice.'

'I've changed the lease.' Ricky removed a burr from her hair with a desperately shaking hand. 'There's a new clause which says you can't stay here any longer if your landlord falls in love with you.'

But Daisy wasn't listening. 'We've got nowhere to go.'

Roughly Ricky turned her round to face the sun, examining her deathly pallor, the hectically reddened cheeks, the swollen eyes spilling over with tears.

'I'm totally repulsive,' she sobbed.

But when she tried to jerk her head away, his hands closed on either side of her face like a clamp.

'Look at me.'

With infinite reluctance Daisy raised her eyes. Even jet lag couldn't ruin his bone structure or the length of his dark eyelashes.

'It's not fair you should be so beautiful,' she mumbled helplessly, 'and we've got nowhere to go.'

'What about R-r-r-robinsgrove?' stammered Ricky. 'You can bring Perdita and Violet and Eddie and Ethel and the puppies, even that inc-c-c-ontinent cat if you like. I love you,' he said desperately. 'Will you marry me?'

'Me marry *you*?' mumbled Daisy incredulously.

His face was suddenly so unbelievably softened that she had to drop her eyes hastily, fearing some cosmic, practical joke.

'Oh, please,' Ricky spoke to the top of her head. 'I couldn't understand why I was so bad-tempered in America. I couldn't sleep – I mean even less than usual. Then I realized I was missing you hopelessly all the time. I had to fight the t-t-temptation to ring you and beg you to come over.' He smiled slightly. 'I searched everywhere for daisies, but the lawns are so perfect over there they don't have any.'

744

The rosiness of her cheeks spread to the whole of Daisy's face, but she simply couldn't get any words out. To save her trouble Ricky bent his head and kissed her, first very shyly and tentatively, then, when she responded with alacrity, very hard indeed, by the end of which Daisy's knees had literally given way for the first time in her life and as she couldn't speak or stand up they collapsed on to the old garden bench she still hadn't got round to painting.

'But what about Chessie?' she mumbled finally.

'Buggered off with Red.'

'What! When?'

'The night of the Westchester. She vanished in the middle of dinner. I went back to the house we'd rented. I couldn't face any more celebrating. Didn't feel there was anything to celebrate. Half an hour later Rupert rolled up with a letter to me that Red had had delivered to the restaurant. He said he was desperately sorry, but he'd been hopelessly in love with Chessie ever since she'd become his stepmother, but had been fighting it because he hadn't wanted to screw up his father. It all falls into place – why he was so irredeemably bloody to her always, why he was so frantic to beat us. He was far more terrified she'd come back to me than Bart was. Then she hurled herself on me after the match and it finished him off completely. So he finally thought, Sod Bart, declared himself and they ran off.'

'Goodness,' said Daisy in awe. 'Just like that?'

'Well, not entirely,' Ricky shrugged. 'They've obviously been sidling round each other for ages. Perdita admitted she caught them in bed after the polo ball.'

'Oh, the poor little duck,' said Daisy appalled. 'Why didn't she tell anyone?'

'She promised Red she wouldn't.'

'Is she absolutely devastated?'

'No, at least not about him. Daisy darling, can we talk about us?'

'Poor you,' said Daisy in horror. 'You must have been . . .'

'Ecstatic, giddy with relief. I'd psyched myself out for so long, obsessed with proving we could win the Westchester, obsessed with getting Chessie back because I felt so guilty about Will. I knew she was miserable with Bart and I'd driven her into his arms in the first place. Suddenly I was free. I felt a great burden falling off my back. Like one of Victor's ponies at the end of a chukka.'

Daisy giggled.

'I got the first plane back,' Ricky went on, 'getting more and more panicky because I couldn't get you on the telephone. Did you know there's been a hurricane? London's out of action. The Stock Exchange has stopped trading. Fifteen million trees have been blown down.'

'That's nothing to losing you,' said Daisy simply. 'When I saw Chessie leaping on you and looking so beautiful, I was so unhappy I just got drunk.'

'I was worried you'd see that,' admitted Ricky, 'and I was worried Drew was in Rutshire, festering because we hadn't asked him to play.'

'Drew?' stammered Daisy, going even pinker.

'Drew,' said Ricky acidly and told her about finding the puppies eating Drew's shoe the day before he left. 'Jesus, I was jealous!'

'Oh, how awful! I'm so sorry.'

'I'll forgive you if you never, never, sleep with him again.' Ricky cut short her frantic apologies with another kiss, then he drew her head against his chest, stroking her hair.

'It's strange,' he said slowly. 'I feel so safe when you're in my arms, but all I want to do is to make you feel safe. You've always reminded me of a stray bitch chucked out for getting in pup, who, although she looked after all her puppies in the wild really well, needed a loving master and a home.'

'Oh, I did,' sighed Daisy.

'It's also a dreadful confession,' said Ricky, 'but it's the first time in my life I've loved something more than polo. My nerve failed me at the beginning of that third match, I didn't want to win because subconsciously I didn't want Chessie back.'

Snuggling her face happily into his chest, Daisy suddenly saw pink spots before her eyes. Could it be her hangover? Then she blinked again and, putting her hand up, realized they were real pink silk spots on a blue background.

'You've left off your black tie,' she said in amazement.

Ricky glanced down. For a second he, too, had difficulty speaking.

'I don't have to wear it any more. The mourning's over.'

Wonderingly, Daisy put her hand up and touched the scar on his face. For a second he flinched, then his hand closed over hers. 'Darling, darling Daisy, are you quite sure you don't mind being a double parent again?'

Suddenly he looked so vulnerable that Daisy put her arms round his neck and kissed him. They were so engrossed they didn't hear the dogs barking or pause for breath until Violet appeared in the doorway.

'Hi, Mum. I'm back. Christ!'

'Bugger off,' ordered Ricky. 'We're busy.'

'Okey'doke,' said Violet.

But two minutes later she put her head round the door with a faint smirk. 'Sorry to interrupt you two love birds, but it's Drew on the telephone for you, Mum.'

Ricky's eyes narrowed. 'It is bloody not,' he howled, loping back into the house. Temporarily blinded after the sunlight, he snatched the receiver from Violet.

'Drew? You can fuck off, and if you ever come within a million miles of Daisy, I'll smash your head in – and break your bloody jaw. Pity Angel didn't do it properly the first time,' and he crashed the receiver back on the hook.

Violet whistled. 'Wowee! Macho man.'

'Don't you get lippy with me, miss,' snapped Ricky. 'I'm going to be your new stepfather.'

For a second they glared at each other, then Violet giggled.

'I *had* guessed. Look, I'm really, really, pleased. Mum adores you so much. She's been madly in love with you for yonks.'

Ricky blushed and was about to return to Daisy in the garden when he knocked over the nude of Drew which had been leaning inward against the kitchen table.

'My God,' he exploded.

'I quite agree,' said Violet. 'That is definitely one for the log basket.'

76

A very subdued Perdita returned from Palm Springs. She was delighted – despite Daisy's apprehension – that her mother and Ricky were getting married, but their almost incandescent happiness only emphasized her utter desolation. The telephone rang constantly with patrons suddenly finding a hole in next year's team for a five-goal player. But she accepted nothing. She just thought about Luke and cursed herself for not having had the courage to tell him how much she loved him. But surely if he'd felt anything he would have come forward. Perhaps he did love that cool, stylish lawyer with the warm eyes. Daisy was spending most of her time up at Robinsgrove which gave Perdita the chance endlessly to watch videos of the Westchester and marvel at Luke's unselfishness and his sheer bloody-minded tenacity.

Ricky and Daisy had wanted a quiet wedding at Rutminster Register Office, but as usual the carnival took over and every polo player in the land – except Drew who'd been banned by Ricky – seemed to have rolled up with polo sticks to form a guard of honour outside Eldercombe Church. Daisy wore a dark green velvet suit with a pillbox hat which kept sliding off her newly washed piled-up hair. She looked so radiant no one noticed the ladder in her tights nor the inch of red silk petticoat hanging beneath her hem, nor the mud on her heels from taking the puppies out in the garden before she left.

Rupert, who, on the Chairman of Revlon's advice, had gone liquid before the stock exchange crash which occurred a few days after the final of the Westchester, insisted on throwing a party for them afterwards. Eddie, euphoric to be out of school and at the prospect of endless fishing and shooting ahead, confided to Perdita in a lull in the service that Taggie and Rupert were planning a surprise party for her twenty-first birthday next week and he hoped to wrangle another day off school. But this did little to raise Perdita's spirits. Then, to crown it, they sang 'Dear Lord and Father of Mankind' during the signing of the register. When they came to the bit about the *'Still Small Voice of Calm'* speaking through the *'Earthquake, Wind and Fire'*, Perdita was so sharply reminded of Luke that she fled out of a side door.

Rupert found her, oblivious of the icy wind and a lurking circle of press, sobbing pitifully against a yew tree and hustled her into his car.

748

'I didn't mean to screw up Mum's wedding,' she choked, 'but I can't bear it.'

Rupert got a hip flask out of the dashboard.

'I brought this to steady Ricky's nerves. Forgot he didn't drink. Have a great slug. Warm you up. Look, I know how ghastly these things are.' He put a hand on her heaving shoulders, appalled by the jagged edges of collarbone and shoulder-blade. 'I never really understood unhappiness until I thought I wouldn't end up with Tag.'

'Luke's like Taggie,' sobbed Perdita. 'They're both seriously good people.'

'And prodigals like you and me are far too insecure to find happiness with any other kind of person. You turned Luke down once – told him never to come near you again. You'll have to make the first move.'

Putting a hand in his inside pocket he drew out a Coutts cheque book and a fountain pen.

'It's your birthday next week. We're both Scorpios.'

'I know. Eddie said you might be giving me a party. It's really kind but I couldn't.'

'Sure,' said Rupert. 'But you can't stop being twenty-one. I've been meaning to settle some money on you. Ricky's always said the thing that you craved most was financial security. This should be a start.'

In his big blue scrawl he wrote her a cheque for £100,000.

Over in Florida, Luke was slowly going out of his mind with misery. Seeing Perdita at Palm Springs had made everything a million times worse. He had finally levelled with Margie, telling her it could never work out. Now he wanted to slink into his lair and die. But, with Red disappearing with Chessie and Angel shoved off with Bibi to play in the Argentine Open, there was no-one to cope with the Herculean task of comforting a maddened, desperately humiliated Bart.

For not only had Bart lost his wife, but his fortune as well. In his obsession with polo he had neglected his business and totally failed to anticipate the stock market collapse. Black Monday had cost him over a billion and chopped the value of Alderton Airlines by ninety-five per cent. Bart had also borrowed heavily to take over oil and property companies, gold mines, theatres and big department stores. Now these had to be sold off for virtually nothing, most of them to a gloating Victor, when the Wall Street merchant banker withdrew a $330,000,000 loan which Bart desperately needed to help lower his enormous interest charges at other banks. He had also had to sell his five houses and put *El Paradiso* on the market.

Bart was very unpopular, so no friends came forward to bail him out, particularly in the polo world. Ponies he had spent $100,000 on were now being sold off for a fifth of the price. He had enough to live on and would no doubt claw his way back one day, but he couldn't support a polo team.

The only good thing that had come out of the whole sorry business, reflected Luke, was that his father and he had at last become friends.

One Friday afternoon at the end of November Luke was down at *El Paradiso* trying to forget Perdita for one second by concentrating on breaking one of Bart's young thoroughbreds which they'd managed to salvage from the wreckage.

A slender, dark brown filly, with one white sock and a white star who turned both ways automatically, she was such a natural she reminded Luke of Fantasma, when he'd ridden her back from the river after her first, maddened bucking-and-bolting spree in Argentina. He wondered, as he wondered every day, how she was and prayed Alejandro's grooms hadn't broken her glorious, cantankerous, tempestuous spirit. A warm breeze shook the 'For Sale' sign hanging forlornly outside the barn and sent a waft of orange blossom towards him.

Oh, Perdita, he thought hopelessly. To him, she truly was the Lost One now.

He was roused from his black musings by a groom telling him that Angel was ringing from Buenos Aires in a complete panic. Alejandro, the captain of the Mendozas' team for which Angel was playing in the Argentine Open, had broken his leg in the semi-final.

'It's the final on Sunday,' begged Angel. 'Alejandro say you only back in zee world who can stand in for heem.'

'I have no horses,' said Luke in despair. 'Alejandro's got my best one.'

'Eef you come and play the Open, Alejandro say you can buy back Fantasma. He say she never go as well for him.'

But, the blissful prospect of getting Fantasma back apart, the moment Luke agreed to play he regretted it. He knew it was every polo player's dream to play in the Open and no American had ever reached the final. But he didn't feel up to it. There was no way the Mendozas' team, which consisted of Angel and Alejandro's two sons, Patricio and Lorenzo, could win without Alejandro, particularly when they were pitted against the might of Juan and Miguel O'Brien and their cousins Kevin and Seamus, all ten-goal players who'd beaten them five years running. The two teams detested each other and there had been endless squabbles over officials and umpires being bribed and both teams threatening to pull out. Fans would turn up on Sunday to see them tear each other apart. No-one ever shook hands at the end of the game.

Besides Luke didn't want to go to Argentina. It reminded him far too poignantly of Perdita. Making matters worse, Bart insisted on coming too to lend support, which was the last thing Luke needed, as Bart, unused to being poor, would make a fuss about travelling Economy and not staying in five-star hotels.

They had great difficulty landing at Buenos Aires because there had been a coup and the airport was on strike. Although the whole town was sky-blue with jacaranda blossom, soldiers with cigarettes hanging out of their handsome mouths were everywhere. Armoured cars patrolled the streets. Bart's wallet was promptly nicked and, when he stormed into the police station an officer with his boots up on the desk told him there was a coup on and no-one had time to bother about stolen goods.

The taxis were also on strike and no-one was there to meet them. Luke was wearily hiring a car to drive out to Alejandro's *estancia* when Angel rolled up, black under the eyes, already in a frightful stew about Sunday and not at all pleased to see his bossy father-in-law whom he disliked intensely.

As Angel negotiated the lunatic traffic out of Buenos Aires, using his horn at red lights rather than his brakes, he deliberately excluded Bart by gabbling incessantly in

Spanish to Luke, who felt burdened by added responsibility as he realized how crucial Sunday's match was for Angel. Having deeply offended his family, his fellow players and his country by taking American citizenship, Angel felt he would only be taken back into the fold again if he played well in the Open.

At General Piran all was pain. Every eucalyptus leaf, every speck of brown dust, the pampas stretching like his love to infinity, reminded Luke of Perdita. Claudia and all the children hugged him, the grooms, gauchos and their wives rushed forward to pump his hand, even Raimundo, whom he'd hit across the café after he'd tried to back Tero by tying her to Angel's car, seemed delighted to see him. Why had Señor Gracias stayed away so long? they demanded and where was Perdita, the little lost one?

But Luke was only interested in seeing Fantasma. Rounding the orange grove, he saw her before she saw him. Flattening her ears, pawing at the floor, she was furiously trying to gnaw wood off her half-door through her muzzle. At least they hadn't broken her spirit.

At the sound of his voice, Fantasma looked up incredulously, stared for a second, whickered like an earthquake, then once again soared over her half-door like a lark in flight. Charging up to Luke, she began rubbing her head against his chest, nuzzling his pockets as though he'd never been away.

Ripping off her muzzle, stroking and hugging her, Luke ran his hands down her legs, still as familiar to him as the pattern on his own bedroom curtains. Thank Christ, she was OK. His hands trembled so much he could hardly undo the packet of Polos he'd bought her at the airport and in the middle he had to get out a handkerchief to blow his nose and wipe his eyes.

Having crunched up every Polo, Fantasma wouldn't let him out of her sight, jumping fences and grazing close by when he lunched under the trees with the family, then insanely, shrilly jealous when he tried out other ponies for the match the next day.

Alejandro, who was in a lot of pain, was very bad-tempered and, yelling instructions from his wheelchair, only succeeded in unnerving the rest of the team. For too many years he had manipulated Patricio and Lorenzo like puppets. How would they take orders from Luke?

Luke and Bart stayed the night with Bibi and Angel, who were restoring a romantic ruin near by with a beautiful deserted garden. But, as the match approached, Angel got more and more nervous and ratty, ending up in having such a row with Bibi that she flatly refused to come and watch him.

Match day dawned. True to form, Fantasma started lashing out with both back legs the moment she saw the polo basket containing all the tack going into the lorry. On the day of last year's final the grooms of the wily O'Briens had reached the Palermo ground three hours early to bag the better stalls on the shadier side of the pitch. This year they were outfoxed by Raimundo and the Mendoza grooms who arrived four hours early to annex the cooler stalls. This so incensed the O'Briens that they started sneering that the Mendozas must be very pushed to include two damned 'Americanos' in their team. Soon both sides were hissing like Montagues and Capulets and only Luke shoving his large shoulders between rival grooms stopped a fight breaking out.

Oblivious of all this, Angel sat on an upturned bucket with his head in his hands, not bothering to check his horses or even warm up.

'She'll show up,' said Luke, resisting the temptation to shake Angel. 'Don't be so goddam histrionic.'

Ten minutes before the parade both captains were giving last minute pep-talks. The Mendozas had speed and the courage of lions, but the O'Briens were technically superior and hit the ball harder and more accurately.

'The only way to beat them,' urged Luke as he pulled on his lucky gloves which were mostly hole now, 'is to stop them opening up and press them all over the field, which means sticking like leeches.'

The O'Briens, who, like Perdita, had been watching videos of the Westchester, realized they must obstruct Luke as much as possible and divert his fusillade of deadly passes away from his young team.

'Don't hang on to the ball,' ordered Miguel, swinging his mallet round and round to loosen up his massive shoulders, 'and don't let the Mendozas see what you're doing.'

Despite being surrounded by the skyscrapers of Buenos

Aires, few grounds are more beautiful or dramatic than the Number One field at Palermo with its forest of white flagpoles, lush tropical trees, green hedges lined with pink roses and huge stands rising like cliff faces to a white-hot sky on either side of a sage-green ground.

Two minutes before the parade Bibi crept into her seat beside Bart. She was almost deafened by the O'Brien supporters with their emerald-green parasols and the Mendoza fans with their primrose-yellow flags and banners, encouraging their teams on with a cacophony of trumpet and drum. Bart, who'd bought a new panama for the occasion, was outraged because he was too far from Luke to bombard him with last-minute instructions. All around him were beautiful, laughing girls unfazed by the heatwave, their shining hair cascading on to slim walnut-brown shoulders. Perhaps there was life after Chessie after all. Bibi was more aware, to the right, of a rampart of Angel's relations, who clearly recognized but studiously ignored her. Only marginally more hostile was Mrs Juan, Sitting Bully in person, whose huge bulk occupied three chairs instead of one.

'Here they come,' said Bibi in a choked voice. 'Oh, come on, Angel! Come on, Luke! Come on, the Mendozas!'

The heat, which had been stifling as the vast crowd began to file through the turnstiles, was now like a cauldron of boiling oil. With people all fanning themselves with programmes, the two stands were like vast swarms of white butterflies. Despite his air of smiling imperturbability, Luke's primrose shirt was drenched with sweat and his hands were propped on his saddle to conceal their trembling as he rode quietly out on Alejandro's most beautiful liver-chestnut mare. Beside him rode Lorenzo, Patricio and Angel, curls flowing out underneath their helmets, long limbs supple as liquorice sticks, faces white as flagposts. At mid-field waited the O'Briens, four, immensely strong, proud men in the prime of life, hell bent on a sixth victory, who would take no prisoners. Everyone had been looking forward to the band who had guarded the President for nearly 200 years, but they had been banned from the ground because of the coup, so a lone trumpeter played the Argentine National Anthem instead. The tantivy of horn and trumpet and the tumbril-beat of drums intensified.

'We are going to be keeled,' said Angel through clattering

teeth, 'and Bibi 'aven't even come and say goodbye to me.'

'Oh, God of battles! steel my soldiers' hearts;

Possess them not with fear,' muttered Luke to himself, but out loud, with a confidence he didn't feel, he said, 'Bullshit, we'll bury them.'

'Now he play bettair,' said Patricio, nudging Lorenzo and looking upwards. Following his gaze, Angel was stunned to see a little plane chugging across the sky trailing a message: 'Good luck, Angel, I love you, Bibi.'

The crowd burst into a collective roar of laughter. Angel went crimson but he was grinning like a pools winner. Now he would play like a king. He could hardly wait for the long-thighed umpire in his bright-blue shirt to chuck the ball in.

Luke found the Palermo Open quite different to any other tournament, not only because eight chukkas were played instead of the usual six, but also because the pace was twice as fast, the bumps three times as violent and the ponies four times as superior. There was no razzmatazz, no cheer leaders, no balloons, no commentary, because everyone in the madly excited crowd knew what was going on and made whistling sounds every time a foul occurred, often anticipating the umpire. All you could hear between the great roars of encouragement and the din of trumpet and drum was the clatter of incessantly galloping hooves, the snorting of the ponies, the desperate shouts of the players and the blind-man's tap, tap, tap of their sticks.

By any standard the first chukka was played on fast forward. To boost morale and rattle the O'Briens Alejandro had mounted his sons and Angel on his best ponies. Exploding on to the field shiny as conkers shot from their husks, they outraced the O'Brien ponies with ease. By the bell the Mendozas were ahead by a staggering 5-1, three of the goals scored by Angel.

The O'Briens' game-plan emerged as they settled down in the second chukka. Seamus O'Brien spent his time either sneakily inserting himself between Luke and the Mendozas' posts or luring Luke away from the goal-mouth so that Miguel and Juan could unleash their thunderbolts from the mid-field which would find the flags immediately or be tipped through by a returning Seamus. Playing with pulverizing attack, changing direction all the time, by the end of the third chukka the O'Briens were leading 10-5 and had plunged the volatile Mendozas into despair.

'Keep your shirts on, guys, you're doing great,' Luke reassured them as he mounted Fantasma, the only grey in the match, for the fourth chukka. As usual her beauty brought gasps of delight from the crowd and once again Luke felt humbled by the combination of courage, competitiveness, steel, intelligence and boundless energy. She always inspired him. Somehow he must try and settle his own side. But almost certainly it was going to be 11-5 as Juan hurtled towards goal on his fastest mare, the legendary Gatto, and like a matador, revelled in plunging another pic into the desperately injured Mendoza bull.

'We'll show them,' muttered Luke, and next moment Fantasma had streaked like a shooting star after Juan. Coming in from the right, Luke waited until her grey shoulder was level with Gatto's gleaming, dark brown quarters. He could also feel Miguel behind him breathing down his neck like a hair-dryer on high. Coolly he leant forward, hooked Juan's stick out of the way and then, with a lightning flick, backed the ball. Instantly Fantasma swivelled round, so, bypassing an astounded Miguel, Luke was able to hit the forehand straight to Angel who was waiting on the boards. Gathering up the ball like a lost lover, Angel dribbled it round, tossed and hit it in the air twice in a contemptuous piece of clowning, then took it upfield, passing to Lorenzo who galloped off and scored. The crowd erupted in delight at such dazzling play. Overjoyed, Bibi hugged Bart. Even Angel's rampart of relations were looking less supercilious.

A lone trumpeter up in the gods struck up the Stars and Stripes; Luke grinned and waved his stick. Two beautiful Argentine girls behind Bibi consulted their programmes and agreed the blond Americano was *muy atractivo*.

'My brother,' Bibi told them proudly.

In the fifth chukka the Mendozas rode their fast ponies again and closed the score to 8-10, but not for nothing did the blood of Irish kings run through the veins of the O'Briens. Refusing to be rattled, they fought back, furiously stampeding the score to 12-8. Having played their trump card to so little effect, the Mendozas started to panic.

Even worse, a second later Miguel pulled up dead on the line bringing down Luke on the beautiful liver-chestnut just behind him. Luke, winded, staggered to his feet. The chestnut stayed put and had to be shot. Channelling his fury into a superhuman effort against the opposition, Luke hit the ensuing penalty through the posts and into the road and a lorry full of soldiers, who, thinking it was part of the coup, reached for their guns.

In the sixth chukka the O'Briens were awarded a penalty four which Luke knocked out of the air to Angel who again took it upfield with three almost languorously contemptuous offside forehands and then scored with an exquisite nearside cut shot. The crowd boiled over; 10-12 and Angel's relations were all shaking Bart and Bibi by the hand. Angel's bay mare had a lot to do with that goal, thought Luke darkly, but no-one told her so. In fact none of those gallant ponies had been patted once in the whole match except by him.

The heat was awful and even the umpires' ponies were white with sweat. He must concentrate. He was exhausted after a long flight, unused to playing eight chukkas, unacclimatized to such punishing heat and the hand smashed earlier in the year was giving him hell. Suddenly the cliffs of yelling faces on either side seemed to be closing in on him and for a terrifying moment he thought he was going to black out.

Respite came horribly. One of Miguel's ponies, racing Angel's to the boards, tripped and, overturning, broke her back. With a delay of ten minutes before her body was taken away, Luke managed to recover in the shade. Then in the next chukka one of Alejandro's most gallant mares broke a leg doing a lightning turn and also had to be shot. Patricio, who had made the mare himself, was in floods of tears. The crowd moaned in sympathy. Again, rage at such senseless waste fuelled Luke's blast-furnace. As Miguel hurtled towards him, blotting out the sun, bringing the ball down for a certain goal, Luke coolly charged him, buffalo for buffalo, and passing him legitimately on the offside, whisked the ball to Angel who passed just in time to Patricio who scored. Twelve all, proclaimed the sea-green scoreboard in vast, white letters. The crowd had nearly yelled themselves hoarse and resorted more and more to their instruments. Two rival supporters, overcome by emotion, started a punch-up. Primrose-yellow flags and banners, emerald-green parasols swooned in the heat.

It was the last chukka. The O'Briens' legendary temper was roused. It was time for Goliath to despatch David. But, by sheer persistence, the Mendozas, each clamped on his opposing player like Jack Russells, managed to keep the score level until, in the last ten seconds, Seamus crossed Luke. Up went the Mendozas' sticks, twirling in triumph and there was a sharp exchange between the O'Briens and one of the long-thighed umpires who'd been looking at his watch at the time, until the third man came out of the bar and confirmed it was a foul.

Grimly the O'Briens lined up behind their goal. The Mendoza supporters (now most of the crowd) bellowed without ceasing and, in the bars below the great stadium, started opening bottles of champagne. Lorenzo, Patricio and Angel exchanged surreptitious but delighted grins. The grooms of the Mendozas rubbed their calloused hands in glee. Señor Gracias never missed a penalty. The Open was going to change hands at last.

The stadium went quiet as slowly Luke circled, a lone figure on an incandescently white horse under the burning sun. Turning Fantasma towards goal, he suddenly panicked. His hand might not hold up and he should have given the penalty to Angel. For a second his concentration flickered. To a man the Mendoza supporters groaned as Luke mis-hit and the ball went wide as the last bell went.

Overwhelmed by shame, Luke slumped in the saddle, resting his tired head on Fantasma's bristling grey neck. He ought to fall on his polo mallet. Then, realizing the match wasn't over, with titanic effort he pulled himself together and cantered back to the pony lines.

'Sorry, you guys,' he called to the rest of the team who were on the verge of tears.

'Sorry,' he shouted to the dead-pan masks of the grooms.

'I thought you never miss a penalty,' snarled a furious Alejandro. 'Why are you bloody well smiling?'

'To stop myself crying,' said Luke.

Only Fantasma seemed to be on his side now. Flattening her ears and striking out at Alejandro, she nudged Luke sympathetically in the ribs as he dismounted, then tried to make him laugh by knocking his hat off.

Waiting to go into a ninth chukka, Luke took a swig of Seven-Up and soaked an entire towel wiping off the sweat. Alejandro wanted him to ride another flashy, beautiful chestnut called Zou Zou who'd been rested for three chukkas. But knowing Fantasma best, Luke opted to ride her a third time, which is allowed in Argentina. Briefly he put his arms round her neck echoing Sir Jacob Astley's prayer at the Battle of Edgehill.

'*Oh Fantasma, thou knowest how busy I must be this day. If I forget thee, do not thou forget me.*'

Fantasma, who was dying to get back into the action, nipped Luke's polo shirt in acquiescence. Three hundred chukkas with him were better than one with Alejandro.

'Come on, you guys,' shouted Luke as they rode back on to the field. 'I know I goofed, but we've got to hold on. We can do it.'

The young Mendozas and Angel, who'd all played their hearts out, were now running on pure adrenalin. The shadows were lengthening, a slight breeze swirled pale blue jacaranda petals across the pitch, but the sun seemed even hotter. It was sudden death now. All that mattered was somehow to get the ball between the O'Briens' posts.

The Mendozas had youth on their side and with kamikaze courage, the three young boys tried to score again and again, until Kevin O'Brien, at back, got fed up and cleared from his own goal. It was a monumental hit, the ball making a huge arc through the air, hurtling towards Luke who was waiting just beyond the halfway line.

Luke had left his back door open and he knew that Fantasma, despite her gallant, gutsy heart, had completely run out of steam. There was no way she could turn, gallop and keep up with Miguel and Juan, nor shake the pair of them off and take the ball back down to the O'Briens' goal. The ball was still hurtling towards him. He was dimly aware of the screaming, excited blur of the crowd, of the leaping mallets of Juan and Miguel trying to halt the ball as it flew over their heads.

Now, bearing down on him, bringing death in the afternoon to the Mendozas' hopes, pounded Juan and Miguel, ready to whip the ball away from him and together take it down the field and blast it into goal.

Despite her utter exhaustion, Fantasma never took her eyes off the ball. Trembling with anticipation, shifting from foot to foot, she was determined to position Luke perfectly for the shot. Dropping his reins on her sodden steel-grey neck, grasping his mallet in two huge hands, Luke took a mighty swipe as the ball passed him at eye-level. It was a complete cowboy shot but perfectly met. There was a tremendous crack, like an elephant's tusk breaking, as he connected.

The crowd gave a great shout of amazement as the ball took off back again. As though carried by the slight breeze and the indrawn breath of everyone in the ground, it flew like a white gull towards the posts. The great shout of amazement had become a greater one of ecstasy and encouragement. Had it gone far enough? Kevin O'Brien bucketed back. But he was so busy looking up in the air and whipping his pony that he didn't give himself enough time to get in position. Swiping at the ball as it thudded to the pavement-hard ground, he missed and the next second it had somehow bounced to the right and sidled in through the posts.

With agonizing slowness, as though the goal-judge couldn't believe his eyes, the red flag suddenly went into a frantic jive of joy.

For a few seconds there was utter silence as it dawned on the vast crowd that the Titans had at long last been toppled. The six-year wait was over. Then followed a mighty explosion of cheering that must have been heard by the foals at General Piran and, just as if the huge stands had leant forward to see better, the fans fell, as though toppled, on to the field. Fantasma's breath was coming in sobbing gasps. Her nostrils flared red as traffic-lights, her pale coat was black with sweat; like cobras, her veins writhed with her heaving body.

'*Gracias, gracias*,' croaked Luke, collapsing on her neck again.

Next moment Juan and Miguel were pumping him by the hand and he had been pulled off Fantasma and was being carried shoulder-high round the stadium.

'Americano, Americano,' shrieked the crowd in ecstasy, over and over again.

They knew Luke had stepped into the boots of the mighty Alejandro at the last moment and they wanted to salute his courage because he had turned the game around and never stopped fighting.

'Americano, Americano,' roared the crowd as, with his widest grin, Luke went up to collect the great Gold Cup with the soaring eagle on its lid and they roared on and on, refusing to let him go. Glancing up at the stands, Luke saw that Bart was yelling his head off, tears of joy coursing down his cheeks.

Another great cheer went up for Angel, olive skin tinged with colour, peacock-blue eyes bloodshot, bronze curls clinging damply to his forehead. All his cousins were shouting, crying and congratulating each other. He knew now that he'd been taken back into the fold.

As Angel brandished his own gold trophy he smiled across at Bibi who was crying as much as Bart and he thought how lovely she looked with her mascara running and her long nose red.

Luke ruffled his hair. 'I guess God looked after his Angel today.'

Luke won the Best Player Award. Fantasma won the two Best Playing Pony prizes and was only just restrained from kicking the President of the Argentine Polo Association when he put the white blanket of honour on her even whiter back. She had never looked more beautiful, thought Luke, shimmying round in her new white rug, ears pricked to hear the cheers, dark eyes searching restlessly for Luke, terrified to let him out of her sight for a second. Soon she would be his again.

Determined to clinch the deal at once, leaving the others swigging champagne and signing autographs, Luke set off to find Alejandro. Post-mortems were already going on in the bars in every language under the sun. The *Buenos Aires Herald* stopped Luke for his views on the match.

'We should remember the horses,' he said, suddenly sombre. 'They played their hearts out in this heat and three of them died. It was the worst I've ever known.'

He found Alejandro ecstatic, tearful and already drunk.

'Well done, *amigo*. I taught you well.'

'And now you can sell me my horse back.'

Suddenly Alejandro looked shifty.

'She play well. I decide I cannot part with 'er. Friend-sheep ees friendsheep, but business ees business.'

'I'll give you one hundred and fifty thousand bucks,' said Luke in desperation. 'It's all I can raise.'

But Alejandro refused to budge. He had put nothing in writing.

'If you hadn't broken your leg, I'd beat you to a pulp, you greasy, double-crossing son of a bitch,' shouted Luke, storming off.

77

Luke was so distraught that he nearly boycotted the massive celebrations afterwards, but he felt it was unfair to his own team who had played so well and to the O'Briens who had defended so gallantly. Everyone wanted to discuss his last goal which seemed to grow in length and splendour by the glass. He was almost more bruised by people clapping him on the back than by the game. He tried to get plastered, but it didn't work, and after a few hours he drove back to Angel's and Bibi's house. Arriving at dawn he found a primrose-yellow banner across the drive to welcome him, and bitterly remembered how he had covered up Perdita with a shawl the same colour when she'd ridden naked into the Casino.

He longed to drive over to Alejandro's to tell Fantasma in private how brilliantly and bravely she had played, but having raised her hopes once, he couldn't bear to raise them again – not if he was no longer going to be able to take her back to Palm Beach.

All the next day it poured with rain and Angel's cousins, still tight from the night before, swarmed through the house and the telephone rang with congratulations and offers for Luke and Angel to play next season anywhere in the world.

By six o'clock the rain had cleared and Luke, desperate to be on his own, went out for a ride with Leroy who had had a boring day confined to barracks. It was a beautiful evening with the turquoise sky reflected in the huge puddles and the acid-yellow and green sweep of the pampas, only interrupted by the occasional windmill or grey fringe of gum trees, stretching to infinity. Luke wished he could ride off the edge of the world.

Every bone in his body ached but not nearly so much as his heart. Tonight the cousins were giving a celebration for him and Angel. But what was the point without Perdita? Even the loss of Fantasma was nothing by comparison. He wondered if there had been a moment in the last three years when he hadn't longed for her or if there would ever be in his life again. Even yesterday's success had already turned to ashes in his mouth.

He had so wanted to go to her after she broke up with Red, and again on the night of the Westchester when Red had bolted with Chessie. She'd looked so desolate that evening in her black dress, he'd longed to help her pick up the pieces. But he knew it would be wrong. His love was so strong he'd never be able to control it and she'd feel claustrophobic. She could never marry anyone she didn't love or survive in captivity like Chessie had for so long.

Down by the river into which Fantasma had once galloped, he dismounted and sat on the bank letting his horse graze and Leroy charge off after hares. He watched a flock of white birds winging slowly homewards, turning pink in the setting sun. In three weeks it would be Christmas and suddenly the pain became unbearable as he remembered that first Christmas in Palm Beach with Perdita when he still had hope.

Luke had always had brilliant eyesight but his eyes were so misted over that at first he couldn't identify the cloud of brown dust on the horizon. Then, as he got to his feet, he heard hoof beats and realized it was a pony and rider going ludicrously fast. He couldn't identify the colour of the horse because they were against the sun. Now they were flashing through a blue puddle, now disappearing behind a field of alfalfa, faster and faster. As they curved round towards him down the rough track, he realized the rider was bareback and guiding the pony in just a headcollar.

Luke recognized the pony first. Rose-pink in the sunset, as she had been in that sunrise after he had saved her life, she was covering the ground at breakneck speed with that beautiful, low, inimitably smooth action. He had a moment of outrage that anyone should ride her so dangerously fast after such a gruelling match yesterday. A split second later he recognized the rider. No, he was hallucinating. No-one rode so aggressively, so gracefully, or in such a hurry to get to goal. It must be a mirage.

Perdita was only wearing a khaki shirt and shorts. Her face was caked with dust, her features set, her whole body trembling as she tugged Fantasma to a halt in front of him. Luke, who had a lump as big as a polo ball in his throat, couldn't speak. Neither could she. They just gazed and gazed at each other. Fantasma, however, had no such reserve. Whickering with delight, she shot forward nudging and licking and nuzzling her old master all over, searching his pockets for Polos.

Still unable to get a word out, Luke put his arms round her lovely head, breathing in the smell of her sweat, fighting back the tears. 'You didn't ride all the way?' he mumbled stupidly.

'Only from the airfield.'

'You didn't steal her?'

'No. I bought her.'

'But Alejandro said she wasn't for sale.'

'Every Argie has his price. Rupert gave me some money,' she added by way of explanation. 'It seemed the only way of spending it.'

'But that was your security,' said Luke, appalled.

Perdita shook her head violently.

'It's for us. You're my security. You're the only person I've ever felt secure with in my life.'

Tears were pouring down her face now, streaking the brown dust.

Frantically she wiped her eyes and nose with both hands like a child, streaking the dust sideways as well.

'I love you,' she sobbed. 'If you love that revoltingly beautiful lawyer and don't love me any more, I shall quite understand. But once you said you did and I hoped you still might. Ricky thought that perhaps . . . and Rupert too . . . we might try again. Oh, Christ' – she gave a wail and put her hands over her face – 'I'm such a cow.'

Next moment Luke had pulled her off Fantasma and into his arms and was kissing her harder than he'd ever hit a sixty-yard penalty.

'I don't believe it,' he groaned. 'I simply don't believe it. I was sure it was still Red.'

'I haven't loved him for ages, not ever really. I always felt as though I was wearing boots on the wrong feet. I loved all the money and the trappings. Then I realized they didn't mean anything. With you it's truly bread and onions.'

'I guess it is,' said Luke ruefully. 'I haven't got a cent.'

'Bullshit,' said Perdita. 'Now you've won the Open everyone wants you, including me. I only came back because you've become such a star.'

Luke grinned. 'Double bullshit! You bought Fantasma before the match. That's why Alejandro wasn't looking nearly as guilty as he should have done yesterday.'

'You're right,' gasped Perdita, when at long last he stopped kissing her. 'I wanted something to cheer you up in case you lost.'

Luke took both her hands in his and kissed them.

'*Gracias*,' he said shakily. 'The only thing better in the world you could have given me is yourself.'

Exactly on cue Leroy bounced up with a mud-caked nose and threw himself on Perdita. For an outraged second, Fantasma flattened her ears and stamped her foot, then, recognizing her old friend, she once more whickered in delight as Leroy barked ecstatically and licked her pink nose.

Luke turned back to Perdita.

'I love you more than anything else in the world.'

'More than Leroy and Fantasma?'

'Don't push your luck.'

'Don't push my Luke,' said Perdita, reaching up to kiss him again. 'I'll have to change my name.' She gave a sigh of happiness. 'I'm not the Lost One any more.'

'You'll have to change your name anyway,' said Luke slowly.

With a trembling hand he tugged out the bit of Fantasma's mane that was left long on the whithers to stop the saddle rubbing and wound it round Perdita's wedding-ring finger.

'I can't go down on one knee because of my cartilage.' For once the deep, Florida drawl was coming out in a rush. 'But d'you figure you could possibly love me enough to . . . ?'

He didn't need to go on. With an instinct that knew that neither Perdita nor Luke would take any notice of her for some time, Fantasma gently started to eat the grass.

THE END

PANDORA
by Jilly Cooper

No picture ever came more beautiful than Raphael's *Pandora*. Discovered by a dashing young lieutenant, Raymond Belvedon, in a Normandy Chateau in 1944, she had cast her spell over his family – all artists and dealers – for fifty years. Hanging in a turret of their lovely Cotswold house, *Pandora* witnessed Raymond's tempestuous wife Galena both entertaining a string of lovers, and giving birth to her four children: Jupiter, Alizarin, Jonathan and superbrat Sienna. Then an exquisite stranger rolls up, claiming to be a long-lost daughter of the family, setting the three Belvedon brothers at each other's throats. Accompanying her is her fatally glamorous boyfriend, whose very different agenda includes an unhealthy interest in the Raphael.

During a fireworks party, the painting is stolen. The hunt to retrieve it takes the reader on a thrilling journey to Vienna, Geneva, Paris, New York and London. After a nail-biting court case and a record-smashing Old Masters sale at Sotheby's, passionate love triumphs and *Pandora* is restored to her rightful home.

'Open the covers of Jilly Cooper's latest novel and you lift the lid of a Pandora's box. From the pages flies a host of delicious and deadly vices . . . Her sheer exuberance and energy are contagious'
The Times

'This is Jilly in top form with her most sparkling novel to date'
Evening Standard

'One reads her for her joie de vivre . . . and her razor-sharp sense of humour. Oh, and the sex'
New Statesman

'She's irresistible . . . she frees you from the daily drudge and deposits you in an alternative universe where love, sex and laughter rule'
Independent on Sunday

'The whole thing is a riot – vastly superior to anything else in a glossy cover'
Daily Telegraph

'A wonderful, romantic spectacular of a novel'
Spectator

0 552 14850 4

A LIST OF OTHER JILLY COOPER TITLES AVAILABLE FROM CORGI BOOKS AND BANTAM PRESS

☐ 12041 3	**LISA & CO**	£5.99
☐ 14696 X	**HARRIET & OCTAVIA**	£6.99
☐ 14697 8	**IMOGEN & PRUDENCE**	£5.99
☐ 14695 1	**EMILY & BELLA**	£6.99
☐ 15055 X	**RIDERS**	£6.99
☐ 15056 8	**RIVALS**	£6.99
☐ 15058 4	**THE MAN WHO MADE HUSBANDS JEALOUS**	£6.99
☐ 15054 1	**APPASSIONATA**	£6.99
☐ 15059 2	**SCORE!**	£6.99
☐ 14850 4	**PANDORA**	£6.99
☐ 14662 5	**CLASS**	£6.99
☐ 14663 3	**THE COMMON YEARS**	£5.99
☐ 04404 5	**ANIMALS IN WAR**	£6.99
☐ 04404 5	**HOW TO SURVIVE CHRISTMAS (Hardback)**	£9.99
☐ 14367 7	**THE MAN WHO MADE HUSBANDS JEALOUS (Audio)**	£12.99*

* including VAT